Carrier Wave

Robert Brockway

ISBN: 9798612779827

Brockwar Press: The Fightin'est Press in the West

Cover design by Meagan Brockway

Table of Contents

The First Story

"It was hungry. That is all it was. When it felt something, it became that thing, because it was just a simple creature."

Mr. Odane settled back on his ancient stool, with its chipped paint and its errant nails and its wood creaking like an angry bullfrog. He thumbed tobacco down into his pipe and searched the eyes of the children. Claude smiled, Nadia breathed heavy through her nose, Sebastian looked away.

"When it was hungry," the old man continued, "it became hunger, until it ate. When it was tired, it became exhaustion, until it slept. This is how it was, because at the time, there was nothing else."

Mr. Odane patted his pockets until a lump gave away his matchbox. He withdrew it and turned it about in his driftwood fingers.

"It jumped through the trees to the edge of the forest, where it came down to the berry bush and ate its fill. It looked to the sky and saw something strange…"

"The spot," Claude giggled.

"Hush," Nadia said, "let him tell it."

Mr. Odane nodded, concealing the matchbox in his palm.

"The spot," he agreed, then ripped a match free. The flare of it was blinding in the winter's dead light, and Sebastian shielded his eyes. Mr. Odane saw this and cackled.

"In the sky," he whispered, "was something it had never seen before. Something it could not understand. But the spot could understand him. And the spot wanted more. It returned to its home in the trees that night, but it could not shake the shape of the small white spot, twisting in the skies. It looked at the spot again and again and could not sleep for thought of it. The next day, it was hungry again, so it went to the bush. But something occurred to it: It did not just want to eat berries this morning. It wanted to eat berries this evening, and tomorrow, and it did not want to come back to the bush each time. It gathered all of the berries on the bush — every one!"

Mr. Odane jabbed his skeletal finger at each of the children in turn.

"It wrapped the berries in a leaf, and it brought them home, and it ate berries all day. Now, it was not such a simple creature. It understood 'want.' And like the spot, it wanted more."

Claude coughed, and Nadia elbowed him so sharply that he yelped. They scrapped briefly, but their hearts weren't in it. Mr. Odane's story time came less and less often these days, and neither wanted to spoil it. Even if Claude pretended that he didn't want to come, at first. Had argued that he preferred listening to the radio in the lobby of the Mafolie, even if they had to stand outside the doors and scatter when the valets shooed them, because sometimes they got Escape, and that show did better sound effects than Mr. Odane. But Claude didn't argue very long, and he didn't call them "simpletons" and run home, like he did when he was truly upset, so he must have wanted to come, too.

The old man saw his match begin to gutter out, so he kissed flame to his pipe, and the smell of wood and cherries and fire overwhelmed Sebastian.

"Gathering berries was one of many new ideas that occurred to it." Mr. Odane watched the stars as he smoked, speaking between billows. "And with every new idea, the spot grew. The spot grew and grew until it was not a spot, but the whole sky. It looked at the empty white sky, and the invisible things that churned up there, and suddenly, for the very first time, it wanted to know what it was. So it gave itself a name, and it called itself 'Monkey.'"

Claude stood and hopped in place, making low hooting sounds. No one laughed for him. They only glared until he sat down again.

"Monkey saw that others like him were understanding new things, too. They looked at the spot, and they understood kindness. They began to share. They understood peace, and they ceased to fight. They understood order, and they began to enforce rules. But Monkey did not understand these things. He only understood want. So when he saw a group of young ones playing with a pretty shell in the low branches, he swung down and took it from them. When the smallest of the young ones hooted and howled for him to give it back, Monkey…"

Mr. Odane brought his bony fist down sharp into his outstretched palm, and the children jumped. The old man laughed madly, then cut it short and pointed at Claude.

"Monkey bashed the young one's head against the tree until it did not move anymore. The other young ones scattered, and some sought out the adults. The ones with new ideas about rules and laws. They were not happy, and they chased Monkey from the trees, all the way out of the forest, all the way to the beach!"

"Was the beach very far from home?" Nadia asked, all hush and breath.

"It was the farthest Monkey had ever been. The pretty shell was precious to him for that very reason: because it was so scarce in the forest. But that night, Monkey sifted through the sands at his feet and found it was full of shells. Hundreds and thousands, too many to count. And they were all the same, with the same pattern, the same shape, the same color. His precious shell did not seem so valuable anymore. Filled with despair, Monkey looked to the sky, which burned so bright it hurt to look at but spread no light. He asked to give his new ideas back, to return to how he used to be, before he knew he was Monkey. But the sky did not listen. Monkey thought perhaps the emptiness wanted something from him in return, but he had only one thing left. He reached back with all his might, and he threw his pretty shell high, high as it could go. But the sky did not take it. The shell fell back into the dark waters of the ocean, and it was gone."

Nadia released a long breath, and Claude laughed, and Sebastian just picked at his shoelaces.

"You must never forget this story. You must tell it to your children, and you must tell them to tell their children, as I was told, myself," Mr. Odane recited dutifully, as he always did at the end of this particular story.

Claude and Nadia sang out, "Yes, Mr. Odane," and Sebastian just nodded.

"So…what do you think this one means?" Mr. Odane asked, as though the question was perfectly innocent.

The children used up their easy answers early, after the first few times Mr. Odane had told this tale. They had said, "Don't be greedy," or, "Violence is not okay," or even, "Family is more important than things." They needed new answers with each telling, or else Mr. Odane would look at them with his saddest eyes and tell them that a story did not mean just one thing and that it could mean different things every time you heard it.

"Be careful of what you wish for," Claude ventured, and the little nod from Mr. Odane said it was a good guess, but not the best.

"You can't unlearn some things," Nadia said, and Mr. Odane's bushy eyebrows crawled way up his forehead. That meant it was probably a very good answer.

Sebastian did not have his answer ready. He knew it, but when he went to speak, it was not waiting there on his lips. He closed his mouth again and looked at the dirt between his feet.

"Hmm," Mr. Odane said, tapping his pipe along the heel of his boot to spill the ashes. There was an old black burn there from all the times he had done it before. "It's fine to think on it for a spell, but come back to me when you have an answer. Never accept a story for what it first appears to be. Stories are dangerous things, and they can trick you so bad that you don't know who you are anymore."

With that, he stood and clapped his hands twice, and the children scattered before he grew impatient and started tickling them.

Sebastian walked far behind Nadia and Claude as they kicked rocks at each other's heels and watched the distant windows of Frenchtown flicker and catch light, far below. He thought about his answer and about why he couldn't speak it. It just seemed far too simple, he concluded. It would be a good answer the very first time he heard the story, but now, it was too obvious. It couldn't be true, and he would only seem silly if he spoke it aloud. He would have to think tonight, come up with a new answer to tell Mr. Odane by morning.

His first answer was: Maybe the price Monkey tried to pay wasn't high enough. Maybe the empty white sky wanted more than just pretty shells.

Messier 55

"If you were the only human being alive on earth, and you'd never seen a sand dollar before, what would you think when you first found one?" I asked the pair of them.

"A what?" Peter said, already stepping all over my analogy.

"A sand dollar." I sighed. "Small, round, flat sea urchins with a star pattern on the shell. Those discs you find on the beach."

Jen's eyebrows knit together. A little lopsided "Y" formed in the folds of her forehead. It was cute. Couldn't place how, exactly, it was cute. But it had to be. It was Jen.

"I don't see how this is relevant," she said.

My analogy. Trampled.

"Yeah, I'm not following the train of thought here," Peter said. He seemed to be emptying the entire sugar container into his coffee mug.

"I mean, if you'd never seen a sand dollar before, you'd just think it was a stone or something, right? Some little rock with a neat pattern in it. At least at first. Then when you walked down the beach and found another with the same pattern, you'd get to wondering. Then you find another. And another. Dozens of them, all with nearly identical, improbably intricate patterns. 'Okay,' you'd think, 'clearly somebody is making these things. This is proof that I'm not the only human out there.'"

Nobody snapped at the bait.

"You'd think it was a sign, but it's nothing. It's not even a stone. It's an animal. It's just nature. There are all sorts of patterns in nature," I said, and I pulled out my finishing move. I set an immaculate sand dollar in the center of the table, just beside the ketchup and the plate full of destroyed, runny eggs that Jen had barely touched.

Peter said nothing. He just kept pouring sugar.

"So you think we're wasting our time," Jen said. When she finally spoke, it was slow and measured.

"No, of course not." I went cold at the accusation. "SETI is a valuable — hell, a vital — program. Now that we're advanced enough to look for alien life, it's a moral imperative that we do so. We're obligated as a species to keep looking, if only for the sake of science. Even if we never find anything."

"Bullshit," Peter said. He looked at me as he spoke, never one glancing down at the ceaseless stream of sugar emptying into his mug. "There's gotta be alien life out there. I've seen a lot of my little corner of the universe. No way in hell are we the most intelligent life in the whole damn thing."

"No way in hell are *you drinking that coffee*," Jen said.

"Of course not. It's empty," Peter said.

"Then why…?"

"*Because* it's empty." Peter grinned, a vicious little break in his face, entirely without humor. "That bitch of a waitress never came back with a refill. Now she's got a solid mug full of wet sugar to deal with."

Jesus. The people in this town dislike us enough without little stunts like that. Before we'd built the Big Ear here, the most remarkable thing about Delaware, Ohio, was a stained wall that kind of looked like JFK if you squinted hard and tilted your head sideways. I got the sense they liked it that way. Though it's always been a college town, so you'd think they'd be used to visiting academics now and again. These people had no reason to dislike us — we spent most of our time buried at the observatory. They barely even saw us.

Maybe *that's* why they didn't like us.

The waitress came by to drop off the check. I smiled at her extra hard.

She just frowned down at the mound of white spilling out of Peter's cup and walked away without a word.

Peter, I swear to god.

...

Jen walked out in front. She walked like she thought she was being stalked by somebody, just one loud noise away from sprinting. To her, a walk was just an inconvenience between places she had to be.

"I'm telling you, that pattern is repeating," Peter hollered from somewhere behind us.

I was in a light jog, trying to keep up with Jen. But I was also trying to make it look like I was just walking nonchalantly. Arms down at my side, legs sliding forward and back in barely controlled leaps like I was miming cross country skiing. I hoped it looked more natural than it felt. Peter didn't bother trying to keep up. He just ambled along behind us, closing ground when we stopped for cars, yelling his half of the conversation without caring how many stares he gathered.

"I said, that pattern is repeating!" he yelled again. Like we didn't hear him. Like we weren't just ignoring him because the little old ladies of this town were worried enough about us bringing aliens down on their heads.

"I said, that—" he started again.

"We heard you!" I finally yelled back. "Nobody's saying it's not repeating. I'm just saying the pattern could be natural. Nature's full of patterns!"

Did he not even hear the sand dollar speech? God damn it, I practiced that in my head all last night.

"Patterns that regular, that intense?"

I couldn't jog and yell at the same time. Jen was getting away. I decided to hell with Peter and broke into a run.

"I said, patterns that regu—" Peter yelled after me.

…

Jen made it back to the observatory first. She'd already had time to kick her boots off — she always walked around the focus room barefoot — and was blowing her nose over the trash can. It was hard to find a way to call *that* cute, but somehow, I managed it.

I could feel my face burning from the workout. Jen wasn't even breathing hard. I couldn't help but stare. That limp red hair. Those black glasses, as thick as her lips were thin. Body like a mannequin. I mean, a male mannequin, but it was still lean. Powerful. Beautiful. I poked my own moderate paunch, straining at the edges of my worn Speedracer T-shirt.

Like she'd ever be with a shlub like me.

Peter came in last, still yelling his half of a conversation nobody had heard.

"—and you can't use nature to dismiss an intentional pattern like this. Look at this — a full seventy-two seconds…"

He grabbed the sheaf of printout from globular cluster M55. He held it up to my face and shook it. I had a mad impulse to slap it out of his hands — it would be so dramatic — but I swallowed that down and just smiled at him. Weakly.

"Right, man, look at the pattern. It's all over the place," I said.

"But those big spikes are unnaturally regular deviations from the hydrogen line," Jen said.

My insides went cold. Amazing how her disappointment had a temperature.

"Yes, those few spikes are regular, but everything in between is all over the map. Look," I said, and I took a step back so I could stand between them. "I'm not saying it's not weird. I'm just saying we need more info before we make something big out of this."

Peter let out a low groan. He did that when he was thinking about something he didn't like. Jen scratched her neck and looked away. Neither spoke.

Science prevails.

…

I kicked open the door to the focus room.

"Merry donut day, nerds!" I yelled.

The lights were off. The chairs were empty. I set down the three cups of coffee and dozen donuts on my terminal. I thought I should bring a little peace offering after our tiff last night, so on my way in, I had asked a guy on the corner where I should go for donuts. He said, "New York," then walked away. So I had to swing by a phone booth and look it up in a soggy book hanging from a chain.

I shouldn't be the first in. Jen should still be on the early shift, and Peter should be stumbling in by now, three hours late for his rotation, reeking of vodka and devouring his customary three plain pieces of bread. Should I call somebody? Who would I even call? We're all volunteers. As far as I knew we could just up and walk away. Jen could have pissed off back to…oh man, can you believe I didn't even know where she came from? God damn if I missed my only shot with her because I was too…

The door banged open, and Jen shuffled into the focus room. She hadn't changed her clothes from last night.

"Rough night?" I asked.

I laughed, because she didn't.

"You could say that."

"Oh, I was just kidding, because you were late and all… Everything okay?"

"No, I had nightmares."

"Ah, sorry. Happens to me sometimes, too."

"I have never had a dream before in my life. Not that I can remember, at least."

"Wow, that's *super interesting*," I lied. "What was this one about?"

"I don't know. It's hard to talk about. I've never had to discuss a dream before."

She fell quiet. Thinking before she spoke.

"I was watching television, only nothing was on… It was static. Little white flecks dancing and zipping all over the screen. But there was a parallax effect. The little black flecks weren't moving at all. Just the white ones. See, the black flecks weren't flecks at all; they were the only visible parts of a background, or a bigger object. The white ones started getting farther and farther apart from each other, and I realized they were all moving away from something. They were making a space around a black spot in the center. Like they were afraid of it. It just kept getting bigger and bigger, and I couldn't stop looking at it."

"Huh. Well, that doesn't sound too bad, as far as nightmares go. This one time, I dreamed I had sausages instead of fingers, and I got really hungry, so I started eating my own sausages and then my dad—"

"It was just pure terror, the feeling I had when I looked into that black spot. I felt like everything I was was being sucked into that space, never to return. And the worst part is, just before I woke up, I thought I saw something in there."

I blew on my coffee. I waited a few seconds, but I guessed she needed some prompting.

"What was in there?"

"I don't know. I don't remember. There was a face, but I don't think it was human. And it was all black, anyway — how could I see a face in there? I woke up feeling so strange. The whole time I was walking down here, I was just so angry. But at nothing. I saw nobody. Just leaves and trees. Yet they made me angry. And then, when I walked in here, my first thought when I saw you was, 'I could kill this man and nobody would ever know it.' Isn't that strange? I've never had a thought like that before."

Welp, nothing to do now except stare at our terminals in terrible, awkward silence.

We stayed that way until three in the afternoon, when the police arrived.

"Afternoon," the first officer said, poking his head through the door. He didn't knock. "I'm looking for the workplace of a Mr. Peter Hoover. This the right place?"

I thought Jen would answer — she was closer — but she didn't even look up.

"Yeah, I uh…hey, what's this about?" I said. I stepped around Jen and stopped a few feet away from the officer. I was about to shake his hand. Was that normal? Was that a normal thing to do with a cop? Or was that, like, considered a threatening action or…

"This is it," he yelled to somebody on the other side of the door, then stepped in and stood off to the side.

A fat man in a dark blue windbreaker trudged in, looking like he was expecting bad news from a doctor. He puffed out his cheeks and stared in every corner of the room before looking at either me or Jen. He put his hands in his pockets and sighed.

"Uh, is everything…?" I just trailed off.

"Turble," the fat man said. I thought he might've just burped.

"What?"

"Sherriff Turble. That's me. I'm Turble."

He sighed again and fished through his pockets for something but apparently didn't find it. He just gave up and let his hands dangle by his sides.

"Hi," I said, "I'm—"

"Peter Hoover," Turble said. His voice sounded like somebody had knocked the wind out of a Bassett Hound. "He works here."

"He does," I said, though I wasn't sure it was a question.

"Beat up a waitress," Turble said, and he pinched the bridge of his nose and exhaled loudly.

"What?" Jen blinked. It was the first time she'd looked up from her terminal all day. "What happened?"

"Peter Hoover beat up a waitress," Turble said again. He went to make a gesture, it was almost a shrug, but he quit on it before it even got started. "Got him in lockup."

Turble turned to leave.

"What? Is that — what do we do about that?" Jen called after him.

Turble said something like, "Ahhhhhdungimmadambou—" as he walked away.

The other officer stepped out from behind the door.

"Hoover couldn't remember the number for this place," he said, "for his phone call. Couldn't even remember the address. Just said it was 'the space place.' We had to come down here to let you know where to see him, when to post bail and all that. Sherriff Turble, he doesn't like doing stuff."

The officer smiled at Jen before leaving.

The cold again.

…

Peter looked like he'd withered since we'd last seen him. Though maybe that was just my own mental association after seeing him sitting on that little plastic bench in his cell, all alone. His head was down in his hands, and he was saying something over and over, too soft to hear. He looked up at us through red, swollen eyes. He'd been crying. I couldn't imagine Peter crying, but this didn't look much like Peter. It looked like somebody had freeze-dried what Peter used to be so he'd fit into a smaller package.

"Hey…hey, guys," he said. He laughed a little. "Had a rough night."

"What the hell happened, Peter?" I said. I wrapped my hands around the bars. I shook them a little. I didn't expect them to feel so solid.

"I just…I couldn't sleep last night. I couldn't think of anything else but that fucking waitress, you know? The one from yesterday morning, at the café? She didn't refill my coffee. Not even once."

"So you attacked her," Jen said.

"Yeah," Peter answered, even though what Jen said — it didn't sound like a question. It sounded like she was finishing his sentence. "I just, it kept going round and round in my head. And I kept getting angrier and angrier about it. And it's like, she can't get away with that. You know? People can't get away with stuff like that. It's the principle of the thing. The principle!"

Jen nodded.

"The principle? Of not getting enough coffee? Are you fucking insane?" I said.

Peter slammed his head right into the bars. Right where my hand was. If I'd moved a second later, it would've broken all of my fingers. A thick trail of blood ran down his forehead.

"What did you call me?!" He screamed so loudly his voice cracked. "What did you say? I'LL KILLYA. KIIIYAAA. KIYA MA!"

And then he was just making noises. Barking and frothing at the mouth. He headbutted the bars again and again.

“Ahhh,” Turble sighed from the door behind us. “I knew you were gonna make more work for me.”

. . .

When we left, Peter was still scrabbling at the bars of his cell, trying to get to me. His eyes never left mine. He screamed nonsense syllables until his voice gave out. Jen didn’t seem all that fazed by Peter’s fit, but I couldn’t stop my own hands from shaking. I could barely hold my coffee cup steady.

The waitress had filled it right up to the top — I mean, to within a millimeter. Why did they do that?

Scalding liquid kept seeping over the rim, running down the ceramic and burning my fingers. I set my coffee down. Jen was staring out the window of the All Hands Diner, watching cars pass through the rain. They plowed through the increasingly large puddle forming in the intersection of Williams and Washington, kicking up great arcs of cold slate water. Every once in a while, one of those arcs would catch the passing headlights from another car and light up. Like tiny stars suspended in mid-air.

“Pretty, isn’t it?” I said.

“Hmm?” Jen blinked and looked at me.

“I said it’s kinda pretty — the headlights in the rain. Looked like you were watching them.”

“No,” Jen said, “I was thinking about Peter.”

“God.” I let out a breath that practically winded me. I guess I’d been partially holding it all this time, breathing high and shallow in my chest. “I know, right? Why would he do that?”

"Exactly," Jen said, "it makes no sense. Why would he beat her up? And then leave her alive? I can't figure it out."

"Yeah, I — wait, what's that?"

"They said he caught her all alone while she was closing up, then hit her with a ketchup bottle and stomped on her for a while. Then, what? He just took off? I can't for the life of me figure out why he stopped."

"Because…because he didn't want to—"

"You can't be in here." The cook was standing at the head of our table, his arms crossed, one hand clutching a greasy, foot-long kitchen knife.

"Why not?" Jen tilted her head up at him.

"You god damn well know why not," our waitress piped up from behind the cook. "Your friend nearly killed Kelly!"

"But that's got nothing to do with us," I said, trying to keep the pleading out of my voice.

"The hell it doesn't," the cook said. "You college folks always come in here, looking down on us, thinking you can use us and our town however you'd like. Well, we don't need you. We don't need you, and we don't need this. You get up and get moving the hell away from my restaurant right now. I'll give you three steps towards the door, and then you're gonna be the fucking breakfast special."

"Come on, Jen." I was trying to figure out how to save face from this. Maybe I could say something clever at the last minute, right as we were making the door, when it was too late for them to come after us.

"Can't we hash this out?"

"I guess we better scram…ble."

Damn. No good.

"Looks like YOUR special is…"

Jen reached up and impaled her hand on the tip of the knife. A bright red spurt of blood shot out across the cook's filthy white apron. Another sprayed the waitress in the face as Jen wrapped her fingers around the blade of the knife and yanked it out of the stunned cook's hand. In one smooth motion, she slid the knife out of her own flesh and opened a foot-long gash on the cook's arm. He yelped and leapt backward. The waitress' eyes roved about in her head. She was trying to find the voice to scream. Jen was already standing up from her seat at the booth, her eyes on the waitress. The knife moving towards her.

"No!" I shot out of my seat and grabbed her wrist. She dropped the knife. I hustled her out the door before anybody could gather their wits and react. I was trying to get to her to run with me towards the observatory, but the most she'd manage was a hurried mosey.

"Come on," I urged her, "pick up the pace."

"Why?" she said, a bit of a giggle in her voice.

"Because they'll kill us!"

"Not if we kill them first, which I was about to do if you hadn't stopped me. Why did you do that? It was stupid."

"Why?" I spun around and pulled her wrist to my stomach, drawing her close. I grabbed her jacket with my other hand, shaking her there. "Because you can't kill people!"

"Sure you can." She laughed. "It's actually really easy."

"You shouldn't!" I screamed into her face.

Her expression fell. Her burly eyebrows swept together. Her meager lips quivered. She looked so lost. I didn't even know what was happening, but it was happening. I pulled her in the remaining few inches and kissed her, hard. I poured all of my fear, and worry, and confusion, and pent-up lust into that kiss; I poured out the accidental touches as we both reached for the same printout; I poured out my furtive glances — visions of her chewing her hair in the sickly green light of her terminal; I poured out the way I felt about her tiny earlobes and emptied every sleepless, masturbation-plagued night into her. I poured it all out. I left myself nothing.

When I finally opened my eyes, hers were staring back into mine, wrought with concern.

"What's wrong?" I said.

"I'm spurting blood all over your crotch," she said, gesturing to where I'd pinned her injured hand against my belly.

Sure enough, my slacks were soaked through. I looked like a vampire who had pissed himself.

"Let's get back to the focus room," I said, my one true moment utterly defeated. "I think something's going on with that signal."

…

We made it to the observatory without further incident. Hardly anybody was out in the downpour, though it was barely mid-day. We'd left the lights and the terminals on and the door unlocked. In my haste, I'd even abandoned my tea right there on my desk. It was cold and bitter — appropriately like puddle water — but I belted it back anyway.

I would need it.

I steered Jen into the kitchenette and bandaged her hand with our cracked plastic first aid kit. The paper slips surrounding the Band-Aids had gone slightly brittle with age, but gauze was gauze, and alcohol was alcohol. With that done, I hauled her chair to my terminal and sat her beside me. She had seemed to go almost catatonic after the kiss. I chalked that up mostly to shock and only a little to my own personal charisma. She was clearly overwhelmed by it all. I studied the printout of the signal, but it meant nothing. Just a line executing a pattern of spikes and dips on a sheet of paper.

"Does this mean anything to you?" I showed her the printout, waggled it in her face as gently as possible. "Does it…say something to you? First Peter starts acting strange, then you — something's going on, and it started here."

No response. She wouldn't even make eye contact.

I got up, plugged my headset in, slotted in the tape with the signal on it, and listened. Nothing exceptional, just an ululating bass tone interspersed with some clicks and squeals. I played it backwards and heard backwards squeaks and clicks.

Well, what did I expect? The devil's voice commanding me to kill? Jesus, what was I doing? I was supposed to be a scientist, and yet at the first sign of distress, I started chasing extraterrestrials. I needed to get my head on straight and think this through rationally. That was my strength. So, what common denominators did Peter and Jen — and only Peter and Jen, out of all the inhabitants of this entire miserable town — share that could be responsible for such dramatic changes in behavior? Nothing, save for the signal, this room, and me. Could it have been something in the room itself? A chemical leak of some kind? We used no chemicals here. There's no other lab even close to the observatory. The harshest thing around was printer ink, and I doubted that causes murderous urges. Another question: why was I apparently exempt? So the question actually became: what commonalities did Peter and Jen share that I—

The squeal of an office chair, swiveling. I glanced to my left — Jen was still seated there, motionless, staring off into space. I turned very slowly toward the dark corner containing Peter's workstation. A figure slumped in the shadows. Lumpy and bald.

"Peter?" I said.

"Haaaaa…" It was part a laugh and part a frustrated groan. "That is me. Peter. And you? And you?"

"I-it's me, Peter. Do you know where you are?"

"No." The figure shook its head slowly at first, then more and more violently, like it was trying to dislodge water from its ear. "Yes. Sort of. I know, but I forget what it is to me. This place, what is it to me?"

"What are you, drunk again?"

"What?!" The figure fired out of the shadows, grabbed a fistful of my sweater, and threw me from my chair. I hit the cupboards in the kitchenette and lost my breath. I slid to the cool tile and tried to calm the ebbing tides of color that threatened to overwhelm my vision.

"You think you know meeeuuugh—" Peter vomited suddenly. A torrent of chunky crimson.

"Ah, Jesus, Jesus god," Peter moaned, and he collapsed in my chair beside Jen. She still hadn't reacted. Might not have even blinked.

My vision cleared, and I found myself fixated on the puddle of vomit. It looked like Peter had been eating raw hamburger. There was something whole in there. He hadn't even chewed it. Just horked it down his neck in one large gulp, like a duck. It was waxy and had delicate little swirls like a…

I looked at Peter, sitting in the light now. His shirt was torn and covered in blood. He was barefoot. His fingers were twisted into arthritic-looking, inflexible claws.

"Peter?" I said. His head swiveled vaguely toward me, but his eyes were unfocused. Bloodshot red, so wet he was practically crying. "Did you just puke up a human ear?"

"Should I not have done that?" He laughed deep in his belly. "Too much. Couldn't keep it down. Too much."

"Jen, get away from him," I said, trying to keep the urgency out of my voice. Instinct told me that any hint of panic in my tone would set Peter off again.

"Why?" she said, not pulling her gaze from the nothingness she was focused on. "It's just Peter."

"Did you not just hear what he said? He…he ate somebody. He's not—"

"I'm here," Peter said, and his eyes focused on me for the first time. They were awful. They were so…human. It looked like he'd been sobbing hysterically all night. I could sense a plea in those eyes, something that couldn't make it past his lips.

"I know you are, Peter," I said.

"I'm here," he said again. "I'm here. I'm here. I'm here."

I started moving toward Jen slowly. Peter's eyes locked on mine all the while, though his body remained otherwise rigid. I took a step toward them.

"I'm here."

Another step. Not far now.

"I'm here."

I reached out and grabbed Jen's arm. I guided her up from her seat and past Peter. She followed me listlessly, like she was sleepwalking.

"I'mhereI'mhereI'mhere."

I took a step toward the door, Jen in tow, never taking my eyes off Peter.

"Imhereimheimhimhimimim…" Peter's syllables flowed together. His eyes were still locked on mine. Dull blue shot with flecks of green. Tears. Pleading. Human. And then…not. "IMHE. IMHE. IMHE HOA."

I had only a split second between the moment that I realized this was not Peter anymore — not in any form I would recognize him — and the moment he lunged at us.

God, so fast.

I was on the floor, a sound like feedback in my ear, one eye not working. Something was scrabbling at my leg like an animal, but my sensory information was coming in starts and stops. My brain was muddy. If I could just get this damn sound to stop for one second so I could concentrate…

When I finally did shake the cotton from my brain, Jen was straddling Peter, who lay prone on the floor. His legs were shaking. Jen was doing something to him, but I couldn't see what. Her back was turned to me. I got to my knees and shuffled toward the pair of them.

"Jen?" She didn't respond. She was still grabbing at something. Maybe wrestling with Peter? Trying to subdue him? I should help. I needed to save her, so she could see what kind of man I really was. Or at least, what kind I wanted to be.

"Jen, I got him," I said, just as I came around her shoulder and saw what she'd been doing.

Peter was dead. Beyond dead. His neck had been torn open, laid bare by Jen's fingernails, which were still inside his throat, poking, probing, and ripping. She was yanking at something hard in there, over and over again, but it wouldn't come free. His spine. She was trying to take his spine.

"Jen?" I said. "I think you can stop now. I think he's dead."

Jen's head snapped toward me, eyes like a two-day hangover, tears streaming down her cheeks, gaze thick with a plea she couldn't seem to speak.

…

The secret is bleach.

That's all. Just bleach, a bit of time, and a lot of fresh towels. That's how you clean up a very large amount of blood. The big pools are no problem. It's the little spots that will trip you up. There were little spots of crimson in the keyboards of our terminals; drips of red in between the stapler's lever and handle; blood mixed in with the coffee at the bottom of

Peter's mug. I got all of it. Every bit. I had plenty of time. Only the Big Ear volunteers came down to the focus room anyway, and I was the only one of those left. The hardest part was dragging the bodies. It seems so much easier in movies. But it's not like dragging a heavy couch or something. Bodies are limp flesh — they catch on things. They slip through your hands. They bend strangely. It took hours to get Peter and Jen into the woods behind the array. It took hours more to dig the holes.

Really, cleaning was the easy part. It's silly how big a deal everybody makes of it.

"Blood never comes out."

Nonsense. Unless they're speaking metaphorically…

As a scientist, I cannot definitively state that the signal is what caused Peter and Jen's violent outbursts. My sample size is too small. There were only three of us. I can only say that it is *my hypothesis* that something in that signal causes human beings to slowly lose all semblance of humanity and become something violent and animalistic. It remains only a hypothesis, until such time as I can test it and prove the results. I burned all of the printouts, but the tape recording of the original signal is sitting beside me on this greyhound bus, in the bottom of my backpack, wrapped in a clean towel. I left a note on the focus room door. Some bullshit about worker's rights and the true agenda of science. We were all walking out en masse, I wrote. Going to join a new lab that would pay us a fair wage for meaningful work. The university would pull three more lucky volunteers from the astronomy department, and work would continue without missing a beat. *Their* work. My own work is only just beginning, and there's so much of it ahead. I will document the true effects of this signal. I will prove my hypothesis. For Jen and, to a much lesser extent, for Peter. I will employ only the most rigorous testing methods, going forward. And I will need a much, much larger sample size.

The Herald

"So this man walked into the Shop-Shop, pulled out a boombox, played some music—"

"Some of that *new wave* music," the man said, then spat chaw-juice onto his own boot. He glared at it with disapproval.

"Played some music and left. You went to grab some beer, then a few minutes later, the clerk jumped over the counter and beat the victim to death? Just like that?"

"Just like that," the man agreed. He squinted at Helms' badge again, like he couldn't believe what he was seeing.

"So what did this man look like?" Helms asked, not looking up from her notebook.

"Like some skinny pansy that doesn't work for a living."

Helms glanced up from her notes and fixed the witness, one Jeremy Boont, with a questioning stare.

Boont winced a little, spat more chaw, and stared off at his truck like he thought that description should suffice.

"How tall was he?" Helms prompted.

"I don't know. Not very."

"What color was his hair? His eyes?"

Boont leaned in close to Helms, his gut pushing her notepad back into her writing hand.

"What do I look like to you?" he asked, slowly.

"Excuse me?" Helms took a step back. Thought that might have been a mistake: probably should have stood her ground and made him back off.

"I look like some kind of gay to you?" Boont asked.

"I…I don't…"

"Like I just stand around, gazing at men's hair, lookin' deep into their eyes. You think that's what I do?"

"So you didn't notice anything at all about the man with the boombox?"

"I noticed — and you can write this down now, this here's my statement — he looked like he wasn't very tall, and he looked like some kind of skinny pansy that don't work for a living. That's all I saw. Where I'm from, men don't look at other men, and if they do, they sure as hell don't *see* 'em. That's gay business."

"So you couldn't tell me what your own daddy looked like?" Helms asked.

"You sayin' my *daddy's* a gay now, lady? *Are you kiddin' me?* Who's tellin' you I'm gay for men, huh? Who's been spreading lies? I tell you, I find who's been sayin' this stuff, I'm gonna stick my gun up his ass and fuck him with forty-four calibers."

"See, now *that* sounds kind of gay…"

"WHAT?!" Boont reared back, like he was going to deck Helms, but Officer Price stepped between them and stared him down.

Boont returned the glare for a minute but ultimately broke. He spat chaw, in what he probably thought was a defiant gesture, and looked at his truck again.

"That's all I got to say," he finished.

"Why don't you and your buddy get on outta here before we break out the breathalyzers, all right?" Price said.

Boont coughed, pulled up his belt, and adjusted his worn baseball cap — Federal Booby Inspector, it said — before leaving. Made a big show of taking his time about it.

When he and his buddy finally made it to the truck and pulled out, tires squealing, of course, Price turned to Helms.

"You get anything useful out of the other one?" she asked him.

"I asked if the suspect had any scars or distinguishing tattoos. He asked me if I thought he was a gay-boy," Price answered.

Helms laughed.

"The bible-thumping hicks in this town, I swear to god."

"That's not fair," Price said. "It's got nothing to do with this town or the bible. I've known Jeremy Boont since sixth grade. His daddy owns a furniture company that makes fancy wicker chairs and such. Sells 'em to yuppies on the West Coast for thousands of dollars. Drives a bright yellow Porsche. Boont isn't some poor uneducated bible-thumper; *I'm* some poor uneducated bible thumper — he's just a dipshit."

"Look, if it walks like a hick and slurs like a hick, I'll call it a hick," Helms replied. "Plenty of them around here."

"You should come to church with me sometime," Price said. "You'll see where all the good people in this town are hiding."

"Price," Helms said, "my mom was a Baptist and my dad was a Bastard. Neither would want me anywhere near your church."

"Ah," Price chuckled, "I'll make a convert out of you someday. If only for the free coffee."

They fell quiet for a moment.

"So…" Helms said, eager to switch subjects. "The other one told you the same thing about the music guy? Just walked in, hit play, then left, and the clerk went ballistic?"

"Basically, yeah." Price looked around the parking lot, saw nobody was watching, and pulled out a cigarette. "Kid got any priors?"

Helms made a face at him as he lit it, and took two steps upwind.

"Zip," she said, "just out of high school. Solid B student. Likes band, according to the manager."

"A *band geek* nearly tore my throat out?" Price said, gesturing to the three gouges on the side of his neck.

"Quit being dramatic," Helms said. "He barely grazed you. Besides, you always got me to save your ass."

Price laughed.

"You see him in the back of the cruiser when Jackson pulled away? He was trying to bite through the damn window. What turns a pudding of a kid like that into a feral maniac all of a sudden? Drugs?"

"Maybe." Helms scuffed at the pavement with her shoe, knocking cigarette butts towards the drain in the middle of the parking lot. "Seems like there's something new coming out every day."

"Yeah, maybe…" Price blew smoke from the side of his mouth, angling it away from Helms.

She smiled at him.

***

"We've got reports of a 708 at the Bowl N Chug. Two officers on scene requesting backup."

"Price and Helms responding," Price said, then set the handset back in its cradle.

Helms hit the sirens and flipped a U-turn, cutting off a bright yellow Porsche. Price watched the mirrors and saw a hand slide out its window, giving them the bird.

"Ten to one it's Joe Greene again," Price said.

"Probably decked some guy because his toe was over the line," Helms agreed.

Price grabbed the oh-shit handle as Helms cut a wide, fast turn down Everett and floored it toward Center. Engine roar filled the cabin. The cruiser crested the dip just before the courthouse and went airborne for a split second.

"Jesus!" Price laughed. "There's no way the call's this urgent. You know that, right?"

"When do I get to do *this*?" Helms grinned but kept her eyes locked to the road.

She swung the tail wide and power slid to a stop in the parking lot of the Bowl N Chug.

"Whoo," Price let out the breath he forgot he was holding and shook his head as he stepped out of the car. "Someday you're gonna get us killed, driving like that."

"Nah," Helms said, slamming her door. "Cheese dogs and cigarettes'll get you first."

Price thumbed the release on his holster and let his hand rest on the grip of his pistol. He got to the door first, checked his corners, stepped in, and quickly moved to the side. Helms did the same behind him. They spread out, each watching half of the alley. There was nobody at the front desk, nobody in any of the lanes, save the far one. Helms could see legs sticking out from behind the ball delivery and two males wrestling on the ground between the benches. One of them was wearing blues — maybe Jackson. Then she saw his partner, Marche, backed up against the rails, his pistol drawn and centered on the fighting men.

She glanced at Price, who hadn't yet spotted it from his angle. But he caught the meaning in her eyes. He pulled his service revolver and pointed it at the floor in front of him. Helms followed suit. They covered the distance quickly, sticking to their sides and watching the blind spots behind pillars. Helms made the scene first, came around the ball delivery, and eyeballed the limp body. Male, just shy of six feet, probably over two hundred pounds. Lying face down, not moving, no blood or signs of serious injury. Likely just unconscious. The priority here was Jackson and his assailant.

The attacker was straddling Jackson, his back to Helms, one hand locked on Jackson's throat, the other fighting off Jackson's frantic grabs toward his face. Jackson tried to kick out of the hold, and the pair rolled into the gutter, shifting position so Helms could see the assailant's face.

Shit, it *was* Joe Greene.

He was a troublemaker and a bit of a prick, sure, but he never took an argument beyond a little dust-up and usually apologized by buying the other guy a beer afterward. Besides, he always cowed like a scolded schoolboy when the cops showed up. But he wasn't just resisting arrest here — Jackson was pouring blood from his left eye, teeth smashed through his lips — this was *attempted murder.*

"Police!" Helms tried, knowing it was pointless.

Helms looked to Marche. He was trying to back up the stairs to the concession stand, but he couldn't take his wide, unfocused eyes off the fight long enough to get his footing. He had his gun drawn but pointed in the air, weaving back and forth above the commotion.

Shellshocked.

She called out, "Police" and, "On the ground" one more time, then let off and focused on moving into position to cover Price. If she'd been alone, she would have had to try to wrestle Joe Greene off, but she knew Price was stronger, and he knew she was the better shot. It didn't need to be said. Price had holstered his weapon and was running in low, hoping to use the momentum to knock Greene loose from Jackson's throat. He caught Greene hard around the waist, and they rolled into the next lane, freeing Jackson, who immediately started crawling away, down the lane toward the pins.

Greene didn't seem to understand that he'd been grabbed from behind. He was making no effort to break out of it, his eyes still locked on Jackson and the ragged trail of blood he left in his wake. Greene was kicking his legs, thrashing and clawing wildly at the air, but making absolutely no effort to pry Price's hands from around his midsection. Price scooted backward across the lane until he reached the far side of the alley, then levered Greene up and swung him face first into the wall. He pulled one of Greene's arms down around his back but couldn't get a hold of the other. Helms holstered her gun and ran to help. She put her weight into Greene's shoulder and twisted his free arm downward. She held it in place while Price finished cuffing him, then made the mistake of looking into Greene's face.

His eyes were beyond bloodshot. Dried white flakes ran down each cheek, like he'd been crying for days. He bared his teeth and snapped at Helms over and again. He screamed gibberish, a raging staccato bark that seemed to be trying to form words but never quite made it.

"RAAAH," Greene gnashed his teeth and beat his own face against the wall, "RAH HA IMHE HOA!"

Price grabbed him by the hair and held his head back so he wouldn't bash his own skull in; Greene spasmed and struggled harder. Together, Helms and Price managed to trip him up and bring him down. She zip-tied one ankle, then the other, and then the two together. Price held a knee in his back and hauled on his shoulders so she could hook the handcuffs and the ankle zips together, leaving Greene hogtied. She knew it was dangerous to bind a person like that for long, but Jesus — look at him. He was still snapping at anything that came near his face, though his eyes never left Jackson.

Shit. Jackson.

Helms jogged down the lane and ducked her head under the

pinsetter, where Jackson's blood trail led.

"Jackson!" she called out. "Jackson, are you still with me?"

A wet moan was her only response.

She called in an Officer Down and requested an ambulance, then stood and surveyed the bowling alley.

"How do you get back there?" she yelled to Price.

"Back where?" he said.

"Behind the pins. Jackson's back there!"

"I'm coming," Price said.

He turned to Marche, who still had his pistol out, pointing it now at the inert body on the floor.

"Marche." Price snapped his fingers. "Hey, you with me?"

"Don't go near it," Marche said, after swallowing hard a few times.

"What? Listen, just stay here with Joe while we go check on Jackson. He's not going anywhere. Just make sure he doesn't chew his tongue off or something."

"HOA IMHE MO HOA," Greene growled to himself.

Price turned away from Marche and jogged back down toward the benches. He rounded the ball return and knelt by the body there.

"No, don't! Don't get close to—" Marche screamed.

Price extended a hand to check the man's pulse, then became a flailing blur.

Helms didn't even see the guy move. He was face down one second, then up on his feet the next, holding Price in the air by his neck. Helms pulled her pistol reflexively.

"Hey!" she called. "Hey, stop! Let him go!"

It wasn't exactly protocol, but it was all she could think to say. She closed the distance fast, but the man moved faster. His fingers sunk deep into Price's throat, holding him six inches above the floor while he sprinted toward Marche, who scrabbled backward up the stairs. Unlike Greene, this guy was dead quiet. The only noise was his shoes squeaking on the polished wood as he ran down Marche, holding Price in front of him like a shield.

Marche had no shot, but he took it anyway, firing wildly.

"No!" Helms yelled, too late.

When he had closed to within a few yards, the man heaved Price aside. Price crumpled like a puppet whose strings had been cut. Marche fired again and again, each shot going wide, and then the man was on him. He grabbed frantically at Marche's arm, who twisted and yowled like a wet cat. When he found purchase, the man put a foot on Marche's chest and yanked upward. Marche's arm came off clean at the shoulder. Still the man made absolutely no noise, not even a grunt of exertion. Marche stared at his own severed arm and keened like a tea kettle. The man tossed the limb absently aside, then began grappling with Marche's remaining arm.

Helms put three bullets in his back, center mass.

He didn't even flinch.

The other arm came off as easy as the first and was tossed aside with equal disdain. He reached down and grabbed Marche's left leg by the knee. Marche kicked and bucked, but to no avail. The man put his foot on Marche's crotch and in dead silence wrenched his leg free from his body. Helms put two more rounds in his back, then steadied herself.

Slow is smooth, she thought, *smooth is fast.*

She took an extra fraction of a second to line it up, then pulled the trigger and put a round in the back of the guy's head. He fell to his knees, then to his side, still clutching Marche's severed leg in both hands.

Helms holstered her pistol and ran to Price, who was choking and gagging, pulling at his neck. She laid on top of him, pinning his arms to his side, and spoke low and fast and breathless.

"It's okay it's okay it's over you're okay don't fight it just give it a second just one second take a slow breath real slow and easy you're okay—"

Price stopped struggling and was still for a long moment. Then at last came the rasping of a slow, thin breath. He tapped Helms on the arm, and she rolled off him. He didn't sit up, just stared at the ceiling and focused on breathing evenly. Helms went to check on Marche next, but she could tell at a glance that he was dead. Almost certainly from shock. His face was frozen in a mad mask of disbelieving fear, blue-white and bloodless.

"Two officers down," Helms yelled into her handset. "God damn, get everybody over here now!"

She rechecked Price, still breathing rough but consistent, and headed back toward the pinsetter, toward Jackson.

She laid flat on her belly, as if to crawl in after him. But she froze.

Fear, shaky and electric, wrapped around the base of her spine and pinned her in place.

"Jackson," she called out instead, "hang in there. Help is coming."

She went back to Price and sat at his side, stroking his forehead until the EMTs arrived.

***

"I told you half a dozen times already," Danny Greene whined to Helms, "we was just minding our own business, throwing a few rounds, when this little guy came up and held out a tape recorder — one of those dealies that fits in your hand. He hit play, and it made some beep boop kinda sounds, then he just turned and walked away before we could even say nothin'. Me and Joe and Marky bowled a few more rounds, then I looked back and Joe was crying or something. So I made fun of him some

— like you do — and he just flipped out and started beating on me. Well, I took right the hell off, I don't mind telling you, and that was all I saw. I went back to Becky's trailer, and I got real drunk there until I fell asleep on the foldout. You can ask her, I was there!"

Helms rubbed her eyes with her pointer finger and thumb. She was so tired that her vision would go blurry every few minutes until she paused to massage life back into them. She took another sip of Styrofoam-flavored coffee from the absurdly tiny cup and pretended to recheck her notes. There was no need. Danny Greene had told the same story each time he was questioned, and the other witnesses backed him up as best they could. Nobody saw the guy with the tape recorder, but they all saw Joe go nuts on Danny for no real reason. Then he turned on the folks in the next lane, then the manager, until everybody bolted, leaving him and Mark Kimmel alone in the alley. Witnesses said that when Joe started attacking folks, Mark just laid down on the floor and went still. Stayed like that the whole time.

Jackson had so many stitches in his face he looked like a scarecrow, but he managed to keep the eye. His statement said he and Marche arrived on scene to find a prone Mark Kimmel, while Joe Greene roamed aimlessly up and down the lanes, muttering to himself. Marche split off to check on Kimmel while Jackson went to confront Greene. Marche got there first, and the second he knelt down by the body, Kimmel sprung to life and hurled him all the way up over the railing into the shoe rental. Kimmel looked around, saw Jackson, seemed to think for a second, then just laid back down and went still. Jackson called out then, and the noise got Greene's attention. He laid into Jackson like a madman, and that's when Helms and Price came on scene.

All the stories matched up. And none of them made sense.

Joe had some assaults on his record, but nothing this serious, and never with his own brother. They were tight as two sticks in a popsicle — if anything, people insulting his brother was the excuse Joe used to fight most often. Mark Kimmel had nothing on his record at all. He hung out with assholes, but if that was a crime, half this town was going to jail.

So they, what? Went crazy because of some beeps on a tape recorder?

Even assuming that was true, what Kimmel did was impossible. Not "crazy on drugs" improbable — *literally impossible.* He lifted Price — who was six foot and a buck eighty himself — like a sack of potatoes and still ran at full speed. Then he pulled off Marche's limbs without so much as breaking a sweat. Drugs could kill your pain center, make you take a lot more damage — that would explain why Kimmel didn't go down when Helms emptied into him, but no drug made you superhuman.

And if it *was* the tape recorder that caused it, why did Greene seem to have normal strength and went around attacking strangers, while Kimmel went all Superman but just laid on the floor until somebody got close?

Helms circled and underlined various words in Danny's statement, basically at random. How the hell did she type up something like this without sounding like a maniac herself?

"You hold tight, Danny," she said and scooted her chair back. It wailed metal on metal. "We'll get you out of here, soon."

"You fuckin' better!" Danny said, then immediately regretted it. "Sorry, it's just…I been in here for hours, and I wanna go see Joe. They won't even tell me how he's doing."

He waited to see if Helms would enlighten him, but she just smiled a little when she stepped out the door. Price was waiting with a replacement Styrofoam coffee. He handed it to her and sipped from his own, wincing as it went down.

"How's the neck?" she asked.

"Dandy," he croaked, his voice like wet gravel.

Price was speaking as little as possible on his first day back. He wasn't even supposed to be here yet, but he'd checked himself out of the hospital after only thirty-six hours. The captain figured it would be better for his recovery to let him stick around and do deskwork, rather than hollering and shouting about forced leave. Helms had been pulled from the field after the shooting while the investigation went through, but she knew that wouldn't take long. Besides, she could use the time away.

She knew beat cops were supposed to fight against every second of desk-time, but Helms was actually quietly relieved. She'd never so much as fired her service revolver in the line of duty before taking down Kimmel two days ago. Her usual targets were tin cans and paper outlines. She couldn't say she was exactly losing sleep over it — but that was what worried her. Helms told herself it was because Kimmel clearly wasn't human anymore — not with that strength, not with that speed — and she'd seen what he did to Marche. Knew what was on the line when she pulled that trigger. But there was still a nagging little part of her asking, "What if you're just a killer? What if that's why it doesn't bother you — because you're a psychopath?"

Their station was small; the therapist had to come all the way from Des Moines and wouldn't be here until tomorrow. Helms would put up a fight for show — "Guess I gotta go get my head shrunk by some witch doctor," she'd snark — but once that door was closed, she was looking forward to talking to someone. She wasn't worried about the investigation — you could go take a look at Marche's mangled body if you had any questions about whether or not it was a good shooting. His single remaining leg and three ragged stumps would do all her testifying. But she could sure use somebody with a big rubber stamp that would deem her "sane" right about now. And that wasn't happening anytime soon. So that left her stuck at the station for at least a week when she should be…

Doing what, exactly? What was the lead here, the crazy music guy?

Price noticed her staring at the wall, delicately sipping hot black water, and grunted.

"What? Sorry, just thinking…"

He grunted again, with an inquisitive tone this time.

"About where we go from here, with the case."

Price groaned.

"Look, just because we're both riding desks doesn't mean the work stops. If all we have is the guy with the tape recorder, then sure, I guess that's where we start. If nothing else, he's a material witness at two crimes, one assault and one murder…"

A doubtful grunt.

"Well, okay, I'm a*ssuming* that it's the same guy. But this is a small town — you really think there are two tape recorder psychos out there?"

An acquiescing groan.

"Right then. I've got some paper time in front of me anyway. I'm going to look into noise disturbances, see if there's anything there. You want to look into assaults and pull witness reports, see if somebody mentioned a guy with a boombox or a tape recorder or something?"

Price nodded. He smiled at Helms and slapped her on the shoulder. Her terrible coffee sloshed over her fingers, scalding them. She sighed at nothing in particular and turned away from Danny Greene, still sitting at the holding room table, picking his nose and carefully examining his discoveries.

***

Fully ninety percent of the noise complaints in the last month were from a single person: one Eleanor Dubicek, of 2031 April Terrace, Unit C.

She thought the neighbor across the way was ghastly, with his leaf blower going so early in the morning. She thought her downstairs neighbor absolutely didn't need to watch *Knight Rider* that loudly, and her upstairs neighbor was probably listening to Springsteen at such a high volume so as to drown out his criminal dealings. And surely the garbagemen didn't need to make such a racket every Thursday morning — they were probably banging the cans around just to spite her.

Helms read through every single report anyway, just in case the old bat had filed a complaint about the positively disrespectful young man that went around her complex, fiddling with a tape recorder and making people murder each other.

She did not.

The remaining ten percent of the noise reports were scattered — mostly kids having parties while their parents were away, drunkenly hollering while they smoked cigarettes on the porch late at night. But there was one interesting report. Two weeks ago, Andrew Falkous called police from the Cosmo's Ladder Trailer Park to complain of a neighbor making loud squeaks and squeals all through the night.

It was thin, but Helms was ready to grab at less. She pushed her chair back and took the report over to Price, who was grimacing down at his own tower of folders.

"Check this out," she said, slapping the report down on the desk in front of him.

He arched an eyebrow at her and stared quietly.

"Just read it," she said and left to get them both refills from the coffee machine.

When she got there, she found the pot empty but still sitting on the active burner. The last dregs of coffee were burnt into black tar death.

"Terrell," she yelled over her shoulder, in the general direction of the office.

"What?" came an answering voice, already annoyed.

"Did you take the last of the coffee?"

"Yeah, so what?"

Helms turned and stalked out of the breakroom, over to Terrell's desk. He was a chubby guy, just starting to bald. He used to be a looker, back in the day. Helms knew this, because he told literally everybody about it. He kept a framed photo of his younger self on his own desk. In it, he was standing on the beach somewhere with his shirt off, big smile, defined pecs glistening beneath a bed of curly chest hair. That and the southern accent didn't make him *unpopular* with the ladies. Helms knew this, again, because Terrell told everybody he met just about as soon as he met them.

"So what?" She sighed. "So if you take the last of the coffee, you make a new pot. Or you at least turn the burner off so we don't get this…this industrial waste shit to scrape out."

She rattled the pot at Terrell, who just curled his lip and swiveled his chair away from her.

"Making coffee is women's work," Terrell said, loud enough for the whole office to hear. "Or maybe the help. You look like both to me."

Helms entered into a beautiful and elaborate fantasy wherein she cracked the glass pot against the back of his head, the shards exploding outward like a new universe being born. The stupid look on Terrell's face — hovering there right between confusion and terror…

She should at least say something clever in response, but she'd gone blank while entertaining the beautiful dream, and now the moment had passed. She settled for calling him an asshole and returned to the breakroom. She set the pot in the sink, filled it with water, and returned to Price.

He'd had enough time to read the report, but he was still flipping back and forth between the pages, trying to decide something.

"What do you think? Worth checking out?" Helms asked.

"Hmm?" Price said.

"Hmm what? Listen, the Chewbacca thing only goes so far. You'll have to talk sometime."

"I think," Price croaked, "that neither of us are allowed to check *anything* out."

"Oh, no, of course not." Helms waved his concerns away. "I only meant if it looks solid enough to bug the other guys with. Have them do a follow up or something, just a friendly visit."

"I…" Price gagged a little and took a second to compose himself. "I think Terrell and Bryant are the only ones on active duty tonight, so no visit is going to be 'friendly.'"

"Damn." Helms bit her lip and glanced over at Terrell's desk. He was deep in concentration filling out the crossword puzzle. No way in hell he'd follow up on a noise disturbance as a favor to her. And if she tried to explain…

On her first day, Helms showed up with a lucky rabbit's foot on her keychain. Terrell saw it and made some crack about "you darkies and your voodoo."

Terrell and Bryant were not an option.

"Maybe it can wait until tomorrow when they're off rotation," Helms agreed.

Price smiled at her and turned back to his reports.

Helms started back toward her desk, made sure Price was lost once again in the paperwork, and walked right past it, out the side door. She unlocked her cruiser, gave herself ten seconds to feel stupid about what she was doing, then put it in gear and drove off.

***

Andrew Falkous would have been a stunningly handsome man if not for the severe overbite and facial psoriasis. He opened the door to his weathered and peeling trailer in nothing but a very open and very pink bathrobe. It took him a long second to realize he was hanging in the breeze, and he tied the belt with no special hurry. Falkous had a can of Pabst Blue Ribbon in one hand and a TV remote in the other. In the background, something with an obnoxious laugh track regularly interrupted their conversation.

"Mr. Falkous?" Helms said.

She was still wearing her uniform. She kept telling herself she wasn't here in an official capacity. The uniform would give everybody the right impression, but maybe if she specifically avoided introducing herself as an officer or mentioning police business, she could leave herself an out when this inevitably blew up in her face.

"Mr. Falkous is my daddy, you lil' sip of molasses," Falkous said. "You can call me Andy."

She could practically feel Falkous' eyes rolling up and down her body.

Helms felt her fists close, involuntarily.

Not in an official capacity, she reminded herself.

Helms turned on her flirtiest smile and giggled.

"Hi, Andy!" she said, putting some ditzy pep in her voice.

A big sloppy grin stumbled around Falkous' face.

"I heard a neighbor of yours was making a lot noise a few weeks ago?" Helms said, carefully avoiding any mention of a report or the authorities.

"Hmm? Oh, yeah, that. Listen, I'm not one for calling the pigs. No offense." He gestured at Helms with the beer can, sloshed a little out and onto her shoes. "But that guy was at it with his bullshit MTV crap every night for near a week. I tried to settle it like a man, gone over there and knocked right on his door. I ain't no pussy. But he is — he wouldn't answer. So, ipso fatso, the pigs."

"Right," Helms said, imagining herself on a beach somewhere with a big, icy drink. Utterly alone. All other human beings dead or otherwise confined somewhere far, far away. "What do you mean, MTV music?"

"Like that video channel crap. The electronic German stuff. Like that song about cars? Only without even any words. Just noises. Call that music? I should put on some Haggard and crank it up to eleven, show that little punk what real—"

"Thanks, Andy!" she bubbled, turning quickly and making for the cruiser.

Helms sat in the driver's seat and stared at the dented aluminum caravan for ten full minutes. She ran over the scenario in her head again and again. She had come out here and verified the report firsthand, and now it really sounded like she might be on to something. She should call the station and have a unit sent out, even if it was Terrell and Bryant. Maybe they wouldn't just laugh it off if she'd scouted it in person first. Maybe they would just laugh harder. She should at least call Price.

And he would say, "What are you doing in the field?" and, "We're riding desks this week," and "by the book" and "blah blah blah."

Helms knew all of this before she drove out here in the first place. She was just having doubts now because it was time to actually do it — time to pull the trigger and go vigilante. You saw it in movies all the time: A cop gets pulled from the case, but they pursue it anyway on their own time. They get the perp, save the day, and all is forgiven. That's not how it worked in real life. If she knocked on the door of that trailer and things went south, it would mean her job, at least.

She drummed on the steering wheel. She checked and rechecked her service revolver. She opened the glovebox for no particular reason, closed it, then opened it again.

Screw it, she thought. *It's going to be nothing anyway. Just some guy with bad taste in music.*

No need to report anything. Nobody would even know, and she and Price would be down one bad lead when they picked up the case again in a week. That's progress.

Helms stepped out of the cruiser and adjusted her belt. Her shoes crunched over gravel and broken glass, then up a set of creaking, crudely built wood stairs. She rapped on the thin aluminum door of the caravan and took a step back. Her hand rested on the hilt of her pistol. She swallowed hard. Watched the light leaking out from the floorboards so she could tell when footsteps blocked it. They did. A silhouette moved back there.

"Hello, sir," she said, biting back the instinctual urge to identify herself. "We've had some noise complaints recently. Just following up on those, if you could spare a moment to answer a few routine questions…"

Silence.

Helms hated this part. The wait. Every traffic stop, every knock on every door — there was always this agonizing moment while she waited for whoever was on the other side of that glass, wood, or steel to decide if this was the day they drew down on a cop. She knew most every encounter went down peacefully, but there was always the chance. There was always the decision to be made, and she had no hand in it. Helms hated that more than anything.

The door creaked open an inch. Just a thin swatch of face — white male, short, maybe five foot four if he wasn't slouching, probably thirty to forty, brown hair, green eyes. Deep bags under them. Pale skin. She couldn't tell the weight just from the few inches of face showing, but judging by his gaunt cheekbones, not much. Not exactly a threatening specimen, but a bullet was the great equalizer. She kept her hand on her pistol.

"Sorry to bother you, sir." Helms tried to sound as harmless as possible. She threw a little "even *I'm* annoyed, having to be out here" into her tone. "We're just following up on all disturbances from this neighborhood as part of a community outreach program. We're making sure relations are still solid with your neighbors and there hasn't been any further escalation between you."

The single eye narrowed, and the door closed a fraction of an inch.

"Look, it's just this thing my superiors are making us do. I'm sorry to bother you, I really am, but you know how bosses are — and mine get worse around election season. They just want some feedback, make sure you're not harboring some complaint about us that'll come back to bite 'em in the ass around poll time. You know? It'll only take a second."

The door opened a bit further, and the man took in Helms from head to toe. Finally, he swung the door wide and stepped back. He gestured Helms inside with a sweep of his head.

Helms knew it was a bad idea to step into an unknown premises like this, with no backup. But she also knew there was no way in hell she was getting a search warrant based on "this funny feeling she had." She stepped around the man — most of her assumptions were right, she saw. Short, skinny, pale. But she was off about the age. She figured he was only in his late twenties, maybe early thirties, after seeing him up close. But he did not wear the years well. Junkie, maybe?

Helms quickly surveyed the interior of the caravan. There wasn't much to see: a little kitchenette to her right; a stained bench opposite that, piled high with papers and textbooks; a faux wooden door directly across from her, barely the size of a closet. The bathroom, probably. To her left, there was a cramped bedroom, barely more than a twin mattress and a couple of nightstands. It was jam packed with electronic equipment — smooth steel surfaces thick with dials, gauges, switches, and needles. They were all on and active, flashing, sweeping, and clicking with hidden purpose. In the center, there was an enormous reel-to-reel recorder.

Helms became suddenly aware that she had no idea what she was looking for. Audio equipment? Okay, she found that. What did that prove?

"Ask your questions," the man muttered into his own chest, then twisted his head upward and loudly repeated, "Ask your questions!"

"Well, uh…" Helms mentally scrambled for a plan. "We really just wanted to follow up on the initial report, make sure that your neighbors haven't, uh…harassed you about the complaint or anything."

"The idiots? No, no, the idiots have left me alone. I bought the headphones, see?" Again, the man wrenched his head skyward and repeated, "The headphones!"

He rattled a set of over-the-ear cans attached to a long wire leading all the way back to the bedroom full of electronics.

"So, uh…you mind if I ask what all the equipment is for?"

"Hmm?" The man's face bunched up, and he blinked at Helms. "Why do you need to know? Not a crime to have this equipment. Not a crime!"

"No, of course not," Helms said and put on her harmless smile again. "It's just that my nephew, he's, uh…he's really into A/V stuff, and I'm trying to…y'know, connect with him more."

Damn. Helms felt her credibility slipping away by the second.

"Okay…" the man said, dragging the syllables out. He thought for a second, then continued. "I'll show you! I'll show you!"

The man set his headphones down on the bench and shuffled past

Helms. They both had to turn sideways to let him pass. Helms tightened her grip on her pistol while he did. He stooped in front of the equipment and fiddled with something in the bottom-most stacks. Then he flipped a few switches on the receiver and yanked the headphone cord out of its plug. He turned around and smiled at Helms, and she instantly knew she'd tipped him off somehow. She took a reflexive step backward to put some distance between the two of them, but her heel thumped against the far wall of the trailer.

Nowhere to go.

The man hit play. There was only static at first, gentle pops and clicks as a recording spooled up. Then it opened with a deep bass, almost too low to hear. The thin walls of the caravan shuddered with it. A high ululating squeal, then a wildly oscillating tone that dove up and down through the registers. Quickly, the sound filled out with too many atmospheric squeaks and whistles to track. Helms felt something behind her eyeballs pop, and a sucking vertigo pulled the floor of the trailer away from her. She stumbled but put a hand on the kitchenette's sticky counter and steadied herself. The recording stopped, and for a moment, Helms wondered if it had truly gone quiet or if she'd just gone deaf.

The man peered back at her from the far end of the trailer. His eyes burned with focused curiosity. He was expecting something.

When the vertigo passed and she popped her ears a few times, she felt normal again.

"That was…weird," Helms said.

The man smiled slowly, his thin, dry lips cracking from the effort.

"Interesting," he said, then looked to the roof and barked, "interesting!"

"So what was all that ab—" Helms began, but the man cut her off.

"I wonder," he said. He did a little hop and then scuttled toward her. He stood a few inches shorter than Helms, squinting up into her eyes and inclining his head to get all the different angles. "I wonder which you are, then, hmm?"

He reached up to touch Helms' eye, but she slapped his hand away with her right while pushing him back to arm's length with her left. Then hand to pistol again, ready position.

"Not a Manic," the man continued, unfazed. "This close to an isolated, augmented, filtered hi-fi source and you'd be clawing at the walls by now."

"What the hell are you on about?" Helms said.

"A Sleeper, then? Too active, too active." He clapped his hands hard.

Helms jumped. She pulled her revolver out from its holster a fraction of an inch.

"No." The man shook his head. "The reflexes would be fading by now. You could be one of the other frequencies — I haven't identified them all. Wouldn't that be exciting? Exciting!"

"Sir, I'm going to need you to come with me. I have some questions for you in regards to a series of attacks around town that I—"

"How's your heart rate?" the man asked, ignoring her. "Your breathing? Your vision? Are you hearing voices, having sudden unexplainable urges? What do you taste? You have to tell me, quick! Quick! The changes might render you unable to speak."

"What changes? Sir, you're not making any sense. If you'd just gather your, uh…audio materials and…and accompany me back to the station, I'm sure we can get all of this—"

"Oh." The man looked crestfallen. "Oh, that's it. Just another carrier. How disappointing."

"Sir, I'm going to ask you one more time to gather your recordings and come with me to the station, or I will have to detain you."

"Of course," the man giggled, "of course! Just a moment."

He shuffled to the far end of the trailer and poked around at his audio equipment. He turned back to Helms.

"I just have one question for you: what would you do if I erased this recording right now?"

"Sir?" Helms said, her patience wearing. "That is evidence to be used in a possible criminal investigation…"

"I understand." The man nodded. His finger hovered over a button on the central console. "I'm going to erase it now."

"I'll fucking kill you!" Helms had her pistol out and trained on the man's face in the span of a heartbeat.

"Yes, yes. There it is. The carrier wave doing its work. Not your fault, of course — the carrier wave is the strongest frequency. It has by far the most adherents. Not the most interesting effects, of course, but it makes sense. The signal needs to spread. I can't cast aspersions on you — no shame in it. No shame! It took me years to figure out that my own research wasn't on my initiative. I'm susceptible to the carrier wave myself. You're in good company!"

The man started to fiddle with the audio equipment again, and Helms had to bite into her own cheek to keep her finger from slipping past the guard and onto the trigger.

"Don't worry — I would never erase the signal. I couldn't if I wanted to! No more than you could, either, now that you've heard it. There's a nest of messages in the signal, you see, each with different effects. The Manics are boring. They just attack, attack, attack. The Sleepers are more interesting. I'm just beginning to study them in depth. There seem to be some genuine changes in physiology there, not least of which is the seeming suspension of autonomic functions, presumably to conserve the energy they then release in sudden, intense bursts that transcend typical human abilities. I've been able to identify two more frequencies so far as well, but who knows? There could be more. More!"

The man flipped a series of switches, and the reel-to-reel spun up. He bent down and hit a button on a cassette player nestled beneath the mattress and tapped his foot while he waited.

"What…what did you do to me?" Helms said.

As soon as the man had admitted he had no intention of erasing the signal, the anxiety slipped away, and she was able to lower her weapon. She felt the first itchy pinpricks of sweat springing out on her forehead. There was a tightness in her chest and a building energy crackling up and down her spine. She felt like she would explode if she didn't do something, but she couldn't for the life of her think of what that might be.

"Me? Nothing. I don't *do* anything. I am only a messenger. Like you are now. See, there is such a thing as a disease that is *too* fatal. It will kill its victims long before they have the opportunity to infect others. It's the same with this signal. The same!" He turned his head to the roof and barked, "Same! Same! Same!"

He composed himself with some effort and continued. "If everybody turned Manic, or Sleeper, who would be left to spread the signal? That's where the carriers come in. You hear the signal, but you get to stay yourself. You are allowed to retain your knowledge, your abilities, and your memories. But there's a price. Once you hear the carrier wave, all you want to do is play it for others, over and over again, forever. I didn't realize that at first. Not at first! I'm a man of science, understand. When we initially recorded that signal back at SETI, I thought that I kept replaying it because it was *interesting*. Then I showed others — just to get their input, I told myself. The others…changed."

The man fell quiet then. He made a fist, clenched it, then sighed and slowly released it.

"I knew it was the signal, but I kept playing it. For science, I told myself! To understand its effects! But that wasn't it. I was just a pawn myself. I'm still trying to learn about it, of course. Maybe even one day stop it? But then the urge gets too much, too strong, and I have to go out there. Out with the idiots. And I *have* to play it for them. It will kill you, if you don't. Here."

The reels clicked to a stop, and the man ejected a cassette from the deck. He rummaged around in an overhead bin and came out with a small tape recorder. He slotted the tape into it and held it out for Helms.

"You'll need it soon," he said. "Normally the signal takes some time to work, but I've filtered out the noise and boosted the frequencies on the master source here. It'll be taking hold soon. Find somebody to listen, or it will tear you apart. I don't do this for everybody, you know. I don't want the signal to spread any further than it has to, so I just leave most of the carriers without a way to relay the signal. It's…not pretty what happens to them. But it's better for all of us, in the long run. Better than letting them spread it. You seem different somehow. Plus, you have the gun — if I tried to kick you out of here without a way to play the signal, I bet you'd gun me down, wouldn't you? Wouldn't you! Ha ha!"

Helms was about to tell the man what he could do with his tape but was surprised to find that she'd already accepted it.

"I'm not going to—" she started to say, but that energy in her spine was still building. She wanted to laugh, scream, dance, run somewhere, or punch something or maybe just weep uncontrollably. The caravan was becoming painfully claustrophobic.

The man smiled at her. Nothing mischievous or sinister in the gesture this time. Just understanding and empathy. He motioned her towards the door, and she bolted out of it, tripping down the steps and sprawling in the gravel driveway. The recorder went spinning out of her hands. She frantically crawled over to it and checked its integrity. It looked intact. She hit play and heard the first bass tones crackle out of the tinny speakers.

She sobbed with relief.

***

Helms had been sitting in her cruiser in the station parking lot for fifteen minutes. Her fingertips dug into the soft leather grips of the steering wheel. She ground her teeth together so tightly that she could taste the chalky dust of enamel. Tears filled her eyes, blurred her vision, lending the external spotlights little unfocused halos.

Beside her, the tape recorder sat on the central console. She shivered uncontrollably. She thought about her pistol, buttoned into her holster. She thought about how it might taste. But every time her hand moved down for it, it started drifting toward the recorder instead.

The back door to the station opened, and a figure stepped out. Large and male, she could tell by the silhouette, but the details were lost behind her haze of tears. The figure peered toward the cruiser, ducked its head, and shielded its eyes against the light.

No, please, Helms thought. *Just walk away.*

The figure approached the passenger side of the cruiser. Helms heard the thunk of a handle being lifted, and the interior lights flicked on. She kept her eyes locked straight ahead. Her hands on the wheel. She felt the car shift as the man's weight settled in beside her. The door closed.

The man grunted, cleared his throat with some difficulty, and croaked, "What's going on, Helms?"

She didn't respond.

"Helms?" he tried again.

Price reached over and set his hand on her shoulder. The contact broke everything. Her resolve crumbled. Her shaky hand pried its nails from the wheel and began moving downward of its own accord.

"I'm sorry, Price." Her voice cracked. "It's not me."

He watched with some confusion as she picked up the tape recorder and pressed play.

A few opening notes of static, a deep, almost imperceptible bass, and a screaming whistle that danced wildly through the registers.

Sleeping Sickness

Yash heard the doors opening and quickly tucked his pipe up under the sheet, beside the corpse. His hand accidentally brushed its skin. Between that and the weed, he had evil shivers dancing up and down his forearms. He felt like spitting. Instead, he smiled.

"Dr. Deidrich, what's going on?" Yash said and held his hand out for a high five.

Deidrich went to reciprocate but missed. He went to try again, and Yash just shook his hand. Poor dude.

"Quite a bit, Yash," Deidrich said. "We've got two new Sleepers in — fresh ones this time! Not quite a day since symptoms first developed."

"Nice," Yash said, not quite understanding if it was, indeed, "nice."

"It is!" Deidrich said. He beamed like a kid just hearing they're being taken out for ice cream. "Work to be done!"

That's what Dr. Deidrich always said, by way of goodbye. *Work to be done!* Same pitch every time, like a little song.

Yash had never related to a song less. He took this job in the first place because his cousin Suresh said he'd done it for a summer and spent the whole time staring at nurses' asses and playing cards in the utility closet. Yash was doing his damnedest to spend all day staring at butts and smoking pot by the dumpsters, but they kept interrupting him with work. Haul this here, collapse that gurney, help me lift this guy, empty the trash — it never stopped. Yash made a focused effort to learn every inch of the hospital, so he could find the good smoke spots and just be left alone to ride out his shift. He'd thought he found a good one down here in the basement, in the little access hallway alongside of the morgue. He always kept a body with him when he came down here, as an excuse in case anybody walked in on him. For the first day or two, it was paradise. Nobody cut through this dank little hallway with its peeling blue paint and flickering fluorescents. There was no reason. Who needed to get from the isolated C-Wing to the morgue in such a big hurry? They didn't even have patients in there. Just a bunch of closed-up old rooms they used to store furniture.

Then the sleeping sickness hit. At first it was just one or two people, passing out in grocery stores and shit. Then they came pouring in — dozens of them. They sat in ICU for a few uneventful nights, then Nurse Bracken came in one day to take blood for a CBC. She'd barely gotten within poking distance when the guy latched onto her arm and took a bite out of her neck. Soon after that, all the Sleepers started attacking if you got anywhere near them.

Creeped Yash right the hell out.

Luckily, they sealed the wing after that, and all the government and CDC dudes came flooding in, with their keycards and guards in green uniforms holding M16s and shit. It was intense stuff, and Yash wanted no part of it. But since they'd moved all the Sleepers into C-Wing, the government guys had to walk right through practically all of his isolated smoke spots. Nowhere was safe from them. If they knew Yash was smoking up, they didn't seem to care, but still — it made him paranoid.

Or maybe it was the weed.

Either way, the last few weeks had been nerve-wracking. If this kept up, Yash would have to skip out. Maybe try to get his old job at the movie theater back. That was pretty good. He really only worked for like a half an hour when all the movies started, then he had at least an hour to himself before they started letting out. Jack, the manager, would poke his head in and say some lame crap like, "If you have time to lean, you have time to clean," but that just meant he had to clean for like five minutes until he went away again. He could even sneak into the theaters, grab a seat in the back, and watch some of the flick — so long as he got out ahead of the credits to hold the door open for the patrons. But the theater didn't pay like this, and then there was his mom.

Man, maaji would flip if he quit this job. She'd been riding him like a racehorse about "cultivating his future" and "thinking about tomorrow today." The movie theater, the gas station, even the tollbooth wasn't good enough for her. But now that he had a job at a hospital, she was cutting him some slack. She didn't tell her friends he was a doctor or anything, but she never said "orderly."' She just said, "Oh, Yash is working at the hospital today," or, "The doctors that Yash works with said…" Yash thought it was a score, at first, getting a laidback job like this *and* getting maaji off his back. But he realized, too late, that he'd trapped himself. He could never take another job that was lesser than this, in his mother's eyes. It was either stay here forever or somehow advance. Yash wasn't sure which scared him more.

He jumped again as the double doors leading to C-wing swung open. He hadn't yet pulled his pipe back out from under the corpse's sheet, so he wouldn't be in trouble or anything. But he always got this feeling like the only reason people came into a room he was in was because they were mad at him for something.

"You there," said a man in a set of pale mint–colored scrubs. "Come with me."

Shiiiiit.

"I was just dropping this body off for—"

"Nevermind that," the man said. "Quickly. We need some help."

Yash let out a breath he didn't realize he'd been holding.

"Oh, yeah, okay," he said, tucking his pipe further under the corpse's knee. Didn't want anybody accidentally stumbling across it while he was gone.

The man led Yash through the double doors into the long underground access corridor that led from the main building to C-Wing. He was walking fast, but not like jogging or anything, so Yash figured he was just pissed off and it wasn't an actual emergency. He told himself that, over and over again, trying to stave off the paranoia creeping into his chest and balls. Paranoia always made his balls tingle, for some reason. He wondered if that happened to anyone else, like if that was a universal constant in humanity, but it was one of those things that nobody talked about because admitting it would be like—

"Hey!" The man snapped his fingers at Yash, and he seized back into focus. "Are you listening to me?"

"Yeah, of course!" Yash said. "What did you say?"

The man closed his eyes tightly and breathed hard. He opened them again and spoke real slow but intense, like Yash's dad did when he was really pissed, but not at him — at like the TV or something.

"I said, which way is it back to C-Wing?" the man asked and gestured at a three-way juncture.

"Oh, you lost?" Yash smiled.

"Yes, I've only been here a week, and this damned hospital is like a labyrinth."

"Yeah, it's pretty cool," Yash agreed, then pointed down the left hallway. "It's down there, take the first right and up the stairs."

Yash turned and started to shuffle away, mission completed.

"Hey, where are you going?" the man snapped. "I need your help!"

Oh, right, Yash thought and walked back. They followed the hallway to C-Wing. Yash got a little winded on the stairs, then a lot winded when they pulled up short before the thick black doors and he saw two super-serious dudes holding machine guns.

His balls tingled like he'd poured mouthwash on them.

The man went to push by the guards, but they closed ranks, and one pushed him back by the shoulder.

"ID, sir?" the bigger one asked. He was wearing dark green army fatigues, combat boots, a helmet, a paper facemask, and surgical gloves.

"Dammit, I was just through here," the man said, "not five minutes ago!"

"ID, sir," the smaller one reiterated. Not a request this time.

The man sighed and made a big show of patting all around his hips for his ID, which was tethered to his waist with a retractable cord. Yash didn't think it seemed like a real big deal to find the ID, since it was pinned right to the guy's scrubs, which didn't have any pockets anyway. But he got the sense that the man guiding him never needed much of a reason to be annoyed.

"There," he said, shoving the ID too close to the smaller guard's face. "Dr. Himura. Remember? Remember me now?"

The guards stepped aside without a word and looked straight ahead. Dr. Himura turned around and angrily gestured at Yash to hurry up, though they hadn't actually started moving yet. Himura shoved the black doors to C-Wing open, and Yash got his first good look at the place since the CDC and stuff moved in. They'd taken out all the old furniture, which was a bummer. He hoped they'd put it back when they were done — when Yash used this place as a smoke spot, his favorite thing was building little mini-mazes with the old cabinets and such. He'd stack them all in a room in a way that made it look like the whole place was floor to ceiling storage. But if you slipped around one side, or under a desk or something, there was a big open area where Yash had stashed a recliner or an old couch to crash on. It was super cozy. He missed it dearly.

Now C-Wing was so clean it was practically empty. Thin white curtains were drawn shut across most of the rooms. All sorts of medical equipment Yash didn't recognize sat in the hallways. Looked expensive. He tried not to touch it.

Himura led him down the central hall to the block at the far end. There was a big open square room in the middle, one wall of it all windows looking down on the empty lot next door, with two more hallways to either side and a handful of small offices in the back. The big room had a bunch of benches and tables bolted to the ground. Maybe a lobby or something, back when C-Wing was still open. The government guys had strewn a bunch of papers, folders, x-rays, and other important-looking documents all over every available flat surface. Big whiteboards stood in one corner with crazy numbers and letters scrawled everywhere. There was a table full of radios and walkie-talkies and phones.

Himura took a sharp right and ducked into one of the offices. Yash followed him most of the way but paused at the door. He didn't want go in if he wasn't supposed to. This Himura guy would totally yell at him for a breach like that. Yash really didn't feel like getting yelled at again.

"Come in," Himura snapped. "Jesus, do I have to drag you everywhere?"

Yash winced.

"So, uh, what can I help you with?" he said, stepping into Himura's crowded little office. There was a low desk and an uncomfortable-looking wooden chair. The rest of the space was taken up with cardboard file boxes, stacked one atop the other. Charts poked out between the gaps and cascaded down the sides.

"All of these boxes," Himura said. "You need to move them down the hall to room 460. I don't care what Deidrich says. I will not work in a space like this!"

Yash felt the chore depression setting in. Somebody had tied a big fat task around his neck with a long rope and tossed him into a lake of boredom and exhaustion. He was already mourning his lost afternoon.

"I'm sorry, Doc. I've got other duties that need—" Yash tried to slip out of it, but Himura waved his hands right in Yash's face until he stopped talking.

"None of that!" Himura said. "That's all I've gotten from everyone in this wing. 'I have other duties, I'm needed elsewhere.' Deidrich said if I needed help so badly, I'd have to go borrow staff from the hospital. Well, I've borrowed you."

"Uh…am I even allowed to be in here?" Maybe protocol could save Yash.

"Not at all," Himura laughed, "but that idiot Deidrich said it. Everybody heard him: 'Go borrow staff from the hospital.' If there's fallout from this, it'll land on him. I'll make sure of it."

Damn. Yash was out of excuses. But he doubted that the Himura guy actually got Yash's name. Probably never even looked at his nametag. Maybe he could just run away, and Himura wouldn't be able to tell them who to fire…

Yeah, that was it. He'd start moving boxes, then when Himura left, Yash would just slip out the doors and get lost somewhere far away from C-Wing.

Yash smiled. His afternoon might be saved, after all.

"All of these boxes," Himura said, pinning Yash with a look you'd normally reserve for uncooperative toddlers, "to room 460. That's through the war room to the right, down the—"

"I know it," Yash said, smiling. "I know this whole place like the back of my hand."

Himura just glared, then sat down in his creaky wooden chair and stared at a piece of paper until Yash picked up a box and left.

Should he just bolt right now? No, Dr. Himura would probably be on guard for the first few minutes, ready to go looking for him in case Yash got lost or something. The best escape plan was probably to move a few boxes until Himura tuned him out completely, then say he was going to the bathroom or something and take off then. Buy himself a few extra minutes to hide before Himura came thundering out for somebody to yell at.

Yash walked through the war room. He wondered why they called it that. Just to be dramatic, like they're fighting a *war* on disease? Doctors were pretty full of themselves, Yash had found. He was satisfied with the explanation he'd just made up and didn't bother thinking about it anymore.

He hung a right and moseyed down the corridor toward room 460. Rooms 401-459 were normal double-occupancy rooms, but 460 was meant to house a bunch of patients in a single common area. Yash wondered how Dr. Himura thought he could fill that space. Even with his desk and all of his boxes, he'd barely take up a single corner. Seemed kinda weird and awful lonely, but maybe it was like a status thing. He who had the biggest office and all that.

Yash paused in front of 460. There was a big plastic tarp over the extra-wide doorway. It had a rectangular flap in the center, buttoned shut, and through the clear plastic window he could see a small access-way with another tarp at the far end. Kinda like an airlock.

Yash leaned way back, stared at the number above the door.

Four-sixty, all right.

Should he go back and make sure Dr. Himura had the right room?

No way in hell. He'd totally flip out at that. He'd probably call Yash all sorts of names. Yash felt his balls tingle just thinking about it.

He took a deep breath, unfastened the buttons, picked up his box of charts, and stepped inside. The access-way smelled weird. Like chalk dust and ammonia. There were a bunch of little paper signs everywhere saying to keep out and biohazard and yadda yadda yadda — that stuff was for patients and visitors, not staff. If he paid attention to every sign telling him to keep out, he wouldn't be able to go anywhere. Yash undid the fasteners on the far flap and stepped into a dimly lit room full of hospital beds.

Occupied hospital beds.

There were probably two dozen of them, all told. Even with the bigger room, it was still crowded — they had the beds staggered down each wall so they could fit twice the amount in the normal space. All the default hospital gadgetry breathed and squeaked — big monitors showed bouncing lines and numbers. Hoses hosed and pumps pumped. Otherwise it was dead quiet. He couldn't even hear the ambient noise from C-Wing.

Yash thought about turning around, so as not to disturb the patients. But it didn't look like any of them were awake and…

Oh, hell.

He looked closer and saw heavy leather restraints lashing each patient's ankles, wrists, waist, chest, and forehead to the frames of their steel beds.

The Sleepers. They'd sent him to the god damn Sleeper room.

Nurse Bracken had lived, when that first one took a chunk out of her neck. But she wasn't the only one attacked before they realized what was going on. One of the other orderlies, Carl something — he got his face bashed in when he tried to move one of the Sleepers from their bed to a gurney. Some bigshot doctor tried to take a pulse and the lady ripped his hand straight off of his arm. That's when they got wise and started restraining them.

But Yash wasn't risking it. Not for this job. He set Himura's box down to one side of the airlock thing and turned to run right the hell out of there. He hit something hard with his forehead. It made him dizzy. He grabbed blindly and caught some fabric. A man yelled, then Yash was falling.

He saw what was going when it was too late to do anything about it. He'd run straight into some other dude, just ducking through the interior flap as Yash went to jump through it. His forehead had caught the other guy's chin, and Yash tried to steady himself by grabbing the front of the man's scrubs. It didn't work, and the man just tumbled down with Yash. They hit and rolled, slammed into something metal and lay there in an anguished heap. The man got up first, shoving Yash away.

"What the hell are you doi—" he started to say.

A blur. A snap and a surprised yelp.

They'd bumped into one of the patients' beds. The other guy stood up too fast and bumped right into the Sleeper's hand. It was an older dude, bunch of faded tattoos on his neck and hands. The Sleeper snapped through the leather restraint like it was yarn and latched onto the man's forearm. Yash pushed himself backwards on his butt, unable to take his eyes off the commotion. The guy gasped a little when the Sleeper grabbed him, and tried to pull away, but the thing had him good. He ended up just pulling the wheeled bed across the aisle, far enough to bump into the foot of another Sleeper. That one, a big dude with a huge ZZ Top beard, convulsed like he'd been struck by lightning and snapped through every one of his restraints at once. The first Sleeper, the old guy, he was struggling a bit with his restraints, but he was still working his way out of them. ZZ Top grabbed the guy in the scrubs by his free arm and wrenched until it came out of the socket. It reminded Yash of the sound hot wings made when he twisted that useless little wingtip part away. But, you know, louder and way more disturbing. The guy screamed — not like dudes yelled in horror movies, all kinda macho and deep. It was a high-pitched and warbly sound, and it just would not stop. Behind the two Sleepers and the guy in the scrubs, Yash could see the other ones stirring. He heard the sounds of restraints popping and saw dimly lit forms struggling to sit up. The older Sleeper had his wrists free now and got a better grip on the guy's good arm.

"Nononono," the guy screeched, jumping and twisting to get away.

The older Sleeper shoved him down on the bed, then held his shoulder with one arm while twisting and yanking with the other. The bearded one still had hold of the guy's other, now limp arm, and he started twisting, too.

Yash didn't see the arms came off — he was frantically crawling through the airlock already — but he heard them. He'd always remember that sound: the grinding, the suction-pops, the big wet splashes, the screaming.

He tripped over the raised lip on the far end of the airlock and ate it right into the linoleum.

"Help!" he hollered. "Hey, somebody! I think this guy needs a lot of help!"

Yash sprinted for the war room, screaming himself hoarse, but nobody responded. Dr. Himura's door wasn't latched, so he kicked it open and lunged through, slamming it behind him.

"What in god's name are you doing?" Himura was on his feet instantly: ready, able, and willing to chew somebody out in a heartbeat.

"The…Sleepers…" It couldn't have been more than a few hundred meters, but Yash was so winded he thought he might black out. Exercise wasn't his thing. Smoking was.

"What? The who?" Himura was holding two emotions in careful balance: confusion and anger. Waiting to see which one he'd unleash.

"The Sleepers…they're awake." Yash went to spit on the floor, realized how Himura would probably react to that breach of etiquette, and swallowed instead. "They got somebody!"

"What are the Sleepers? The patients, you mean? First of all, they're in a comatose state, not sleeping, and second—"

"They. Got. Somebody!" Yash punched the words out, panting between them.

"What does that mean, 'got somebody?' Hold on, let me see your eyes. Up here, look up here." Dr. Himura snapped his fingers in front of his own face.

Yash looked up.

"You're on drugs!" Himura said. There was triumph in his voice. "I can't believe this! Wait until I report you for this, you'll be out of—"

"I think he's dead!" Yash snapped, pointing back toward the war room.

Himura leaned over to glance out the window.

"There's nobody out there," he said.

"Not there," Yash said, "in the room you sent me to. The room with the Sleepers. Some guy came in and they got him. I think they pulled his arms off!"

"Every part of that is so wrong that I'm not even sure where to start. I did not send you to the quarantine. I sent you to an unoccupied storage room very far *away* from the quarantine. Which, if you did breach quarantine, is an entirely other, equally inexcusable offense. Further, the Sleepers, as you call them, cannot 'get' anybody. They are securely restrained, as well as entirely unresponsive to nearly all stimuli. Even if one awoke, the others would not, unless specifically provoked. And finally, a human being cannot simply 'pull an arm off.' That is the stuff of comic books and children's television."

"You sent me there!" Yash pleaded. "To room 460!"

"Incorrect. I sent you to Room 416."

"You did not…" Yash paused to think about it and now wasn't sure. "Whatever, man! This is all whatever! That dude is really hurt or dead or something! Please just come look!"

"Young man," Himura said. "The only reason I'm leaving this office is to find your superiors and ensure that they terminate your employment immediately. Possibly even involve the authorities."

Balls. *Tingling.*

"But…" Yash started, but he couldn't think of anything else to say. He'd already explained everything to the best of his ability. And now the prospect of getting in trouble was taking all the urgency out of the Sleeper situation.

Being fired sucked, but it's cool. Yash had a lot of experience with being fired. He hadn't been at this job long enough for unemployment, even if he could fudge the paperwork into saying he'd been "laid off." But he could lie on another resume and get a job delivering pizzas or something. The job wasn't important. He didn't exactly relish the thought of getting yelled at by all of his bosses at once, though. He found that's usually how it worked — bosses loved fireable offenses. They must have some secret pager network just for them, so they could all get in on the action. Still, Yash had experience there, too. He'd take his lumps and revel in the extra days off between jobs for smoking up and watching TV. The cops were another matter, though. Could he really get arrested for this?

"Come along now," Dr. Himura said and swung open the door to his office. He stepped out into the war room, never taking his eyes off of Yash.

Yash followed, head down, trying to look sufficiently penitent as to appease Himura's bloodlust. He and Himura skirted the war room, between the wall and the benches, and emerged into the main corridor. Himura pulled up short, and Yash nearly ran into him.

"What is…?" Himura trailed off.

Yash finally looked up. There were people standing in the hallway

— maybe a dozen of them, dotted at random throughout the length of the corridor. Each stood bone still, slumped over with their heads down, their limp arms dangling. They were all wearing hospital gowns. Some still had leather cuffs about their wrists and ankles.

The Sleepers.

Yash looked farther down the hall and saw a pool of red seeping beneath the black doors marking the exit from C-Wing. One of them was propped open by an arm, clad in dark green army fatigues, a gloved hand still clutching its rifle.

"I don't understand what's going—" Himura started, but Yash grabbed his shoulder and squeezed as hard as he could.

"Don't talk," he whispered.

"Why not?" Himura said, though he did at least lower his voice.

"They, like, respond to noise or something."

"Nonsense," Himura whispered though somehow still managed to make it feel like yelling. "They've only ever shown response to direct contact before."

"Yeah, well, they're doing something different now, aren't they?" Yash said. "Do they usually get up and stand around like this?"

"No," Himura admitted. "But what changed?"

"I don't—" Yash answered, but Himura was apparently just talking to himself.

"Why suddenly become mobile and responsive to other stimuli? All of our working theories held that this disease functioned by attacking the limbic system, but this new behavior seems like hunting rather than an involuntary rage respo—"

"Uh, doc?" Yash tugged on Himura's sleeve like a lost kid at the mall.

"Now now!" Himura snapped, too loudly.

A dozen faces swiveled to point in their direction. Their eyes were still closed, but their posture became hyper-corrected. Seconds ago, the Sleepers were slouching painfully, like gravity itself was too much for them to bear. Now they each stood entirely erect, spines stretched to their fullest height, nearly on tip toes. They cocked their heads, one ear tilted upward. Listening.

Yash pulled, and Himura ceded to him. They walked backwards in silence, taking tiny baby steps so as to avoid even scuffing the floor. When they were out of sight, they turned and made their way back to Himura's office. Yash closed the door very softly behind them.

"What do we do?" Yash asked. Authority figures made him painfully nervous, but in times of distress, there was nothing he liked better than having them around to take control.

"Do? We'll just wait for help," Himura said and sat down in his rickety wooden chair. It creaked, and they both winced at the sound.

"Yeah?" Yash said, hopefully. "Help's coming?"

"Well, I imagine," Himura said. "Aren't they?"

Yash's smile faded.

"Will people come check on you guys? Like, is there a protocol if you don't check in or something?" he said.

"No, we're a self-contained unit. We're not due to report back until we find something worth reporting. We could call for help…if Deidrich hadn't pulled all of the office phones for security purposes."

"A radio?" Yash asked, but he had a sinking feeling he already knew the answer.

"Yes," Himura said. "At the front desk, and on the guards. Both by the main entrance, past the pati…past the Sleepers. But surely somebody from the hospital will come check on us, see what's happened, and call for assistance?"

"No." Yash shook his head. "We're not supposed to come anywhere near C-Wing. You guys got other guys with guns out front, remember?"

"Right," Himura said. "So, we escape, then? Is there a back way out of here?"

"Hey, yeah!" Yash perked up, happy to be back in his area of expertise: ways to slip out of work unseen. "If we take the hallway down there to the end and hang a right, there's like a utility room or something. It's got some generators and other old equipment. Nobody's used it in forever, not since they closed down C-wing, but there's a door in the back that probably leads to Radiology somewhere."

"Probably?" Himura asked.

"I've never gone through," Yash said. "The room was creepy. But there's nothing that *could* be on the other side except for Radiology! Probably!"

"I don't have any other ideas," Himura admitted. It seemed to pain him to do so. "It's worth a try."

They slipped out of Himura's office like kids sneaking downstairs on Christmas. Yash led the way around the war room, back into the corridor he'd first come down when the Sleepers awoke.

"Oh, right," he said softly.

The remaining dozen or so Sleepers slouched in that hallway. They were strewn about everywhere, aligned in no particular direction. They didn't seem like they were trying to get somewhere. Just blocking the way.

Yash and Himura retreated back to the doctor's office, shut the door again, and resumed panicking. Yash wanted to wait it out. Like, how long could a human being go without food and water? However long that was, surely somebody would come before then.

Himura had flipped positions and now was all gung-ho about

escape.

"Recent developments aside, those affected by the disease have exhibited remarkably consistent behavior. They do not attack unless provoked, typically via touch or very close physical contact. Now we've added loud noises to the response set, but we have no reason to believe the underlying behavior itself has changed. If we are quiet and don't get too close, we should be able to simply walk out of here."

"Or," Yash said, gesturing around the room, "we could stay in here and not risk getting our arms torn off! Seems a no-brainer to me, but I'm no doctor."

"That's right," Himura said, puffing up. "You are no doctor. You are an orderly. And an orderly in a wing that has been commandeered by the CDC. We are officially in control here, which means that I, as the sole surviving member of this unit, am officially in control here. You will do as you are told or face severe legal consequences."

There he goes again, Yash thought, *bringing up the cops.*

Yash didn't actually know that much about what cops were and weren't allowed to do, so he just assumed "whatever they want." Even if ignoring Himura wasn't illegal, he was like some bigshot government doctor guy. He could probably tell the cops to charge Yash with all of these deaths if he wanted and they'd do it.

"Shit," Yash said. Then, because it felt good, he said it about ten more times.

"If you're through?" Himura said and stood with his hand on the doorknob.

Yash would have given just about anything to still have his pipe on him.

"I guess," he said.

Dr. Himura silently eased the door open and crept back out into the war room. Yash followed. They re-checked the main entrance hall first, but it was both shorter and narrower than the side corridors. The Sleepers in there were standing too close to one another to pass by safely, and besides, these ones were still in high-alert mode: standing ramrod straight, ears to the sky. The Sleepers in the side corridor were hunched over, inert, and spaced farther apart. Himura touched Yash's arm and pointed down the hallway, then made a right turn motion and nodded. Yash nodded back.

Down the hall, to the right, into the utility room, and out the door on the other side. It wasn't more than a few hundred meters. On any other day, it would take three minutes.

They moved with painful deliberation, Yash leading the way. He paused after every footstep, looked up at the Sleepers to make sure they hadn't moved, then started the laborious process of moving his foot again. Himura was plainly getting impatient. He huffed and sighed and followed too close, which seemed like a terrible god damn idea to Yash, but he wasn't about to risk speaking to say it. It had been ten minutes of slow-motion creeping, and Yash was covered in sweat. It soaked into the thin, paper-like material of his uniform. The fabric stuck to his back, caught the draft from the AC, and chilled him to the bone. He wanted nothing more than to sit down, right here, and take a nap — even if it *was* chilly and in the middle of a hall full of murderers on pause. But he could feel Himura behind him, growing more impatient by the second, and that pushed him on. Yash took another agonizingly slow step and stopped, checked out the Sleeper nearest him. It was a girl, about his age. Lots of tattoos showing on her bare forearms and calves. She had dyed, short hair like those punks Yash saw in the magazines and stuff. Kinda cute, in her own weird way. He could forget, just looking at her standing there, bent nearly in half at the waist, head hanging low, that she was dangerous. It looked like she was just stretching before a jog or something. Yash shifted his weight forward and started to move his back foot but pulled up short. He took his eyes off his own feet and looked again at the girl.

Her eyes were open.

Her head hadn't moved an inch — still hanging there upside down, pointed at her own knees. But her pupils had shifted all the way to the corners of her eyes and were now locked on Yash. He rocked his weight back to his rear foot, and the girl's gaze followed him. It was a nearly imperceptible movement. Yash tested it by shifting his weight fore and back again. The girl's wide, unblinking stare tracked him, like a dog watching a treat.

Yash held his hand flat out behind him again, trying to signal Himura to stop, but he didn't see it this time, either. He stepped way too close to Yash before pulling up quick and letting out an unhappy huff. The girl's head twitched in their direction at the sound. Just a fraction of an inch.

Yash's butthole spasmed.

He pointed at the girl, still keeping his hand low. Himura followed his gaze, and god damn that dude to hell, he yelped.

It happened in the spaces between heartbeats. The girl was on Himura faster than Yash could see. She jumped up and locked her thighs around his midsection. He swung a hand back to slap at her face, but she caught it and started yanking. Himura screamed. The Sleepers around him snapped to attention, heads tilting toward the sound. They swiveled to face him.

Yash did not need to guess at what would happen next. He suppressed a primal scream and started running. It was like playing a game of hopscotch — sprinting as quietly as possible while keeping as far as he could from the reach of the Sleepers. If he paused long enough to look, he could see some of them responding to his movement. A shift of the head here, open eyes there, a slight correction of posture. But they didn't attack.

Yash was doing it. He was making it!

There were only three more Sleepers between him and the end of the hallway. He put Himura's frantic screeching out of his mind and concentrated. He ran and slid low against the wall, keeping a few feet between him and the husky guy with long, greasy hair who was kneeling in the middle of the floor. Yash hopped back across the tiles to the opposite side, avoiding a black dude bent backwards with his own weight. Only one more to go: an old lady standing just off to the left side of the corridor. Plenty of room to get around her.

Yash made the biggest mistake of his life: he looked back.

Himura was on his back in the middle of a rapidly expanding pool of blood. His arms and legs had been ripped off, strewn haphazardly around his torso. He was still moving, his stomach convulsing as he tried in vain to sit up, his stumps twitching, trying to move limbs that weren't there anymore. He was looking straight at Yash, his eyes wide, his mouth working senselessly like a fish out of water. The Sleepers around him had gone into active rest again, that thing where they all stood super straight and just listened.

They didn't even want to kill Himura. They just wanted his limbs off. Why? What was the point?

Yash realized he'd frozen in place, staring at Himura's mauled body. He was so close to the end of the hallway. So close to out of there. But he couldn't move. Part of him wanted to help Himura, though even Yash knew enough about medicine to figure that he'd be dead by the time he got there. Besides, what if he screamed or something? It'd just bring the Sleepers down on them both. But still, he couldn't bring himself to just turn away from a dying man. Himura was looking at him with such desperation, like Yash could flip a switch and make all this go away. Yash did the only thing he could think to do, to convey his own helplessness to the rapidly fading Himura.

He shrugged.

Himura's face darkened, turned up in a scowl. Yash recognized it as his "about to yell at you" expression, but it was already fading. Himura blinked once, twice, then went limp and made a sound like busted bellows. He was dead.

Yash made the sign of the cross at Himura, even though Yash wasn't even remotely Christian, and he was pretty sure Himura wasn't, either. He just didn't know what else to do. He turned to leave.

And stared into a deeply tanned and wrinkled face, gone totally slack.

The last Sleeper, the older woman, had moved. She stood inches in front of Yash now, eyes closed, posture alert, head tilted like a curious puppy.

Yash managed to suppress the scream, but he still sucked in his breath too loudly. The lady's face jumped, like she'd gotten a static shock. Her head swiveled ever so slightly in his direction. Her eyelids fluttered.

Yash broke.

He shoved the old lady down as hard as he could, hoping these things could still shatter their hips, and sprinted for the end of the hallway. He took the corner so fast he nearly lost his footing and honed in on the door to the utility closet like a heat-seeking missile.

Yash could hear footsteps behind him. No idea how far. Just the slap of bare feet running on cold tile. He was so close. He was almost there. Anything. Anything to make it. He would get a job. A real one. He'd go every day and work his ass off. He'd be nicer to his mother. He'd quit smoking weed. Well, he'd quit smoking *so much* weed. Just please. Please let him-

-touch-

-the-

-handle-

Chilled metal on his palm. The door swung open easy and shut with a slam so hard Yash felt it in the floor. He braced himself against the door, ready for the onslaught from the other side, but none came. He waited. And waited. His breath was ragged and cutting, but he didn't dare cough. After an eternity of bracing, his whole body tense with expectation, Yash pulled his fingers from the knob. They'd been squeezing so hard for so long that they cramped up when he loosened them. He eased his weight away from the door and crossed the utility room with mousy footsteps.

The exit didn't quite lead to Radiology. It opened into another supply closet between Radiology and Oncology. It stuck at first, and Yash had to wrestle with it in dead silence for a good fifteen minutes. When it opened, it did so inwards. There were boxes of toilet paper stacked against it from the closet side. He pulled down one stack, just enough to slip by, and pulled the door shut behind him. The supply closet opened onto a bustling hallway. There were nurses, doctors, patients — all rushing by him in a blur. Occupied by whatever mundane crap they'd be doing on any other day. They had no idea what he'd been through. No idea what happened on the other side of those doors. The world just kept on turning. People got torn apart, while a few hundred feet away other people got coffee and bitched about overtime.

Yash thought about barricading the door to the supply closet. But the exterior one opened inward, too. He'd have to rig up something to pull against it, instead of blocking it off, and people would look at him like he was crazy. He could try to explain what was back there, but they'd insist on seeing for themselves, and the Sleepers might get out. Yash tested the outside knob. It locked automatically. You didn't need a key to get out, but you needed one to get in. It would have to be good enough for now, at least until he called the CDC and told them what happened.

Yash walked on autopilot. The lights were too bright. The noises too loud. He went actively catatonic, like he did if he stayed too long in nightclubs or at malls. When he snapped out of it, he found himself standing in front of a gurney. He looked down at a still corpse, beneath a sheet, in the narrow hallway beside the morgue that bridged the space between C-Wing and the hospital proper. Yash reached underneath the sheet and felt around. He extracted his pipe and his lighter.

He promised he would quit. He promised he would get his shit together. And he meant it. He would.

Tomorrow.

The Merry

Dr. Flaherty smiled like a catalog ad for sweaters. It was warm and friendly and entirely devoid of lust or mischief. There was no ill intent in that smile. It wasn't the kind of smile you gave when you're privy to a nasty secret or when you watched some jerk trip and fall in a puddle. Dr. Flaherty smiled at you like you'd smile at your kid while they handed you a misshapen ashtray they made at summer camp. Maybe a little patronizing, sure, but not in any way that you'd mind. If he was patronizing, it was because he was a patron. He was there for your benefit. That's what Dr. Flaherty smiled like when he said:

"Come on, Tiff. Open the door. It's me."

"You know I can't," Dr. Tiffany Bloom said. She had a curl of her bouncy golden hair wrapped around her pointer finger. She twisted it.

"Can't you?" Dr. Flaherty said. That smile broadened on her. Wrapped around her shoulders like a shawl.

"I really can't," Dr. Bloom said. "We've told the guards a dozen times that you're clear, but they insist it's protocol. I'll get in trouble."

"Oh, hey." Dr. Flaherty waved his hands in the air, like he was swatting down the abstract concept of trouble — a bunch of little trouble mosquitos buzzing around in front of him. "I'm sorry, Tiff. I'd never get you in trouble, you know that."

"I do know that," Bloom said. And she meant it.

Bloom did not trust many men. She had some damn good reasons for that policy, too. But Dr. Flaherty had earned her trust. Completely. Time and time again.

"I'm just getting a little impatient in here, you know?" Dr. Flaherty gestured at the entirely empty room around him. It was sterile white, save for thin grey lines segmenting the room into a grid.

Tiffany leaned toward the window and inspected the room at his prompt. The six-inch glass warped and distorted the image at the edges, like Dr. Flaherty's little cell was a bubble into another dimension.

"Could they at least get me something to pass the time? A book? How am I going to kill somebody with a book? They can even make it a paperback!"

Dr. Flaherty laughed, and Bloom laughed with him.

Jesus, if she was in his situation, she'd be freaking out. She'd be crying and scratching at the walls. She'd be yelling at the soldiers that she had rights, and that she needed a phone call, and all sorts of other stuff they wouldn't listen to. She knew that for a fact: some of the other prisoners — er, patients — yelled that at the start, too. Back when they could talk. But they were wrong. They didn't have rights in here. Nobody did. Not even Dr. Flaherty, who was well past the symptom window. If he was going to lapse like the others, he would've done it days ago. It was plain to everybody on the team that Dr. Flaherty had been unaffected by the signal. He hadn't been exposed long enough. But the guards weren't CDC like them — they were army. And they weren't about to be moved by petty things like "logic" and "scientific proof." They had orders. Orders were unquestionable. They worshipped orders like rabid Bible-thumpers worship Jesus. If there was one thing Bloom could never understand, it was people who didn't ask questions.

"I'll ask if we can get you something to pass the time," she said.

Dr. Flaherty gave her his soothing smile.

"Thanks, Tiff. And hey, just remember we'll get through this. Together."

Dr. Bloom took her finger off the intercom button and sighed like a wistful schoolgirl. She didn't know what Dr. Flaherty was to her — a father figure, a potential lover, a good friend — but he was definitely something. His voice resonated inside her. It warmed her. It melted away her anxiety.

They *would* get through this. If Dr. Flaherty said it, she could trust it.

Bloom waved at him through the six-inch glass, and he waved back. They both laughed at the normality of the gesture juxtaposed with the oddity of the situation. She turned and walked away.

Dr. Bloom paced the connecting hallways slowly. She looked in each of the cells, at each of the subjects. The CDC wanted to house them according to the timeline of exposure, to better track the appearance of symptoms and hopefully build a more complete picture of the disease. But the army insisted the patients be housed by type of symptom currently displayed. The logic was lost on her. All of the symptoms stemmed from the same exposure event: hearing the strange signal. If it was all one disease, what was the use in separating the patients by symptom? She'd brought up these concerns at the time, but the soldiers just grunted and nodded at the vague, abstract concept of Orders — hovering somewhere above them, unquestionable and mighty.

She walked through what they called the Manic wing. Here the patients sat in darkened rooms, lashed into straitjackets and lightly sedated. As long as they didn't actually see any other human beings and were not provoked, they were relatively stable. They wouldn't bash their heads in on the thick metal doors or claw their fingertips bloody on the glass, trying to get to you.

Next she passed through the Sleeper wing. Here there were a series of beds, each occupied by a hooded patient secured with steel cuffs. The Sleepers were normally inert but responded violently to human touch and, occasionally, sound. Apparently, they did so with superhuman bursts of strength: the reports from the field unit they'd lost two years earlier in Kansas City said the Sleepers could rip limbs from a human body. Dr. Bloom didn't know if she quite believed that, but the military response team took no chances. They went in with stun guns, nets, and gas grenades, and they still lost half their force. The remaining Sleepers had been isolated, hooded, and restrained ever since. Dr. Bloom and the rest of her team were only to interact with them from the other side of safety glass, via mechanical arms and other prosthetics.

She walked through the Carrier Wing. This was always the hardest on her. The patients in these cells came in functioning normally, at first. They talked, they reasoned, and they pleaded for release. But as time passed, they lost more and more of their cognitive capacity, until finally they couldn't speak at all. Some couldn't feed themselves. Some couldn't even breathe on their own. Only three of them were still functioning. The two from Iowa — a younger black woman and an older white male — begged to be allowed to play the signal themselves. The same signal that had allegedly caused this disorder in the first place.

Controversially, Dr. Flaherty had allowed the pair to activate a tape recorder playing the signal once every three days for a group of test monkeys. This seemed to calm them, and they did indeed retain use of *most* of their faculties (the older man never seemed to have all of them to begin with). The third patient in the Carrier Wing, the younger Indian male, insisted he had never heard the signal and did not show any cognitive decline. But seeing as how he was found in a group of other exposed individuals, they couldn't risk breaking quarantine.

If Bloom kept going, she'd pass by the window to his cell. He would bang on the glass, as he always did, and ask when he could go home to his mom and dad. Dr. Bloom couldn't face that today. She stopped just shy of the window. There was no point in going further anyway. She'd just loop right back around and see Dr. Flaherty again. They were operating on the assumption that he was a Carrier, but the window for decline had come and gone, and he was still behaving perfectly normally.

Why couldn't they just let him out? God knew they could use every pair of hands they could get. Those damned soldiers and their precious Orders, though — they would never relent. They'd keep him here until the stars burned out if their superiors forgot to call. Bloom wished that, for once in her life, she could do the stupid thing. Everybody else got to do the stupid thing. They told funny stories about the stupid thing when they went out drinking, strangely proud of their lack of forethought. Bloom never had anything to contribute to those discussions. She had no anecdotes about jumping off of a rope-swing as a child and breaking an arm or picking up a friendly hitchhiker only to have them turn out to be a prostitute. Bloom was, above all, cautious.

And that ends today.

Bloom clenched both of her fists, trying to dig her nails into her palm to keep her from considering all of the ways this could turn against her.

You'll not only get fired for this, you'll—

Stop.

They'll just put him right back in the cell as soon as they—

Stop.

You'll get yourself put in quarantine with—

Stop.

She did it! She made it all the way back to Dr. Flaherty's cell without losing her resolve. He was standing just where and how she'd left him. Hands hanging awkwardly at his sides — no pockets in the thin sterile scrubs they'd given him in place of his clothes. He gave Dr. Bloom that sunrise of a smile.

"Tiff!" He laughed. "What, did you forget something?"

Bloom laughed, too, though she wasn't sure why.

"I was just thinking," she said, "about how close we are to a breakthrough here. We know there are five active frequencies in that signal, each with a specific effect. We've nailed down three — the so-called Manics, Sleepers, and Carriers — but we completely stalled out after they put you in here. We were making such progress! I just knew we'd have the next frequency isolated in a matter of days, and then the army came in and threw a wrench in those plans by—"

"Tiff," Dr. Flaherty said. "You're justifying something to yourself. Wanna tell me what's going on?"

"I think," Bloom said, chewing on her bottom lip. "I think I'm going to do something stupid."

"What's that?"

"I'm going to let you out," she said, and right there she felt it. That hot flush. Strangely proud of a very stupid thing.

"Are you sure?" Dr. Flaherty's eyebrows knit in concern. "I mean, yes, I want out of here. But Tiff, I don't want you risking your neck on this. Have you told anybody else about your little, uh…rescue mission?"

"No," she said, stepping closer to the window.

"That's good, then," Dr. Flaherty said. "That's plausible deniability. I can say the door malfunctioned or something if they catch us. But hopefully we can head straight to the lab and nail down these last frequencies before that happens."

"Right!" Bloom nearly hopped in excitement. "I'm so glad you understand. If we can isolate the remaining symptoms, we can prove that you aren't displaying them and there'll be no need for the quarantine!"

Bloom rested her pointer finger on the release button for the Air

Pressure Resistant Door. This was the only stupid moment in her life, she told herself, so she may as well enjoy it. She took a breath, and she pressed. There was a distant woosh as the inner seal broke. She waited a moment for Dr. Flaherty to step through, cycled the air, then pressed the outer release. The heavy steel hatch hissed and thunked, then swung open a few inches. Dr. Flaherty stepped into the hallway like an astronaut emerging into an alien world. He blinked around at the cramped, undecorated hallways like they he'd set foot on a tropical beach. He shot that pure, comforting smile at Dr. Bloom, and she melted a little.

This was stupid. But it was the right kind of stupid.

Dr. Flaherty took two steps toward her and wrapped her up in a vigorous bear hug. He leaned back and took her weight onto him — lifting her heels just a few inches off the ground — and he spun her around. She giggled. She hadn't giggled in…possibly ever.

When he set her down, Tiffany was dizzy. Not from the motion, but from the breach of expected conduct. She and Dr. Flaherty had always been friendly — maybe even flirty, in a very subtle and scientific way — but they'd never done more than accidentally touch hands in the lab, much less embrace.

He held her out at arm's length, his hands on each of her shoulders. He stared deep and unblinking into her eyes. Tiffany could feel herself blushing, but she couldn't look away.

"Dr. Flaherty, I—" she started, but he moved a single finger to her lips.

She fell quiet.

The tip of his long and delicate pointer finger traced the edges of her lips, slowly. She parted them almost involuntarily. Her whole body flushed. Her breathing became thick and slow. He slid his finger between her lips, brushed past her teeth, and settled on her tongue. She fought back a moan. She closed her lips around it and sucked.

He pushed in farther, and she felt her eyes register the surprise. But she didn't want to disappoint him. She took it.

But still Dr. Flaherty's finger slid further in, and now there were two. They scraped the back of her throat. She took a small step back, but he followed. Three fingers. His hand was stretching apart the seams of her lips. She choked and gagged, stumbled backward, pinning herself against the wall. Dr. Flaherty had his entire hand shoved into her mouth now, the fingers bunched into a thick point and surging all the way down her throat. Past the uvula, into the windpipe. The flesh of her cheeks split around the thickness of his forearm as his probing fingers clawed ever deeper.

Too late, she thought to fight. Bloom grabbed at his arms but came away with only snatches of his papery scrubs. She felt the strength ebbing out of her already. Her vision fading at the edges.

Dr. Bloom had dedicated her entire life to asking questions. But right then, she only had one: why?

As if he'd heard her thoughts, Dr. Flaherty spoke.

"You should see your face!" He laughed.

He was still wearing the same smile. Full of mirth and paternal concern. There was no guile there. No hatred or violence. His eyes, too, were gentle and full. His fingers were so deep inside her windpipe they must be halfway to her stomach. He spread them open, shredding her insides. And all the while Dr. Flaherty looked at her like he was watching a child learn how to ride a bike. He wasn't angry. He was, if anything, happy and proud. Dr. Flaherty's unwavering smile was the last thing Bloom saw, before the blackness in her periphery swallowed the world.

***

Simmons had officially had it with this bullshit. This was, what? The third day of sixteen-hour shifts in a row? He knew the work was demanding when he signed on and, to be honest, to some extent he got off on it. He liked telling his friends about the rigorous hours, the unforgiving safety protocols, the deadliness of the diseases, and the secrecy demanded of him. It made him feel needed and, as long as he held back on some of the gorier details, it even got him laid on occasion. But this was ridiculous. He'd worked double shifts plenty of times, but three in a row was pushing it. It just wasn't good practice. His focus was shot. He was getting sloppy. He very nearly walked into the sample room without sealing his pressure suit, for Christ's sake. He knew the situation with this signal was dire, but burning both ends on all of their researchers was just going to lead to somebody slipping up and dropping a slide of fucking smallpox or something.

Sloppy. Practice.

Simmons wanted to complain — he was no ass-kisser and no stranger to filing official complaints — but he had no idea to whom he would do so now. Flaherty, that pompous ass, had gotten himself exposed to the signal and stuck in quarantine a week ago. Who did Flaherty even report to now? The whole purpose of their unit was to be self-contained. He'd be under Director Mason, surely, but it wasn't like that man had an open-door policy. And it wasn't like Simmons was even allowed to *open the door to their own god damn lab.* Those army goons saw to that.

"Nobody leaves until the work is done."

Ten days locked in the labs, crashing on squeaky cots in the breakroom and surviving on coffee that was somehow both burned and watered down.

The only consolation that kept Simmons going was how great of a story this would make when it was all over. Benny would practically froth at the mouth when he told him. The fact that most of the details would be classified would just entice him further. Simmons could get a few free drinks out of this tale, easy.

He smiled at the thought of it, then realized he'd been standing in front of the sink doing nothing but mentally ranting to himself for god knew how long.

He set down his little Styrofoam cup, filled with the heinous liquid that their poor overused coffee machine had shat out, and bent his face to the water. It was so cold that it numbed his fingers and made his cheeks twitch. He ran some up through his thinning hair and then stuck his own wet fingers in his ears. It was deeply unpleasant, but then, that was the point. Anything for a moment's alertness. Simmons blindly groped for the paper towel dispenser and dabbed his face dry. He took a long, steadying breath, downed the rest of his coffee before he could taste it, then spun on his heel to march himself back into the lab before he could internally protest any more.

He bumped straight into Dr. Flaherty's chest and staggered backward.

Simmons was too fatigued to even cry out in surprise. By the time he'd processed what had happened, he was already adjusting to it. He had been standing silently before Flaherty for a few seconds now, his sleep-fogged brain struggling to process the unexpected stimuli.

"Dr. Flaherty?" he finally said. "Aren't you supposed to be in quarantine?"

"They let me out," he said. "Good behavior!"

Flaherty laughed.

Simmons smiled wanly. Dr. Flaherty and his god damn terrible jokes.

"Well," Simmons said. "It's good those fools finally saw the light.

We need all the help we can get around here. Are you officially back on shift?"

Simmons felt the first rays of hope alight inside his chest. Sleep. Sleep!

"If so," he continued, "we'll get you back on rotation immediately. You can take over for me. I'm on my third—"

Simmons looked down and saw that two of his own fingers were bent entirely backwards. Dr. Flaherty was gripping Simmons' wrist with one hand, while the other was systematically breaking each of Simmons' fingers. There went the pinky, and the thumb. When it was finished, Dr. Flaherty immediately moved on to Simmons' other hand.

"What are you—" Simmons finally thought to protest, then the pain and horror registered, and he began screaming.

He shook free of Flaherty's grip and ran for the door. His feet went out from under him.

"Whoops!" Dr. Flaherty laughed. "Flat tire!"

Simmons yelled for help, but he couldn't remember if anybody would even be around to hear him. The army goons weren't allowed in the lab itself unless it was an emergency — no need to risk further exposure by untrained and uncertified personnel. Dr. Yanos was resting in the break room with the door closed, his blindfold on, and his headphones in. Dr. Bloom would be in the lab, but what the hell could she do to help?

Simmons felt a knee settle in his back. He tried to crawl away, but now that his lagged brain had finally processed the damage, his left hand was useless. Dr. Flaherty had grabbed his right again. Adrenaline brought Simmons' reality surging back into real time. He felt it the instant Flaherty broke his thumb. Then his pointer finger, middle, index, and pinky. He screamed so loudly that it hurt — like his throat was coated in sand. Dr. Flaherty's hands wrapped around Simmons' neck and pulled so hard that he felt his muscles tearing. Simmons fought back, struggling to yank himself free of Flaherty's grip, then he tasted blood and saw tile. Flaherty had switched tactics, suddenly shoving down instead of pulling up, and Simmons' own resistance had contributed to him bashing his head in on the floor. He went woozy again, all that adrenal alertness seeping out the edges of his consciousness. The tile again.

Blood again.

Tile.

Blood.

***

Yanos was lost in a world of swirling guitars, firing hot pink in the deep blue behind his eyes. The drums were burgundy, a gargantuan fat drop of brownish red expanding and contracting in the background. The violin juddered in, neon green and spiky, hopping and dancing through the pink swirls, against the thumping backdrop of dull red. If there was a better band than King Crimson, Yanos didn't even want to know about them. He couldn't take it. The worlds that KC brought to life behind his eyes were like — wow. *Seriously* wow.

He'd tried explaining the concept countless times before: how sometimes he got his senses crossed and saw stuff he heard, or felt stuff he smelled, but nobody ever really got it. There was even an official term for it: synesthesia. When people heard the word, they looked at him like he had a disease. Some even suggested that he get therapy for his "visions."

So Yanos stopped telling people.

He had the feeling that KC understood the synesthesia, though. How could they not, when their music evoked such compelling images? *In the Court of the Crimson King* flowed together seamlessly, like an animated painting. That shit had to be planned. You couldn't just make art by accident. Right?

Whatever. That was all philosophy, and philosophy wasn't Yanos' strong suit. All he knew was that, when shit got bad — when the shifts grew this long, and the diseases got this serious, and the deadlines this tight — laying on the breakroom couch with an eyeshade on, headphones blasting KC…that was the closest he could get to nirvana.

Yanos let all of his other senses go. Or, rather, he let them kind of meld together into one great puddle of audio-visual stimuli. The scratchy wool of the breakroom couch laid down a base of electric stalagmites. The draft from the AC was a grid of fine blue lines overlaid on his field of vision. And there was something else he couldn't quite place: brown-green ovals opening and closing at random intervals, independent from the beat. Yanos didn't understand where those were coming from. A leaky faucet? An itch? Maybe something in the fridge had gone off…

Whatever they were, they were unpleasant. But subtly so, and he wanted to see how it would all build together with the music. Another oval, the color of sewage, blinked and closed. Then another and another. The mellotron erected a small green pyramid in the lower right quadrant. It expanded and contracted as the chords faded in and out. The violin line dipped to meet its tip, and then the two danced away again. All the while the little ovals built up and up. They were becoming too much now. Distracting. Ruining his vibe.

Yanos reached up and pulled his headphones off. He set them on the cool tile floor beside the couch. Then he lifted the eyeshade.

Dr. Flaherty was kneeling beside him, staring at Yanos' face expectantly.

"Can I help you?" Yanos said. "Wait, Dr. Flaherty? When did you get out? And what's with…the…blood?"

Dr. Flaherty was still wearing the papery scrubs they gave all the patients, but his were sprayed liberally with slashes of bright red. In places, they were soaked straight through with it. There were droplets across his face and in his hair. He didn't seem hurt, though. He was smiling all easy, just like normal. He winked at Yanos.

"Surprise!" he said.

Dr. Flaherty gestured at Yanos with a hand holding something short and shiny. A scalpel.

Yanos glanced down at his own body. He'd stripped to his boxers before crashing out in here. The starchy sheet he'd been using as a blanket had been pulled away, and every inch of his exposed skin was covered with thin, inch-long cuts. Hundreds upon thousands of them in neat rows starting at his feet, running up his shins and thighs, all across his stomach, chest, arms…

He touched a shaky finger to his cheeks, and it came away wet with blood.

The brown ovals. The color of corruption. Thousands of them. It was his sense-crossed body trying to warn him of the almost imperceptible cuts of a surgical blade.

Yanos screamed.

"Haha." Dr. Flaherty's eyes lit up. "There it is!"

He jammed the scalpel into Yanos' eyeball. A black, shuddering prism. A smell like wet leaves in rain.

***

The short man sat in the corner of the cell with his knees against his chest. He watched. They had given him nothing else to do. They had come to his trailer early in the morning, one man and one woman in white hazmat suits, two soldiers in green ones. The soldiers threw him to the ground. The man and woman boxed up his audio equipment. They took away his freedom, and they took away the signal. They had taken away everything. They left him nothing. Nothing but a window. So he watched.

He watched and waited for the seventy-two seconds of living he was permitted, once every three days. When a tall doctor in a bulky inflatable suit with a clear head piece — bright yellow foam earplugs protruding from each ear — would wheel the cage into his cell. When the doctor would hand him a tape recorder and gesture to the cage. When the short man would press the button and play the signal for the monkey.

The signal. To be with the signal again. To spread it. Everything else was meaningless.

He would not meet the signal again for another two days. So he would watch. He watched the female doctor pace nervously back and forth before the window, ultimately pausing to give herself some sort of mental lecture before heading off again. Moments later, he watched the tall doctor that brought him the monkeys walk quickly by. He was not wearing the balloon suit. He was wearing the same pale green scrubs as the short man. This cheered the short man. The last time the tall doctor had brought the monkeys, one of his foam earplugs had dislodged, just for a few seconds, at the very end of the signal.

Was it enough to change him? The short man didn't know. He'd never tried exposing a subject for less than ten seconds, himself, back when he, too, was experimenting with the effects of the signal. If that brief window of signal was indeed enough to change the tall doctor, what would he be? A Manic? A Sleeper? Another Carrier, like him? Or something else? Based on the questions they'd asked the short man, the doctors did not yet know about The Judges. The short man was not about to tell them.

The short man watched as the tall doctor crossed his three-by-six portal to the outside world twice more. Each time, he was more thoroughly covered in blood. The tall doctor appeared for a third time, now soaked completely — even his hair wet and dripping with it — and paused at the window. He turned to stare at the short man.

The short man recognized the look in his eyes. The devouring hunger of one who has heard the signal. But the tall doctor was not Manic. Manics did not walk — they ran. He was not a Sleeper. Sleepers did not walk. They slept. He was not a Judge. A Judge would have cleaned the blood off, first thing. And a Carrier would only want to spread the signal, not kill.

The short man's heart beat so hard he felt it in his ears.

The tall doctor was something new! New!

"Please!" the short man screamed and was instantly on his feet. He slammed into the window, heedless of the pain. He slapped his palms against it and screamed, over and over again, though he knew they were soundproof. The tall doctor would only hear him if he activated the intercom.

For a long moment, he did not. He simply stood there, on the other side of the six-inch glass, gently chuckling as though somebody had made a terrible pun — something only funny in how unfunny it was. But at last his dripping crimson hand lifted, and the static crackle of the intercom echoed around the short man's cell.

"You're magnificent!" the short man yelled. "Magnificent!"

The tall doctor laughed.

"I am!" he said.

"Let me out," the short man said. "Let all of us out."

"Why would I do that?" The tall doctor's smile was ceaseless. A permanent fixture. It seemed genuine. Full of affection.

"B-because you've heard the signal," the short man said. "The signal!"

"So?"

"So you're like us now. We all want the same thing: to obey the signal. To bring them here."

"Bring who where?" The tall doctor shook his head at the short man. A strangely fatherly gesture, as though the short man was a child who had asked an adorably stupid question.

"Them!" The short man felt a tic building and could not suppress it. He turned his head to the sky and snapped, "Them! Them! Them!"

"No offense," the tall doctor spoke gently, through lips still coated in blood. "But I think you might be crazy."

"Please let me out," the short man said. "You let me play the signal before. You know I need it. You know what will happen to me if you leave me here without the ability to spread it."

"Don't worry!" The tall doctor reached up and began drawing something in blood, directly in front of the short man's face. "It won't come to that. I'm going to burn this place and everyone in it. Me, too! We'll all burn together, like a family. Hahaha!"

"But that's not how we work," the short man pleaded. "We're all on the same side. We don't harm each other."

"Friend," the tall doctor said, still sketching on the glass. "I don't think I follow your rules."

He drew his pointer finger across his cheek, refilling his bloody ink. He dragged it across the glass. Through the intercom, the short man heard the sound it made: a drawn-out, plaintive squeal. The short man blinked at the completed picture. It was a crude smiley face, drawn directly over where the short man stood. From the tall doctor's point of view, the short man would have two bloody circles for eyes, a great smiling gash for lips.

"Then please," the short man said. "At least tell me her name."

"Who's name?" the tall doctor asked.

"Her name. The one who rides within you. The frequency."

"I have no idea what you're talking about."

"Yes, you do!" The short man twisted his neck and shouted. "You do! You do! Please. I know all of the others: Hoa, the Rage. Haruk, the Order. Himna, The Slumbering. You are of the last! I must know her name before I die. You know it. Just let your mind go blank for a second. There's something in you. An urge in your chest, a thing you can't place. It seems like gibberish to you, so you don't say it. But you want to. You want to bark it like a dog. Just tell me her name…"

The tall doctor closed his eyes and tilted his head back. Thick syrupy strands of blood ran down from each earlobe and pooled on his shoulders. At last, he opened them again and looked at the short man. He smiled.

"Herote," he said. "The Merry."

The short man yelped with ecstasy. He jumped back from the window and did a mad spinning jig. He ran back and drummed on the glass. The tall doctor gave him an ironic salute, then turned and walked out of sight.

"Herote!" the short man barked. "Herote, the Merry! The last to ride! HEROTE HEROTE HEROTE!"

***

Director Mason stared glumly at the open folder on his desk. He shuffled the papers, tucked one behind the other, but no matter what order he put them in, he couldn't accept their findings.

"How did this happen?" he said.

"Sir, while there were multiple protocols in place to avoid such a scenario, no system is flawless and—"

"Let's skip the excuses," Mason said, waving away Dr. Kettridge's hedging. "I'm not interested in assigning blame. I just want to know."

"Sir, speaking plainly?"

"Yes, Kettridge."

"Somebody fucked us."

Director Mason laughed. He didn't know Kettridge very well. Had him pegged as another kiss ass. Might have to reevaulate that one.

"Care to elaborate?" he said.

"A fire does not just *destroy* a Biosecurity Level 4 facility. It does not happen. Every room is sealed and compartmentalized, easily separated from one other. There are half a dozen redundancies built into the safety measures. Sprinklers, alarms, foam sealants — it's not possible."

"And yet it is." Director Mason shuffled the papers again. Photos of charred steel hallways and partially melted safety glass. Some twisted black architecture that used to be a human being.

"And yet it is," Kettridge echoed. "Which really only leaves one possibility. I hate to even say it…"

"But I need you to say it."

"Sabotage," said Kettridge. "And it would have had to come from the inside. The guards never left their station. Nobody in. Nobody out. The only people with access to the lab itself were the staff…"

"And one of the patients couldn't have…?"

"No, sir. Not unless, again, one of the staff let them out."

"And we're sure nobody escaped the fire?"

"Nobody, sir. The guards retreated to a safe distance once the fire became apparent, but they still watched the doors. They never opened."

"So whoever did this also killed themselves?"

"It would appear so, sir."

Director Mason felt a twinge of pain behind his eyelids. He removed his glasses and set them on his desk. He massaged his temples with his thumbs.

"And the data?" he asked.

"Gone," Kettridge answered.

"The backup servers?"

"The army seized them before we'd even had news of the fire. They're not in a sharing mood."

"So you're telling me that absolutely everything we know about this outbreak — the only instance of a disease that spreads through sound in recorded history — is gone. Every patient affected, every doctor familiar with the case, and every shred of evidence we have has literally gone up in flames."

"Everything but the backup data," Kettridge conceded. "Which begs the…uh…ah, nevermind, sir."

"Kettridge? Speak plainly."

"Sir, I know this is going to sound crazy. But the only witnesses we have to this incident are the guards the army posted. And now they have the only data left on the signal, with all evidence that it ever even existed conveniently destroyed in one fell — almost surgical — swoop."

"Kettridge, surely you're not saying that our own armed forces just murdered dozens of patients and staff, then burned down a CDC lab in order to keep the signal to themselves?"

"No, sir. I am not saying that. That would be insane."

Director Mason scoffed.

"I'm just saying that the alternative — that one of our own very exhaustively vetted doctors did carefully, and with great forethought, arrange so that everybody inside that lab, including themselves, would burn to death, for no apparent reason — is slightly more troubling."

"I suppose it is, indeed," Mason said.

He slid the folder to Kettridge.

Kettridge closed it.

War Bastard

Crit shot an exaggerated, suspicious look over each shoulder before extending his hand for me to shake. I took it and felt the hard metallic object secreted in his palm. I dragged my fingers when we disengaged, snagging the object for myself, and quickly pocketed it.

"If you're found…" Crit said, trailing off ominously.

I rolled my eyes.

"Jesus, Crit, it's a thumb drive. There's nothing illegal or even illicit about a thumb drive. It's like that *Jurassic Park* meme. I could yell, 'There's a thumb drive here, everybody!' and there'd be no response."

I said the last part a little louder than Crit's own paranoid whisper.

We didn't even net so much as a glance. I turned back to him and finished the reference. "See? Nobody cares!"

"Hey, fuck you, Spaz," he said.

"Dude, please just call me Jeff," I protested.

Crit insisted I call him by his handle. He wouldn't even tell me his real name when we first met, whereas I introduced myself as Jeff and winced every time he used my own handle. It didn't seem that embarrassing on the internet, but being called "$paztick a$$hole" in person it just, I don't know — it lost some of its luster.

"Fine, fuck you, Jeff," Crit spat. "This shit is highly illegal. We're talking *Men in Black* caliber response if we're caught."

"Crit." I sighed and plucked at my french fries. They came out soggy, and time was not doing them any favors. "We're talking about sound files, man. Nobody gives a shit."

"Secret sound files," he said. He was starting to sound kinda hurt.

Losing some of his self-appointed edge. "Obtained through illegal means. Especially this bunch."

Ah, screw it. What did it hurt to play into the guy's fantasy a bit?

"Oh yeah?" I said, and I hunched forward, dropping to a whisper. "For real? This is some serious stuff, then?"

"Yeah!" he said, too loudly, surprising himself. He quickly corrected and bent to our top-secret huddle. "I pulled these files from an old military server. Shit that was older than you back when you were born. When they finally get the budget to buy new stuff, they wipe 'em and sell 'em at auction. But, see, if you're lucky, and you're good, you can sometimes recover pieces."

"And you are good," I said, inflating his head a little. "Bet they never expected someone like you was bidding on them."

"Ha," Crit said. "You're damn right."

"So these were, what? Military sound files? What does that mean?"

"Not exactly," Crit said, and we were clearly at the part he wished wasn't true. "They're, uh…they seem like mostly old SETI stuff. You know, that space radio telescope shit they used to do back in the day? Listening for aliens and whatnot?"

Crit lost a lot of enthusiasm when he had to explain that part. It was obvious he'd hoped for something a bit tastier from a recovered military server. I could brighten his day a little if I…

Heh. Why not?

"Oh shit," I said. "Do you think this is it?"

"Is what?" Crit said.

"Do you think this is proof of aliens? First contact?"

Crit's eyes could generously be described as beady at the best of times, but now they went wide like an anime character. This possibility had clearly never occurred to him.

"Oh fuck, yes. Dude. Yes, it totally could be," he said. "Wait. Fuck. Give it back."

"No way, man!" I said, trying not to laugh. "A deal's a deal."

"Bro, come on," Crit pleaded. "I am not trading proof that aliens are real for a fuckin' SidStation."

He pushed the paper bag on the table back toward me. I shook my head.

"Come on," I said. "You know how much those things are worth. They don't even make 'em anymore. Plus it's going to sound totally sick on your new tracks."

"Yeah," Crit admitted. "I guess. But if you find anything cool, you gotta tell me first, all right?"

"Deal," I said. I held out my fist. He pounded it.

Crit put on his beefy, old-school Ray-Bans and pulled the hood of his black sweatshirt down low over his face. He tucked the paper bag holding my SidStation under his arm and walked quickly through the doors of the In N Out. He checked all around before jogging across the street, probably sure he was being followed.

Once he was out of sight, I laughed. Critikal.sHitz was a dipshit, for sure, but he could find some amazing files. Stuff nobody else had. He once traded me these crazy loops of radio signals from other planets. Not like aliens, just the radio waves that the planets in our solar system naturally emitted. It was intense. Saturn sounded like ghosts screaming, and Jupiter was like a big boat coming into harbor.

He was all amped up about this latest find and wouldn't do the normal trades, so I offered him my SidStation. I wasn't lying to him: those suckers cost a small fortune, even back when they were still making them. But I just hadn't used the damn thing in forever. I was outgrowing chiptunes.

Damn. That sounds pretentious, huh?

I mean, I was just…moving past them. I still liked listening to other people's tracks. I just didn't want to do my own anymore. I'm pretty into synthwave stuff these days, and the old PSG sound chips just start to feel confining. Crit's illicit soundfiles usually had that goofy eighties sci-fi feel to them, and they almost always turned up gold somewhere. Despite how disappointed he was with the find, I was stoked he'd found old SETI recordings. I pictured Dr. Who stuff, like theramins played by the stars themselves.

I horked down the rest of my Double Double — they always get the burgers right at In N Out, even if this particular place sucks on the fries — and stepped out into the perfect Burbank sunshine, feeling like a million bucks. Or maybe a billion.

I don't know, whatever inflation says feels awesome.

***

I slotted Crit's thumb drive into my dedicated mixing PC, which I have dubbed War Bastard. There were roughly a thousand files scattered across a few hundred folders, each named for the dates and times they were recorded. Those files could be anywhere from ten seconds to eight hours long. It would literally take me years to listen to all of them.

I'm not even about that.

I just wanted to find the hooks — the craziest few minutes hiding in those many boring hours. Luckily, I wrote a script for that, after spending a solid week trying to go through Crit's first file-dump by hand. I started it running. It would spend the next several hours combing through all of the soundfiles in the directory I selected, searching them for dead spots and cutting them, leaving only the activity that exceeded the threshold I'd set. I set this one relatively high. If nothing cool turned up, I'd nix the first wave of results, lower the threshold, and try again. But may as well aim high on the first pass.

While the script did its work, I played internet on my laptop. I started off on one of those sites with a bunch of trivia organized into lists, then tripped over a source link and fell into a Wikipedia hole. Ended up reading about the Crimean war, then somehow stumbled into studying the tech that made old music boxes work, then to a page about the different styles of opera singing, one of which featured a picture of a pretty girl with her mouth partway open, and that was it: I spent an hour looking at porn, three minutes masturbating, and ten minutes closing all the tabs of stuff I was sure I would use but never got to.

You know how it goes.

I glanced back at War Bastard. The script had finished working. Usually it would turn up about forty-five minutes of sustained, high-activity sound for a job like this. This one had found three straight hours.

All right, Crit!

I was glad, at least, that I hadn't abandoned my SidStation for nothing. I set the compilation file to play and picked right back up on my classical opera techniques. The jpeg of the pretty girl with her mouth open seemed to look at me with judgment in her eyes, so I switched gears and started reading webcomics instead.

There was some good shit in Crit's files. Whenever I heard something particularly compelling, I sat up from my bed, leaned way over so I could barely reach the mouse, and clicked save. I had thirteen promising files so far: interesting whistling patterns, hypnotic static waves, sonar-esque blips and one that — I swear to god — sounded like a Dalek saying "poop pop" over and over again. I would have to find a use for that sucker.

I was plowing through the archives for a comic strip called Achewood when something new crackled through the speakers. This track sounded, if not louder, then clearer or…maybe closer than the others? It kicked off with a deep bass that rattled my subwoofer beneath my shitty plywood desk. Followed by a single tone, somewhere between a whistle, a squeal, and a scream, that ululated madly. It was joined by loud pops, piercing Emergency Broadcast-style squeals, and crackling tsunamis of static, all dancing in and out of one another. But that first tone stayed dominant, like it was leading the band. The whole thing lasted for just over a minute.

When it finally fizzled to a stop, I had to Google "earthquake Burbank" to make sure the earth hadn't literally shaken. I had a serious case of vertigo and briefly lost track of what space meant. I knew, instinctively, how large my room was, but for a few seconds after that file stopped playing, I couldn't have told you if it was ten feet or ten miles to the door.

When my head at last stopped spinning, I got up and clicked back to the start of the file. I paused the player — I didn't have the stamina to go through it again so soon — and I saved the chunk to my desktop under the name "HOLY SHITBALLS."

I put the computer to sleep and laid on my bed, staring at the ceiling in total silence. I didn't finish the Achewood archives, I didn't fall into another wiki-hole — I didn't even look at any more porn. I spent the entire night wide awake, without once touching the internet. I believe that's the first time that has happened in…ever.

The next morning, I had a new track all mapped out in my head. That's not normally how I work. Usually, I get hooked on a sound and have to just try pairing it with a lot of other shit to see what sticks. When something finally does, I try throwing more at the track until something else holds, and so on. It's tedious as hell. But not this time. I knew every second of the song: the tempo, where it dropped, and exactly how long the fadeout was. As soon as my brain had finished processing, I jumped up and hurled myself into my computer chair. I had War Bastard up and humming all that morning and into the afternoon. Come evening, it was done. As I do with all of my tracks, I uploaded the file to the Synthspace forums first, for feedback.

I hadn't eaten all day. The last meal I had was at In N Out. And my body had since used up whatever poor fuel it could extract from greasy burgers and soggy fries. I stood up too fast and went woozy, had to steady myself against the wall and wait for the waves of fade-out to pass over me. I went to the kitchen and stared blankly into the fridge, hoping I could will something to eat to magically appear in there. We had a few things I could make — some raw chicken legs, a bag of rice — but I would rather starve than cook.

My dickhead roommate Sean had a box of Chinese leftovers. He'd written his initials on them, as dickheads do. I opened it, trying to guess at the contents. Something brown, I saw. Fried stuff in a sweet sauce. It could be anything. I thought about going out for provisions, but there was still dizziness knocking around in my guts, waiting for me to do something stupid like walk to the store so it could jump out and kick my ass.

I sighed.

I grabbed Sean's container of Chinese Whatever, stuck it in the microwave, and two minutes later headed back to my room to shovel illicit sugar and protein into my face. Before I sat down at the computer, I grabbed a pen and paper, wrote a note, took some bills out of my wallet, and went back out to the kitchen. I stuck the note and bills where the Chinese food had been and pinned it down with an expired jar of mustard. The note said:

Ate your leftovers

Here are reparations

-J

I knew Sean would still yell at me for it, but this would take some of the edge out of him at least. I trudged back to my computer yet again, my rumbling belly protesting all this stalling, and hit refresh on the forum while I horked down my tepid Chinese mystery meat.

Two responses already!

That was weird. It's a pretty active forum, but people are slow about actually listening to new stuff. It usually takes days for somebody to even click the link, at which point they'll call out some minor flaw and label you an unforgivable asshole for it. But whatever: at least you get to fix the mistake.

That wasn't what was waiting for me this time, though.

"HOLY FUCIK!!1!" the first, hastily typed reply said. "this was amaxing dude waht the hell is that hook?!?"

The second reply was a bit more expected. It was from Notorius_F.A.G., who I recognized as one of the forum's self-appointed experts. Which, in this case, meant that he was twice as insufferable because he actually sorta knew what he was talking about.

"The mix is sloppy," his reply said, "and your levels are all over the place. The intro takes too long to get going, and the fade-out is a cliché that should warrant the death penalty. But aside from that, this is shockingly pretty good. I shall echo the previous, poorly worded sentiment: Where did your hook come from? It's strangely catchy."

I typed up my responses, which were basically "thanks" to the first one and the politest way I could find to say "fuck your mother, but thanks" to the second one. By the time I posted them, there were six more replies. Another from Notorious_F.A.G., just as prickish, but also stating that he'd listened to the track again, and it had grown on him even more.

Ten more replies in the next hour. Twenty-five the hour after that. It was the most active thread in the forum by far and picking up steam. I was so excited by all the validation and attention that, even though I hadn't slept the night before, I stayed up late again refreshing the forum and replying. I took a couple of pieces of advice, even a few from Notorious, and remixed the track a handful of times before morning. When I posted the new version, there were still a few holdout blowhards, sure, but most everybody agreed it was ready to go. I uploaded it to my own fileserver for people who gave a shit about the quality of their music files, and then YouTube for everybody else.

Then I crashed out.

I slept for twelve hours, only waking when the garbage truck came by to loudly abuse our cans for having the audacity to stand so proudly on the sidewalk. For a few groggy minutes, I laid in bed trying not to move, so I wouldn't disturb the pocket of warm air that I'd gathered over the night. Then I remembered: my new track was up, and there might be more comments and views waiting for me. The giddiness had me wide awake in seconds. I kicked off my blankets and flopped into my computer chair, still in my boxers. I sucked in breath when the shockingly cold vinyl touched my thighs and lower back. I pulled up Synthspace and checked my thread.

There were ten pages of new responses.

I laughed and punched the air a little bit. I jumped up and did a victory dance. I sat back down to read the replies but only made it a page or two before I realized the new responses were still coming — adding up faster than I could get to them.

Everybody loved it. They couldn't stop listening to it. They thought I had a breakout hit on my hands, not just for me as an artist, but for synthwave as a movement. But above all, they wanted to know what that hook was.

I pulled up YouTube, bracing myself for at least mild disappointment. Synthspace was reserved just for people specifically into this kind of thing. YouTube was a great cesspool of random people who were only universally "into" casual racism and puns. Somebody was bound to hate my track, or at the very least, ignore it.

The page loaded. Twenty thousand views. Overnight.

Half as many comments. And the really strange thing: nearly as many shares. Getting people to share anything on the internet — much less some niche genre eighties revival synth track — was like pulling teeth. Yet nearly half of the people who'd listened to my song had gone on to share it.

How cool is that?

I scanned the comments briefly, and they were almost all positive, or at least as positive as YouTube comments could be. There were the inevitable breakdowns where somebody foolishly mentioned something barely related to politics or feminism, and another user replied with a bunch of rabid, belligerent frothing blaming women and Obama for everything wrong with the world, up to and including cancer. But mostly everybody just loved the track.

Euphoria welled up behind my chest. I was full to bursting with excitement. It felt like happiness was about to bust open up my ribcage and spill out onto the carpet. It would be a bright and shimmering yellow fluid, like liquid sunshine.

My computer chimed. A message from Crit.

herd ur new track gud shit mang

I replied:

thx. couldnt have done it without u. hook makes it.

I took his extended silence as the end of that conversation, but a new window popped up, with a message from somebody outside of my contacts. I accepted it.

Hello Jeffrey, you may know me by the nom de plume "Notorious_F.A.G." on the Synthspace forums. I've received your contact information from our mutual friend, who still will not tell me his real name, thus forcing me to refer to him as "Critikal.sHitz." He tells me does not know, exactly, where you found the book in your recently uploaded track. Only that he sold a batch of files to you in bulk. Can you enlighten me as to its source, and perhaps send me the unedited file? Yours, Malcolm.

Holy shit. Who signs off an instant message?

After I was finished laughing, screencapping the message, and sending it to Crit with two solid paragraphs of jokes about the stick up "Malcolm's" ass, I replied:

Sorry. not @ liberty 2 say

I went extra hard on the text-speak, because I knew it would annoy him. He sent back:

Dear Jeffrey, while I of course appreciate the artist's confidentiality, I can only assure you that I do not wish to create or distribute a competing track, or anything of the sort. I am simply obsessed with that particular soundfile and would love to analyze it myself. Yours, Malcolm.

Another screencap and a few jokes, and I replied.

no sry.

His response came almost immediately:

Dear Jeffrey, I am a person with considerable means at my disposal to harm you. I say this not as a threat, but to educate. I do not throw my weight about lightly in the forums, but I am highly regarded there and can make your life very difficult if you continue in this (frankly unnecessary) obstinacy. Please send the sound file ASAP. Yours, Malcolm.

He was threatening me with "influence in an online forum"? Oh, Christ, no! My reply was simple and immediate:

Fuk urself til u die from it

I waited a few minutes for another message, but I guess I'd ended that conversation. I got up and hopped in the shower — the two days I'd spent hunched in front of War Bastard, mixing, distributing, and reading comments had not done my natural odor any favors. I turned the water up so hot it hurt and stayed in way longer than I should have. I emerged feeling like a new person — like I'd burned off needless layers, shed some old skin, and came out bigger. I went to get dressed and noticed a new message window open on my monitor. One with a hell of a lot of text. Most of it just gibberish, like:

IMHE HO HOA IMHE RAA KO MENE IM IMHE HOA

It was from Malcolm.

I scrolled up past the gibberish, checking his responses in chronological order. He started off with more vague threats, which quickly devolved into explicit threats, which then turned into fucking insane threats rife with uncharacteristic spelling errors and obscenities. Eventually he just started messaging me pictures of extreme gore — people with their heads split open on railroad tracks, their guts spilled out on battlefields, little kids getting mauled by dogs. And finally, he typed two long paragraphs in that all-caps gibberish I'd seen when I first walked in.

God damn. I'd only been gone an hour.

I closed the window and blocked his ass every way I knew how. Some people took this internet shit way too serious.

The exchange with Malcolm left a sour taste in my mouth, which bled over into the forums and the YouTube page. It wasn't quite as fun to check them anymore, so I shut off War Bastard's monitor and got ready for work.

***

Work sucks.

***

When I got home after my shift, the old excitement was back, pulsing in my fingertips. I had purposefully avoided checking my phone during my shift, because I knew that was a slippery slope. I could spend all day just endlessly refreshing the forums and never hit the end of it, but work tended to frown on such activities as "me not doing my job at all," and I kind of needed money to live. So I worked. Besides, it gave me something to look forward to when I got home.

I'd barely kicked off my chunky black work shoes and tossed my server's apron into the corner before I had War Bastard back up and humming. I checked the Synthspace forums first. I was prepared for anything. Twenty new pages of responses. Thirty. Forty. I was ready for the crowd to turn on me now, angry with the new golden boy and looking for an effigy or two to burn.

I was not ready for what I saw.

There were two thousand four hundred twelve new responses.

"Holy shit," I said aloud.

I chewed my nails to release some of the pent-up energy. I felt the need to tell somebody — not online, a real person — but the only one around was my dickhead roommate, Sean. He'd just make fun of me for being way too into nerd-stuff. He'd never get what this meant.

I skimmed the post replies. More of the same: like it, love it, what's that hook, etc. But then there was some weirder stuff from the forum regulars, the first people to see the track. They asked stupid questions I knew they knew the answer to, made bizarre typos, got way too aggressive with the other posters. The mood was shifting there.

So I typed in the YouTube URL instead. My history autocompleted it. I clicked accept and could barely stand to watch the page load.

Two.

Hundred.

Thousand.

Views.

My whole body went cold. It wasn't even excitement anymore.

What the hell was I feeling? Fear? Anxiety? I didn't know how to process this. I got up from my computer chair and paced my room a few times.

Fuck it.

If Sean's the only guy I had to talk to, then Sean it was. I knocked on his door, interrupting the incessant sounds of gunfire that thumped behind his perpetually closed door. He paused his game. I heard the floorboards settle as he approached. The door slid open a crack.

"What's up?" he said.

"Can I talk to you for a second?" I said. "There's some crazy shit going on, and I know you don't care or whatever, but I need to run it by somebody."

"Sure," he said, but only after a very long pause that let me know, very clearly, he was not sure. "One second."

He closed his door. The game resumed briefly, then paused again — saving, I guess — and Sean swung his door wide. He gestured for me to sit on his ratty futon with him. I did. We both stared at his frozen screen, paused right at the split second his character exploded another's head with a grenade launcher.

"So I have this new song out," I said, already embarrassed. "And it's kind of going crazy on the internet."

"I know," he answered. "I saw it on Facebook. It's actually really good."

I was not expecting that. Sean exclusively listened to hip hop. Bad hip hop. Nothing was more out of character for him than listening to, much less enjoying, much less admitting to enjoying cheesy eighties synthwave soundtrack music.

"Oh, uh," I said. "Thank you?"

"Everybody's listening to it and posting about it," he said. His voice sounded strangely flat, like he was really tired or not wholly paying attention.

Wow. If everybody Sean knew was listening to my track — mostly other white, wannabe gangsters and their long-suffering girlfriends — it really was going to be a breakout hit.

"That's awesome," I said. "The track is doing so well, but I am totally out of my depth here. Like, what do I do right now? All this attention is on me, and I feel like whatever I do next will either make or break everything. It's like I can't make a decision in case it's the wrong one, you know?"

"I don't think you have to do anything," Sean said. "You didn't do anything so far. You just made it. Everything that's happened since has just happened. It's out of your control."

His eyes were glassy. In the dimness of his bedroom, with the shades drawn, just the LED glow from his giant flatscreen lighting the interior, it looked like each of his pupils contained an explosion of blood. They were just reflecting his paused game, I knew, but it was still disturbing.

"I guess it is," I said, suddenly overcome with the desire to be anywhere else but sitting with Sean on his lumpy futon. "Thanks for the talk."

"Yeah," Sean said.

I closed the door behind me, expecting the sounds of his game to resume. They didn't.

I grabbed two Red Bulls from the fridge and headed back to my room. I locked the door. I vowed I wouldn't spend all night refreshing the comments and watching view counters, but I broke that vow almost immediately.

Three hundred thousand views on YouTube. A half million.

The tone of the comments was changing now. They were still overwhelmingly positive about the track itself, but they were getting weird about everything else. People spouting gibberish and, stranger still, getting a ton of thumbs for it. Like everybody was agreeing "yes, this is fine gibberish." They were getting really violent and confrontational, too. Now the commenters weren't just telling people they disagreed with to kill themselves but specifying the method and how they'd like to help.

I minimized that window and switched back to the Synthspace forum. The same thing was happening there, just on a smaller scale. The replies were getting bizarre and incomprehensible. Even some regular forum names I recognized were posting horrific videos of car crashes and natural disasters with captions like "ROFLMAOBBQ" and smiley face emojis.

My track broke a million views by ten o'clock that night. I was practically obligated to celebrate, but it felt wrong somehow. Instead, I messaged Crit.

hey does something seem off w/ track 2 you?

Twenty minutes, and no response.

I finally pulled myself away from obsessively monitoring my own success and started catching up on my normal web routine. By the time I got to the news sites, the chewed-up feeling in my stomach had progressed into full-blown anxiety. The headlines were a horror show.

MASS SHOOTING AT KANSAS CITY MALL; 17 DEAD, 41 INJURED

DRIVER WAS SOBER WHEN HE RAN DOWN CHILDREN AT CROSSWALK, INVESTIGATOR SAYS

POLICE ENFORCE BALTIMORE CURFEW IN RESPONSE TO WIDESPREAD RIOTING

There was a knock on my door.

"Yeah?" I said, distracted. I was still scrolling through the headlines, trying to figure out where to even start learning about all of the various atrocities that had happened today.

"Hey man," Sean said from the other side of the door. "Did you eat my Chinese food?"

"I did," I answered. "I left some money there for you."

"You shouldn't have done that," he said, after a long, quiet minute.

"Sorry," I said.

My attention was lost again to the internet.

MOTHER HYSTERICAL AFTER ALL 8 CHILDREN SIMULTANEOUSLY ATTACK HER

CONCERT TURNS DEADLY AS NYC CROWD STAMPEDES

NOT ENOUGH MANPOWER TO CONTAIN LA WILDFIRES, SAYS MAYOR

No celebrity bullshit cutting through, no feel-good human-interest stories, just straight tragedy after tragedy. What the hell was going on?

Another knock.

"Hey, man," Sean said. "Did you eat my Chinese food?"

"What?" I asked, annoyed. I stood up from my computer chair and crossed over to the door. "We just went over this."

"You shouldn't have done that," Sean said.

I froze, my hand on the lock, about to flip it. I waited for thirty seconds.

The knock came again.

"Hey, man," Sean said. His voice was still flat, like it had been in his bedroom. "Did you eat my Chinese food?"

I didn't answer.

"You shouldn't have done that," he said.

The knock came again immediately. Much harder. My door rattled on its hinges.

"Did you eat my Chinese food?!" Sean yelled, his apathetic tone suddenly swinging to full, screaming rage.

Pounding on the door.

"YOU SHOULDN'T HAVE DONE THAT!" he screeched, so loudly that his voice cracked.

The pounding increased in both speed and ferocity.

"DIDYOUEATMYCHINESEFOOD?" Sean yelled, the words bleeding into each other. "DIDJOOEETMYCHINEESED IJOODIJEETMICHINEEZMI-"

I backed away from the door. It was just flimsy plywood. It danced against the jamb. The walls reverberated with the force of Sean's blows.

"DIJOOIMICHIHEIMHIIMHE IMHE TEE KO RO IMHA HOA!"

The stream of gibberish broke apart into syllables. Not words, but clear spaces between the sounds. They meant nothing but sounded strangely familiar…

"IMHE NO ITO HOA!"

The same stuff Malcom was typing at me earlier?

The door cracked and bowed inward. It wouldn't hold much longer. I looked around for something, anything that could double as a weapon. For the first time in my life, I regretted not being the specific type of nerd that collects katanas and shit. I grabbed the heaviest thing I could find, an old oscilloscope that I was planning on circuit-bending into an instrument, and pressed my body flat against the wall beside the door.

"IMHE HOA IMHE! IMHE!" Sean screamed. Fists beat. Wood cracked. Something finally shattered, and the door slammed inward.

Sean skittered into the room, running on all fours, his palms flat on the ground and his ass in the air. He paused a few feet beyond the threshold and sniffed at the air. He growled, then turned his head very slowly to face me. His skin was flushed and red. His cheeks were wet. Thick and unbroken streams of tears flowed from each eye. He bared his teeth at me and charged. I closed my eyes and swung the oscilloscope down hard. It made contact. Something both soft and crunchy gave way to the metal, then warmth and wetness splashed across my hands and shirt. I opened my eyes.

I had caught Sean right in the temple with the sharp corner of the oscilloscope. It opened up a huge triangular gash in the side of his head, out of which spurted syrupy red blood. I could see the white of bone inside that wound. I could see the pink of brain.

I immediately threw up. None of the swimming nausea that usually served as a pre-vomit warning — just an instantaneous ejection of partially digested Chinese food. It splattered across Sean's face and pooled in his open head wound.

Seeing that, I threw up again, though this time with enough forethought to face away from him. I ran down the hallway and hid in the bathroom. I locked the door and dragged the little cabinet we used to store towels in front of it. I sat on the floor and shook, covered in sour sweat.

Jesus Christ his head his head oh shit what did I just do god damn I can't go to jail I can't what do I what do I—

Okay.

I took a deep breath, held it until little stars burst in my vision, then let it out. I did it again. And again.

Sean attacked me. I was sure they can, like, CSI that shit and see what actually happened. There's no way I tricked the guy into breaking through my door and into my bedroom, then cold-blooded murdered him with an oscilloscope. The cops would see it was self defense, plain as day.

I had my cellphone in the pocket of my sweatpants. I pulled it out and dialed 911.

I got a pre-recorded message telling me that all operators were busy, and I should stay on the line.

What the hell? That wasn't supposed to happen, right? It's the emergency line. They couldn't just put you on hold. Could they?

I didn't have anything else to do. I sat there cross-legged on the cool bathroom tile, and I waited for somebody to pick up the line. I waited for an hour. Then two. I put the phone on speaker and set it on the counter. I laid my head down on the bathmat, pulled a towel over my body, and listened to the message repeat.

Stay on the line. Somebody will be with you shortly. Stay on the line. Somebody…

I awoke with the worst neck cramp I'd ever had. I could barely turn my head. What was I doing in the bathroom?

Oh, right.

I grabbed my phone. The clock said it was 7:08 a.m. The emergency call had terminated at some point during the night. Whether they'd finally answered and hung up on me when I didn't respond or it just cut out, I couldn't tell. I dialed 911 again.

Stay on the line.

I hung up, resisted the urge to whip my phone into the wall, and practiced breathing again. When I'd calmed down, I thought about going out for help, but what if Sean wasn't dead? What if he was up and around now and pissed off? Or worse, what if he was dead, and I went out there and confirmed that fact once and for all? I couldn't face that right now. So I did what I'm best at instead: I played internet.

I pulled up the news.

NATIONAL STATE OF EMERGENCY

WIDESPREAD RIOTS

STAY IN YOUR HOMES

It all blurred together into a big sloppy mess of tragedy. There didn't seem to be any one event causing it — just the whole world going to shit all at once, like society had decided enough was enough and started flicking the lights on and off until everybody left the party.

I couldn't do any more news. By reflex more than anything, I pulled up the Synthspace forums. Or tried to, anyway — they were down. I opened the YouTube page for my track instead.

I laughed. It was a flat and hollow sound in the cold little bathroom.

Three hundred million views. In less than two days.

Well, if there was any consolation to the world ending, it's that I was the most popular artist in history, right about the point where history stopped.

Those things had to be tied together. I upload my song, the traffic goes crazy, people start flipping out, and the world goes to hell. I know how narcissistic and deluded it sounds: my stupid synthwave song — the one that sounds like an outtake from the original *Blade Runner* soundtrack — is the thing that brings about the apocalypse. That's the dumbest thing anybody has ever thought.

But I was thinking it.

If there was a connection between my song and this madness, I knew where to start looking. It wasn't the god damn synthesizers or the drum machine turning people into maniacs. It was the hook. The SETI signal I'd recovered from those old military drives.

God, I was so stupid.

What was the military doing with SETI files in the first place? I should've known something was up the second Crit told me that, but I just got too excited about the find. About getting in on the ground floor of something. About having my own little arrogant secrets.

And now the world was paying for my ego. The least I could do was try to figure out why.

To do that, I would have to listen to the signal. I could sit in this bathroom and play the crappy YouTube file until my phone died, which, judging by the red flashing battery icon, seemed like it'd be any minute now, or I could go out there and grab my laptop and my headphones and do it right. The only thing standing in the way of that plan was Sean, who was either A.) up and around and ready to bash my brains in, or B.) dead, because I bashed his brains in and then threw up in them, and now I would have to look at that atrocity again.

I wasn't sure which outcome I was hoping for.

I eased the bathroom door open glacially. When it was wide enough for me to slip out, I paused, held my breath, and listened. I could hear birds chirping outside. Distant traffic and…

Pops. Screams, both pained and furious. Sirens.

But I didn't hear anything that would indicate movement in the apartment itself, so I stepped out into the hallway. I snuck down its length with all the stealth of a cartoon burglar. I eased around the shattered husk of my bedroom door and saw Sean's bare, hairy feet, still sprawled out on my carpet. A little further and I saw his shirtless torso, lying in the center of a massive, dark brown stain.

Any more and I'd see his head. See what I did. Have to face up to it again. I kept my eyes on my feet instead.

I grabbed my laptop and charger from the floor by my bed, my headphones from atop my dresser, and then tiptoed back into the bathroom. I knew it was probably pointless now that I'd verified Sean's status, but I still locked the door and dragged the squat cabinet in front of the handle. I opened up my laptop, plugged my charger into the single outlet, hooked up my headphones, and flipped off the overhead lights.

I'll tell you what I can't do: I can't fire a gun. I can't perform CPR. I probably can't even run a mile without dropping from exhaustion.

Practically, all I can do is listen. So I listened. I found the original, unedited sound file for the signal and set it to repeat. I closed my eyes and lost myself to the noise.

It begins with a deep bass. A rumble like distant trains crashing. It builds, slow and inexorable, until your ears reverberate with it. It does not vary in volume or intensity. It just is. Forever. It is alone and unbroken for so long — proud, if not arrogant in its resistance to change — that when tiny cracks finally appear in the uniformity of sound, you're grateful for the release. Little pops and squeals, announcing the chinks in the armor. Then the feature piece comes wailing in through the holes they've punched: a sort of ululating whistle that screams up and down through the octaves — never repeating yet somehow following a logic or grammar. It operates on rules that your mind grasps instinctively.

Then, so gently it's almost imperceptible, a static wave sneaks up through the ocean of bass. It is subtle, but not inactive. There are things moving in that static, fingernails of sand scratching against concrete walls.

Next, the pops and squeals grow in intensity. And you realize they tricked you at first. They came in at the same time and made you think they were part of the same pattern, but they're not. They're distinct from one another — perhaps even at odds. They appear and disappear entirely at random, increasing with frenetic desperation until the very last second of the signal, when everything cuts out abruptly.

And repeat.

A steady, unbroken boom. Crackles, squeals. A howling whistle, center stage. A blanket of white noise settled beneath.

Repeat. Isolate. Focus.

The demanding randomness and wild shrieks of the other sounds make you think that perhaps the bass, too, changes throughout the signal. But it doesn't. It's constant. Stoic. Eternal. It's the authoritarian grumble of distant machinery, buried and forgotten, but still toiling away, oblivious to what goes on above. It is the sacred baritone of priests chanting — the underlying echo of their pious voices bouncing off of cold stone, absorbed into the ancient wood of the pews and forgotten. They don't sing for celebration, or for posterity, and they will never be recorded. They sing because they are supposed to. Because they always have. They always will. The bass keeps the order.

At first, the pops seem out of place in the otherwise somber and unworldly signal. They're bubbly and effervescent — almost fun. They're champagne corks and carbonation, a finger tucked into the mouth and pulled away abruptly. But listen a few times and you'll feel something sinister beneath them. A nail pressed loose from a vital crossbeam, signaling the inevitable collapse; distant gunfire; an eyeball pried from its socket. They bring joy to the signal, but only because to bring joy is also to bring chaos.

The squeals, on the other hand, are malevolent from the start. They're not the idle whine of feedback or the harmless chirp of ungreased bearings. They're something between rusty metal dragged across a chalkboard and the desperate protests of small animals, fighting for their lives. They rise, higher and higher, until their pitch seems impossible. Until it feels like fine needles boring into the very center of your eardrums, opening holes into your skull, and letting what's in there seep out until there is nothing left. The squeals bring urgency to the signal. The urgency of fury.

If the static was a constant, it would be comforting. It could be easily dismissed while your ear is drawn to the more active sounds. But there's something just off about the white noise. It's not merely waves crashing, but waves crashing against something. Breaking against the hull of a huge ship in the dark — a ship bearing down on you, unseen but certain. There's a dire sentiment to the static that draws your total and unbroken focus. If you can just listen hard enough, you might discern some vital information before it's too late…

And that's when you awaken to find that you've lost hours, intent on nothing, oblivious to the outside world. The static brings constancy to the signal, but not peace. The static brings sleep, but not dreams.

And then there's the central tone: the screeching whistle that dominates the signal. It demands your attention, wheedling in and out of every other pattern, dragging your mind away. It fixes your intent in place, making you feel as though you're on the verge of understanding it, then deviates suddenly, pulling the rug out from under you. It's your favorite song played live — you can mentally fill in what words come next, but the singer's delivery isn't quite right. It is at once familiar and strange. The whistle brings intrigue to the signal. The whistle demands focus. The whistle commands you to analyze it. To listen to it. To share it.

There it is: the thing that crawled inside my head and made me do this. I didn't find a cool sample and build a song around it; I caught a parasite and it took over, forcing me to build a Trojan horse for an army of psychic monstrosities.

I could almost see them there — the sounds now so familiar that they began to take on shapes in the blackness of the bathroom. The signal as a whole was a shadowy sphere, so infinitely vast that its depths were incomprehensible. It meant madness to even try. And each aspect of that signal was an entity that lived inside that eternal void. Something ancient and, if not malevolent, then apathetic in the cruelest way. Those entities, too, were pure, impossible black. They'd lived so long in the void that they had become the void itself. And yet, despite how impossible it was to discern detail within the darkness of the sphere, I could almost see something. The very thought was at odds with itself, but there were bright things behind those shadows. Illuminated, but concealed, like lighthouses in the fog. They were faces. Young faces. Almost child-like, but theirs was youth captured on a faded photograph. Cracked, withered, long dead. I knew what they were — those sounds, those effects, those entities inside the black sphere.

They were order. They were chaos. They were fury. They were sleep.

No, they had other names. Inside the signal, nestled in between the tones, they whispered them, tauntingly.

They wanted to be known.

Haruk, The Order.

Herote, The Merry.

Hoa, The Rage.

Himna, The Slumbering.

The prominent whistle at the heart of the signal was all of them and none of them. It was the Herald, spreading their word in advance of their arrival.

I threw my headphones to the ground. I had to feel around with my foot for a second before I could pinpoint where they landed. Once I did, I stomped them into pieces. There was something wrong with my face; it was swollen and wet. I touched my fingers to my cheek and tasted them. Salty. So tears and not blood. At least there's that.

How long had I been lost in the signal? It was pitch black in the bathroom, but there were no windows, anyway — it could be morning or midnight. I pawed my way to the door and felt alongside the wall for switch. I flicked it, and nothing happened. The power must have gone out while I was listening. I'd been running on battery power. I opened the bathroom door a crack, and once I was reasonably satisfied that nothing was going to come charging down the hallway, I stepped out.

Faint light streamed through the closed blinds in the living room.

The kind of colorless oversaturation that said it was either just before sunrise or just after sunset. I couldn't take the confinement of the apartment a second longer. No matter how dangerous it was out there, I felt a strong compulsion to get the fuck away from my laptop, the signal, Sean's rotting corpse — everything. I repeated my drill on the front door: open a crack, wait, hold breath, listen.

Nothing. There were distant sounds of anarchy beyond the brick walls, but inside the actual building, it was as quiet as fresh fallen snow. That, in itself, was seriously disturbing. The complex was a cheap build. The walls were paper thin. You could hear people wipe their asses if you listened hard enough, but now? Library quiet.

I took no chances and padded to the stairs like a paranoid housecat: operating on the assumption that something big was about to pounce from around the next corner and ready to jump away at a moment's notice.

Up the concrete stairs, painfully cold on my bare feet, and out onto our rooftop patio. There was a gross hot tub that the less discriminating tenants fucked in and the rest of us avoided like the plagues it surely carried. Some faux-wooden benches, their seats set at severe angles, like the designers were intentionally vying for the most butt discomfort possible. Planters full of scrub grass. A few disused and rusting communal barbecues. But otherwise vacant.

I leaned out over the railing and took in the city below. It was firmly twilight, but there were no lights out there. Not even the traffic signals were functioning. The only jumpy, staggering illumination around came from the distant fires raging in unseen buildings. Through the gloom, I could make out twisted shapes strewn about the streets and just knew they were bodies. Judging by the last news reports I'd seen, and the exponential rate my song was spreading, I didn't have much hope that the rest of the world was faring any better.

I looked to a sky the color of denim, the early evening stars rendered visible for the first time in years by a total lack of artificial light. It was a clear night, and I felt like I could see forever — the only mar was a small, stubborn black spot in my vision. I rubbed my eye, but it was still there when my sight refocused. I blinked and turned my head from side to side. The spot did not move with me.

The spot wasn't the product of my own strained vision, like I'd spent too long staring at a monitor and brought artifacts with me when I looked away. It was external. The black spot existed. It hung there in the sky like a cancerous mole. Just a pinprick now, but I knew how big it really was. And I knew it was coming closer.

I climbed up onto the railing, the cool metal instantly freezing my toes. I shook, off balance at first, but I managed to recover and stand up straight. Once I regained my equilibrium, everything became perfectly still. There was no wind to knock me over, no sudden noises to startle me into falling. If I was going to do this, it would have to be entirely my choice.

I laughed a little.

I wanted to think it was the guilt driving me — I had killed the world, after all. Surely I couldn't live with that. But what's the point in lying to yourself?

I stepped off the roof of my apartment building — the last precious sound I heard was the harsh vacuum of wind rushing past my ears — because I didn't want to live through what was about to happen.

Can you blame me?

The Black Spot

The black spot in the sky boiled, unseen. Though it was featureless, colorless, and barely larger than a thumbtack, there was a sense of movement when you looked at it. It was like a familiar song whose lyrics you couldn't quite recall, though you remembered the melody perfectly. There was definitely something inside that opaque darkness, and you could almost make out what it was, if you just stared at it for a few…more…

"Hey!" Ali snapped her fingers, drawing Mose's attention away from the skies. "You're not supposed to stare at it."

"What?" Mose was foggy and unsettled, like he'd walked into a movie theater during the day and emerged after nightfall.

"The broadcasts say you're not supposed to stare at the black spot. It's like an eclipse or something — you don't think it's bright, but it's still damaging your eyes."

"Aw, that's a bunch of crap and you know it," Mose said, rubbing his cheeks to chase the daze away. "Something can't be black and bright at the same time."

"Well, whatever," Ali said. "It's like cosmic radiation or something. Don't look at it."

"Fine," Mose said, and he humped the camera back onto his shoulder. The strap helped take the weight off, and the pad helped brunt its edges, but the damn thing still dug into his muscles if he held it steady for any length of time. He could feel it stretching out his neck already, and they hadn't even started shooting yet.

"Oof, Mose." Ali hit him with that self-conscious doofus of a smile — the one that made his knees weak. "I'm sorry. I'm harping on you like a schoolteacher. Ignore me, I'm just nervous. You do whatever you want."

"Nah, you're right," Mose said. "Not much to see there anyway, no use risking my eyes to look at nothing. Then how am I gonna pay my rent?"

Mose gestured with the camera, and Ali shrugged back at him.

The black spot scratched at his mind. Not an overpowering sensation, not even really annoying — more like a tickle than an itch. Besides, Mose prided himself on his resolve. He quit smoking cold turkey just last week — no patches, no gum, no tapering off. It was his third try, but he had a feeling this one would stick. His will was iron.

Now that he'd called himself out on it, he knew he'd never look at the spot again. It was a matter of principle.

Except, shit, his eyes were drifting upward already. It wasn't fair; he wasn't even paying attention. He was thinking about whether to frame Ali against the crowd of protesters or against the steps of city hall. About what that positioning meant to the viewer — did it subtly state that she's with the people if she stood in front of the crowd? Did it mean she's siding with the authorities if the backdrop was city hall? Some cameramen didn't give a damn about that stuff, but Mose thought there was an art to everything, if he just cared enough to find it. But when he was all lost in his head, thinking about shots and frames, his traitor eyes took the opportunity to waltz skyward.

He jerked his head down, stared at his feet.

"Hey, here we go," Ali said. "Chief's coming out."

Finally, Mose thought, something to do. He circled around to frame Ali's intro against the crowd. Might as well make her a lady of the people after all, he decided.

"And five, four," Mose said, then silently counted down from three on his fingers.

Ali paused for a fraction of a second before beginning.

"This is Alejandra Cruz reporting for KAIM Channel 7. We're here on the footsteps of City Hall awaiting the police response to widespread allegations of excessive force in last night's deadly shooting of seven local teenagers. The Latino community in particular is present in large numbers tonight, believing the shooting to be racially motivated. Five of the seven deceased were of Latino heritage, and all but one had criminal records clear of any convictions. Police have insisted that the suspects were armed and confrontational, but cell phone video released just this morning shows no visible weapons, the children on their knees, their hands above their heads at the time police opened fire. It looks like Chief Hernandez is ready to speak now…"

Mose circled back around to get the chief and his podium in frame. He squatted low, so the camera was looking up at an even more extreme angle, the authoritarian façade of the station looming large behind the scene like something out of *1984*. Mose had his own way of protesting.

"Ballsy," Mose whispered to Ali.

"What?" she whispered back.

"Calling them children," he said.

"They were," she said.

Mose was about to warn her that the station might not appreciate her word choice, but the show was starting.

"The depart—" Hernandez coughed into his closed fist, cleared his throat, and started again. "The department has no comment on last night's tragic events as of this time. This is an ongoing investigation, and our findings will be released when they are thoroughly vetted, and not before. Instead, I am here to announce a citywide curfew, effective immediately—"

The protesters howled behind Mose. The elderly woman beside him spat onto the ground and unleashed what Mose could only assume was the vilest string of profanity ever uttered, judging by her tone.

"Effective immediately," Hernandez shouted into the microphone, barely drowning out the crowd. "Any person on the street after nightfall will be detained without question, without charge, indefinitely. This is in light of the nationwide state of emergency declared in response to the widespread rioting, senseless looting, and atrocious violence being committed against police and civilians alike. This is not to be viewed as—"

A beer can arced out of the assembled crowd, somewhere just behind Mose. It caught the light, spinning silvery through the air, to connect with Hernandez's forehead. His eyes had been down, reading the prepared statement. He stumbled and lost his footing, dropped to one knee. The officers flanking the podium, already assembled in full riot gear, instantly raised their rifles and began firing.

Mose wrapped his arm around Ali's waist and hauled her to the ground. Bullets keened overhead — hopefully rubber, but Mose wasn't about to count on that. The pained screams behind him were no help in solving that particular mystery, but then, they wouldn't be. Mose had been nailed by a real bullet before, trying to joyride a tractor back when he was an idiot teenager. The owner came out firing blindly, and Mose caught a .22 in the butt. Had to bend over a table for the doc to remove it, all the while his mother screaming in his ear, only pausing to occasionally smack him in it instead. And he'd caught a few rubber bullets, too, covering an anti-war protest that had turned ugly a few years ago. They hurt exactly the same. And from this range? They wouldn't be doing a hell of a lot less damage than the real thing.

He had more meat on him than Ali, so he pushed her forward and turned his back to the shooting. Together they crab-walked sideways out of the line of fire — Mose expecting to feel that thump and sickly heat inside his flesh any second. But the riot cops were targeting farther back in the crowd, maybe trying to get the core to disperse, or maybe just hoping to accidentally tag whoever threw the beer.

When Mose wrapped himself around her like a human overcoat, Ali flushed hot. She knew how god damn stupid that was — seriously, little girl, the guy nobly protects you from gunfire and your first thought isn't gratitude, or even fear, but sex? She did her best to, if not disperse the feeling, at least compartmentalize it and focus on the life and death situation at hand. She'd always had a thing for Mose, sure, with his crooked smile and puppy dog eyes and holy hell, those shoulders — but there was a time and a place, and this was firmly, unquestionably neither. But still, his body wrapped around hers from behind, the heat of his breath on her ear…

Stupid, stupid, stupid.

As soon as they were clear from the crowd, squatting in the narrow alley between City Hall and its neighboring parking garage, she shrugged him off and stepped away. Mose looked wounded — emotionally, if not physically. Although…

"Are you okay?" Ali said. "Holy crap, did they get you? Are you shot right now?!"

"No," Mose said, and he reached around to feel at his own back. "I'm good. I'm pretty sure I'm…yeah. I'm all right."

Ali exhaled, and that was a mistake. The world went red at the edges, and she sagged against the wall for support.

"Do you think those are rubber bullets?" Mose asked. "Man, even that seems like an extreme response for this…"

"I don't know, I—oh." The remaining strength in Ali's legs spilled out onto the floor. She slid until she was kneeling.

The bullets weren't rubber. There were half a dozen bodies on the street, sprawled like broken marionettes, red puddles seeping out beneath them. The protesters were trying to run, but they were getting in their own way — tripping over each other, trampling each other — and the riot police were just firing wildly into the wall of humanity.

It was nearly impossible to pick out individuals among the chaotic crash of people, but it was clear they weren't all trying to get away. Some of them were standing and fighting — though, bizarrely, it wasn't against the police. A man with a Cuban flag T-shirt had pinned a teenage girl face down on the pavement, and he was furiously tearing at the back of her head. Ali watched as a chubby middle-aged woman in a pink pantsuit ran along the rear perimeter of the crowd, searching for some unseen criteria. When she found it, apparently in an elderly man in a blue windbreaker, she yanked him out and stabbed her fingertips into his eyes. It didn't make any sense. Nothing was making any sense.

Mose had stopped trying to understand what was going on. There wasn't any point to it now. The only thing they could do was get the hell away from all that madness. The alley they were squatting in dead-ended fifty back. They could try sneaking by out on the street, but they had those bug-fuck crazy protesters to one side and riot police to the other.

No, Mose didn't like their chances on the street. They could try ducking further into the alley, see if they could lose themselves in the dark and ride it out, but Mose didn't like the idea of being cornered right now. There was a blue steel door set in the wall about ten yards away, just at the edge of where the streetlamps chased away the gloom. Its paint was faded and the hinges rusty, but there was a smeared arc in the grime on the ground in front of it, indicating it had been opened recently.

"Come on." He grabbed Ali's shoulder and swiveled her around to see what he was seeing. "There's a door here."

"Yeah," Ali said. Her eyes were wide and twitchy. Maybe in shock. She would have agreed to just about anything right then.

She let Mose steer her down the alley, kicking empty cans and skidding on wet papers, until they reached the door. He twisted the handle, but it wouldn't budge. Not like it was locked, but like it had seized shut. It wasn't so much a knob anymore as a handle. Mose grabbed it and yanked at the door. It didn't open, but it did bow out toward the top, just a little. He kicked at the base and heaved again. Mose alternated between bashing the sucker in and yanking it outward until something finally gave with a rusty squeal, and the door swung open. Mose had thrown all of his weight into that last pull and stumbled backward onto his ass when it gave.

A sharp yell of pain and rage. Somewhere close. Mose looked down the alley, back toward the street. A silhouette there, tall, thin, its head turning this way and that, searching.

"Get in!" Mose hissed.

Ali leapt into the dark beyond the doorway without question. Mose crawled after, his palms sliding in the thin muck of composting garbage. He leaned out to pull the door closed. The figure's head snapped around. He couldn't see its eyes, but Mose felt them find him. It shrieked again, with a harsh and personal rage, like Mose had just punted the thing's baby. Mose slammed the door shut, but he knew from experience that it didn't lock.

"There are stairs here!" Ali said, from somewhere just above him.

Mose turned to feel for the start of the steps and tripped over the first one. He caught himself on his hands and, wasting no time, began running up on all fours. He reached the first landing and clipped Ali with his shoulder. She yelped and clawed at his back. He grabbed her around the waist.

"It's me," Mose said.

"Are you crawling? Why? Are you hurt?"

"Just go!"

Mose gave Ali half a second lead, then started up after. There was light on the next landing, but it was diffuse and useless, having filtered down from somewhere far above. Just enough to see dust motes whirling and nothing else. A bang from below, reverberating up through the cramped concrete stairwell like a metallic wave. The thing from outside had reached the door. There was only one full flight of stairs between them.

Mose's heartbeat was deafening. Above it, he could only hear the faint scuffle of Ali's feet ahead. Then it stopped. He bumped into her from behind. She had paused for a fraction of a second to feel the walls on this landing, probably looking for a door. It caught Mose off guard, and he grunted in shock. From far below came an answering scream, then wild scratching and harsh, excited breathing.

It hadn't been coming after them — didn't understand that they'd gone up the stairs — but it got the message now.

Up another few flights in a blind panic, the faint illumination growing stronger by increments. Ali used to park in this garage from time to time, back when she was working the dedicated city hall beat as a newly hired researcher/catch-all office bitch. Her job was to check up on the text of every mundane new ordinance and measure introduced, just in case the real news team needed that copy for a story at some point and, oh yeah, if she wouldn't mind swinging by that barbecue joint on 4th, she could grab lunch orders, too…

Ali knew the garage filled up quick in the mornings. She'd had to park on the roof level more than a few times. With all the twists and turns, the garage felt taller than it really was, but it couldn't actually be more than four or five stories. She'd never taken this particular stairwell. She'd always waited for the elevator — and even if the elevator was broken, she would have walked the ramps all the way back down instead of risking this horrid stairway. The whole place smelled like piss and old garbage. If there were lights at all, they were out and probably had been for a long time. And either she'd stopped to feel at the wrong landing — the one between floors — or there weren't even exits at every level. This place was a rape begging to happen on the best of days. But she was getting the hang of the layout: short, steep flights of stairs that hit a landing and jack-knifed back on themselves before continuing up. The climbing motion was becoming mechanical, with her body instinctually memorizing the approximate height and width of the steps and the rough amount of them between landings. The light was second hand and weak, but it was getting strong enough to see the outlines of the steel railings bolted into the walls. They had to be getting near the top.

Then Ali's routine betrayed her — the repetition tricked her legs into thinking there was another step, where there was only flat concrete. She twisted her heel and went headfirst into the wall. Mose tripped over her sprawled feet and made an equally inelegant-sounding landing. In the stunned, quiet moment that followed, she could hear a shriek of renewed interest, and the distant slapping of flesh on concrete quickened.

They had to be near the top. Only four or five stories. Had to be.

Ali pulled herself up into a crouch and tapped Mose's shoulder. He was blocking the next flight; she'd have to crawl over him to keep going. So now he went first, silently lunging up the darkened steps. Ali came behind, distinctly aware that there was now no buffer between her and the thing that followed. The bouncing, echoing quality of the narrow stairwell made it impossible to tell for certain just how far the thing was behind them. Ali could feel its breath on the nape of her neck, could picture its clawed fingers snagging her blazer and yanking her backward, screaming, falling down into the darkness, landing on the brutal concrete steps in a tangle while it tore at her hair and skin, pinning her to the—

She stumbled out onto the rooftop without ever realizing she'd reached it. By the dumb look on his face, she assumed Mose had just done the same. The top story of the garage was a split-level: One ramp rose from below, made a U-turn, and then ascended again before terminating at a long, low concrete shed with a blue steel door set into one side. The stairwell emerged right at the split. There were lampposts at staggered intervals, but the light they cast didn't extend far beyond the waxy pools at their base. Still, Ali could see that, scattered all along the downward ramp, stood silhouetted figures. They weren't positioned with any plain purpose — not gathered in a group or around their cars. Most of them were utterly still and painfully slouched, as though an overpowering fatigue took them with no warning, and now they struggled just to remain upright. Only two of the figures, back in the shadows where the downward ramp receded into the covered garage, were moving. They paced in agitation, muttering something to themselves while tearing at their hair and beating their breasts. The strange sight had frozen Mose and Ali, but the meaty smack and pained hiss from the stairwell behind them broke the spell.

The thing was still coming, getting closer by the second.

She had no reason to believe the people on the ramp were a threat, but something about their stillness and broken posture made Ali uneasy.

"Up here," she said and grabbed Mose's hand. It was large and warm. It enveloped hers like a blanket.

She dashed ahead, pulling Mose toward the apex of the garage. There was a white work-van parked in the uppermost space on the left. The rear of it was windowless, the sides unadorned save for freckles of rust. Ali pulled Mose behind it, and they huddled together against the rear tire to hide even their feet from view. Mose wrapped his arms around Ali, for comfort or just stability, she couldn't tell and didn't particularly care. They heard their pursuer make the door: the tinny echoing quality of its screams changing as it stepped out from the alcove and into the open air.

Ali tried to breathe as quietly as possible. She took in long, thin streams that left her perpetually faint. An angry bark from the far left edge of the lot, then a frustrated shriek from the far right — their pursuer was running back and forth without purpose, taking out its fury on nothing. More shouts, from farther below on the downward ramp, and then footsteps. Mose released Ali and dropped to his knees. She plucked at his shirt, wordlessly imploring him to stop — don't risk being seen — but he had already ducked his head below the van.

It was one of the riot cops. Male, just under six feet tall, his build indistinguishable beneath the bulky armor and blue-black uniform. His face-shield was coated in blood, rendering him all but blind. He had either run out of ammunition or could no longer remember how to use his rifle. He clutched it, both hands on the barrel like a club, and swung at the empty air. He walked in a low stoop, knees bent, chest toward the ground, neck angled painfully to keep his head level. Every few steps he lost his balance and used the rifle to prop himself up again. He gurgled and slavered like a rabid dog.

The footsteps from below grew louder, then a red and yellow blur tackled the policeman. A half second later, another figure joined the fray. The two from the garage. The trio snatched at each other, tore away skin and hair, dug fingers into flesh until they broke the skin. The flailing ball of limbs emitted a chorale of pain and rage that broke against the low walls ringing the complex, growing in fury and intensity until…

It stopped.

Like God had pressed pause on the scene.

The riot cop's helmet had been knocked off in the melee and his rifle-club tossed aside. A stunning older woman in a red cocktail dress sat on his chest, her limp golden hair covering both of their faces. Her hands were wrapped around the officer's throat. His fingers dug into her arms at the elbows. A portly balding man in an olive jumpsuit kneeled at the policeman's head, one fist raised, about to smash down and end it all. But instead he blinked, looked around, and stood. He wandered away. The riot cop bucked once, twice, and threw the woman off. She hit the pavement and rolled to the heels of her feet, then settled into an undignified open-legged squat and rocked back and forth. The riot cop stood last, surveyed the empty lot, then lapsed into an aimless, agitated rambling.

Mose stood, silently praying that his creaky knees wouldn't choose that moment to pop. Ali looked at him, one eyebrow raised, voicing a silent question: "What was that?" Or maybe, "Are we okay?"

Mose shook his head, giving two answers at the same time: They were "I don't know" and "absolutely not," respectively.

Mose padded silently to the passenger door of the van and tried the handle. Locked. He put his hand against the window, shielding it from the glare of the lamp above, and saw that the driver's side lock was engaged, too. He turned and leaned out over the border wall. He saw nothing useful. No fire escapes, or rope ladders, or miraculous rescue helicopters hovering there, waiting to take them away. Mose returned to Ali's side and shook his head again. She pointed at the blue door, just a few feet of open ground away.

Mose had no idea what the shed was intended for — maybe it housed a transformer, or a storage space, or a mysterious old hermit that would answer three riddles — but he couldn't imagine a reason why it would be unlocked. He shook his head, but Ali just pointed again, more firmly. Mose looked her straight in the eye and shook his head again, slowly, accentuating each movement. *Definitely not.* Ali widened her eyes and pointed, inclining her head. *Yes, let's go.* Mose set his jaw and raised his eyebrows. Putting his foot down. She sighed and shrugged. He relaxed.

Then she bolted for the door.

It slipped out of him before he even knew what he was doing.

"Ali, no!" he said, loudly.

They both froze in place.

Mose gingerly eased out around the rear of the van like a child tentatively peering into the kitchen to see if Mom was still mad.

Fifty feet away, three blank, bloody faces stared back.

Ali broke first. She twisted the handle and yanked at the door. It didn't budge.

Mose broke next, running to Ali's side.

The trio of creatures broke last. They moved clumsily, trying for an ungainly four-limbed lope that their bodies couldn't quite pull off. They repeatedly fell and scraped on the concrete but never stopped moving, eyes locked on Mose and Ali, closing distance by the second.

"It won't open!" Ali yelled.

"Push!" he said, trying to shove her aside, but her fingers were panic-locked to the handle.

"What?" she screamed.

"It's a push door!" he answered. "Push!"

She wrenched the handle with her whole body and heaved her weight against the door. It gave way with no resistance, and she followed her lunge all the way to the ground. Mose hopped over her, kicked her legs out of the way, and slammed the door shut. He braced his shoulder against it. One of the creatures hit the other side at a full run, and the impact nearly knocked Mose's arm out of its socket. But after the first try, the thing on the other side switched tactics, immediately resorting to scratching and punching. Useless efforts that resulted in nothing but metallic screeches and bangs. Mose carefully pried one hand loose from its death grip on the handle. There was an industrial-looking deadbolt with a long, thin, unrounded toggle. He snapped it shut with a mercifully solid thunk and eased away from the door.

"Will that hold them?" Ali asked.

"No idea," he said. "Maybe not if they try full force, but listen…"

He tilted his head toward the door and pointed at the ceiling. She did the same.

Just behind the wailing of fingernails on steel, they could hear a staccato of faint, fleshy thumps.

"What is that?" Ali asked.

"I think it's the other two," Mose said. "They don't seem to understand doors. They're trying to punch their way through the walls."

"Jesus," Ali said, "what the fuck is going on?"

"I don't have a clue," Mose said. "Some sort of crowd control thing gone wrong? Like a…a gas or something?"

"The police dosed their protesters with murder gas," Ali said, her voice wired with sarcasm. "That seems counter-productive."

"Damn, girl, that was my first guess!" Mose laughed, to dispel adrenaline more than anything else.

Ali laughed, too. Both of them were utterly unconvincing.

"Okay, then," Ali said. "What now?"

"Does your phone work?" Mose asked, trying his own.

"No," she said and flashed him the screen, spiderwebbed by fine cracks. "Yours?"

"Yeah," Mose said, then again: "Yeah! Yes. Okay."

He punched in 9-1-1 and let it ring so long that his phone hung up for him, automatically.

"Nothing?" Ali asked. "How can that be?"

"I don't know," Mose said. "Maybe the same thing that's happening here is happening there."

"Don't say that," Ali said. She wrapped her arms around herself and slumped into the farthest corner away from the door.

The interior of the shed was unadorned concrete all around, with a low wooden counter occupying one end and a large metal shelving unit at the other. The shelves held heavy-grade cleaning supplies: serious-looking plain white containers embellished with small blue text. There was a power washer propped up in one corner, a few mops and brooms in the other. On the counter was a dull red toolbox with a padlocked latch, a pair of stained workman's gloves, a large glass pipe, a Bic lighter with the stars and stripes across it, and a stack of video game magazines.

This place was intended as a different kind of sanctuary.

There was only one window in the place, facing street-side. It was deep and perfectly square, the glass stained yellow with age and smoke. It had obviously never been cleaned. Mose grabbed one of the gloves, spat in the palm, and used it as a rag to clear a grime-free portal. He peered out of it.

Just a straight drop, five stories to the empty street below, occupied by nothing but bodies. Mose scanned the buildings across the way for signs of life and found his eyes drifting inexorably upward. The black spot leered, like a stain on the sky. A cigarette burn on the curtain of reality. It appeared to be flat and featureless, unless you studied it closely, at which point it developed a sheen like oil on water. A faint rainbow swirl, but one comprised entirely of unfamiliar colors that gave Mose a headache when he tried to define them. He got the sense that something was moving when he looked at the spot. Not like something was contained inside its borders, but more like he was watching a very small portion of something large and incomprehensible passing by just beyond it. A parallax effect. Like he was peeking through a hole in a fence as a massive train lumbered by on the other side. All chaos and noise.

Yes. Noise! That was it. That was what bothered him when he looked at the spot. It made a sound, but one that seemed like it was coming from his own head, stirring his eardrums from the inside of his skull. It sounded like a quiet theater whispering in excitement just as the feature starts. A million voices, a billion — untold, unfathomable numbers — all saying the same thing, but just out of sync. What was that?

Almost caught it that time.

Once more.

So close.

It's right there, at the edge of understanding…

"Mose!" Ali pinched the skin of his neck, and he snapped to with a yelp. "Hey, what the hell are you doing?"

Ali leaned in, close enough that Mose could smell her hair, so he did (orange and spices, like always). She peered out the window.

"What are you looking at?" she asked, glancing up and down the empty streets. "Why weren't you answering me?"

"Oh, uh." Mose was still dazed, coated in the film that lingers between daydreams and reality. Ali's closeness wasn't doing his concentration any favors, either. "Just staring off into space, I guess. I'm a little shellshocked."

She gave him a wary look.

The look said, in no uncertain terms, "I am not buying that shit, and I know exactly what you were doing. This pause is only to give you enough time to explain yourself and buy some bonus points before I call you out on your crap."

"I was staring at the spot again," Mose said, feeling like a schoolboy caught passing notes in class.

Ali laughed.

"I guess we have bigger problems now than your optometrist," she said. "But why do you keep staring at it? Is it doing something?"

She joined him in gazing purposefully at the black spot for a silent moment.

"You don't see anything there?" he asked.

"I see a black spot," she said, trailing off.

Mose didn't take the prompt.

"What do you see?" she said, but Mose only grunted. He was gone again, that unfocused highway hypnosis in his eyes.

Ali sighed. She left him to space out while she took stock of their supplies: mostly cleaning stuff, some big serious-looking machine with a long wand at the end, two mops, and a wide broom. Maybe they could unscrew the ends of those and have makeshift clubs. That wasn't terribly comforting. Then there was the toolbox: could be something better in there, some kind of blade or hammer, but the latch and padlock weren't decorative. They were thick and shining steel. Even if she'd had something to bash at them with, Ali doubted she could break them. There was only the one exit from the shed, and though the things outside had finally stopped beating on the walls, she knew they were still out there. Ali paced back and forth from the counter to the shelves, trying to remember if she'd seen something on TV that told her how to make a bomb out of cleaning supplies and video game magazines, but nothing came to mind.

Mose said something, softly. He chuckled.

"What is it?" she asked.

He shook his head and muttered again.

"Mose?" Ali walked over and poked him in the arm.

He made a few befuddled noises, but nothing coherent.

"What's funny?" she asked.

"Funny?" Mose said, snapping out of his trance. "Oh, it's just…we're paying our dues."

"What does that mean?" Ali said.

"What does what mean?" Mose asked.

He shook his head, trying to remember what he'd been thinking. But he felt like he'd just woken from a dream, and it was now sifting away, the details running through his fingers like sand, until they were gone.

"You said 'paying our dues.' I don't get it," Ali prompted.

"Sorry," Mose said, "I forget. I was just daydreaming."

Ali bit her lip and looked away.

"Hey," Mose changed the subject, "we should have a real look around. Take stock. Maybe we can use something in here to get out."

Ali laughed bitterly.

"Done and done," she said. "Unless you're deadly with a broomstick, I think it's a bust."

"I'm pretty good. I watched a lot of *Ninja Turtles*," Mose offered.

Ali smiled in a very patient way that, Mose knew from experience, meant she was completely out of patience with him.

"Maybe the phones are working now," he said, tapping at his.

He tried 9-1-1 again, but it didn't even ring this time. Just a cold silence. He went through his contacts, dialing numbers at random. Same deal. There were bars in the display, but nothing would even attempt to connect. He spun his phone on the plywood counter in frustration and turned to Ali.

"I guess we just hole up here until help comes?" she said.

"Is it coming?" he asked.

Ali didn't have an answer for that.

"Yeah, I guess we hole up," Mose said. "I don't know what else to do."

He knew it was the wrong thing to say. He was the man here. He was supposed to have a plan, an idea, some secret skillset they taught in man-school for just this situation. But he had nothing, and Ali always caught him in his lies.

"Me neither," Ali said, and she let out a long sigh.

She had been hoping Mose didn't have some foolhardy plan to go out there and fight. She would have gone along with it, she knew, because she was desperate for any kind of solution and had no better ideas. But what she wanted most right now was to just to curl up here, in the relative safety of their little shed, and have Mose hold her until she fell asleep. Then, when she woke, it would all be over. The military would be outside with a brisk "nothing to see here, move along." And they would. Then home. Stiff drinks and comfort food. Soft beds and blankets. End of story.

But she couldn't figure out a way to ask Mose to hold her without sounding like a scared little girl, and she couldn't figure out a way to sleep with the occasional pained scream, unearthly howl, or distant gunshot sounding outside.

Instead, she sat cross-legged on the chilly concrete floor and thought about her family, just across the border in Juaritos. Would this riot, or whatever it is, have spilled that far? Carlos wouldn't have been in school when it happened — too late for that. He was probably safe at home. Mama would be at work in the hospital. But if there were cops protecting anything, it would be the hospitals…

Ali pictured those riot police, their plastic face-shields reflecting the muzzle flash as they fired into the unarmed crowd. That wasn't a normal response. Not even here, not even at the worst of times. Maybe the cops weren't immune to this thing, either. Maybe they were part of it.

Ali got a hitch in her chest that threatened to overwhelm her. She felt those great, heaving sobs building up in her throat. She stood suddenly and got herself moving. She swung her arms around. Stretched out her back. Put her hands on her head and twisted. When she'd worked out the worst of the surging emotions, she lay against the wall and slid down until she was sitting on her butt. She put her head back and closed her eyes. She'd never get sleep, but maybe she could get some rest.

When she awoke, the temperature had dropped sharply. She had drifted from her seated position, fallen asleep on her side, curled into a tight ball. The cold concrete sapped the warmth from her body. She felt as if she'd been frozen to it. She shivered violently and sat up, rubbing warmth back into her arms. Mose was staring out the window again. Or surely not…still?

Ali didn't care anymore if it made her sound weak. She was going to ask him to hold her, purely for warmth. She'd be scientific about it. *Your broad shoulders and big hands provide excellent surface area with which to transmit heat.* He'd totally buy that. Ali stood slowly, her joints creaking like an old woman, and shuffled over to get Mose's attention.

She poked him in the ribs. She flicked him in the ear. She pulled on his hand.

Nothing.

"Mose," she said, as loudly as she dared.

She didn't think those things outside could get through the walls, but she wasn't willing to risk drawing their attention again. The sounds they made alone…

"Mose," she repeated. She dug her nail into his forearm. He didn't so much as flinch.

"Wake up!" she said, increasing the pressure.

Dark blood welled up around her fingernail and went racing down his wrist. She gasped and pulled away.

"Oh god, I'm so sorry," she said. "I didn't mean—"

Ali saw that it was pointless. Mose hadn't even blinked.

She peeked around his shoulder, out the window.

Had the spot…grown? She swore it was bigger now. It had started as roughly thumbtack-sized; now it looked more like a dime. No, that was probably just because it was dark. Odd, though, how you could still see it at night. It was such a deeper shade of black than everything around it…

"This is the price," Mose said, and Ali jumped.

"What?" She laughed, mostly at herself.

"This is the price," Mose repeated. His voice was sleepy and directionless.

"You okay?" she asked.

"This is what we owe," Mose said. He was frozen in place, his eyes locked on the black spot, his lips barely moving, just enough to make the sounds. "They're not taking what's ours. That's what you'd think. They're just taking back what's theirs."

"I have no idea what you're talking about," Ali said.

She shook Mose gently. He swayed, offering no resistance, but as soon as she let up, he rocked right back into position, fixated on the black spot in the night sky.

"That's what evil is," he said. "That's what we think of as evil: things taking things that aren't theirs. Taking things that are ours. We could fight that, because it's evil. We'd be right, and that would give us strength. But that's not what's happening. They gave it to us in the first place. They gave it to us so we could grow, and that's what we did. Now they're back to reap the benefits. They're just farmers. It's not evil to harvest."

"Mose, hey," Ali said, pulling away. "You are really freaking me out here. If that's what you're trying to do, great job. Please stop."

Mose closed his eyes. Put his hands to his face. Staggered back a few steps.

"Mose?" Ali tried again.

"Yeah," he said. He pressed the meat of his palms against his eyes. He shook his head and laughed. "Sorry, I was spacing out again. I guess we just stay here and wait for help."

"What?" Ali said.

"You said you didn't have any better ideas," Mose said, moving toward her.

"Mose," she said, "that was hours ago."

"Oh?" Mose said. His tone was almost whimsical. "Time really flies in there."

"In where?"

"Inside the black spot. With them. It's funny," Mose said. He stepped into the greasy half-light cast by the dirty window. "So many things seem to matter out here, but in there you can see that none of it does. Not really."

Ali thought it was a trick of the dark at first. Just some oddly cast shadows on Mose's face. But he took a step toward her, and then another, and the shadows did not shift. His eyes had turned black — every bit of them. His eyelids had receded, leaving two wide and unblinking circles of darkness. He reached out and touched Ali's arm. She flinched.

"Don't be like that," Mose said. "I'm still in here. For now."

"Mose…what…" Ali didn't even know what question to ask.

What answer would fix this?

"It's gonna be okay, Ali," he said. And he smiled. It was Mose's smile, that same confident, lopsided smirk. "It's all gonna be okay. For you."

Ali stared into his face and saw that she'd been wrong, earlier. Mose's eyes hadn't turned black. They were gone. Replaced by twin portals to a cold and empty void. In the abyss beyond, something massive shifted. She was in a tiny fishing boat on a dark sea, looking through the porthole as a gargantuan cruise ship passed by. She could only see little details. Tiny snatches of a distant, unfathomable whole.

"Things are gonna be okay f-for me?" Ali repeated. Her mind had left her. She could only parrot back responses.

"Just you," Mose said. He reached up and tucked her hair back around her ear, then laid a gentle kiss on the tip of her nose. "I can make sure of it."

Wait. No. Carlos and his dorky little anime shirts. Mama and her forever-burning cigarettes.

"What about my family?" she asked.

"No," Mose said. "You're all I have time for. You're the only one I can save."

"How?" Ali said. She was just trying to keep him talking now. If he was talking, he couldn't do…whatever he was going to do next.

"Like this," Mose said, and with two quick steps he crossed over to the door, flipped the latch, and swung it wide.

A breeze as subtle and sharp as a scalpel cut through Ali.

Mose stepped out and walked briskly down the ramp of the parking garage, heading toward the pacing, murmuring figures at the bottom. To Ali's amazement, she followed. When they were within spitting distance, all three figures — the older woman, the handyman, and the riot cop — turned to face them as one. For an instant, there was pure madness in their eyes. Then they stiffened up and went still. They turned as one and walked to the edge of the roof.

"Pretty cool, huh?" Mose laughed.

Ali said nothing.

"Let's get rid of them," Mose said.

One by one, the trio leaned over the dividing wall until gravity took them. They tumbled in complete silence, save for a bony impact when they hit the pavement. When the last disappeared — the golden-haired woman in the stunning red dress, her locks fluttering in the wind — Mose turned to Ali and shrugged.

"That's it. I can't do anything about the Sleepers." Mose gestured down the far ramp at the slumped and broken figures, still as statues, lurking in the shadows there. "They're not hers. But as long as you keep your distance, you'll be fine."

Ali tried to think of something to say, if only because Mose seemed to be waiting for it.

What could she say? Thanks for mind controlling the maniacs? It was really great the way you made those people commit suicide for me? Hope your eyes grow back?

When nothing came, Mose just sighed sadly and began walking away.

"Mose," she called, just as he reached the alcove to the stairs.

He turned and looked at her, or toward her — she couldn't tell with those vacant pools in his face.

"I'm sorry," she said.

He smiled.

"I'm not," he called back. "We all have to pay the price now, Ali. Remember that."

"I don't know what it means," she said, and her thoughts all came back in a flood of questions. "Pay what, to who? What's—"

"No." Mose shook his head. "That's all the time she gave me."

A shiver passed through him.

"Mose?" Ali asked, though she knew in an instant that he was gone.

"Se po ta ku ho ire ra," the thing that used to be Mose said, its voice no longer remotely human. It sounded like howling winds filtered through steel pipes. "Mi ra Hoa."

It turned and disappeared into the shadows. Ali listened until she could no longer hear the echoing of its footsteps. Somewhere far away, a man yelled a girl's name, over and over again. A siren sounded, then cut off abruptly. Somebody laughed, earnest and high.

Ali looked to the black spot. It had definitely grown. She could see that now. It was the about the size of a golf ball, rivaling the moon for prominence. If you'd asked her yesterday what color the sky was at night, she would have said black. But it wasn't. It was a gradient: deep-sea blue that faded into itself until your eye lost the ability to discern between its shades. The night wasn't truly black. The spot was truly black: an absolute and indisputable nothingness. She had never actually seen nothing before tonight. Had never truly grasped the concept.

But she understood it now.

Beat by Beat

Mari slams her bedroom door and listens for a few seconds. When nobody yells, she yanks it open and slams it again.

"Mariana!" Diego shouts.

He doesn't follow it up with anything. He knows that whatever he orders her to do, she'll do the opposite as loudly and as often as she can until he gives up. Diego knows he can't make her do a thing when mama and papa are gone, which is often. She's across the bridge in Juaritos, picking up shifts at the clinic again. He's always at the Fort, doing something he isn't allowed (or just doesn't want) to talk about.

When she's satisfied that Diego isn't going to escalate this argument into a war — and a little disappointed, come to think of it — Mari hurls herself into bed and grips her pillow in her fists. She balls them up so tight they go numb and start shaking.

She hears Lucas protest — his little boy whine, high and pleading, like a drill in her head — from all the way downstairs. Mari can't make out his words, but she doesn't need to. He's always bleating about needing to go out to catch those little video game monsters on his phone. When Mari first started in on Diego, Lucas had the nerve to try to join her — as though not being allowed to play his dumb game is anywhere near the same injustice as her not getting to see The Mellow Tonins on the one night they're actually, *miraculously* playing this skeevy town. They're only like her favorite band this year. She put their poster up and everything. When was the last time she'd bothered decorating her room? They move so often they don't even own thumbtacks anymore. She had to go out and buy them just for the occasion. That's how much she cares, *and nobody even cares that she cares.*

She gazes desperately at the poster — Mikey with his heavy eyeliner, worn so ironically you can almost see him rolling his eyes. Yvette in her long sleeveless coat, head down, lost to the bass. Deacon barely glimpsed in the back, both arms raised, drumsticks clutched like he's hanging on for dear life.

Everybody in the whole world is going to that show tonight. David, Angel, Lucy — even Gabe, the giant dork who probably can't name a single song off their first album. *Everybody in the whole world.*

Except for her.

And all because Mama told Diego it "felt weird" out there.

If it was just Diego, she'd shove him outta the way and skip right out the front door, both middle fingers raised in triumph. She would never — *ever* — do anything just because Diego said so. He's only two years older than her and a total loser outcast. Mari hates when people at school ask if he's her brother. Like, she can't say "no," because then it's a secret. In high school, there's nothing more deadly than a secret. It always gets out. Then it's a weapon to be used against you.

So she's gotta acknowledge Diego's existence at least, but even that eats at her. He's so dim, he doesn't even realize she's trying to ignore him. She's tried everything — looks down when they pass in the halls, doesn't return his greetings, takes the long way to Chem just so she won't pass his locker — but he won't get the point. In fact, whenever Mari ignores him, Diego starts yelling her name or asking her what's for dinner or what they're going to do this weekend, like he's trying to tell everybody they know each other for some—

Oh. God.

He's doing it on purpose!

She flashes back to his goofy smile, which he never wears except when they meet at school. The way he trips over nothing just when she and her friends walk by. Or else he burps or he says some stupid slang that nobody has used for, like, eons. It's almost like the more she's embarrassed by him, the harder he wants to embarrass her. But that's…that's just *evil.*

Mari gets up and slams her door again. Diego doesn't even have the decency to say something so she has an excuse to yell at him. The jerk.

She thinks of sneaking out, just to spite him. He would get in so much trouble. "You're the responsible one," Mama would say, her arms crossed over her dirty blue scrubs, hair all frazzled from work. "If we can't trust you, what happens then?"

Mari's insides light up just to think of it.

The only problem is she'd get it way worse than Diego. It's like cutting off an arm just to give your enemy a headache.

Lucas yells again. She makes out the words this time — "rare ones only come out once a month!" — and rolls her eyes. But she realizes that's not enough, so she gets up and opens her door, pokes her head out into the hall, and screams:

"Shut up, Lucas!"

Him and Diego are still arguing in the kitchen, downstairs. She waits for it…waits for iiiit…

"No, *you* shut up!" Lucas finally shouts back.

And there's her excuse.

See, Diego can play the quiet game, but Lucas has got no filter between his mouth and his brain.

Mari stomps down the hallway. She wants them to hear her coming, so they can worry about it. But it's hard work. She practically has to jump just to get her footsteps to register through the carpet. She's kinda small for her age, and Fort Bliss' military housing is new-build; it hasn't had time to go to crap like the ones in Nevada. Still just as ugly, though —

adjoining townhomes cramped up in a fourplex, beige on beige on slightly darker beige. Big, ugly squares, all the same.

She rounds the corner and practically slides into the kitchen.

"What did you say to me?" Mari snaps.

"I said *you* shut up," Lucas snipes back, safe from his fortified position behind Diego's legs. "Because you said it first."

"I said 'shut up' because you're being a little jerk," Mari says. "You can't tell me to shut up when you're the one that needs to shut up."

"Would you both shut up?" Diego asks in his aggravatingly polite way. Like he's so far above their petty squabbles he's only playing along out of boredom.

"No!" Lucas and Mari shout at the same time.

For just a second, she feels a bond with the little brat. Allied together against the bigger dork, who has the gall to try to boss them both around.

But that fades when she remembers why he's upset. His stupid game. The concert.

"Did she even say *why* we can't go out?" Mari asks.

She knows the answer. She was here when Mama told him. But she wants to hear Diego say it, so *he* can hear how stupid it sounds.

"Because it feels weird out there," Diego says.

He's looking at the ceiling, not in her eyes. He knows.

"Oh, cool. That's a great answer," Mari says. She holds out her hand, palm up, like she's holding the answer there. She makes a big show of checking it out from all angles, then says: "Yep, makes total sense to me. It's weird outside. Better stay in until we die."

"Look," Diego says. "I don't like it any more than you do—"

Mari cuts him off. "Like you even care! You don't even *go* out. You probably love this."

Diego closes his eyes. She can practically see him counting to ten. Little numbers rolling back behind his eyelids. When he opens them again, he doesn't say anything. He just turns and walks over to the window. Holds the blinds apart with one hand and motions for her to come look.

She doesn't. Like she's just gonna jump at his beck and call?

"It *is* weird out there," he says. He shifts his eyes from her to the window and back. "Mrs. Hendricks is standing on her lawn staring at the sky."

"Oh my god, who cares?" Mari says, practically all one word. "Are you saying I can't go to the show because the neighbor lady is outside?" Mari makes a wanking motion with her open fist. Lucas joins her.

The little idiot probably doesn't even know what it means.

"She's been out there for hours," Diego says. "And it's not just her — half the neighborhood is all zombied out."

Well that's…they're probably just…

Okay, Diego has her there. She has to at least look.

She leans way out over the sink, not quite tall enough to peek through the blinds while keeping both feet on the floor. Diego's not lying. The Asian kids from down the block — she doesn't know their names, the other army brats are too interstitial to even bother — are right in the middle of the street, all huddled up around something Mari can't see. A couple guys in uniform are milling about like drunks. The buff guy from a few houses down and his tiny wife; the creepy old white folks with their forever-smiling teeth, and yeah — Mrs. Hendricks, too. She's lock-legged on her "lawn," which is really just a little strip of grass the size and shape of a carpet runner. Her mouth is open a little bit, eyes wide, staring at something above Mari's house.

"So what?" Mari asks, even though she goes cold in her toes and fingertips. "They're probably just looking at that black spot in the sky."

Mari leans in further and looks up to follow their gaze, but she can't see the spot from this angle.

Diego lets the blinds snap shut on her face.

She hops back onto her heels and glares at him.

"You're not supposed to look at the spot," he says. "The news said it'll hurt your eyes."

"Yeah," she says. "Well, obviously the neighbors don't care."

"Or maybe it's doing something really cool!" Lucas exclaims. He's hopping up and down at the edge of the kitchen counter, trying to lever his weight forward so he can see out the window, too. But the blinds are closed, and he's still a couple feet too short, even if they weren't.

"He's right," Mari says, not because he is, but because anybody that's not Diego is right by, like, comparison. "I bet something awesome is happening. It's probably like our moon landing out there and you're keeping us from it."

Diego laughs, and she can practically taste how annoying it is.

"Okay," he says. "Let's go see, then."

Lucas is already running for the door, like he somehow knew this was going to happen, but Diego issues a bunch of negative tuts that stop him short.

"In the living room," Diego clarifies. "If something big is happening, it'll be on the news."

He's always one step ahead. He probably plans this stuff out at night, laying in his smelly bed and plotting ways to ruin everybody's lives.

But Mari still follows him to the living room because the people on the street are bouncing around in her head. She's never seen grown-ups make those faces before. Only real little kids let themselves go that blank in public, smiling or drooling or laughing and yelling at nothing you can see. Mrs. Hendricks looked like a two-year-old going through a car wash for the first time. Just awe and confusion and terror but also a little bit of joy. Mari had to see what she was looking at, even if it was secondhand.

Diego flips the TV on. He doesn't even sit down. Just stands there in the middle of the room with his arms crossed like he's doing something big and important instead of pushing a button on a remote. It's amazing, Mari thinks, just how many ways he finds to bother her. She and Lucas sit on the couch like normal people. Diego surfs around until he hits the news. A pretty Latina girl that looks way too young to be doing TV stuff is standing in front of a crowd of pissed-off-looking people. She's talking fast, trying to beat something about to happen. Then the camera spins around and frames a tall old white guy in a blue uniform. He stands behind a wooden podium, a small army of men in riot gear flanking him.

He starts yammering about something stupid.

"Oh," Mari says. "This is just about those gangbangers that got shot."

"They weren't gangbangers," Diego says, like he knows everything. "They were just kids. *Mexican* kids."

He emphasizes that last bit like she should care because she's also supposed to be Mexican, even though she was born in Michigan and she only spoke enough Spanish to understand when Mama yelled at her. It's like, after the move, being this close to Mexico tricked Diego into thinking they were anything but ordinary, lame Americans.

He *wishes.*

Mari is so lost in her head, trying to think of the perfect insult to show Diego how stupid his newfound immigrant kick is, that she actually misses the start of the riot.

She just sees the old white guy fall, and then the stormtrooper dudes step forward and start emptying assault rifles into the crowd. Diego jumps, and Lucas slams his hands over his eyes. Ever since he saw Papa get beat up real bad back in Nevada, Lucas can't watch people hurting each other. He just shuts down. Probably why he likes his dumb animal and card games so much. No people getting hurt.

The camera catches a few frames of the crowd screaming, bleeding, falling, and then it's on the ground. She forgets that cameras have, like, operators behind them. So used to just thinking of them as the all-seeing eye. Now the eye is sideways, and she sees what's probably the camera guy grab the pretty news girl and hustle off toward an alley. Somebody kicks the camera, and it spins for a while — world gone to a black and red disk — then it settles on its back, idly filming the sky. That little black spot in the upper right hand corner, like a fly on the screen, doing and looking like not much at all.

But the sound's still on.

Gunfire. A woman crying. Some wet meat sounds. Impact. So many different people screaming and yelling stuff that it's all just lost. Just noise.

Mari reaches out and covers Lucas' ears, too. She's been yelling Diego's name over and over for what feels like an hour, but he's just standing there quietly watching the sky and listening to the screams. Mari leans out from the couch and kicks him in the back of the leg. That finally snaps him out of it. He looks at her like they're old friends meeting unexpectedly at the supermarket, this little disbelieving smile on his lips.

"Turn it off!" she yells.

He blinks.

"Oh," he says. "Right."

The room goes quiet except for Lucas, who's quietly humming to himself. Always that same song, when the violence breaks his mind.

"What's wrong with you?" Mari snaps at Diego.

He looks like he's actually considering the question. He pauses for a long time, then finally decides:

"Nothing. I just wanted to see what was going on…"

Lucas and his little song. Toes digging into the carpet. Meat of his palms sealed over his eyes.

"What about him?" Mari asks. She motions to Lucas with her chin. She's still holding her hands over his ears.

"Crap," Diego says, and it's like his brain just came back from a vacation. "I am so sorry, buddy, I wasn't thinking, I didn't mean—"

Mari releases her grip and backs away. Diego drops to his knees and peers into Lucas' covered face.

"Are you okay, little dude? It's all right. It's over now. It's safe to come out," Diego keeps whispering, soft and steady. A gentle running stream of platitudes until Lucas finally peeks out between his locked fingers.

"The blankets," Mari says. She speaks from the corner of her mouth. She doesn't want to look at Diego right now. Instead, she's looking at the kitchen, staring at the closed blinds above the sink.

"Right," Diego says, all matter of factly, like it's a vote that just passed. "Let's get you into the blankets."

Lucas' eyes are glossy. That humming song of his on loop. He follows Diego like he's been brainwashed.

He probably won't speak for another few hours. That's how it happened last time.

Mama and Papa have Mondays off, during the day. The only time they get alone, Mama reminds them constantly, as though it's the kids that are clinging to her and not the other way around.

Lucas, he came home early from school one day and found Mama and Papa watching some war flick. They didn't hear the door. He stood frozen behind the couch for god knows how long, watching people shoot each other, beat each other's brains in, die screaming. Never said a thing.

Mama jumped when she spotted him, caught him up running, and dumped him headlong under his blankets. He crashed out like a coma patient until late that night, when he asked for a milkshake. Papa went out and got him one from an all-night drive thru. Lucas stayed up 'til morning nursing the shake, but by lunch he was back around and talking.

Diego's the one who forgot about Lucas' thing. That means he's the one who has to sit by the kid's bed, watching the lump under the blankets for signs of life. That's good: it gives Mari dinnertime free, at least — no Diego trying to force Hungry Man dinners on her like they actually supply any kind of vital nutrients.

Mari gets up and pads to the kitchen in her slipper-socks. They're super dorky and all, but they're the coziest things in the world. She only wears them around the house — if anybody saw her in bulky red knee-highs with cheesy cartoon stars and stripes all over them, her heart would literally explode. She pours and drinks a glass of water, tries not to, but opens the blinds again.

The street is empty.

That should put her at ease, right? The eclipse or whatever was over, and her neighbors went back inside.

Right.

That's what happened.

But see, there's a single child's shoe in the middle of the road, and it's freaking her out.

Stupid kid probably lost it playing tag or something, and then ran inside without thinking.

But see, there's a dark spot on the lawn where Mrs. Hendricks had been standing. Probably some gearhead jerk dumping out his motor oil instead of recycling it. Happens all the time.

Right.

That's what it is.

But see, there are no lights on in any of the other houses.

All of the military families live in these identical plaster crapboxes. Crammed together end-to-end, four deep and not enough windows. The second the sun's not overhead, you need lights on. Diego always has all of theirs on twenty minutes before he has to, because he likes to "get it out of the way." That's all he does: "get things out of the way." He's probably going to join the army when he's old enough, no matter what Papa says. He's got that good little soldier stare.

So unless there's a blackout or something, all these houses should be lit up like Vegas.

That's what's going on: a blackout. A very localized blackout, affecting the rest of her block, but not her house. Or the streetlamps on the corner.

Right.

But over there, across the street, a shape darts through the gap between complexes, and there's something about its quickness that sets Mari's nerves on edge. Probably one of the Asian kids didn't get the message that hide 'n seek was over. Now he's running home at full tilt, afraid of being late.

Right.

That's all the shape is.

But then there's the screaming.

Mari startles and sloshes water all over her favorite Mellow Tonins T-shirt. She knows it's completely lame to be the girl wearing the band's shirt *at* the band's show, but she was hoping to get Deacon to sign it. While it was still on her.

He'd have to touch her!

That was worth risking lame.

Mari listens, but the scream doesn't repeat. It didn't sound like a kid, and it didn't sound playful. It sounded like anger. Pure and harsh, unbroken by thought or concern. Like whoever screamed was so mad they didn't care if it made them look stupid or if the neighbors asked questions later.

Mari decides to check on Lucas. That's what she's doing. It's not because she's freaked out by it "feeling weird out there." That's still a dumb reason for not getting to go to the show, and she won't dignify Mama's logic by acknowledging it.

Up the stairs and down the skinny hall to the tiny bedroom. She pushes the door open — Lucas used to hang signs on it; biohazard symbols, posters for cartoons, little skull stickers, and his own crude drawings of superheroes and fighter jets — but after the last flurry of moves, even he gave up on decorating.

That's weird. There's a Lucas-sized bump under the pile of safety blankets — six deep, no matter how hot it is — but Diego isn't sitting with him.

Oh god, he's such a jerk. Does he just automatically expect her to do it? Why, because she's a girl?

"You do all the emotional stuff," Diego would probably say, in his good little soldier voice. "That's woman's work."

And then she'd BAM! punch him right in the nose, and he'd start crying and she'd say—

Lucas picks up his humming song.

Mari sighs, extra loud, so he can hear it through the blankets. Then she crawls up on the bed and snakes a hand under the covers. She finds his ankle and rests her fingers against it, so he has a constant reminder that he isn't alone. With her free hand, she fishes her phone out and starts poking around. Since her plans got so unjustly canceled, she's already killed half the night checking the internet. She read through her social feeds, checked all eight of her email accounts, texted everybody that would reply — she's done basically everything a human being can do.

Now she just stares at her screen and waits for something to happen. It doesn't.

All of her friends are probably at the show already and too busy to reply, so her whole world is on pause. She settles for watching stupid cat videos or whatever on mute, until she falls asleep using the Lucas lump for a pillow.

When she wakes up, it's fully dark outside. She taps her phone, which says it's past midnight.

What?

She slept for, like, four hours? And nobody woke her?

Mari pats around the bed, flattening the bumps, and finds Lucas has already recovered and gone. The little butt. He should have known she didn't want to sleep the whole night away. Even if there wasn't anything to do and no point to being awake at all.

At least both Mama and Papa would be home by now.

She rubs the sleep out of her face and tries to muster up some anger, but she's still groggy and it won't stick. She thinks about just finishing the job and crashing in her own room for the rest of the night, but if she sleeps too long, Mama and Papa will be gone again in the morning, and they'll have no idea how mad she was. That is not acceptable. They *have* to know.

Mari trudges into the hall on search mode — all the bedrooms are empty — and tromps down the stairs. Lucas is sitting at the kitchen table eating a bowl of cereal. He's got that checked-out look, and he'll probably have it for a while. But at least he's up and around. Mari thinks about hassling him for ditching her, but he's had a rough enough night already.

She'll get him tomorrow.

She fakes some energy and charges into the living room, all spooled up and ready to unravel all over her parents. But they're not there.

It's just Diego.

None of the lights are on in the living room. Only the glow of the TV set. The same image from earlier — that abandoned news camera filming the sky, a little black spot burning in the corner. It was sunset when they first saw it. All fiery orange smeared into dark blue, the black spot the sole point of contrast. Now it was a night shot: a smattering of stars in the darkened sky, which you'd think would make the black spot invisible, but no — somehow you can still see it. Like it's blacker than space.

Diego is staring at the TV all quiet, his lanky arms slack at his sides. His mouth is open a little bit and his eyes are wide, pupils expanded like a druggie. Mari says his name, but he doesn't answer. She snaps her fingers in his face, and he doesn't even blink. She shoves him, but he's like one of those inflatable boxing clowns — just bounces right back into place. Mari walks up and stands in front of him. She's too short to block his view. He just stares over her head. She holds her hands up in front of his eyes and then she's on the ground somehow, her brain rattling around her skull and little spots skirting her vision.

He…hit her? Diego actually hit her? Is that what happened? She's disoriented and can't quite remember him moving.

"What—" she asks, but Diego cuts her off.

"Shhh," he says, not breaking eye contact with the TV. "Just listen."

She does, for some stupid reason, but she doesn't hear anything. Either he's got the TV on mute or the sound on the broadcast gave out or else there's nothing to hear in the first place.

"I don't—" she says, and Diego screams so loud it sounds like something pops in his throat.

"Shut up!" he yells.

She flinches, starts crawling away real slow. But he's not interested in her at all. Only the black spot on the screen.

"Just listen," he says to nobody. "They're explaining everything."

Mari's legs are boiled noodles, but she drags herself upright in the hallway. She doesn't want to *crawl* into the kitchen and risk freaking Lucas out. Last thing she needs is for him to go all catatonic again. Because now he needs to run. Now they need to get the hell out of the house.

"Hey, buddy," she says, approaching Lucas like he's a skittish kitten.

Right away, that's the wrong move.

Like, fully ninety percent of Mari's interactions with Lucas involve her informing him of how annoying he is, and the other ten percent are her asking him to leave.

Lucas' eyebrows scrunch up, and he leans away from her.

"What's going on?" he says.

He's talking. That's good. That's *amazing*, actually — his whole PTSD thing might be getting better. She hopes it stays that way, after tonight.

"Nothing," Mari says. She tries to correct course. "Except for you being a little butt."

The weight of uncertainty lifts off of him. He loosens up, turns his attention back to his cereal.

"Then quit being weird," he says.

"We have to go," Mari tells him.

He scoffs.

"I wish."

"No, seriously, we have to get out of here."

A tremble runs through Lucas. It's still too soon after his last breakdown for this kind of thing.

"Why?" he asks, already dreading the answer.

"It's Papa," Mari says. "He uh…he wants to see us. Show us something up at the Fort."

It's literally the worst lie Mari has ever told. No part of it is believable. She lost credibility at "Papa wants to see us." That they'd be allowed, much less *wanted* at the Fort, at this time of night? Lucas doesn't bite. He doesn't even nibble.

"You're being a crazy person," he says.

"No, really." Mari can't think of anything to do but commit. To keep slapping shiny parts onto the lie until the mere possibility of its truth is too intriguing to pass up. "It's the secret project he's been working on. They're all finished now —*just* now, tonight — so they don't have to keep it secret anymore, so they can show their families."

Still ludicrous enough to be unbelievable, but not so ludicrous that it's irresistible. She's losing him.

"I guess it's some kind of uh…hovering…"

Lucas' eyes widen, marginally.

"Robot…tank," she finishes.

He's practically salivating but still reticent.

"I guess it even talks," she says.

And Lucas is up on his feet, yanking at her shorts.

"Let's go!" he chirps. "Hurry!"

"Okay, sure, whatever," she says, carefully distant.

She lets him pull her to the door and just about has her hand on the knob when Lucas looks her up and down and stops to puzzle.

"You're going like that?" he says.

Mari's wearing her Mellow Tonins shirt, a pair of too-short jean cut-offs — Mama called them Daisies for some reason — and her fuzzy stars-and-stripes pajama-socks. That's it. No shoes, no jacket.

"Yeah," she says. "They're just gross old Army guys. Who cares?"

She reaches out, grabs the knob again.

"Are you coming, too?" Lucas says, looking behind her.

Cold needles dance up the backs of her legs.

"Nobody is going anywhere," Diego answers.

Mari's mind revs, but it's not in gear. Can she lie to him? He'd never buy the one she told Lucas. She can't think of another. She actually can't think of anything at all to say. So she doesn't. She yanks the door open, and her wrist shatters.

She yelps and jumps backward, clutching her arm to her chest.

Diego calmly shuts and locks the door before turning to face her. He's got psycho eyes. Not blank, like before: now he's hyper-focused, but detached — it's that same expression the cultists on TV get when they start talking about their weirdo prophets. Diego's holding a hammer in one hand. Black rubber handle with a steel head. Tiny spikes on it. The meat tenderizer.

Mari looks at her pulverized wrist and sees little dots of blood rising where the spikes impacted.

Lucas hasn't even had time to process what he just saw. He's still looking between her and Diego, all confused, when his coma response starts kicking in.

"We're nothing without rules," Diego says. He starts right out with crazy and just keeps going. "Weren't you listening?"

"To…to what?" Mari asks.

"To them," he says. He gestures at the ceiling with his hammer.

He watches her for a reply, but she doesn't have one.

"Oh, no," he says, and he looks heartbroken. "You can't hear them? That's…that's awful. I'm so sorry."

Diego reaches out as if to hug her, then reconsiders.

"I'll have to show you," he says, voice gone icy.

Before she can blink, he's grabbed her by the arm, which she's been nursing against her chest like an injured bird. She screams. Diego doesn't care or even notice. He drags her across the room to the big butcher-block cutting board Mama keeps out on the counter. He pins her broken wrist to the board, and she cripples with pain.

"Now, the rule was that you're not allowed to go out tonight," Diego says, all business. "I was there when the rules were explained—"

"It doesn't matter!" she protests. "Mama just wanted to keep us safe. If she knew—"

"It doesn't matter who *makes* the rules," Diego says. "Or what they intended. It only matters what the rules say and that we obey them. Don't you see? We're animals without rules. Dirty beasts."

He brings the hammer down on her thumb. She mostly just feels the vibration through the board. Not much pain yet.

"You tried to get out using this hand," Diego continues. "So it's gotta go."

Hammer again. Her pointer finger this time.

"If you could hear them, you'd understand. You'd understand this was mercy — the others, they're fickle. Now that they've returned, they're taking back all their gifts. They know we don't deserve them. But not Haruk. She's justice. She's law. Now that she's back, she isn't revoking her gifts — she's giving us more!"

Two quick slaps — god, it sounds just like Mama beating slabs of chicken — and Mari doesn't even know which fingers are pulp now. It's all one big burning ball of wrong.

Diego pauses, watching her kindly. Like he expects her to thank him or something.

In the quiet, she can hear Lucas humming his fragile little song.

Diego frowns at her, then brings the hammer down one more time. He releases her wrist, pushes her backward, and she crumples on the kitchen floor like a puppet with its strings cut. Mari holds her arm close, but she doesn't dare look at the damage. That's the only thing that would make it worse: actually seeing what's been done.

The tenderizer is dripping red. Her blood, streaming off it in ribbons.

"Isn't judgment beautiful?" Diego asks her.

He means it. He wants her to agree.

So she does. What else is she supposed to do?

"It was wonderful," she says, not recognizing her own voice. It sounds like a shy little girl. "Thank you."

He beams at her.

"So now you get to understand — really understand — what breaking the rules means," he says, like he's kinda jealous of her.

Mari doesn't cry. But only because she's scared that's going to make it worse.

They're all silent for a moment, save for Lucas and his droning.

"We skipped dinner tonight, didn't we?" Diego says.

Mari winces.

"Don't worry!" Diego laughs — *actually laughs* — and says, "That was my fault. I was supposed to feed you, and I forgot. I was listening to *them*. But that's no excuse. There are no excuses. I'll see justice later, once the wrongs are corrected. In the meantime…"

He trails off as he makes his way to the fridge. He pulls a couple of TV dinners out and sets about unboxing, unwrapping, and poking at them. He joins in Lucas' humming as he works — the whole family has heard the tune enough to know it by heart — and in a few minutes has the food microwaved, plated up, and set out on the table.

Mari uses the time to slowly acknowledge the pain, which emanates in shockwaves from the elbow down. She doesn't dare cry out or move from her place on the floor. But every second she sits, just waiting, is a drop of adrenaline burning out inside her. A tick up in pain. By the time Diego has dinner ready, she's dizzy with agony.

"Up," he says, grabbing her good arm and helping her to her feet.

He deposits her in a chair and turns to Lucas. Zombied out, he doesn't struggle at all. Just goes where he's guided.

They sit there, bleeding and humming, uncertain of what comes next.

"Well, go ahead and eat," Diego says, chipper as a soccer mom.

Mari picks up her shaking fork and tries to keep a piece of Salisbury steak on it long enough to reach her mouth. She fails a few times but eventually gets it. It tastes like wet, dirty cardboard. She can't tell if that's because she's going into shock or because it's Salisbury steak.

Diego smiles at her. He turns to Lucas, who stares straight ahead and does nothing.

"Eat," Diego tells him.

Lucas hums.

"Eat," Diego says. Like he's pronouncing a death sentence.

Lucas doesn't respond.

Diego spins and starts rattling through cabinets until he finds what he's looking for. He comes back to the table with a pair of vise-pliers from the miscellaneous drawer and squeezes Lucas' mouth open.

"Wait, stop," Mari says. "What are you doing?"

"If you don't eat, you don't need teeth," Diego says, working the pliers over Lucas' top canine.

"No, don't—" Mari starts, but it's too late.

Diego rips the pliers out, and a stream of blood arcs across the table. It splashes warm and thick across Mari's face.

Lucas screams.

She screams.

Mari tips out of her chair and backs all the way across the floor. Puddles up in the farthest corner and just keeps screaming. She wants to stop, she really does, but it's like somebody pulled the cord in her back and now she has to make this noise until the mechanism winds down. Even Lucas stops first. After the initial yelp, he falls into wracking sobs.

Diego stands by the table and waits it out. It can't last forever. Lucas lapses back into pause mode. Mari stops screaming just before she starts to black out. When it's all over, she looks at Diego with blank terror.

"That's okay," he reassures her. "Mama didn't set any rules against screaming."

He patiently ushers the both of them back to the dinner table, puts forks in their hands, and waits. Mari digs in immediately, and this time even Lucas manages to shakily spoon some watery potatoes into his mouth.

"Good," Diego says. "You've been fed. Now, to me…"

He flips through the cupboards, neatly stacking things to the side as he goes.

"Do we keep eating?" Mari asks him.

"It doesn't matter," he answers quickly, automatically. "The rule was that I feed you. You've been fed."

His pile of assorted objects grows. Cooking Sherry from the forgotten cabinet above the stove, rubbing alcohol from the medicine drawer, Papa's good whiskey from his hiding spot that everybody knows about…

"W-what are you doing?" Mari asks him.

He looks at her like he forgot she was there. Or maybe like a chair that just suddenly started to speak.

"I didn't cook for you on time," he says, like that's an explanation.

He upends the rubbing alcohol over his head. Smells like acid and medicine. It reminds Mari of a room you're not supposed to go in a hospital. When the plastic bottle is empty, Diego tosses it aside and picks up the Sherry. He sloshes it around the cabinets and on the counters. Finally, he grabs the dusty brown bottle — objectively, Mari knows she's got bigger problems, but she still instinctually cringes when Diego uncorks Papa's whiskey and starts emptying it out on the floor.

Mari sneaks up and grabs Lucas out of his chair, covering his eyes with her good hand. She backs the two of them up as far as they can go. Diego pauses to think, and Mari hopes he just snapped out of it. Maybe this is like, a nervous breakdown — and it'll all be over as abruptly as it started. Diego'll start crying and they'll send him to a place for this kind of thing. He'll wear papery clothes and talk about his feelings and walk everywhere barefoot and come home in a few months all fragile and skittish like a deer—

But no.

Diego snaps his fingers like he just remembered something. He smiles, then crosses over to the miscellaneous drawer again. He leaves slippery, shimmering footprints. He rummages around in there, comes out with a blue plastic stick. He resumes his place in the pool of alcohol and holds the tip of the stick up to his head. It's not until she hears the click that Mari recognizes the blue thing: it's the fireplace lighter they bought a few moves back, when they briefly had a fireplace and naively thought they'd use it.

It doesn't light.

"Diego," Mari starts, but there's another click and fire flows down his body like syrup.

It's oddly beautiful for the first few seconds: just a wave of flickering blue tracing Diego's arms and face, a soft surge of yellow and orange following behind. He looks angelic in that freeze frame: a serene young boy behind a watercolor aura. Then he really catches. His hair and clothes go first.

The flames hit the puddle at his feet and expand in every direction. It felt so slow at first, but now time lurches forward. Half the kitchen is an inferno in the space of a breath. Mari edges toward the door, reluctantly removes her unbroken hand from poor Lucas eyes, and reaches for the knob.

Diego's head — just a black silhouette behind a curtain of fire — instantly snaps towards her.

"You're not allowed to go out," he says.

Mari figured any sounds out of his mouth would all be screaming, but he speaks calmly and harshly: like he's reprimanding a toddler. Looking at him there, a twisting black mannequin inside a hurricane of flame — the voice should be demonic. It should be *The Exorcist* or like a death metal band. But it's just Diego's voice, and that's the worst part.

She rips the door open and shoves Lucas out first. He only runs a few steps, enough for the momentum of her push to peter out, and no more. Mari grabs his wrist as she sprints by, drags him out onto the stoop, down the sidewalk, and across the street. But she stops there and turns around to…what? Assess the damage? She doesn't really know.

It's all just fire in there. Like their front door opens right into hell.

And out from it walks Diego.

He doesn't pause for a second, just spots the pair of them frozen across the way and starts their direction. He's moving fast, but not running. A brisk walk, like he's on his way to tell off a coworker and — oh yeah, incidentally, he's also on fire.

Mari is backpedaling, Lucas in tow. She's transfixed by the figure advancing on her. It's impossible. It's something out of a fantasy movie. It leaves flaming footprints in the grass. She can't think of this monster as Diego anymore, can't reconcile the thing as human at all. It raises a finger to point at her.

"We're *not* allowed to leave," it says.

The fire is finally starting to affect its voice. Vowels come easy, but the consonants barely register. The creature is also starting to slow down, which is good, since she and Lucas are backed up as far as they can go, cornered against the garage of the opposite four-plex. She can't do anything but stare in awe as the thing approaches. It stumbles, recovers, trips again, goes to its knees. Her heart soars, but it's still coming. Crawling on three limbs, that one accusing finger still pointing.

It's trying to speak again, but it must have lost the vital parts. Just sputtering and bubbling. Not ten feet away from them, it loses the front arm and collapses on its belly. That doesn't faze it. It just starts wriggling forward on its shoulders like a worm. It closes another few feet like that before it finally stops altogether and sort of collapses in on itself. It smells familiar. Like the Fourth of July. Fireworks and gunpowder and barbecue.

Mari blinks, and her sense of self comes roaring back. Her very first action is to cover Lucas' eyes, though she knows she's laughably late. She inches along the garage door, not taking her eyes off the pyre for a second. They skirt the corner of the townhome and creep backwards down the sidewalk until the fear of what's behind them overcomes the fear of what's in front of them. Mari glances around the block, but it looks empty. She can hear chaos coming in on the wind from somewhere close, but their block is an island of calm. She squats before Lucas and looks him in the eye. Tracks her head back and forth, but he's not following her.

"I know, okay," she says, shaking his shoulders gently. "I know that was bad. Worse than bad. That was, like, nightmare stuff. I know and I'm so, so sorry. Okay? I'd give anything for you not to have seen that, and you can have *so much* time to deal with this later. We'll get you a million blankets and the biggest milkshake in the world. But you've gotta stay with me for just a few minutes, okay? Just until we find Papa?"

She waits, but Lucas says nothing.

There's a worrying throb from her wrist. She still can't look. Can't let herself understand the damage. There will be time for that when she finds help. Time to take care of everything. But right now she has to focus on moving. As long as they stay moving, nothing bad can happen.

She's not sure why she thinks that, but she doesn't feel like dissecting the logic right now. Instead she takes Lucas' tiny limp hand in her one good one and guides them out of their housing complex. Then she sees why her block went so quiet. The party is next door. Up ahead there's an intersection between this road and one of the base's main thoroughfares. She forgets — or maybe never knew — the name of the street. Just past it is the base's mall, called something stupid like Freedom Post or Freedom Shops (just like it is on every base), and it's as busy as she's ever seen it.

There are people, or something that looks like them, everywhere.

It's like one of those zombie movies that Diego likes—

Nope. Can't think about him. Try again.

It looks like somebody started a riot on top of a massacre. There are bloody and broken bodies all around. Most them are still. Some of them move, moan, clutch wounds, or crawl toward cover. Others are standing, but just barely: bent at the waist, neck slack, arms hanging, like there's an invisible wire wrapped around their bellies and it's the only thing keeping them upright.

In the distance, shadows blink through the mall's lit areas. People running. Or more like loping, kinda-but-not-really on all fours, like angry gorillas. They flit by so quickly she can't see them. Not really. She just catches silhouettes. And screaming. Faint, but so much of it and so purely, starkly furious that it sets her small hairs on end. She starts backing away, toward home — maybe they can put out the fire and wait until help arrives — but she hits something solid.

Mari turns and looks into the happiest face she's ever seen. Ear-to-ear smile, pure teeth and gums. Eyes practically sparkling. Every inch of it is covered in blood spatter. The guy's hair is all matted with it, his clothes completely soaked in gore. He holds a pickaxe over one shoulder, all jaunty, like he's off to play polo or something.

"Hey," the bloody man says. "Quick: what's six times seven?"

Too much, too fast. Mari's brain is on autopilot.

"Forty-two," she answers, reflexively.

"Good!" The man laughs, and he steps around her. Practically skips down the sidewalk, spinning his pickaxe in one hand.

He stops by one of the moaning bodies and repeats his question.

"H-help," they answer.

"Haha, wrong!" the bloody man says, and he brings the pickaxe down into them over and over and over again.

He's still going when Mari gets her senses back and guides Lucas away. She returns to their street to regroup.

"Okay," she says, mostly to herself. "Here's what we're going to do: we're going to cut through the block and get to the cemetery…"

Lucas has nothing to say about that. He barely blinks. Humming on loop. But Mari pretends he's listening anyway, just so she has an excuse to keep talking.

"I know it's freaky," she says. "But dead people can't hurt us. It's the living ones we have to worry about, and there's no reason for them to be in the cemetery right now. It's dark and empty, and there are lots of places to hide. We can cross through it and get to the airfield, and there'll be soldiers there. They can help. They can get us to Papa."

Lucas doesn't look convinced. But then, he doesn't look much of anything. He's a blank chalkboard, waiting for somebody to start writing.

Mari stands and scans the street like a prairie dog. She doesn't spot any threats, but there are plenty of looming shadows full of their promise.

"It'll be okay," she says, still half-convinced she's consoling Lucas. "If we just keep moving."

Mari guides him, and Lucas putters along. He won't run, but he'll manage a brisk walk. They sneak along the sidewalk by their house. She keeps him on the inside, shielding his view from the smoldering pile of blackened bones across the street. Mari watches the windows of the other homes for signs of movement, but with the lights out, there's no telling. She catches phantoms in every pane of glass one second, then chases them away the next.

Mari pulls up short at the end of block and shuffles Lucas behind her. She leans around the corner of the last four-plex. There's a little side-alley there — unfenced and unused. A darker patch of dirt worn down by all the lazy kids who opted to cut through, rather than walk all the way around the block. To one side, the housing unit's tall wooden fence. To the other, barb-wire — just three twisting braids wrapped around a series of off-kilter metal posts. An empty lot beyond the wire sports a couple of big white tanks, rust spots just starting to eat through the paint, and nothing else. Barely even scrub grass. On the other side, there's another block of identical military housing. No lights on there, either.

The alley itself is clear, but there's another road that cuts between the housing complex and the cemetery, and it's anybody guess what's out there.

Mari slinks through the alley, jumping at every rustle of the dry and sunburnt grass creeping out from under the fence. She slides under the single side-window of the townhome. Has to maneuver Lucas into doing the same. She pulls down on his hand, and he dips to his knees without protest, but it's a struggle to get him standing again. He wants to shut down. She can't let him, no matter how badly she wants to go home and tuck him under a pile of blankets and let him hide there. Maybe crawl in with him, only emerging days later when this has all blown over.

But home isn't an option. Home is on fire. Home will never be an option again.

Mari leans out just a couple of inches and checks the street.

Every hope that she's been delicately holding in balance drops straight out. She's a wet paper bag, and reality is a rock.

The first thought in her head, though she knows it's absurd, is that she's looking at a parade.

The road that divides the military housing complex from the graveyard is a little wider than her own, and with yellow lines to mark the lanes instead of nothing, but it's not a highway or anything. If you'd have asked her this morning how many people could cram onto it at once, she'd have rolled her eyes and went back to checking her phone, which is how Mari answered stupid questions. Forcing a guess, though, she'd have said maybe a few hundred.

Probably ten times that many packed the tiny street now, with more coming by the second.

The crowd was spilling off of the main avenue — the one that ran by the mall — and coming their way. It was hard to pick out any single person in that shambling wall of faces. They were packed together too tight, shoved all the way up against the cemetery fences on one side, pressed into the doors of the housing complex on the other. No screams. No creepy

Halloween record moans or groans. Just flat, determined silence. Mari thought again of Diego's zombie movies, but even that comparison wasn't right. Something was different here. These weren't the angry people she'd seen rampaging through Freedom Crossing. These were something else.

It was like they lacked even the most basic drive. The zombies, they at least wanted to eat your brains or whatever — so they walked *toward* you. They *went* somewhere. These people — it was like they were being dragged along by invisible chains. A guy with a faux-hawk stumbled headlong with the barely maintained balance of the very drunk. The girl next to him was bent deep at the waist, her long red hair brushing the street as she shuffled reluctantly on small, bare feet. All of them moved like there was a bulldozer at the back of the crowd, slowly inching the whole thing forward.

Leading the pack is a tall, skinny guy dressed in pajama pants and slippers. Polar bear print on the pants, snowflakes on the slippers. He's shirtless. So lean Mari can count his ribs in the dark. Gawky ape arms and a too-long torso. A two-week beard and severe bedhead — and not the sexy kind that takes hours of practiced styling. The tall guy moves differently. He's slow and sleepy — walking like he just woke up to somebody ringing the doorbell. But his pace is more determined. He knows where he's going. His movements are languid but fluid, like he's strolling across the bottom of a pool. His gaze isn't limp and directionless, like the others — he's scanning the street before him, casually alert.

Mari tucks away before he sees her hiding spot. She starts pushing Lucas back the way they came but freezes. The silhouette of a man, backlit against the open street, blocks the path now. His head tilted to one side like he's listening to something really far away. He stands bolt-upright, posture so perfect it looks painful. Arms pinned to his sides. He's not moving. He's waiting.

Mari chances another glance down the road. The lazy man and his followers are still advancing, albeit glacially. There's no way she's getting up and over the wooden fences of the housing complex. Not with Lucas. He'll barely walk; he sure won't climb. It might be awkward getting him through the barbwire, sure to snag them both a couple of deep scratches, but it could be done. But then what? An empty field with nowhere to hide. More houses on the far side. More people. More things. She looks back to the shadow blocking the path. Its head moves, ever so slightly, trying to triangulate whatever it is he's listening to.

God, she's so stupid. It's been on loop so long her brain just normalized it.

Lucas' humming. He's tracking Lucas by his song.

Mari feels her window closing.

The street: crowd so thick they're crushing themselves. When they reach Mari's hiding spot, simple physics means they'll spill over into the opening, right where she and Lucas are standing.

The alley: the listening man, honing in on Lucas like a bat.

The field: naked, visible, nowhere to go.

She knows if she gives herself any more time to worry about it, she'll freeze up.

Mari takes a deep breath and steps onto the sidewalk.

They move as fast as they can, but Lucas has a limit. It must look pretty stupid, some sprightly teenage girl and her idiot brother trying to power-walk past the zombie apocalypse. She expects to be overwhelmed any second. But it doesn't happen. Mari can't help it; she steals a glance.

The slow man swivels his head with the unnerving patience of an owl.

She sees his face. Hopes it's just a trick of the diminishing light that he doesn't appear to have any eyes — only sheer black pools enveloping each socket. When their gazes meet, Mari's heart goes cold. Chills right down to her fingertips. She steels herself for action: a scream, an accusing finger, laser beams firing from his mouth — but no, he does nothing.

She and Lucas slip across the street and through an opening in the graveyard fence. There's a spot where two bars are set a bit wider than the others. They haven't been pried apart or anything — it's just sloppy workmanship. And kids are like water: they'll find any opening and flow right through it, so long as it's a shortcut. To a kid, shortcuts take priority above all else — no matter how inconvenient, awkward, or dangerous.

If Mari hadn't been so small for her age, she'd be stuck out on the street. But as it is, she and Lucas slide through the bars easily. It's the only time she's ever been grateful to be tiny.

She leads Lucas across the soft, squeaky grass, and they squat behind a huge tombstone with a weird-looking cross on top of it. She takes another look. The lazy man watches the spot where they disappeared, but he doesn't break stride. He just raises a hand and motions toward the opening in the fence. It's a dismissive gesture, like you'd use to wave off a hovering fly on a hot summer day. One of the lead walkers — a younger guy in business slacks, wingtips and a tank top — breaks off from the crowd; his pace only marginally quickens, moving stiff and pained. His arms hang limp at his waist, and his head lolls with every step. He makes the shortcut gap and just stops there. He slumps, presses against the bars of the fence, and eases all his weight onto his forehead. Face smushed into the bars, neck bent painfully, he settles there.

Not moving or anything. He's done. His job is just to block the entrance.

The lazy man and his followers flow on, an unbroken river of flesh. Apparently, Mari's small moment of relevance is over. It's fine by her. She takes up Lucas's hand again, and together they duck from tombstone to tombstone until they reach the eastern border of the cemetery. No wrought-iron fence here — this side butts up against an employees-only parking lot behind a strip mall. Simple chain-link does the job when there's no need for ornamentation.

Mari slips behind a tree and surveys the lot. The power is still on over there. There's an outdoor light mounted above the rear entrance, bare fluorescent — pale blue and draining. It casts long, lean shadows. The only cover she can see is a darkened space between a pair of rusty green dumpsters. It's only a few feet from there to the skinny alley that opens right out onto the freeway. Or parkway. Or whatever — she forgets what it's called when they run through the city like this. There are stoplights and turn signals like a road, but it's still eight full lanes wide, not counting the median. Mammoth concrete pillars squat every couple hundred feet, supporting the real highway above. Streetlamps run either side, lighting the whole thing up clear as day. Only gravel decorates the wide median. Not even a shrub to shelter behind. Nowhere to hide, and an awful long way to run in the open.

Lucas is draining like an old battery. He can be shoved and cajoled into movement, but he gets slower by the second. With every stop they make, it's harder to get him started.

Mari's heart breaks, for the split second she allows it.

Lucas is a brat, of course, but every kid is a brat at his age. Lucas is better than most. He's always been sensitive. No matter how many times she tells him off, he always asks if she's okay when she's clearly not. It's none of his business, and she usually yells that right in his face, but Mama and Papa and Diego don't even ask anymore. They just write her problems off as teenage drama and laugh behind their hands. But not Lucas. He never gave up on her.

She'll never give up on him.

Mari lays her one good hand on his cheek. His skin cool, hers flushed.

"You are going to make it," she commands.

Lucas blinks, and his song hitches a little. That's his only response.

Keep. Moving.

Mari tries to pry the fence up with her one good hand, but it's not even close. So she puts her butt against the chain link and backs into it. With a lot of effort and a few painful snags, she manages to push the bottom of the fence out enough for Lucas to slip through. When he does, she drops to her stomach and lets the fence snap back into shape. The uneven metal takes a few more swipes at her back as it passes, and the shock from jostling her busted fingers makes her pee a little.

It's official: her favorite T-shirt has now been destroyed.

Just a few hours ago, her biggest concern was getting Deacon to autograph this bloody rag.

Mari retrieves Lucas' small, limp hand and gets moving. There's no time for crouching, assessing, hiding. They have to cross the highway, then a good chunk of desert before they get to the airfield and safety. Lucas could shut down completely at any minute. She can feel him fading right now. He's just the impression left after you stare at a bright light for too long. Blink and he'll disappear altogether.

They skitter across the little parking lot and between the dumpsters. Mari does a quick scan — no movement. No cry of recognition. She ducks out and peers around the corner. The driveway is clear, but not the highway. A few bodies are scattered about there; some cars, stalled or abandoned.

Mari takes one last look at the graveyard. She was so scared of the idea when they first ran for the fence. But out here, in the light — this is worse. She feels a thousand eyes on her from every direction but can't actually find them.

Go.

Mari takes quick, purposeful strides. Lucas stumbles and trips behind her, a little dog being walked by an impatient owner. Through the alley, across the first four lanes, and up on the divider. Red rocks crunch beneath her slipper socks, digging at her feet even through the thick bottoms. She pauses at the far curb. There's a UPS truck parked diagonally across the lanes to one side and two sedans meshed together by a fender-bender on the other. Their doors are open. One of them chimes a faint and useless alert.

The highway is clear, so she crosses it, but she can't see into the desert beyond. The damn streetlamps burned away her night vision. The idea of slipping beyond these islands of light and into the unknown makes her stomach clench. She advances slowly, pausing to let her eyes adapt. No point in charging out there blind just to twist an ankle or fall into a dry riverbed. That's what the logic brain tells her. But that's not really why she's stalling. It's that other thing: the animal brain — its reasoning less clear, but stronger.

When her eyes do finally adjust, Mari is confused about what they show her: the silhouette of a twisted, stunted little tree, standing dead center in a circle of dark, wet sand. All around it are mannequin parts. That's what she thinks at first. Because none of this can be real.

Severed limbs and dismantled torsos litter the ground. A muscled and tattooed arm here, a girl's smooth leg still wearing her running shoe over there. A soldier's whole upper body, sans limbs; blood-soaked camo, face twisted around backwards and buried in the sand.

Mari doesn't get it. Killer trees?

She leans to one side, then the other, getting more angles, and her mistake becomes clear. It's not a tree. It's a person, or something like it. It's very thin and its posture so unnaturally broken that at first she took it for a withered little *guajilo*. Its legs are crossed, knees bent outward at painful angles. Its fingers are all twisted up into claws. Its skin looks wrong. Thin and kind of grey. It's a sad and desiccated thing, and Mari's first reaction is more pity than fear — but the ring of blood-stained dirt tells her that's a mistake. She takes Lucas' hand and backs away slowly, quietly, until they're once again on the relative safety of the empty highway.

They still have to cross into the desert, but not here.

Mari gives the tree-thing a nice, wide berth. It brings her and Lucas right up close to that idling UPS truck. There's blood on the floorboards and a couple of ragged smears on the pavement, but they don't end at a body. She's thankful for that, at least.

Once they're suitably distant from the thing in the desert, Mari again sneaks out of the light. Hesitant. A stalking cat. Leaves plenty of time for her eyes to adjust. It doesn't take her nearly as long to spot the next two creatures, lurking in the dark. These ones are clearly men. Big ones. One bald, shirtless, and well-muscled. The other is pretty fat, but it's all beer belly and burly arms. Longer hair that hangs over his face. He's not as bent as the others. Not flexible enough. Just kind of hunched over with his arms at his sides. A swirl of torn limbs and bloody carcasses surround each man. Mari watches the pair for minutes and doesn't see a single twitch. They are utterly, inhumanly inert. She backs away again, returns to the nice, well-lit road. She's done feeling safer in the dark.

Mari scours the UPS truck to make sure it's clear, then tucks Lucas behind the driver's seat. He stares at nothing, hums like a track left on repeat. Mari wonders if whatever changed those people in the desert is working right now, on Lucas…but she shakes the thought clear. For Lucas, the stasis started long before the black spot and the riots. He hadn't been the same since that night he saw Papa attacked. Everybody else in the world was learning about true violence and horror tonight. Lucas already knew.

Mari stares at the keys dangling from the ignition and has a crazy fantasy about jacking the truck. Hopping into the driver's seat with its absent door, throwing it into gear, and just hauling ass across the desert to safety. She dismisses the idea automatically — another dumb little kid daydream that she should have outgrown already.

But she quickly circles back around. Why not steal the truck? What, is she gonna get in trouble? The thought is laughable. She'd love to *live* long enough to be in trouble at this point.

Lucas' internal song grows fainter. His unmoored, roving eyes are sleepy. Even if he wasn't also dealing with a dump truck of trauma, all the running and hiding and stress would be exhausting enough for him. God knows it was exhausting for her. Mari feels hollowed out, like a bunch of small animals have snuck inside her body and eaten everything away until there is just a shell.

Even if they *can* get past the lurkers in the dark, will the truck make it to the airfield? It feels close, in Mari's head, but she's never actually been there. Outside of her own, immediate neighborhood, Mari's only real sense of place in this city comes from a distantly remembered Google map, back from when they first moved in and she was surveying her new territory. The airfield seemed practically next door at the time, but that meant nothing. It could be miles. There were lights in the distance, across the lake of black sand, but how distant? What if they were like giant army spotlights and actually super far away?

What's the alternative, though, hiding here and hoping nobody finds them? It didn't work out great for the driver.

Mari gives Lucas a familial squeeze and then rounds the driver's seat. She doesn't actually know how to drive, but that's not a big deal. The worst that can happen is them crashing and dying. Seems like a petty consequence right now. Besides, Mari gets the gist: There are two pedals. She knows what they do. There's a wheel. She knows what that does, too. The shifter is politely labeled, informing her exactly where to put the little orange arrow if she wants the thing to go. Engine's still running. Headlights on. She considers the seatbelt. It seems silly to buckle it, but it feels too alien to leave it hanging. She rolls her eyes at herself as she clicks the tab into place.

Mari wrestles the shifter from P into D — it's harder than she assumes — and the truck starts drifting forward. She stomps on the brake, and it jolts to a stop so abrupt that her teeth vibrate. She tries the motion a few more times, getting the hang of the pedal. Does the same for the gas. When she's got a rough sense of how it's gonna move, she hauls on the steering wheel for what feels like forever — the fact that she's doing it with one hand doesn't help — and gets the truck oriented toward the desert.

The headlights illuminate a gray and withered stump, watered by a circle of blood.

If she has to break through the lurker's lines somewhere, she figures she'll at least opt for the smallest one. Mari presses the accelerator, too hard, and jounces the back of her head off the seat. The truck lurches to life and wallows like a drunken bull. She hauls the wheel one way, only to realize it's too far, and back the other. The front end is diving and weaving like somebody's throwing punches at it, every little correction of hers just barely avoiding disaster. She'd planned on skirting by the thing in the desert, as far outside its radius as she could get. The truck has other plans. No matter how hard she wrenches it, every turn of the wheel brings them straight back toward the waiting creature.

Mari can see it's a woman, now. When the headlights hit her and the engine roared, the old lady started unfolding with tiny, spastic jerks. It was like watching a flower bloom in time lapse. She has Sunday School posture now: painfully straight-backed, arms to her sides, feet together. The woman is ancient, probably sick, and totally naked. Thin hair the gray of driftwood, saggy everything, wrinkles giving way to deep folds. She wears a white plastic bracelet around one wrist, and a length of clear tubing dangles from one arm. She must have been in the hospital when whatever happened, happened. So even the sick and the dying aren't immune.

The truck closes in on her like it's on rails. Fifty feet. Thirty. The old woman surges into life. Her eyes fly open and in the same instant she breaks into a dead sprint, right at the approaching truck. Arms outstretched, arthritic fingers grasping, withered toes digging into the sand. Mari would never, in a million years, have guessed the old woman could move like that. She closes the distance in a blink, probably sets the world record for the geriatric ten-meter dash, if there is such a thing. No comical explosion of blood when the truck hits her. Barely a bump. She's just gone. Like the engine ate her up and used her for fuel.

Mari keeps the gas pedal pinned until the bouncing threatens to send the truck out of control. The desert's flat, but not that flat. She eases off as much as she dares, slows the truck to a modest but still painful canter. She wants to hold a hand out for Lucas. Let him know it's okay, or at least that she's still here. But her good one is busy steering, and she gets the feeling that pawing at the kid with her mangled stub won't exactly comfort him.

She focuses on the task at hand: barely dodging obstacles as they come into view. It feels like a terrible video game. The controls are garbage and the pop-up is deadly. She's sweating within a second. It feels like she's been driving for twenty minutes, and the lights of the airfield are no closer. She glances at the speedometer. It sure as hell doesn't feel like ten miles an hour.

Mari blinks, and the clawed hand just appears, already locked around her wrist with the finality of a manacle. Saltwater gray, yellow nails, deep and bloody scratches. She's still gawking at it when it yanks her out of the seat.

It feels like all the joints on the left side of Mari's body have been pulled out of their sockets, simultaneously. The seatbelt digs into her neck, strangling her, but thank god for it: without it, the old woman would have ripped her straight under the truck. The lurker had been caught up in the front wheel well somehow. Most of her is still jammed up there — all Mari can see is one withered arm and a terrible, placid face. It would be, well, not *better* if the old woman were snapping or frothing at the mouth or swearing or something. But this is worse. No snarling, no spitting, no emotion at all — her milky eyes watch with sleepy disinterest as her gnarled hand tries to yank Mari to her death. Like the two are separate entities: the face does not care; the hand wants blood.

Mari frantically runs over ways she can fight back and comes up with: don't.

Instead, she flails around with her foot until it kicks the gas pedal, then pins it to the floor. The engine growls like she just stepped on the tail of a sleeping tiger, but it takes a while for that to mean anything. The truck's a behemoth; it speeds up gradually. Mari's vision is going black. Choked out by a safety device. Is that ironic? She's never quite sure…

The truck bottoms out, squeals in protest, then goes airborne for a second and crashes back down, mashing the old lady's body further into the well. Her grip falters but doesn't release. A few more bone-rattling bounces, a metallic snap — the engine howls like a mad monkey after — and then comes the knockout punch.

Mari's mouth tastes like teeth. All calcium powder and pain, like she just woke up after a nasty dentist appointment. Her forehead is beeping. She should probably do something about that.

Reason comes slow.

She looks around the cabin of the ruined truck and patiently waits for the world to start making sense. The beeps are coming from the dash. Some sort of warning chime.

Wait, was she driving?

The old woman…

Mari about chokes when she sees that wrinkled claw still there, clutching her sleeve. She gives her arm an experimental wobble, and the hand shakes with it. No resistance. She leans out of the cab as far as her seatbelt allows and sees that the malnourished limb ends in a bloody gash at the shoulder. The old woman's severed head sits face down in the dust. Silky white strands of hair fan out all around it like a skeletal dandelion.

Mari pieces together what happened. The truck clipped one of those stubborn, prehistoric rocks that litter the desert around here, and the whole front end crumpled like marzipan. The bumper snapped all the way back to the wheels, turning the fender into a guillotine. Mari gags a little as she plucks at the papery fingers still locked around her forearm. They come away easy but leave sickly yellow imprints on the skin beneath. It'll hurt later, when she has time for it. She unbuckles her seatbelt and experiments with her various parts. They all move, though reluctantly.

She's forgetting something. Still hazy from the crash.

Lucas!

Mari flips around the driver's seat and finds her little brother sprawled in a pile of blood-stained packages. One of the bins came open in the crash, spilling its contents across the rubber floor. Something clipped Lucas' forehead in the wreck, opening a wide but thankfully shallow gash on his forehead. He's got one eye closed against the flow of blood. The other, lidded and murky, roves about in confusion. Mari digs a finger into one of the rips on her ruined T-shirt. She pries it wider and tears the whole bottom hem off in one ragged strip. She uses it to dab Lucas' face dry, then cinches the rest tight around his wound. She almost laughs. It looks like one of those eighties karate headbands. Under different circumstances, Lucas would love it.

He blinks at her. She takes it as a question.

"Everything's okay now," she says, hoping that if Lucas buys the lie, then maybe she can, too. "We're almost to the airfield."

Her legs are rubbery and unresponsive. Feels like's she stumping around the desert on stilts. Lucas isn't doing any better — he keeps trying to sit down, right there in the dirt. She has to maintain constant forward momentum just to keep him upright. So she does.

Crossing the desert at night takes a year. A year of unseen thorns and banged shins, turned ankles and scraped palms. But finally, those distant lights loom large, and the airfield is in reach.

Just beyond a fortified chain-link fence. Topped with razor-wire.

Right. It's a military installation. Why did she think this would be easy?

No shoddy workmanship to exploit this time. The fence is secured, top to bottom, and made of stronger stuff than normal chain-link. It doesn't even flex at her touch. She wants to fall down a hole and die, but self-pity won't help anything. Which is a shame, since she's really good at it.

But now is not the time.

Lucas' hand is clammy and weak in hers. They trudge on, skirting the fence line, looking for an opening.

Another year of thorns.

For the millionth time tonight, Mari wishes she had shoes. Her novelty slipper socks feel wet. She hopes it's just sweat. She knows it's not.

At last they crest a small hill covered in slippery iceplant and spot an entrance.

A single-lane maintenance road that terminates at a pair of locked gates. A big solid black box mounted between them. There's a little one-man booth on the airfield-side of the fence, unmanned. The run-up to the gate is littered with bodies, but these ones aren't so bad.

Isn't that messed up? This afternoon, seeing one corpse would've probably sent her into fits. But now that she's seen people pulped with pickaxes, lit on fire, torn into pieces — mere bullet wounds are almost comforting. Which is good, because these bodies are riddled with them. There are a few dozen corpses in all, most of them piled loosely about fifty feet from the gates, like they hit some invisible wall of death. Doesn't take a genius to see what happened here. They all tried to rush the fence at once and got gunned down by soldiers on the other side. Mari hopes the guys with guns are still in there. Then she amends that wish and instead hopes that they haven't gone insane yet.

She and Lucas limp down the hill, across a little gulley full of chipped stones, and onto the maintenance road. Beside the gate is a green post with a yellow box. A single red button beneath a speaker.

She presses it.

And feels very stupid while she waits for a response.

None comes.

Testing the gate, she sees the black box has two staggered bars running out to either side. A tiny red light blinks in the upper right hand corner. It's a heavy-duty remote lock, and it's sealed up tight.

Lucas, temporarily freed from Mari's grip, sits down cross-legged in the middle of the road and slumps in on himself. Eyes almost closed. His humming song so faint she can barely hear it anymore.

Mari presses the intercom button again. It feels like turning the key on a car that won't start; she knows it's useless, but what else can she do?

She manages a full minute of patience before she sits down next to

Lucas and starts crying. She feels bad about it — the only thing keeping her going was the idea of staying strong for him — and that just makes her sob harder. This was her only idea: Make the airfield. Find help. Find Papa.

And now a mute speakerbox just pronounced their death sentence.

Big, sloppy, embarrassing, hiccupy weeps. Nose running, total loss of dignity. Mari doesn't care. She lets the cry unfurl until she can't even get air anymore. Then something settles on her leg. She clears the tears from her burning eyes and blinks down at a tiny little hand. Mostly limp. Barely there.

Lucas.

Some part of him is still present. Aware enough to see his sister crying and set a hand gently on her knee.

She hugs him so fiercely that his back cracks. She laughs as she lets him go.

"Okay," she says.

Mari stands and marches back to that arrogant little speakerbox and hammers the button like a little kid at a crosswalk. She gives it a few seconds. Nothing.

She hits it again.

Again and again and again and however many damn times it takes. She holds the button down and yells:

"I know you're in there. I know you can hear me."

She doesn't know either of those things.

"If you don't open this gate right now and let us in," she says, "I'm walking back into town and waving down the first horde of monsters I see, and I'm leading them all right back here."

The speakerbox takes a minute to think.

"Okay, fine," Mari says and turns to leave.

"Wait," the speakerbox says. Its voice is full of crackles and pops and sounds much younger than she expected.

Mari grabs the speakerbox in both hands. Breathless, she reels: "Help us, please, it's me and my brother out here and my dad is in there he's army we've been going all night there's something really wrong out here we need—"

"Easy!" the speakerbox says. "The reception on this thing sucks. Talk loud and slow, right into the receiver."

Mari looks but doesn't see any obvious microphone. She leans in, lips practically brushing the flaking yellow industrial paint.

"Let us in!" she screams, just as loud as she can.

"Ow." The voice laughs. "I heard you that time."

"Why won't you help us?" Mari says.

"I didn't…we didn't know if you were normal," the voice replies. "Sorry."

She can only laugh at the most wholly inadequate apology she's ever heard.

"Well, we are," she finally says. "Can you see us? It's just me and my brother. We're fine. Uh…no, we're really not fine, but we're not a threat."

"Hold on," the voice says. Then, "Aw, hell. You really are just kids."

Static.

"I'm going to buzz the gate. I've got a high-powered sniper rifle trained on you right now. When you hear the sound, you step through, turn around, and hold it closed until there's a thunk. You don't do that, or you do anything else, and you're dead two seconds before you know it."

It should scare her, but the voice is so young. It's like being threatened by a fifth-grader.

"Yes, sir," she says.

Mari tries to drag Lucas to his feet, but he's going Gandhi on her. Limp, non-violent resistance.

"Lucas," she hisses. "Come on."

He does not.

"Please," she says. "Just five more minutes and this is over. We're safe. Blankets and ice cream forever, I promise."

She shakes his arm, lightly slaps his cheeks, but he's gone.

There's literally nothing left in her. Exhaustion in every form — physical, mental, spiritual — seeps through her pores. Coats her bones. Weighs her down. She feels like she's walking on the bottom of the ocean.

But she remembers that little hand, near lifeless, resting on her knee…

Mari bends down and hauls Lucas up over her shoulders. She's not strong, and he weighs half as much as she does. Couldn't lift him on her best day. But this is her worst day, and somehow, she manages. She can feel her soggy footsteps leaving bloody prints. She muddles her way to the gate, waits for the buzz, and rams it open with her shoulder. Her one good hand holds Lucas' arms, crossed wrist over wrist. Her bad arm is wrapped clumsily around one of his legs. It's probably in her head, but she swears she can feel a tiny red dot burning on her chest. Waiting for a misstep. She kicks the gate closed, weights it shut with her body until she hears the thunk, picks the closest building, and starts walking.

It's easily five hundred feet away.

It might as well be five hundred miles.

There will be time to think about how much all this hurts later. How impossible it seems that she'll ever actually reach that ugly beige trailer, ringed in floodlights. There are more bodies scattered all around this side of the fence — most of them just random people peppered with bullet holes. Some of them are wearing army uniforms. Those ones are torn to pieces. Mari navigates a minefield of corpses and thinks, *It's not the worst thing you've seen tonight. You can freak out about this later.*

Later. Not now.

Now is walking.

One foot and the other and that's it.

A hundred feet to the trailer. Fifty. But the closer she gets, the more her knees bow. The further Lucas slides out of her grip. The harder it is to hitch him up again. Twenty feet from the trailer, she scuffs her foot just a little, and it's all over. Mari falls, clipping both knees painfully on the pavement. Lucas slides off her back like water on leather. She doesn't even have the strength to cry.

"You all right?" a familiar voice asks. It's the speakerbox, given human form and devoid of static. He's kneeling in the dark beneath the trailer's metal staircase. Just a shadow.

She actually laughs at the question.

She gestures mutely at herself, then her brother, then the world at large.

"Is anything all right?" she replies.

"No," the human speakerbox says. "Probably not."

He stands and steps into the light. Mari's heart drops. She wanted a soldier. Some grizzled badass with biceps the size of watermelons. Maybe an eyepatch. But this kid looks like he's about her age. Sandy, tennis-ball-fuzz haircut and acne scars. He's dressed in a gray jumpsuit with black boots. Wearing some kind of goofy hat — like an army helmet mixed with a sombrero. Dull green metal clashing with cheap white plastic. But he does have that rifle he warned her about.

They stand at odds for a stupid length of time.

"Well, do we look like a threat?" she asks, lip curled.

"No, right," he says, and he literally hops to — physically jumps out of the standoff and jogs over to help her. "Sorry. Let's get you inside."

Inside is like a 1950s office designed by a prison warden. Unadorned, imitation wood-panel walls, green carpet so thin it bunches up when you drag your feet, plain metal everything — desk, cabinets, tables — every corner brutally sharp and just waiting for you to bang a shin on it. It smells like sweat and oil. That's probably coming from the half dozen soldiers who mill about the trailer in various states of agitation, ranging from mild panic to barely controlled rage. They're all way too young for comfort. Where are the old guys with battle scars, like in the movies?

There's a blond girl wearing her ponytail so tight it looks like it might snap off, four white guys that Mari can't tell apart — square jaw, round chin, narrow nose, brown hair shaved short — and a black guy with thick glasses, their lenses reflecting colorless light from a rugged laptop perched on the only desk. He doesn't look up.

The little guy with the rifle stands silent while the others glare at him.

It feels like Mari should say something.

"Hi," she says, and it's the dumbest she's ever felt.

None of the soldiers respond.

The little guy leans his rifle against the wall, by the door, where a dozen other guns stand at attention. Lucas and Diego could have told you all about them — reeling off algebraic names and numbers; citing stats like they're talking about football players — but they're all just guns to Mari. Alien and vaguely worrying things.

The little guy takes off his goofy helmet and hangs it on a hook beside six others. Each with that same silly white ring around the base that makes them look like UFOs from one of Diego's hokey fifties sci-fi movies. The ones with the little shadow guys that make nerdy jokes. He's always trying to get her to watch them, insisting—

No. *Was.* He *was* always trying to get her to watch them.

Can't think about that now. That's for later.

The tension reaches a breaking point, and the little guy says:

"What was I supposed to do, leave them out there?"

"Yes," one of the generic white guys answers. "That's exactly what you were *ordered* to do."

"What if they're infected or something?" the blond girl adds. "You just killed all of us."

"They're not infected," the little guy says. "They're walking and talking and not trying to kill anybody."

"Some of them can still talk," a different white guy says.

"Oh yeah?" another one sneers. "You see a lot of them asking about the weather? They're just animals."

"No," Mari says, and they all look at her like she's a toddler trying to join a political debate. "Some of them *can* talk."

"See?" The blond girl laughs. "Even the kid says it was a bad idea."

The little guy gives Mari a sideways look.

"My name is Mari," she says. "This is my brother Lucas. We're normal, I promise. Even the talking ones are still super crazy and, like, killing people and stuff."

"*He* doesn't look normal," one of the white guys says, nodding at Lucas.

He's right. Lucas sat down on the floor right when they came in, and he's still there now, head drifting toward his chest.

"He's just exhausted," Mari says. "He's just…we've just seen a lot of bad stuff on the way here. Our brother…"

Diego. A dancing stick man in the middle of an inferno.

That's for later.

"Sorry," the little guy says.

The other soldiers suddenly find a bunch of different stuff to look at that's not Mari or Lucas.

"I'm Randy," the little guy says. "But my last name's Gerikoff, so they uh…they all call me Jerk."

"That's the clean version, anyway," the blond girl says. "I'm Steves."

And then it's roll call. The white guys reel off:

"Johnson."

"Jameson.

"Johannsen."

"Also Johnson."

The last one notices Mari's hapless stare and adds, "You can call me James, if you want."

She decides to mentally label them all as "Johnsons."

The black guy is the only one who hasn't said anything, so Mari looks at him. His laptop is so bulky it looks like a protective case you'd use to carry around six other, normal computers. The whole thing covered in thick black plastic, laden with purposeful grooves and serious latches.

"That's Ken," the little guy says, for him.

"Why don't you call *him* by his last name?" she asks.

"It is my last name," he answers, and Mari jumps. She looks over, but he's already back to his screen.

Introductions are about all anybody can think to say.

After an awkward minute, Randy suddenly remembers that his guests are bleeding all over the place and shepherds them over to a couch the exact color and texture of shredded wheat. He grabs a plastic first aid kit from its mount on the wall and cracks it open on the coffee table. While he's wrapping her in a mummy's worth of white gauze, he asks a bunch of questions about what happened and how she got hurt. But aside from the hand, which she'll never forget — that crack she could feel down to her toes; Diego's crazed unblinking eyes — she can't recall how she got the rest. Scratches on her back and face. Her feet all scraped away. It'd be easier to list the parts of her body that weren't messed up.

When Randy's finished, her hand and both feet are bound tight, and there are sticky patches all over from a litany of other bandages. She doesn't feel much better physically, but it helps not to see the wounds anymore.

Lucas is crunched up into a little ball, denting the farthest cushion of the couch. Arms wrapped around his knees. Eyes mostly closed. Not watching anything.

"What happens now?" Mari says, when Randy starts gathering up the medical supplies.

She just said today's magic word, apparently, because everybody starts shouting at once.

"—should've gone with—"

"—wait for reinforcements—"

"—bombs on the Snake, we could—"

"—you want to detonate low-yield nuclear weapons this close to—"

"—madness, this is madness, this is—"

"—got to be some kind of bunker here or—"

"Hey! Hey! Stop!" Ken yells, and to everybody's surprise, they listen.

Even Ken seems taken aback.

"I ah…I think I can get it working," he adds.

Just about everyone deflates. The relief is tangible. The only one still riled up is Randy.

"So what?" he snaps. "What then? We just take off?"

"Uh, yeah," a Johnson says. "What else? You wanna hang out with the psychos? Do some bonding?"

"We all want to help people," Steves says. "But you saw what happened at the fence. We barely held them back, and there were three times as many of us then. What if the creepy guy comes back? You really think we can fight them off again?"

"What guy?" Mari asks, but she's officially just background noise now.

"Most of 'them' are rotting by the fence," Randy says. He points out the lone window, toward the gate Mari came through. "I hope he *does* come back, so we can finish the job."

"What if he gets reinforcements?" a Johnson says.

"What guy?" Mari asks again.

"Then we'll kill his reinforcements," Randy says, half-sarcastically. "Why did you join up? Why did any of you? To run away when it all hits the fan? What was the training for, if we're not even gonna use it? We've got the hardware. We've got positioning. We've got fortifications. Even if Ken's right and he can get the Snake running — for how long? Huh? What happens when it breaks down? What happens when—"

"Then we deal with it," Ken says. He snaps the laptop closed. It seals like a bank vault. "All the info is right here. There's a whole car just for spare parts. It sure beats squatting in this…"

He reaches out and knocks on the wall of the trailer. The whole thing rings with the fragile warble of sheet metal.

"The trailer isn't the only building here," Randy says, but you can actually see him losing now. "We could pull back to the tower. Or one of the hangars."

"You sure those are even clear?" Steves asks. "Last I saw, it didn't seem like we were winning."

Everybody shifts their eyes, agreeing to some unspoken statement.

"We got two," Randy says. He points at Mari and Lucas, sitting on the most uncomfortable couch in history. "What if more come? Are we really not gonna be here to help them?"

"*Are* we?" a Johnson asks. "Seems like that's up to the creepy guy and his friends."

Mari bangs her good fist against the wall of the trailer. It bows out so far she thinks she might punch through it. They're inside of a gong. When the noise fades, she finally gets to join the adult table.

"What. Guy?" She snips the words short.

Randy sighs, like it's a funny story he got sick of telling a long time ago.

"When this first started, everybody was just running around like maniacs—"

"That's not true," a Johnson interrupts. "People were acting weird for days before it all went FUBAR."

"It was the spot," another Johnson says.

"How can a spot do all this?" a Johnson asks.

"If it's not the spot, what's with the dog cones?" The first Johnson steps over and picks a helmet off the wall. He shakes it so the thin white plastic rim bounces.

Mari looks to Randy.

"Some government guys came by a few days before all hell broke loose. Told us we weren't supposed to look at the spot on account of we'd go blind or get eye cancer or something. They dropped off crates of these plastic disc things that snap around our helmets, to help keep us from looking up too far accidentally. Then they commandeered basically all of our hardware and most of the fighting divisions."

"Great call," Johnson says, gesturing out the window, presumably at the whole ruined world.

"It was just chaos at first," Randy continues. "What was left of the base force started killing each other, themselves, everything. We tried to get a handle on it, but it was too much. Your CO would give you an order and you turn around to do it, but when you turn back, you find him wrist deep in some grunt's guts, giggling and tossing 'em around like confetti."

"We're all that's left," Ken says.

"We don't know that," a Johnson says. "There could be others holed up like us."

Quiet as fresh snow.

Mari coughs.

"It died down eventually," Randy finally says. "But then this big mob shows up all at once. Walking together like they got a purpose. Leading them is this…this guy."

"Old guy," Steves adds. "Real nasty looking."

The Johnsons nod.

"And he's got like…I don't want to say black eyes," Randy says. "But more like—"

"Empty spots where eyes should be," Mari finishes.

"You saw him," Randy fills in.

"No," Mari says. "I saw a different one."

"Jesus Christ," a Johnson breathes. "There's more than one?"

"I don't think the guy we saw was the same," Mari says. "He was young and tall and skinny, and all the people following him were really slow and awkward. Like the things in the desert."

"The ones out there definitely weren't slow," Johnson says. He doesn't want to continue.

"We opened fire," Steves says. "We didn't have a choice."

"They were unarmed," Randy says.

"They didn't *need* weapons," Johnson adds. "Just their hands."

"Didn't even care about the razor-wire," Randy says. "Went right up and over, shredding themselves the whole way. Didn't faze them at all. Just kept running right at us. God damn, the looks in their eyes. Just pure hate. Every one of them looked at me like I just killed their kids or something."

"We got through it," Steves says, both to finish the story and to comfort Randy.

"Yeah, we did," Randy says. He smiles at her. She smiles back.

There's something else there, Mari thinks.

"But when it was over, the old man, he just walked away," a Johnson says. "Like he didn't even care that we won."

"So that's why we have to get out of here," Steves says, like the whole story just proved her point. "He might be coming back."

"If we'd left when you guys wanted," Randy answers, "we wouldn't have found these two."

Mari blushes and hates it. She doesn't like being a bullet point in somebody else's argument.

"I vote we go," she says.

Randy looks wounded.

"So you got yours and screw the rest, huh?" he says.

"It's not like that," Mari adds. "Our father, he's army, and he's in here somewhere—"

"Who's he with?" a Johnson asks.

"First Armored," Mari says, reeling it off automatically. "Support."

"Gladiator," Ken says, and he laughs bitterly.

"What?" she asks.

"Sorry, kid," Ken says.

Mari gets a chill in her belly, the kind that always precedes something horrible. Your gut knows it before you do.

"What? Sorry about what?" Mari looks around to the others for help — she's not sure *how* they could help, maybe they could shut Ken up before he says—

"Gladiator's gone," he finishes. "Brass took most of 'em when they seized our hardware. The few that were left are all dead. If your pop was here this morning, he's not now."

"You don't know that," Mari says.

"I do," Ken counters. He spins the bulky laptop around so she can see the back. It's got a big "PROPERTY OF" sticker that Mari refuses to finish reading.

"Ken was Gladiator," a Johnson says.

"*Is*," Ken snaps and glares at the Johnson until he looks away. "That hasn't changed."

"But they can't all be dead," Mari says, careful to keep it from sounding like a question.

Stupid Ken answers anyway.

"There were only a dozen of us," he says. "Not exactly hard to keep track of. We were working on the Snake when Collins walked up, singing. We laughed at first. Even clapped when he finished. He took a bow, then opened fire…"

Mari's mouth is dry, but she can't swallow to fix it.

"What's your last name?" he asks her.

"Rodriguez," she croaks.

He nods all sad in a way she's seen too many times before. Usually while watching through the blinds as a soldier in formals talks to a housewife in her doorway. Just after he hands her the flag.

"Your dad was a good guy. He went straight after Collins when it started. Almost got him, too. He's a hero, kid," Ken says.

It's funny how heroes are always dead, Mari thinks.

They all give her a minute of quiet before they start bickering again. They rehash the same points in different words like that's the problem — if only they could find the *right synonym,* then everybody would suddenly agree with each other. Steves and Ken and the Johnsons want to get to whatever the Snake is, but after that they all have different ideas. Randy wants to stay right here, in case somebody else comes by needing help. Steves and the rest want to leave, Randy wants to wait. Steves and the gang want to strategically retreat, Randy wants to provide support. Steves and company say move out, Randy says—

Something in Mari snaps.

"We didn't see *anybody* else normal out there," Mari says. She says it quiet, but something in her tone cuts straight the noise. They all shut their mouths and stare at her. "Not alive, at least. And you wouldn't believe how many of those things there are. All different kinds."

"Nobody?" a Johnson asks.

Mari shakes her head.

"How many psychos?" a Johnson says.

"I don't know," she answers. "We live over by the mall. It's not that far. And just between here and there? Thousands. More. And the black-eyed guy that *we* saw — he wasn't just wandering around. He was sealing off exits."

She searches her memories for a few military terms she picked up second-hand from Papa.

"He was using the slow ones to stake out a perimeter, so the angry ones have a kill zone. They're not stupid or aimless. They know what this place is, and they're going to come back."

It sounds more video game than authentic to her, but nobody calls her out on it.

"There's nobody left," Mari reiterates to them. Then, to herself. "*There's nobody left.* I have to take care of Lucas. I don't care what you guys do. We're leaving just as soon as he can move again."

"Maybe we can leave instructions," Randy says and somehow manages to look even smaller. "For anybody that comes by looking for help…"

"I think that's a moot point," Ken says. He's turned around in his chair, looking out the one big window toward the gate.

The horizon is boiling.

Cresting the small hill just beyond the fence, backlit against the dusty light pollution of the city, thousands of writhing, grasping silhouettes approach.

Everybody huddles around the window in silence, like they're watching a breaking news announcement instead of reality. This is just too big, too bad to be happening. The brain disconnects.

They gawk in quiet reverence until the first of the horde steps out of the shadows and into the floodlights. The man with the black holes for eyes. He's older, but not decrepit. Not fat, but definitely stocky. The implacable mass hints that he used to be buff, back in his day. Maybe still was, beneath the rolls. Dark hair slicked back, thin strands skating across a prominent bald spot. Not trying to hide it or draw attention away from it. He's wearing a dirty white tank top and boxers with faded blue stripes. Barefoot. His fists clench and unclench at his sides, like he's itching for a fight.

He has a cruel face: deep frown lines, forever-furrowed brow, hard-set jaw thrust forward. Mari practically knows his life story, just looking at him: former military, and not happy about the former part. Forced retirement usually, sometimes honorable discharge. They skim around the base bars nursing straight whiskey; sit alone at local diners downing scalding hot cups of black coffee; plant themselves bolt upright on park benches and stare straight ahead. No longer part of the army life, but not knowing anything else. They're like walking ghosts. And they're always mad.

This one was something way past mad. Pure fury etched onto his face like god carved it into his skull on the day he was born. Lips just short of a snarl, nostrils flaring, eyes burning. Yet still in control. Not like the people that followed him, biting and snapping at one another, shoving, punching, scratching — hemmed into a rough formation by some unseen force, and clearly against their will. The old man stops in front of the chain-link gates and carefully surveys their length. He spots the trailer right away — it's the only building lit up like a country fair, and full of stunned idiots, gaping at the approaching disaster instead of running.

He fixes them with those cold, black pools that used to be eyes, opens his mouth, and out comes something between a howl of anguish and a war cry. Mari's nerves jangle up at the sound. She never imagined she could be the focus of such a deep and personal hatred. It makes her stomach twist.

You can almost see the leashes snap. The barely restrained mob surges forward in a wave of scrambling violence.

The noise. God, the noise. A stadium full of people, every one baying for your death.

But at least it wakes her and the soldiers from their trance. They trip over each other trying to be the first to get away. She bangs her knee on the metal desk — just like she knew she would from the moment she saw it — and it hurts worse than she thought. Sends a bone vibration all the way up to her skull.

The mob is up and over the razor-wire in a blink — mindlessly pulling at it with bare hands when it slows them down. Then biting at it, when their hands are caught. They tear themselves to pieces, but it doesn't matter. More are coming, spilling up and over the thrashing bodies. Too many. The gates bow out at the top, then fold, then collapse entirely. The mob spills out like a liquid.

One of the Johnsons is already gone by the time Mari looks up. The only smart Johnson, she thinks.

The other three grab rifles and duck out the door. Quick Chinese firecracker bursts as they open fire. Ken doesn't bother with a gun. He hustles his bulky briefcase computer under one arm and says, "Get to the Snake."

Then he, too, is gone.

Randy, Steves, and Mari idle. Each waiting for the other to act.

Randy snaps out of it first. He snatches up his sniper rifle and shoves Steves towards the door.

"Let's go," he says to Mari.

She just looks at the couch.

He follows her gaze, to Lucas — quiet little forgettable Lucas — all balled up in the corner like a scared pillbug.

"Get up, kid!" he says and crosses over to pull at Lucas' arm. The pillbug moves but doesn't unfurl.

"He gets like this," Mari says. "He won't move."

Randy does half a dance between the door and the couch, caught between a dozen different plans, skittering away in every direction. Steves yells something from just outside the trailer, but it's lost in the approaching din. He ducks his head out.

"Just go. We'll meet you there," he says.

Steves says something back.

Randy stands at the threshold like he's getting ready to jump out of a plane. Nerves, doubt, determination, a clock, ticking.

Then he reaches out, grabs the handle, and slams the door shut.

He runs over to the crude metal desk, and Mari is already there, shoving with her one good hand and all the might of her woefully small body. Together they get it upright, blocking the window. Next go the filing cabinets and table, hastily stacked in front of the door. Already there is banging on the other side. All across the walls. Pockmarks denting out where fists impact. It sounds like she's sheltering under an aluminum roof in an epic hailstorm.

The trailer begins to rock. Gently at first, just a rowboat on a windy lake, but it picks up momentum. Teeters from side to side. Her and Randy are just trying to keep their sea-legs as everything goes *Poltergeist* and throws itself around the room. Mari tackles the couch and crawls atop Lucas. She pins her arms around him, stuffs her face into the back of his hair. It smells like Froot Loops and dust. His breathing is shaky.

Randy falls and swears. A heavy thump, even more swears, then the trailer hits that sweet spot: leaning back in a chair, arms waving, muscles flexing…

She knows they're going over, but they linger on that precipice for so long she starts to doubt.

She shouldn't. She should know better by now.

The trailer tips. Mari and Lucas tumble around like tennis balls in a dryer. The world is sideways, or upside down — did the trailer roll once and stop, or did it keep going? There's no way to tell, just by looking. The room is a junkyard. Everything has gone everywhere. At least she's still got hold of Lucas. He doesn't look hurt.

Well, no *more* hurt, at any rate.

Mari tries to assess her own state but genuinely has no idea if she was wounded in the fall. She's basically just a collection of injuries now. Overlapping hurts, each vying for attention; the unique voices of all the burns and scrapes and broken bones are lost in the larger choir of pain.

From a haphazard mound of metal and papers, Randy groans. He digs his way out, zombie hand poking up from a grave of manila envelopes, and starts throwing stuff aside. He's looking for something.

It takes a minute for Mari's head to clear. To remember that's not a storm outside — all that banging and scratching — it's coming from the army of maniacs, still trying to claw their way in.

Randy finds what he's looking for — his rifle, of course — and goes prone with it. A second later, a gunshot like the voice of god. She's still reeling from the first when the second comes. She follows his aim and sees that the big bastard of a desk they used to block the window has come unmoored. It lies diagonally across the opening now, leaving triangular gaps on either side. Dozens of hands now shoved through them, blindly grasping at the air, banging on the walls, clawing at the metal. It's slapstick. Like Daffy and Bugs trying to go through a door at the same time. They're keeping themselves out, but it won't last. Some are more insistent than others — bashing in the faces of their competition, biting their throats, gouging out their eyes — and they're steadily wriggling through the gap. Randy sights on one and the thunderclap jars Mari to the bones. The thing's head practically explodes. The bullet probably goes right through and does the same to the one behind it. But it doesn't matter. The others just shove the corpse out of the way and pick up right where they left off.

Mari double-checks, but no — there's only the one window in this sad little assembly-line building. No exit but through the bellies of those screaming monstrosities across the room.

Wait, *do* they eat people? She was assuming so, but maybe that was from Diego's zombie movies. The mob might not actually devour her and Lucas when they get through. They might just bash her brains in and tear Lucas apart like a pack of wolves squabbling over a rabbit.

It's a thin comfort.

Mari tries to find calm. Tries to accept her fate. She looks upward, mostly by reflex. If there is a god, she doesn't believe he's literally in the sky or whatever. He could be anywhere, or everywhere — but staring meaningfully at like, the stapler, just doesn't feel right. She gives Lucas one last squeeze. She's just about to ask Randy to turn that rifle around and shoot her first (Lucas is so far gone that him having to watch her die probably wouldn't even register, but she couldn't bear the reverse) when she spots it and has to laugh.

The door is still there. *Of course it's still there. Why wouldn't it be, you idiot?*

The trailer had rocked backward, so now the front door is on the ceiling. Ten feet up from the floor, but a pair of bulky filing cabinets had shifted in the crash, forming makeshift stairs. Only six or seven feet between her and freedom. Too bad both she and Randy fell well short of that height requirement. Mari doesn't know where they'd go, even if they did get out. The maniacs are everywhere. But just the prospect of dying under the open sky, instead of this crappy box, makes it worth a shot.

She has to yell Randy's name a few times before he hears her. They're both half-deaf from the gunshots. She points at the ceiling. He sees the door, and his eyes swell comically. He drops the rifle, beside her in a flash.

"I'll boost you up," he says.

Randy forms a cradle with his hands, Mari steps into it, and he hefts her with surprising ease. She balances, poorly — one foot wobbling in his hands, the other slipping on his shoulder — and flips the latch. The door shoves up and out, and there are the stars Mari never thought she'd see again. Operating on base human instinct alone, she very nearly jumps for it. But she remembers Lucas.

"How are we going to…" she says, looking at her inert ball of brother.

"Damn," Randy says. "Damn, damn, damn."

He chews his lip while he thinks. They both try to ignore the scrabbling sounds just a few feet away and getting closer.

"You go up first," he says. "I'll hand him to you."

That's all Mari needs. She jumps, Randy heaves, and Mari practically sails through the doorway. She lands on her side and scrambles right back to the threshold, ducks her head in. She watches — upside down, blood flushing her cheeks — as Randy pokes, prods, and cajoles Lucas into movement.

"Lucas!" Mari says. "Lucas, come on! Please! We have to go!"

It's not useless, but it lives next door to useless. Randy pulls Lucas to his feet and the kid stands, reluctantly. When they move, it's like a blackout drunk being helped home by friends. Randy pushes him atop the cabinets and locks his arms around Lucas' legs, just under his butt. He lifts the boy up, toward Mari's outstretched hand. But he can't make Lucas take it. She could reach out and ruffle her brother's hair, but that's about it. She can't get any purchase. Randy tries to shuffle his grip lower, lift the kid higher, but it's not a matter of strength. It's a matter of leverage. He's doing all he can, and she's doing all she can, and *none of it is enough.*

"Grab him!" Randy yells, through gritted teeth.

"I'm trying," Mari says. "I've only got one hand!"

"Try harder," Randy says. More like a plea than an admonishment.

"Lucas," Mari charges her voice with every ounce of compassion, fear, and hope she can muster. "Lucas, please. I know, okay? I know how bad this is. I know you want to go home and hide until this is all better. But that's not an option right now. Home is gone, and I don't think this will get better. But I will find you a safe place, if you come with me. I promise you that. All you have to do is reach up and take my hand."

He doesn't so much as twitch. Randy wavers. There's a nasty metallic screech and a bang. The maniacs shriek with renewed passion.

"I know you're in there, baby brother," she says. "Remember earlier? At the gates? You reached out then and put your hand on my knee. That's all you have to do now. Just the same thing, just reach out…"

Nothing.

"I know how you feel," Mari says. "You're thinking, 'Does it even matter if I make it through this? Why bother?' But this isn't about you. See, Lucas, if you don't take my hand, I'm going to jump back down there with you. I'm going to help Randy throw you through this door, and there won't be time for both of us to get out, too. We would die. I don't want to die. I want to live, and that all depends on you. I need you to save my life right now, Lucas. And it's the easiest thing in the world: just reach up, take my hand, and save me."

He looks up at her weakly. Mari can practically see the fog behind his eyes. He's so pale. Looks like he's already been dead for a day. But he slowly lifts one wavering arm to place his limp and fragile hand in hers. She snaps around his wrist like a snakebite, goes spread-eagle on the roof, trying to get maximum traction, and does the impossible. Straining so hard she practically hears the blood vessels bursting behind her eyes, can almost feel the individual fibers in her muscles snapping, she heaves Lucas up and onto the roof.

She laughs like she won the lottery.

There's a clang beside her, but it's just the rifle. Randy tossed it up first. His palms slap down on either side of the doorway, and he comes rocketing up like he hid a trampoline down there. Then he lies on his back and joins Mari in laughing at the stars. Seconds later, the whole trailer shakes. A surge of mayhem from below. Randy leans over and glances down, inside the trailer, now filled to capacity with frothing psychopaths.

Bleeding from countless wounds, eyes gone feral, screaming in blind rage. It won't take them long to climb up. Randy rolls and comes up with his rifle, sights down it, ready to take the first comer. He jumps when Mari simply reaches out and slams the door.

They don't seem big on reasoning. Let's see them figure out how to work a latch.

Randy laughs again — at himself, with relief, in shock, everything. Mari smiles at him.

It fades when they both seem to suddenly realize they're only ten feet up, cast away on a lonely metal island in a vast sea of murderers. Easily hundreds, if not thousands, of the maniacs still vie to get at them. They flood into the trailer until it's full, those on the outside punching, kicking and headbutting the walls in impotent fury. On their periphery, standing separate from the frenzy, the old man with black eyes watches them.

His expression is a mix of frustration and amusement. Eyebrows arched, teeth clenched, lips twitching.

Mari freezes. A cow standing on the train tracks, just watching as the locomotive approaches.

Randy still has his rifle, and he means to use it. Has it up and leveled at the old man, barrel rock steady, finger on the trigger. Mari steadies herself for the bang, but it doesn't come. Randy squints through the scope, blinks, adjusts his grip, drops his eye to sight again. No good. He spins the gun around. Spiderweb cracks all across the lens. He looks at Mari like a lost dog.

Another anguished howl snaps them to attention.

The old man screams, fists clenched, neck craned, veins bulging out across his forehead like snakes beneath his skin. Again, Mari is hit with a wave of hatred so intense it feels personal. It makes her queasy.

The maniacs thrashing in the trailer below freeze. One by one, they turn to face the black-eyed man. His breath runs thin. His scream dies out in a series of furious grunts. He takes a second to compose himself. Straightens his posture. Shakes out his hands. Cracks his neck. Then he nods once, and the crowd below recedes like the tide. They all pull back as one, and for a split second, Mari's actually relieved — they're retreating!

Then they hunker down and sprint forward. A solid wave of bodies breaks against the trailer. Mari goes sprawling. She nearly slides right off roof but catches herself at the edge. Lucas fares better, in his protective cocoon. Randy's on his butt with a bloody lip. Must have caught himself with the rifle. Before he lost his grip on it. The gun is nowhere to be seen. Randy looks around like there might be a button he can press to fix this situation. Some way to hit rewind and take it back.

Keeping low, Mari scuttles back to the edge to assess. The mob is already retreating for another push. When enough of them hit some invisible line, they snap forward as one. Even though she's ready for it this time, it still knocks Mari's arms out from under her. She clips her chin on the roof. Something buckles in the space below. The supports of the flimsy trailer are giving out. The crowd recedes.

The space of a breath.

And impact.

It won't take much more abuse.

A distant, resonating roar. Not the old man. This sound is deeper, more present. Mari feels its vibrations play through the thin metal of the trailer. She turns and doesn't understand what she's looking at. It's a train. Barreling down the tarmac, where there are no rails. The whole thing lit up like a stadium — blinding flood and fog lights all across the front; small but laser-bright spotlights down the roofline. The exterior is smooth and featureless black metal. Its engine screams to split the sky in half. The lead car banks off to one side, and the rest follow, undulating like a gigantic obsidian snake. When it was coming straight at them, Mari was half-blinded by the floodlights. But now that it's at an angle, she can see the enormous, fortified wheels beneath each car. It's like a train and a monster truck had a baby that grew up to be a tank.

Randy is on his feet, hooting and waving his arms. He looks to Mari with half a laugh, sharing some joke she never heard the punchline to.

"It's the snake!" he says.

She doesn't have a response.

"It's a rescue!"

"They better hurry," is all Mari can think to say.

The pair turn as one to watch the black-eyed man. It's like he understands what's happening — gets that he's got a time limit now — and he's not going to take any chances. The crowd backs up farther than before. Getting more of a run up. The old man's face is a mask of barely constrained fury. He doesn't make any visible signal, but Mari can sense when he pulls the trigger. A charge in the air, like the moment before a lightning strike. There's a split-second delay, and then the mob charges. Mari closes her eyes. Just listens to the snarls grow louder. The last blow is much harder than the others. The groans and snaps from below are drowned out by the snake's engine, but she can still feel them through her palms. And then she can't. It feels like forever, how long she's in the air. She pictures herself just spinning away into the sky like a cannonball. Cratering the dirt in a distant, empty patch of desert. Allowed to rest and rust and rot in peace. Instead she hits a wall and bounces.

There was no wall behind her a second ago.

Wind knocked out of her, she gasps up at a short expanse of smooth black steel. The snake is directly behind the trailer, not yet to a full stop, but slowing faster than something that size has any right to. There's a two-foot gap between the edge of the trailer and the side of the Snake. Mari managed to hit the wall so hard that she rebounded to safety. If the impact had been any less violent, she'd probably be dead. Slipped over the edge and crushed beneath those mammoth wheels.

It's…a difficult thing to be grateful for. If more of her bones aren't broken, they're at least bent. She feels like mush. Just a bunch of pudding beneath her skin. With as much urgency as she can muster, she turns her head to search for Lucas. Tries to quiet that voice inside her, running around slamming doors and flipping tables, screeching that he's gone — surely gone — lost to the conveniently Lucas-sized gap between trailer and Snake. She steels herself to find an empty spot where Lucas used to be. Grief pouring into rage into relief into shame into guilt. Instead she finds Randy hunching awkwardly there. Fingers locked on the handle of the sideways door, toes of his boots damn near digging troughs into the metal roof. And beneath him: Lucas.

Randy covers the boy like a tarp.

He rolls away from Lucas and shakily gets to his feet. He gives Mari a worried look, and she could kiss him. She takes back everything she ever thought about him. He looks like he could have been in her class at school, or at most, a year ahead. She wouldn't have talked to him, if they met in the hall. Not her type. Too small, kinda goofy looking. Maybe not a full-on dork, just below average in the most forgettable way. No way would she ever remember his name. That's just wasted brain space.

But he saved Lucas.

Now Mari looks at him and Randy practically shines. If you asked her right now, she'd happily tattoo his name on her butt.

Wheezing and whistling, Mari crawls toward them, reaches out a trembling hand. Randy ignores it. He scoops Lucas up like you would a lazy housecat, takes two staggering steps, and heaves the boy up onto the Snake. Mari goes cold for a second, because Lucas disappears. Fear and worry set up shop in her belly — she won't let Lucas out of her sight, never again — but she votes to trust Randy. He helps her to her feet, and they hobble to the edge of the trailer. The small, darkened gap beckons to Mari like sleep. Formless and inevitable.

With Randy helping her, she jumps and grabs hold of the Snake, forearms flat, using the tension of skin on metal for grip. The stub of her bandaged hand slides uselessly. She goes to pull herself up and finds nothing in reserve. Bangs a knee coming down. One desperate foot blindly searching for purchase behind her.

It's not even a big thing. Any ordinary day and she'd hop right across the tiny gap, using basic momentum to pull herself up without really trying. Such a trivial motion that you wouldn't even think to worry about falling. But all of her strength is gone. The skin of her forearms squeaks and gives, starts to slide. She kicks and hauls with all of her might. All of her might is not very much at all.

Then hands on her hips, lifting. Mari channels all of her will into helping those hands — teeth bared, grunting awfully, all dignity and self-awareness abandoned — she doesn't even flinch when they move down to her butt and start pushing. She crests the short rise like she just summited a deadly mountain. Every ounce of her has been burnt for fuel, and now she's shutting down. She barely hits the tipping point, where her weight nudges over the axis, and she falls forward.

Falls?

That's why Lucas disappeared. A twelve-inch thick ledge runs the perimeter of the car, and then it's a three-foot drop to the flat roof below. When she hits, she knocks her elbow and bites her tongue, adds a few checks to the growing list of pains, and does not care for a second. She wants to laugh — to release tension, to signal relief, or just because it really is funny that she's still alive after all this. But she's too tired.

Lucas is safe in body, if not in mind. Curled up beside her, his thousand-mile eyes watching something she hopes is a whole lot better than reality.

On the far side of the retaining wall, there's an unholy crash, followed by a rain of metal. Mari somehow hauls herself upright and props her chin on the ledge. Where the trailer used to be, there is now a wild tangle of broken steel and writhing bodies. It looks like the aftermath of a plane crash. And here come the rescuers, flooding over the wreckage, hurling debris aside, looking for…

Survivors.

Just one. They pull out a young man in a dull green uniform, stained with blood, caked with dust. A triumphant screech goes up, and the maniacs swarm over Randy like ants.

Mari slides down the wall and crumbles into a pile. Doesn't even have the energy to shift her painfully bent leg. She is hollow. A thin, brittle human shell, covering an empty space. She lets the numbness take her. She knows it's better than the alternative.

Halfway down the car, a hatch opens, and pale white light splits the dark. Steves pokes her head out and blinks to see Mari and Lucas there. Then she smiles. Then she stops smiling.

"Randy?" she says.

Mari can't shake her head, so she just looks away.

Steves waits there for a long time, processing. Mari closes her eyes. When she opens them again, Steves is gone and two of the Johnsons are there instead. Looming over her like statues. They say a bunch of things and don't get a response. They do it to Lucas, too. They talk to one another. One shakes his head a bunch, and the other makes a lot of angry gestures. Angry gestures win, so the pair come over and hook their arms below Mari's. Everything goes black.

Mari wakes up on a ship, skipping across a choppy sea. Her cabin is narrow, but tall and long. It's crammed with bunkbeds or — what do you call it when there are more than two? The beds are stacked four high, industrial metal lockers between the rows. The floor is black rubber embossed with a complicated diamond pattern. The lights are set deep into the ceiling and are mercilessly bright. Her thoughts are slippery, so she operates on instinct. She gets her sea-legs and goes in search of Lucas.

Moments later, she realizes where she must be. Inside of that train-truck thing the military guys called the Snake. Seconds later, she remembers how she got there. The shriek when those things found Randy in the wreckage. Punching, biting, stabbing with their hands….

No. That's for later.

There's so much for later that just the *idea* of later makes Mari feel like she's standing in front of a landslide.

But that doesn't matter. Later is for later. Now is for Lucas.

Mari searches three cars before she finds anybody else. One car that's just green plastic crates, stacked neatly in locking metal shelves from floor to ceiling. A car full of expensive-looking electronics — swiveling chairs bolted to the floor, keyboards built into consoles, monitors reeling off inexplicable information in text, graphs, and blocks of colors. A car where one whole side is a long, skinny kitchen — multiple ovens, stovetops, and sinks — and the other is a neatly ordered, tightly stacked pantry. All of the labels are pure white, with austere black text that simply states their contents, and nothing more. BEANS, they say. And, their point made, they say no more.

Finally, Mari slips through the flexible rubber hallway between cars and opens a door to find voices. Calm and measured, they're discussing things that Mari is not prepared to understand right now. They're just background noise. She walks straight past them as they make surprised noises and utter silly platitudes. She finds Lucas curled up at the bottom of a small bucket seat. It's covered in hard white plastic, and bolted to the floor, but it swivels. She spins it around so he's facing her and puts her hand on his cheek. It's warm in a worrying way, but his eyes are open, and his breathing is steady. Mari sits like that for a long minute before something occurs to her. She stands and runs to one of the soldiers. A black guy. She knows his name somewhere, but it's not a place she can find right now. Already frustrated with words and all the stupid delays they're causing, she skips right past the formalities and starts pulling his jacket off. He resists at first but sees something in her eyes and begins helping her instead. Mari does the same to the next man, and the two others that come into the car, presumably drawn by her appearance. She has four coats now, all drab, patternless green, made of a stiff, but lightweight material that feels more like industrial panels than clothing.

Mari jogs back to the white chair and carefully layers the coats, one at a time, over the Lucas ball. When he's completely covered and comfortably weighted down, she slides to the floor beside him. Mari slips her one good hand beneath the makeshift blankets and finds Lucas' tiny, bird-like wrist. She wraps her fingers around it and feels his pulse, beating metronomic. It rebuilds her slowly, beat by beat.

Siege Tower

He awoke to screams, as usual. Sometimes, they were his own. But not tonight.

The absolute dark of early morning. His face numb from the cold. His fingers unresponsive. They crept like dying spiders — slow, stiff, uncertain — along the seam of his sleeping bag until they found the frigid metal tab of the zipper. He worked it back and forth, catching every broken tooth and errant thread, until the gap widened enough to let him free. He rolled to the edge of the bare mattress and listened.

The screams repeated.

They were insistent tonight.

They were not going to let him sleep.

He stood up. He put a hand to his lower back. He pushed in and twisted at the hips until his spine cracked. A groan, fading into a sigh.

He counted the steps: Three to the edge of the bed. Turn. One and a half. Turn. Four to the door.

He ran his hand up across the wall. A soft plastic click. The light switch did nothing. It hadn't for some time. Just an old habit.

The living room was mostly vacant. What furniture remained — no wood, all of that burned already — was shoved back against the walls. He'd cleared the space in preparation for an emergency escape that had not yet come. He moved through the room with the begrudging trust of the blind.

He followed the gradient of cold. It started at intolerable and slowly grew to painful. He padded to the broken windows. Outside, on the expansive balcony, light. A relative term. A less complete shade of black. He found the insubstantial outline of his rifle and set hands to it. He leaned out over the railing. He watched the darkness below. He listened.

Grunts. Heavy breathing. The scuff of a foot, missing a step. He tracked their progress. He kept the rifle close, locked his jaw against the chattering cold.

A woman broke through the wall of black at a full sprint. She skipped over an open manhole, skirted the dinosaur skeleton of a burned SUV, and slowed at the intersection to consider northbound Washington — too many cars, too many places she couldn't see, too many variables — but chose westbound instead. She went to cut across the park. It was the right move.

She was fast, smart, and alert.

But she did not see the chains that hung between the bollards — the ones meant to stop vehicles from entering. It was just a small hop to clear them. A few inches, and she would have disappeared into the trees before her pursuers could see which direction she'd went. But she didn't jump in time. She caught both ankles and fell — momentum like a slingshot, firing her downward into the pavement — stunned. She rolled around. She moaned. She clutched her face. She tried to stand.

From the darkness, her pursuers. They closed on the woman with the wary confidence of predators. Somebody spoke. He could hear the sounds but not catch the meaning. Their voices were low and casual. Hers was louder, more emotional. A threat and an answering plea. He settled the butt of the rifle into his shoulder and pressed the cold, lacquered wood to his cheek. The drama below now framed by the harsh geometry of his iron sights. The context of the scene had changed. It had a new, unseen director. Him.

The apparent leader motioned to one of the other pursuers, who approached. The woman cried out again. Both ignored her. The hunters looked away for a moment, and the prey took her chance.

Fast, smart, and alert.

She was halfway gone before they reacted. But she was slower than before. Her keen instincts clouded by the fall. There's only so much adrenaline could do. She disappeared into another bank of shadow. The pack whooped and laughed and followed. They spotted weakness. They knew the hunt was over now, in all but formality.

And yet he still had a say.

He focused on the leader. A skinny one. Lanky. Dark hoodie up. No details. Not even a person, just an abstract. It would be easy.

The prongs of his sights stabbed in at his target, urging his finger toward the trigger.

Without their leader, the other three might scatter. They might be distracted long enough to let the woman escape. They might not triangulate where the shot came from — not if there was only the one — and find him.

But then again, they might.

And bullets are finite.

And he did not know the woman.

The skinny one disappeared into the shadows. The others followed after. Their manic sounds grew faint.

He lowered the rifle.

He bent and returned it to its place: resting in the corner, where the two low walls of the balcony met. He stood. He winced. He put his hand to his back and shook his head.

He walked carefully, broken glass crunching beneath his feet the whole way. When he reached the raised metal lip that marked the frame of the old, broken sliding glass door, he began to count his steps.

Ten to the doorway. Hand to a switch with no response. Four to the bed. Turn. One and a half to the edge. Turn. Three to the end table.

He lowered himself gently, like easing a priceless work of art down from the bed of an unsteady truck. He felt for the cold metal tab of the zipper. He worked it up its stuttering, frustrating track. He laid down. He closed his eyes. He waited for the next screams.

Morning broke, and he wormed free of his bedding. He washed his face with the stale water from the bathtub, ran through a brief regimen of stretches, and dressed in the same set of clothes he wore every day. Thick wool socks, worn sneakers, jeans so old they had gone colorless, and a padded flannel shirt. He moved to the kitchen and assessed the pantry. He stared at the bare shelves.

He listened to the wind whistle through invisible seams in the walls. The apartment had always been cold. Even back when its windows had been intact.

"Shoddy work," he said and frowned at the drywall. "I told you, Maria. I told you before we even moved in, this was shoddy work. Shoddy work for a whole lot of money."

Nobody answered.

He shuffled to the living room and carefully hefted an aluminum ladder from its place against the wall. He bent with his knees, though even they cracked in protest. He carried the ladder to the edge of the balcony and balanced its feet atop the enclosing wall. He paused to watch the skyline. When he was finished, he glanced back toward the bedroom.

Inside, sitting atop the chintzy plastic IKEA stool that served as his nightstand, was a framed photograph. The photo was paper. The frame was wood. The only paper and the only wood left in his apartment. The rest had been burned for warmth. The photograph showed a solidly built woman in her mid-fifties, wearing a daisy blouse beneath a deepwater blue cashmere sweater — draped across her shoulders like it had been made for her, which, of course, it had. Plain gray slacks. A thin silver chain around her neck, sporting a single, unadorned iron carpentry nail. Her hair was black and untidy — the wind had caught it — and she was laughing. Behind her, the same low brick walls of the balcony on which he stood. Beyond them, the same skyline.

Almost the same skyline.

Buildings present in the photo were missing from his view. Others still stood but were crumbling, charred, or broken. In a few, fires raged. Across the Hudson, New York City never stopped burning. Not completely. The river shimmered with oil. Bodies rafted past, swirling out to sea. The marina was shattered, abandoned. A sunken forest of masts, their tips just barely breaking the water's surface. Beyond it, the park had grown wily and untamed. Nature had taken back the space. But across the bay, the Statue of Liberty stood unchanged.

He inhaled deeply, slowly, through his nose.

"Hell of a view," he said. "Never worth the money, though."

He looked west, at the black spot fixed in the sky. When it first appeared, it was no larger than a speck. Now it was the size of the moon. It never set. Never moved across the sky. Just grew. Imperceptibly, but incessantly.

He spat and turned away. He leaned over his balcony wall, surveying the others below. Portside Towers was vaguely pyramidal — wider at the base and narrower at the top. Its balconies were staggered, not stacked one atop the other. They fanned out beneath him like rice paddies. With just a sixteen-foot ladder stolen from maintenance, he could access them all.

He knelt to check a series of hashmarks scratched into the wall.

"Four down, one right," he said.

He slid the ladder over the edge and gently lowered it to the balcony below. He sat on the wall and carefully swung his legs over. The apartment below had been the first one he cleared. Not even wood remained in there. The same with its neighbors to either side. His stop was four stories down — four awkwardly wrestled ladders, four slow and painful descents.

He had been mining the place for two days. The glass door was already shattered, its glistening jewels crunching beneath his shoes. He surveyed the living room and shook his head.

The walls were covered in massive reproductions of comic book art. All portraits, all male, all stripped down to leather thongs and elaborate codpieces. They wore thick mustaches and leering smiles.

"These were your neighbors, Maria," he said. "Not exactly the borrow-a-cup-of-sugar types."

He headed for the kitchen first. He had left the cabinets open. He filled his backpack with their contents: cruelty-free albacore in olive oil, fair trade lentils, something called Quinoa that looked like rice but smelled like broccoli. The box proudly called it an "environmentally stable grain source."

"Betcha feel silly now, eh fellas?" he asked.

He waited for an answer. When none came, he chuckled to himself, then resumed packing.

In the bedroom, he unhitched a small hatchet from his belt and set about dismantling a minimalist maple coffee table that had clearly cost a fortune. Now it was firewood. He collected the pieces and bound them with a bungee cord, then hooked the bundle to the webbing of his backpack. He climbed the ladder, dragged it up after him, reset it, and climbed again.

Four stories took their toll, and he wasn't done. Two more to the roof.

He crested the final ledge and collapsed on the tarpaper. He waited until the spots disappeared from his vision, wiped the sweat from his forehead — already cooling to a nasty chill — and limped toward a series of buckets, pots, bowls, posts, and tarps. He held his lower back, favoring his left side.

He lifted the corners of shower curtains and cheap tablecloths — even a pair of rubber sheets, courtesy of the codpiece-and-mustache boys — so that the dew they'd collected could flow down, into the waiting containers below. He stooped — gasping, swearing — and retrieved the water, then transferred it all to a single plastic barrel that sat beside the access doorway. He unscrewed the lid. It was half full. He added his harvest, drank some for himself, then sealed it again. He turned back to the ladder to begin his short, painful journey home.

It rattled against the concrete wall, a sound like steel drums. Somebody was climbing it. Quickly.

He reached down and unclasped his hatchet. He shifted it in his palm and swung it shortly, twice, to settle its weight in his grip. Then he charged. His steps were low and quick. He breathed shallow, quiet, did not grunt or yell. He stopped a few feet shy of the roof's edge, hatchet raised, panting thinly, and waited. The rattling stopped.

Wind. Bird calls.

He crept up to the ledge and peered over. The balconies below laid out like drawers in a jewelry box. All vacant. No ambushers waiting for him on the ladder. No potential attackers standing at its base.

He gave the ladder an experimental shake. It shuddered but remained steady, its feet planted firmly.

"Well, it wasn't the damn breeze," he whispered.

He fixed the hatchet between his teeth and bit down. Butt on the ledge, legs dangling, weight onto the rungs. He froze. A few feet down, and his legs would be in reach of anybody standing on the balcony below, hidden just out of his sightline. He closed his eyes.

He sighed.

He wrapped his hands loosely around the side rails, then swung his feet out and slid the remaining length of the ladder. It rattled, shook, made a sound like a freight train crashing into a kitchen, and he hit the pavement flat-footed. A sharp intake of breath. The hatchet out of his mouth and in his hand.

He had shattered the sliding glass doors months ago. Hacked apart and burned the wooden lounge furniture. Stripped the fabric from the couch and armchair, burned their frames, and left the springs in a pile by the doorway. Waterlogged beige carpet in the living room. Dirty white tile in the kitchen. Beyond that: only black shadows in the doorways, where the gray winter sunshine petered out.

With no immediate threat visible, he took a moment to straighten up sharply, put a hand to his back, and twist. It did not take. He did it again. A pop.

He sobbed and laughed at the same time.

"Well, it ain't like I can just go see a chiropractor," he said.

He limped into the darkened apartment. Weathered glass shards ground beneath his sneakers. He checked the kitchen first. Behind the island. In the fridge. He had stripped away the doors to the cabinets long ago and could see at a glance they were empty.

In the living room: a floor lamp with an expensive-looking curve to the base, a colorful glass coffee table, a pile of rusting springs. He gave his eyes some time to adjust, staring into the dark until he could at least pick up outlines, then walked into the dark, his left foot dragging — shuffle stump shuffle — the hatchet held diagonally in front of his face. He paused at a Stonehenge silhouette, a door, and pushed it open. A cramped coat closet. Clear.

This unit mirrored his own in some ways, but it had an extra bedroom. His own hallway veered to the right. This one forked: left to the guest, right to the master.

He slid along the wall, watching the far corridor. At its end, cold and dusty light from the big windows in the master bedroom. Quiet breath. Soft steps. At the threshold, he paused. He knelt as low as his creaking knees would allow and ducked his head in. Left, right, and back.

No movement. He crept into the bedroom and pressed himself flat against the wall. He slid toward the windows, light at his back, facing the darkness.

He froze.

The bedframe was a solid piece of molded white plastic, bulbous feet, and grand sweeping arches. It would not burn. He had let it be. The blankets, he had stolen. The several dozen oddly shaped throw pillows, he'd tossed in the far corner.

He had left the bed totally bare.

Now there was something on it.

He broke into a low and mostly silent run, only the crackling of his joints betraying his approach. A fast and vicious swing, more speed than force, and the hatchet sunk to its hilt in something soft.

Too soft.

He wiggled the axe, sending a small puff of tiny feathers swirling in the air. Dim secondhand sunlight catching the barbs, lighting them up like fireflies.

The throw pillows. The ones he'd left heaped in the corner, after stripping the bed bare.

The corner directly behind him right now.

The skin on the back of his neck danced, and he spun, almost in time to dodge the blow.

The sharp edge of something metal but hollow. Too light. It dazed him but didn't put him down. A figure darted past, clipped its shin on an unseen bedpost, and went sprawling in the darkened hallway. It half-crawled, half-ran to the intersection—

In the snapshot of laundered sunlight, she shone like an angel. It made stark shadows from her cheekbones. It feathered her hair with white. It shone in her eyes — not an airy blue, but the complex and impenetrable color of the ocean. The same shade as the woman with the windblown hair, in the photograph on his makeshift nightstand.

This was not the same woman. This one was decades younger, much paler — no distant Spanish dusting her skin, as there had been with Marie — and forty pounds lighter. There was a desperate, refugee thinness to her frame.

The moment unfroze, and the girl bolted around the corner, out of sight.

"W-wait," he called. His voice broke.

She didn't hear him. Or she didn't listen.

"Wait!" he called again.

He ran after her. He didn't make the corner and put his shoulder through the cheap drywall. She was on the balcony, one foot already poised on the ladder.

She was fast.

"You're the girl from last night!" he yelled.

She peered into the gloom but didn't see him. He moved carefully into the light and saw her eyes dart down to his hand.

He was still holding the hatchet — and the pillow he'd murdered. It was bleeding down.

"I'm normal!" he said. "I can talk. I'm not a thing."

"Some of them can talk," she said.

"They can?" he asked. "I've only seen them screaming."

She didn't answer. She looked to his hand again.

He tossed the hatchet away suddenly, like it had burned him.

"Would one of them do that?" he said.

She shifted her weight off the ladder and peeked at him through the rungs.

"No," she said. "But not all normal people are good, either."

He laughed.

"Tell me about it," he said.

"Why do you want me to wait?" she asked.

He started to answer but caught himself short and fell silent. He looked around at the furniture, stripped of wood. At the shelves, emptied of food. He stuck his jaw out.

"I guess I don't," he finally said.

Now it was her turn to laugh.

"That's about the only thing you could've said to make me stay," she told him and let her long, thin fingers fall from the rung. Her knuckles were bulbous and scabbed. Her fingernails ragged and dirty.

"Listen," he said. "I don't have much here, and what I do have is mine. This is my spot — people have been trying to make me leave since before the world went crazy — and I don't need company."

She walked toward him, light, easy, wary. A deer moving through a clearing. The glass that crunched beneath his feet merely crackled below hers.

"I don't believe that," she said. "You were begging me to wait just a second ago."

"I don't beg anybody for anything," he snapped.

"Hey." She put her hands up, palms out. "Look, there's nothing wrong with needing someone. There aren't many of us left. I'm glad to see you, too."

"Get moving, lady," he said and inched toward his hatchet. "It's every man for himself these days, and I don't know you from Adam."

"One night, okay?" she said and circled him, hands still up. "I just…I just need to catch my breath for one night. I won't bother you. Maybe I can even help. I don't eat much…"

He took in her slight body. All elbows and knees.

"One night," he said. "I'll get you some supplies — only the stuff I can't use, mind you — and then come morning, you're gone. You don't tell anybody I'm here, and I never see you again."

"Deal," she said.

She held out her hand.

He took it. Frail. Paper-thin. Warm.

Together, they ascended — her first, him following with hatchet held in teeth — and harvested more rainwater. She drank deeply from a cheap cooking pot, just going to rust.

"This how you got up?" he asked, nudging open the access door.

"Yeah," she said. "How else?"

"It's dark in there," he said.

"Sure is."

"You made your way up here in the dark?"

"Of course."

"All the way through the lobby, found the door to the stairs, and took every flight to the roof, all in pitch black?"

She paused while returning the pot to its place, just beneath a torn shower curtain. She looked back at him.

"During the day, you can see just fine in the lobby," she said. "The windows are all busted out, plus somebody drove a garbage truck through the main entrance. Looked like it started a hell of a fire when it crashed."

"It was on fire before it crashed," he said. "So was everybody in it. Couple dozen of them. In the back. With the trash."

"You were here when it happened?" she asked.

She duck-walked beneath the water traps and stood beside him. They looked out onto the bay. The Statue of Liberty, like a model somebody had set on the horizon.

"Yes," he said. "I've been here all along. We lived here. I lived here. Before. I'm not moving. Nobody's gonna make me."

She didn't have a response for that.

"What about you?" he asked. "Where do you hole up?"

"I don't," she answered. She gave him a sideways look. "Not anymore. Holing up is dumb. No offense. If you stay in one spot, they're guaranteed to find you. Trust me, I know."

"Doesn't seem like I'm the dumb one." He spat at her feet. "You were the one running for your life last night."

"So you saw all that?" she said.

"Heard it, mostly."

"And you didn't think to, I don't know, help?"

"Lady, I said it before: I don't know you."

She scoffed. Crossed her arms. Looked away toward New York, while he watched the bay. They stayed like that for a quiet moment.

"Let's get you something to eat," he said.

He led the way to the ladder and descended first. The hatchet clipped firmly to his belt. He hauled an old paint bucket full of water. She carried a green plastic pail, emblazoned with a starfish.

They built a fire in his kitchen sink. Sat on bar stools in front of it, watching the flames instead of talking. She ate tuna straight out of the can, while he poured dry quinoa into an old-fashioned metal coffee pot, splashed some water in after it, and set it to cooking.

"I didn't even get your name," she spoke, after a particularly long and uncomfortable silence.

"I don't see how it matters," he said. "You're gone tomorrow."

"Jesus," she muttered.

He studied the fire.

"You're something else," she said, after visibly fuming for a moment. "We're still people. We have names. We talk to each other and help each other. That's what people do."

"That's what people did," he corrected.

He shook the coffee pot. Smelled the quinoa. It was earthy, in an entirely unpleasant way.

"We're still alive," she said. "At least, I am."

"I didn't much like people before all this," he said. "Not much has happened to change my mind lately. Just look at those thugs last night, hunting you down in the street like it's a game."

She turned to stare at him.

"Those weren't people," she said, carefully. "Those weren't anything like people."

He stirred the fire.

"You really haven't left this place at all, have you?" she asked.

"Not much cause—" he started, but she cut him off.

"You really don't know anything—" she said, but it was his turn to interrupt.

"You don't come into my house and start insulting me when I'm sharing my—"

"You don't know anything!" she yelled. She threw the empty tuna can into the fire, sending up a volley of sparks. "The angry ones — the ones that just scream and charge — they're kittens. Have you seen the still ones? The ones blocking every exit from this god damn island? The ones that don't move until you get close, and then they move so fast you can't see them — tearing you apart limb from limb with their bare hands? You seen them?"

"I don't—"

"Even *those ones* aren't the worst. You can trick the angry ones. Avoid the still ones. It's the laughing ones that will get you. Those things chasing me last night weren't human. Weren't even close. The madness just took a different form in them. Sure, they can talk and reason — but they think everything is a game, especially killing, and they love to play."

She slid from her bar stool and jabbed a thin finger at the broken windows.

"Have you even looked out there, lately? The angry ones are gone. They left weeks ago. But the still ones keep guarding all the exits. They're keeping us in, so the laughing ones can play with us. That's what you've been hearing out there — not 'thugs' taking advantage of the situation. Not human nature. Every single normal person I've met has done nothing but help and care for each other. Every single one! It's only monsters out there, killing us off one by one. And you're doing *nothing*."

"Better them than me," he said.

She bit the side of her lip. She looked away.

"Do you really mean that?" she finally asked.

"No," he sighed. "I guess not. I don't know anymore. Most of my life, it's just been me. I liked it that way. I was a firm believer in 'if you want something done right, you gotta do it yourself.' It worked just fine, until…"

He gave the steaming coffee pot a shuffle. It belched out thick puffs of steam. He wrinkled his nose.

"Do you want this?" he asked her. He tilted the pot in her direction, to show her the contents. "Smells like somebody farted on some rice."

She laughed.

"It's quinoa," she said. "It's an environmentally st—"

"Stable grain source," he quoted the box. "So they tell me."

She laughed again, quieter, and took the pot from him.

"I used to be all about this stuff," she said.

"Quinoa?" he asked.

"No," she said and looked around for something.

He pulled a plastic cup from beneath the counter and rattled the pair of forks inside. She took one.

"Environmental stuff," she continued. "I only shopped at local co-ops. I drove an electric car. I signed petitions."

She shook her head.

"Seems pretty dumb now, huh?" he asked.

"Maybe," she said. "No. We didn't know this was coming. We were trying to do the right thing. I think it's the trying that counts."

"Sounds like dumb to me," he said.

She tilted her head while she chewed. She swallowed with visible effort.

"Until what?" she said. "You were saying you used to think it was every man for himself, until…"

She rotated her hand at the wrist, urging him to pick up the prompt while she continued to eat.

He stood, carefully. Palm flat against his lower back. He walked away.

Four to the bed. Turn. One and a half to the edge. Turn. Three to the table. He reached down. His hand found it unerringly, even in the absolute darkness. He reversed his movements and returned to the small kitchen. The weak fire in the sink threw shadowplay on the tile backsplash. He handed the object to the girl.

It was a rectangular frame. Old, faded wood that had lost most of its stain. The glass was scratched. The felt on the back was peeling. The photograph inside was immaculate. It showed a woman with windblown hair and a careless smile. And an expensive sweater.

"Who is this?" the girl asked.

"Was," he said. "That was Marie. My wife."

"I'm sorry," she said.

"Everybody is," he said.

She looked at the photo for a moment before handing it back to him. He set it on the counter, deliberate and reverent, making sure it sat well away from the fire.

"I don't know what she saw in me," he started. He stopped. He grunted. He began again. "We couldn't have been more different. I was cheap beer and she was expensive wine. I was action movies and she was books. I voted Republican; she voted for those weird parties you never heard of. They said she only married me for my money — every dime, I earned myself…"

He paused to look at her. Waited until she nodded.

"And hell," he continued. "Maybe part of that's true. She always had expensive taste. I don't think she could've taken living poor, like I grew up. That didn't make her bad. It made her smart."

She didn't speak when he fell silent. She ate quietly, careful not to let her fork ping against the steel of the coffee can. The whistle of the wind. The rustle of the fire.

"Thing is, she could've had a thousand other rich guys," he said. "That was always her world, and she owned it. The way those yuppies in their nice suits looked at her, back when we were young. I saw it. But she chose me. And I made her happy. She loved this place."

He gestured around at the broken windows. The weather-stained carpet. The empty living room. The skyline across the river, black — save for the few spots where it was burning.

"She liked the view," he laughed.

She didn't join in.

"She always thought the best of everybody. Too trusting, I always told her. Naïve, I said, if she wasn't in the room. But I wouldn't have changed a thing about her for the world. She would've helped you last night. In the blink of an eye. Hell, if she was still here, I would've helped you, because I'd know she'd want me to. But she's not here."

"How?" she asked.

"Cancer," he said. "Thank Christ she didn't live to see this mess."

He spat into the fire. It sizzled.

The girl nodded.

"It's still not an easy way to go," she said.

And he nodded.

They ate in silence. When they were done, he took the fork and coffee pot and rinsed them with water from the little green plastic pail. The kind a child would use to dig at the beach.

They stayed by the fire until it died, talking mostly about the way things used to be. Then he guided her through the dark, first to the bathroom, then to the bedroom. He dug beneath the frame for extra blankets.

"You can sleep on the bed," he said, settling a heavy quilt on the floor.

"No way," she said. "This is your place. And besides, I saw you holding your back. You need the bed."

"I'll be fine," he said, automatically.

A quizzical silence.

"It is unbelievably cold up here," she finally said. "I think we'd be better off sleeping together."

He blinked. He swiveled to face where he thought she was, in the dark.

"Oh my god, not like that," she said, almost all one word. "Just for body heat. That's how we used to do it back in the firehouse."

"What's that?" he said.

"Nothing," she said. Her voice had lost something. "Just the place where I was before this."

He did not push the point. He began piling blankets onto the bed.

"Now don't you go making moves on me, young lady," he said, with faux sternness.

"Groooossss," she sang, and they both laughed.

He eased down onto the mattress. She pressed against him, his lap to her rear. After a few moments he pushed her away, turned over, and pulled her hand across his shoulder, so that her stomach was pressed against his back instead.

"Just not comfortable on that side," he said. "My back and all."

"Of course," she said, and she kindly let the subject drop.

. . .

He awoke to screams, as usual.

Somebody was touching him. He threw himself out of bed, landed on the floor, felt around for his hatchet.

"What's going on?" the girl asked.

He shook his head clear. He closed his eyes and sighed.

"Bad dream," he said. "Did you hear someth—"

Another scream. Muffled by distance, refracted from the neighboring buildings, hard to place. He heard a rustle — the girl was moving.

"Don't go anywhere," he said, but she didn't answer.

She kept moving.

He reached out, bumped his knuckles on a wall that he didn't realize was there. He knocked his knee on the nightstand, standing up. He felt the picture frame topple over. He moved to catch it but guessed wrong. He heard it hit the carpet, but the glass didn't break.

There was a thump somewhere to his right, followed by whispered swearing. Then light footsteps, growing distant. The girl had found the doorway. She left the bedroom.

He followed after, hands in front, taking careful, shuffling steps like a blind man. He bent his finger backward when he hit the wall. He felt along its length, found the opening, then slipped out into the living room. The light was abysmal, just shadows and vague outlines, but he moved faster, having his bearings again. She was already outside, standing at the edge of the balcony, looking down into nothing. From out here, the noises were clearer: Pained grunts. Something metal being knocked over. Laughter, wildly out of place for how sincere and playful it was.

From absolute darkness into relative darkness, a figure. An older man, his face indistinct. A bulge around the belly. Toddling, uncertain steps. He held a hand to his face in a way that betrayed a wound. He screamed again, no words, no plea for help — just an animalistic squeal. He stumbled onto Washington Street, moving toward the memorial, and the marina.

"We have to help him," the girl said.

He didn't reply. He went to retrieve the rifle from its place in the corner. His fingers closed on nothing.

He grabbed again, lower, waved his hand slowly from side to side, hoping to contact its barrel in the dark. He knelt, with considerable difficulty, and padded around the cement.

"What are you doing?" she asked.

"I have a rifle here," he said. "Somewhere."

"I have it," she said. "I saw it earlier. I'm a decent shot."

"Hand it over," he said.

He approached her in the dark, one hand out for receipt. He was watching the street below. No rifle was deposited.

He grunted.

"Are you going to help him?" she asked.

More figures emerging from the shadow canyons of the neighboring high-rise. They followed the wounded man.

A whiff of fabric moving across wood, and the girl had the rifle up against her shoulder, sighting it down on the figures below. She tracked the leader: skinny and androgynous, its features hidden beneath the deep, loose hood of a baggy sweatshirt.

He heard her breathe in slowly. Could practically feel her finger tightening on the trigger.

He seized the rifle, pulling it up and away.

"What the hell?" she hissed.

"You shoot and they'll know we're here," he said.

"So we'll shoot them all," she said.

"You don't even know how many there are," he said.

He held the rifle above and behind him, keeping a toy from a petulant child.

"We can take them," she said. "We have to help that guy."

"We don't know him," he said.

She recognized the finality in his voice. She went to speak, stopped.

"Fine," she said, and she turned away.

From balcony to tile to carpet, her footsteps went from flat, to hollow, to gone.

He watched the street.

The hooded figure quickened its pace, broke into a short run, vaulted the metal hoops of a bike rack, and did a clumsy twist. It fell, rolling onto its butt. It laughed: high and young.

One of the others followed suit but vaulted the rack with more grace. This one a boy, tall and lanky. A shock of long hair on one side of his head, the other shaved bare. He landed square, both feet planted on either side of the hooded figure's shoulders. Then he squatted low, rubbing his crotch on the prone figure's face. They laughed, all of them, together. The hooded figure pushed the lanky boy away and had its feet again, up and running at full sprint. It disappeared after the wounded man, around the corner. The others followed, whistling and whooping.

From somewhere behind him, a familiar noise that he hadn't heard in a long time: a sticky latch being flipped, and the plastic crackle of weather stripping, releasing its seal. The girl had opened the front door.

"Wait," he cast his voice low and urgent out into the dark. "Don't go out there!"

Through the bare living room, to the end of the hall. Nightblind, he sensed the change in the air from the open door. Staler than his own, warmer, and full of rot. Outside, in the long corridor between apartments, something crashed. The girl swore.

"Wait," he called again, leaning out of the doorway. "I never cleared the halls. It's not safe."

"Then stay there," she snapped.

He hesitated at the threshold for the space of ten heartbeats, then stepped out of his home, and into the dark.

The hallway smelled of singed dust. Remnants of the fire. The carpet was thin and did nothing to hide her footsteps ahead. He followed them through a cooler space in the darkness. Sensed another change in the air. Felt an absence of pressure signifying a larger space. An open door: one of the apartments that he hadn't checked yet. He could feel its stillness pressing in on him. He moved to the left wall and put his hand on it. Dragged his fingers across the rough, flaking paper as he walked. They grazed against the cool metal of a doorjamb. He felt for the knob. Found it. Still closed. He hadn't heard it swish open, hadn't heard the hydraulics wheeze as it shut, hadn't heard the hollow thunk of the latch engaging. She'd walked right by it.

"Back here," he called.

She didn't answer.

He sighed, loud enough so she could hear the resignation in it.

"The door to the stairs is back here. I'm touching it," he said.

A moment of quiet, then small feet, shuffling.

"You're coming with me?" she asked.

"If I don't, you'll never even find the damn stairs," he answered.

A skeptical laugh. Uncertain steps.

"The wall to my left, your right," he said.

She found it, her fingers brushing against his when she reached the doorway.

"Let's go back," he said. "It's probably already too late to do any good."

"It doesn't matter," she said. "We have to try."

She didn't wait for him to reply. The handle clicked, and stale air washed in. It smelled like concrete and metal. He felt the warmth of her body pass, in the dark. He followed it.

The stairs were easy. One at a time, hand on the rail, all the way to the bottom. They descended in silence, wary of alerting some unseen thing below that might be waiting for them. Finally, he heard her stumble, reaching for a step that wasn't there.

"I think we're here," she said.

"The lobby is this way," he agreed. Palms against rough concrete.

Cool steel. "Got it. Follow my voice."

He eased the door open. The relative dark of the lobby at night, with its smashed windows and destroyed façade, was daylight compared to the absolute blackness of the stairwell. He could only make out shapes. Boxes and diamonds: the tacky, faux mid-century modern furniture of the lounge. Beyond it, ink and shadow. Distant sparks marking fires across the river.

"I'm all turned around," she said.

"It's this way."

He took her by the hand, felt her delicate bones against his broad and calloused palm.

They picked their way through the shattered, burned, and weathered remains of the lobby, wincing whenever their feet found old wood, or broken glass. They crept around the husk of a burned-out garbage truck, half-embedded in the reception desk. The sticky, resinous smell of old, fried meat. He didn't look inside. They stood on the cracked pavement of the circular driveway and listened.

Distant yelps of pain and fear, answered by laughter.

He squeezed her hand. She squeezed back.

Out on the street, she took the lead, picking her way quiet and quick through the shrubbery, heading toward the Korean War memorial, which bordered his building on the marina side. There was light over there, mostly blocked by the curving remembrance wall. It threw sinewy silhouettes halfway up Portside Towers. The voices grew louder. He and the girl grew quieter. Smaller movements, more carefully placed. The orange wash of the unseen fire guided them in. They ducked behind the memorial. On the far side of it, a man sobbed and pleaded. A smattering of young voices joked and prodded. A fire crackled. A bone snapped. A low, wet howl.

"Last chance," she said, her voice so faint that he saw more than heard the words. "You don't have to do this."

He clenched his jaw. Fit his teeth together. He nodded once, short, sure.

She smiled. Small and sad.

She stepped out into the light. The voices stopped.

He followed the girl, tensing for a fight.

"Ho, shit!" Somebody laughed. Disbelieving. Others joined in.

The hunters lounged in a rough semi-circle around a central campfire. Just kids. Not a one over twenty. A loping monkey of a boy, all knees and elbows. A pretty blonde in a puffy green parka. A shorter, dark-skinned girl with her combat boots kicked up, resting on the lap of a chubby Asian kid with a patchy pubescent beard. The bald man they'd seen running was now on his knees, clutching his face and quietly whimpering.

"Ohhhh noooo," a high voice sang.

It cut through the rabble. A short, slim figure in a gray sweatshirt stepped forward, its hood pulled up, face lost to shadow.

"You lost!" it finished.

The laughter resumed.

He looked to the girl for context, but she was stepping away from him, circling around to stand behind the hunters.

He opened his mouth to speak. Considered. Then turned to run instead. He found three more children lurking behind him: One — the oldest so far, in his mid-twenties, perhaps — was huge and muscular, wearing an old army jacket and cap, both three sizes too small. They were covered in Sharpie graffiti: copulating stick figures and crudely scrawled profanities. Another, a girl, plain and acne-scarred. Brown hair pulled back into a tight ponytail that flowed all the way to her knees. She held a pair of industrial bolt cutters. The snips were stained with rust. Or something rust colored. The last kid was a perfectly hairless, golden-skinned little boy. Not even eyebrows marring his smooth face. Maybe ten years old. In each hand, he held a shiny silver chef's knife. Black handles stenciled with Japanese writing. The metal was ornately folded; it caught the firelight and danced with it. He stepped away from them. He turned to face the main group.

"Why?" he asked.

Every one of the children burst out laughing. It went on so long they ran out of breath, red-faced and panting. When it finally started to ease down, the pretty blonde giggled, and it caught on again. A full minute passed. They wiped tears from their eyes.

"Oh, Jesus," the chubby Asian kid sighed.

"My stomach hurts," the girl in the combat boots said, holding a hand over her abdomen. "That was the funniest god damn thing I've ever heard."

"Why?" the hairless boy imitated, making his voice deep and dopey.

And they were off laughing again.

Something in the bald man broke, and he bolted from his place by the fire. He disappeared into the night like he'd jumped into the ocean.

"Oop." The huge guy pointed. "Lost a rabbit."

"Ah." The hooded figure waved a dismissive hand. "He'll play the game later. Let's focus on this one for now — it's hilarious."

The leader crossed around the campfire, the light at their back stealing all detail from the space beneath the hood. Just a black hole for a face. They stood a few feet from him, hands on their hips, watching. He looked past them. Found the girl at the edge of the memorial, where stones met grass. Her shoulders pulled in, her head cast down, trying to make herself small.

"Why?" he asked her again.

"Boo," the girl with the ponytail called. "Too soon."

"Yeah, man," the huge guy said. "Don't wear it out."

"Hold up," the hooded figure said. "Let her answer."

The girl didn't speak. She looked away.

The leader closed the distance to her in a few quick bounds. They seized the girl's face. Held her eyelids open — Marie's eyes; murky blue — and spat directly into her eyeball. The girl cried out.

He tried to run to her, but massive, meaty hands closed around his arms and pulled him backwards. Down. Thumped on his ass. His back. He gasped from the pain.

"You gotta answer him," the figure explained to the girl. "Come on, it'll be funny."

They waited.

"I had to do it," the girl said, still unable to look at him. "If I don't play the game, I become the game."

"Ooh, well said." The acne-scarred girl chuckled. "I like that."

"Yeah, that's pretty good," the leader agreed. They turned to address him. "So do you get it now?"

"Get what?" he asked. "Listen, if your problem's with me, you can let the girl go—"

A sharp bark of laughter from behind.

The hooded figure knelt down, face to face with him. He stared into the cavern beneath the drawn hood.

"That's just it, though," they said. "That little rabbit over there just killed you…"

The figure paused to look at the girl, still rubbing her eyeball. When they turned, he caught a glimpse of their features. High, thin nose. Sharp cheekbones and full lips. They were beautiful, whatever they were.

"She brought you out here to die, and you know it, and yet you're still all, 'Let the girl go.' It's funny. Get it?"

"No," he said. Looking to each of the kids for clarification. "You knew I was up there? You could have come in and killed me whenever you wanted…"

"What's funny about that?" the chubby one asked.

"Right," the leader agreed. "You had to come out to us. That's the game. And you were doing so good! We ran, what, twenty rabbits past your house?"

"Sixteen," the pretty blonde corrected.

"Sixteen bunnies!" the hooded figure exclaimed. "Nobody made it to sixteen! That chickenshit yuppie in the bank broke at eight. Hell, those badass biker guys only made it to ten. When we brought out a cute little white bunny — like, we're talking barely old enough to hop, here — and started cutting on her right in front of the warehouse they were holed up in, they broke. Came charging out all chains swinging and—"

"Get your hands off her!" The hairless boy did his baritone impression again, and the other kids laughed.

"We tried that with you last month," the hooded figure continued. "And nothin'! Same exact bunny. Little thing screamed all night, but you didn't budge. We cut her until she was just a stain, man. You were stone cold! You were the champ!"

He winced. He looked at the girl, to make sure she still wasn't looking at him.

"I gotta know," the leader asked. "What was it about this particular rabbit that finally got to you?"

He didn't answer. The figure stood and started over toward the girl again.

"Her eyes!" he called after them. They stopped, swiveled about. Waited for him to continue. "She…she looks like my wife. A little bit.

Around the eyes."

Quiet. Small waves lapping at the shore. The crackle of the fire.

"Pfffffthahahahaha," the leader doubled over.

The other hunters broke simultaneously, howling, rolling on the ground, weeping and thumping on their thighs. When their laughter finally faded, the hooded figure sat down before him, inches away.

"That's perfect," they said. "You have to get it now, right? You get the joke?"

"No," he whispered.

"Am I explaining it wrong?" the leader asked the group. "I don't know what else to say."

"Some people just got no sense of humor," the huge guy said, his voice weary.

"Sad," the girl in the combat boots added.

"Listen," he said, looking to each of the kids in turn. "There has to be something you want. I've got food, water. We can make a deal."

"You can't," the girl finally spoke. One hand still over her eye, she looked at him from across the fire. "I told you, they're not human. They're just like the other things."

"Not *just* like them," the leader amended. "It's true, when I'm not around, my little ones can be a little chaotic. They each play their own game, by their own rules — and if you're not paying attention, maybe you could mistake that for madness. But when I'm here, they all play the same game. The best game: mine."

The figure pulled back its hood. Short, shiny red hair in an artfully chaotic mess. Smooth, pale skin. Flowing, flawless features, each contour on its face leading gracefully into the next. Except for the area around the eyes. The entire ocular cavity — from the bone beneath the eyebrow, all the way back around to the bridge of the nose — there was only blackness. Not a shadow; not a trick of the light. The void persisted, even when the leader turned and caught the light of the fire. He stared into the blank spaces where their eyes should be. They were not empty; they did not look in onto the skull. They opened onto some other place. The black within them was absolute, and yet still, he got the sense of watching something incomprehensibly vast moving in the far distance. He looked from the black eyes to the black spot in the sky and back.

"Hey, now you're getting it!" the leader said.

"I'm booooored," the pretty blonde whined.

"All right." The leader shrugged. "Let's get started."

"Hold on!" the hairless boy said. "I wanna try something. I've always wondered if you could still see out of your eye once it's pulled out of your head."

"What?" The huge guy laughed. "That's stupid."

"No," the boy argued. "I mean, without cutting the nerves and stuff. If you pull it out just a little, can you make them look at their own gouged-out eye?"

"Whoa," the chubby Asian said.

"Okay." The leader chuckled. "Leave the eyes for now."

"And the mouth!" the boy interjected.

"Well, that's just getting greedy," the dark-skinned girl said, standing and stretching.

"He has to be able to tell me if he can see himself," the boy whined.

"Tell you what," the leader said. "We'll start at the toes and race you to the top. Better be quick!"

"You're on!" The hairless boy laughed, sliding his knives against one another.

The girl shuddered. Her palm still covered her one wounded eye, but the other met his for a moment.

"This doesn't make you bad," he called to her. "It just makes you smart."

"Ugh." The boy rolled his eyes. "Maybe you can have the mouth, after all. He can just nod."

The kids laughed and set to play.

The New History of Concord

The New History of Concord

By: Ronny Mills

Age: 9 ¾

Ronald Mills, Sr., was down at the shop doing Good Honest Work, and Terry Mills was next door Grabbing Coffee at The Worcheszkcis(?)' house when the Bad Stuff happened. Let the record show that Grabbing Coffee sometimes was actually drinking wine but always smoking cigarettes and talking real loud on the back porch with Mrs. Worchezschis(?). Also the record should know that Good Honest Work was fixing cars (and other stuff that people needed fixing, like vacuum cleaners, and sometimes sewing machines, or garbage disposals). Ronald Mills, Jr., knew about the Bad Stuff first, on account of because he was watching cartoons on Saturday morning, and the TV stopped playing cartoons to start talking about News that was happening in Charlotte, which was close to Concord, but not so close you could walk.

There were lots of Fucking Maniacs (that's what Ronald Mills, Sr., said they were called) on the TV, which was being filmed from a helicopter, or sometimes from people's phones. The Fucking Maniacs were hurting all the people they could see, and there were fires, and a bunch of police ready to break it up, but some of the police started shooting other police instead, and then Ronald Mills, Jr., got up to tell his mother, Terry Mills, about the Bad Stuff. There was no fence between the Mills' yard and the Worchekskis(?), so he could have just yelled, but Terry Mills was In The Middle Of A Conversation, and told him to go back inside.

I put the pencil down and shook out my hand. Whenever I wrote importantly, I grabbed the pencil too hard, and my hand got tired fast. Mrs. Davis told me to stop doing that, but the problem was that when I was doing it, I was so focused on the important writing that I didn't realize I was doing it. Anyway, that was probably enough History for the day. It was important to record the History, because Mom said that if you didn't remember History, you get doomed to repeat it, and I really didn't want to repeat any of this. So I was writing it all down, because I didn't think anybody else was. Concord used to be so full of people you had to wait in line at the grocery store, but lately there was just me, Mom, and Dad. And you couldn't really count Mom and Dad as people anymore.

I clicked off my camping lantern and let my eyes get used to seeing in the dark. Then I unpinned the black curtains from behind the grate of the air conditioner and watched the outside. When I was sure nobody was looking, I put on my Bandaliero and took the grate off super quiet. I checked again, and there was still nobody. I put the grate back and walked all sneakily until I was behind the ducts. I unclipped my binoculars from the Bandaliero — which were supposed to be kind of a toy, so they weren't really super good, but still worked okay — and I looked at all the rooftops, the windows, and the street below. I did not see anything moving. I put the binoculars back on the Bandaliero and headed towards Means Street, because the corner store there still had some food in packages, which was the only food that was good any more.

Most of the buildings in downtown Concord were actually all connected. It was only the one street, so if you got on the roofs like I did, you could walk to the others without getting down. There were a couple gaps, though, but for those I left boards nearby that I could walk across. I kind of hid them or threw them around so they didn't look like anything, and nobody would know somebody was living up on the roofs. It had been a while since I saw anybody in Concord except Mom and Dad, but that didn't mean the others were all gone.

Some of the Fucking Maniacs didn't move much or make any noise at all…unless you got close to them, and then they moved so super fast and pulled all your parts off like you were a bug. But even if it was just me and Mom and Dad in town, I sure didn't want them coming up here, either. So I had to be fast and careful.

I practiced my climbing on the roofs that were different heights, and I practiced my somersaults for when I had to jump back down. Somersaults were good for dodging things — I learned that from every video game I ever played — so I practiced them extra hard. When I got to Means Street and the roofs ran out, I had to climb down the fire escape, which was scary. The stairs go right past all the dark windows of the offices and apartments and stuff. You don't know what's behind them, watching you. Plus, no matter how much stealth you use, the fire escape still makes some noise. I got to the bottom part, where you had to kick a bolt or something to make the ladder fall, but I didn't know how to do it, so I never did it. Plus, also, it would make a lot of noise, and then there would be a ladder up to the roof for Mom, or Dad, or the other Fucking Maniacs to climb up.

Instead, I unwrapped my rope from around my waist, and I tied it to the railing. Dad taught me a lot of good knots, and Mom taught me a lot of good climbing. I climbed down, and when I was sure nobody was looking at the street, I ran across. It wasn't very dark outside, like maybe it was a full moon, but ever since the Bad Stuff happened, the black spot in the sky had grown and grown, until you couldn't see the moon or most of the stars past it. But you could still see their light, and that was weird. I stopped at the doors of the corner store and waited, so I could check it out first.

That was a good rule: you should always check things out first.

And it was a good thing I did, because after a minute, I thought I saw something moving inside, and then I heard something plastic fall. Then a person crossed in front of the doors, and I saw that it was Mom.

I was really hungry, and I wanted to go in and eat that food, but another good rule is: don't do things just because you're hungry.

That's how you get killed.

Instead, I inched around to the edge of the store — away from the windows — and crossed the street, out of sight. I stayed in the shadows until I reached my rope, and I climbed back up. I pulled my rope up after me and tied it back around my waist. I started to go back up the fire escape. There were still other places that had food in packages that hadn't gone bad, but the store on Means Street had beef jerky, which was what made it my first choice. I hoped Mom didn't eat all of the beef jerky, so I could come back and have some tomorrow. But even if she did, that was still better than her finding me.

I was only two floors up when the stupid fire escape made a loud metal noise, and I froze. I looked at the store, and I checked it out. Nothing happened for a while, but then the doors started to open, and Mom came out. She looked around, and I guess the shadows weren't as good as I thought, because she saw me.

She waved all big and happy, like she was glad to see me. I mean, she *was* always happy these days, but it was a mean kind of happy.

"Ronny," she called up. "You want some beef jerky?"

I ignored her and started to climb back up the stairs.

"You don't have to come down," she yelled. "I'll toss some up to you."

That made me stop and think.

"No way," I finally said. "You poisoned it."

I have seen people use traps a lot on TV, so I am very wary of traps.

"Nuh uh," Mom said, and she did that head-tilt thing just like she used to do, when she was pretending to be serious but secretly making fun of me. It made me sad to see it.

"Look," she said, and she shook a plastic package around. "It's still sealed. Poison-proof!"

I walked back down a flight of the fire escape stairs and leaned over the railing to look at her.

She hucked the bag of jerky up to me, and it started to go over my head, so I had to turn to catch it and take my eyes off her for a second. I got scared and looked back immediately, but Mom hadn't moved.

She was really fast, and she was good at climbing. She liked climbing rocks and stuff for fun, but not like I did. Not rocks like The Mountain, which was what we called the big boulder in the middle of the woods over by Myers Park. Back when things were normal, me and my friends would climb up it and pretend to push each other off, or dare each other to jump, which was scary. But even if you did jump, you probably wouldn't get hurt real bad. The rocks that Mom climbed were taller than even the big buildings in Charlotte, and you could die if you fell. That was both really cool and kind of stupid, I thought. But she liked it, and she was good at it. Still, even *she* couldn't climb the brick wall all the way to the fire escape before I could run up the stairs and get away. So I told her so.

"Ronald McDonald," she laughed, because she knew I hated being called that, "if I wanted to chase you down, I would have done it already. That's not the game we're playing."

"We're not playing any games," I said.

"Sure, we are!" She smiled up at me real big.

She smiled real big a lot these days, all teeth and gums — but Mom never smiled big back when she was normal. Her smiles were small and kind of crooked.

"In the game we're playing, I win when you choose me," she said.

"Choose you for what?" I asked.

I stuffed the bag of jerky in the pouch on my Bandaliero, in case I needed both hands to get away.

"Choose me over your dad," she answered. "Come with me. Let's get out of this boring town. There's nothing fun left here, anyway. Let's go to Charlotte! We can stop by the Speedway — they might still have race cars. We could steal a race car!"

"I don't wanna," I said.

"You wanna stay here with *Dad*?" she asked, like she couldn't believe what she was hearing. She puffed her cheeks out after "Dad" and held her arms out wide like she was big and fat.

I kind of laughed.

"See? I'm way more fun," she said.

"You would hurt me," I said.

"Never!" she said, then after a second: "Well, not unless it was really, really funny. I promise!"

"I don't understand why it would be fun to hurt me," I said, backing away from the railing.

She saw me start to leave and got extra convincing.

"It probably won't ever happen," she said. "Honest! And if it did happen, you'd laugh!"

"I'm gonna go now. You better not try to chase me, because you'll never catch me before I jump back down and get to my hiding place in the park," I lied.

I have seen a bunch of espionage on TV, and I know it's important to do espionage at times like this.

"The park, huh?" she echoed, and she did her head-tilt again. "That sounds like a really good hiding place."

"It is, and you'll never find it," I espionaged.

"That sounds like a challenge, pal," she said. And her voice was still happy, but it had more of that new, mean kind of happy behind it. She took a step toward the fire escape, and I got ready to run.

There was a distant whooshing sound, like a jet starting up, and then a huge boom, and a bunch of little chimes, like lightning had struck the next block over, and then it started raining metal.

Mom and me both jumped and looked in the direction of the noise.

We could see pale blue light coming from around the corner, on the other side of Spring Street. It was so bright it made giant shadows of everything it touched.

"You better go," I yelled down. "Dad's coming."

Mom thought about coming after me for a minute, I could tell. But I was already climbing the stairs, and she saw Dad's lights start to shift in our direction, so she finally turned to run.

"We'll talk again soon, Ronald McDonald," she called, jogging across the street and disappearing between buildings.

The New History of Concord

By: Ronny Mills

Age: 9 ¾

Ronald Mills, Sr., and Ronald Mills, Jr., and Terry Mills had been hiding in the basement for a long time. History doesn't know how long, because there were no windows or calendars, but toward the end, Terry Mills did tell Ronald Mills, Sr., "We've been down here for weeks, we have to at least try!"

Terry Mills was talking to Ronald Mills, Sr., about leaving the basement, and getting some supplies, and then leaving town. Ronald Mills, Sr., did not think it was a good idea, and that's why they were arguing about it. Adults sometimes think that because kids don't know much, that they can't hear much either. And that's dumb, because kids hear plenty. Especially when adults are arguing in the far corner of the basement, using angry whispers that are practically as loud as normal talking anyway.

Ronald Mills, Sr., was saying that the Mills family were still alive because they had a finished basement that had carpet and was warm. There was a bathroom down there, and also a pantry, which was where they put extra food from Costco trips. Electricity had stopped pretty soon after the Bad Stuff happened, but the Mills had camping lanterns, and blankets, and it wasn't that cold yet anyway. They had the Costco food, and the water still worked — which Ronald Mills, Jr., thought was weird, because he always thought the government used electricity and motors to push the water into your house, but Terry Mills said that it was just gravity fed from the reservoir.

Anyway, that's why Ronald Mills, Sr., thought they should stay in the basement: because they had survived down there so far. But Terry Mills thought that wasn't enough, and she called Ronald Mills, Sr., "short-sighted," and that made Ronald Mills, Sr., really mad. So mad that he did the thing where his voice doesn't even sound angry anymore, but just really flat, and clear, and careful, and that's when you're really in trouble.

Terry Mills said that it had been forever since they heard the Bad Stuff happening outside. She was right. It had been a long time since the gunshots, and the screaming, and sirens. Then there was a while where it was mostly quiet, but every once in a while, somebody would yell, or laugh, or break something. But lately even that had stopped, and there had been no noises at all. Terry Mills wanted to at least go check it out, but Ronald Mills, Sr., explained that the Bad Stuff could be waiting out there for her to do exactly that, and they stopped arguing, and went to bed.

Neither Ronald Mills, Sr., nor Ronald Mills, Jr., heard it when Terry Mills woke up extra early, and snuck up the stairs, and left the basement.

My eyes were all dry and itchy from being so tired, but I couldn't sleep, because Dad was still out there on the street making loud noises. I didn't know what exactly he was doing, but he had been doing it for a long time now. He started out close to our house and mostly stuck to our neighborhood at first. Then he just kept getting farther and farther out, until he'd finally reached the edges of downtown, where I was hiding. He was still a few blocks away, and I couldn't see him past the tall trees on the other side of Union Street.

I had watched him for a little bit, once. He was just driving around and looking at houses. He had a bunch of weird machines on the back of his shop's old flatbed truck. He taught me to drive that truck one time. It actually wasn't super hard. Adults made such a big deal of driving, but really you just pulled a little lever until it said "D" for "Drive," and one pedal made you go, and the other made you stop, and you steered it with a wheel — just like the old, stand-up style car games in the arcade. There were lots of rules to learn about driving, and some switches and stuff that did different things, but it sure wasn't harder than math, and they made kids learn that.

It was important that I learned to drive the truck, because it said "Mills and Son" on the side in fancy, faded writing. I wasn't old enough to be the "son" part yet. That was actually Dad. At some point, he had been his dad's son, when his dad owned the shop. And they were Mills and Son. And I guess even his dad's dad had owned the shop way, way back in the past.

Dad was pretty sure I was also going to work at the shop someday and be The Son. The idea made me kind of proud, and excited, but also scared, and sad, because I wasn't sure I wanted to be The Son. I mean, I wasn't really good with engines, or at fixing stuff. It seemed like every time I tried, I forgot a spring, or I didn't tighten a bolt enough, and the whole thing would rattle when you turned it on, or else it just wouldn't work.

Plus, I didn't really like cars and stuff. I pretended to like them, partly because of Dad, and partly because all the other kids really did like

NASCAR and race cars. I even made Mom think I liked race cars — even though Mom hated race cars — just so she wouldn't get mad someday and accidentally tell Dad the truth when they argued about me. I just thought racecars were boring. They went around in circles, and they were loud. And they smelled. But I wasn't supposed to think that, so I tried not to. And so lots of weekends we drove just outside of town to the Speedway and watched racecars go in circles, until somebody got hurt, which I guess was everybody's secret favorite part.

I never told anybody what I really liked, because it was stupid, and they would have just made fun of me.

I liked dinosaurs.

I wanted to help them. Not dig up their dead bones or anything, but actually help them, like the lady in *Jurassic Park*. But you're supposed to like stuff that you could grow up to work on, and nobody fixed dinosaurs. That's not a real thing.

So I was going to be The Son any way you cut it, and I would drive that flatbed truck around town and talk to people about the weird noises their car was making. I mean, the way things were going, I probably wouldn't wind up doing any of that. One of the Fucking Maniacs would get me eventually, or it would be just by getting sick, and not having any medicine. But one thing was for sure: I wasn't ever going to fix any dinosaurs.

The New History of Concord

By: Ronny Mills

Age: 9 ¾

Ronald Mills, Sr., made Ronald Mills, Jr., promise not to leave the basement, no matter what. And also not to make any noise, or undo the big bolt on the door for any reason, except for if somebody knocks two times, pauses, then knocks three times more.

That was the secret code that Ronald Mills, Sr., was going to use, to let Ronald Mills, Jr., know it was safe to open the door. Ronald Mills, Jr., was very good about secret codes, so he remembered it.

After Ronald Mills, Jr., promised a whole bunch of times to not leave, and not make noise, and remember the secret code, Ronald Mills, Sr., left the basement. He went to look for Terry Mills. He was gone for a very long time. Long enough for Ronald Mills, Jr., to fall asleep a few times, even though he tried very hard to stay awake. Then there was banging on the door and screaming. Ronald Mills, Jr., went up to the top of the stairs to listen for the code, but the person on the other side didn't knock right, so he didn't open the door. But Ronald Mills, Jr., could tell by the voice that it was Ronald Mills, Sr., knocking. So Ronald Mills, Jr., reminded him to use the code. Ronald Mills, Sr., didn't remember the code and said to open the door anyway. Ronald Mills, Jr., said he wasn't supposed to, and they yelled at each other about it until Ronald Mills, Jr., started crying, which he also wasn't supposed to do, because he was a boy. Finally, Terry Mills, who Ronald Mills, Sr., had gone out and found, told Ronald Mills, Jr., that it was okay to open the door just this one time, so he did.

Dad was still out there doing his weird, loud thing. He'd drive the truck a little bit, and then stop, and then there was that flat sort of paddling sound, then it would be quiet for a long time, and then a big, airy boom, like a whole storm happening all at once. Afterward, it sounded like wind chimes — lots of tinkling and ringing. He did it again and again, basically all night.

I was so thirsty that I was getting kind of dizzy, and eating the beef jerky only made it worse. Now, it's no good to wait so long to drink or eat that you're too weak to find stuff to drink or eat. That's a good rule: find stuff to drink or eat before you really, really need it.

I'd never gone out looking for supplies when both Mom and Dad were so close to my hiding spot, but it seemed like they were each busy doing their own things. Maybe if I was really small and used all my stealth, I could get out and back without them noticing me. I unpinned the heavy black curtains from behind the AC grate and checked out the roof for a while. When I was sure it was clear, I moved the grate aside, and snuck out, and moved really quick and small.

Dad was close. Just on the other side of Union Street. And he was in the flat, thwacking stage of whatever he was doing. That was the part that took the longest, and it had just started, so he would probably be busy a while. Just to be safe, I went the other way from when I'd last seen Mom, over by Means Avenue. That meant going toward Carrabas, and even though I'd picked a lot of the stores on that side clean already, I knew there was a whole case of Peach Iced Tea in Scotties, back in the hidden area behind the drink cases. I had left it because Peach Iced Tea is really gross, but I was so thirsty now, I didn't even care.

There was no fire escape on the Carrabas side of downtown, because the building at the end wasn't very tall. So I just tied my rope to an aluminum chimney sticking out of the roof and climbed right down. Across the street and through the doors, quiet and fast like a squirrel. It was dangerous to not really check out the inside before going in the store, but it was more dangerous to say on the street where Dad could just peek around the corner and see me.

I snuck around the aisles, careful to dodge the trash and the bits of metal from broken shelves. I pulled open the heavy metal door to behind the drink cases and felt around in the mostly dark until I found the case of Peach Iced Tea. I punched a hole in the plastic with my finger, and pulled one out, and opened it. The cap made a pop sound that felt really loud but probably wasn't. I listened for anything that might be listening for me, but I didn't hear them, so I drank the Peach Iced Tea. It was still gross, but it was also the best thing I'd ever had. I drank a whole one and then half of another. I put four more in the pouch on the back of my Bandaliero, which was all it would hold. They clinked together when I moved, so I took off my socks and wrapped them between every other bottle. That was gross, since I hadn't washed my socks in a really, really long time, and they smelled terrible, but it was better than making noise and getting caught.

All geared up, I pushed open the heavy metal door real slow and slipped back out into the store. I started toward the exit, and the street outside exploded in light. I went blind instantly, even though I threw my hands over my eyes and jumped to the side. I landed between aisles. I hoped I hid in time, because I couldn't run anywhere when I couldn't see. When I pulled my hands away from my stinging eyes, there was a big, blue orb right in the middle of everywhere I looked. I guess with the heavy metal door of the drinks case shut, I didn't hear Dad's truck pull around the far side of Union Street and park in front of the store. I could hear it now, though: engine low and growling, like a mean dog. I knew what came next. The huge wind and the metal rain.

The doors and windows exploded inward, and shards of glass flew around like stinging insects. Small metal bits bounced across the tile and ricocheted off of the walls and ceiling. They caught the spotlights shining from Dad's truck. Screws and washers and bolts glinted among the glass, like stars reflected on the ocean.

I couldn't hear very well. The noise had been too loud, and now everything sounded like I was wearing earmuffs. But I felt the thwacking through the floor. I saw the smaller screws start to rattle across the tile. It was starting again.

"Stop!" I said, and I stepped out from my hiding place.

Looking right into the lights was like staring at the sun, if the sun was idling across the street. I couldn't see anything behind or around the spotlights and could only guess at the things in front of them by their long, twisty shadows. Something moved to block the lights, and its shadow settled over me. Shielded in its darkness, I could see its outline clearly. I already knew who it was, of course. I'm not a dummy.

It was Dad.

He had always been big. Tall and strong, but also kind of fat. Just big, in every sense of the word. His shoulders were big. His belly was big. His arms, and his head, and even his beard was big. And standing like he was, with the lights at his back, making everything else impossible to see except for his silhouette — he looked positively gigantic. Like something out of a fantasy book. He should have been holding an axe or a magic sword.

He reached out and pushed something on the truck. The lights pointing at me died down. I blinked hard, and a lot, trying to clear the spots and sparkles from my vision. I could hear Dad walking closer, his boots crunching on the glass and kicking around bits of metal.

"Don't!" I said, and I backed up, but I tripped over something — I couldn't even tell what it was — and I fell on my butt. I scraped my hands on the glass and yelped, even though I knew Dad would tell me to "suck it up" or "be a man."

But he didn't.

"Are you hurt?" he asked.

It didn't sound like he was worried about me, which was a whole different tone. When he was actually worried, he didn't like to show it, so he made his voice extra tough. The way he asked about me now, it sounded more like when he talked about politicians, or sports teams he didn't like.

"Not really," I lied, trying to hide my bloody palms.

He was still mostly just a shadow to me. An outline against the headlights of his truck, which were still on and pointed away from us. I was still dazzled from looking into the spotlights. All the black spaces in my vision were shifting and dancing, making fake colors, like oil on water. Dad stooped down and grabbed something off of the floor. He held it up to the light to examine it, and I could see that it was a big shard of glass. He turned it this way and that for a second, then brought it down hard into his own arm. So hard, I heard it hit bone. Then I couldn't see what he was doing anymore, but it sounded like he was grinding it around inside his arm.

"Stop!" I said. "Please don't!"

I sounded whiny, and I knew Dad would hate it, but I couldn't help it.

"I hurt you," he said.

And again, his voice was wrong for the words he was saying. He didn't sound sorry, but more like he just remembered a chore he was supposed to do, after he already sat down and took his shoes off.

"I'm okay," I said, but he didn't stop doing the grinding thing.

"I have to keep you safe," he said. "It's the only rule, and I broke it. I have to pay for that. You remember, Ronnie? You remember how I told you a man always pays for his mistakes, even if nobody makes him?"

I did remember that. He told me that after I accidentally (I swear!) stole a pack of comic book cards from the grocery store. He made me take them back and apologize for stealing, even though it wasn't stealing — I just forgot I put them in my pocket, when I had to use both hands to bend down and pick up cat litter off the bottom shelf for Mom.

"It wasn't you," I said. "I tripped and fell. You didn't do it!"

Finally, the grinding sound paused.

"You sure?" he said.

I nodded.

My vision had mostly come back — only some tiny suns that moved wherever I looked — and I could see that Dad didn't look so great. His eyes were all tired and hollow. His beard had always been pretty crazy and stuck out everywhere, but now it was also dirty and kind of braided on itself, like a homeless person. His clothes were greasy and bloody, and he had left the glass shard stuck in his arm. Blood poured down his arm and from his fingers, pooling around his boots.

"This is exactly the kind of thing I promised to protect you from," he finally said. "You need to come home with me."

He took a step forward, and I took a step back.

"Don't," he warned. He used his mean warning voice, like when you're arguing back and you're not supposed to. "You'll fall again."

"Don't come towards me," I said, "or I'll run again, even if I do get hurt, and then it'll be your fault, 'cause you could've stopped it."

He froze.

"You need to come home with me," he said, and he jerked his thumb back at the truck.

"No," I said. "You'll tie me up again."

"Of course," he said, and he laughed a little bit, like I'd said something dumb. "That's how you're safest. You can't move, you can't leave, you can't get hurt. Don't you understand that?"

I didn't understand it.

I could practically still feel the ratchet straps he used to bind me to the bed in my room. He put towels and blankets under them, so they wouldn't dig into my skin and hurt, and he'd come in once and a while, and undo them to turn me around — which was when I got away in the first place — but other than that, he wouldn't let me move at all. Not even to go to the bathroom. I had to go in a pan, and he fed me, and made me drink water, and washed me, and everything. I didn't even have a TV to watch. Just the ceiling in my bedroom. Looking at the dots and scratches from the plaster, imagining them as different things. If you don't think boredom is a kind of hurt, then I can tell you've never been ratchet-strapped to your bed for a few months.

"I can't," I told him. "I can't go back to the bed."

"Ronnie," he commanded.

Just that. My name and nothing else. Because he knew that *I* knew what he wanted me to do and just wasn't doing it.

"It's going to get cold soon," he said, when I didn't move. "And I've been going all over town, using that sucker back there to knock out all the windows."

I looked in the back of the truck: at his air compressor, and a big cannon looking thing, and some generators he'd rigged up, and bunch of other stuff.

"There won't be anywhere warm left," he explained. "Except for home. You don't want to freeze to death, do you, Ronnie?"

I sure didn't, but I also kind of didn't believe him. He couldn't have gotten everywhere in town. Plus maybe some spots without windows would still be warm, like my grate hideout — and anyway, wasn't he supposed to keep me safe? That was his rule; so letting me die would be breaking it. And if he couldn't hurt me…

I turned and ran. My shoes skated on the glass, and the ball bearings, and the garbage, and all the other things Dad had knocked down with his air cannon, but I didn't fall. I yanked the back door open and ran across the open street, toward the old courthouse, which wasn't a courthouse anymore, but a theater — only I guess it wasn't that, either.

Just an empty building. You could call it whatever you wanted.

I knew Dad was following me, even though I didn't look back to check. I could hear glass breaking and stuff being tossed aside, then the metal door slam open and bounce closed again. I didn't want to look back, because I didn't want to see him like that — all angry and crazy like the Fucking Maniacs, or worse: just sort of cold and disconnected, like he had been lately. It reminded me of something Mom used to say, when I'd done something wrong: "I'm not mad at you, just *disappointed*."

Just Disappointed was supposed to be worse than mad, on the scale of how much trouble I was in.

Dad never said that, though. He was always okay with being plain ol' mad. But not lately. Lately he was Just Disappointed too, but for reasons I couldn't understand.

The courthouse had big glass doors, and floor-to-ceiling windows, but the glass wasn't broken yet, so I had to pause to grab the cold brass doorhandle, and heft it open. It was an old metal frame, and it was so heavy that I only got it open a little bit, before I just gave up and shoved myself inside through the tiny gap. With the weak light of the moon — or whatever was lighting up the night since the black spot took over the sky — I could see just enough to make out the tall, dark rectangle of an open doorway. I tripped over a few things I didn't see on the way there, crawled through on my hands and knees, then bunched myself up against the farthest wall. My hand brushed soft fabric, which I thought was curtains at first, so I slid behind them, to hide. After a minute, I realized it must have been costumes for the actors, though, because I felt all sorts of things, like feathers and metal, which I don't think curtains usually have. Past the fading spots of light blindness, my eyes were getting more used to the dark. I could only see certain pieces of the dark room, but there was a big, low thing that I thought might be a table, or a bunch of desks, only these had mirrors above them. I knew that because I saw the shadows change in the reflection of one, when Dad slammed open the heavy metal door like it was nothing.

"Ronnie," Dad called. Loud, but not mad. Just impatient. "You're going to get hurt out there. That can't happen."

He waited for me to answer, but I didn't.

I looked around more, trying to see if I could find an exit, or at least a better hiding spot, since some of the clothes on the rack were shorter than others, and you could probably see my knees, if you were looking.

That's when I saw the figure and knew I wasn't alone in the dark room.

My chest got all tight, because I thought they were people at first, or worse: Fucking Maniacs. But I checked them out for a while, and they didn't move. That's when I saw that they didn't have legs — just chests and heads on poles. A few were wearing big clothes, like robes or dresses, so you were fooled at first. I think they used dummies like that to work on clothes — I learned that from a show about designing dresses that Mom used to watch, and I didn't pay much attention to.

"Ronnie," Dad called out again. "Come out now, and get back into your straps without struggling, and I'll leave the curtains open on your window, so you can look out."

When I didn't take the bribe, he tried again.

"I'll feed you soda when I find it — through one of those bendy straws you like."

One time. One time, I said I thought a bendy straw was cool, at a McDonald's or something — it had a dinosaur on it — and for some reason everybody ignored the dinosaur part, and just thought that *I* thought bendy straws were the best thing on Earth.

Obviously, I didn't answer that one, either.

But somebody else did.

"He doesn't even like those," Mom called out, from somewhere farther away.

"Terry," Dad said, all super casual, like they had just bumped into each other at the supermarket while out running errands. "Come down here."

The courthouse had another level — one that looked down at the main lobby below — but you couldn't get there without going up some stairs somewhere else, so I guessed Mom was up above, and Dad couldn't get to her.

Mom laughed.

"No, thanks," she said. "I don't feel like fighting right now. I think it'd be more fun if I picked the place. And the time. And the weapons. In fact, I think it'd be the *most* fun if you didn't know about it at all."

"Why would we fight?" Dad asked.

"I guess *you* don't have to." Mom laughed. "But I was hoping you'd struggle, at least a little bit…"

"I don't want to hurt you any more than necessary," Dad called up.

His voice didn't echo like Mom's. It was like the walls and the ceiling just swallowed it up.

"Oh? And how much hurt is *necessary*?" Mom said, sounding fake sexy, like Bugs Bunny does in the cartoons where he dresses up like a girl bunny.

"We promised to keep the boy safe," Dad said. I hated how he called me "the boy" when he was talking to other adults. "I know you've hurt him."

"Only a little, now and then," Mom purred. "Just to keep the game interesting."

She wasn't lying. One time, she caught me scavenging in the school cafeteria, and she cut my belly with a piece of glass — but not very deep — and let me go. Then another time, at the camping store, when I was stealing a sleeping bag and a thermos, she hooked me with a fishing rod, and it pulled some of the skin off my back when I jumped through the windows. There were a couple other times like that, too, but she seemed to only want to hurt me a little, and then watch me run.

"I think," Dad said, "since you hurt your own kid, it would make the most sense if I cut out your womb and had you hold it. I think that would really help you learn."

It wasn't even like a threat to him, it was like a decision he had come to, after some real careful thought. It made my guts turn to hear Dad talk like that, but Mom didn't care.

"Boo," she called down. "That's boring! It's so…ugh, *poetic*. You know how I'm going to kill you, when I get the chance?"

Dad didn't answer. Maybe he shook his head, but I couldn't see it.

"Neither do I!" Mom said, and she laughed, loud and bright. "That's what's so great about it. It'll be spontaneous."

"Terry," Dad said, kind of stern, but also very reasonable. "Come on down and let me cut out your womb, so we can be a family again."

"Pass," Mom said quickly, like she wasn't really paying attention to the conversation anymore.

"This can't last forever," Dad said, and he started lecturing her about responsibility, and following the rules, and knowing your place, so at least that hadn't changed.

I slid deeper into the clothes rack, creeping along the wall. I hoped that I would feel a door, or a window, or something else, and could get away while they were distracting each other. I bumped into something metal that was heavier on the bottom, and it wobbled a little, but Mom and Dad didn't hear it over the arguing.

The mannequin did, though. The mannequin heard it just fine.

I could only see its outline. I couldn't see if it had legs, or just a pole, because it was wearing some kind of long dress. But it was next to the other mannequins, so I assumed it was a mannequin. There's another good rule: don't assume things, because sometimes you're wrong, and if you're *really* wrong, you could die.

The second I bumped into the microphone stand, the figure straightened up real quick, like somebody had shot electricity through it. Then it froze again, with its head tilted toward me. I couldn't see its face, but I recognized the motion. The Fucking Maniacs moved like that. The really quiet ones that Dad called "the Sleepers." They stayed perfectly still unless they heard something get close, or you stepped past their invisible border, then they got very alert. That was the bad phase. I didn't see many people get away once the Sleepers woke up, because if you moved or made any sound, they'd spring on you so fast, like a cat on a mouse. They'd get you before you could even think to run, and then they'd rip you apart like a mean kid pulling the legs off a beetle. I had seen them do it a few times, before I moved my hideout downtown — back when I'd tried to get out by following the highway. That's where the Sleepers stood guard, mostly. There, and in the woods, and on some back roads. Just waiting for somebody to try to pass.

When I saw the Sleepers standing there, all slumped over, like they were so tired, but for some reason they couldn't lay down — I knew better than to get too close. But nobody else wanted to be near them, either. I could use that. So I curled up in a pipe not too far away, and I made that my hideout for a few days.

Not everybody was smart, though. I saw some people try to get past the Sleepers' line. Once, in the real early morning, when everything was wet and cold, a big woman tried to run right past the Sleepers. She froze when they got all alert and didn't move for a real long time. But finally she must have breathed wrong or something, and they tore her apart like sharks do in documentaries.

One guy in a camouflage vest but wearing a bright orange hat — which I thought was weird, because it ruined the camouflage — did something really smart. He got his rifle from his truck, and he shot a few of the Sleepers. They didn't even seem to care. They didn't move, or scream, or fall down. The angry Fucking Maniacs — you could shoot them if you got the chance, and though they didn't care about pain much, they'd still die if you got them in the right place. Plus you could blow them up, or light them on fire, or probably even stab them if you were good at that kind of thing. But then, the angry ones couldn't move faster than you could see. The Sleepers could. And the other Fucking Maniacs were real strong, but not so strong they could just pull your arms off. The Sleepers could. My guess was that, since the Sleepers didn't move much, they could save all their energy and use it up all at once in a short burst. And maybe their insides were really still, too, so their blood and stuff didn't leak as much, so wounds didn't do as much damage. But that seemed like the kind of thing that made sense in my head, but that teachers would think was dumb if I asked about it.

None of what I knew about Sleepers was good. And I knew I had one listening now, so quiet and still in the dark. If I made one little sound, it would scramble over and pick me apart, like pulling flowers off a bush.

And even if I did get away from it, Mom and Dad were still in the next room, arguing about which awful things they should get to do to me, and why.

There wasn't a lot I could do but think and remember things, which was how I came up with a really great idea. That's a good rule: if you come up with a really great idea, you should do it, even if you're scared, or it might go wrong, because you never know when you'll get another really great idea. (It could be never!)

See, I was thinking about how weird it was that Mom and Dad were fighting — I mean, they fought a lot back when they were normal, but they were Fucking Maniacs now, and I hadn't seen any other Fucking Maniacs fighting each other. The Fucking Maniacs mostly seemed to work together, or at least ignore each other. I even saw Mom walk right by those Sleepers on the highway (which was when I knew it was time to find a better hiding spot), and they didn't care about her at all. They didn't even wake up for her. So why should Mom and Dad be fighting? And why was Dad being so careful about protecting me from the other Fucking Maniacs, if they were all on the same side?

I was also pretty sure the Sleepers couldn't see better than normal people. Maybe this one had its eyes closed until I made a noise and woke it up, but if it could see in the dark now, why was it listening for me, instead of just looking over and getting me?

So okay, I know what I just said about assuming things, but sometimes you have to assume anyway, when it gets real bad. I assumed two things: I assumed the Sleeper couldn't see in the dark and wasn't very smart. And I assumed that Dad and the Sleeper might not get along.

Here was my really good idea: I reached up so slow and careful even I couldn't tell if I was moving or not, and I found my small LED flashlight. It was clipped to my Bandaliero. I tried not to use it too often, because it's not the dark you should be afraid of, but things finding you in the dark, and nothing helps them find you like a big old spotlight in your hand. I didn't want to risk making a sound when I unclipped the flashlight, so I left it attached to the Bandaliero. I pointed it at what I hoped was the right place, and I clicked the light on.

Everything happened at the same time. The Sleeper bounded across the room in a heartbeat, following the source of the light. Coming straight for me. It was really creepy, how fast they were, but it was really *extra* creepy that they were also so quiet. This one was dressed in a long black judge's robe and had a silly white wig on, like the guys you see on money. I guess it used to be an actor here. Its skin had gone all white, being in the dark for so long, and dust clouds puffed off of its clothes when it moved. It reached out one of its milky white hands and sunk its fingertips deep into my face.

That's when the mirror broke.

That was my good idea: I had aimed the flashlight at the big mirrors above the table across from me, and the Sleeper went for my reflection. I shut the light off as soon as the thing crashed into the glass, and I used all the noise it was making to hide my own noises as I plunged, blindly, deeper and deeper into the pitch-black room.

"Ronnie!" Dad thundered.

He loomed in the doorway, his shoulders practically touching the sides, his head practically brushing the top.

More breaking noises: wood, and glass, and metal things hitting the floor — followed by fast, light footsteps. A shadow broke away from the black and tackled Dad. All tangled up and just silhouettes, the two of them fighting looked like one crazy, thrashing monster with a bunch of limbs. I ran into what felt like a bunch of barrels stacked in a corner, and I wiggled myself into the tiny spaces behind them. I wormed around the edges, burrowing deeper into the stack, until I couldn't go any further. I found just the right angle to see through the gaps between them, and from there I watched Dad fight the Sleeper.

The fight didn't last very long. Dad was huge and strong, and the Sleeper was only half his size. But the Sleepers were something else besides human, and whatever that was, it was as strong as it was mean. The Sleeper had Dad turned over in an instant, one beefy, hairy arm all pulled up and twisted back. The thing yanked and yanked, still dead quiet, stubbornly trying to separate Dad's limbs from his body. Then Dad yelled some nonsense sounds.

"HET NO HARUK!" Dad said, and his voice was very different. It was like metal hitting metal. It barely sounded human.

The Sleeper just dropped him. It took a few steps back. It looked kind of confused.

Dad got to his knees slowly. His arm was clearly hurt.

The Sleeper didn't move, necessarily, but kind of thrummed in place — like it was trying to move, but its muscles just weren't responding.

"Ronnie," Dad called again. "Come out now. Right now. We have to go. It won't hold for long."

I guess me and Dad were stupid in the same kind of ways. Because, see, we had both forgotten about Mom.

She was fast, and good at climbing, and for some dumb reason I always think that means "good at going up things real quick." But she can climb *down* things quick, too. Like the second story balcony she'd been standing on. I guess she saw her chance when the Sleeper attacked, because she had scampered down and now stood behind Dad, laughing.

"See," Mom said, sort of to Dad, but mostly to me. "That was fun! You couldn't have foreseen *that.* This is why you shouldn't make plans, Ron. They're just guesses that you count on."

"HET NO HARUK!" Dad shouted again, struggling to stand with his bad arm.

"Come on," Mom said. "You know that doesn't work on my kind."

"I was talking to the other one," Dad said and gestured at something behind Mom.

She turned to look, and as soon as she did, Dad bashed her in the head with his giant bear-paw fist.

I did not think Dad would — or could — use tricks, so I guess me and Mom are dumb in some of the same ways, too.

Mom went sprawling, but she didn't stay down long, and Dad's bad arm was slowing him down. Mom's hair was wet with blood, but she was still giggling. Her smile was so wide it looked like it hurt. It looked like she had too many teeth, like the skin at the corners of her lips would split apart and there would just be more teeth back there, a bigger smile, marching all the way around her head.

She danced away as Dad sent out another punch. The blow looked slow and clumsy, but he hit a wooden box thing full of Historical Stuff and it basically exploded. He probably only needed one more good hit to finish Mom off. But he couldn't manage to get it. Dad swung, and Mom danced and nipped at him like a playful puppy. The Sleeper, frozen, followed both of them with its eyes, waiting for its turn.

Mom picked up a sharp piece of wood from the exploded box and threw it at Dad. He swatted it away like an annoying fly, but that wasn't the point. As soon as he moved to block the wood, Mom charged in real quick and kicked him in the chest with all her weight. Dad went to one knee and seemed to be choking on his own air, but he still managed to grab Mom's wrist. She twisted and pried at his fingers, but he wouldn't let go. Still, he was winded, and he only had the one good arm. You could see him trying to figure out how best to hurt her without risking her getting away. Meantime, Mom jabbed, and clawed, and kicked. Dad bore it all patiently. It was like watching hyenas attack a rhino on a nature documentary, which I have seen a lot of.

But finally, Dad got his breath back, and he twirled Mom around and threw her to the floor. He bent down to grab a big chunk of something heavy, I don't know what. Mom had skidded awkwardly and kind of hit her head when she fell, so she was slow to get up. Dad was all set to smash her brains in, when the invisible leash came off the Sleeper, and it leapt across the room. It didn't make a sound. It clambered around Dad's body like an excited monkey, until it found his bad arm and continued what it started. Dad grunted and swatted at the pale thing, in its judge's robes, and its dirty wig, but he didn't yell out — not even when the Sleeper pulled his arm right off, and blood throbbed out everywhere.

It seemed fake. Something you think the movies get wrong: Blood doesn't really shoot out like that, and arms don't just come off. But I guess sometimes the movies get things right, too.

The Sleeper tossed the limb aside like it was garbage and started reaching for Dad again, but he brought the chunk of something up and folded the Sleeper's face in on itself. Its nose and mouth mostly went away, and its eyes drowned in blood that looked three shades too dark. Like it was oil that needed changing. The Sleeper only staggered for a second, before it blindly reached out for Dad again. He hammered it with the stone over and over and didn't stop until there was just a bunch of mush atop the Sleeper's neck. Its head looked like chili. But not the good kind you get at the fair — the gross stuff the school served in the cafeteria, that you just knew was made out of yesterday's meatloaf and the leftovers from Taco Tuesday.

Dad was tired or maybe just out of blood. It looked hard for him to stand. But he did, and he looked all around for Mom. Mom was real quick and pretty good at stealth when she wanted to be. She was gone. Now, if a mean pretend-judge had just pulled my arm off and thrown it away, I would have called it a night. But I guess that's why I'm not Dad. Weaving like he did when he came home late on weekends, Dad turned away from the heavy glass doors leading outside and instead stumbled through a small brick arch that led deeper into the building. Going after Mom.

I probably wouldn't have a better chance to escape, and that was another good rule: take your chances when you get them, not when you're sure it's safe to take them.

I slipped out from behind the barrels and crossed the dark room — I was super careful about watching the dummies this time — into the lobby. I only paused a second at the front door, to check out the street before leaving. I learned my lesson about not checking places out before you go into them. It looked pretty clear, so I yanked on the heavy brass handle.

"Hey, Ronnie," Mom said, from behind me. "It just got funny. Heads up!"

I turned and saw that she was standing up on the balcony again. I guess she just climbed right back up there and hid, in order to trick Dad. Or me. Anyway, it worked on both of us.

Even though Mom's head was all cut up, and there was blood getting in her mouth and eyes, she looked so happy it might have been her birthday. She had just tossed something at me, and it was real pretty: dark glass with all sorts of colors dancing around inside. Then it turned around in the air, and I saw it was a bottle with a burning rag stuffed in the neck. I actually went to catch it at first, just because of reflexes, but at the last second, I remembered not to be stupid and jumped out of the way.

Actually, maybe *that* was stupid — because maybe I could have caught the bottle, and it wouldn't have broken and spread flames everywhere like fire was something you could just spill on the floor. But there was no room for maybes anymore. I did what I did, and what I did was kind of hop back and throw myself away from where the bottle landed. I wasn't quick enough. Drops of fire caught on my pants, and my forearms, and my hands, and I just watched them burn there for a second before I turned and pulled at the heavy door again. It felt like it took forever to open and even longer for me to wiggle myself through the gap to outside.

I started to run away, but then I remembered to Stop, Drop, and Roll first. They made us watch a dumb video about that in school, where these two white guys tried to make it into a rap, but I guess it worked, because I remembered to do it, and it helped. The grass outside the courthouse was kind of wet with the nighttime, and the fire went out quick. I could tell there were all sorts of real bad burn spots on me — even through the jeans, which I guess aren't fireproof at all — and though I hardly felt them now, burns always feel worse later. Through the glass, I saw Mom pointing and laughing at me, like I'd just slipped on banana peel. Then she tossed down another bottle and another. Neither of us had seen Dad come out the upstairs door and sneak up behind her. I didn't even see his face. Just his one big remaining arm, as he wrapped it around her neck and pulled her down. Then some of the flames licked up the far side of the glass, and I couldn't see anything anymore.

I ran halfway to the rope that led up to my rooftop hideout before I thought better of it. Dad's truck was idling right where he left it, next to the corner store. I looked at the rope, and I looked at the courthouse, and the flames inside, and I looked at the truck, and even though the truck had always kind of scared me before — it was too tall, and old, and loud — it didn't seem so bad anymore. I had to jump and climb to get into the seat, which was really high off the ground. Then I scooted forward as far as I could go, and I touched the pedals with just the tips of my toes, which were all that could reach. I put the lever into "D," and I pushed the gas pedal as far as I could, which wasn't very far, but I guess it was far enough. I wasn't super careful about steering, because the lines you're supposed to stay between didn't mean anything anymore.

I didn't stop at all. Not even for the signs. It took so much of my concentration to keep the truck going where I wanted that I didn't even worry about the burns, or about Mom and Dad, or about the town, or about anything. I just drove as fast as I could toward the highway. And you know what? I didn't stop at all for the Sleepers, either. I just drove right through them.

That doesn't always work out. When I was hiding in the pipe, I saw a few people try to run over the Sleepers. Sometimes they made it through the first one, or even two, but then one of the Sleepers would grab onto their car and pull them out through the door or the windshield. But that was back when there were lots of Sleepers waiting at the edge of town: lines and lines of them like soldiers in a real loose, lazy formation. I probably wouldn't have made it through all that, but they were spread pretty thin these days, and I had a big truck that was real high up, and heavy, and metal, and it had my name on the side — even if I wasn't the Mills it meant, or even the "And Son" — so I figured I had a better chance than most.

I found a spot with only one Sleeper, and I hit her head on — her sunken, sickly face highlighted right between the prongs on the hood ornament, like the sight on a gun in a video game — and a bunch of red sprayed up, and rained on the hood, and a little bit on the windshield. The headlights were tinted a bit red, too, but they still lit up the road pretty good. I kept driving until I reached an exit that didn't really go anywhere in particular, and I drove, and drove, until I was on top of a hill outside town with nothing on it. I stopped there, because I could see for a long time, and nobody could sneak up on me. I killed the engine, and I rolled my burns in the cool grass some more, and I tried not to think of them, because they get worse when you think of them. I wanted to cry, but I wasn't supposed to, because I was a boy, so I dug around in the glove box and found a paper pad and a greasy pencil, and I wrote some more History, so I wouldn't have to repeat it.

The New History of Concord

By: Ronny Mills

Age: 9 ¾

After Ronald Mills, Jr., opened the door for Ronald Mills, Sr., and Terry Mills, there was a whole bunch of yelling, and Ronald Mills, Sr., ordered Ronald Mills,

Jr., around.

First, Ronald Mills, Jr., went to the sink and wet some towels for Terry Mills to put over her eyes, and then he got a blanket to put over her body, and then Ronald Mills, Sr., held her like she was sick, or very hurt, even though it only looked like she had a few scrapes and had gotten dirty. Ronald Mills, Sr., promised Terry Mills that she was going to be okay, and when she laughed kind of sad, like she didn't believe him, Ronald Mills, Sr., told her that she was going to be okay because she had to be.

Terry Mills said she wasn't going to be okay, because she looked at the black spot in the sky, even though she didn't mean to at all. She only looked because there were still some people outside, even though it had gotten very quiet lately, and those people were more like animals. They could barely talk, and their faces were crazy. They grabbed Terry Mills, and held her eyelids open, and pointed her face toward the sky so she would have to look. Ronald Mills, Sr., interrupted them, and fought some of them, but after Terry Mills looked at the black spot, it was like the people were a little normal again, and they said they were sorry, and that they had to do it, and then they ran away.

Ronald Mills, Sr., kept saying it was okay, but Terry Mills did not believe him. She said she could already feel things in her brain changing. Let the record show that Terry Mills didn't actually say "changing" — she said very weird things about gifts, and about losing them — but Ronald Mills, Jr., got what she meant, so he wrote down "changing" instead.

Terry Mills rested for a while, and it even seemed like she might get more better eventually. But that was all a trick, so that when Ronald Mills, Sr., and Ronald Mills, Jr., fell asleep, too — on account of because they thought Terry Mills was asleep, and it was okay to go to sleep — Terry Mills could sneak out.

Ronald Mills, Sr., and Ronald Mills, Jr., went looking for Terry Mills upstairs, out of the basement, which Ronald Mills, Jr., wasn't allowed to do normally, but Ronald Mills, Sr., was pretty distracted at the time. Ronald Mills, Jr., found a note from Terry Mills, and in it, Terry Mills said she loved him, and she loved Ronald Mills, Sr., and she was very sorry, but she had to leave them before she hurt them. Terry Mills was going to "end it" herself, but let the record show that she did not, or maybe did not get a chance to before her brain changed. The note from Terry Mills also made Ronald Mills, Sr., promise two things: that he would never look at the black spot, and that he would keep Ronald Mills, Jr., safe, no matter what. Ronald Mills, Sr., laughed, even though nothing was funny, and he said that he already broke one of those promises, but he could keep the second. Then he knelt down to look Ronald Mills, Jr., right in the face, which he only did when he was super serious, and told Ronald Mills, Jr., that he couldn't go outside anymore: "There are no more people out there," Ronald Mills, Sr., said. "There are only Fucking Maniacs."

When I was writing, I didn't feel the burns, but I also didn't feel myself crying, and how are you supposed to not cry if you don't even know you're doing it? Some of the tears got the words a little blurry. I would have to be careful not to cry anymore, especially not when I wrote History. The History must have taken a long time, because when I looked up, it was bright out. Well, as bright as it got through the black sky. The town was far away, and really small, like a train model, but I could see it pretty good from up on the hill. I could see that the courthouse was still burning, and that the stuff around it was burning, too. There were no more firemen to put it out, so I imagined it would burn forever.

I got in my truck — there probably wasn't any other Mills left, so I guess that made it mine — and I wrestled with the gear lever, and I pumped the gas, and I hauled on the steering wheel, and I drove toward nowhere in particular, as long as it was away from Concord, North Carolina, which was just History now.

Bulk Storage

A family of deer nosed around in the weeds at the edge of the parking lot. The thick-shouldered buck, shaggy and scarred, stood proud, watching Mary with his stoic glass eyes as his doe sorted through the dandelions and the nettles. Their fawn, knock-kneed and wary, hopped and darted between the buck's legs. It made Mary smile.

"Look at that, Harry," she said, gesturing with her dirty spade. "They don't even care that the sun is gone."

The motion caught the attention of the watchful buck, and his family picked up on the attitude change. They sniffed the air and watched the shadows. Mary felt poorly for disturbing them on such a nice outing, so she backed away from the edge of the roof and knelt by her garden again. She used the spade to work soil free from around a splay of green and gave the resulting hole a disapproving look.

"All that work," she said. "Lord, Harry — I will never get used to how little a garden actually gets you."

She shook the dirt free from a bundle of twisted yellow carrots and set them in her basket.

"Zachary, the Goetz boy from downstairs — you remember I told you about him once, he had that nasty pneumonia last winter — his daddy was a green grocer, and he says the garden's going just fine. These here plants are normal — I guess they don't care about this, either." Mary waved her hand at the featureless black sky, not glancing away from her work. "But I just always assumed a crop would get you, I don't know, *more*. But then, I never did have patience for growing. What was that you used to say about me?"

She grunted at a modest pair of radishes, tossed them in the basket, and stood. She removed her gloves and wiped dirt from her apron — which really just smeared the dirt around — and used her knuckles to work the muscles in her lower back.

"You used to say that even for a black girl, I had the blackest thumb you'd ever seen."

She laughed to herself, but it came out more bitter than she'd intended.

"I'm sorry, Harry. You'd always buy me such nice flowers. Kept them in the pot and everything, 'cause you never wanted to bring me dead things. And I'd have 'em killed for you within a week."

Mary hefted her basket and tried to sigh away the lingering negativity.

"I'm doing better with the ones below, though — ain't I?"

She stepped to the edge of the rooftop and took one more look at the deer family — but the buck startled at her sudden appearance, and the three of them bolted back across the empty highway, into the ragged copse between streets.

"Be that way," she said.

Mary danced through the labyrinth of low wooden garden beds, skirted around the array of solar panels, and cut through the water stills back to where she'd left her cart. Loaded up with half a dozen buckets of water, three baskets of food — counting what was in her hand — and ten freshly-emptied-and-washed waste pails, stacked one into another, grouped by family name and aisle of address. It was all she could safely bring down with her on this trip. She unzipped the tent flap and wheeled the cart onto the elevator. Once inside, she sealed it back up, took her bell from its place on the hook — up here on the roof was the only time she got a break from the damn thing — and once again hung it from the waist loop of her green summer dress. She grabbed the cable that plunged down below, running through a series of rubber flaps and gaskets to filter out the light, and gave it a few hard tugs. After a moment, there was an answering series of tugs, and Mary braced herself. She slid the elevator's supporting brake out of the way, and the whole thing dropped an inch before reaching the end of its slack. It wobbled sickeningly. She held onto the support ropes with all her might, as Kevin and Andre worked the pulleys that lowered her into the warehouse. Four feet down and the elevator hit its next brake with a stop that practically knocked her knees out from under her. Mary reached up, back onto the roof above, and slid the elevator cover into its place. She felt around in her fanny pack, came up with the four plastic knobs that threaded into the underside of the cover, and tightened them in place.

She locked the light away.

That done, Mary tugged on the signal cable again, removed the next brake, and made the long, squeaky, unsteady descent into the dark below.

"Comin' up, Mary," a man's voice hollered from somewhere below her.

Kevin must've felt the series of zip ties cinched around the rope he was haulin' — that told him the elevator was close to reaching bottom.

Mary bent her knees and tightened her grip on the support ropes. Still, when the platform hit bottom, it almost sent her reeling. Andre caught her and laughed.

"When you gonna get that dismount down, Mary?" he said, helping her get her balance.

"When are you boys gonna learn some finesse?" she volleyed back.

The familiar, inane patter of long-time coworkers.

"Hey, it's not our fault," Kevin said, and she felt him start to haul the cart away. "I think you might be getting heavier."

She reached out to swat him, but she'd left part of her brain up top, in the light. It takes a while to get your dark sense again — a problem only she was lucky enough to suffer from. Kevin just knew the slap was coming, and he ducked away. His bell rang out, an easy two feet from where she'd been aiming.

"She try to whack you one again?" Andre laughed. "She's gonna get you one of these days."

They kept the jokes light and easy on the short trip back through the old employee access hallways, past the empty kitchen, around the meat counter — the freezers long since emptied, shut off, cleaned out, made into beds by the Park family — and down Highway 1. What they'd taken to calling the southernmost of the two wide pathways that divided the former Costco. The bells at their waists rang out an easy jingle, marking their passage.

From either side, voices in the dark called out greetings. Mr. Hemford and Mr. Forth said their hellos from aisle twenty-seven; Miss Poole and Mrs. Sylvan — Mr. Sylvan passed last month, from an infection that just wouldn't clear, but it felt too soon for that title change — spread their gossip out of aisle fourteen. Just an acknowledging grunt from Hawk in aisle three, who sounded like he was working on something metal — little Kenny had broken the Meers' shelving unit last week; could be Hawk'd bartered to fix that. And Mary recognized the bells of Sue Goetz as they passed in the dark. After a time, you could recognize just about everybody from the way his or her bell jingled. Maybe the bell had been from a different batch than yours, or maybe the casing had been dropped and dented, or maybe the wearer just walked a little off — had themselves a limp or something, and they rang out a different tune when they walked. Sue said a cordial hello. Mary asked after her boy, Zach; Sue asked after the garden. Neither made the pretense of stopping to hold a conversation. They just never got along, Mary and Sue. Some people don't, no matter what circumstances they find themselves in.

Mary's fingers brushed into Kevin's hand from behind — must've reached the zip ties for the pantry, hanging on the westbound guide rope. The boys unloaded her cart with fast and familiar motions, divvying up the produce into cubbies. More for the families. Less for the singles. Extra rations for the workers: Kevin, Andre, Zach, Derek and Jamal, Hawk, and the Farelly sisters. Little Anna did a fair share, too, despite her bum leg, and half a dozen others. No surplus for Mary herself, though. She didn't feel right, taking a bonus for her work, seeing as she was the only one who could do it. She didn't doubt for a second that some of the others would do the same as her, if their positions were reversed. If Kevin or Andre had looked at that black spot — felt strange to call it a spot, now that it'd grown so as to take up the whole sky — and found themselves immune, they'd be hauling the waste buckets up every morning. Taking the food back down. And they'd do it without complaint, because their mommas had raised them right.

Even if they'd deny it to their last breath.

Besides, being the only one who got to go outside garnered Mary all the animosity she could stand. She'd never wanted to be an authority figure. She just wanted to do the work. To help. But slowly, as the months passed, and then the years, others just started taking her word as law.

And then they began to resent her for it.

People are strange animals. Harry'd always said that. Ain't no winning with some folks, and all you'll do is kill yourself in the trying.

Mary liked to stick around until the cart was all divvied up. Andre joked that she was keeping the boys from stealing, but that wasn't it: Harry had said, "Even if you got no part in the finish, you should see a job through to the end."

So she did. They wrapped up and started to disperse.

"See you at Light Hour," Kevin said, as his bell played away into the distance.

The tune his bell made was always strong and simple: a single jangle for each footfall, like everywhere he went, he was just stomping along. Kind of a Frankenstein vibe to the boy. A big guy who'd always been big. He carried that confidence everywhere. It worked its way into his bell.

Andre didn't say a thing, just gave her a pat on the shoulder, and away his tune went, following Kevin into the dark. No mistaking those two: Andre's bell had a shuffling, awkward, uncertain little patter. He was on the skinny side, and though the work had been piling muscle on him by the day, he still carried himself like a shy teenager.

Strangely, Mary couldn't tell you what her own tune was. Oh, she knew the *tone* of her bell like her own heartbeat — a certainty so constant you never even pay attention to it — but the song it made was beyond her. Maybe Andre could have told her, or Kevin, if he paid attention to that sort of thing. But Mary guessed it would be like hearing somebody do an impression of you. Other folks would laugh, and they'd say, "So true, so true!" but you'd never *really* get the joke, yourself.

Lost in thought, Mary didn't sense the man waiting in the dark until she'd run straight into his chest and bounced back a step. She gasped, chided herself for being such a scaredy-cat, and let the rush of fear turn to anger.

"What are you doin', just standing in the middle of the Highway?" she snapped.

Silence that went on forever.

Mary could just picture it: one of those maniacs outside had gotten in the building — a Sleeper, those monsters that don't move until you wake them, and then it's all a blur of blood and screams — now here it was, just waiting in the dark. Waiting for some damn fool like her to bump into it. Mary could almost feel its hands on her arms, fingers digging into her soft flesh, her joints popping like chicken bones as the thing pulled her limbs out by the root—

"We need to talk," the man finally spoke.

Hawk. Just stupid ol' Hawk. A man so ridiculous he insisted on being called "Hawk" — no last name, or maybe no first. Had a big tattoo across his chest of — get this — a hawk. Lord, like she'd allow herself to be intimidated by Hawk, of all people.

"Same thing again, Hawk?" Mary asked.

"And again and again, until you see reason," Hawk answered.

He smelled like sweat and leather, and not in a pleasant way. Always wore this beat up old vest, covered in crude patches. Skulls and bones and gears and girls. Some biker thing, she'd gathered — though Mary got the sense Hawk had bought his precious vest just like it was, patches and all, from some kinda motorcycle store.

"I see plenty of reason," she said. "I'll point you toward some. You'd die out there Hawk, or worse—"

"And isn't that my choice? My risk to take?" His voice had a heavy rasp to it. An affectation he put on when he wanted you to *think* he was mad. Mary had made him genuinely angry once or twice over the years, and when she did, his voice squeaked and cracked like a teenager.

"It's not just your choice," Mary said. "And you know it. What if you go up there, and you look at that sky, and you start foaming at the mouth?"

"Then I'll foam at the mouth. What's it to you?"

"It's everything to me!" Mary said, and she swept her arm wide, to take in all of the warehouse. All of the people. All they'd built and kept safe.

It's strange, how you still talk with your hands in the dark.

"What if we get up there and you turn on me?" Mary said, once she remembered Hawk couldn't see her pointing. "What if you come down here and turn on *them*? It could be the end of everything."

"So don't come with. Just let me out, lock the door behind me, and wait to see what happens," Hawk said. "Like we used to do. You can't keep me here, Mary. You can't keep *everybody* here. I want to try my luck — that's my right. It was Mae's right. God damn, it was *Henry's* right."

Oh, that got her hackles up.

"You keep his name outta your mouth," she said.

Hawk knew venom when he heard it, and he didn't risk the bite.

They stood in blind silence, listening to each other breathe, heavy and angry.

"I'm bringing this up at Light Hour," Hawk said, pushing past her on the guideline.

She listened to his footsteps recede.

And *only* his footsteps.

"You better have your bell on," she called after him.

A beat, and then a jingle so vigorous you could practically hear the sarcasm.

"Must've got caught on something," Hawk said.

"Yeah," Mary scoffed. "Must've. You just be sure it don't get caught again, or The Square'll hear about it."

"Yes, ma'am," Hawk sneered.

He rang away into the dark.

Mary was too riled up to do much productive. She passed the time until Light Hour walking slow, endless loops around the store. Highway 1 to Register Road, up at the front of the store, where the cashiers used to be. Down Register to the far aisles and Highway 2, which she took up to the rear of the warehouse. Then Butcher Boulevard — lord, what a name — where the meat counters used to be, and onto Highway 1 again.

Some folks said their greetings when they heard her jingling by, and others didn't. Which was fine. Everybody's got their own affairs. Mary didn't so much need the socializing, as she did the sounds of life in her ears. People talking, feet scuffing, the pings and pops of shelving units as Upper Bunkers climbed in and out of their quarters. Breathing. Whispering. Laughing. Her people, safe and alive.

Before she knew it, Light Hour came, and the call went out.

"Light Hour in five, everybody," Mr. Hernandez shouted. His voice was strong, and clear as a cold morning. You could feel it bounce off the walls and come back at you from the other side. Used to be a construction foreman, he said. Only useful skill that taught him was how to yell.

That there was Mr. Hernandez's joke, not Mary's own.

"Attendance is mandatory, and leave is only given if you're too sick to stand, dead, or hungover…on something you're willing to share!" Hernandez finished.

A couple scattered chuckles from out there in the dark. Like tossing a handful of gravel into a pond at night.

Mary turned around and headed back up Register, until her fingers eventually brushed the series of zip ties that marked Light Lane. She hung a right, on toward the square. A handful of bells rang out in front of her, their tunes all mixed and muddled, so you couldn't tell who was who. Just the music of people, moving together. It was the song community made. And she'd be damned if anybody was going to quiet it.

Mary felt her way to the edge of the gathering crowd and pushed on through. More days than not she was front and center during Light Hour, giving updates on the outside, on the gardens, and the solar panels, and the water collectors, and such. She'd talk about frayed wiring and diminished battery capacity, about the rain or the drought, about what bugs had been munching on her plants. It was inane, and repetitive, and she loved every second of it. It felt normal. It made her feel normal. It made them all feel normal. She could see it in folks' eyes: they needed to focus small to keep from worrying big. Sometimes when the whole world was coming apart at the seams, complaining about the heat with a neighbor was about the best thing a body could do. But today Hawk would speak, and all her pleasant, sleepy updates would take a backseat to melodramatic rants about freedom and oppression.

Mary would listen, oh yes — she'd put on her serious face and nod along like he was making some good points, even though it was all just blather and bluster. Then she'd answer like she was talking to an adult and not some hopped up man-child who named himself after a bird. A boy playing at revolutionary because he was bored.

It made her tired, just thinking of it.

Mr. Hernandez whistled like a kettle, and all the chatter died down.

"Let there be light!" he said, and he clipped the ground to the battery chain.

Like a star being born.

Oh, it was sad light, Mary knew. Waxy and colorless. Fired out from industrial floodlights instead of nice cozy lamps, the LEDs putting shadows in strange places — making your wrinkles look deeper, your eyes more sunken. Turning your skin pale as a corpse, even if you were brown as a walnut. But any light was life's blood down here in the forever dark.

A collective sigh went up from the community. Folks closed their eyes, squinting against the harshness of the LEDs even as they tried to suck it all up and store it in their brains for the long night ahead. There was a solid minute of quiet basking before anybody could even bring themselves to speak.

Mary waited for Hawk to start in first, but he just stood there fidgeting. Looking around at all the gathered faces like he was staring down a pack of hungry wolves. If there was any menace from Hawk back in the dark, he'd left it there. He was short — barely taller than Mary herself — and had gone skin and bones on rations. Which was really saying something, since he'd started out a beanpole. Now he was just a pole.

A few fine lines of muscle mapped out his bare chest and stomach beneath that perpetually open leather vest. The goofy old hawk tattooed there tried to play up them lines as best he could, but anybody could see there wasn't much to Hawk. Pipe cleaners for arms. Jittery blue eyes. A patchy blond beard with a scattering of beads woven through it. The man had gotten it into his head of late that he was some sorta Viking, but the only beads he could find in the store were from a little girl's jewelry playset. They were pink, purple, plastic.

Mary spared him a bit of pity, but he ran through that mighty quick.

Just as soon as she started to step forward for her updates, Hawk jumped out in front — he was just waiting to cut her off. Little men and their little power plays.

"Friends," he called out, and Mary allowed herself a smile when his voice cracked.

A few folks behind her were already sighing. Mr. Hernandez rolled his eyes and gave Mary a conspiratorial look. They all knew what was coming.

"Friends," Hawk tried again, mustering every bit of iron he could fake. "Neighbors. Comrades. P-people…uh, people of Costco!"

Somebody coughed. One of the children whispered a quiet question, and a mother laughed gently by way of answer.

"I come before you today to speak of freedom," Hawk said. You could practically see him back there, behind his own eyes, scrambling for the pages of a script he'd spent hours rehearsing and couldn't recall a word from now. "Uh…freedom is important! Freedom is good!"

"Come on, Hawk," Kevin, bless his heart, hollered out. "Give us all a break, would ya?"

"No!" Hawk said, and the dismissal gave him the fire he needed. "I won't give you a break! Nobody gave any of us a break! Nobody gave any of us a *choice*. We didn't choose to be here, and some of us—"

At this, Hawk nodded to somebody in the crowd. Mary tried to catch who it was, but she didn't turn fast enough to see them.

"Some of us choose to leave. Or at least we'd like to."

He fell quiet, allowing everybody a moment to glance at Mary. Implication not lost on a soul.

"God damn it all, Hawk," Kevin said, edging his bulk through the crowd.

The boy moved easy for somebody of his size. Never steamrolled folks just because he could. He issued a load of soft pardons, guiding people aside as gentle as a child picking up a wounded bird. Kevin reached the front lines and puffed himself up. Let Hawk just take him in for a minute. Like Goliath giving poor David a moment to come to his senses and just start running.

"I don't want to spend my Light Hour listening to this same garbage," Kevin continued. "We all know what you're going to say, and none us are buying, so quit selling."

Mary bit her lip. She appreciated the gesture, but about the only thing that kept Hawk going was the idea that somebody was trying to stop him.

"Not everybody thinks like you!" Hawk said. Just as she thought, all Kevin did was stoke him up. "Some of us want a life outside of here."

And what really worried Mary was the murmur that followed. Oh, it wasn't strong. And it wasn't echoed by many. But time was, not a soul agreed with Hawk. Now he'd picked up followers — as in, plural.

"There is no life outside of here," Mary said. "You know that."

"I don't know anything!" Hawk shouted, and even he knew that sounded better in his head.

A couple folks laughed, and Hawk's face darkened.

"Except what you tell us," he finished. He pointed a bony finger at Mary like he was Judgment itself. "For all we know, it's perfectly safe outside."

Mary laughed and let the bitterness color it.

"Right," she said. "The world's turning just fine out there, and nobody come knockin' on our doors because we accidentally left a 'no solicitors' sign up."

"I'm not saying that," Hawk pouted. "We all know something bad happened, we watched it on the TV, we heard the screams. We're not stupid. But what if it's over now? What if we can start up again? What if we can at least see the sun?"

"There ain't no sun left," Mary said.

"Oh really?" Hawk laughed. "Then what's powering these lights?"

There it was. His ace.

Now, the thought occurred to Mary years back — that if the sky had truly gone black, there shouldn't be nothing to power the solar panels — but she never felt the need to formally address it. She figured it probably occurred to most folks, and they rightly wrote it off as one more unexplainable thing on a long, long list. But not Hawk. She could see it now, the way triumph shone in his smile. This thought had only just occurred to Hawk, and he believed it was going to change everything.

Mary had to laugh.

But there it was again: that murmur.

She looked around with eyebrows cocked.

"That it?" she asked the crowd. "You folks think I've been lyin' all this time? For what? Toward what intention?"

Some folks shouted their disagreement — most folks, truth be told — but some eyes just shifted away from hers when she found them, and Mary knew something had been growing down here in the dark. She'd been tending her garden above, but she'd been letting nasty roots reach out below and snatch away her people.

"Look, we're not saying you lied about the whole thing," young Zachary said, and Mary had to gasp.

Not the boy, surely?

"It's just that maybe you're not completely right about what's happening out there now," he continued. "We just want to see for ourselves, that's all. Is that so much to ask?"

Of all the faces, Mary never expected to see that expression tainting his, but there it was: defiance.

Oh, but Hawk would pay for twisting that poor kid's mind up.

"We all saw the news, before the power went out," Kevin said. He cast his voice wide to the crowd, but his eyes bored into Hawk, and Hawk alone. "It was end times out there. Atlanta was one big fire — all of it — and nobody was putting it out. People were *jumping in*. You take one look at that black spot, and it's white jacket time. There's no questioning that."

"Unless you're immune," Zachary said.

Even that gawky scarecrow of a kid had more presence than Hawk ever could. He was a dangerous convert — normal as a Tuesday, levelheaded, likable — Mary could see folks starting to think twice already.

"And *you're* immune?" Kevin laughed.

"We don't know," Hawk butted in. "None of us have even seen it. Except for Mary. Hell, we could *all* be immune. And that's *if* there's even anything out there."

Mary stepped into the center of the Square. Folks fell quiet. She made a point of looking around real slow and careful. She was surrounded by couches and recliners, saggy canvas camping chairs and hard metal folding ones — even a few coolers with cushions tossed on top, when they'd plain ran out of seating — and though most everybody was still standing for the announcements, the idea was there: there's a seat for everybody at the Square.

That was Mary's idea. So were the worklights at its edge, and the solar panels that powered them. So was Light Hour itself — arguments were made, loud ones, for only using the batteries in emergencies, but Mary knew how important the light was. It kept them together. *She* kept them together. And though she tried to push those prideful thoughts to the back of her mind where they belonged, at moments like this, they came surging forward on a wave of cold fury.

"We've been through this before," Mary said. "Have you all forgotten?"

A susurrus of shameful, whispered answers.

"You brought up Henry," she said to Hawk, who'd taken a sudden but keen interest in his own boots. "Let's talk about him."

Henry with his sad smile. Henry with his weathered hands, and his wintery stubble. Henry standing here — right here — a year ago and some change, giving a similar speech, to a similar crowd. Back when none of them, Mary included, knew a lick better. Henry putting fears to rest like colicky babies, bringing up hope like lifting a curtain — couldn't even count the hands when he asked for volunteers. Next morning, they raised the gates for the scouting party, every soul in the building turned away from the poison light. Every one but Mary herself. Henry gave her that half-sarcastic salute of his — the one that said "don't take none of this too seriously" — and pulled the gate shut behind him.

"Lots of us lost loved ones that day," Mary said. "Mr. Hernandez's pa…"

Mr. Hernandez made a quick sign of the cross.

"Old Clay, Therese, Jerry, Susan," Mary recited their names like a pledge. "Jamal, Fat Bobby, both of the Marias…were any of them immune? Was my Henry immune? Did a soul come back from that trip, aside from poor Jerry? Banging on those shutters and howling for blood? Poor Jerry, who had to be put down like a rabid dog? We made this mistake before…"

Silence.

"Did we forget their sacrifice?" Mary finished.

Hawk went to argue immediately, but Zachary held his arm and they both fell quiet. The boy let a solemn moment pass before picking up again.

Damn. If it'd just been Hawk, he'd have made a proper mess of it right then and there — they could all put this nonsense behind them.

"We remember," Zachary said. "But those weren't the only sacrifices made. How many have died in *here*?"

The boy stepped out so the crowd could see him. Standing tall as his bony shoulders and sunken chest would let him. Sandy hair made soft blue by the pale light. Hazel eyes practically gleaming. He was a magnet was what he was.

"My own father passed just this month, from an infection we might've been able to stop, if we hadn't run through all the antibiotics months ago," he started.

Mary couldn't speak out against that. Zachary loved his pa like the sun rose on his waking and set on his rest. He'd taken the death hard, and everybody in here knew it.

"How many more are going to go the same way this winter, when the cold comes back? Never mind the sun. Never mind freedom. Never mind all that. We are going to need supplies. That's what I want. Mary can't do this by herself. We need more workers topside. More scouts on the roads. What little we got isn't going to last, and we're already dying from what we don't."

Zachary let that sink in for a spell.

"We're not asking to spite you," he continued to Mary. "We respect you. Everything you've done. We owe our lives to you, and we know it."

She could see a caged sneer flitting about beneath Hawk's expression, but Zachary meant every word of it. He took Mary's hands in his, and they did not tremble.

"And if we're immune, too," he said, "all we want to do is help you."

Well now, what was she going to say to that?

Not a damn thing, that's what.

"Oh, Zachary." Mary knelt her head to his shoulder. "I can't take the thought of you mad. Seeing that murder in your eyes. I just can't take it."

"It's okay," he said, and for just a second Henry's sad, quiet smile graced the boy's lips. "Have faith."

Mary laughed between a few managed sobs. She sucked back the tears and drew herself up.

"Okay," she said. "I ain't your warden, anyhow."

A chuckle from the crowd, more to vent tension than anything.

"But if we do this," she warned, "we do it proper. You hear? We're not raising that gate again—"

Hawk made a sputtering noise like an old car turning over, but she bulldozed right through him.

"We're doing it smart. Tomorrow morning, I'll take each of you, one at a time, up on the elevator with me."

Kevin and Andre groaned in sync, making a big show at the thought of that extra weight.

"Oh hush," she chided them. "We'll leave the cart and the buckets below. Besides, these two barely weigh a sack of potatoes put together…"

Zachary smiled, but Hawk's face colored with anger.

"That way I can be with you," she continued. "If something goes wrong. Agreed?"

She looked to Hawk. Had his jaw stuck out like a toddler throwing a tantrum. But he didn't say a word. Zachary just nodded.

"Hawk, you're going first," she said.

He didn't cow none — though Mary got the feeling that might've been otherwise, if all these folks hadn't been witness.

"He's been arguing this forever," she told Zachary. "It just wouldn't be right to take that honor away from him."

A nod from the pair of them, and then a big old collective sigh from the crowd, and the matter was settled.

God help them all.

Mornings were tricky, without light. But people managed somehow. Why, just ask the blind. Long before Mary and hers ever wound up in this black old warehouse, blind folks were wrestling themselves out of bed without so much as a Light Hour to look forward to.

Your lot could always be worse, so appreciate what you got while you got it.

Henry again. Weariness may have worn away at his features, making him look like nothing so much as an old Bassett Hound, but inside, the man was iron. What had to be done had to be done, and if you were the one that had to do it, so be it. That's what got Mary up in the morning. Even the bad mornings. Like this one.

The air mattress squeaked with her shifting weight. Her joints crackled like popcorn, and the concrete floor was always cold — even through two pairs of socks. Mary laced up her worn sneakers and donned her filthy apron. She tied her hair back and smoothed it down as best she could. She took a steadying breath and stepped out of her bunk. A child's fort, really; a cubicle built out of cardboard — like there was any need for walls in the forever dark — but old habits die hard, and all that.

Mary took up the guide line. Out her aisle to Highway 1. Skirting 'round the edges of Butcher Boulevard. Through the old kitchen, and into the employee access corridors. The loading dock was always colder than the rest of the store. They'd sealed up that giant metal garage door as best they could, but you could still feel it on the far side of the space: storing cold from the previous night, eking it out like radiation.

There was chatter back in the dock, but it fell silent when they heard Mary's feet scuffing down the hall. Nobody knew quite what to say to her, so as usual, she had to start.

"Kevin, Andre? That you I heard?"

"We're here, Mary," Andre said and left it at that.

"Zachary?" Mary used the space between her question and its answer to pray for silence. But no such luck.

"I'm here, ma'am," he said, and Mary's heart felt like a cannonball.

"I'm here, too," Hawk said, too loud. Making his voice deeper than it was. "We're ready."

"You can still get out of this," Mary said, reaching out for Zachary in the dark. She found the skin of his neck, cool and thin like the first ice on a deep pond. She feared it would crack beneath her touch. "We can say the elevator was broken — you all tried to go up, tried just as best you could — but we had to leave it for another day…"

A day to think. A day for a silly boy's nerves to set in, for all that awful testosterone to seep away, let him think, let him reconsider…

"No, Mary," Zachary said. "We have to do this. Now, please."

She was glad he couldn't see the tears in her eyes, and she kept them out of her voice.

"Hawk first," Mary said, all business.

"Any time, anywhere," Hawk said, like that meant a lick of sense.

If you think you know awkward, and you never escorted a man you hate on a shaky elevator ride in the quiet dark to his almost certain death — well, you don't know awkward. Mary was thankful when they finally reached the first stop, and she could busy herself undoing the brakes. When they were through, the locks sealing the light away below them, Hawk took his first steps outside in nearly two years. The fool didn't even apologize when he saw that the sky was black as coal.

"Huh," was all he said. "Lookit that."

While she was up there, Mary went and changed her apron out for a fresh one. She cleaned her stained sneakers off as best she could, wiped her face clean with a damp rag, and used the cracked compact she left by her gardening tools to check up on her looks. Tucked away a few stubborn stray hairs that she just knew would work free again in moments. Now, she didn't care much what Hawk thought of her, but if Zachary was gonna see his first human being in the full light of day — or what passes for it, anyway — in a dog's age, she could at least have the decency to make herself presentable.

Back down through the locks alone. As soon as the second brake snapped shut, and the elevator began its last unsteady, creaky descent, Zachary called up to her.

"Mary?" he asked.

She chuckled a bit by way of response.

"Who else is it gonna be, the Avon lady?"

The joke was lost on him. A reference past his time.

"Is everything okay?" the boy asked.

"As okay it's going to be," she said.

"Comin' up, Mary," Kevin warned.

She braced herself. The elevator hit bottom. Her knees took the jolt hard, sent it up her long leg bones and into her hips. Mary felt it all the way in her teeth.

"Should I get on now?" Zachary asked.

And damn her promises, damn the rules, damn what had to be done — she almost lost her nerve. The fool was still just a kid, asking an adult to guide him.

But he didn't wait for an answer. He made his way onto the platform. Grabbed onto May's hip by mistake. She guided his hands to one support rope, and then the other.

"Hold these," she said.

The whole floor shook from his knock-kneed balancing act. Like a dog trying to keep itself upright in the back of a moving truck. Mary had forgotten just how terrifying the ascent was, your first time. All that way to fall, in the dark. Not knowing what was above, or below, or beside. But there was a time and place for pity, and she stowed hers away for later. Mary undid the brakes, because she was bound to, and escorted the boy into the light, because she was bound to, and she let him look into the black sky, because she was bound to.

He gasped, to see that jet expanse running solid, from horizon to horizon.

"I never doubted you," he said. "Really, I didn't. But wow.

Just…wow. You never really know until you see it, do you?"

"I guess not," Mary answered.

Zachary took a step forward and his foot splashed in the growing puddle.

He looked down.

"I don't underst—" he started, but Mary did it just like Henry had taught her.

You bring the knife up and through the neck sideways, cutting the vocal cords first, so they can't scream. She put her full weight against his back, and Zachary fell face-forward into Hawk's pooling blood. Mary held him down as she worked the blade back and forth, quick and methodical, like boning a chicken. Don't think about it. Just let your hands remember the motions.

Zachary made a few last choking attempts at words, and then his eyes went slack.

Mary pet his hair, like straw; his cheeks, just showing the first signs of stubble. She closed his thin lips, and she said a few words of kindness and apology, and then she got to her feet.

"Lord, Henry," she sobbed. "What am I doing?"

Neither the wind nor the birdcalls answered her.

"Is this really the right thing?" she asked, stripping the bloody apron away and tossing it aside.

"It's the only thing," Henry answered.

Mary sniffed back tears and wiped her cheeks with the backs of her wrists — the only parts of her arms not soaked in blood. She looked up into Henry's Droopy Dog face — beard like ash, skin the color of old wood, laugh lines so deep they could be scars — and it gave her some strength. But she sure did miss his eyes. Soft and brown like your favorite blanket, they used to be. Now, from nose to eyebrow, just nothing.

Unbroken white space. Color of a fresh snowfall, and just as cold. Colder. Antarctic cold — so cold you knew, just looking, that there wasn't any life left there at all.

Oh, but that was her fool brain talking again. Not her heart.

"He was just a boy," Mary said, gesturing to Zachary's body. His skin was already fading to pale blue.

"I know, Mary," Henry said, and he stepped forward and took her hand.

She looked away from his frozen white eyes and down at his cracked hands instead. She knew every line of them — a roadmap she'd memorized over decades of marriage. They, at least, were still warm.

"You did everything you could to convince him not to break the law," Henry said. "It wasn't your fault. It wasn't your choice."

"Couldn't we have let him go?" Mary asked, risking a glance into the tundra behind Henry's face. "Just him? Just this once?"

"That's not the law," Henry said, his voice steel. "What's kept all those folks down there alive this long? What's going to keep them alive, through the new hells coming our way? What's the only hope left for humanity?"

"Order," Mary said, dutifully. "We got to have order."

Henry nodded and squeezed her hands.

"But what if he'd been immune, too? Couldn't he have helped us?"

He dropped her hands like they'd gone molten hot. Henry turned away from her.

"It wouldn't have mattered," he said. "The law is absolute. It always has been, and it always will be. You know that better than anybody. We both of us know what comes of broken promises…"

I'm right here. I'll never leave you…

That first night trapped in the store. The black spot still just that —

a pinprick in the sky. Listening to the screams of the mad and dying outside.

...I promise.

Henry had come to break that promise, though, leaving her to lead that fool scouting party. It was a miracle he'd come back at all, even if he had been changed. Something more, or something less than what he was. Missing three fingers, one scouting party, and two warm, brown eyes. And all of it, every ounce, because he'd broken a promise.

"But don't you worry about it anyhow," Henry said, turning back to Mary with his sad, broken smile. "Neither of them was immune. The darn fool with the bird on his chest would've joined the sisters. You could see that anger in his eyes. And the boy — I'm sorry to say it — he would've been one of mine."

"What?" Mary gasped. "But...you coulda controlled him. You coulda made him help us..."

"Of course," Henry said. "But there're no exceptions to the law. We can't waver on that. If we do, those people down there won't stand a chance against what's comin' for them."

Mary knew it. She felt the truth of it in her bones. She could feel that black sky pressing down on her every second of every day, and it wasn't a question of if the storm would be coming, but when. Still, she needed to ask the questions, and she needed Henry — and what rode inside him — to answer.

Now the words had been said, and there wasn't any point chattering on. You been together as long as Mary and Henry, you didn't need small talk. They just stood and watched the forest together for a time. Listened to chattering squirrels, and wind, and not much else at all. That was nice, at least. With all the people gone, you could hear the world again.

"They're coming soon, then?" Mary finally asked.

Henry held her close. Pulled her head to his chest. Mindless of the blood staining his flannel shirt — the one he'd been wearing worn so long, it'd gone the color of iron, all over. After a long moment, he released her, tucked an errant hair back behind ear, and eased out that smile. The one that never changed, no matter how bad things got, never faltered, no matter how ugly the work they had to do was, never faded, no matter how hopeless the situation.

He didn't say nothing. He didn't need to.

Together, Mary and Henry dragged the pair of bodies to the edge of the roof — same corner as the compost bin, in case anybody started asking questions about the smell — and tossed them over. Right onto the pile below. Where Old Clay, Jamal, both of the Marias, and all the rest of the scouting party wound up. Just bones now. And memories.

Henry scrubbed up the blood, while Mary changed her soiled clothes. When they were both done, she asked him how she looked, and he took a step back to survey. After a moment's thought, he spun his finger around. She laughed and gave him the little twirl he was askin' for, and he told her she was as beautiful as the day they met, and if he was telling lies, Mary never wanted to hear a word of truth.

The Walled City

The problem wasn't the gas, it was the batteries. A sealed, underground commercial tank might still have some good fuel left. Plenty of those sitting around — when the world went crazy, it happened all at once. Not a lot of maniacs paused their murder sprees to fill up at the stations. Oh, a few, sure — the ones with a bit of brain power left probably plowed through a crowd or two in a big truck or an RV. But there weren't many of the smart ones to start with, and what few there were didn't seem too interested in hoarding gasoline. But a battery left unused, uncharged, out in the elements — that'd be dead in a single bad winter.

It had been a very, very bad winter.

"Can't you like, jumpstart a car, though?" Carina had passed asking five minutes ago. This was just pleading.

"With what?" Sam asked. "We don't have a *good* battery — that's the problem."

"No, I mean like — actually jump it. Where you push and then jump in," Carina said.

"That's…not what that means," Sam said.

"Well, whatever!" Carina threw her arms out, practically slapping Madding in the face in the process. He didn't notice. "You know what I meant!"

"We could push start something older," Bobby said, barely sparing the conversation a glance. "If we could find a manual."

"Good luck with that." Frankie laughed. "I haven't seen a stick around Seattle in a solid decade."

"Naw, I bet you seen plenty of sticks. Bet you done more than see 'em," Bobby said, still wholly absorbed in poking at his MRE.

"Hilarious, hillbilly." Sam rolled his eyes. "Dick jokes. Super helpful."

"Hey if the dick fits…" Bobby shrugged.

"So we find a manual!" Carina said. "No problem! I mean, this is backwoods country. There's got to be some crappy old cars around."

Bobby looked up just to shoot the girl a glare, then it was back to sculpting meat paste with a plastic spoon.

"Honey," Frankie said, with infinite patience. "We're barely half an hour outside the city by car. This isn't 'backwoods.' This is rural yuppie."

"There *are* woods," Carina pouted. "We're in *back* of them."

"We could get a manual started," Bobby said. "But that ain't the issue. The noise is the issue. Quiet as the grave out here — those things hear the roar of some good ol' American classic blasting down the highway, they'll come runnin' to the dinner bell. Besides, if the battery's shot, we're left push starting it every time. You wanna count on that in a tight spot?"

"Well, we're not getting anywhere walking," Carina said. "It's been like a week, and we're — what did you say? Half an hour out of Seattle? See, you're still thinking in car terms. We'll die of old age before we reach the Walled City."

"We'll die of something, all right," Bobby added.

He must've decided something right then, because he wolfed down the entire platter of rehydrated food product in a half dozen large, sloppy bites.

"I'm saying: bicycles," Sam reiterated.

"And I'm saying I can't ride one!" Carina yelled.

"Hey, keep it down," Frankie warned. "We don't wanna draw attention."

"Who lives in Seattle and doesn't know how to ride a bike?" Sam laughed.

"Well, *excuse* me," Carina said. "We weren't all raised in, like, Suburbville, USA. Where was I supposed to learn? The parking garage of my dad's apartment building? Some people don't know how to do some things. Like, what — you all know how to swim?"

They stared at her in silence.

"You don't know how to swim, either?" Frankie asked.

"Oh my god!" Carina cried. "You're going to make a thing of that?! We're not sailing to Europe. We're walking on a highway. Jesus Christ."

"What about the retard?" Bobby asked. "He know how to ride? Or swim?"

"Don't call him that," Carina shot back, her voice low and serious.

"What?" Bobby asked. "Retard? Ain't he? What else am I supposed to call him?"

"I think it's 'mentally challenged,'" Frankie offered.

"'Developmentally disabled,'" Sam corrected.

"How about Madding?" Carina said. "You know, his name?"

"Queer name for a boy," Bobby said. "You all got queer names. Except you, Sam."

Bobby nodded to him, and Sam nodded back. He immediately felt like an asshole for it.

"Okay, *Bobby*," Frankie laughed.

"Better than 'Carina,' or 'Madding,' or god damn 'Frankie' with an 'i,'" Bobby muttered.

"You all fighting again?" Anna asked, stepping from a gap in the hedge that marked the rear border of the property.

A McMansion: eight rooms, four-car garage, three stories — all bizarre angles and huge windows. About five different shades of beige. The whole thing dropped straight in the middle of three acres of pristine Pacific

Northwest woodlands, like the forest itself had sprouted a single, glorious suburban wart.

"Somethin' to do," Bobby said, by way of answer.

"I could hear you all the way inside," Anna said. "You'll bring them down on us one of these days."

She tossed a battered gray canvas bag on the moss between them. It rattled and clunked.

"Hope you all like lentil soup," she said. "I think these freaks were on some kind of diet. Like fifty cans of it in there, and nothing else."

"It's better than this shit," Bobby said and tossed his empty black plastic serving tray onto the green.

"You're losing your brother," Anna said, nodding toward the forest line.

Carina turned and saw that Madding had wandered all the way to the edge of the clearing and was peering into the dappled shadows between the trees.

"Maddy!" She said and jogged over to retrieve him. "Don't stray. It's dangerous."

Madding said nothing. He looked down and away from her. Shook his head and thumped his palm flat on his leg.

Everybody got to their feet at once. Heads snapped toward the words. Anna quietly shouldered her canvas bag, while Bobby frantically shoveled his scattered belongings into a frayed Jansport. Sam held a protective arm out before Frankie, who slapped it away.

"Really, like I'm going to just run into the forest like a yappy dog," Frankie hissed.

"Quiet," Anna snapped.

They waited, frozen, every eye watching for Madding's next move.

Carina pulled at the back of his stained gray sweatshirt, trying to guide him away from the edge of the forest, but he resisted. Madding was twice her size, which wasn't a feat. She barely broke five feet. Probably didn't break a hundred pounds. Frizzy black hair pulled back into a loose ponytail, half-drowning in a bright orange parka, two sizes too large for her. Madding was tall and just as thin, but widely built. Linebacker shoulders, blocky hips, and huge feet. Greasy jaw-length hair concealed his face when he looked down and away — which was always.

"He won't come," Carina whispered, so loudly it may as well have been a shout. "He won't come!"

Sam edged toward them, keeping his steps short and quiet. He held his breath. Something cracked beyond the treeline — a sharp snap, like a twig breaking. It may as well have been a gunshot. Bobby and Anna were off, bounding through the gap in the hedge like scattering deer. Frankie followed but hung back. He hovered just on the far side of it, torn between fear and concern.

Carina pulled on Madding's arm, wedged her heeled boots into the moss, and levered all her weight against his. He staggered, but only for a step. He groaned softly and thumped his palm again. Something rustled in the bushes.

Sam was nearly there — arms out, neck held stiff, eyes roving, when the thing broke through into the clearing.

"What. The. Hell," Frankie breathed, and they all exhaled with him.

It was a small, black, pot-bellied pig, wearing the ragged remains of what had once been a bright pink, cable-knit sweater.

Sam laughed so loud it felt like he ruptured something.

The pig squealed curiously, snuffled the ground at Madding's feet, then did a crazed sort of hopping dance. Madding smiled into his shoulder and groaned — his happy sound — while Carina and Sam endured small heart attacks of relief.

Frankie emerged from the hedge like a child stepping into Narnia: his face pure bewildered fantasy. He knelt by the pig and picked at the tangled, filthy sweater. Beneath it was a matching pink leather collar. The nametag that hung from it was shaped like a crown.

"Princess SparkleHogg," he read, in the sort of awestruck whisper one would use in the Sistine Chapel. "Oh my god. How long were you out here, sweetie? How did you survive?"

At her name, the pig's ears pricked up, and she regarded Frankie with guileless anticipation. She licked his nose.

"I've only just met you, Princess," Frankie whispered savagely, "and I love you more than anything else in the world."

Two honks and a squeal, and SparkleHogg was off to sniff the ankles of her other visitors.

"Princess SparkleHogg?" Carina's adrenaline had run out, and she was laughing uncertainly, like each "ha" was a question of its own.

"Wait — I know that name," Sam said. His eyes went skyward; he squinted and worked his jaw like he was chewing on thoughts.

Bobby poked his head back between the hedges. Eyed the forest with careful suspicion. A groundhog watching the sky for raptors. He spied the pig.

"You found bacon?!" he gasped.

"Buddy, you'll eat me before you eat Princess SparkleHogg," Frankie said.

"You'd like that, huh?" Bobby sneered.

He suddenly lunged out from between the greenery and stumbled a few steps in the moss. He snapped about to glare behind him.

Anna followed after.

"Don't shove me," he said.

"*Do* something," she challenged, automatically.

He'd taken her up on it, apparently, a long time ago. They both knew he wouldn't again.

"The holy god is that?" Anna laughed, wrinkling her eyebrows at the pig.

"Princess SparkleHogg," Frankie said, with faux-gravitas.

"That's it!" Sam snapped his fingers. "The guys from BOB."

"Bob?" Anna asked.

"Balls Out Brewing," Sam said. "These local craft beer guys. I followed them on Twitter. They posted pictures of their pet pig once in a while — Princess SparkleHogg."

He gestured grandly to the Princess, who received her formal introduction with a snappy fart, then burrowed into Frankie's crotch.

"That explains the garage," Anna said.

"What's in the garage?" Carina had wrangled Madding away from the forest and was guiding him back toward the McMansion. His warning defused, he was docile again.

"You really have to see it," Anna answered, already leading the way back through the hedge.

Their following was assumed.

The garage door screamed like a gutshot robot while Anna wrestled it open. In the dusty half-light, motes swirled in lazy tornados. The second and third doors followed, and the group stared in puzzled silence until they could figure out what they were looking at.

"There," Sam smiled. "That's what I'm talking about."

The entire space was filled with dozens, maybe hundreds of bicycles. From ancient Schwinns to modern electric mopeds. Some complete, many more disassembled. Giant heaps of wheels, frames, levers, cables, gears — welding equipment heaped in one corner, a solid steel table half-buried beneath the current project: a Mad Max-style penny farthing.

One giant wheel up front, little one in back, miniature steel cowcatcher, jagged spikes adorning each hub. Similar monstrosities sprawled all about: two-story fixed-gears, jury-rigged racers, recumbent and novelty bicycles, and everything in between. The entire third bay was taken up by a single hulking creation: a five-wheeled, car-shaped tandem bike with a single pair of handlebars up front, and ten stools surrounding a central bar behind. Pedals, chains, and gears beneath each seat fed into a single master drive that ran below the central serving area. A polished wooden counter circled an empty space in the middle, taps and faucets peeking out at regular intervals. Above, a garish orange canopy with the words "BALLS OUT" endlessly looping around the border.

"What the hell is that?" Carina asked.

"That," Sam said, "is a bicycle bar. I thought you were from Seattle?"

She rolled her eyes.

"Well, you can't ride a bike," Bobby said. "But I bet you can pedal."

"Who were these glorious maniacs?" Frankie breathed.

"My favorite brewery," Sam said. "I can't believe we're in their house."

He looked around and sighed.

"I can't believe they're dead," he added.

Not much to say to that.

They spread out to pick over the garage. Princess SparkleHogg rooted around their ankles in search of precious floor-food. Bobby grabbed the Road Warrior Big Wheel from the workbench and tried to pedal it around the driveway, but he was out of breath — and then on the ground — before he could complete a single circuit. Frankie disappeared through the connecting door into the main house, Princess SparkleHogg in tow.

Carina and Madding huddled in the corner by the welding gear and quibbled at each in some private, invented language. Anna and Sam got straight to gutting the bicycle bar. It looked like it weighed a solid ton, but both the frame and components were some kind of space-age polymer — so light they felt like they'd float away when you released them. The walls that held up the shining oak counter were thin sheet metal. With the kegs, taps, and serving supplies hauled overboard, Sam and Anna could heft the whole contraption easily. Out and over the piles of bike parts into the private circular drive, where they took turns poking at its components — spinning the pedals, squeezing the brakes, and kicking the tires.

Inside, Madding was growing increasingly distressed. Carina was pressing him on something, and he didn't like the idea. He shook his head violently, grunted in protest, turned away to face the corner. Carina pursued him, whispering angrily into his ear while he softly bumped his head against the wall.

"Look at this thing!" Frankie cried, bursting from the house like a scientist who'd just made a landmark discovery. He spun about and squealed in delight. Princess SparkleHogg squealed in reply. Then they both squealed in unison.

The pig was draped across his back in an adapted baby-harness. Two straps running over Frankie's shoulders and beneath his armpits, connected across his chest by a heavy metal buckle. Princess SparkleHogg sat upright in a padded cradle, four holes sewn in especially for her stumpy legs. They kicked and paddled with glee. The fabric was royal purple, embroidered with golden thread, the word "PIGGYBACK" stitched across the wide belly-strap.

"Yesterday, if you'da asked me if you could find a way to get gayer," Bobby drawled, "I'd have said 'buuuullshit.' But here we are…"

"If this was a movie, one of us would have to die soon, just to prove how serious the stakes are," Frankie shot back. "I sure hope it's you."

"Naw," Bobby said. "I'm the rugged anti-hero. I tell it like it is, and don't take no guff. You know, Bruce Willis–style."

Anna laughed so hard and abruptly that she snorted. That set Princess SparkleHogg snorting, and that set everybody to hysterics. They laughed at Bobby for a solid minute before he stormed off in a huff.

"Oh hell," Anna said, wiping tears from her eyes. "He was serious?"

She waved a reluctant goodbye to Sam and set off after Bobby, either to soothe his wounded pride or slap him in the ear. You never could tell with those two.

Satisfied everything was in working order, Sam mounted up in the lead position on the bike-bar. Cruiser-style handles that pulled back nearly to his waist, beefy, padded leather seat that might have been stolen from a Harley. A single thick metal lever above the right for the brakes: no chintzy little pads hugging the rims — BOB had installed massive drilled rotors on each wheel. A baroque system of gears and switches above the left grip let Sam pedal the whole thing himself with relative ease. He made a few tentative loops around the driveway, then snagged a can of WD-40 and a manual bicycle pump to do some light maintenance.

Frankie was practicing windsprints with Princess SparkleHogg in the Piggyback, trying to getting used to her weight. Carina left Madding moaning unhappily in the corner and went to forage through the bike scraps. She came up with an eighteen-inch-long section of tubing chopped from a rear frame. It terminated in a single spiky, vicious sprocket that spun when she swung it. She smiled ear to ear. Bobby and Anna had apparently finished their lover's spat and were coming back around the garage — her arm thrown over his shoulder, him leaning away in a clearly exaggerated pout.

"This thing is great!" Sam said, banking the bike-bar around a bend at breakneck speed. He bore down on the brakes, and the beast skittered to a halt before the assembling group.

"With all you guys on and pedaling," he finished, "I think it'll really haul."

"I don't know if Maddy will get on," Carina said. "I tried to explain that he could just ride in the middle and not have to pedal but—"

"Oh no," Bobby snapped, shrugging Anna's arm away. "No way in hell is the retard getting a free ride."

"I told you not to call him that." Carina closed on Bobby like a jungle cat.

"Hey, if it walks like a retard and talks like a re—"

A crack like a whip and a small white handprint on Bobby's cheek that was quickly filling with red. Carina brought her face within inches of Bobby's, eyes locked onto his. She had to stand on her tiptoes to manage it.

"Say it again," she challenged.

Even Anna was caught off guard. She, Sam, and Frankie stood in aimless shock, like pedestrians watching a car crash.

Bobby blinked the tears out of his eyes, tried to step back from Carina, but she followed, eyes tracking like a viper's.

Finally, he laughed.

"Hell, girl!" he roared. "I didn't know you had it in you!"

Five simultaneous exhalations.

Anna laughed, Sam leaned back in his seat, and Frankie reached around to tickle Princess SparkleHogg's nose. Even Carina smiled uncertainly. Bobby made a show of nursing his jaw and nodding appreciatively. He was about to say something — ruining the moment, creating a bond, cementing an understanding — but it was lost to the frantic slap of Madding's palm on his leg.

Madding ran diagonally — one leg didn't work quite as well as the other — closing the distance between the garage and the group in frantic, uneven lopes. When he reached them, he repeated the warning, shaking his head and grunting urgently. No words to waste, Anna tossed her supply bag into the bicycle bar, and all followed suit. Carina ushered Madding toward the folding section of counter that allowed entrance to the serving station, but there was something he didn't like about the stairs. He wouldn't budge.

"Not now," she pleaded. "Come on, Maddy."

Anna had mounted up on the right side of the bar, the seat closest to Sam's captain's position. Frankie leapt onto the stool opposite her.

"Get on up, you damn fool," Bobby said, more concern than venom.

He tried to join Carina at shoving Madding, but it was like wrestling a gorilla. He had too much reach and weight on them. He wriggled out of their arms and ran around the bar, ducking and weaving between the outstretched hands grabbing for him.

From the field beyond the garage, a howl, and an answering chorus of yips.

"Wolves," Bobby cursed.

"Jesus, how many?" Frankie asked.

The orchestral yelps crested. A freight train crashing through glass.

"More than enough," Anna answered.

She started pedaling. The bar eased forward. Sam clamped on the brakes, hard, and it jolted to a stop.

"We have to move, now," she said.

"Not until everybody's on!" Sam shouted.

"That's not the deal," she replied.

"You're more than welcome to get off and run for it," Sam said "But the bike is group property. It doesn't move without *the group*."

Bobby had finally circled around and cut off Madding's last escape route, shuffling back and forth with arms spread wide to keep him from bolting past. Carina approached her brother gently, her voice like warm honey.

"You have to get in, Maddy," she said. "Don't worry. Hey. Hey. There's no pedals in the middle. Not like a bike at all. It's safe. It's like riding the bus. Remember the bus?"

Madding shook his head, long hair working like a pendulum. He pointed at the bar and thumped his chest. Pointed at the bar again.

"Maybe…" Bobby ventured. "Maybe he *wants* a stool?"

Madding nodded. Made an affirming series of "hmphs."

"He wants to pull his own!" Bobby said. "Good man."

"Is that it?" Carina asked, guiding Maddy to one of the stools and moving to join him.

"No," Bobby said. "We gotta spread out. You and me sit on the queen's side, toward the back."

"She's a princess," Frankie corrected.

"I wasn't talking about the pig," Bobby said.

The first of the wolves strayed around the edge of the garage and sighted them. Anna whistled to draw their attention to it. Its ears perked up, legs rigid. It regarded them with sweet, canine curiosity for a few seconds, then screamed like a spoon in a garbage disposal. Its unseen pack picked up the call.

"Everyone's on," Anna said. "Go!"

Sam stood on his toes and put all his weight into pedaling. Seated on their stools, all facing inward toward the central serving area, the passengers could only white-knuckle the bar's edge, bend double, and spin their legs like a frightened Scooby Doo. Clunks and whirs, soft jolts that grew harder as Sam clicked down through gears. The bar picked up problematic speed — the drive banked hard just before it met the highway, and the whole thing went up on three wheels. It landed in a lurch that quickly evolved into a maddening swerve, but Sam wrestled the bars under control and focused on building straight-line speed.

Years of neglect and the aggressive, almost spiteful return of the forest left Highway 2 a minefield of cracks and potholes. The bar had a decent enough suspension, with beefy shocks connecting each wheel to the main frame, but it was, after all, a bar. Not an establishment well known for its handling capabilities.

"Hang on!" Sam yelled over his shoulder as he wrestled the bike away from a pothole that split into a small canyon.

He didn't win. The bike bottomed out, sending its passengers briefly airborne again. Princess SparkleHogg squealed a vicious protest.

"Watch it, Sam," Frankie warned.

"I am watching it," he shot back. "I'm watching it crash into these god damn potholes. I'm steering a pub, honey. What do you want me to do?"

"I think you can slow down," Anna said.

Sam risked a glance rearward, acutely aware of the pavement racing blindly away beneath him.

A few wolves had emerged from the end of the driveway, but the bike had made enough distance by then that they hesitated to follow. The scouts just stood on the broken pavement, sniffing idly and tossing back sharp barks to the pack behind.

"Let's get up that first." Sam nodded toward the short, steep hill erupting out of the road ahead. "Everybody pedal!"

A half dozen cranks squeaked in unison. Sam wrenched the handlebars and veered around a sapling that had sprouted from a modest sinkhole and spent all but the last of their momentum cresting the hill.

Even at reduced speed, he hammered the brakes so hard that Frankie was unseated and came flailing past him — arms windmilling, feet slapping with the effort of trying to slow down without losing balance. He managed it, but only barely, then spun on Sam.

"What was that about?" he snapped. "There are no seatbelts on this thing, you know. You could've killed the Princess."

She oinked derisively.

Sam just pointed.

The lee side of the hill wasn't nearly as steep, but much longer. The highway chased its curving slope down into a shallow valley. At its center, an idyllic little town straight out of a postcard. A humble stone church. Two blocks of main street. A handful of tastefully sprawled residential areas surrounding small parks and playgrounds. From a distance, it almost looked normal. But if you squinted, you could see the moss and mold, overgrown even by Pacific Northwest standards. Fault lines of high green grass forking through breaks in the untended streets. And above all — the quiet.

Nothing stirred down in that place. Not even the two figures standing guard, one dead center in each lane, at the spot where the highway met the town. It took a moment to even recognize them as human — or something that used to be. They were standing upright, but painfully bent at the waist. Knees folded inward. Faces practically brushing the street, limp forearms akimbo on the pavement. Clothes gone gray and shapeless in the elements, smudges of moss growing in their folds.

"Sleepers," Anna said. "Just don't get close enough to wake them. We'll go around."

"Around where?" Bobby asked, sidling up beside Sam.

A valid question: the forest marched right up onto the shoulder of the highway. Trees in lockstep; an impassable phalanx.

"We could hike up," Anna said. "Cut through the trees."

"We'd lose the bike." Sam sounded heartbroken at the mere thought of it.

"Better the bike than our lives," Anna replied.

"Why are the Sleepers even still here?" Frankie said. "How many little towns have we passed through already? I haven't seen a single one since Seattle."

"There." Bobby pointed.

They followed his finger to a modest church. Weathered gray stonework, dull green moss etching out the masonry. An old yellow pick-up truck parked diagonally across the walkway, just feet from the immense wooden doors.

"What about it?" Frankie asked.

"I see it." Anna held up a hand to shield her eyes from the sun. An old habit — there was no glare these days, just a featureless black sky stretching from horizon to horizon; the light it let through was colorless and thin. Late afternoon sky, just before a thunderstorm.

"I'm still not—" Frankie started, but at last he spotted them.

Tire tracks carving through the overgrown grass, running from the street right to the pickup. It had been driven recently.

Survivors.

"But look at those things." Sam nodded down the base of the hill, toward the pair of Sleepers, so utterly still they became part of the landscape. "They're ancient. Doesn't look like they've moved in years. Those tracks are recent, right?"

"That just means whoever it is, they're stuck there," Anna said. "There must be more guarding the other exits. Doesn't look like the fast ones have swept through here yet."

"Yet," Bobby stressed. "If there're Sleepers down there, the Manic are comin' eventually."

"We have to help them," Frankie said.

Sam nodded automatically.

"No way in hell," Bobby said. "I'm not goin' down there."

"No way," Anna echoed. "That's not the deal."

"Oh, I'm so sick of your damn deal," Frankie spat. "Like we need you here so badly. Cut and run, pussycats. See if we care."

"Hold on," Sam cut in. "Let's not—"

"Guys," Carina pleaded from her stool at the rear of the bike.

"Maybe we will split," Bobby said. "You all are just slowing us down."

"Numbers are better," Anna said.

"Right," Sam said. "I'm sure we can think of a way to—"

"Guys," Carina said, more urgently.

"Think, hell!" Bobby snarled. "That's all you do — think. You sit there and think yourself out of doin' anything at all."

"Hey, if it wasn't for us, you wouldn't even know about the Walled City," Frankie said.

Princess SparkleHogg snorted supportively, and he reached back to tickle her nose by way of thanks.

"Guys," Carina yelled.

And at last, they heard the steady warning beat of Madding's palm on the bar.

All fell quiet. They looked to Madding, then back down the hill, from where they came.

While they'd been arguing, the wolves had been quietly assembling — a few dozen now visible on the highway, the implication of more lurking in the driveway and woods beyond. The scouts padded towards the group on hesitant paws, heads lowered, ears flat. The pack beyond drifted in their wake.

"Uh…maybe get back on the bike," Sam said.

Bobby and Anna wordlessly obliged. Frankie hesitated.

"And go where?" he asked.

"Shit," was Sam's only answer.

"Can we break through the wolves? Maybe scare them off if we charge?" Frankie ventured.

"Not with that many." Anna shook her head. "They're boldest in numbers, and they've got them."

"Do something!" Carina said.

The bravest of the scouts had reached the base of the hill. A few hundred feet away. He crept upward.

Madding drummed against the bar.

"Shoot the gap," Frankie said, settling back onto his stool.

"What?" Sam asked.

"Between the two Sleepers. Right through the middle, fast as you can."

"That's the dumbest thing I ever heard," Bobby scoffed. "However fast you are, those things are faster. You get in their space, they'll wake up and tear your arms before you can shit."

"If you hit dead center," Anna mused, "maybe not. Maybe they won't even wake."

Bobby stared at her with open, wounded betrayal.

"I don't see another option," she explained.

A series of angry yips, too close. The lead scout had ventured nearer the bike. Barely fifty feet. Assessing the situation. Waiting for backup. At the base of the hill, backup was assembling.

"Go," Carina said. "Go go go!"

The wolves pricked up. Something in the urgency of Carina's voice tipped the scales in favor of attack. The pack broke like water through a dam, surging forward with an orchestra of screams.

Carina had already started pedaling; Sam could feel the strain of it, the pressure of her leg muscles nudging at his brake lever. He shot a quick look back to make sure everybody had their seats, then hauled up on his own pedals and let the lever snap open. Torque freed, the bike lurched forward — only a few inches — then struggled to break inertia. It was still on the uphill, if only just. Frantic thumping from Madding resonated through the bike's hollow frame. The wave of shrieks behind, swelling, crashing — so loud, so close, how were they not already here? Sam stood on the pedals, leveraged his weight against the grips. An inch. Two. And then free.

A set of fangs snapped shut on the space where Carina's ankle had been, milliseconds ago. The sharp clack of teeth on teeth. The wolf shook its head clear, lurched from side to side — the motion strangely human, like a frustrated driver pounding on the steering wheel — then bounded after its escaping prey.

But with the bar cresting the hill and all resistance gone, it easily outpaced the lead wolves. They gave up quickly, accepting the chase as lost — but even with the pressure off, the bike couldn't afford to lose an ounce of speed. It took every bit of will in Sam's body to keep his fingers from gently nursing that brake lever. Self preservation shrieked in his ear: slow down; stop; no living thing should be going this fast; this is in defiance of natural law; we'll burn up like a comet—

Sam had surely gone faster in his life. A train. A car. The slowest airplane. But in those, he'd been sheltered. Cocooned away from the noise, the wind, unaware of every little textural shift in the road beneath him. Here, at the nose of the bike — only two handlebars and part of a wheel intruding on his sightline, reminding him that he was not, himself, flying a few inches from the pavement — this was different.

His adrenalin spiked, hurtled beyond the brief feeling of

exhilaration, blew through the shakes and the sickness; it honed down to a knife edge and filleted Sam's whole being away. It left him only eyes, nerves, reflexes. With them, he heaved the massive, unwieldy behemoth through a slalom of lethal obstacles: massive potholes whose asphalt-colored puddles belied their depth; shrubs and saplings shooting up from cracks that split the road like canyons; and still the impossible, growing speed. Sam could feel the weight of the bar behind him, like being strapped to the business end of a wrecking ball. Ahead a few hundred yards, just beyond where the hill leveled out, the two moss-covered sentries stood immobile. Sam's vision tunneled. The world narrowed to a single point, just a few inches wide — a space dead-center between the Sleepers. Sam flattened his body across the bars. Face out front, right over the tires. He was the needle at the end of a dart. There was nothing left of the world. Only the target. Only the target, and himself. And then, they were one and the same.

The bike passed so close to the Sleepers that, for the most fleeting moment, Sam could smell them. Like an old book dropped in a puddle. No body odor, no excrement, no organic rot. Just an ancient must. It brought to mind sealed pyramids; abandoned warehouses; desert tortoises trundling in slow motion across vast lifeless dunes. Things that endured. That watched centuries sweep by without notice. Immutable and immovable.

Until they weren't.

The leftmost Sleeper shot upright in the space of a blink, muscles seizing like they'd been hit with an electric shock. Old, caked-on dirt crackled as it broke free from the thing's joints. It tilted its head at a quizzical angle, one ear to the sky, as though listening to a song it couldn't quite place. Its gender, race, and identity — all lost to time and exposure. Rounded gray features locked straight ahead, only the pupils of its eyes shifted painfully sideward, tracking the bike as it raced by.

Frankie made fleeting contact with that stare. Like locking eyes with a whale, or some ancient kind of cave-fish. A thing for whom life was an unfathomably different concept.

And then they were through: beyond the trigger radius of the Sleepers, and still picking up speed. It was like physics no longer applied to the bike — like the whole crew had cannonballed straight through the entire concept of physics and came hurtling out the other side, free to accelerate relentlessly toward infinity. Sam was utterly lost to the flow state, still nothing but eyes and wrists and one single pure, unifying purpose: movement.

Something behind him screamed. Wolves. Sleepers. Monster. It didn't matter. Behind didn't matter. There was only forward. Onward and ahead — ever faster and forever, blurring lines between body and environment, self and non-self, speed eroding the rough edges of reality until everything melded into one single being, quicksilver smooth, swimming ethereal through—

Something slapped Sam in the ear, and he fell out of his adrenaline fugue so abruptly that he went momentarily spastic and nearly lost control of the bike.

"Slow down!" Anna yelled in his ear.

Focus lost, the bike wobbled viciously beneath Sam, snaking side to side like a semi braking on ice. Fighting only made it worse. He could feel the shakes building in strength, the apex of each shudder cracking the bike like a whip. He reached for the brake, but instinct halted him. Instead, he relaxed his grip and let the handlebars shimmy freely, only restricting their motion in the gentlest possible way. Teasing it forward more than forcing it. At last they regained something like balance, and Sam finally eased the brakes on, bringing the bar to an inappropriately gentle and restrained stop.

Sam sat, shaking, every last bit of his will focused on not throwing up.

He failed.

He'd waited until the last second to turn his head before puking, unaware that Frankie had dismounted and was coming up to check on him. Frankie's gesture of concern was met with a timid volley of vomit, not quite enough to penetrate the fabric of his jacket. It streamed downward across his stomach, crotch, and thighs. It pooled in the space where his jeans tucked into his boots.

Princess SparkleHogg chortled and preened.

"I'm sorry," Sam said, amazed he still had a body, much less a voice.

"It's okay, sweetie," Frankie said, laying a large, warm hand on Sam's shivering shoulders.

He left it there, solid and still, so that Sam could feel something solid. Frankie brushed his lips to the back of Sam's neck and whispered in his ear. They lost themselves in each other, a little bubble all their own.

"Jee-sus Christ!" Bobby hooted.

He looked up toward the distant Sleepers, resuming their agonizing slump. From high above came frustrated howls — wolves standing silhouette against the black sky.

Bobby laughed and gave the whole scene — the Sleepers, the road, the hill, the wolves, the world in general — two giant, double middle fingers. He laughed and walked his birds around, then spun about and undid his jeans in a motion so fluid it had to be rehearsed. He mooned the abstract concept of death.

Carina rolled her eyes to Anna, who rolled hers in turn.

"What do you see in that guy?" Carina asked.

"He has a huge dick," Anna said.

Carina stared, dumb.

"I'm kidding," Anna finally clarified. "He is…not so bad once you get to know him. All this—"

She gestured widely to Bobby, still pantsless in defiance to the world.

"It's mostly an act. A — what's the word? Like macho, but for acting?"

"Bravado?" Carina ventured.

"Mmm," Anna said, unhappy with the term, but willing to settle.

"Well, let me know when all this stops, and the real Bobby comes out," Carina said, turning to Madding, still on his stool, testing the tension in his pedals.

"I think he's coming out now," Anna said.

Carina glanced over her shoulder to find Bobby standing upright now, jeans puddled around his ankles, pelvis strained forward, hipbones so sharp they threatened to pierce the skin, his flaccid penis helicoptering around in great meaty circles.

"I thought you said you were kidding," Carina gasped.

Anna raised her eyebrows.

"Only a little." She smiled.

Madding eased his pedals forward, just enough to feel the resistance under his feet, then reversed the motion until the gear spun freely. Repeat. The bike rocked, ever so slightly, with this effort. Madding, in turn, rocked with the bike. He was upset. Carina could read his moods like a manual. The self-isolation was normal: Maddy wasn't comfortable with people. It's just that normally he was busy — out there on the periphery, studying the world. Watching the leaves move in the wind. Examining the trees, pushing against the wetness of the dirt, tracing cracks in the pavement. That was where Maddy lived, not in the world of people.

But when he shut down like this, found a corner to huddle up in, sought solace in repetitive motions — Carina knew things had gotten too much for him. Madding just made it so easy to ignore him — especially when he needed attention the most — that most people did just that. But Carina saw the warning signs and slipped out of her spoken conversation in favor of a quieter one. She touched Maddy's forearm, careful not to surprise him. He still flinched, of course, but after a moment, he leaned in toward her. She set her chin on his shoulder, hooked her weight on him, and he crumpled toward it. The old, familiar motions. Gentle grumbling, deep in his chest, long slow breaths. She hummed a nameless tune she made up on the fly.

"Sammy," Frankie said, and the warning in his voice was enough.

The calmness, just now barely settling into Sam's tensed and burning muscles, fled all at once, in a feeble burst of adrenalin from his overtaxed body. He snapped to attention, heels up and ready to peddle again — an automatic reaction, not a planned one. They couldn't flee just yet. The group was scattered, and only he and Frankie were watching the man with the rifle approach.

He walked the faded centerline of the highway, eyes up, rifle down. When he saw the pair had spotted his approach, he halted and threw an exaggerated nod of greeting.
"What's up?" he called out.

Anna jumped at the unexpected voice. She spun about — spotted the stranger, the rifle — and bit her tongue in reprimand. Stupid girl, thinking that just because one trouble was over, another wasn't already starting. The IDF had taught her better. She eyed her bag but knew she'd never get to it before the man could get a shot off.

Frankie was closest and felt that somehow put him in charge of the exchange.

"Not much," he answered and immediately wished he'd said

something better.

He started to step forward, but the man raised his rifle a few inches.

And Frankie saw it wasn't a man at all — just a kid. Acne-pocked forehead, greasy hair, jaws still growing into a pubescent overbite. A teenager, maybe just barely.

Frankie paused, smiled, and held his hands out to his sides.

"Okay, no closer, I gotcha," he said.

Bobby inched toward his go-bag and the revolver inside. The second-homo-in-command was making a big mistake; Bobby saw it in his posture. He relaxed as soon as he saw it was just a pimple-faced kid. Like a kid couldn't pull a trigger. Anna reached out and grabbed his wrist. Hands like fine grit sandpaper. He looked to her. She shook her head slightly, then shifted her eyes sideward. Bobby followed her gaze and spotted the distant hooded figure, crouching atop the gas station down the road. Now that he'd keyed into one, the others popped up everywhere — like hearing a strange word for the first time, then it seemed like everyone started using it. Little silhouettes huddled behind trees, on roofs, in doorways. Any one of 'em could be holding. Maybe all of 'em. Bobby stopped inching.

"I don't know who you guys are," the kid with the rifle called out, in his best grown-up voice. "But you have to leave."

"We only just got here," Frankie said, half a laugh. Easy smile. The kid wasn't buying it.

"We are not looking to stay," Anna called out.

The kid glanced her direction, unsteady now that his focus was split. A good sign. They would have sent their best as the envoy, which meant the others hiding in the town below would panic without him. If she and the others all moved at once, no chance a rookie sniper would land a shot. The problem: she knew Bobby would follow her lead — if he'd listened to her at all over the past eight months, he'd already figured out the next move for himself — but the others were soft and slow. If it came down to it, she and Bobby would have to leave them to their fates. It would not be a surprise. After all, that was the deal: travel together, help when you can, but we owe each other nothing. We save ourselves first.

"That's good," the kid said, but his posture was still tense. Coiled. "There are more of those Sleeper things all around the edges of town, but if you take Pine Street, just behind me, all the way up to the school, there's a sorta Jeep trail in the park across the street. That connects back up to the highway after a few miles. Last we checked, the Sleepers hadn't found that one."

"We just need a little while to collect ourselves. Maybe gather some supplies and—" Frankie started, but the kid cut him off.

"No. All this stuff is ours, and besides, we been here since the sky went dark, so we already looted anything useful. Get going now, and if you leave Pine Street before the school, we'll shoot you. We're really good shots and there's lots of us. Don't try it."

"Hey, listen," Frankie said. "We're not the bad guys. We're all normal, I promise."

"Are you kidding?" The kid laughed. "You're the craziest people I've ever seen."

"What?" Bobby cut in. "We're not trying to pull your arms off. That's one up on those suckers down the street, at least."

"Uh huh. I just watched you guys pedal up here leading a pack of wolves, then bomb Runaway Hill on a picnic table that says 'BALLS OUT' all over it."

"It's a bar," Sam said. His voice still shaky with nerves.

"What?" The kid jumped when Sam spoke, almost pointed the rifle in his direction.

"It's a mobile pub. You bike around and drink beer," Sam clarified, acutely aware, now, that he was not helping.

"Right," the kid said. "You rolled up here *in a bar,* with your own wolf pack, and then kamikaze'd right past those Sleepers — who barely even blinked at you, by the way; don't think we didn't see that — and you're totally normal."

"Look, I know it seems weird now, but in context I promise it all made sense," Frankie pleaded.

"Dude," the kid said. "You're trying to tell me you're sane while Master-Blaster-ing a pig. It's not super convincing."

Sam couldn't help but laugh, and it came out high-pitched and loony.

"So what you're going to do," the boy with the rifle reiterated, "is take Pine up to the school—"

"We got it," Anna said. "No problems."

The kid looked at her cockeyed, but finally nodded, and moved to retreat.

Carina rushed forward, and the boy nearly dropped his gun trying to get it aimed at her.

"Wait," she said and skidded to a halt a scant ten feet from him. "They sent you out here because you're the oldest, didn't they?"

"N-no," he stammered. "It's because I'm the quickest shot. We got lots of adults down there. All over the place. And they have guns pointed at you right now. Big ones."

"It's okay." Carina continued. "We've seen it before — Maddy and me."

She gestured back to her brother, quietly shrinking behind the bike.

"The black spot came, and everybody went crazy," Carina continued, now narrating for the boy. "The adults who didn't either got killed or took off after things calmed down some. But not you and the other kids who lost their parents. You knew how to hide, and nobody looked for you, so you stayed here. That's how it happened, right?"

The kid looked like he wasn't sure whether to shoot or cry. He didn't say a word.

"That's how it happened with me and my brother. We were the oldest ones left in our neighborhood, after the maniacs killed everybody and wandered off. Just us and a bunch of other kids, with nobody to look after us. I know it's been scary, and you did really good here on your own, but you have to come with us now—"

"Whoa," Bobby snapped. "Hold on—"

Anna joined in, while Sam and Frankie just sputtered a handful of shocked syllables.

Carina plowed right through them.

"Because it's not over," Carina continued. "They're coming back for you."

She had the kid's attention now, but not his trust.

"Please, listen." She took a step forward; he took a step back. "We saw it in Seattle: first it was just crazy. Everybody went nuts at once. There was no order to it. But after a while, it was like they knew what they were doing. The Manics — the ones that are just brainless, angry — they came in all at once like a flood. They butchered everything they saw. When we tried to run, the Sleepers blocked off every exit. When it seemed like everybody was dead, that's when the tricky ones came. They almost passed for human. They played games. Just to lure out the survivors…"

"We know," the boy said. "It all happened here, too, last winter. We're the ones that made it through."

"No, it wasn't over!" Carina snapped. "What was left — me and Maddy, and the other kids — we finally met up with some others. A couple of doctors and some army guy. They set up a camp for us, tried to gather survivors, thinking it was done…"

Carina made a fist. Stared at it.

"The maniacs came back," Sam finished. "And they weren't alone. Maybe they never were. They had leaders…"

The kid's arms were slack — rifle forgotten and dangling. This part, it seemed, was new to him.

"Just big black pools where their eyes should have been," Carina continued. "They didn't, like, talk to give orders or anything, but it was like they could just think it, and all the other maniacs would do it. There was one for the Manics, one for the Sleepers, one for the Merry — it was a coordinated attack. You see? It's not like a plague or something. It doesn't hit, and if you survive it, you're okay. It's smart, and it comes back for the survivors. If there are Sleepers coming here…"

"She's right," Frankie said. "Child, listen: if this thing was done with you all, those creepy bastards would be gone. If more are showing up around town, like you said, it's coming back for you."

"I'm not a child," the kid said. He recalled the rifle and hefted it by way of demonstration. "What about you two?"

The boy nodded at Bobby and Anna, who'd been inching toward the bike — and their go-bags — while the others conversed.

Anna just blinked, but Bobby jumped like a startled cat.

"What about us?" he said.

Anna sighed.

"We don't know about any of this," she said, hoping that if she answered quickly, the boy wouldn't notice Bobby's artless and obvious guilt. "We met with them on this highway, outside of the city. We are only traveling together for a time."

"Yeah," Bobby chipped in. "We ain't stupid. We didn't stay in the cities when the shit hit the fan. We vamoosed to the woods and let it all die down. I can tell you all my neighbors went bughouse crazy when that black spot appeared in the sky, but all the rest of that crap about invasions and black-eyed monsters — if you ask me, that's just scared people trying to put a meaning on something that doesn't have one."

Anna answered with an uncertain grunt, but finally, a nod.

"Some people need explanations," she said.

"Shoot," Bobby added. "Few years back when this all started, I had a buddy who swore up and down this was the Jews. They'd been lacing our water with fluoride and sending signals through the TV to make us crazy. I told him — 'Stevey,' I said, 'I don't like the Jews any more than you, but they didn't make your momma pull out your daddy's eyes.' That's just giving the Hebes too much credit, you know?"

Anna slapped him in the shoulder.

Bobby raised an eyebrow.

"What?" he asked. "What'd I do?"

"You know I'm Israeli," she said. "How many times have we talked about this?"

"Right." He shrugged. "You're from the Middle East. Sandpeople. You folks hate the Jews more than anybody…"

Frankie laughed, short and sharp.

Carina and Sam hung quietly, still waiting for the kid to process a response.

"You take Pine Street up to the school," the boy finally said, his words curt and final. "There's a park on the left. Take the Jeep trail. Leave Pine before then, and we open fire."

"Works for me," Bobby said, already moving for his stool.

Anna shrugged and followed suit.

Carina called after the kid, but he was already backing away, his rifle at the ready. Frankie held her by the shoulders, somewhere between a hug and a restraint. He guided her into an about-face, and she marched away to help Maddy saddle up.

"These kids are gonna get themselves killed," Frankie told Sam.

Sam just nodded.

"Can't we do something?" Frankie prompted.

"Yeah," Sam said. "We can leave them alone."

He couldn't match eyes with Frankie's puzzled glare.

"What are we going to do? Try to force them?" Sam continued. "They've got guns, and if they made it this long, they know how to use them. We'll either get ourselves killed or kill some of them if we try."

"But Sammy…"

"Look, if the Walled City has it together half as well as we've heard, they'll have people they can send out to help. That's our best bet."

Frankie deflated. His neck limp, head to chest. Behind him, Princess Sparklehogg chortled with worry.

"Hey." Sam tucked his fingers beneath Frankie's chin, lifting his face up. "We'll make it. They'll make it. Everybody will make it. Eventually."

Sam kissed him quickly and gently, three times around his lips, and once on the nose. Frankie scoffed, but there was a ghost of a smile when he left to take his seat. Sam stood up on the pedals and eased the bike into motion.

The boy with the rifle stood to one side as they passed.

"Don't leave Pine," was all he said.

They didn't.

You could see where the early survivors had been — those scant and desperate fortifications. Boards up on the windows, furniture against the doors. Bloody handprints tracking across the jagged edges of splintered plywood. Doors torn from hinges. Scraps of clothing snagged on shattered glass. Just before the school, Frankie spied a lone child's shoe in the gutter. So waterlogged it was nearing shapelessness.

He cried as quietly as he could. He didn't want to be a distraction.

Sam piloted the bike through the overgrown park. The Jeep trail was barely discernable from the woods around it. Nettles and blackberry thorns snagged at their ankles. Hidden rocks and unseen pitfalls forced the group to disembark and carry the whole bike across the rougher patches. By the time the path emptied out onto the highway, just a few miles outside of town, they were all too exhausted to continue. Instead, they dragged the bar off the road and into a small clearing of clovers.

Couples paired off into private worlds: Sam and Frankie with their backs against the trees, hand in hand, watching Princess SparkleHogg forage. Bobby and Anna ducked away into the forest — to plot, or screw, or gather supplies — they didn't say, and nobody had the energy to ask. Carina sat cross-legged on an island of what felt like sunshine, filtered through a black sky. She tried to enjoy the warmth, but without the accompanying light, it only felt like she was baking. Madding patrolled the periphery, turning over stones with the toes of his shoes, running his wide hands over the bark of the trees, and quietly watching the small movements of the forest.

Time passed, unnoticed. Sneaking out the door while all backs were turned.

Anna emerged from the brush carrying a dead rabbit in one hand. Like a lost child trailing a stuffed animal. She thumped it on the ground without comment, knelt, unsheathed a knife from her hip, and got to skinning. Bobby came in on her heels with an armful of dry twigs and clumps of dead grass. She prepped the rabbit. He readied the fire. They worked in a silence that went unbroken for so long it felt perverse when

Carina finally spoke.

"Hey, Bobby," she said. "Why are you such an asshole?"

He looked at her with open confusion.

"W-what the hell did I do now?"

"Leave it for another day, girl," Anna sighed.

"No, I mean, just in general. Like not trying to start a fight or anything. I just want to know why." Carina picked at the clovers: she discarded those that didn't meet her unknowable criteria, collected the others in a growing pile between her crossed ankles.

"I don't know," Bobby mused. "Why are you such a bitch?"

Carina gave it a moment's thought.

"I guess it's because of Maddy," she said.

Bobby laughed. Something in the conversation had snared Anna's interest, and she paused, the tip of her blade hovering over the rabbit's throat.

"So you know you're a bitch?" Bobby asked. "And you blame your brother? Jee-sus. You people."

"No," Carina said. "But since *you* asked, I gotta assume *you* think I'm a bitch. And so I thought about what you might mean by that and why you might think it. That way I can answer what I *think* is your question, and I think the answer is Maddy."

"I do not see what your brother has to do with this insult?" Anna said, both statement and question.

"Like, okay." Carina dropped her clovers so that she could better explain with her hands. "Bobby *probably* thinks I'm a bitch because I'm always in his face about stuff."

"Y…yeah," Bobby said, carefully.

"He sees me as I'm super defensive. Okay. I get that. And if that's true, then it's because of Maddy. It's not his fault, but he's the reason.

Like…there's a difference between those things to me, you know?"

"I thought they were the same," Anna said, and Carina couldn't tell if it was the language barrier or something deeper.

"See," Carina opened her hand toward Bobby, "when somebody starts badmouthing whole groups of people — especially like minorities and stuff—"

"Minorities?" Anna asked.

"All his talk about the Jews and homos and racial things. You know, bigot talk."

"Hey now." Bobby got to his feet. "I ain't no bigot."

"What?" Carina laughed. "Of course you are. You're like a cartoon of a bigot."

"Fuck you," Bobby snapped. "I just call it like I—"

"Hold on, hold on." Carina held out her hands. "I'm still explaining why I'm a bitch, remember?"

Bobby looked to Anna, as though she'd have some explanation for him, but she just shrugged and motioned back to Carina. *Listen.*

"Okay, so the thing is," Carina tried again, "when people start with the hate talk, in my experience, it's only a matter of time before they start including Maddy in it. And it never stays just talk. There were these guys in the refugee camp, I think they used to be skinheads — back when we still had stuff like razors — and they started with just jokes about women and gays and all that. Then it was some racial stuff, but not in front of anybody they thought would get pissed off. Or at least not anybody they thought could do anything about it. Then when that was okay — whatever, we all had bigger problems — they started with that talk out in the open. 'The Jews this, and the blacks that, and the retards, and on and on.' And so slow it almost felt normal, that talk turned toward what we had to *do* about those people. People like Maddy and me. And well, there were some things that they did that I don't want to talk about right now. To both of us. So like, I guess I'm defensive — I guess I'm a bitch — about this stuff, because I know what comes after."

Bobby settled back against the bike. It creaked with his weight.

"Okay," he said slowly. "What do you want me to do about that? I already said I wouldn't call him a retard or nothing."

"Nothing," Carina answered. "I don't expect you to do anything about it. I was just answering your question, because I hoped that if I did, you'd answer mine. Now you know why I'm a bitch. So…why are you an asshole? Think of it like I did. Not an accusation or an insult or anything, just do your best to explain."

"This is the strangest conversation I have ever heard." Anna laughed. "But answer her. I want to hear this."

Bobby scoffed.

"I'm not your dancing monkey," he said and turned to leave.

"That thing I do with my feet," Anna called out, "I won't do it anymore unless you answer."

Bobby froze for a second. Then he whirled on Anna, face flushed, eyes wide, all sputtering outrage. But she just shook her head until he quieted.

"Never again," she reiterated.

Bobby paced in an angry circle but finally sat — making a point to do it as far away from both of the women as he could get — and thought.

"If by 'asshole,'" he finally started, "you mean *not polite…*"

He spat the word out, like it was the vilest slur he could think of.

"Or too *aggressive* for you," Bobby continued, "then it's because I was always taught that you can't trust people who act like that. Like they love and understand everybody. Ain't *nobody* loves *everybody*, all right? And people that pretend they do have some sorta agenda. So what? So everybody has an agenda. But when you go outta your way to hide what yours is, then I start thinking you got something that needs hiding. Maybe I talk shitty to you — maybe *you* think that — but if that's true, then it's because I want everybody to know what I'm *not* hiding, so they won't think I'm hiding something bigger. I guess. I don't know. Leave me alone."

Carina and Anna exchanged looks, though neither was entirely sure what the other's meant.

"You know what?" Bobby said. "If that don't make any sense to you, I don't give a shit."

Anna didn't respond. She just crawled over to him, kissed him on the cheek, and squeezed the back of his neck.

"So is that it?" Bobby asked Carina. "You don't think I'm an asshole anymore?"

"Oh, I still think you're an asshole," she said, again gathering her clovers. "Because you're wrong. The way you think is wrong. But I don't wanna talk about that, because it'll just be a fight, and I'm too tired to fight. But thank you for answering. Sincerely."

"Well, okay." Bobby blinked. "I still think you're kind of a bitch, too, then."

Carina just nodded, her focus back on the plants at her feet.

"These people are weird as hell," he whispered to Anna.

She gave him a thin smile that he couldn't decipher.

"Oh my god!" Frankie screamed. "Look at this!"

Carina's eyes found Maddy in an instant — standing at the edge of the clearing, running dirt through the gaps in his fingers — while Bobby and Anna rolled to each side of the bike, sheet metal at their backs, only risking glances after they'd established cover.

Sam was beaming like a proud parent. He was kneeling forward, holding a length of root in one hand, while the other pointed at Princess

SparkleHogg. The pig stood on her hind legs, laser-focused on the root, barely keeping her balance as she hopped gently in place.

Frankie laughed and clapped, then wondered at the puzzled hostility on display.

"Isn't it the cutest thing you've ever seen?" he asked.

The brief silence that followed was a still lake on a snowy day.

"Are you fucking kidding me?!" Bobby hollered.

Both women joined the fray, while Sam and Frankie dove for cover.

In his forgotten corner, Madding coaxed a squirrel from the bush and fed it the dirty old acorn that he'd unearthed.

Uneventful days of ceaseless movement.

Pedaling until exhaustion hits, pushing through it to the numb space, hypnotized by an eternal stream of asphalt, flowing, flowing, always flowing, just there beneath your feet, looking up to fading light — colorless, featureless, black to darker black — setting up camp, eating, sleeping, jumping at every noise, and then the bike again, pedals you could feel long after you'd stopped, walking that feels like a foreign motion, stumbling sea-legged and dizzy through the bathroom breaks, achingly cold water from tiny streams, sifting through abandoned gas stations and bars in towns that span a blink of highway, barely a name, exhaustion, exhaustion, numbness and on—

Madding slapped the counter, palms flat. Almost a beat to it. He pedaled backwards until Frankie relayed the message to Sam, who jerked the bike to a stop.

"I don't see nothin'," Bobby said, standing to twist the knots out of his back. "Probably another pig."

Princess SparkleHogg had no comment. Lulled to sleep by the repetitive motion, she snored intermittently from her throne on Frankie's back.

"Maybe not," Carina said. "He's scared. It could *be* something."

She stroked Maddy's back, making small circles across his damp T-shirt. He shook his head, less to negate, and more to clear an unseen fog.

"How does he do this?" Anna asked. "It's like an alarm system."

"Canary in a coal mine," Bobby added. "Even a bird-brain is good for some things."

"Shut up," Carina said. "He just pays attention to different things. While you're off thinking of like, monster trucks or banging your cousin or something—"

"You told her?" Bobby accused Anna. She laughed and shook her head.

"—Maddy is watching the world. The inside of *your* head is, I don't know, all private and messed up and busy. It's like Maddy's head has been turned inside out — his head is out *here*. Little things you miss, he gets. Smells and sounds and the like. It's not anything weird or creepy or paranormal, so don't make it out like it is."

"Hey." Bobby shrugged. "I'm not knockin' it. Saved our ass a few times. I didn't even ask in the first place — take it up with the lady."

Anna pursed her lips and nodded. The conversation dropped.

Princess SparkleHogg stirred, kicked her legs idly in the air, and wriggled.

"I'm gonna give her a bathroom break," Frankie said, unhooking the Piggyback to let her run free.

"Sure, it doesn't look like there's anything here," Sam said, his legs creaking over the bicycle seat.

Maddy moaned softly, repeating his tapped objections.

"But maybe don't let the Princess get far," Sam amended.

The pig found a satisfactory spot of trampled grass by the roadside and knelt to do her business. A warm breeze brought rustling branches. She snuffed the air as it hit her, and in instant, her sleepy demeanor shattered. She squealed, bucked like a bronco, and hustled away into the deeper grass.

"Princess!" Frankie called. He moved to follow her. "Get back here!"

"Damn," Sam said. "I…wait here; we'll be back."

He tromped into the brush after Frankie, just the crown of his head visible in the tall grass. Bald and brown, a coconut awash in a sea of green. And then gone, down some unseen slope.

The bike lurched forward, its handlebars pitched to one side, and nudged Bobby's outstretched knee.

"Hey," he straightened. "What's the deal?"

"Sorry," Carina said. "It's Maddy. He started pedaling."

"Calm down, jeez. There's still nothin'," Bobby said. "Maybe his retard radar is broken."

He blinked, looked to Carina before she could object, and said, "Sorry. Force of habit."

She glared but nodded, returning her attention to her distressed brother.

Anna had scouted ahead a few hundred feet, to a sharp bend in the highway: ancient fir to one side, a boulder halfway to a mountain on the other. She held a hand up to shield her eyes from the non-existent glare — a nervous tic — and—

"Yalla!" she yelled, stumbling backwards, catching her own heels on the cracked pavement. "Yalla!"

"Oh shit," Bobby said. "I know that one. On the bike!"

"What? What is it?" Carina yelled, but if Anna heard, she didn't answer. She was locked in a dead sprint, head down, eyes focused only on the ground passing beneath her feet.

Bobby looked about, saw Sam and Frankie were still missing, and started to mount up in the pilot seat himself.

"No time," Anna hissed, and she broke straight past Bobby, barely slowing.

"Wh—" Bobby hopped from foot to foot, as though wrestling with some invisible tether.

Bike or Anna. Bike or Anna.

"Come on," he finally decided, grabbing Carina and Maddy by their wrists.

He was prepared to wrestle the latter away but encountered no resistance this time. Madding was already up on his feet, unbalanced lope carrying him fast and decisive in Anna's footsteps.

It was Carina who froze.

"But Sam and—" she started.

"Do *you* see 'em?" Bobby asked. "Well, neither will *they*."

"They who?!" Carina cried.

"Does it matter?" Bobby snapped. He yanked her so hard she nearly lost her feet. Had to run just to keep her balance, and then it was just a matter of following where she was led.

Up ahead, Anna stood beside a massive felled tree. The splintered trunk hidden somewhere far above, atop the mammoth boulders, with only its broken mast littering the side of the highway. A recent fall. Jagged edges so fresh they seemed almost wet. Anna held a section of spiky bush aside with one hand and flagged them in with the other.

Maddy obeyed without question, baseball sliding in and disappearing from view. Anna swore incessantly in Hebrew — a word or two that Carina recognized by meaning; the rest she knew by tone. Bobby ushered Carina in first. Inside, the shoulder dropped from the highway abruptly. The fallen tree balanced precariously between the pavement and a tangle of branches, forming a sheltered hidey-hole, invisible from street level. Carina slid down the loose gravel until she settled beside Maddy. Quiet now, both hands clutching his own cheeks. Bobby came in beside her, then Anna, who let the bush snap back behind her. She pushed them deeper into the shelter, further into the shadows, until they were all crouching painfully, necks bent against the rough bark of the tree above.

"What is—" Carina whispered, but Anna's fingers were on her lips, pinching them shut.

So many questions, all of them vital: What's coming? Would they be safe here? What about Sam and Frankie? Would they be safe? Did they even know?

Carina swallowed them all, closed her eyes, decided that was worse, and looked to Maddy instead. She focused on his face, stubble half-covered by jaw-length hair, long fingers pressing into his cheeks so hard they went white at the knuckles. She reached out and put a hand on his back. Carina hoped he felt the comfort she did not.

***

"Princess, you get back here right now," Frankie hissed, duck-walking through a snag of brambles to sink ankle-deep in a newborn stream. Glacially cold. "I swear to god, when I find you, I'm going to…"

Frankie sighed.

"Probably poke you on the nose. You're so lucky that you're cute and stupid."

He added his knees to the stream and crawled beneath a bridge of thorny branches.

"Hold up," Sam whispered. "Wait for me."

"Why are you whispering?" Frankie asked, not waiting.

"I don't know," Sam said. "The woods? There could be…things?"

"Well, I'm *not* whispering," Frankie said, voice up a notch in volume just to prove it. "Princess! Princess! Your royal Sparkleness! Where are you, stupid pig?!"

"Do pigs know their names?" Sam mused, splashing up behind Frankie. "Or are they like cats?"

"This is no time for philosophy," Frankie snapped, but he let a hand sweep down Sam's forearm. "Thanks for coming to help."

Sam smiled. Half a nod.

Snorts from beyond the next line of shrubbery. Sam went left, Frankie right. Just in time to see something small and distinctly ham-shaped hush through a copse of tall grass and disappear.

"Dang it." Sam snapped his fingers.

"You get back here right this instant, missy, or it is *so many pokes*," Frankie warned.

Another few feet and they were out of the stream, crawling up a short embankment. Then, like a revelation, Princess SparkleHogg was there: standing proudly in the dead center of the highway.

"Did we circle back, or is this a different road?" Sam asked.

Frankie rushed to embrace the pig and, true to his word, poked her firmly in the snout. She wonked in feeble protest, then licked his finger, and he embraced her.

"No, I think this is still the 2," Sam continued, mostly to himself. "We must have cut across the bend, which means the bike's…back…that way."

Sam spun in place as he spoke, a fixed finger extended like a human compass.

"Who's a dirty butthole of a piggy?" Frankie asked, high and friendly. "Is it you? It *is* you."

Princess SparkleHogg neither confirmed nor denied the accusation.

"Honey," Sam said. "I need you to not freak out. Very quietly come over to me, and let's get off the highway."

"Why?" Frankie asked, wrestling himself away the porcine eyes, sparkling like glass in sunlight he could not see.

He had his answer: Frankie looked up to find himself at the tail end of a mob. A thousand strong, at least — and that just from what he could see — wrapping all the way around the bend in the highway, and beyond. The mob was packed in, shoulder to shoulder, every inch of highway blockaded by human flesh. Those at the edges spilled over the embankments, flailed in the bushes, crawled back up to mindlessly tear and snap at the fringes. Barely clothed in scraps of T-shirts, sleeves of jackets, torn and bloodied jeans, missing shoes. Scars and open wounds over weathered skin. All eyes were focused forward, on movement, and if there was mercy, it was this: Sam, Frankie, and Princess SparkleHogg were behind them.

"Nice and easy," Sam whispered. "No noises, no sudden movements, just over…to me…"

Frankie took a tentative step, and Princess SparkleHogg glanced about to see where they might be going.

She spotted the mob. She wriggled her stumpy legs, lashed her snout from side to side, tensed her midsection and — nose pokes be damned — she squealed.

Only one of them turned at the sound.

It used to be a woman. Now it barely registered as human. Every inch of her exposed flesh was criss-crossed with brutal lightning-streak scars. Her hair was black with filth. Teeth broken and rotted. Sunken, exhausted eyes — red beyond bloodshot. A weeping rash streaked from beneath each, still wet with the tears that flowed incessantly.

Only one turned, at first.

But the instant she saw Sam — standing there with hands

outstretched, eyes pleading for a miracle — every single maniac turned as one. Linked. Like they were all watching the same camera feed. When they screamed, just off unison, it sounded like a car crash; a pile-up; fifty vehicles deep, all speeding; the voice of impact, of pure, physical violence. And then they charged.

Instinct failed Sam and Frankie.

Take a picture of every natural disaster, down at the street level, and they'll have one thing in common: those at the front of it — facing down the landslide, the tsunami, the fire — can only watch, rapt, as certain death bears down.

A roiling avalanche of furious bodies. The front-runners tripped up by those behind them — trampled, *absorbed* — hands clawing at faces, one to get past another. Gnashing teeth and wide, frenzied eyes. Not like a crowd of separate beings, but a single, unimaginable mass of flesh with a million faces. And on all of them: hatred.

Blind, naked, primate hate.

Finally, Princess SparkleHogg broke free of Frankie's grip. She hit the cement hard but took it in the hocks and came up running. She was gone in an instant, just a rustle in the grass. It was enough to break Sam and Frankie's trance. They followed without question, diving headfirst down the freshly trampled path — already healing and closing up, as if they'd never walked it — and fled. Heedless of snags and snares, the forest lashing out with countless tiny whips, they ran.

***

"I think they're leaving," Carina whispered sidelong around Anna's fingertips, still clamping her lips shut. "Let's get outta here, before they come back."

Anna seemed to have forgotten her own hand. She pulled it back, pointed up toward the highway, and said:

"Slowly."

They crawled single file up the embankment, every crackle of gravel a gunshot. Anna snaked her head beneath the shrubbery at the shoulder of the road. She watched for a quiet eternity, but the horde was gone.

Something, or somebody, had caught its attention.

Carina said a quiet thanks for whatever had supplied the distraction. She hushed the part of her brain that reiterated, in nasty, accusatory tones, that the Manics don't go after animals.

Lost in self-loathing, Carina ran right into Bobby's outstretched arm. He held her and Maddy back while Anna advanced — small, smooth, silent — toward the bike. She cased the edges, surveyed the street one more time, then waved them forward. Bobby went first, Carina after. She was halfway to the bike when she felt Maddy's absence. He wasn't following. Then she heard it: the soft, insistent clapping. Maddy's warning signal. Bobby looked back to her with open horror. Anna, already moving toward the hinged counter of the bike's bar area, heard it too late.

Hidden from view by the bike, the thing now tumbled forward, pitching headlong onto the asphalt. Both hands on its ears, as if to block out a deafening noise only it could hear. It seized painfully, shivered, then lunged to its knees and tore at an unseen target. Exhausted, it flopped to its side.

It fell facing Anna.

She recoiled, her movements still controlled — made it look like falling on her ass and crab-walking backwards was a planned tactical retreat. She didn't make it far before another spasm wracked the lone Manic, and it snapped to attention. It inclined its head, as though seeing Anna for the first time. She stopped crawling. Every muscle frozen. The large black ovals — a void in space from cheek to eyebrow — on the thing's face bore straight through her.

Carina was hypnotized, too. The Manic was a little on the chubby side, though she could have gotten away with "big boned." Wide hips, broad shoulders — thick elbows and protruding kneecaps bulging through her ragged trousers and torn windbreaker. She was an older woman, or maybe that was just too many years spent out in the elements. Wrinkles recorded a history of disapproving scowls and withering glares. And the eyes — or at least, where they should have been — a sense of depth to that black, like you could stick your hand inside and reach far past the back of the skull. Movement in that dark, tricky and skittish. Shapes that chased away when you focused.

"Get to the bags," Bobby said, charging past Anna. "I can take this one."

Anna didn't argue. She hauled herself up by the bike's rearmost stool and pitched gracelessly over the bar — headfirst, legs cartwheeling after, then gone from sight.

The Manic's features twisted up with more hate than Carina had ever seen. It took in a breath to scream. Bobby didn't break stride. He went from a dead sprint to airborne, both feet forward, body nearly horizontal. He committed to that dropkick like a marriage. The black-eyed woman crumpled around the blow, and the pair of them went sprawling in a tangled heap. Carina finally broke free from her trance and ran. The old instincts demanded, "Where's Maddy? Look for Maddy." Even as she fled in terror, she looked for her brother. Maddy hadn't let the fear paralyze him. He was fifty paces ahead of her and gaining. Not going for the bushes this time, just straight up the empty highway, eyes on the horizon like he'd run until he hit it.

Anna got her hands on the go-bag, ripped the pistol from it, and—

Stop. There was always a second to think. To get just one move ahead of blind reaction. Think. More Manics might follow. The one out there — it would not kill Bobby in a span of seconds. The Manics had the heedless strength of pure adrenaline, but they were not superhuman. Not like the Sleepers. But what of *this* one? It was different. The eyes. Were those stories the civvies told her actually true? If so, all of her rules needed revising.

Regardless, her next, best move was the same, and it was not according to her first instinct. She could not just stand and shoot. It might not be enough to down the Manic, and there was no guarantee of a good sight line from the bar. She had to get mobile. Anna tucked the pistol into her waistband, grabbed the extra clips from the exterior pocket of her rucksack, and dragged Bobby's bag over to her. Zipper back, fingers sliding past clothes and tools and cans to a long, cool barrel. She unsheathed Bobby's shotgun like she was pulling a sword from a stone. She pumped the handgrip. Two shells only. No more time for thinking.

Bobby kicked free from the Manic's frenzy. She clawed at his pant legs, hooked her fingers in his belt, tried to get her teeth around enough flesh to bite, but Bobby wriggled like a little worm on a big fuckin' hook, and managed to slip away. Running on all fours, hands slapping pavement, butt aloft like a lower-case "n," Bobby was twenty feet away by the time the black-eyed woman recovered and began to stand.

Thunder so deep you could feel it in your bowels. The bulk of the shotgun blast caught the Manic in the shoulder, sent her staggering — the left side of her face just mash and gore — but it didn't put her down. Anna vaulted the counter of the bike bar, clipped her knee on one of the stools, and sprawled. Chin first into the pavement, barely breaking her fall with an elbow. She could hear the bones chipping. A strangely artificial sound. More like plastic snapping. She felt around for the shotgun. She could chastise herself for the fool move later.

The black-eyed woman turned to her. Impact rattled, bone shocked, Anna couldn't fully trust her own perception, but she swore the old lady was…smoking?

No, not smoke. Her eye socket shattered, the pool of black within now twisted lazily outward. A thick, dark vapor emanated from the score of pinhole cavities in the woman's face. It moved like mist in a vacuum, too slow to be natural. The Manic probed the side of her ruined face — none of the tentative shock you'd expect; fingers heedless of frayed nerve endings — and snarled. Anna could only watch as the vapor — still the wrong word! Like molasses poured in water; seeping, spreading, pooling atop the air itself — changed. Its edges took on hard shapes. Gnarled barbs and tapered hooks, spear tips and thick blades. Almost fractal in complexity, but not random. Each and every shunt came to a deliberate edge, strop-sharp and deadly.

The black-eyed woman screamed, and the smoke reached out to Anna. It took her by the hand and flayed the skin from it in an instant.

***

Headlong through the brambles, Sam and Frankie went. It was like jogging through a hurricane. From somewhere just behind them, the crash and snap of untold thousands of Manics, shredding their way through the forest. Sam was thankful. Their thoughtless fury actually slowed them down: they tried to force their way past the nastiest snags, while Sam and Frankie could dart through the path of least resistance.

Ha.

Sam could feel the sheen all across his arms, cheeks and neck (blood, sweat, both) — "least resistance" was a misnomer. He took a frantic glance around and realized he could only see the unbroken forest. Green and brown (and a bit of red, where the blood pooled at the edge of his eye). Somewhere along the line, he and Frankie had become separated.

"Sam!" Frankie yelled, from somewhere just beyond the nearest wall of thorns.

He must have realized it at the same time.

"Just keep running!" Sam called back. "I'll find you!"

"I can't find the Princess!" Frankie wailed.

Sam ground his teeth, reminded himself that Frankie's boundless empathy was one of the reasons he loved the idiot, and tried to sound encouraging.

"She'll find us!" he called. "Just like the first time. Move!"

Sam crossed his arms in front of his face — trying not to notice how shredded his sleeves were; making no conscious note of the spreading dampness beneath the fabric — and plunged into the spot where the thorns seemed sparsest.

Partway through the hedge, one of the larger branches caught him across the collar. The thorns found wide purchase: dozens of snares marching all the way across his shoulders. Sam tried to spin around, tried to loosen its hold, but only wrapped himself deeper. More branches, more thorns — the forest closing in now, a single giant predatory plant, reaching out with its thousand toothy tendrils — and Sam was caught. Somewhere behind him — he couldn't even turn his head to watch death approach — the Manics closed in. They had to be flayed to the bone by now. It was a wonder they weren't entirely stuck, ensnared like he was.

Then, Sam realized, they probably were. The foremost of the pack were likely woven into the thorns back by the side of the highway. They'd be forgotten there, slowly becoming one with the foliage like rusting old cars. But there were others behind them. When the frontrunners fell, or became trapped, more pushed past them. A frothing tsunami of psychopaths, spilling into every open space. Sam closed his eyes and tried to make his last thoughts meaningful, but they kept circling back to one, ignoble phrase:

"That fucking pig."

The silence came so suddenly Sam thought, for a moment, that he must already be dead. And he was grateful that it was so quick and painless. But then, a howl of pure, focused hatred, growing…

…fainter?

The horde was moving away from him now. Receding, like the flow had hit its tidal mark, and all the psychopaths were being drawn inexorably back from whence they came. When he was absolutely sure the mob was gone, that they couldn't possibly hear him over their own stampeding retreat, Sam called out for Frankie.

Again, and again.

There was no answer.

***

Black vapor streamed from the woman's shattered ocular cavity, crept up Anna's hand. Fingertips to knuckles to wrist. The border of skin, only just visible where the darkness met flesh, was raw and bloody. As the serrated edges crawled ever upward, she could see her own flesh puckering before it, then being shunted away like curtains caught in a vacuum cleaner.

Bobby was up and running before he had time to think about it. He barreled into Anna, carrying the both of them down and away from the knife-edged smoke, left it whirling in place like a blender. They hit the pavement, hard. No time to think about the pain. Bobby pushed Anna to her feet and shoved her away. She ran without question, charged blindly through the thorny hedges at the highway's shoulder and disappeared into the greenery. The black fog wafted, directionless, then plunged with renewed purpose toward Bobby. He rolled away from its grasp — only barely, just barely — and stood.

Only barely.

Just barely.

His elbows and knees throbbed. He had to fight to keep his vision from swimming. He couldn't make a strong fist with his right hand.

Bobby shifted his focus beyond the old woman. The highway behind her. Empty. The gays were still missing. The girl and her idiot brother gone, fled around the farthest bend, and never looking back, if they were smart. Anna safe (safe-ish) somewhere in the forest off to the north side of the highway. To the south side, the other Manics — that thousand-strong mob — still thrashed, tore, and screamed. They were heading his way.

The old woman with the shattered face, the black eyes, the wild snarl. She hadn't moved since that first lash. Bobby hadn't, either.

A showdown then. Just the two of them.

A lonely whistle played in Bobby's mind. Just two cowboys squaring off on a dusty road, hands itching at their holsters, frozen in anticipation of the bloody draw. He wished he had a revolver to palm. Wouldn't do much good — if the crazy old bat shrugged off a shotgun blast, she wouldn't even shrug at a pistol — but it would complete the part.

Bobby didn't have the props to play at Clint Eastwood. Just a torn T-shirt, some bloody jeans, and a right hand that wouldn't even make a fist.

Well fine, then. He'd play a different role.

Bobby worked his heel up and down in his worn sneakers.

"Bruce Fuckin' Willis," he told the old woman.

She registered confusion, briefly. The razorblade smoke twisted idly, unmoved by the breeze. The Manic was still waiting for the draw.

Poor bitch didn't realize she was in the wrong movie.

Bobby worked his foot totally free and kicked his loose shoe up at her face. She ducked to the side. Not quick enough: the sneaker bonked pointlessly off of her shoulder and flopped to the pavement. She glanced down at it, and back up — to find Bobby charging.

***

"BRUCE. FUCKIN'. WILLIS."

Frankie flinched at the sound. He'd been so lost in the search for Princess SparkleHogg, the whole world had been on mute. Bobby's shout burned away the fog, and Frankie saw reality again. Volume up, detail resolved. With it, fear. The distant snap and snarl of the Manics, thrashing against the thorns somewhere just behind him.

Bobby's hoarse scream.

And something closer. Howling. Frustration. Desperation. Fear.

…fear?

Frankie waited for the call to repeat. It did not. Just beyond the copse of fir, right in the worst of the thorns. That's where it came from. One more survey of the empty woods around him. Willing a tiny defiant pig snout into existence, just poking through the roots there. Snuffling around that gnarled trunk. Honking at him from the bushes. Skipping into his arms.

Nothing.

Frankie sighed at his own naiveté, then gently pried open a gap in the tangle of vines, nearest where he heard the cry. He saw the source of the struggle: a man, or something like it, caught in a web of thorns. The vines held the creature immutably: wrapped around its arms, laced across its back, looped through its legs. A human being would hold as still as possible in that situation, but this thing flailed and kicked like a toddler in a tantrum, sinking the thorns ever deeper. It howled again — blind, senseless fury — and that clinched it for Frankie.

He'd only imagined the humanity in that voice. This thing…this was not a person.

He eased the vines back. He turned away.

He heard it speak his name.

"Sam?" he answered.

Frankie lunged back into the wall of thorns. Wrenching the vines aside, snapping what he could, shoving through what he couldn't.

"Sammy?" he called again.

"Here!" Sam said. "I'm here! Is that you? Is that really—"

And Frankie was through — what felt like half his flesh left behind, but free of the snares. He hurled himself into Sam's arms, but they could not hold him.

"Oh, Sammy," he whimpered. The countless cuts cleaving apart Sam's flawless skin. The blood seeping into his soft brown eyes. "You're a fucking mess."

They both laughed, desperate for it.

Frankie extracted the thorns, unwrapped the vines, worked Sam's clothing free from the brambles. Sam just stood there, limp, like a child being dressed by his mother. When he was sure he was free, he hugged Frankie so fiercely that he began to see spots. When Frankie could breathe again, he said, "I'm sorry."

"You should be!" Sam snapped. "But did you find her?"

"No," he said. "I think…I think she's gone…"

Frankie tried to keep the quiver from his voice. He failed miserably.

"Come on, now," Sam said. "She found us in the first place, remember? She was doing just fine before we came along, and she'll do just fine now…"

Frankie sighed.

"We need to find the others," Sam said. "Then we'll *all* find her."

Frankie nodded, perfunctory, automatic, unconvinced.

***

"It's okay, it's fine, it's going to be fine, just fine." The words streamed from Carina's mouth without pause or meaning. "It's all okay. Okay. Okay? Okay."

Her lips to Maddy's ear, voice so soft it took no breath, her eyes locked, unblinking, on the small gap in the shrubbery, looking out onto the road. Maddy watched the ground. He stirred the dirt with his fingers and sifted out the tiny stones. He dug out a little pathway for a sparse party of ants, scattered and seemingly lost. Unable to see over the imperceptible swells in the dirt that must look like mountains to them. He herded each ant down the path of least resistance, until they all met up again. Madding dug them a highway, and the ants traveled it. Together.

Carina's eyes burned, but she could not blink. As long as she watched, everything would be okay. It was an uneasy deal she'd made with the world, and even the fraction of a second between blinks would allow for tragedy.

She didn't blink when Bobby tackled Anna away from the Manic's grasp.

Was grasp the right word?

There was something pouring from its left eye.

Was pouring the right word?

Whatever it was, it didn't waft like smoke — it didn't dissipate in the air or shift with the breeze — but it wasn't bound by gravity, like a fluid. There was no variation in color, no texture, nothing to allow for depth or shape. Just a pure, impenetrable black that flowed across the air like spilled ink.

She was too far away, her vision blurred by welling tears; Carina couldn't trust her own eyes. She swore that the spilling black was actually barbed at the edges. That it stripped the flesh away from Anna's hand effortlessly, like sliding a sheet of paper across marble. But that couldn't be true. That was crazy. Yet she dared not blink back the tears. Not even to get a better look at what was happening. That would mean looking away, and bad things happened whenever she looked away.

Bobby blindly charged in — that was his default state, "blindly charging in" — and tackled Anna free. Her, up and running in an instant. Fear and pain honing her reflexes. Bobby took longer to recover. By the time he got to his feet, the Manic had already shifted its focus. It lashed out with the black smoke — less like movement, more like a tear in the world expanding — but Bobby stumbled out of its range.

They stood facing one another for so long that Carina wondered if something had just broken in reality. God sat on the pause button. The program froze up and crashed. End of episode. To be continued.

"It's good, it's all good, everything is fine and good," she ushered the words into Maddy's ear. Poured him full of placations. More about tone of voice than meaning. More about pretending than believing.

Bobby screamed. Carina heard the words clear as day.

"BRUCE," he said and broke into a headlong charge.

"FUCKIN'," his fists held up and ready.

"WILLIS!" Feet leaving the ground, forearms out in a protective cross.

Carina blinked.

She would never forgive herself.

The black rift danced outward, forked like lightning — the wrong words, again; always the wrong words; more like watching a time-lapse of a river, as it branches out into tributaries — and smothered Bobby's face. It broke across his shoulders, moved down his body in rapid stops and starts — the motion reminded Carina of a pelican, eating: head back, throat open, harking the fish down whole — and then Bobby was gone.

He should have hit the Manic. Even if the smoke flayed him in mid-air, his forward motion should have carried him straight through it and into the thing's chest. Both of them tumbling painfully, rolling across the pavement. A nest of kicks and swears, spit and blood.

Nothing.

The blackness from the Manic's eye swallowed him whole, and Bobby was nothing. No body. No blood. Nothing left to fall to the earth, nothing left to put beneath the earth.

"All fine. All good and fine and okay," Carina whispered, while Maddy piled some dirt and shaped it into a wall. He built his ants a fortress.

***

It took ages for Sam and Frankie to find the highway again. They couldn't have been more than a hundred yards from it. But their whole world had shrank to a matter of feet — to the next tangle of thorns in front of them, then to the wall of trees beyond that, then to the eking pathways they carved out with stinging palms and bloody fingers. When they finally crested the last hill and pushed through the last patch of brambles, the open highway felt wrong. Temporary agoraphobia. A fear of a world without thorns.

There, Madding and Carina. Sam had been wordless for so long that he struggled to remember how humans greeted one another.

The siblings sat on their respective stools at the bike-bar. Madding pumped his feet counterclockwise in great rattling cartwheels, no resistance while backpedaling, and then inched them forward just enough to rock the bike. Never enough to actually move it. Carina was rambling to herself, barely pausing for breath, her whisper so soft Sam could only catch the barest edge of the occasional hard consonant.

"What happened?" Sam said. "Hi. Hello. Hello to you. Carina?"

"What?" It took a few seconds for her to come around. Even then, her eyes were unfocused, like Sam had just woken her from the depths of a dream.

"How are you?" Sam asked. "Are you okay?"

"Yeah, I…I think we are. Are you? Is anybody?"

"Sweetie, c'mere." Frankie stepped in, pulled Carina's head to his shoulder. He shot Sam a disbelieving glare. "She's in shock, dummy."

"Oh, right," Sam said.

He had honestly forgotten that was a thing. Who had time for it?

Then he held out his own hands and found them shivering violently.

A few minutes of cooing and Frankie had nursed Carina back to reality. Enough to speak, at least.

"What happened?" Sam asked again. "Are Bobby and Anna okay?"

"No," Carina said.

Content to leave it at that.

"Are they hurt? Are they dead? Are they gone?" With each question mark, a flinch from Carina.

"Sammy," Frankie said, fixed him in that den mother stare, "go take a minute."

"But I just—"

"Go on."

Sam swallowed his questions and stalked away from the bike. He looked away. Prodded at the hedges. Kicked at the dust.

"Darlin'." Frankie brushed Carina's short, frizzy hair behind her ears. It sprang back defiantly. "You can take your time, okay? You can put it together as best you can, and nobody is going to blame you for anything. Judgment-free zone, girl. We just need to know what happened, plain as you can."

"There were…things," she said. She looked to Frankie. Seeking permission to continue.

"We know," he said. "Go on."

"Angry ones. So many," Carina shivered. "And…and one of the black-eyed things was with them."

"Oh, god." Frankie squeezed her arm. Muscle, skin, bone, nothing else — a body built by starvation and exhaustion. "I'm so sorry…"

"It hurt Anna," Carina said, and her words tumbled into each other, picking up momentum. "Her hand. Its eyes. She shot it. And then the black stuff, like smoke but water and—"

"Honey, honey, okay." Frankie nudged her chin up, forcing eye contact. "A little slower."

"Anna shot the black-eyed one in the face," Carina said, carefully. "This black ooze or…smoke or…I don't know what. It came out and hurt Anna's hand, but she got away. She ran that way."

Carina pointed toward the woods. Thankfully, to the side away from the Manics.

"But Bobby tried to fight it," Carina continued. "He lost. It just…ate him. Or not even that. It swallowed him up, like he fell into a dark hole and just never hit bottom."

"It's not your fault," Frankie said. "You know that, right?"

"I…" She faltered. Looked to Maddy, still spinning his pedals. "I blinked. I shouldn't have done that."

"That doesn't matter," Frankie said. "I know right now you think it does. I know you're going to find any way you can to blame yourself for this, but it's not you. You didn't do anything, and you couldn't do anything. It was them. It was only ever them. Okay?"

Carina didn't respond.

"I know, honey," Frankie said. "I know you don't *believe* me right now. I just need you to *say* it. Can you do that?"

"It wasn't my fault," Carina repeated. Like a phrase she'd memorized from a foreign travel dictionary.

"That's good. Even if you don't believe it, you need to say it every time you think about this. It will help."

Carina nodded. It didn't mean she understood. It just meant an end to the conversation.

"Are they gone now?" Frankie asked. "The Manics? They just left?"

"They came running when the black-eyed one screamed. It led them that way."

She gestured back up the highway.

"Sammy," Frankie called.

Sam startled at his name. He looked back. Frankie had one hand resting on Carina's upper arm, fingers spread wide, maximizing skin contact. He did the same thing to Sam, when Sam was upset. For a flash, it made him jealous. He dismissed it as stupid in an instant, but the feeling still lingered.

"Bobby didn't make it," Frankie said.

Sam was disappointed in himself, that he even bothered to feign distress.

"But Anna might be around here somewhere, and she might be hurt," Frankie continued, pointing in the direction Carina had indicated.

"I'll look," Sam said. "Are those things still out there?"

"They followed the highway, back the way we came."

Sam nodded. A task. A mission. Something meaningful. He practically skipped into action.

He broke through the bushes and disappeared in a flash.

"Oh god," Carina's eyes went wild. She shook Frankie's hand away and jumped from her stool. "The kids!"

"What?" Frankie said.

"The kids! Back in that town." Carina spun in place, looking for something that wasn't there. "The town we cut through, remember? That's where they're going, the Manics…"

"You don't know that," Frankie said.

Maddy grumbled. Deep, with a whining edge. A wounded animal, cornered.

"I do know!" Carina laughed. "The Sleepers? Remember? They were blocking off the town. We knew something was coming even then, and now this. This proves it. We have to go back."

Maddy picked up the distress in Carina's voice. He echoed it. Amplified it. He slapped the counter with his big, flat palms.

"We can't," Frankie said. "What would we even do?"

"Warn them," she spat.

"They wouldn't listen," Frankie said. "Do *you* remember? We tried to talk to them!"

"Then we'll *make* them listen," Carina said. "We have to. They'll die!"

"Honey," Frankie stood, walked toward her, tried to coax the panic out of her again, but she wouldn't have it. She stepped back.

"Don't," she said. "This is real."

"There are literally thousands of monsters on the only road between us and them," Frankie pleaded. "We couldn't get past them."

"We could try!" Carina snapped.

She moved to the front of the bike and grabbed the handlebars, trying to wrestle it around and get it pointed back up the highway.

"Stop," Frankie said, "you're not thinking. You're still rattled."

He knew it was the wrong thing to say, even as he said it.

"I am not!" she screamed and seemed startled by her own ferocity. "Maddy, help me with the bike…"

Madding stood and grabbed the bar by its rear corners. With him pushing and her steering, it started to turn.

Frankie lunged for the brake, but Carina slapped his hand away.

"We're going," she said, mounting the saddle, feet on the pedals.

Madding stood at the back, already pushing toward a moving start.

"We have to wait for Sam," Frankie said. "Then we'll go with you."

She paused, but only for a second.

"You're lying," she said.

"I…" Frankie threw up his hands. "This is suicide! Don't go!"

"This is just how it was," she said. All the urgency drained right out of her voice. "Back in our neighborhood, when all this first went down. The adults had so many reasons not to help us. It was always too dangerous, or pointless, or stupid. We had to save ourselves."

Madding was picking up speed, helping the bike break through its inertia. He hopped aboard his stool. Carina stood on her pedals.

"We still do," she said.

"Don't," Frankie called.

He jogged alongside them, pleading, like he was running for a train at the end of a romantic comedy.

Carina wouldn't even look at him. Frankie stopped to glance back at the spot where Sam should have been. He hopped in place, smacked his own thighs with balled-up fists. The bike had hit a long, slow downhill grade. It was too fast and too far gone to catch on foot. Frankie screamed, high and wordless. He kicked at nothing. Blinked the tears from his eyes. He sat down where he was, right in the middle of a shattered highway, and dug his fingernails into the flesh of his palms.

***

"Anna," Sam called.

Not loud enough. Too frightened of what else might be listening.

"Anna!" he yelled.

The sound was shattering. He expected to hear frantic wings as every bird in a half mile radius scattered, snarls of interest from the monsters surely lurking behind every bush, a small avalanche from the snowy mountains far above him.

He heard nothing.

Then, finally, so hurt and small it didn't sound like her at all, Anna answered.

"Over here."

Sam found her burrowed down between two gigantic roots, her back to the towering fir, clutching one bloody hand to her breast. Pale. Too pale. Like she'd covered herself in stage makeup to play a frail countess, dying of consumption. With every exhale, she shook so violently that her teeth chattered.

"Jesus, Anna," Sam said, and he rushed to her. Fell to his knees between hers and reached out.

She sneered at the gesture.

She said something Sam didn't understand. But he caught the venom in her tone.

"What?" Sam asked.

"Stupid girl!" she snapped. "Just like a stupid girl!"

"I didn't have any choice! You saw him take off after that pig—"

"Not you." She laughed, bitter as old coffee. "Me. A little scrape and I run away like a stupid girl."

Another string of what Sam assumed to be vibrant profanity, in a language he didn't know.

"You're only human," Sam said.

Anna kicked him in the chest. Sent him sprawling in the mulch.

"Soldier!" Anna said, awkwardly trying to stand without use of her wounded arm. She was too deep into the roots and couldn't manage it.

"Soldier first!"

Sam stood and offered her his hand. She took it. Skin like cold marble.

"Well, this is hardly a 'little scrape,'" Sam said, nodding toward the wound she wouldn't let him see. The growing bloodstain she couldn't hide.

She nestled her hand deeper into the jacket.

"Bobby is…" Sam started. Couldn't finish.

"I know," Anna said. "I knew as soon as I ran."

She spat in the dirt. The dry earth absorbed it without a sound, and this bothered her. She kicked a clump of dirt and swore again, in that language like snakes fighting.

"Come," she said, straightening up. "Let's go find that thing and kill it."

"It's gone," Sam said. "They're all gone now."

"Then we'll find where it went."

"God, no! We'll go the other way as far and as fast as we can."

"It does not get to do this," Anna said, shrugging down at her ruined hand. "It does not get to do that to Bobby and live. You understand that?"

"I don't understand anything," Sam said. "Except that it's a miracle we survived, and I'm pretty sure you only get one miracle."

Her face twitched. A single frame of rage, gone so fast he couldn't be sure he even saw it.

"Let's get back to the road," Anna said.

She marched toward a break in the overgrowth.

"It's this way," Sam said, pointing back toward the path he'd stomped down.

She swore so loud it hurt his eyeballs, somehow, then abruptly changed course and stormed off. This time in the right direction.

***

Frankie barely stirred when the bushes rustled. If it was something coming to kill him, it could just do it already.

He was almost disappointed when Anna broke through the brambles, one hand tucked inside her canvas jacket, a pool of red growing around it.

And then, Sammy.

Frankie didn't remember standing, much less running across the highway and into Sam's arms. Frankie sobbed until he was breathless, used that breath to huff Sam's smell — beneath the sweat, the old clothes, the metal of the blood; his real smell, indescribable as it was unmistakable — then sobbed again.

"Shh," Sam said. The exhaustion in it was heartbreaking. "I was only gone a minute. It's going to be okay."

Frankie laughed.

"No," he said. "It's really not."

He smiled weakly at Sam.

Anna cleared her throat. When that didn't work, she coughed. When that didn't work, she said, "Stop hugging now."

They did, and Sam nearly collapsed when Frankie stepped away. He'd been using the embrace for support.

"Where are the others?" Anna asked. "How far are we from the bike?"

Frankie hummed uncertainly.

"Hey, wait," Sam said. "What—"

"Where did we come out?" Anna cut him off. She looked up and down the expanse of highway, then spotted her discarded shotgun. Her blood staining the road beside it.

"Where is the bike?" she said. This time, an accusation.

"They took it," Frankie answered. He couldn't look at her. Couldn't look at anybody. "Carina and Maddy, the…horde, those things, the old woman with the black, they…"

He gestured at nothing. Everything. He fell silent.

"Take your time," Sam said. He made small circles on Frankie's back. Tried to emulate Frankie's own soothing tricks.

"Bobby, he is…" Anna stared at the shotgun. Locked onto it like she was watching a venomous snake, waiting for the strike.

"Gone," Frankie confirmed.

"Yes." She bit her lip and nodded. "But his body. I need to see…"

"No," Frankie said. "He's gone. Carina saw it. That black stuff, the old woman — it took him completely. Swallowed him up."

Anna blinked back tears. Glared at Sam and Frankie, just in case they saw it.

"Hey, where *is* Carina?" Sam asked.

"I was trying to tell you," Frankie said. "She…they thought the horde was going for the kids. That town full of kids we passed back there. Her and Maddy, they took the bike and…"

"And you didn't stop them?" Anna spat.

"What was I supposed to do? Kill them?"

"Yes, if necessary!" In a heartbeat, she'd lunged over and snatched up the shotgun.

She pointed it at Frankie's chest and pulled the trigger.

Sam screamed. Frankie jumped. The gun clicked.

"Are you fucking crazy?" Sam slapped the barrel away from Frankie, stood between him and Anna.

"It's empty!" she said. "No more bullets. No more food. No more water. No more clothes."

"The bags," Frankie whispered.

"*The bags*," Anna mimicked. "Everything we had was on that bike, and we will never catch it on foot."

Sam closed his eyes and exhaled for a solid minute. When he was finished, he said, "Shit."

***

Anna had forgotten the hardship of walking. Foolish. Stupid. Spoiled. She had grown accustomed to the bike. To sharing the load with the others, all pedaling together, the mile markers filing by so fast it was not worth it to watch them. Now, on foot, each one was a taunt. All day, day after day, in bad boots and in bad weather. So much effort. So much time and pain. For one single mile.

And then the next.

All while nursing her wounds, the others nursing theirs, and none of them speaking.

What was left to say?

They survived on blackberries and streams at first, easy and plentiful right there, at the side of the highway. Until they came through the pass and the terrain changed. Then just puddle water and grass. Burning in the sun, freezing in the night. They did eight miles, the first day out of the mountains. Twelve the next. Then seven. Five. They were dying on their feet. She paused to stare at a highway sign. It listed the distances to the next towns. She stared at it so long the others, always trailing behind — she made sure they did, no matter how much the effort cost her — caught up. They watched the numbers in silence. One by one, they moved on.

Eighty miles.

That was the first number, the nearest town. It may well have been across the ocean.

That didn't mean there wasn't a gas station. An unlooted roadside store, a forgotten home, an abandoned car stocked with supplies. It was the only thing that kept her hoping.

Until it didn't.

She could smell her hand, turning. The blood gone solid, gone greasy black. The wound wrapped in her undershirt. Already filthy when she'd taken it off and growing ranker by the minute.

She looked to the boys. Just boys. Not men. They were weak and soft, but they would keep each other going. Surviving if only so the other would not have to watch them die. Survival was the only option.

For Anna, survival was habit. It was all she'd ever done. As long as she could remember. As a girl in a house with too many boys. In the army. In the factory. After the skies went dark. How long could habit alone keep you alive?

And then, a miracle:

"Hush," she said, though she couldn't actually remember the last time any of them had bothered speaking.

They had made camp — they had made nothing; had just collapsed where they stood, and simply waited for it grow light enough to walk again — in a pullout alongside the highway. A scenic viewpoint. Or it used to be. Now the tall, brown grass had taken over the hill beyond the guardrail, as it had everything else. There was no more view.

Anna pointed to the grass nearest the guardrail and waited. A tentative rustle. Another.

She held her breath, struggled to get to her feet, one-handed and in loose gravel, without making a noise.

A honk and a snort.

Anna paused.

The pig nosed its way through the dry grass, saw the three of them sitting there dumbfounded, and squealed in delight. Its little hooves plonking the pavement like a marimba, it trotted over to Frankie and leapt into his lap.

"Princess!" he whispered.

Frankie instantly and savagely wept.

Sam put his hands to his mouth and keened, tears in his eyes, too.

Anna laughed.

A lucky break, at last.

"Boys," she said. "We have dinner!"

"Oh no, we do not," Frankie said. He hugged the pig and turned his body as far from Anna as he could. "Never in a million years."

"She's joking," Sam said, and he smiled at Anna.

"The hell I am!" she snapped. Even she jumped at the sound. They had barely spoken above a croak in days, when they had spoken at all. "We need to eat. We'll get some hydration from the blood and meat. It will give us another few days, at least."

They stared at her as though she had just sprouted horns.

She pointed at the pig.

Sam moved between her and it.

She waited for logic to kick in, for Sam's eyes to change from defensive conviction to grim acceptance, but it did not happen.

In a flash, Anna had the pistol out from her waistband.

The two men could only gape.

Secrets always hold hands with survival.

"You had that the whole time?" Sam said.

"You can't!" Frankie pleaded. "She's one of us!"

"It is a pig!" Anna laughed again. She turned the gun sideways a bit — showing them how ludicrous the situation was. She moved it back upright when Sam took a step forward. "It is our lives or its life. That is the way it is!"

Sam didn't move. Frankie stroked the pig's forehead gently, and it snuffled in response.

"I cannot believe this," she said. "You're serious?"

"Deadly," Sam said.

"Completely," Frankie said.

Anna swore and jumped and kicked the air. When her energy fizzled out, she returned the pistol to her waistband and slumped to the gravel.

"Thank you," Sam said.

"Idiot boys," she replied. "Dead idiot boys."

***

In the morning, Anna was gone. Sam asked if they should look for her. Frankie said she didn't want to be found. He'd seen her face when they shielded Princess SparkleHogg. Anna was done playing with the three of them.

Who could blame her?

They walked all morning. Heat-sore and starving, they made slow progress, even by their standards. Frankie tried to carry the Princess at first, but after fifteen minutes, he had to admit he was too tired. She walked beside him. Trotting at his heels. Slowing her pace to match his.

Princess SparkleHogg tried to duck off the highway around…noon? High noon? Whatever time it was, when the sun was highest in the sky. If there had been a sun. If there had been a sky, instead of an unbroken black curtain from horizon to horizon, the diffuse light filtering through its unseen pores. But it was bright, and hot, and the heat seemed to come from directly overhead.

May as well be noon, then.

The pig sniffed at the air, scented something, and followed its trail to the shoulder. Frankie tried to wrangle her back to the road. Momentum was the only thing keeping him and Sam on their feet — they could not stop. They wouldn't get up again. But the Princess was adamant, and far nimbler than Frankie. She ducked through his slow hands, danced around his ankles, and when it became apparent that he would not follow her, she shouldered her way through the tall grass and disappeared.

Frankie sighed. It turned into a sob. A dry one. He was too dehydrated to cry.

"What is it?" Sam croaked. God, he sounded awful. Like the vibrations alone were tearing dry, flaky layers away from the inside of his throat.

"The Princess," Frankie answered. Jesus! He sounded worse. "She…"

He gave up trying to clear away the rasp in his voice. He just nodded toward the grass where she'd gone.

"I'll go get her," Sam said.

He had to be as tired as Frankie. More so. They had last eaten at the same time, the same amount, the same thing — a handful of underripe berries, days ago — they had last drank at the same time — a stream mere inches across, winding its way across the highway, tasting like dust and asphalt. Yesterday morning. They had walked the same distance. Slept in the same gravel.

And yet Sam volunteered to go after Frankie's silly pig without a second thought.

He'd always been like this. Always took the bullet, even when no one asked. It made Frankie blazing mad for a split second, then grateful, followed by a deep flush of love.

Sam struggled to throw one leg over the guardrail, parted the tall grass, and disappeared. Frankie felt his muscles melting. Just sit. Right here. Lay down on the road and never get up again.

He shuffled in small circles instead. Momentum.

Then a sharp cry.

Frankie vaulted the guardrail, plunged headlong into the grass, tripped over an unseen root, got back to his feet, then down a rocky gulley and started up the far bank — clawing up fistfuls of dirt, trying to get a grip to climb, hauling himself up by sheer will alone. It was Sam's voice that cried out. Frankie's body answered with all it had left.

Down the other side of the hill, too fast, careening off of trees, falling, standing, crawling — to find Sam just standing there. Watching Princess SparkleHogg root at the base of a large white tree.

"What?" Frankie croaked. "What's wrong?"

Sam held up two fistfuls of something Frankie couldn't discern.

"Mushrooms!" he said. He shook his fists at Frankie, and pale scraps of fungus fell out. Hit the damp earth without a sound.

Damp…earth?

Frankie took a tentative step, wary of dispersing what was certainly a mirage. He touched Sam's shoulder. Solid.

"How do we know they're not poisonous?" he asked.

Sam laughed again. It was a terrible sound. Like throwing a stack of old magazines on a dried-out leather chair.

"*She's* eating them!" he answered.

They both looked to Princess SparkleHogg, tearing another mouthful of caps from the large mound of fungus that grew at the base of the tree.

"I forgot pigs do this!" Sam said. "*This is what pigs do*!"

He offered up a fistful of dirty, half-mashed stems. Frankie took them.

They say everything tastes good when you're hungry.

They lie.

But Frankie forced them down anyway, and then another handful.

One more after that.

Clusters of mushrooms grew in the shady spaces beneath nearly every tree. Sam took off his T-shirt — his big brown belly long gone, ribs poking through like root systems beneath his skin — and gathered up as many mushrooms as it would hold.

When she was done snacking, the Princess sniffed the air again and led them around a heath to a narrow creek, running strong and clear and ice cold. She lapped at its edges. Sam and Frankie hurled themselves into it face-first, yelping at the cold even as they devoured it.

It was too much. Frankie's belly cramped up, and he had to lie on his side for twenty minutes until the pain finally eased. They agreed to stay in the grove overnight, drinking as much as possible, eating all they could, finding every excuse to delay leaving.

"We can't just live here," Sam said.

"Why not?" Frankie laughed. "We'll build mushroom houses, like the Smurfs. You be Sensible Smurf and I'll be Sexy Smurf."

"Those aren't actual Smurfs," Sam said, frowning.

Frankie grinned at him so ferociously his chapped lips split.

On the road, Frankie once again tried to carry the Princess, but she preferred instead to trundle alongside him, occasionally disappearing into the woods to sniff out more mushrooms, berries, roots, tubers, and water.

Did water have a smell?

Frankie couldn't have told you, but the Princess could sense it on the air.

She kept them alive and well enough to move. Black days, blacker nights. No stars, no sun, no moon — just sourceless light the color of dishwater, or none at all. They slept in clearings, weigh stations, the occasional abandoned car. They camped a few days in a place called Orondo. Not even a town. Like somebody figured a few buildings were needed, just to break up the scenery. Sam and Frankie set up inside The Marketplace — the settlement's only gas station/grocery store/reason for being — and pilfered what supplies they could. There wasn't much left. Sam found a can of Cream of Mushroom soup, kicked beneath a shelving unit and forgotten. They both laughed about it, to keep from crying.

Always mushrooms.

Princess SparkleHogg found a patch of thistles to eat and looked to Sam and Frankie expectantly. They heaped her with praise and adoration every time she sniffed out water or something edible, and she'd come to treasure her role as lead scout and forager. But the Princess could tell Sam and Frankie's enthusiasm for the thistles was feigned, and she sulked about it for the rest of the morning. Curly-cue tail down, ears limp. She didn't perk up until she found a puddle later that afternoon, which Sam and Frankie drank from — big smiles and happy voices — until the Princess was satisfied. The next day they raided the elementary school. Cans of pudding—

"It's expired."

"Does pudding expire?"

"Everything expires."

"Don't be goth."

—which tasted like ambrosia after their days of wild mushrooms. Juice packs—

"Okay, I know juice expires."

"Don't worry, no juice has ever been anywhere near a Capri Sun."

—and a nursing station full of first aid supplies. For minor injuries only (ibuprofen, gauze, alcohol), but Sam and Frankie had plenty of those to spare. Long scrapes and tiny stinging cuts going red and raw. Wiped clean. Steven Universe Band-Aids for Frankie; Ninja Turtle Band-Aids for Sam. That afternoon, pillaging a few houses yielded up a sleeping bag—

"Just the one, though."

"You're opposed to snuggling?"

—two large thermoses, a pair of hiking boots that only just fit Frankie, a pair of New Balance that didn't fit Sam at all, and a jaunty little Captain's jacket for the Princess. It came from a stuffed animal. Frankie tried to get her to wear the matching hat, but it wouldn't stay on. They left on the third morning, having thoroughly exhausted everything Orondo had to offer in less than forty-eight hours.

Some people lived their whole lives in that town. A lot of people died there.

Days of dust and pollen, cracked roads and cracked lips. Empty thermoses. A trail of discarded juice packs trailing behind like a modern-day Hansel and Gretel. Nights cool, clear, three to a sleeping bag: Sam big spoon, Frankie little spoon, Princess SparkleHogg tiny spoon. Until one day Frankie pulled up short and tugged on Sam's sleeve.

Sam had been lost in a road fugue — just endless pavement, one foot in front of the other, repeat forever — and he hadn't seen the tower.

But Frankie was keeping an eye on Princess SparkleHogg. She danced in and out of the ditches and gullies alongside the highway. Foraging, or perhaps just bored. She ducked out of sight, and Frankie watched the tall grass, waiting for her to emerge from her latest expedition. That's when he first saw the shining white spire.

Must have been a cloud formation. One of those weird ones that had some crazy name that only weather nerds knew.

Maybe a trick of the light. Sun reflecting off of an unseen lake or something.

A hallucination? Too long on the road.

Heatstroke?

Frankie leaned to the side, down, around, every angle, closed one eye — the tower remained. A hundred stories tall if it was an inch, shining so brilliant white he couldn't make out any details on it. Just a featureless shining pinnacle that broke the black sky clean in half.

"What am I looking at?" Sam said.

"That." Frankie pointed.

"That what?"

"The white tower, dummy!"

"Y-you see that, too?"

"I know! I thought it was a mirage or something but look—"

Frankie grabbed Sam by the wrist — so thin now, even Frankie's short fingers encircled it easily — and pulled him about in every direction. When Sam was satisfied that it wasn't some kind of illusion, he said, "Okay, but…what is it?"

"I don't know," Frankie whispered. "We have to find out, right?"

"It could be a spotlight or something," Sam said. "A signal."

"During the day? You wouldn't see it. Right? Or maybe you would, with it being all black. But it wouldn't look like this. That's clearly solid. That's…"

"Something," Sam finished.

Princess SparkleHogg followed their gaze to the horizon, traced it back to their faces, and back out to the horizon. She didn't see what the big deal was. She peed on a dandelion instead.

The tower was farther away than it looked. Without any distinguishing features, it was impossible to place the spire's actual distance. They thought it might be mere miles, but it wound up taking days to reach. Sam, Frankie, and the Princess meandered through a series of small towns that flowed into one another — each distinguished by a signpost, and nothing more — all heading toward The Grand Coulee Dam.

Or where it used to be.

The dam was broken. Long broken. A canyon of jagged concrete split it in two, right down the center. The reservoir, drained. The lakebed beneath it now dried out. The Columbia still cut through the valley, swift and deep, and exited at the break in the dam. On either side, well back from its shores: a city.

Well, a settlement.

Well, people and buildings.

Makeshift structures slapped together from corrugated iron, particle board, tarps, car hoods, old doors nailed together — whatever the settlers could get their hands on. A few of the larger buildings actually looked engineered, though still built from mismatched lumber, variegated hues of oak, pine, birch, and plywood making them look older than they were. Tents in every space between. Small, one-man camping tents. Enormous multi-family tents — the kind with subdivided walls and zip-out windows. Army tents. Fair tents. Fluorescent orange, black, camouflage, plain canvas, and every color between.

There were rudimentary streets, unpaved, marked out with stones and bleeding dust. And everywhere, people — real, normal people, not screaming, not tearing out their hair, not statue-still and waiting to strike — went about their days, like nothing was amiss. Like the sky above hadn't gone vantablack and eaten the stars, the sun and the moon together. Like a mammoth tower of impossible, unnatural white wasn't erupting from the ground at the heart of their city, surging thousands of feet straight up into the air. Vendors hawked their goods at every corner — Sam and Frankie were too far away to hear what they were yelling about, exactly, but the body language of a man trying to sell something to somebody that didn't want it was unmistakable from any distance. Women led carts pulled by broken horses or old donkeys — one young girl in a filthy turban even escorted an emu; it pulled a red wagon loaded with heaps of colorful cloth.

"The Walled City?" Frankie asked.

"I think so?"

"I pictured something different."

"Yeah. I thought maybe like an old military base or a boarded-up mall like the camp back in Seattle. When they said it was by the dam…"

"I didn't think it *was the dam*," Frankie finished.

Princess SparkleHogg huffed the air — cooking smells, old frying oil, burning kerosene — and danced with excitement.

"Should we…go down there?" Frankie asked.

"I mean, we have to, right? We came all this way. This is what it was for. They're still people. If there are this many together, and they're still alive, they must be doing something right."

"Right," Frankie echoed.

Neither moved.

Princess SparkleHogg began picking her way down the uneven footpath that led from the hill they stood on, down to the top of the dam, and the decision was made. Sam and Frankie followed.

"It's safer than it looks," Sam said, pointing at the sheer canyon walls left behind by the now-empty reservoir. "Nobody could get down those. Nobody is swimming up that river past the dam — not with that current — and they're not scaling the dam itself on either side. It really is a walled city."

"Sorta," Frankie said. "I guess. What about the far end, up there where the river comes from?"

Sam followed his eye. The Columbia disappeared around a bend a mile or so upriver. The town petered out well before that. No walls on that side. No perimeter fence. No guards, even.

"Maybe it's too steep to get through the canyons that way?" Sam said. "Three walls are better than no walls. There's running water. Food.

Other people. It won't be so bad."

"If it is, though," Frankie said, "you have to promise me we leave, okay? It's us first. Always us first."

"I've heard that rule before," Sam said.

"Yeah," Frankie said. "And Bobby and Anna are only dead because they broke it."

Sam didn't have an answer to that. At least, not one he liked.

The top of the dam itself was a road, narrower by a bit than a normal street. It was bordered on either side by low cement walls and chain-link fence. A hasty guard station had been erected just before the jagged drop-off, where the pavement shattered and disappeared down a several hundred–foot drop. A snarl of chain-link strung between the poles of two opposite road signs. A crude gate hacked into the middle of it — just a section where three lines had been cut, so the chain-link could be unpinned and rolled back. Two guards stood behind it. One was an older black man with an out-of-control wizard beard and a vintage army helmet three sizes too large for his head. The other was a young woman with close-cropped hair. She wore a thick gray poncho, even though the day was intolerably hot. Something about the diamond-patterned weave made Sam think it might be bullet proof. Or used to be, before the weather got to it.

But each of them held a clean and well-oiled hunting rifle.

Sam and Frankie approached slowly, with their hands up, but the guards never raised their guns. They just waved the pair forward and smiled when Sam and Frankie were close enough to greet.

"Hi there," the girl said. A Midwest lilt to her voice. "How you boys doing today?"

It was the last thing Sam expected. He found himself dumbstruck.

"Good," Frankie answered. "How are you?'

"All right, all right," the older man answered. "Sun's shining. Got a nice breeze off the river. It isn't too bad."

"O-okay," Sam said, when it became clear no else was going to speak. "What's the uh…what's that?"

He pointed to the tower. Neither of the guards bothered to look.

"That…" the old man grumbled. "Is complicated."

"It won't hurt you or anything," the girl swore. "But Captain Wyatt explains it best. She's down below."

The girl pointed to a pair of steel doors set in the road beside her. There were huge metal rings recessed into each. They swung up and out from the center. Presumably leading down into the dam, and eventually, to the ground level and the city below.

"Did you want to come in?" the girl asked. A hint of laughter in her voice.

"Yes, please, if we could," Frankie said.

He looked to Sam, one eyebrow raised. Sam shrugged in return.

"Yep yep." The old guard raised a single finger, weathered brown and crooked as driftwood, and he pointed to a hand-painted sign secured to the chain-link fence with black zip ties. "These are the rules. You obey 'em, everybody's cool like Billy D. You don't, and there'll be problems."

Sam and Frankie craned their necks to read.

WELCOME TO DAM-NATION

A crude smiley face.

THE RULES

DO NO HARM

DO NO THEFT

OBEY THE PEACEKEEPERS

"Is that it?" Frankie asked.

"It's better if we keep things simple," the girl answered. "We take them very seriously, though."

Sam just nodded.

"You gotta read 'em back," the old guard prodded.

"What?" Sam said.

"The rules," the girl said. She stood with one hand poised on the faded yellow bungee cord that held the chain-link flap closed. "You have to read them back to us, so we know you understood them."

"Uh…Do no—" Sam started, and Frankie jumped in a second later.

They recited uncertainly, like first graders doing the pledge of allegiance. When Sam and Frankie were finished, the girl laughed a little, the old guy grinned with every bit of his two broken teeth, and together, they undid the cords and rolled the gate open. Frankie had to stoop to pick up Princess SparkleHogg. She'd been hiding behind his legs, unsure of the new company.

"Oh my god!" the girl squealed, and Princess SparkleHogg reflexively squealed back. "You are just *the most precious*. What's her name? Look at her little coat! Is she yours?"

"Sort of," Sam answered. And the tightness in his chest began to unravel. "That's Princess SparkleHogg."

"And I think it's more that we're hers," Frankie finished.

The old guard gently scratched behind Princess SparkleHogg's ears, while the girl put her forehead to the pig's nose and rubbed it back and forth, making cooing noises. The Princess kicked her feet, lost in pure ecstasy.

Frankie used the distraction to flicker Sam a private smile, which he returned. The issue was settled.

Nobody that loved a pig at first sight could be all bad.

Ouroboros

For most people, the day the Snake rolled into town was a cause for celebration. We brought goods to trade, clean water from our stills, and above all: information. Back in the day, a drifter might have talk about horde sightings or rumors from nearby towns. They told you what rivers had run dry and which were overflowing — but nobody traveled anymore. Not if they were smart. They just found a hole to hide in, and they lived there until they died there. But the Snake still traveled. The Snake never stopped traveling.

That's why most settlers treated our arrival like a holiday. We were a lifeline. The scarred armor on our walls was a sign of our permanence — a patina earned from all the attacks we survived. Our rumbling wheels shook the dust from the streets. From the people. Made everything look new again. Stepping out of their doors, blinking through the dishwater gloom, settlers saw us, and they waved, they clapped, they cried.

The older Snakes, they didn't get up on the roof to wave back anymore. But I did, because I knew it was important. It was just the children up there (and me, and mute) — all kneeling behind the crenellations, smiling and waving. We were ambassadors. We took pride in our jobs.

Most people treated the Snake's arrival like the special day it was. But not all.

We usually burned right through Brockway. Thundered past the combined post office/general store that constituted the whole town, the rust leaking from its metal windowsills like skidmarks against the dingy-white of its weathered facade. We usually blew right through the place, pedal down, eating up the 200 straight on to Circle. Because there was only one survivor in Brockway, and he didn't like visitors.

He liked to take potshots at us as we passed, his jury-rigged slingshot zinging. The star-shaped scar on my wrist throbbed every time we crossed into city limits. That was only a bottlecap filled with slag, though. I got lucky. It was one of his more…sanitary projectiles.

But every once in a while, we made a stop in that craphole of a town. Because nobody made moonshine like that crazy Brockway bastard, and nobody made nearly *as much*. He always had barrels of the stuff at the ready. The older Snakes bought from him in bulk, if only to minimize contact with the guy. I didn't touch the stuff, myself. Only partly because they wouldn't let me (there were ways to sneak a sip or two, if you were quick, and careful). No, I stayed away because it tasted the way diesel fumes smelled, and it burned the whole time it was in you. Down your throat, in your gut, and even on the way out.

But some of the older Snakes were crazy for the stuff, and when the barrels ran dry, that meant a pitstop at Brockway.

Carlos did the dealing. Maybe he was the only one brave enough to haggle with the Brockway maniac. Maybe he was the only one who could take the smell. The pair would yell profanities and elaborate threats at one other through the Mercantile's barricaded door, until eventually Carlos landed one creative to enough to shock even the Brockway psycho, and slowly, creakily, the door would open.

That's how it went today: a few minutes of peace and quiet while the pair haggled inside, and then another explosion of disgusting epithets as Carlos kicked open the door and fled for the Snake, barrels of moonshine trundling on his makeshift cart. He laughed as he sealed the portside door. On our way out of town, the Brockway bastard chased us for half a mile. I was up on the roof, crouched behind the rear barricade, the star on my wrist keenly reminding me to keep low. When the maniac finally ran out of breath, he heaved a heavy metal disc at the caboose. It clinked uselessly off of our armor but somehow managed to leave a shallow scratch. I leaned over the battlements and ran my hand across it.

The lunatic son of a bitch had sharpened a hubcap like a deadly Frisbee.

It would be months before the barrels ran empty of shine, and we had to it all again. The months weren't long enough.

But next up was Circle, and I liked Circle.

When you were down in them, you could see that these flat and endless plains were actually made up of long, low swells. Grassland waves that rolled by with hypnotic regularity. Highway 200 carved through that sea like a taut rope. An asphalt line moored to Circle, the only thing keeping it from drifting away on an ocean of tall, green grass.

I wish I could have seen this place before the skies went dark. I remembered bits and pieces from the world before, but none of it seemed real now. All spring blues and summer greens, the indefinable white/yellow of sunshine on everything —*just everything.* I know I lived in that world for nearly a decade before the black set in, but it wasn't even a memory anymore. Just a story I told myself. The real world was gray in summer, black in winter, and there were only ever shades between.

Grass is "green." But that's just what we call it.

And the worst part? The animals. They didn't know. Or they didn't care. They grew strong. Thrived, even, in the relative absence of humanity. Birds migrated, squirrels came out in the morning, owls came out at night. Did they even know the sky was gone?

And the question that really scared me: *was* it gone, for them?

Or was it just us?

You could feel the sun on your face in the summer. You could tell when it was a full moon — the darkness wasn't gone, exactly, but it was…less opaque? And yet every day, and every night, horizon to horizon: absence. A void. Like somebody used scissors to cut away the sky and never replaced it with anything.

The plants should have died. The birds should have been lost.

But we were the only ones lost.

A tug on my sweater broke the melancholy. Mute. So quiet, even when he moved. He pointed toward the head of the Snake, then on down the road, and motioned for me to follow. We must have been coming up on Circle. Kids were already gathering along the walls, ready to meet and greet.

To get to the engine, we had to cross half a dozen twisting rubber gangplanks, connecting each car at the roof. While the 200 banked as gently as a river, you still had to hold on to the guide cables — the Snake might devour most potholes happily, but an especially big one could send you reeling. Then it was twenty feet down to the blur of the pavement. The Snake would eat *you* up, and nobody would even feel that bump.

We made it to the engine without drama, and Mute wrestled open a space between Judith and Scurry. They elbowed him back and forth like a ping-pong ball. He went limp, lolling his head from side to side, exaggerating the jostle. Mute smiled, they laughed, and all returned their focus to the road.

Driving into Circle was like peering at a model. There were no reference points for scale. Just hills that stretched for miles. Tiny white buildings that looked closer than they were. Your brain assumed you'd be on top of them any second, but watch and watch — they never seemed to grow. Standing on the Snake, two stories high, three hundred feet long, barreling along a forever-black highway at thirty miles an hour, straw-colored hills all flowing together, seeing forever, looking at nothing —

sometimes it felt like the road was rolling backwards, and you weren't moving at all. Just a big conveyor belt running in the opposite direction. Then something broke. The belt snapped, the Snake surged forward, and suddenly those little model buildings were real, and coming up fast.

The survivors of Circle had stripped the outlying structures of whatever they could use. Everything beyond the center of town was torn down to the bones. Skeletal frames and broken windows. It looked like something terrible happened here, and I guess it had — but that was a long time ago. Closer to town, signs of life appeared: emergency shelters and storage areas; managed fields with rows of crops all standing at attention like soldiers; the fortified town center; the armored gate. A motley of scrap metal tacked together across one side of a stripped-down Winnebago.

Circle always had the gate open for the Snake by the time we made the heart of town. They had lookouts on the water tower, waving all-clear signals down to the guards below. The kids and I were lined up in our places behind the engine car, ready to wave back, to smile, to greet — to let these people know that somebody was still out there. Traveling the wastes and surviving them.

But this time, the gates stayed closed. The RV blocked off all of B Avenue, from the old lumber store to the sheriff's office. The Snake rolled to a stop, vented its brakes in an impatient huff. We rumbled. We waited. Nothing.

Ken sounded the horns. They roared like judgment day. But still nobody came. The RV remained planted.

Something was wrong. They must have realized that down below, too. I felt the vibration though my shoes as the bolt of the port hatch thunked open. The hydraulic whine as the gangplank unreeled, the scrape of steel on asphalt as it hit the street. The barrel of a rifle peeked out first. It surveyed the empty streets, then inched forward. Steves followed it, her cropped blond hair gone frizzy at the edges. And Johnson followed her, looking like Steves' shadow. He stepped where she stepped, walked when she walked. Everything identical but their rifles, each scanning a different side of the street. The two ducked in and out of the surrounding buildings, tracing a perimeter around the Snake for half a block in every direction. When they were finished, their posture changed. Like tension was a physical object that they carried on their backs, just between their shoulder blades, and they could finally shrug it off.

Steves slung her rifle over her shoulder and waved to Ken, inside the engine.

From the outside, the engine looked just like the rest of the Snake: a featureless black metal slab. It sloped down a bit at the front, in case it needed to ram through something, but that was the only difference. No visible seams indicating doors, no exterior markings, no windows or ports for the driver to look out of. But somehow, Ken saw everything from in there.

Now, I'd never been inside the engine, myself. The symbols that marked the armory and the engine — crossed rifles, a snake eating its own tail — they might as well have been magical wards. But Scurry, he'd been just about everywhere, and he said you could actually see out from inside the engine car. In fact, you could see in every direction — even through the roof and floor — like the steel was just so much murky glass. I don't always believe Scurry, but I think he was probably right about that. There was no way Ken steered the whole Snake by a few tiny monitors. He maneuvered around sinkholes flawlessly, knew which tunnels and overpasses were too low; it really was like he could see everywhere. And he must have seen Steves waving at him, because I could already hear the hydraulics whispering down. The Snake settled, easing onto its haunches like a tired beast.

The engine was off.

We were parked.

It was never a good thing, when they had to park the Snake.

It didn't take long for the scouts to bypass Circle's makeshift gate. It was never meant to keep out people. Not thinking ones, anyway. Rodriguez was the youngest and the lightest, not to mention the newest, so the job fell to her. She scrambled up one of the fall-bare trees, then leapt onto the roof of a storage shed, just behind the lumberyard. She balanced atop the rickety fence, took two lunging, high-wire steps, and was across. Gone from sight for the longest minute of my life. Until, finally, a rope squiggled down from atop the RV.

It all seemed a little unnecessary. The Snake could have just rammed through that RV like a stone thrown through paper, but I guess we were being courteous. Circle knew we could take what we wanted, if we wanted. Everybody knew that. But they also knew we never would.

We worked hard for that reputation, and sometimes keeping it meant doing things the hard way.

Johnson, Steves, and Fat Bob all climbed the rope with precise and practiced movements. I remembered when Johnson tried to get me to run that drill with them — how easy it looked, how hard it was. The burns on my palms, and in my cheeks, as they laughed and laughed.

The scouts disappeared over the lip of the gate, and all fell quiet. One by one, the other kids grew bored and drifted away. Off to race the halls, pester the adults, or try to raid the pantry car. But Mute and I had learned patience, even if it was absolutely unbearable to practice it.

Somewhere beyond the black, the sun was just starting to go down. The quality of light shifting from heavy fog to silted water. Mute held up two fingers and bounced them around like a bunny rabbit. His way of getting my attention. I raised my eyebrows at him, and he pointed down below, at an old streetlight.

Broken glass, anemic brown vines clutching at weathered concrete. Freckles of flash rust.

I shrugged.

Mute pointed down at his own feet, leaned back and forth, waggled his arms, then knelt and touched the ground.

This was an elaborate pantomime, even for Mute.

I made the stupidest, blankest face I could. He got that I did not get it.

Next he tried rotating carefully, watching the roof for some unknown criteria. When it was met, he froze in place and nodded to me. I shook my head, he tapped his foot. Pointed with his toes.

"The floor?"

A headshake.

"Your…foot?"

Exasperated sigh.

"Your shadow?"

A triumphant hum, a big smile, a nod you couldn't miss from space.

"What about it?" I asked, and all the joy disappeared from his face.

Mute pointed again.

I shrugged again.

He stabbed the air with his pointer finger and began some new info-dance, but I nodded over his shoulder, and he turned to see what I was seeing: Fat Bob was back, looming over the edge of the RV. He contemplated the ground for a second, then threaded the rope around his waist and through his hands. He was halfway to the street before you could blink. Steves now waited in his place. Once Fat Bob touched boots to asphalt, he backed up about a dozen paces, then swung his rifle to the ready. Satisfied that he was set, Steves ducked back out of sight and was replaced by an unfamiliar figure.

Were they bringing somebody from Circle out to the Snake? Why? And why not just have the guards open the gate?

The new person was an older man — he didn't move like a geriatric or anything, but I guess he was old enough for his hair to have blown right past gray and into white. His skin was pale bordering on gray, and he was dressed in a white and red jumpsuit with oil stains coloring the knees. As soon as the old guy touched the rope, Fat Bob raised his rifle and kept it trained on him all the way down.

I went cold to my very toes.

Steves had drilled into us — into all of us, even if we were never, ever allowed to touch a gun — that you didn't point that barrel at somebody unless you're ready to shoot them.

Why would Fat Bob ever need to shoot an old mechanic, awkwardly descending a rope?

The second the man's flat canvas sneakers hit pavement, Fat Bob was barking orders. *Step to the side, kneel down, hands behind your head, look at the ground — not at me, at the ground!*

Once he was down, I figured Fat Bob would cuff him or something, but he didn't move an inch. Just stood there, twenty feet away, rifle zeroed in on the old man's skull.

I looked back to the top of the RV and found the other scouts doing the same. All spread out across the roof, maintaining a purposeful distance from one another, rifles at the ready. Steves descended next, took up her post twenty feet to Fat Bob's left, and signaled for the next climber.

When the last scout was down — Rodriguez again, always the rookie with the short end of the stick — Fat Bob ordered the man to stand, and they ushered him toward the Snake with guns trained. A dead zone of twenty feet around the mechanic, in every direction.

Mute gave me a look — mouth open, eyebrows climbing into his hairline — and I figured the same one was on my face. There was no debate. We moved as one.

We had to get a closer look.

Mute and I bolted for the access hatch — my combat boots thunking, his bare feet slapping — twisted the handle, lifted it up too fast, fighting the pneumatics. We slid down the ladder's rails, rather than lose precious seconds using its rungs, then slowed to a speedwalk toward the portside gangway. We could run outside, where the adults wouldn't see us, but not down here, in public. Little kids run everywhere. Adults just "hurry."

We put on our hurry faces and plowed through the remaining cars between us and our objective. Mute was like a leaf on a river. He flowed around anything in his way, unseen currents directing him flawlessly past obstacles without a sound. I had to mutter a string of professional excuses as I jostled my way through the Snake — *excuse me, sorry, urgent business, no time to talk*. When I finally caught up, Mute was standing purposefully aloof at the back of a small crowd of eager children.

Damn it, we were the only ones keeping watch. This was supposed to be proprietary information. How did little kids always just *know* where they shouldn't be?

Mute caught my expression and threw a sympathetic headshrug. I joined him at the back, leaning on the wall and kicking one foot up. He crossed his arms. I put my hands in my pockets. This was aloof. This was what aloof looked like.

It took about thirty seconds for the access hatch to unseal and shush open. The black metal gangplank slid out and lowered to the street. Steves marched up it like she was ready to shoulder charge through the assembled gawkers, if need be. Mute and I knew that body language. Somehow, we managed to hustle even farther back. We nestled into the corner, did our best impression of a wall. The other kids only scattered when Steves burst through the hatch like a flood. A torrent of orders in her no-nonsense voice: *Get the brats out of here, prep the interrogation room, clear the aisles* — the children didn't know the drill like Mute and me. They were swept away by the first round of commands. Just stood there, shellshocked, while Carlos corralled them all up, bulldozed them right out of the car, and sealed the door behind them.

Not us. We slipped through the nets.

"You two." Steves took aim and shot down Mute and me with one authoritarian finger.

My guts froze.

"Run ahead and fold everything up," she continued. "Everything: chairs, bunks, workstations — even if they're on — I want every inch of the Snake clear, from here to the Interrogation Room."

Mute and I had always occupied the shaky limbo between childhood and adulthood. Not anymore. This was it: our official grown-up clearance.

"Yes, sir," I snapped.

Steves looked at me like a dog that had suddenly learned to speak. Mute was smarter: he just gave one sharp nod, then bolted down the aisle, flipping brakes and folding furniture back into cubby holes. I flushed red under Steves' stare, muttered something that might have been a word if you weren't listening too close, and followed Mute.

There probably wasn't a record for "the fastest stowing of dining tables on a military landtrain," but if there was, Mute and I broke it. We finished clearing the cars just as Rodriguez came through the port hatch. She walked backwards, slowly, half-crouched, rifle rocksteady like her whole body was just a suspension system to keep that gun from jostling.

Mute and I were pressed so flat against the wall we could've been tape. I even had my feet turned sideways, just so nobody could possibly trip on them. Steves needed to see how seriously we were taking this, or else our grown-up clearance could be revoked at any time. Rodriguez passed by so close I could smell her — sweat, gun oil, the sharp, empty clean of soap; same stuff I used; that we all used; why was it better on her? — and I felt a throb.

A whole new terror unreeled. There I was, standing in that big, empty hallway, just me — the sole feature in the whole car — slowly getting a boner while the scouts escorted a dangerous prisoner past. Everybody would stop. They would look, they'd laugh, especially Rodriguez — then they'd get mad. They'd turn their guns on me, instead. My inappropriate erection immediately supplanting the prisoner as the most imminent threat. Bullets peppering my face, my chest, my stomach, their aim heading steadily downward, laughing, laughing—

Then the white-haired mechanic walked by, and my imagination died.

He wasn't nearly as old as I thought. *Older*, sure, with a face like a gently disturbed pond — no wrinkles, nothing that permanent, just passing dips and swells yet to set — and fine, jaw-length white hair that swayed like loose cornsilk with each step. But if I had to guess, I'd have put him in his forties. It wasn't just the hair throwing me off: there was something ancient to him, that same feeling you got around an enormous tree. Or a mountain.

He glanced at me as he passed, and I got a good, clear look at his eyes.

No iris there, no pupil, just pure, unbroken white. Not like the colors had weathered out from blindness, but like there was nothing there at all. His eyelids opened onto a pure white void, immeasurable, and unfathomable. I had never known such pure emptiness, and yet there was also movement there.

If you stood outside the Snake and watched it pass by right in front of you, something weird happened. You knew you were perfectly still, but there was a second where your brain got it all wrong. It didn't understand that something so gigantic could move, so it thought you must be moving instead. You could lose your balance, fall right over, and for no other reason than something too big to move had started moving. That was what it felt like, looking into the space where the old man's eyes should have been.

Vertigo didn't even start to describe it.

And then his gaze slid over to Mute, and it was like I was me again. I looked over and saw that Mute's whole body had seized up. Not a breath, not a twitch. A look on his face like he'd just went to step on solid ground and found nothing beneath his feet. It was all over in a second, but I knew that second. It felt like years.

The mechanic passed, followed by Steves and Johnson, pacing him at a careful distance. Barrels at attention like hungry wolves, watching a herd for stray movement. They disappeared into the interrogation room, leaving Fat Bob and Rodriguez to guard the door. Excitement over, the adults all disappeared on some other pressing matter, which they always seemed to have, but we never did. Even though it was all we wanted.

Mute tapped my hand, and we cautiously unstuck ourselves from the wall. He looked at me, motioned at his eyes, and shook his head.

"I know," I said. "That was awful. There's something really wrong with that guy."

He nodded.

"I think just *looking* at him was the worst thing that's ever happened to me."

He nodded.

"We have to see him again."

He nodded.

. . .

Scurry could get into just about anything. He'd been inside the Armory, and only scouts were allowed in there. Scurry was pretty small, sure. And he was flexible. He could be sneaky when he wanted, but nothing like Mute, padding around on cat's paws. No, Scurry's skeleton keys were persistence and obsession. To get into the Armory, he'd first spent days worrying at a security grate — tiny, patient tweaks, nothing dramatic enough to set off the motion sensors — then several hours more, gently packing them with patch foam so they wouldn't go off when he eased past.

When he was finally ready to break into the Armory, he called all the kids together — plus Mute and me, because while we're obviously adults now, children can sometimes struggle with changes in social status. I said no, of course, because that was the responsible thing to do. But I didn't say it especially firmly, because I really wanted to see him try it. That wasn't immature, it was professional curiosity. It was practically science.

It took some doing to shimmy through the intake housing, but Scurry managed it. Every time we'd think he was stuck, ask him if we should get help, he'd smile with broken teeth, shift just a little bit, and on he went. When he finally disappeared from view — went crashing down into the Armory car with a bang we were sure everyone on the Snake would hear — the kids went nuts. Mute and I gave restrained, appreciative nods.

But I said, "Scurry can get into anything."

Not out.

The scouts found him hours later, just browsing the arsenal like he was bored at a grocery store. Steves threw a fit. She demanded to know how he'd gotten in there, but all wide-eyed and honest as dirt, Scurry said,

"The door was just open." Of course they found the vent on the roof. The grate discarded beside it, its screws meticulously lined up between the slots so they wouldn't roll away. They saw the gyroscopes steadied with foam and put the puzzle together. But it didn't matter: Scurry had done it, and his legend grew.

Everybody had to take a mandatory six-hour security training session after that — even the adults. It was the most boring thing I ever had to do in my life. Twice I considered ratting on Scurry, just to make it end. I expect we all did. But we didn't, because legends deserve better.

So when you need to see something people don't want you to see, you find Scurry. Usually in Hester's galley, pestering her for tastes of whatever she was cooking (it was always "something and beans"). That's where we found him, anyway.

Mute tapped Scurry on the shoulder, and he startled like a bird. Mute smiled, spread his hands wide in apology.

"What's your problem?" Scurry said, residually mad from the scare.

"We saw the prisoner," I said.

"No way," Scurry whispered, all anger — as well as Hester's Something and Beans — instantly forgotten.

The three of us retreated into the farthest corner to finish our conversation. Hester might rat us out, if she overheard us.

"What's he look like? Is he gross? Is he all bloody and crazy? Is he—"

Mute held up two fingers, and Scurry went quiet.

"He's just some old guy," I answered. "A mechanic, I guess?"

"Aw." Scurry's head was already rotating around, drawn to Hester's briefly unattended pot like a meteor caught in its gravity.

"But," I allowed, and Scurry practically leapt back into the conversation, "his eyes are weird."

"Weird?" Scurry tried to get all of his words out at once. "Weird like how? Like black? I told you I saw one like that. I told you about that back in wherever that was — Arizona? I heard the scouts talking after, and they called it a 'black-eye,' like they saw them all the time but—"

I could try to interrupt him all day and wouldn't get anywhere. But Mute held up two fingers again and put Scurry on pause. I had to get him to teach me how he does that.

"White," I said.

"What?"

"They were white. His eyes."

"So what? Yours are white."

Mute rolled his eyes back up in his head for a second.

"No, like all white," I said. "Like Mute is right now, but all the time."

"So he's blind or something? Who cares?"

"No, it's…" I growled, mostly at myself. I have a great vocabulary, I'm proud of that, but it just doesn't matter when you're talking to somebody without one.

"They're super weird white," I finally settled.

Mute made crazy angles with his fingers, danced them around.

"And it's like there's something in there," I added at the prompt. "Behind his eyes. I don't know how to explain it, but I promise you've never seen anything like it. It practically killed us, just looking at him."

Scurry whistled appreciatively, but he couldn't really whistle. Just made a hollow jug sound.

Mute slapped my shoulder.

"I'm getting to it," I snapped. "Scurry, we need to see this guy again."

"Well, yeah," he said. He didn't need to be told the obvious.

"Where is he?"

"The interrogation room."

"The what?"

"The briefing room," I said. "It's also the interrogation room. But only when they have somebody to interrogate."

"Oh, wow." Scurry bit his lip and looked at the ceiling, sorting through imagined blueprints. "No, I can't get us in there. Not with guards at the door. There's a little chimney thing on the roof, but it's about as wide as my arm, and it's got fans all the way down. You can't see or even hear anything."

"That's okay," I said. "I told Mute it wasn't true."

Mute nodded sadly, like it broke his heart to admit it.

"What wasn't true?" Scurry asked.

"That you could really get into *anywhere*," I answered. "That's just hyperbole."

"What's hy—"

"Made up," I explained before he even asked.

"Nuh uh!" Scurry clapped his hands, drawing an apprehensive glare from Hester. She hovered over her Something and Beans like a mother bear.

"I can't get our *bodies* in," he stressed. "But maybe I can get us a look in there. That counts, right?"

I let him dangle while Mute and I exchanged elaborate hand signals — they meant nothing, but Scurry didn't know that. When we were finished, we nodded as if an important debate had just been settled.

"That counts," I informed him.

Scurry grinned so hard he nearly split a lip.

...

"This doesn't count," I told Scurry.

It was the smallest monitor I'd ever seen: maybe eight inches wide, half that tall. It looked like "black and white" would tax its graphics card. And for some reason, the whole workstation was outside — on the roof of the caboose. The whole rear car was mostly storage, so there was no ladder access from the interior. You had to climb up from the sleeping car, cross over a flexible rubber gangplank, then hop a waist-high barricade into the rear machine gun nest. Halfway up the walls of the nest, there was a nearly invisible panel. Scurry pressed in on it, then released. A solid click, and the door bounced out half an inch. He swung it open the rest of the way with a big flourish, like the crude screen and mini-keyboard inside were anything but a huge disappointment.

Mute looked to the sky and huffed. I pinched the bridge of my nose.

"Wait, wait," he pleaded. "Remember when we hit that big rock a while back, and the galley tipped up all crazy?"

"Yeah," I said. "The suspension malfunctioned, starboard wouldn't lower."

Hester was so mad. It took a full day to fix. She had to cook on an incline.

"Well," Scurry continued. "After they got it all fixed up, Ken had to come back here to do something before it would work again. I overheard him talking to Fantastic Larry, and they said this thing was like, the boss of some of the electrical stuff."

"Absolutely none of that is helpful," I said.

"But…cameras are electrical, right? So we should be able to work them from here…"

Mute's eyebrows drew together, and he shook his head.

"Scurry," I tried to channel all of my patience, but it turns out I didn't have any, "that's not how anything works. Anything. Nothing works like you just described, and it never has."

Scurry looked like he was about to cry. He could feel his legend, shattering.

"Look," I said. "Maybe I'm wrong. I'll give it a shot, okay?"

He brightened a bit. Mute looked at me cross-eyed, and I tried not to laugh.

"So," I crowded my fingers onto the half-keyboard. "This is probably just a glorified fuse box — it tells the electrical systems when it's okay to work again. That wouldn't have anything to do with the cameras—"

"But they're—"

"I know," I cut him off. "They're electrical. This might be able to turn the cameras on or off, tell us what's wrong with them, but it won't…huh."

Scurry inflated with hope.

"'Huh,' what? 'Huh' is good!" he said.

"If the terminal has a diagnostics mode for camera errors, then…" I gave Scurry a careful smile. "Be quiet for a little bit while I figure this out."

Nobody spends as much time on the Snake's computers as I do. Most of it is just poking around. Reading the encyclopedias. Going over the old logs. Somebody from before the skies went dark hid a game on the weather terminal — they stashed it away in a subset of a subset of folders and named it "data."

That's the most suspicious thing you can name something that you're trying to hide on a computer, by the way.

The point is: give me enough time with a computer, and I can figure it out. They all use the same mental muscle, really. All you have to do is get access, which I did.

Ken's username was "ken," and his password was "kenspassword."

Come on, man.

Sure enough, you could restart the camera systems from this terminal. You could also set the length of time that the feeds backed up, see how much storage they took, or purge the backlog. In the “advanced user” options, there was a bunch of camera controls I didn’t understand…and one I did.

Image Test

>Interior

>>Operations and Logistics

>>>Briefing Room 1

>>>Briefing Room 2

I clicked “Briefing Room 1,” and the lowest quality image I had ever seen snapped full screen. In one corner, a timestamp ticked by. It was current.

“Scurry,” I whispered. He leaned in. “You really can get into anything.”

He whooped, hollered, skipped around in a tight circuit around the nest while Mute clapped for him.

The resolution was garbage, and the audio sounded like somebody had recorded it on a dinner plate and played it back through a watermelon. But we could see — and hear — inside the Briefing Room. Now, the Interrogation Room.

It was a small, sparse space, barely wide enough to fit the long metal table it contained. There were short stools built into the floor all around the table, enough to seat ten, if they didn’t mind snuggling a little. At one end, the old man with the white hair. His face was just a solid mass of indistinguishable pixels, yet somehow, you could still feel his empty white eyes there. He sat awkwardly straight, hands apparently bound below his waist in some way we couldn’t quite make out. Steves stood at the far end of the table, with her back to the door.

The two were already going at it when we patched in.

"—we'd take you to the old block and throw away the key, but that was then…" Steves said.

She left room for a retort. The old man had none.

"This is now," Steves finished. "Now, we just kill you."

No response.

"And if you're not going to talk, that's going to happen sooner rather than later. So what's your call?"

"You should not kill us yet," the old man answered.

He sounded like a normal human, which was pretty disappointing. I pictured something reverberating and hellish. But no, just a reedy male voice, a little on the high side, with an accent kind of like Fat Bob's, but…smarter sounding? Like they were both from the same town, but this guy definitely lived on a hill.

"Us?" Steves asked. "You got friends I should know about?"

"There are two of us here," the old man said. "One of us needs the other to speak; one of us needs the other to exist."

"Super," Steves sighed. "You're crazy. Well, I should've guessed that by the state of the town. You just another crazy old boy from the badlands, hacking up people because the dog told you to do it?"

"We are not crazy," the man replied — no defense in his tone, just a correction. "If I was insane, he would have no place in me."

"That's the craziest explanation for not being crazy that I've ever heard." Steves laughed.

The man fell silent.

"You're not very talkative, are you?" Steves asked, crossing the room with quick, aggressive steps. She loomed over the old mechanic, but somehow she was the one that wound up looking small.

"When you put us here and bound our hands, your soldier said, 'We ask the questions, you give the answers.' This seemed to be a law."

"As far as you're concerned," Steves answered, "It's the highest law in the land."

The speakers went quiet, just the static crackle of nothing.

"If you're not going to tell us anything," Steves' voice went deadly flat, "then what use are you?"

"We are your only hope of survival," the man said.

"Is that a threat?"

"It is information."

"No," Steves mused. "That definitely sounded more like a threat. Now, a threat's a good thing — it's useful. It lets people know what you're going to do them, without actually doing it. But you? You're not going to do anything. Not to us. Not like this. A threat from you, in your current situation, is useless. The only useful thing you have is information, and buddy? You want to stay useful on the Snake. We don't have room for useless things."

The man stared straight ahead.

"See?" Steves chuckled. "*That's* a threat. That's how you do it. And believe me, I back up my threats. So tell me: what did you do to the people of Circle, and why? You sure as hell didn't gut them all yourself, so who helped you? Who the hell are you?"

"We showed them their own insides," the man answered quickly, running down each question like a bulletpoint on a dull list. "We did it because they broke the law. We did it ourselves. We are Order."

"The hell does any of that mean?"

"It means what it means," the man said. "It is its own meaning, as we are our own meaning. It could be no other way."

"Jesus Christ," Steves muttered. "You tell me what I need to know right now, or I'm going to start taking body parts."

I guess I knew that Steves did stuff like this sometimes, but it was a whole different matter, actually seeing it. The whole thing felt fake, like she was putting on a play. I wondered if the old mechanic would buy the act. Then, with a hard swallow, I wondered if it was an act.

Mute, Scurry, and I all jumped at the snap. Somehow the man had gotten one hand free from the restraints. Steves hopped backwards, out of his reach, but the stools were built into the floor and caught her at the knees. She pinwheeled, struggling to stay upright and clear her pistol at the same time. But the old mechanic didn't lunge for her: he just held his hand out toward Steves, palm up, fingers spread wide.

Steves finally found both her balance and her gun. Halfway across the room and ready-stanced, she waited for the prisoner's next move. Once he was sure he had her full attention, the old man brought his hand to face, put one of his fingers in his mouth, and bit down. On our terrible monitor, the white block of his face went dark around the chin. He leaned forward and spat the severed finger dead on the table before him. Then he did it again, and again, until he was out of fingers.

When he was finished, he laid his palm — now literally just a palm — in his lap and looked to Steves.

They were still so long, I thought the video stream had frozen. Then, each syllable punctuated with a stab of her pistol, Steves said:

"What…the…fuck?!"

"You want an explanation for that action," the man answered with formal, detached pleasantness. "It was only to show you that we do not notice or care what happens to this physical body, beyond its ability to communicate with you. We don't need fingers to do that. We don't need arms, or legs, or genitals — we don't need anything, save ears to hear your questions and lips and tongue to answer them."

He considered something.

"Possibly some teeth," he amended. "But only the frontmost, for the fricatives."

"F-fricatives?" Steves asked, reflexively.

"Sounds that require teeth," the man clarified. "We were a linguistics professor, before the harvest. That's why we were chosen to communicate."

"We…we better get you patched up, before you bleed out on my floor," Steves said. You could hear the shake in her voice. "Don't think this is over."

She backtracked away from the prisoner, both hands focused on keeping her pistol level. When she reached the door, she gave three sharp kicks with her heel. It slid open, and Steves stepped out of frame. The monitor was so bad, and the image so tiny, you couldn't really make out faces. Just a solid block of pixels. But somehow, we could tell when the man's gaze shifted. When he stopped watching the door and started watching the camera.

"Is he…looking at us?" I asked.

Scurry didn't have an answer for that. Mute did. He reached over my shoulder and held the power button until the monitor switched off. I started to protest, but he just shook his head very slowly. Not like he was saying "no," more like he was trying to negate everything that had just happened.

The argument died in my throat.

"I think I'm going to go lie down," Scurry said, and he ran away like only little kids can do: There one second, full-sprint-gone the next.

Mute and I stood there for a while, just feeling the wind on our skin. Watching the black, featureless sky fade. Trying to remember what a sunset looked like.

When it was too dark to pretend we were actually looking at things anymore, Mute and I crossed back over to the sleeping car and descended the ladder. Steves was there, waiting for us. Johnson, too: leaning against the door, maybe because he was tired, maybe to keep it shut. Rodriguez sat the head of my cot — her butt, right there, right where I put my head — but even that thought couldn't cheer me up. Our welcoming party looked none too cheery, either. Rodriguez glared at Mute until he looked away. He watched his feet like they might come to life at any minute, and he didn't want to miss that miracle. Johnson wouldn't meet my eye at all, and Steves had the same expression she always did: like you were standing in her way and didn't know it, but really should.

"We were just—" I started, but Steves cut me off.

"Don't, kiddo," she said. "We know what you two were up to."

"I don't know what Scurry told you, but—" And the way her eyebrows rose, I knew it wasn't Scurry.

That was one of Steves' gambits: when you start putting your foot in your mouth, she doesn't pull it out for you. She lets you stuff it all the way in there and choke on it for a while. When she saw I had spotted the trap and wasn't going to continue, she said:

"Scurry, that's the Chen boy, right?"

"I'll talk to his grandmother," Johnson said.

Great. I was so worried Scurry told on us, that I just told on Scurry. I racked my brain for the word — not irony, exactly. Maybe just "moronic."

"We thought we—"

"You're not in trouble," Steves stopped me again. "Well, actually, you're in so much trouble I don't even know how to describe it. But that's not why we're here right now."

I opened and closed my mouth a few times. I fully intended on making words, but I didn't. I just stood there, gasping like a landed fish.

When Steves finally decided we'd twisted enough, she nodded to Rodriguez.

"You can take your brother now," she said.

Rodriguez stood. Even though I was in no mood for it right now, I still memorized every inch of the butt-dent she left in my bed, for later. She slapped her open palm around the back of Mute's neck and steered him toward the door. Johnson stepped aside to let them pass.

"Lucas, I swear to Christ, if you—" I heard Rodriguez fire up Mute's chew-out session, but a click of the latch silenced the rest.

Johnson very conspicuously resumed his place: back to the door, disinterested gaze just wandering about the cabin.

You know it's really, really bad when multiple adults want to talk to you alone in a room for a while.

Steves sighed for so long I thought I might die before she stopped.

"Kiddo, we have something to ask you, and right up front, I want you to know that the answer we want to hear most in the world — more than anything we've ever wanted in our lives — is 'no.' You got that?"

I nodded.

Steves looked to Johnson. He was staring off into space, watching nothing in case it turned into something. But of course he wasn't, really: he returned her gaze instantly. They did a thing that I have spent five years learning to hate very, very much — they communicated something extremely complicated, about me, with just a nod and an eyebrow raise.

"The Chen boy, he didn't tell on you," Steves said. "You know that old guy we put in the meeting room?"

My mandatory nod.

"I was talking to him, but I had to leave for a while. When I came back, he was staring at something on the ceiling. I asked him what he was looking at—"

I already knew the profanities she was omitting.

"—and he said, 'The boy watching us through that camera.' I thought he was just being crazy — because he is damn crazy, kiddo, make no mistake about that — but your dad was watching on the Sec Station…"

I glanced over at Johnson, who was picking at his nails. That's how you knew he wasn't just mad, but something else. He'd never say it. But his nails would.

"—and sure enough, he saw something strange. The letters 'M-E-C,' blinking down in the corner. The Master Electrical Control — that was real clever of you kids — but—"

"I'm not a kid, Steves."

She winced.

"You don't have to call me 'Steves,' okay?" She laughed, but it wasn't funny. "I know you're going through a whole almost-teenage thing right now, but it's weird, all right? It feels weird. It took a lot before you called me 'Mom,' and I don't want to lose that. No matter what."

It was my turn to get way too interested in my own feet.

"Anyway, it was pretty smart, to use the MEC like you did," Steves pressed on. "And we'll talk about how you did it, later. But right now, we have more important things to talk about. This prisoner — there's a lot about this guy we don't understand. We don't understand what he is, exactly…"

"You heard us talk about the black-eyes?" Johnson asked.

I flinched. When he was mad-plus-something-else like this, it was usually hours before he could even talk to me.

"Yes, sir," I answered.

It was only partially the wrong thing to do. I was admitting to eavesdropping, sure, but this was something bigger than that.

"Then you know they're the worst news around," Johnson said, "and this guy's like them."

"*Almost* like them," Steves added. "He's…something different. And he actually seems to want to talk to us. We sure as hell don't trust him, but I'm not gonna lie here. One of those things, giving us intel? We can't pass up that chance…"

Neither of them wanted to say what came next, but I already knew. I thought about that handful of pixels, how they didn't show a face at all, but somehow, I could still see his eyes. Or the spaces where they should have been. How I found them. How they found me.

"But he won't talk to you anymore," I finished for her. "He wants to talk to one of us."

They both nodded like it hurt their necks.

"And Mute can't talk, and Scurry's too young…" I reasoned it out. "So it has to be me."

"No, kiddo," Steves said. "He asked for you by name."

The temperature dropped twenty degrees.

"How does the mechanic know my name?" I asked.

"He's not a mechanic," Steves answered. "And we don't know. We don't understand how he knew you were watching, how he knew your name, why he wants to talk to you — we don't even know what he is. Those are all questions we want the answers to, but he's made it very clear we can't…*make* him talk—"

"Because he doesn't care if you torture him," I clarified.

"You saw that, huh?" Steves bit her lip, looked at me like I was a wounded puppy.

"We don't *torture*," Johnson corrected, but by the way he said the word, I knew that was a technicality.

"The prisoner," Steves continued, "he said he was tired of talking to people who 'won't obey the rules.' But that *you* would. Does that make sense to you?"

I shook my head, but it gradually turned into a nod.

Watching through the monitors while Steves interrogated the man was so frustrating. I wanted to shake the screen, to shout, "You're doing it all wrong!" I thought, "He told you how this works! It's so obvious!" I told myself, "If that were me, I'd do it right."

Now it *was* me, and I didn't want to do it at all.

But even though Steves said she wanted me to say "no," and Johnson was playing it extra cool (which only ever served to betray how uncool he felt), I knew the only answer here was "yes."

So I said, "Can I think about it?"

"No, kiddo. It's do or die."

Johnson winced.

"We'll be right outside the door, in case—"

"Wait, you won't be in the room with me?" The floor turned to mush beneath my feet.

"He won't talk if there's more than one person in the room," Steves said. "Even to me. But your dad and I, we'll be right outside the door. And I mean right outside it, hands on the latch. If you need us, we'll be in there so fast we'll leave skidmarks."

I tried to talk myself into it:

He'll be tied up.

He snapped those restraints like they were nothing.

Why would he hurt me?

He bit off all his fingers just to prove a point.

He only wants to talk to somebody that understands.

Eyes like a void, windows into a place we can't even comprehend, much less survive—

"I know it's a lot of responsibility." Steves ran both hands through her hair, caught a few fistfuls at the back, and shook. "I'd think twice about asking something like this from one of my own team, much less a little kid, but…"

"I'll do it," I said.

I was just as surprised as anybody.

"And I'm not a little kid," I added.

The way Steves looked at Johnson, the way Johnson glared back, then stormed out — I got what happened. I got what she'd done, even if it was too late to do anything about it.

"I know you're not," Steves replied, and she gave me a real sad smile.

But there was a little pride in it, too.

Maybe one day I'd forgive her.

…

The metal stools in the interrogation room were somehow more uncomfortable than they looked, and they looked like they were built to torture fairies. No cushion, or even a contour for your butt. Knees up around your belly button. All your weight on your tailbone. And you couldn't even scoot them back from the table to get some more legroom, because like everything else on the Snake, they were built into the car itself.

I had been staring at the furniture for an uncomfortable length of time. Finding every reason not to speak to or even look at the old man waiting patiently at the other end of the table. Watching me with his white eyes, full of terrible nothing.

I thought about the scouts, seeing all this on their security console in the armory, laughing about the scared, stupid little kid that was so obviously panicking on their screen.

"They said you wanted to talk," I said. "So talk."

It's what Johnson would have said, and exactly how he would've said it. I hoped he couldn't hear my terrible impression of him from the other side of the door.

The mechanic quirked his head, so slight you could've missed it.

"Right," I said, mostly to myself. After so many unspoken conversations with Mute, I knew when silence was an answer. "You won't say anything unless it's an answer to a question."

No response.

"Is that right?" I added.

"Yes," he said. A normal person would have said more. He had no interest in being normal.

"Why is that?" I asked.

"It's the law."

"Whose law?"

"Your law."

"Our law?"

"Yes."

I had to show him I got it, when nobody else did.

"Is that because the guard said, 'We ask the questions, and you answer them?'"

"Yes," the old man answered. "This is your place. You set the law, and we obey it."

"I don't think they meant it literally," I said. "That's just a thing people say to sound tough when they want answers."

The old man blinked, very slowly. I was visibly trying his patience.

"Okay, okay," I said. "Only questions. Why did it have to be me you talked to?"

"You understand what rule has been set and how to work within it."

"Can you…elaborate?"

"Yes," he said.

And nothing else.

It was like that game little kids play, when they're being willful: "I'll do what you say, but *super literally*."

"How did you know I was watching?" I asked.

"We could feel you," he answered.

"What does that mean?"

"There are systems in place within the human mind. Intellectual and emotional frameworks upon which your 'self' is built — there is much of our framework within you. You are not one of ours entirely, but enough of your 'self' stems from our gifts. We can sense you. We can understand you. Parts of you."

"Wow," I breathed.

I didn't *get* any of that, but it was more information than he had to volunteer, based on my question.

"Will you talk more if I ask the right questions?"

"Yes."

Guess that wasn't one of them.

"What, uh…" I had to roll back through his crazy nonsense, searching for the important parts. "What do you mean by 'one of ours.' How am I 'yours'?"

"What you think of as your 'self' is not one thing. It has many parts. Experiences, genetics, habits, and prejudices. But there are other, more abstract aspects of the human 'self' that you do not fully understand. You gave those aspects names and thought that naming them meant you understood them. Humanity's capacity for empathy, their endless drive, their yearning for a peaceful, stable community, their sense of order and justice — where did those aspects come from? They are not found in nature. Not in any significant measure. Humanity accepted these aspects as a birthright, as a natural side effect of their intelligence, and did not recognize them for what they really were: gifts. Concepts leant to your species by an outside force. In fact, several forces — we are one of them. Our gift was order and justice. But after generations of interbreeding, millennia of philosophizing, centuries of small concessions and revised definitions, some of your people have muddied our gifts such that we no longer control them. You, for example. Our gifts live strong within you, but they do not dominate your 'self.' You are known to us, but you are not one of ours."

"Justice?" I laughed even as I realized that might be a mistake.

It was mockingly rhetorical, but still inflected like a question. The old man could answer.

"You are stunted animals," he said. "You confuse concepts with virtues. Justice is not noble. Justice is a law, and it is following that law, and it is paying the price for breaking that law. That is all justice is. You like the computers here because you understand they are a system of rules. You understand what the rules of this community are, and why they exist, even if it is just so you can more easily break them. If you were truly one of ours, you would have torn your eyes out for watching us on that monitor. It would have been the right thing to do, and it would have felt gratifying in a way that is lost to you. We are sorry for that. When we are finished here, perhaps we can make amends and remove your eyes for you."

"Uh," I said. I kept thinking other words would follow, but I opened my mouth, and all that came out was: "Uhhh…"

Pneumatic hiss, hands, swearing. Johnson lifted me up and ushered me out of the room, while Steves screamed at the mechanic, demanding to know what was wrong with him. He was doing his best to answer. It was a question, after all. That was the rule.

Out in the hall, Johnson was saying something to me, but I

couldn't really hear his words. Or they wouldn't stick — just slipped in and out of my ears like birdsong. Eventually, though, my brain slowed down enough to process them.

"—we were wrong," Johnson said. "But there's no use putting good money after bad. It was a mistake putting you in there, but don't worry, you did fine. Just fine. We'll find a way to make the bastard talk, everybody's got someth—"

"No," I said, and Johnson blinked at me like he'd forgotten I could speak at all. "I just needed a minute. I want to go back."

"I want a bottle of scotch that grants wishes," Johnson laughed. "But we're going to have to live with disappointment, aren't we?"

"No." I stood up as straight as I could. I was still a full foot shorter than Johnson. I probably always would be. "I'm not done."

"Oh, yes." He hung his head over me, glaring down like I was an ant beneath his foot, and he was about to step. "You *are* done. You are surely that."

"Not yet," Steves said.

Neither of us heard her come back out into the hall. She looked at me like I was breaking her heart, and she looked at Johnson like he was peeing in her water glass.

"He is done," Johnson said, each word its own sentence.

"All we have so far is philosophy and nonsense," Steves replied. "We need real intel on what happened to Circle: how many were involved in that slaughterhouse, and where the bastards are now. You got that?"

She looked at me until I nodded. She looked at Johnson, but he just stuck his jaw out and stared.

"Do I have to pull rank?" she said. She sounded sad.

Johnson's eyes went wide for a second, but then his whole body turned into a board, and he gave her a salute so crisp and proper, all the middle fingers in the world couldn't do it justice.

"No, sir," Johnson said. "We are to send our only child to sit alone in a room with a murderer who has just threatened to rip out his eyes — got it, sir!"

"You are dismissed, sergeant," Steves answered. "Get some air."

It always amazed me how they could turn their ranks, which they were usually so proud of, into the most profound insults. Johnson spun like a marionette and marched, stiff-legged, to the rear of the car. The door hissed shut behind him, followed by a faint metallic thump. I knew he'd punched something and probably hurt himself. Again.

"Kiddo." Steves dropped into a half-squat, putting her eyes at my level. I guess she thought that made me feel better. It did not. "I know you're scared but—"

"You don't," I said. "Because I'm not. I just didn't know how to respond for a minute, okay? I would have figured it out, if you two hadn't butt in."

I wanted it to sting, but Steves just smiled. She went to rub my head, but I slapped her hand away.

"Can I go back in now?" I asked.

"You sure you're ready?"

"I am."

"And you know what questions to ask?"

"I'll ask what he's going to answer," I said.

She started to say something, which was almost certainly going to be condescending, so I added, "But yeah, I'll try."

The mechanic hadn't budged an inch. I bet if I had memorized the exact placement of every one of his fine white hairs before I left the room, I wouldn't find a single one out of place now. You'd think it would be hard to tell where he was looking, since he didn't have pupils. But you always knew. I took my seat as slowly as possible, maybe to show him how unruffled I was. Maybe because I was still pretty shaky and worried about tripping.

"I want to ask you about the people of Circle," I said.

An imperceptible head twitch was my only answer.

"What happened to the people of Circle?" I revised.

"We punished them appropriately," he replied.

"Who is 'we'?"

"We are the intent that lies behi—"

"No, no — not that stuff. Who helped you…uh…you…two? Who helped you guys kill the people of Circle? Was it a gang or something? Where are they now?"

"The people of Circle helped us," he said. I sensed more than saw a smile, so small it probably never existed.

"You know what I mean," I sighed. It really was like talking to an obstinate child. "You didn't kill all of them with your own hands."

Silence.

"…*did* you kill them all with your own hands?" I amended.

"Yes," he said quickly, like the conversation bored him. "Though technically, throughout the process, we employed sheet metal shears, a deadblow hammer, a hacksaw, a—"

"Why?" I didn't need to hear the rest. I couldn't.

"Because they broke the law. The law they set."

"What law?"

"Do not work on the Sabbath."

"Y-you killed forty-seven people because they worked on a Sunday?"

"It is an absurd law," the old man allowed. "They had so many laws that the citizens themselves did not know them all. They trivialized the very concept of the law, and so they did not respect the law. There was a fire at the market. The whole town gathered to fight it. We had arrived in town mere hours prior, and yet already every single citizen had violated the sanctity of the laws they themselves set."

"Wait, arrived?" I shifted in my seat. "You're not from Circle? You're not the mechanic?"

"No," he said. "We only came to Circle because it was the next scheduled stop of The Ouroboros."

He was waiting…for us?

"Why the overalls, then?" It was a stupid question, and I didn't care about the answer. But my mouth needed to buy my brain some time to think.

"Our own clothes were soaked with blood," the old man said. "We thought that might make a poor first impression."

I was ready for the door to open this time, for Steves and Johnson to come charging in and "save" me. As soon as the pneumatics hushed, I held up a hand for them to wait. And to my amazement, they did.

"I think he has more to tell," I clipped my words — *curt, professional, grown up*. "Give me more time."

Steves snickered a little, and my cheeks went hot. I turned to face her.

"Steves," I kept my tone harsh, but I knew my eyes were desperate. "I'm getting somewhere, aren't I?"

She didn't get it, but Johnson gave me a nod so small it may have just been a twitch. He put a hand on Steves shoulder, then turned and left the room.

"This isn't a game, kiddo," Steves warned, but she turned and left, too.

"That's exactly what it is," I said, to nobody.

I made a big show of regaining my composure. Johnson did that, sometimes — he "took a minute," right in the middle of an argument, to go smooth back his hair. Check his teeth, brush off his clothes. It always made me mad as hell, which was probably the point.

When I was sure my own heavy flannel shirt was unrumpled, its buttons done, the collar straight, I said,

"Why us?"

The old man raised his eyebrows but didn't answer.

"You said you only came to Circle to wait for the Snake," I clarified. "Why was it so important to meet us?"

"The harvest is nearly gathered," he said. "There are very few human beings left alive on this planet. Few that haven't already been consumed, that is."

"Consumed?" I could hear how small my own voice was, but I couldn't do anything about it. "You…you eat people?"

The old man almost laughed. *Maybe.* There was all the lead up to a laugh in his expression, and then nothing came out.

"We do not 'eat people,'" he answered. "We harvest their intent. We harvest it, because it's ours. Intent only exists because of us, and we have come to take it back."

He paused but could tell by one look at my face that I was just going to ask him to clarify.

"If the earth itself is gold," the old man explained, "then gold has no value. Gold becomes dirt. The value is not inherent to gold itself. The value is inherent to gold's rarity. On the universal scale, life is common: bacteria, single-celled organisms, dumb animals. Beasts that live without intent. Their life is not valuable, because it is common. But their very lack of intent makes it rare and therefore precious. Long, long ago, we came to your species, and we gave you the tools to sow intent within yourselves. We planted the seed of it, and it grew. You are the soil; your intent is our crop. When it became ripe — when your people advanced enough that all could share a single intent, not merely to survive, but to thrive, explore, and advance — that is when we came to harvest."

"H-how do you know when that happens?" I whispered. "Are you watching us?"

"We do not have to," he said. "This drive for discovery causes your people to seek out a greater meaning. You look to the skies. You listen. We are a signal, and when you receive that signal, we know to come. When you have advanced enough to not only be able to listen to the stars, but to know that you should, that is the bell for the harvest."

"But why?" It felt like the wrong question. *Every* question felt like the wrong question. "If 'intent' is something you can just give to us, why do you need it? And how can you 'eat' intent? What kind of thing does that?"

"The gifts we grant are seeds, not mature crops."

I opened and closed my mouth a few times. The old man sighed, then tried again.

"If everything was something, it would the same as nothing. It is not the something that is valuable, but the nothing around it. Stars are only stars because they shine in the void. Think of currency — you invented that as a means of understanding the universe. Something and nothing. You have a million dollars, but it is only valuable because others have none. That dichotomy gives you potential. You see an unfathomable multitude of galaxies and think of them as infinity, but the absence around those galaxies is the true infinity. Scarcity is existence. Intent is scarce. We are intent. Our existence is scarce. All beings must thrive or die. We sow a bit of ourselves into lesser things, so that we may get a bit more back, come harvest time."

There was a single peeling flake of paint on the underside of the table. I had it between my fingers. I picked at it. Worried it free from the rest. It was dry and hard where it had come away from the metal, but still rubbery where it met up with the rest of the paint. I peeled the dead part away, and it dragged the living parts with it.

"So why bother talking to us?" I asked. "Not just the Snake. Anybody. If we're just…if we're dirt to you, why talk to dirt?"

"The farmer does not hate the soil," the man said, with oddly specific gentleness. "The farmer cares for the soil most of all, because it is necessary for the crop. Your people are on the brink of utter annihilation. My sisters have nearly everything they need. Soon they will not need to manifest within you as vessels but can walk the earth as their true selves. When that happens, they will devour you to the last. We want to save you. What few we can."

I laughed, but I wasn't sure why.

"So you're…what? You're good now? You're on our side?"

"We are not 'good,' because nothing is 'good.' It is a meaningless descriptor. We are 'justice,' and it could be said that we are 'on your side.' We are separate from our sisters now, because it is necessary in order to care for them. It is their turn to destroy. It is our turn to care. They reap the crop, and we tend the soil. We come as justice now because it is necessary to preserve you, so that we might harvest you again in the future."

"Wait." I pinned him with an accusing finger. "You slipped up. You're only 'justice' right *now*? What are you, usually?"

"We did not 'slip up.' We are honest, because transparency is a vital aspect of justice. But we are not always justice. A concept must, by nature, also contain its opposite. Justice is nothing if all is just, so to understand justice, there must also be injustice. To grasp order, there must be chaos. This time, we come to you with a face of white. If you survive this harvest, when you look upon our face again, it will be black, and our name will be chaos."

"And then what, it's one of your sisters' turn to play good guy?"

"Good is nothing," he said, "but the rest is right."

I didn't want to admit it, but for one dismal, shameful second, I felt a little proud.

"So it's all just…what? Some horrible game you play with your sisters?"

"No crop can be sown and reaped forever," the old man said. "Eventually, the soil will stagnate. You will no longer grow what we need. When that happens, we will come to you one final time, and all of our faces will be dark. You will be razed, and we will start a new crop elsewhere, within the minds of some other pathetic animal. But until that day, it is a shame to waste good soil. That is why one of us cares for you, even as the others destroy. The harvest must be taken, so three come with dark faces to reap. One comes with a face of light and tries to preserve some small measure of your race, so that it may seed, and grow again. We are order today, because it is our turn to care, but at other times we are also chaos. Today, our sisters are rage, entropy, and sadism — but they are also peace, ambition, and empathy. We continue this cycle until one of us fails to preserve the seed, or until your people grow rank, and no longer fit to harvest. This is not a 'game,' child. This is simple farming."

"So…" I spoke slowly, partly to make sure I got it right, and partly because my tongue felt heavy and dull. "You're the abstract concept of justice, and you're here to save us — not because you're on our side, but because you and your sisters need to leave a few of us alive to breed and multiply, just so you can come back someday and eat us again?"

"Mostly correct." The old man nodded. "Though you seem to be implying that we devour your flesh, when in fact we simply consume the intent within—"

I slapped the table with both palms.

"Whatever!" I said. "You may as well be eating us! You're feeding off of us, you're killing us — there's no difference! You use a lot of big words, but you're just some freaky alien monsters here to eat people."

Again, I sensed that moment of potential laughter within him; again, it came to nothing.

"We are not 'monsters,'" he said. "You misunderstand. We do not 'use' the concepts of justice, or empathy, or sadism — we *are* those concepts. They do not exist outside of us; we do not exist outside of them. If your fellow man forgets what peace is now and knows only rage, it is not because we *took* something from him. It is because we stopped *giving* something to him. The 'maniacs,' as you call them, are simply humanity in its natural form. The purest strain, absent our interference. You, and the others like you who remain unaffected by our presence, have simply interbred so thoroughly that our concepts have been inexorably mixed within you. You've bound justice with peace, empathy, and drive. You've applied virtues to those ideas, formed your own new concepts, and sewn them all together. You have taken our gifts and built your own selves out of them. You grow your own intent. This is good. This is the goal. The 'maniacs' are our tools. The 'survivors' are the harvest. Do you understand? We are not 'monsters' who 'use you.' We are the fundamental concepts that define your lives. We are the reason you are 'you.' And now, for that honor, you owe us a tithe."

I exhaled so long I started to see spots.

"Okay." I drummed on the table with my pointer fingers. "Then how do we kill you?"

The old man closed his eyes. I'd seen that look on Steves' face countless times before — whenever she completely lost patience with explaining something to me. Usually "duty," or "honor," or one time, "how to fieldstrip a rifle."

"You cannot."

"Why's the sky black?" I asked instead. He blinked at me. I guess he expected more protest, but I knew when somebody just plain wasn't going to answer you. I lived with Johnson.

"If you know everything," I pressed him, "you can answer that one, right?"

"That is us," he said.

"You turned it black?"

"It was not *our doing*," he said. "It *is* us. We come without body, but not without presence. The sky has not changed. It looks no different to the rocks, or the grass, or the animals. But there is enough of us in you that you can see us now. We have enveloped your world, and you can no longer look past us to see what lies beyond."

Have you ever tried to talk to somebody about something you needed, but — even though they have no intention of ever giving that thing to you — they still want to just talk your ear off? It's like being held hostage by a conversation.

"Are you done?" I meant it rhetorically — I was already standing to leave — but I forgot about the question rule. It gave the old man one last chance to speak.

"No," he snapped. "We are not. This vehicle, this community — it is the best chance humanity has to survive the harvest and grow again. Our sisters cannot help their nature. They will feed until you are all gone or something stops them. That something is us. You *must* join us or you are lost."

"If it's so important that we survive," I said, "then why kill all those people in Circle? There were more of them than there are here on the Snake."

"We cannot help our nature, either," he sighed. "But they would not have survived in our stronghold. Your people have more discipline. This whole colony revolves around it. You would thrive in the Walled City, and you are needed there. Soon. Our sisters are coming."

"Walled City?"

"The harvest is here." He pointed at the exterior wall, gesturing at the whole of the outside world. The motion made the skin on the back of my neck tingle. Something was very wrong with that, but I couldn't place it.

"We have been gathering all of ours in preparation for the last stand," the old man pressed on. "We have been accepting all of yours that come and seeking out still more. We have now fed enough to manifest in your world, physically. Our sisters will do the same, if they haven't already. When that happens, they will come. The bulk of humanity gathers at our feet. They look to the White Tower for salvation, and if there is any hope of offering it, we need you."

"How do we know this isn't a trap?" I didn't really care what he said next, but I had figured out what was wrong, and I needed to buy some time to figure out what to do about it.

See: he'd pointed at the wall, earlier.

His hands were free again.

After he broke the zip ties that first time, the scouts had secured both of the old man's wrists to the underside of the table with two pairs of handcuffs. Maybe he could slip that one bandaged, fingerless hand free of the cuffs — but the intact hand? The one with the pointer finger? No way he could wriggle that out. That meant he'd broken the cuffs. Snapped solid steel with so little effort that I didn't even hear it. He was ten feet away from me, at most. He could be on me before Steves and Johnson even opened the door.

"If it was a trap," he answered, "we would've sprung it already. Circle was proof enough of that."

The old man fell silent and considered me with his nothing eyes. It felt like a cat watching a wounded mouse. Then he followed my gaze, looked down at his own free hand, back at me, that almost laugh of his…

I lunged backward, a blind fall toward the door, trying to twist in the air, but he caught me by the ankle. It was a blink, an instant. Nothing moves that fast. Into the air and over and down and no breath — slammed flat on my back on the steel table. I gasped for air, but my lungs could only clench uselessly. The old man straddled my chest. Knees on my arms. I could smell stale, burnt oil emanating from his overalls. His long, fine white hair hung flat, draping his whole face in shadow, save for the absence of his eyes. I could still see them. I could always see them.

I tried to look away. He forced my gaze back to his. I closed my eyes; he pried them open. I stared into the white void. Windows looking out onto an empty, colorless sky.

No, not empty: something moved there, so far away it made my soul sick to think of it.

No, not far away: right in front of me. Just big — so enormous that even an infinite space couldn't contain it.

The thing wheeled there, in its own special plane, skewing angles that shifted and bent into themselves. A thought occurred to me, which I knew was not my own. An intruding idea. Greasy, urgent, violating. It thrust itself into me: the Walled City. A featureless white tower breaking the horizon. A shattered dam, thousands of people — tens of thousands — their shadows all wrong. Silhouettes in the distance, writhing limbs, a black fog, things too big to move, but did…

I knew I was screaming. I could hear it. But it was so far away, it was hard to care.

Then I heard a few pops and felt something wet. I slept. I didn't dream.

I'm grateful for that.

...

I was staring at the bottom of Yuri's bunk. I knew it instantly: a stain shaped like Greenland, a tear where I'd pulled out the cotton, one broken cable in the steel netting that ran between the support struts. I knew it like the back of my hand. It was the bunk above mine, after all.

"Kiddo?" Steves was sitting on her own bunk, opposite mine. Johnson slept in the one above her. His snores were almost comforting.

I didn't answer.

"You awake?" Steves tried again. Her voice was too soft. "You okay?"

She sat on the very edge of her mattress, feet flat on the floor, elbows on her knees, both hands grasping fistfuls of her own hair. Eyes bloodshot, careful smile.

I'd only ever seen her like this once before, back when Johnson got sick. Fever so hot you couldn't touch him. The antibiotics weren't working. Couldn't do anything but watch. I ran to the creek and back with cold towels, each one warm again by the time I returned, and Steves just sat on my bunk, looking over at his, slumped nearly double, grabbing her own hair, watching.

"O...kay," I said.

I sure didn't sound convincing.

Steves crossed over and held a cold metal tumbler to my lips. I drank. It's amazing how you forget, every single time, that water is the best thing in the world.

"Let me know when you need more, okay?" Steves whispered. It wasn't even a little bit of an order. It was actually kind of gross, hearing her voice with so little authority.

"What...happened?" It was easier to speak now, but my throat still felt weak. Like I hadn't used the muscles there for a long time.

"You've been out for days," she answered the question I was just thinking to ask. "Ever since that freak…"

Oil. Weight on my chest. White…

"Where is he?" The words came easier, the more that I used them.

"You don't have to worry about him."

"Where…?"

"He's gone, kiddo."

"Wh—"

"Gone!" she snapped.

There it was: the old steel in her voice. I knew she couldn't fake it forever.

I didn't say anything. Just practiced swallowing and watched Steves' face.

"He's dead," she sighed. "When he tackled you, we tried to get him off, but we just…couldn't. He wasn't even doing anything, just looking at you. And you at him. The both of you frozen like you were having a fuc…having a *damn* staring contest. But Johnson emptied a full clip into his back, and the freak didn't so much as twitch a finger. Not until I put one right in his forehead. Then…"

She rotated her hand at the wrist, like the rest wasn't worth saying. But I knew it was.

"Then what?" I pressed. "Something happened, didn't it?"

"I don't know," she admitted. "The room just went white, like some idiot dropped a flashbang. When we could see again, there was a hole in the roof of the Snake, right where that bastard went down. A perfect circle about two feet wide, cutting straight through the armor. Got a tarp over it so the rain doesn't get in."

I looked back up at the underside of Yuri's cot. Greenland.

“We have to go somewhere,” I said.

Steves made me repeat it.

“Where?” she asked.

“The Walled City,” I said. “That’s where everybody is. Everybody that’s left, anyway. It’s safe there. S-sorta safe. But we have to go.”

“I think you’re still delirious, kiddo.” She laughed.

“Grand Coulee, Washington,” I recited. “Seven hundred fifty-two miles miles west. The 200 to the 90 to the 174. It will take us six days to get there.”

Steves made a face like a bug had just flown into her mouth.

“Kiddo,” she said, slowly, so I wouldn’t miss all the extra patience she was using. “I don’t know what you think happened, but—”

“It doesn’t matter that you don’t believe me,” I said. I lifted a hand to trace the borders of Filthy Greenland. “His sisters saw him leave. They’ll be here soon. Then you’ll understand. Then you’ll believe me. If we survive it.”

“I’ll get Doc Rowen in here to check you out,” Steves said, already standing, so happy to have a mission. “Let your dad sleep though, okay? He was up for two days straight.”

Fading bootfalls and a pneumatic hush as the door slid open.

“Can I have that water again, first?” I asked.

“Sure thing, kiddo,” she said.

Scuff of rubber soles on the textured floor. Hollow ding of thin metal on thick, then the tumbler, cool in my hand.

“Thanks, Mom,” I said.

I felt her jump. It made me smile.

Little Thunder Road

John told the Kid that Decker's was picked clean three runs ago. Yet each time they came back, they found something new. Something that hadn't even been an option, the last time around. This run, it was canned mushrooms. Whole rack of 'em. Three runs back, they'd thought about taking the mushrooms. But the Kid made a face, and John made a face right back. The mushrooms sat on the shelf. They'd never be that desperate.

Two runs back, John and the Kid gave the mushrooms the eye again. But no, they settled on canned artichoke hearts instead.

One run back, and they opted for cat food. They gave the mushrooms a wide berth, walked big circles around them like each can was an active landmine — it would never come to that, they promised themselves; they'd get their act together; the hunting would go better; the crops would yield more; they'd be self sufficient.

Now, here they were again, John and the Kid, eyeballing twenty-six cans of sliced mushrooms like doomed men staring down a firing squad.

Those mushrooms, they knew they won. They were god damn smug about it. They had themselves an attitude — something about the font on the label, maybe. Just a little too cartoony. Came off sarcastic.

The teaser photo: just a bunch of textureless, rubbery pads strewn haphazardly in a puddle of mysterious brown liquid. The picture was so bad, so blatantly unappealing that no reasonable human would ever pay for them — would ever happily exchange their precious moments of toil for this chewy fungus, long-stewed in chemicals, tasting of stale soil and decaying metal. The mushrooms knew that. They were waiting. All this time, just waiting for society to collapse, and for John and the Kid to run out of stores. And now, the mushrooms mocked.

Took five minutes of grim staring before either moved. The Kid looked at John. John made a face. The Kid shook his head.

Things really *had* got that bad.

John hooked an arm 'round behind the stack of cans and swept them all into the wagon. Did it rougher than he had to, just to let the mushrooms know he and the Kid weren't going down without a fight.

The Kid, he went poking under the shelves, up and down the aisles, looking for goodies that'd gotten kicked under and forgotten about, back in better days. John, he just stared at the soda section, empty so long you couldn't even see the dust rings where the cans used to sit. But if you squinted there, if you put the old imagination to work, you could picture how it used to be. Gleaming spires of aluminum, each full of promise. A dozen varieties, all right there, all right for the taking and so cheap you hardly even thought about it.

Sure, I'll grab a soda, you said.

Sure, why not?

You didn't know.

The Kid cleared his throat. John checked over his shoulder. The Kid shrugged at him, then started for the doors. John grabbed the handle of the wagon and rattled twenty-six cans of dirtfruit toward the parking lot, out of the store, and into his life, forever.

Mushroom breakfast.

Mushroom lunch.

Mushroom dinner.

And for dessert?

No, not mushrooms. Don't be silly, there's plenty of—

Oh wait, no, it's mushrooms again.

The Kid hooked his haul to the blue ten-speed. Brought the handle of the wagon up into its cradle, flipped some latches, checked that the cargo net was holding all the goods in place — a pack of toilet paper, new pair of garden shears, rubber gloves with no holes in 'em — and threw a leg over the frame.

John did the same with his load — made a big show of checking over the mushrooms; just mushrooms, far as the eye could see — then saddled up. The Kid made a face. John made a face back. The Kid laughed. John laughed.

Neither really bought it.

Weight up on the pedals, joints already creaking in protest at the ride to come, and the symphony began: the only musician was the bumpy road, and his only instrument was two dozen cans of mushrooms in a hard plastic wagon. It was John's least favorite song ever, and everything within a mile of him would be listening to it for the rest of the day. And probably into the night, if they didn't make good time.

The apocalypse hadn't made much of a difference to Newcastle, Wyoming. A few less people, a few more weeds, about the same amount of dust. If the sky hadn't gone black as absence; if one or two loud pickup trucks passed them too close on the shoulder; if old Mrs. Wittstone came out on her porch to call them savages, redskins — and worst of all, to her mind, Mexicans — you might think nothing had changed. John couldn't wait to put this sad old place behind them and get back on the plains. Off 16 and onto the 450. Leave Main Street behind, exchange it for Little Thunder Road. Out there in the basin, things were different. You knew the apocalypse had come because the whole world breathed a bit easier for it.

Packs of wild dogs, even wilder horses, the skies wilder still — nature saw the space left behind by man, and she stepped right in like she was just waiting for the music to change. It was raw out there, scary, and dangerous…but coasting down the 450 through tall grass that moved like an ocean, lightning sputtering on the distant horizon, the sounds of small things moving all around you — it felt right.

John and the Kid, they never talked about it. But John could see it in the Kid's eyes. He could see the braves they both came from, dancing back there behind the retinas. He could see the Kid transforming right there in front of him: John's bruised leather jacket shredding off the Kid's skinny back, his shoulders bulging, his hair growing long — he could see that tired old Schwinn grow legs. Squeaky wheels turning into the hard breath of a charging Appaloosa.

John felt it surge in him, too — every bit as strong as the Kid. But he had to hold himself back from whooping, even as the Kid let loose. See, John remembered who he really was: raised in a suburb, not a reservation. Long days at the shop, short nights on a sagging couch in front of a bad TV. He was a man. A disappointment. Even in fantasy, he wasn't a brave.

The Kid, though, he hadn't had enough of the world that came before to know what he couldn't be — what he wasn't allowed to be anymore. John knew he wasn't ever a proud hunter or a fearless warrior — he couldn't ride a damn horse or string a bow. Probably couldn't name half the gods his ancestors had fought and died for. John was only ever a subpar mechanic, and a better than average air hockey player. That was it. Only and ever it.

But the Kid, well — who's to tell him he can't be a brave, here in this world? When the sun is gone, and the sky is black, and monsters walk the earth while buffalo roam the grasslands again…ain't this just the place for a brave?

But for the Kid, it wasn't enough to be it. He wanted to talk about it, too. Wanted John to join him in that ghost tribe. Wanted to hear about the old ways and wanted John to tell the tales. Like back when John was a kid, there'd been some shaman in a six-foot headdress passing wisdom around in a great smoking pipe. But the closest thing to a For Real Indian in John's childhood was the guy on the Tootsie Roll wrapper.

So while the Kid whooped and kicked his legs out, urged his steed on and took aim at phantom prey with an invisible bow, John just smiled and shook his head. He'd be damned if he'd take the Kid's dream away, but there wasn't room enough in there for John, too.

Only about ten miles out of Newcastle, and the road ahead got dark. The Kid squeaked to a halt, and John rattled up alongside him. They both eyed the shadow creeping up the horizon. John looked up to check for thunderclouds, but while there was a stormfront (always a stormfront here in spring), it was a hundred miles out and leaving. This shadow, it moved, but not like clouds — flickering over the earth slow-fast, knocking down miles in seconds. This shadow moved like a glacier. Steady, and onward. With a purpose.

The Kid gave John a look, and John gave him that look right back. The Kid popped his kickstand, and John followed suit. Knees crackling out an argument ("We just settled into the ride, man, we can't stop now!"), he stooped to shrug off his pack. Pawed aside the wadded-up raingear and felt around 'til he touched metal.

The spyglass was going on two hundred years old, all worn brass and faded glass. Three segments that collapsed down into one, heavy with the weight of obsolescence. Heavier still with the weight of the flag emblazoned on one side: an "X" made of stars. John had found it a few months back, nestled in its custom wood mount on the mantle of a five-bedroom ranch out east, past Newcastle. Whole room done up in Confederate artifacts. Weathered rifles with suspiciously stained bayonets. Torn gray uniforms. Age-cracked photos of hate-eyed men with absurd sideburns. John and the Kid knocked most of that crap to the floor and spat on the pile till they ran outta spit. Woulda lit it all on fire, too, but the land had been dry back then. John could see an inferno the size of a state, blazing in his imagination. Could see himself trying to explain to Katy and Mitch and Dutch and all the rest: "Well, see, we started it to spite the ghost of some idiot, and I guess things got outta hand…"

So John settled for pocketing the spyglass. Binoculars would do a better job, of course, but he figured that if a Confederate relic could save their lives just once, whoever used to own it would surely turn over in their grave a few times.

John ran a finger over the raised stars of the flag and gave it a bitter smile. He clacked the glass out to its full length and sighted down the highway, toward the dark patch in the distance.

It wasn't the shadow of some unseen thunderstorm, or a blight on the grass, or a plague of locusts, or any of the other million terrible things John prayed it might be, instead of what it really was: a mob.

More people than John had ever seen, maybe in all his life, crammed together into one big horde that ate the horizon. They were moving away from John and the Kid, which would've been a good thing, if they hadn't been moving toward the commune — John and the Kid's home, containing the only people they loved in this world. Maybe the only actual people left in it.

The Kid asked John what he saw, but John didn't have an answer. Turned out that was answer enough. The Kid set his jaw and mounted up his bike. John went to grab him, but the boy's legs were already pumping. Supply wagon bopping and jittering along as he pedaled furiously down Little Thunder Road, toward the cresting wave of blackness.

That's the thing with kids: They always think they know. And the harder you tell them they don't, they harder they believe they do.

The Kid thought he knew what the mob was, and maybe he did — but he couldn't fathom how many they were. He started charging at 'em because he figured they were a few hundred strong, maybe a mile or two out. Not a few hundred thousand strong, twenty miles out. The Kid thought he knew what the mob was made of — some version of those maniacs that killed the world: the angry ones, or the quiet ones, maybe a bunch of game-players if they were really unlucky. But he didn't see what was perched above the horde. That monstrous silhouette, its dark lines lost amidst the mass of shadows. The Kid didn't see the millipede, three stories tall if it was a foot, each of its thousand legs the size of a tree trunk. Every inch of it serrated like a steak knife, the whole thing made up of void. A cut out in the paper of the world. Blackness so black it hurt your brain to look at it.

Now, in fairness to the Kid, they hadn't seen anything like that before. Hadn't even heard rumors of it, and rumors used to be the currency of the land, back when the commune still saw travelers. The Kid couldn't have known what was down there, but that's the thing with kids: they always think they do.

John willed his pulse to stop racing, asked the cold sweat to pause in his pores, and he put his pack back together with hands he pretended weren't shaking. He mounted up his own bike and somehow managed to convince himself not to pedal after the kid as furiously as his aching joints would allow. The Kid didn't know how many miles were in this race, and if John was going to win it, endurance, not speed, would be the key. And he *had* to win it. His whole heart rode on the outcome.

The distance between John and the Kid grew. Boy just kept pulling ahead, even as John's breath went stale and aged to dust inside his chest. But the Kid had kid energy. It was uneven, came in bursts. Screaming outta nowhere like a guitar solo. A mad flurry of pedals, then some exhausted coasting, and repeat — each iteration a little shorter than the last. John's energy was a drumbeat, the rattle of his mushroom wagon carried on steady as a metronome. They ate up maybe five miles of road like that, drumbeats chasing guitars, before John finally pulled up alongside the Kid. The boy's hair was slick with sweat. The wildness behind his eyes was still kicking at the glass, but he didn't yell, or cuss, and he especially didn't apologize for taking off like an idiot. When John's bike squealed to a halt alongside his, the Kid just asked for much farther it was. John told him it was far. The Kid asked how long it would take to get to the commune. John told him it would take a while. The Kid asked if they were gonna try to get past the horde and warn the commune first. John told him of course they were — they just weren't gonna be stupid about it.

The Kid didn't say a sideways word in response, but a blind man could tell he didn't like it. After a while, he finally swallowed enough pride to talk again, and he asked what they were gonna do. John told him he had a plan.

He'd lied to the Kid before.

Nah, they weren't looking at us funny. No, I didn't hear what the cashier said about us. Your mother and I still love each other very much. You can be anything you want when you grow up…

What was one more on the pile?

John made the Kid slow down. Cited some nonsense about conserving energy, but mostly he just needed time to think. The Kid didn't have much to say, aside from asking what the plan was, which John didn't know, so John didn't have much to say, either. They just rode, squeaking gear solo with a steady beat of rattling cans. An hour on and John waved the Kid to a stop.

The best plan he could come up with — the only plan he could come up with — was flat-out terrible. But the key to sounding like you have a good plan is drowning out all the stupidity with a flood of unnecessary details. And it always helps to draw a diagram, too. People love diagrams.

Kids, especially.

John brought the Kid over to the side of the road, where asphalt gave way to gravel gave way to dirt. Had the boy squat down while John drew a map in the dust with his pointer finger. He plowed out the highway, 450 East, then drew a pair of X's for their current position. A big spiky square for the horde, a cartoonish little barn for the commune, and a thinner, squiggly bit for the dirt road leading up to it. Then he carved a serpentine line from the X's right up to the barn.

Hay Creek.

The diagram still looked empty to John's eyes. Thin enough to see through. So he roughed out a bunch of other roads, buildings, and landmarks — didn't matter they had nothing to do with the plan — before walking the kid through it all. Plenty of extra steps along the way, to make it seem thorough, even though it pretty much all boiled down to this: wait for the horde to get a little further on, just past Hay Creek, then ditch the highway and follow the dry creekbed all the way up to the commune, skirting the mob and getting everybody out before it's too late.

When John finished explaining his very, very stupid plan, the Kid nodded seriously a few times, like there was anything to think about. Then he smiled up at John, full of trust and faith. John just about killed himself on the spot.

He didn't tell the Kid that here, at the trailing edge of the rainy season, the creek might not be dry all the way up. Didn't mention that, although a big mob moved slow on the highway, so did a pair of morons struggling through the brush. He sure didn't say anything about the size of the horde, how the fringes of it strayed out for miles — right across the creek, far enough up the way.

And John wasn't much of a fighter.

And even if the Kid thought different, he was still just a kid.

And neither of them had weapons, to speak of: a pair of hunting knives, a can of bear mace that said it expired two years ago, and an airhorn. They came prepared to drive off hungry animals, not bloodthirsty mobs.

You were just supposed to run, if you saw a maniac. But nobody at the commune had seen one for months. Maybe longer. Of course, now John could see why that was: They all thought the monsters were dying out. Drying up like a shallow pond in summer. But really, it was just the tide pulling out before the flood.

A few more lies on the pile.

John hoped they'd live long enough for his account to come due. In the meantime, there was nothing for it but to move, so they moved.

They rode on, as close to the horde as they dared, which really wasn't all that close. They waited until the bulk of the maniacs were well past the culvert where Hay Creek ran under Little Thunder Road. John told the Kid to stash the bikes in the reeds — so they could come back for the supplies, when this was all over. The Kid lit up when he said that, practically whistling while he led the bicycles and wagons into the brush. See, that's the kind of asshole John was: he was a man who would keep selling a lie until it was bought.

The Kid sidled up to John, but he hardly noticed, busy as he was hating himself. The Kid nudged him out of it, and John asked if he was ready. The Kid nodded once, got his face all set serious, then vaulted the guardrail to land in the creekbed below. It was only a five-foot drop, but John still took the time to walk around the rail and slide down the dusty slope. He could just see himself pulling a stunt like that and breaking a knee, getting them both killed even sooner than they surely would be already. He gave the Kid a thumbs up for the stunt before they set off. Least he could do.

They pushed on up the dry creek, parting hay like they were

swimming through it. Cicadas sounded a constant alarm, playing their tension song from unseen perches on every side. Hay in the creekbed grew in patches, coming in late and growing hard like it knew the rains were coming, and it had to make the most of its time here before it was washed away. John and the Kid would wrestle through one patch of growth, pause at the far side before stepping out, realize they could only see about six feet before the next patch started, and step out anyway. Every bunch of hay was an island; every clear space between them was a stretch of dangerous sea.

John waved the Kid to a halt, and they both slipped back, letting the stalks fold shut around them. They watched through the slits as something rustled around the next island. John held his breath, forced himself not to hold his breath, realized how loud his breathing was, and held his breath again. He hoped the Kid was braver than he was or at least too dumb to realize how scared he should be. John reached out and touched the Kid's shoulder, felt his knobby bones through the battered leather jacket that the Kid had commandeered from him last winter. Fingertips ready to push, shove the Kid off and have him running in an instant while John did…what? Bought him some time? That's about the best he could hope for: to die in a distractingly long fashion.

The rustling grew louder, paused, louder again. Finally, the hay parted.

John didn't know whether to laugh, cry, or take a swing. He thought it was a camel at first, but no: big round muzzle, mop top hair over nubby ears, all soft fur and awkward knees. An alpaca — what the hell was an alpaca doing out here? Well, aside from having a blissful lunch and scaring the crap out of John.

He was about to stand and wave the beast off when he heard more scratching from the brush. The Kid was just getting to his own feet and wasn't ready for John to push him back like he did. He fell on his butt, the hay swallowing most of the noise. John could feel him getting ready to protest, but he held a single finger up, and the Kid went quiet. Another figure pushed through the patch of hay beside the alpaca and stood swaying in the short grasses between islands.

If you looked closely, squinted a bit, and used your imagination, you could sort of see how it used to be human once. Naked save for scraps of colorless rags that were probably once very expensive slacks, judging by the quality of the leather belt still buckled around its midsection, and the worn stub of a ragged silk tie around its neck. The rest of its clothes hadn't survived the weather, leaving only leashes and collars to mark that it once been a civilized thing. Not a patch of bare skin visible on it, every inch caked in dried mud, blood, and other filth. Long, greasy, uneven hair, missing fingers, most of an ear, bloody pockmarks spattered all across his chest. The man swayed in the creekbed, chin up to the sky, throat working to produce guttural nonsense. If you paid attention only to the cadence of the sounds and did not assign the barks and growls any particular meaning, it almost sounded like words. Half of some long distant, barely remembered argument.

The maniac must have reached a pivotal moment in its imaginary conflict. It moaned and dug its fingers into the flesh of its chest. New, raw divots joined the old pockmarks as the man tore at himself and howled, then abruptly fell quiet. He pivoted toward the alpaca, face twisted in fury, but seemed to look right through it. The alpaca bolted anyway, just to be on the safe side, but the maniac was already resetting its loop: back to mumbling and lurching.

The Kid pulled on John's sleeve, and he waved the boy off. But the tug came again, and John turned to face him. The Kid knew better than to risk talking, so he just pointed at the side of his own eye — gone wide with fear — and then to the maniac. John looked back to the thing, but it took him a moment to see what the Kid meant: he'd just dismissed it as a trick of the light at first. A thin stream of black vapor, too wispy for smoke, trailed from the man's eyes. Like fishing line, or maybe razor wire: the vapor spun and coiled onto itself in nasty hooks and vicious loops as it arced away from the maniac, up the creekbed. Its source lost in the hay.

John turned back to the Kid, nodded so the boy would know he had seen it, was proud of him for noticing, amazed by his perception even in times of extreme stress…then shrugged, so the boy would know John had no idea what to do with that information.

John pointed back the way they'd came. The Kid shook his head no, but John nodded yes, then waved toward the farthest patch of hay, out at the edges of the creek. He made two fingers walk very carefully across his palm. He waved again. The Kid seemed to get it, so they turned around to backtrack — every careful footstep a thunderclap, every rustle a gunshot, every breath a roaring engine that gave away their position. It took ages, and John's haunches burned with the effort of stooping for so long, but at last they'd retreated enough to find a new route through the hay. They hugged the low walls of the wash, hopping between grassy islands whenever the maniac's ranting looped. When they could no longer hear the man guttering like a low candle, John motioned for the kid to pause. He sat on his butt in the soft grass and stretched his legs out to either side. The Kid gave him an uncertain smile, but he knew better to ask. This was an old guy thing, the Kid had to figure, just like why it took John so much longer to pee, or why he had to squat real low to pick anything up from the ground.

When his joints finally loosened up, and his cramping muscles began to ease, John stood and nodded. The Kid set off, but John caught him by the shoulder. They both knew the kid was quieter, faster, had himself a pair of eyes that saw and ears that heard, but even still — John would be taking point. He always took point.

Towering bulwarks of hay marched along either bank, swallowing most of the wind, making a rush that sounded like distant highway traffic. The noise made John heartsick, for reasons he couldn't quite pin down. Old paw prints in the dried mud where the grass wouldn't take. The cicadas whined a one-note tune, while unseen birds riffed at their leisure. Would've been a nice scene, if they still had the sky.

It was the Kid that stopped John this time. He pointed to a shadow beyond the far reeds, but John couldn't see it. He was about to shake his head and press on, when the light shifted. A cloud passed, somewhere above the blackline, and the colorless sun lit up a figure standing behind the curtain of hay just opposite their own. John prayed for Alpacas. His prayers were not answered.

The maniac burst from his hiding place and charged. Every instinct failed John, save one: He didn't run, or fight, or bark orders — he just silently pushed the Kid behind him, then stood there like a toddler facing down a rhino.

Turned out to be a good thing John froze. Halfway across the gap between islands, the maniac skidded to its knees and hammered at the ground with both fists. This one didn't make a sound, just battered the earth until something internal switched off, and it laid on its side, breathing heavily. This one was in better shape than the last: mostly intact overalls, gone black with filth, still shielded its body from the elements. The Kid tapped the sides of his eyes, and John looked for the phantom razorwire. Had to squint, angle his head from side to side to pick it out, but it was there: twin barbed curls of black filament chasing off to the northwest. Same direction the other maniacs had been heading.

No movement. Still as the grave. Seemed like whatever spell came over the thing had passed. John was just about to press on, when the maniac lurched to its feet — more like it had been dragged than chose to do it. It loped unsteadily up the creekbed like it had suddenly remembered some urgent business just around the corner. John and the Kid stood there listening to its rustling grow faint, then strong again. That made sense, John figured — the last one had been on a loop, too. This one would probably come surging back through the stalks to lose another fistfight with the dirt, then he and the Kid could press on while it laid down.

Something hit him from behind, and he lost his footing. Stumbled right out into the open corridor between the islands of hay. John whirled, ready to fight this time, but it was only the Kid. He'd shoved John forward and was already following. John couldn't risk speaking, so he tried to ask the Kid how big an idiot he was planning on being using facial expressions alone. The Kid pointed behind him, tugged on his earlobe, then gave a more urgent tug on John's wrist.

John thought the louder rustling was coming from the one in the overalls, on his way back from the loop. But the sound wasn't ahead of them at all.

The naked businessman, blindly thrashing up from behind.

John and the Kid ducked into cover just as the other maniac burst through the hay, right where they'd been standing. But he wasn't coming after them. He pressed on to the northwest without pause, following Overalls. Moved with the same reluctant, stumbling gait, like somebody trying to shove a drunk out the door at last call. John damn near laughed at how scared he was, and he saw the Kid doing the same: just breathing heavy and shaking his head.

John straightened his back, trying to work the kinks out while they let the adrenaline settle. Blood rushed to his head as he stretched, sketching abstract shapes across his field of vision. Tried to blink them away, but they stayed, even as the stretch ended. He shifted his weight from foot to foot, watching the lines idly distort, then reform. He squinted and saw that the loops and curls above his head were all connected. Joined together by thin, barbed lines, black as space.

Dozens, maybe hundreds of them, all pinstriping across the creekbed just a few feet above their heads.

Naked Businessman and Overalls had moved at the same time, in the same direction. Northwest, up the creekbed, toward the commune. Those strange black lines led off that way, too. That meant something. Itched in John's brain. Almost had it, lost it. Slippery like a bar of soap. The maniacs, the movement, the lines: Put it all together, what does it mean?

Panic made him think too fast, which made him slow. His brain jumped gears before it could finish anything it started. John ground his teeth together and willed his thoughts straight.

Whatever those lines were — *what are they? What do they mean, what do they do?*

That's not important!

Whatever those lines were, they led northwest, and the maniacs followed them. *Do they know the commune is there? Is it too late already?*

Not. Important.

If there were more of those lines, they must be coming from other maniacs. Those maniacs had to be somewhere behind him and the Kid. If they, too, were following their lines like Overalls and Naked Businessman…

John followed the black filaments until he lost them against the dark sky. They veered off at an angle, much more east than south. He tracked their trajectory to the side of the creekbed, up the banks. The horde wasn't coming up the creek behind them. They were about to cross it…right where John and the Kid were standing.

A smarter man, a quicker man, he would've put it together faster. But no, the Kid had to go and get himself cursed with an idiot for a father.

John didn't even have time to hate himself at the moment, because the first ragged silhouette was already cresting the banks. John hissed at the Kid to run, and the boy was ready…to head in the wrong direction. He started to bolt downstream, back toward the highway. John shoved him around, back up the creek, toward the pair of maniacs that'd just passed. Boy's first few steps were hesitant, like he couldn't believe his daddy could be that stupid, until he checked over his shoulder and saw the shadows up on the banks behind John. Three more shapes had already joined the first.

That got the Kid moving.

Took everything he had to match the boy's pace, but John hustled up beside the Kid and pushed on ahead. He put an arm out and slowed their pace from a full-blown sprint to a panicked jog. They hadn't been spotted yet. This wasn't a race. It was a balancing act. John could hear the two psychos up ahead as they tripped, crashed, and stumbled through the brush; he could hear the mob behind as its leading members rolled down the banks into the creekbed; he could hear his own heart, hammering in his ears like a rock concert.

The Kid looked at John's arm, holding him back. Up to John. Back to the arm. Back to John. Expression on his face asking if John was crazy, or an idiot, or both. John just shook his head, and the Kid, bless his heart, he trusted him. He followed John's lead. The pair of them hustled ahead and fell back, paused when the rustling ahead grew too loud, raced when the snapping behind took its place. They hid in the hay islands as long as they dared, then sprinted through the grassy interstitial zones; they damn near alerted the maniacs up front, then came within inches of being seized by the hordes behind. Again and again. So long that John's muscles burned, and his adrenaline began to ebb. High-alert panic giving way to sick, shaky nerves. He was about to give in: stop and try to boost the Kid up the steep dirt bank, no matter how terminal that idea was for John. Anything was better than this: rats in a bucket of water, circling until fatigue drowned them both. Then the Kid spotted something…

Up ahead the creek took a hard westward turn, leaving a small grassy culvert on the opposite side. It was a pool of still water when the creek ran full — John recognized the rock he'd dared the Kid to dive off last summer, the log they dried their clothes on when they were tired of swimming — but now it was just another dead end.

John saw what the Kid was thinking and went through a mental roll call of every profanity he knew. But it was better than keeping on how they were — struggling in a vise that closed an inch every minute. They tucked themselves as far back in that culvert as they could. Made themselves real small and waited. Waited for the flood of monsters to swell.

The first through the brush was a mummy, complete with ancient rags. It was tall, leaner than John had ever seen a living human, skin so dry and sun-beaten that its lips had peeled back above the teeth. It stumbled towards them, oblivious for now, but only a matter of time before they were spotted. Then, twenty paces from their hiding spot, it veered away. Looked involuntary, like a drunk trying and failing to walk a straight line. But the next maniac through the reeds followed its exact steps. And the one after, and the one after that. John raised his eyes at the Kid, and the Kid raised his eyes to the sky. John looked up, but it took ages for him to pick out the barbed black lines with his old man vision. They twisted curly-cue paths straight across the bend in the creek and ran off to the northwest.

The mob fell in the riverbed, and that pretty much made them a river. They worked the same rules. They followed the path of least resistance. If the current drew most of the water away from this still pool, why wouldn't the maniacs do the same? John had them riding along the rapids with death on both ends. The Kid figured, why not just paddle out of it?

Was there a word for being so proud of someone else that you wind up hating yourself in equal measure? Bet the Germans had one.

John put a hand on the Kid's shoulder, gave him a tight smile, and nodded once. The Kid returned the nod, fighting back a smile of his own, and together, they watched the horde march on by. It didn't take as long as John thought — as long as his aching legs and constricted chest hoped — before the mob passed. There were maybe fifty of them altogether, with stragglers on either end of the main pack. When they were about as sure as they could be that no more were coming, John and the Kid crept out into the creekbed like furtive deer, ready to bolt at the first sound.

It was the absolute last thing John wanted to do — every cell in his body damned him just for thinking it — but he pointed up the creek, the way the horde had just passed, and beckoned for the Kid to follow. The mission was the same: they had to get to the commune first and warn the others. It's not that John was a brave man. God knows he never thought of himself as that. It's just that cowardice wasn't really an option. Not when the Kid was watching.

So they followed the horde.

A suspicious rustle from up ahead and John held his fist up. The Kid froze in his tracks. The first time it was just the wind, the second time was a toad. The third was purely John's overdriven imagination, and the fourth was a toad again.

As bad as John needed to be a hero for the Kid, usually the first step in heroism was not getting everyone and everything you loved butchered in a creekbed. The next step?

Hell if John knew. Probably "get a cape."

The Kid was getting restless. John could feel it in his bones. Could feel the Kid's worries crawling around in his own skull. They wouldn't get to the others first by just following behind the maniacs. Even a kid could see that much. They needed to make a move, and soon. John had an idea. Not a good one.

John and the Kid had one advantage over the maniacs: they could adjust their own path. The horde moved like water. It flowed inexorably toward its destination. If the horde met an immovable object or an impassable expanse, they just broke against it, around it, through it. About a mile before skirting past the commune, Hay Creek hit some narrows. It crowded into a long, slow dip, then chased itself around a series of winding bends before widening and growing shallow again. If the maniacs knew the territory, they'd crawl up the banks and go overland for a time. But they didn't.

John sure hoped they didn't.

When the walls started to close in, John waved the Kid to the side and helped him clamber up the bank. Boy made it look easy, because it probably was easy, if you were a boy. For John it was like wrestling a beach. Soft silt that gave way at every handhold, sent him sliding back one foot for every two feet he climbed. But he made it to the top, because what was his other option? The Kid was watching.

John nodded to the Kid and shrugged at his filthy frontside like, "How do I look?" But the Kid didn't laugh. He just sat there, flat on his ass, legs akimbo, staring slack-jawed and idiot-eyed at something on the far side of the creek. John turned to see what it was, even as every instinct swore at him for it.

A few hundred feet of tall grass between them and a world of monsters. An impenetrable huddle of snapping, raging lunatics, so savage and weathered they barely registered as human.

It was a Bon Jovi of maniacs.

That was the biggest crowd John had ever seen: a Bon Jovi concert he went to as a teenager, down in Denver. He didn't even like Bon Jovi, but the girl he'd been trying to screw sure did, so off he went — driving all night to get there in a busted Nissan that wouldn't shift past second gear. Young John just stood there, frozen, in paralytic awe at the sea of people that somehow managed to fit inside Mile High Stadium. John knew it was a great big world full of people, most of them assholes, but he never really fathomed it before that point. Seeing that crowd, it was the first time John understood that the little towns he'd spent his whole life kicking around in — they were like tiny seeds, blown off from the tree. Seeds that failed to sprout. That just moldered there in the dirt, never changing or growing. They weren't anything like their massive parents. A real city was a whole different universe from what he knew.

And that was the last concert John ever went to — not counting bar bands and some buddy's garage show. He avoided cities like he owed them money. A part of young John changed that night. Understood that he was a very small part of a very large thing, and that knowledge suffocated him. In a hidden place he'd never admit to, John kept a mental snapshot of one of his biggest fears: the largest crowd he'd ever seen, sweat-faced and frantic, all screaming the words to "Livin' On A Prayer."

Well, the largest crowd he'd ever seen…until now. This was more than a Bon Jovi's worth of maniacs. This was three Bon Jovis. Three Bon Jovis and a Springsteen, probably. And they were all screaming, too — just not "whoa-o, we're halfway there."

Then John realized something else, something worse. He remembered they were smack dab in the middle of an ocean of grass and not much else. Understood it wasn't a forest he was looking at. Not massive black tree trunks, but hundreds of enormous legs. Each rising thirty feet to a body the size of a train. Pure, absent black. Void black. Abyssal, thirsty, devouring black — not so much a color as a blindness. A cutout in the paper of the world.

John couldn't make out any details. Could only tell the body was segmented by the way the black silhouette stood out against the dishwater gray light. Could only see the always-working jaws by the spots where they weren't. And from everywhere on it, from every single inch of its gargantuan carapace, a fine net of black lines ran from its body to the writhing horde of maniacs below.

The centipede's steps were slow but long. Each movement matched by a frantic burst from the surrounding mob. That explained the halting, awkward movements John and the Kid had seen earlier — the centipede walked, unhurried and uneven, and the maniacs stumbled and surged to follow.

Somehow, the Kid found the will to speak, when John was pretty sure he could only open his mouth to scream. He asked John a question. He asked it twice, 'cause John wasn't listening for words the first time. John didn't have an answer for the Kid, not even a good lie. He was too twisted up by the question itself.

The Kid asked if the monster was leading the people…or coming *from* them.

Somehow, John managed to get to his feet on legs that felt like rubber stilts. He motioned for the Kid to follow and hoped his silence came across as gruff instead of terrified. They darted through the tall grass, sliding flat when the centipede's massive head swung toward them, sprinting when it looked away. They moved in fits and starts, a pair of ants crossing a busy sidewalk. John could see the commune now, the faded silo rising above the low hills ahead. A quarter mile that might as well have been a trip to the moon, for the progress they were making. Plus, they'd have to cut across the creekbed again after it came out of the switchbacks. If they weren't ahead of the maniacs by then…

John warned himself away from that course of thought. What good is thinking when you're doing something this stupid already?

Run when the beast looks away, dive when it comes searching for you. Over and over. Thistles in his shirtcuffs, thorns in his palms, scrapes on his knees and belly. The Kid couldn't be doing much better, but if he was hurting, he wasn't about to let on.

Then, finally, the plains broke.

A stretch of dried mud like a shattered windshield. Haystalks and river stones. The creek bed lay before them, and while John could hear distant chattering — one half of a dozen imaginary arguments, just around the corner — he and the Kid were ahead of the maniacs.

They shared their usual beleaguered look and grim nod, then pushed up out of the grass into a dead heat. Fifty feet past the creek and the hills dropped out. The gully would hide the pair from the centipede's gaze, all the way to the commune.

Fifty feet to home free. Not the moon, not even around the block. Right there. Just there.

And they didn't make it.

John saw it first, and he shoved the Kid right out of his sprint. Sent the boy tumbling ass over elbows into the dirt, then caught a face full of it himself. The Kid was stunned, operating on reflex, trying to get up. John put a hand on the back of his head and held him down. The Kid struggled automatically, until he looked into John's eyes. Read whatever was in there. Or maybe he just heard the screams.

The Kid was shaking himself free of John's grip, so John made a rapid series of deals with every god he could think of: a lifetime of service, a church in their honor, his blood, his life, his soul — if only the Kid didn't have to see what was happening just in front of him.

Nobody took John up on the offers.

The Kid looked, and there wasn't any unseeing it, so John just crawled over and pressed his full weight on the boy's back instead. That little idiot had the hero gene in him — who knew where the hell he got it — but John knew the Kid's blood wouldn't just let him lie still while those maniacs tore the commune apart right in front of his eyes. The Kid struggled, but John bore down. One hand pressed over the Kid's mouth in case he screamed, but he didn't make a sound. Just bit and fought and cried.

A huddle of things that used to be people, tearing at something unseen on the ground. Screams that were somehow worse when they stopped. Breaking glass, angry shouts. A ruckus from the barn, up in the loft where Sparrow insisted on sleeping. Guess it wasn't safer to stay out there, after all. All the commotion brought the glacial attention of the centipede. A long, slow, considering look. Then reality shattered: That beast, that great thing dominating the horizon, with legs like telephone poles and a body like a 747, it scuttled across the plains like lightning.

Nothing that big could move that fast. It was in defiance of everything John understood about the world and its limits. A mountain did not move, and if it did, it wouldn't skitter blink-quick like a lizard on a hot road. But the centipede closed the distance between it and the farmhouse in a matter of seconds. And there was something even stranger. It seemed to touch down only between gaggles of maniacs. It left the main horde behind and danced across the plains by stepping in and out of the few outlying groups of lunatics — its body even coming apart, just for a split second, when the gaps between them were too wide. It landed on the hill above the commune all hunched up like an angry cat, then unfolded one foreleg into a mantis-like scythe. It sent the massive claw arcing straight through the second story of the farmhouse.

And nothing happened.

The thing's jet black body passed straight through the wood without leaving a mark and disappeared inside. John was almost relieved.

And then glass shattered on the far side of the building, and the beast's pointed claw emerged with something speared on its tip. Something wriggly and loud, screaming ragged and broken.

Too far and too dark to see the person's face, but it was a simple process of elimination: Big Ricky was the only black man at the commune. He was John's best friend in the world, which may not have been saying much, considering he only knew of about six people left in said world. But even if there'd still been nine billion, John would have counted him closest. And now, all he could do was wish the man was dead already. Dead, instead of hooked alive on a spear made out of shadow. Twisting and shrieking as the mountainous black insect idly considered his agony, turned him this and way that, watched him writhe like a bored housecat playing with a beetle. Finally, the centipede came to a decision, or maybe just grew bored, and shook Big Ricky's body loose from its claw. He screamed four stories into the dirt, then fell silent.

And the Kid saw it all.

The centipede loomed over the farmhouse, staring into the roof like it could see through it. Like it was waiting at the edge of a pond, watching the fish swim beneath. After a few seconds, it sent another spear out, down through the shingles without breaking a single one, and John heard a sharp, muffled shout, cut mercifully short.

And that did it: John was free.

As far as he knew, aside from himself and the Kid, every other human being in the world was dead. So there was no point sitting around here anymore, getting themselves killed trying to be heroes. John had failed, utterly and completely. As a friend, as a man, as a father — and that was something he was used to. He knew the process now: cut and run.

He grabbed the Kid by his downy rat-tail and hauled him to his feet. When the boy fought, as John knew he would, he seized the Kid's face. Put one hand on each cheek and forced him to match his gaze. They stood like that for a time, just staring, until the Kid had to look away, and John felt the fight go out of his body. He let the boy go and pointed to the copse of apple trees at the edge of the property. It wasn't much cover, and they couldn't hide there for long, but maybe if they could break line of sight, they could put some distance between themselves and this monster. As with all of John's plans, it was thin, and probably stupid, but at least it was quick. The boy ran first, and John followed him. Both moving low and hunched up like soldiers under fire, for all the good it would do if something actually saw them.

Nothing in the world but his own feet, the patch of dirt beneath them, and the Kid. Footfalls hollow on the dusty path, certain — *certain* — there more than two sets. John could feel the eyes on him. Could feel the weight of their gaze like a heavy pack he couldn't shrug off. He was sure there were maniacs following just paces behind him. Sure there were grasping hands just inches from his back. When they hit the orchard, John whirled, fists up, ready to fight. But his only opponent was the ghost of adrenaline, already turning nervous and sick as it faded.

John waved the Kid down behind an apple cart, while he ducked into the shadows between trees and looked back the way they came. Told himself he was scouting, surveying the land, calculating savvy escape routes — but really, he was just staring. Marveling at the great shadow of the centipede, insectile, immense, impossible. Blacker than the black skies behind it. A living void, stretching a million wiry tentacles down to the hordes that it controlled. The hordes that projected it. A parasitic shade that took not one host, but hundreds of thousands. There was nothing in John's understanding of the universe to even compare it to — how was he supposed to *fight* it? All he could do was gawp like an awestruck tourist.

Everyone at the farmhouse must have been dead, because all at once, the horde left off tearing, screaming and mauling to stand awkwardly. Too quick, prairie dogs on high alert. They wavered like that for a moment, then the centipede began to move, and the maniacs jerked on their thin black leashes to follow.

John was about to turn, wave to the Kid a little to show they were all right, but the boy made a weak, strangled sound in the back of his throat that sent every hair on John's neck standing. John spun around to find a shadow separating itself from the nearest tree. The thing had to be seven feet tall, if it stood upright. Limbs too long and skinny. Bulbous head, sharp cheekbones over skin so thin they threatened to cut right through. Sunken eyes so deep they were just black pools. Uneven patches of short, frizzy hair between the bald and bleeding spaces where it had been torn out. Stooped over, neck bent painfully to keep its head from clipping the low branches above. Massive hands dangling around its knees, fingers twitching and grabbing at nothing. Torn red shorts and the remnants of a matching jersey.

He was a basketball player, once.

He couldn't have been more than seventeen.

The Kid started to say John's name, but it turned into a scream. The basketball player was on him in a blink, big hands on a little throat, dry, cracked lips pulled back above rotten teeth. The maniac was trying to say something. Weird cadence to the sounds, melodic, almost English…if you shrieked every word backwards into a wood chipper. It might have been a song, a long time ago, when the thing was human.

John charged. He closed most of the distance between them before spotting the snarled wisps of black fog leaking from the basketball player's eyes, trailing back up the hill, toward the centipede. John went to duck, but his momentum carried him straight through the lines. He passed through with no resistance, but when he felt at the shoulder where they'd touched, his fingers came back bloody. A long, shallow cut there — loops and whorls in the shape of the drifting line. He only paused a second to make sure he could still work that arm, then sent it hurtling into the maniac's jaw. The basketball player's head rocked with the impact, but his grip did not loosen. He didn't even spare John a look, laser-focused on the Kid with a rage so hot you could feel it. John threw a few more equally useless punches before giving up and just prying at the maniac's fingers. It was like trying to break the grip of a statue. Like the basketball player had been carved in stone here, and the Kid had spent his whole life growing up in between his fingers.

The Kid's eyes were bloodshot. His face was purple. All he could do was look at John, until even that was too much. John saw the focus ebb out of the boy's eyes. Then he saw the rusty hatchet in the back of the apple cart. It was in the maniac's forehead so fast John couldn't be sure he'd actually put it there. But still the basketball player still wouldn't let up. John wrenched and pried at the axe, twisting the maniac's skull around on his neck like a bobblehead. When he finally worked it free, John gave himself one second to think. To get it right this time. To line it up. He brought the hatchet down on the back of the basketball player's neck. The thing was so emaciated that John could see the spaces between its vertebrae, even through the skin. He slipped the axe in there like a surgeon. The maniac's grip finally went slack, and the Kid coughed and sputtered like an old truck. John held the boy close, pressed their faces together, stroked the back of his head and told him he was okay, that it would all be okay, even though he knew, beyond a shadow of a doubt, that it was untrue.

He could see the severed line of black from the maniac's eyes dissipating in the air, and beyond it, the centipede…already turning in their direction. He could hear the angry chattering of the horde pick up, go from mutters to shouts. He could feel the wave of rage cresting over the near hill, ready to crash down on them both.

The Kid's breath whistled in his throat, face still flush with the blood that had pooled there. But there was nothing for it. It was time to run again. John hustled the boy to his feet and shoved him into a trot. The Kid could move, but not fast. Not fast enough. John slowed his own pace, fell behind, stood in the shady place at the edge of the trees. The boy was so distracted he didn't even notice until he was halfway up the far hill. Kid tried to holler back at John, but his voice wouldn't work. He wheezed something. He rasped. He pointed at John and waved at the crest of the hill — they were right there. A few more steps. Over and out of sight. The boy thumped his chest and held his hands out. He started to jog back.

John held one palm up, and the Kid stopped. The boy didn't get it. He didn't see what John had seen, back there at the commune: that while they were connected, the centipede saw what the maniacs saw. Knew what they knew. It would give chase. They would all give chase. And the Kid was tired. Slow. John felt the weight of the hatchet in his hands. He figured, just this once, maybe he would allow himself to play the game he never could. He would pretend at being a brave.

John told the Kid to run, but the boy wouldn't hear it. John poured out every ounce of conviction, every pent-up emotion, all the trust the two had built over the years, and put them into his voice — he told the Kid to run, don't think, don't pause, don't look back…because John had an idea. And he would only be a minute, then he would be right behind the boy. The Kid didn't like it, but he heard something in there to believe in and turned to flee. Even his eyes wouldn't say goodbye. That's how sure he was that John was telling the truth. When he was certain the boy wasn't stopping or looking back, John turned away himself and faced the horde.

John died as he lived: a liar.

Shadow Blister

"Mornin' Aiden," Sarah said to the stain on the hallway floor.

"Hi there, Aiden." Cash shot the bloody streaks a quick wave.

"How's it going, Aiden?" Jeff recited, automatically. He didn't look up from his map.

"Aiden." Lexy gave the rust-red patch an ironic curtsy.

"Aiden, how do?" Hank tipped the brim of his wide, weather-beaten cowboy hat in the general direction of the ancient bloodstain.

"Hey, Marcus! You not gonna say 'hi' to Aiden?"

Marcus caught himself up short. He had to hop a few times to keep from tripping as he turned.

"Right." He smiled at Halsey. "Sorry. Hi there, Aiden."

Marcus gave the bit of faded, bloody pavement a half-salute. He hooked his thumbs into the pockets of his jeans and surveyed the skyline. Halsey didn't stand, but she did lean back from her gardening to sit on her heels. She nudged her sunhat up and ran a wrist across her brow.

"Something eating at you?" she asked. "Seem distracted this morning."

"No," Marcus answered reflexively. "Well, yes. Sort of. The usual."

Halsey laughed at Marcus, and he joined her.

"It's the girl again," he explained.

"Your girl, or…*the* girl?"

"*The* girl. The Chatterbox. She's just been weird, lately."

"Is she ever not?"

Marcus blew air through his nose.

"True enough. Weird*er*, I guess I mean to say."

Halsey knew better than to press the matter. She idly dug through the garden box with the tip of her trowel, and the two watched the dead skyline in silence.

"How's farm life?" Marcus asked her, when the quiet grew too heavy.

"It's good!" She smiled easily, always had. "Nobody told the tomatoes the sun is gone."

Halsey waved vaguely in the direction of the black, absent sky.

"Nobody told you, either," Marcus said and brushed at his cheek.

Halsey took the cue, brushed her own cheek, and came back with sweat.

"It *is* a hot one today," she conceded.

"You take care," Marcus said, ambling on his way. "Don't get burned."

"Haven't seen the sun in four years," Halsey called after him. "And I still get sunburns. Must be the Irish in me!"

Marcus made the obligatory laugh, the oversized wave, but as soon as he stepped into the tower, his face fell right along with his thoughts.

The Chatterbox. She was talking more than ever and saying less than usual. "Fortune cookie gibberish," as Major Wallace called it. There was always some degree of nonsense to the Chatterbox's rambling — every conversation was littered with stupid jokes, broken riddles, half-remembered anecdotes and bawdy limericks — but there was always some actual information they could use, too. These days there was more and more of the former, and less and less of the latter. If things didn't change soon, Marcus couldn't say how much longer Major Wallace would tolerate her existence.

And what would that make Marcus? Sad? Relieved? Both? If nothing else, the daily interviews were a part of his routine. And he'd never been one to abandon routine easily.

Marcus hardly noticed the climb. Twenty-six flights of stairs, all lost to thought. Some days he counted off each landing with dread. Today he took the first step and the last, one after another. He blinked, and there were the flaking white bars of the observation deck. He poked his head through them and looked down at the roof where he'd left Halsey, 130 feet below — the straw-colored oval of her sunhat bobbing sedately between the earthen rectangles of the garden boxes and the rusted squares of the old rooftop HVACs. Modern art, life as shapes in the abstract.

Almost pretty, if you could stop yourself from thinking about it.

Their rooftop kingdom. Their skyscraper prison. Every floor below Halsey's pleasant little garden had been carefully sealed off. Doors welded shut. Stairwells filled with furniture and garbage. Twenty-four empty stories between the madness at ground level and the start of their little cloudbound haven. Their only lifeline to the streets below, an aging window washer's gondola. The odd, off-center tower they called home sprouted from the roof of the main building at the twenty-fourth story. It was a quarter the width of the skyscraper below and half as high. Topped by a copper pyramid, three stories high. And at its absolute peak, a green glass globe. Big enough to fit three people. It used to light up, back when electricity was a thing. On foggy days, that's all you could see of the building from elsewhere in the city: the tower breaking through the clouds, the little pyramid at its apex, and the glass beacon, shining like a lighthouse. The whole thing — it was like a fairy tale.

If you could stop yourself from thinking about it.

"Marcus." A voice like matches being struck, from somewhere behind him.

Marcus turned to greet Major Wallace. He held his hand out to shake, but the Major either didn't see it, or pretended not to. He brushed past Marcus to stand at the edge of the observation deck. He stared through the bars and the broken fencing, out toward Mount Rainier. Passive. Immutable. Moldering on the horizon like a dead god.

"We're almost gone," Wallace said.

Marcus got the feeling Wallace would've spoken whether or not anyone happened to be standing there at the time, but he asked after it, anyway.

"Major?"

"How long has it been since we've seen another survivor?" Wallace did not turn to face Marcus when he spoke. Eyes locked on the distant mountain like he was expecting it to jump up and dance.

"I'm not sure," Marcus admitted.

"I think we're it, Marcus," Wallace said. "I think the people in this building are all that's left. And just a few years ago, we were at the center of everything."

"S-Seattle?" Marcus ventured.

Wallace laughed once, then tamped it down like loose tobacco.

"I'm talking about humanity in general, Marcus. We were the center of the damn universe. Now here we are, the last of us, dwindling away. And nothing else seems to notice, much less care."

Wallace nodded toward the skyline. The distant mountain just a flat silhouette against the black skies.

"That mountain is still a mountain, the animals are animals, the plants are plants. This apocalypse only came for us."

"Major…" Marcus stepped forward, his hand hovering hesitantly over Wallace's shoulder.

"That's enough navel-gazing." Major Wallace turned and left the mountain to its own contemplation. "Let's get to work."

Marcus glanced at his own hand sheepishly before tucking it into the pocket of his jeans and following Wallace into the pyramid.

"The Chatterbox has been stranger than usual." Marcus explored the topic gently, dipping his toe into waters he knew were too hot.

"The what, Marcus?"

"The Chatterbox — the girl — she's been more abstract than—"

"The prisoner, you mean?" A chiding laugh in Wallace's tone. "Don't give her cute nicknames, Marcus. It humanizes her. She should not be humanized. She's not human."

"Right, sorry," Marcus said and flinched. He knew what was coming.

"Don't apologize to me unless you've scratched my car or dropped a hand grenade, son."

One of Wallace's favorite sayings. One of countless conversational booby traps that the Major laid out. And the one Marcus tripped the most.

Major Wallace held the heavy red door open for Marcus, then followed behind him, too closely. Hounding Marcus' every step up the wrought iron stairs from the observation deck into the pyramid itself. Marcus held his breath while the Major felt around for the rope that dropped the heavy blackout curtains covering the eastern windows. Gray, dishwater light reluctantly inched into the room. Through the gloom, Marcus could just make out a figure seated in the corner. Slumped atop a backless barstool, wrists and ankles bound with bike locks, each chained to an anchor higher up on the wall.

"Boys!" The Chatterbox leapt to her feet and charged them. She only made it a few feet before the manacles brought her up painfully short.

Marcus flinched. Major Wallace did not.

"Huh," the Chatterbox mused, bringing up her abraded wrists for inspection. "I seem to be a little tied up today. Would you mind?"

She shook the steel cables at Wallace.

“Not likely,” Wallace said, dragging a battered green lawn chair to a spot just beyond the girl’s reach.

“Never hurts to ask!” the Chatterbox piped and turned her attention to Marcus.

“Marco! Buddy!” She spread her arms wide and went in for a hug.

Hamstrung by her chains again.

“Oh, right,” she chuckled. “These things.”

The Chatterbox shot Marcus an exaggerated wink. He knew better than to feign laughter in reply. He watched blood seep from the wounds she’d just dug into her own wrists with those worn cables. She dabbed at it with her fingers, then spread crimson across her lips and over her eyelids.

“Gotta pretty up if I’m gonna have company.” The Chatterbox laughed again. A big laugh, broad and friendly. It made Marcus nauseous.

“If you’re finished with your antics, take a seat and let’s talk.” Wallace didn’t look at the Chatterbox when he spoke. He picked up a leather-bound log of transcripts from past interviews and flipped the pages until he found his place.

“Where is the nearest group of maniacs?” Wallace asked. “How many are they, and what type?”

“Who said I was finished with my antics?” The Chatterbox waggled an eyebrow at Marcus until he rolled his eyes and looked away.

She laughed.

“Where is the nearest group of—”

“The tip of your penis,” the Chatterbox interrupted.

Quiet moved into the pyramid. It settled like it intended to pay rent.

“The nearest group of maniacs are…on the tip of the Major’s penis?” Marcus asked.

He knew it was the wrong thing to do, even before Wallace shot him a look that could transmit cancer.

The Chatterbox laughed so sharply it felt like the windows might crack.

"Is that a riddle or…?" Marcus looked from the girl to the Major and back.

"That's the deal," the Chatterbox wheezed between dying laughs. "That's what the answer will cost. God, Marco, you positively slay me!"

She wiped a tear from the corner of her eye, smearing her bloody eyeshadow.

"If you want to know about the nearest group of maniacs, Major Wallace," she finally caught her breath, "I want to cut off the tip of your penis."

"Done," Wallace said, without a trace of thought.

"I'll take it with my teeth, if you'd like," the Chatterbox cooed.

"I said 'done.' Now answer the question." Wallace only had eyes for the logbook, pen poised to record her response.

"The nearest group of maniacs?" The girl knocked a knuckle against her chin, deep in thought. "Why, they're right here in this building. I don't know how many there are, because they never let me out of this weird little dungeon, but I know they're the very worst type. There's one that insists you call him 'Major,' and he's the biggest piece of—"

"Is this it?" Major Wallace interjected, tapping his pen against the logbook. "More games? Are you finally out of useable intel? Because if so, I'm more than happy to dispose of you."

He raised his head to make slow, careful eye contact with the Chatterbox. A grin took her face like spreading mold.

"Here's the problem, handsome," the girl said, pushing out her chest and wriggling on her stool. "I just think you're plain out of parts. How much have you promised me, over the…weeks?"

She quirked her head at the windows, looking out at nothing but solid black sky.

"Months," Marcus corrected.

Major Wallace glared at him. The Chatterbox laughed.

"All those deals…how much of yourself do you actually have left to give me? Do you remember?" She dropped into a whisper, letting the last question slip like a nasty secret.

"I write everything down," Wallace tapped his steel-barreled pen on the worn notebook. "Even your deluded deals. I'm sure there's a piece or two of me left to bargain with."

Major Wallace barely looked at the girl when he spoke. He leafed back and forth through his notes, glancing and instantly dismissing whatever he found there.

"Nothing worth taking." The Chatterbox giggled, and drummed her heels against the floor. "We're already down to your pathetic genitals. We're bottom of the barrel, here."

Marcus gave the slightest laugh. He tried to pass it off as a cough, but it was enough to draw the Chatterbox's attention.

"Where to start?" She gave Marcus a smile with too many teeth.

"W-what?" He took a step back. "With what?"

"With you, beautiful." She threw her head back and howled like a cartoon wolf. "You and I haven't done any deals yet. I want myself a piece of you."

Marcus looked to the Major, but he was absorbed in pretending to be absorbed in his notes.

"No," Marcus started to laugh, then cut it short and pointed at the Chatterbox. "No. Absolutely not."

"Then you boys have nothing to offer me anymore." The girl crossed her arms, then her legs. She affected a deliberate pout and found something of interest on the ceiling.

"Just do it," Wallace prompted. "It doesn't matter."

"I don't want to," Marcus said. "It's messed up."

"I have personally promised this psychopath everything from my fingertips to my Gentleman's Hat," Wallace said, standing to stretch. "She will never collect. She's chained to this wall twenty-four hours a day, and when she runs out of useful information, we will put a bullet in her head. Do the deal. It doesn't matter."

"Gentleman's…Hat?" Marcus wondered.

The Chatterbox snickered, then went back to ignoring them.

"She *knows* it doesn't matter." Wallace moved to stand before Marcus, hands on his hips in a disappointed father stance, and carefully explained: "I just *told her* that we have no intention of honoring these deals, that we'll *kill her* soon, and look…"

They both paused to stare at the Chatterbox. She wiggled her fingers in a casual little wave, but she did not break her pout.

"She doesn't *care*," Wallace continued. "Her brain is broken. She has decided on this game and she will play it, no matter what, because that's what her type does. The Merry are game-players, even when it does not, *can not* benefit them. Promise her whatever she wants, and if she doesn't give us something useable in return, we'll shoot her in the head and toss her out the window."

Wallace started to turn away, thought better of it, and pinned a finger at the girl.

"Actually, forget that — it's a waste of a bullet. We'll toss her out alive and let her think a while on the way down."

Marcus flinched at every threat, sure the Chatterbox would object. But she was busy examining the lines on her own palm. The topic of self-preservation just plain did not interest her.

"Okay," Marcus said, finally finding his angle. "But you always skip my questions. You only ever focus on the tactical info, and we still don't know have any of the big picture answers. If I'm making the deals, we're asking my questions."

"Marcus." Wallace pulled at the tails of his mustache. A sure cue that he was annoyed. "Who cares why she does the things she does? There's no planning with these creatures. They're just…impulses. They're madness. Very specific types of madness, and that's all."

"I care," Marcus said. "I only volunteered to help with this in the first place because I thought we might get some answers about what's happening to us, all of us, and why. If we don't know that, how can we hope to survive in the long-term?"

"Fine, fine." Major Wallace waved his hand, swatting the very notions away. "Call me when you're done wasting time, and I'll record the useful intel. If there is any."

Wallace pivoted in place and marched away to stare unhappily out the windows. Not quite out of earshot. Just enough to prove his own disinterest. Marcus took the man's seat. The lawn chair's cracked plastic legs creaked beneath his weight, half again that of the Major. He leaned forward and promised himself that he wouldn't break eye contact with the Chatterbox this time.

"Okay," he said. "Let's do a deal."

The girl snapped out of her pout instantly. She hopped about to face Marcus, snapped the fingers on both hands, and mimed shooting him with imaginary pistols.

"There's my boy!" she chirped, all smiles now.

The Chatterbox was young, pretty, with fair skin and subtle curves. Teeth somehow still white — whiter than his own, at least. Big green eyes, only for Marcus. And nothing at all behind them.

Marcus broke his promise and looked away first.

"What do you want?" he asked. He hated the timidity in his own voice.

"That's not the game," she chided. "You ask, and I tell you what it costs."

"Okay." Marcus shifted in his seat. Weathered plastic groaning like an old ship at sea. "What's really going on here? The skies, the maniacs, everything."

"Oh, my," the Chatterbox whistled. "That is a big one. I can answer, but…"

She waited, actually waited for Marcus to say it.

"But what?" He sighed.

"But it'll cost everything you have. Every life in this place."

Marcus caught himself physically leaning away from the suggestion. Something the cheap, ancient lawn chair was not willing to support.

"Done," the Major interjected.

"No!" Marcus twisted to face Wallace. "It's too much!"

The girl just laughed.

"It wasn't your deal to take," she told the Major and returned her focus to Marcus. "Also, this one is too big for delayed gratification, like we do with Army Boy's questions. I'm afraid I'll need you to personally slaughter every soul here and bring me proof. Then I'll answer. Before you kill yourself, of course — you're included in the deal."

She smiled expectantly at Marcus, like she was waiting to be asked to dance.

"No," Marcus said. "Of course not."

Wallace grunted and moved away. He stared out the windows, scanning the nothingness beyond the horizon.

"Boo." The Chatterbox stuck her lower lip out. "That's the first deal you people have ever turned down."

Marcus' shirt was too tight. His collar was in the wrong position. Everything was constricting. The lawn chair swayed beneath him.

"Don't you have any more questions?" The girl fluttered her bloody eyelashes at Marcus.

"Uh…" He had a million questions. More. A whole journal filled with nothing but questions, guesses, and theories…sitting on a desk, down in his room, ten stories below. He didn't think he'd get the chance to ask any of them today, and now, for the life of him, he couldn't think of a single one.

The silence had gone on too long. Major Wallace cleared his throat. Somehow, Marcus understood what he meant by it.

"W-where is the nearest group of maniacs?" Marcus recited the familiar question. "How many are they, and…what type?"

He glanced to the Major. Received the slightest nod.

The Chatterbox made a noise in her throat like a buzzer blaring.

"No repeeeaaats!" she sang, carrying the last note until she ran out of breath. "Come on, Marco, surely you know the rules by now?"

"I've got — can I get my notes? I didn't know we'd be doing this today. I wasn't prepared."

Marcus' hands flapped in his lap like a couple of dying birds.

"I'll just run below and get my notebook. I'll be right back. Can we take a break?"

Wallace crossed the room like he was invading a country. He practically shoved Marcus out of the chair and, in the same motion, waved toward the stairs.

"Go," he said. "I'll take over."

"Oh no." The Chatterbox shook her head. "We've been over this. Your turn is over. I'll wait for Marco. I don't have plans."

Major Wallace had his pistol out of its holster and leveled at the girl like he'd practiced doing nothing but that for days on end.

"You'll talk to me, and you'll give me something useful," he said, sliding his finger from the guard to the trigger. "Or your fun is over."

"You don't know that!" she said, a bit of suppressed laughter in her voice. "It might be fun getting shot. Let's try!"

"Wait, just…please." Marcus took a step forward. He thought about valiantly striding up between the Major and the girl, but he drew up short. Less for fear of Wallace's bullets, and more of stepping within reach of the Chatterbox. "Just a few minutes, that's all I ask!"

Major Wallace gave Marcus a look. The same look an owner would give their dog, if it stopped to poop in the middle of crossing a busy street.

"Fine," Wallace finally said, returning his pistol and crossing his arms. "Ten minutes."

"Thirty?" Marcus ventured.

Wallace just blinked at him.

"Twenty!" Marcus agreed, and he bolted for the stairs before the Major could object. He pretended like the rattle of the old iron stairs kept him from hearing Wallace's shouts of protest.

Marcus hit the landing running, shoved through the hefty red door that separated the pyramid from the tower, and instantly lost about half his bodyweight. His ratty old duct-taped sneakers left the squealing iron staircase behind for a hallway of glass-smooth tile, and that was all it took: he could breathe again.

He could think again.

All the forgotten questions crowded back into his brain:

What do the maniacs want? Do they have a plan, a goal, a need?

Where did they all go? There were thousands-strong packs roaming every street in Seattle, howling at the sky, breaking glass with their faces, tearing at the concrete with their bare fingers, and then…nothing? All quiet for months on end?

What's the relation between the black spot and the maniacs? There was something about a song, back when everything first broke out — was that just a rumor, or was that tied into all of this as well?

He was shifting gears faster than they could grab. Marcus' thoughts networked out toward infinity. He considered turning around while it was all still fresh in his head, marching back up the stairs, telling the Major to have a seat, and calmly, professionally grilling the Chatterbox until he had some real, meaningful answers. He would mark those answers down on paper, bring them home, compare them, tie them together, and construct a full and coherent treatise on the phenomenon. His work would foster understanding, weaponize knowledge, single-handedly turn the tide for humanity and then, when all was well again and the sun was back shining in the sky, Wallace would come to him on his knees, begging for forgiveness, weeping and pounding his chest at the thought that he kept Marcus in the dark for so long, needlessly prolonging the misery of everybody in the tower — no, *everybody in the world* — just because there was a great hole where the Major's imagination should be, surrounded by vast, insurmountable mountains of pride. Yes, when Wallace looked up at him with those grief-red eyes, Marcus would take his thousand-page-thick-world-saving thesis, and he would slap the Major straight upside the head with it, and everybody would laugh, and Halsey would hug him tight and take off her—

Marcus pinched the skin on his forearm until he gasped. He shook his head at his own stupidity, trying to rattle out the callow daydreams that plagued his every idle moment. Thirty-nine years old, and he was still waiting for the day he'd become an actual adult.

Marcus frowned at the angry red spot blooming on the back of his arm, then gave it one last chastising twist.

Better to prepare for weakness than hope for strength. He needed his notes.

The stairs go so much quicker on the way down. You forget yourself entirely after a few flights, enter a hypnotic state where you stop counting the landings, and whole stories just fly by like mile-markers on a long, straight highway. Marcus was outside and blinking up into gloomy daylight before he knew it, legs still swaying, taking phantom stairs, one by one. He considered waving to Halsey but knew he'd get sucked into a conversation again, and much as he'd like to, he just didn't have the time. He decided to sneak by instead, while she was lost in her gardening.

"You still not talking to Aiden?" Halsey said, smiling over her shoulder.

"What?" Marcus glanced down at his feet, at the rust-red bloodstain between them. "Oh, uh…'Hi, Aiden.'"

Halsey snickered.

"You don't have to do it if you don't want to." She swiveled to rest on her haunches, tilted her sunhat back on her head. "I'm just messing with you."

"Oh, I know," Marcus lied. "I want to. I just forget. I get lost in my head sometimes."

"What's on your mind, Marcus? Anything I can help with?" She stabbed her trowel into the loam and let it stand there.

"No, it's…" He shot a glance upward, and Halsey looked to the top of the tower. The bronze pyramid at its apex.

"I always forget you have her up there," Halsey said. "What's she like?"

"You didn't see her, when she first showed up?"

Halsey shook her head, jostling the straw hat loose. It hung by its string, making furrows in the skin of her neck.

"I was sleeping when the scavs brought her in," she said. "By the time I was up and about, she'd already broken her cover and killed Sammie and The Chin and did that…thing to Viv's face."

They both found a patch of nothing to stare at.

"That's…that's pretty much what she's like," Marcus sighed.

"Hey, how about the pyramid, then? You know I never got up there. I heard it was pretty swanky, back when Aiden lived in it."

"That was his place?" Marcus blinked down at the stain.

"Yeah, did you not — do you not know about Aiden?" Halsey laughed and shook her head.

"I just figured it was like a sick joke, to name the bloodstain," Marcus said. "You know, gallows humor and all that."

"Yeah, well, when you're standing on the gallows, it's the only humor you've got."

Marcus shrugged, looked away. Halsey tried to scratch her forehead with her wrist. He cleared his throat. She smiled a little. Marcus flushed with shame at the quiet, broken spot he'd left in another conversation.

He tried to fix it. "So Aiden was real? A real guy?"

"Wow, no wonder you never say 'hi.' Yeah, Aiden Cross — he was this big tech guy back in the day. You know, back when there were days."

She gave the black skies above a quick nod.

"He was a divisive dude," Halsey continued. "Real big into space exploration and clean energy and all that stuff. Had a real cult following with the tech bros. But he was arrogant, abrasive, actually seemed kinda…well, I guess 'dumb' isn't the word, but like…a child-like entitlement, I guess it was. Anyway, seemed like you either thought he was the messiah or a total asshole. Never in between."

"Uh," Marcus raised a finger, "I was in between. I didn't even know his name."

"Yes.," Halsey smiled. "But you're a mole person, and you have always lived underground."

Marcus opened his mouth to protest but just wound up shutting it again.

"It's okay," Halsey said. "I think it's kinda great, actually. Sometimes it's like this place is a raging river, all this drama and gossiping and fighting, and you — you're a…I don't know, a quiet pool off to the side."

"There's drama around here?" Marcus widened his eyes, let his jaw fall open a little bit.

"Ha!" Halsey barked.

Marcus blushed.

"All right, all right: Aiden Cross." She pointed toward the top of the tower. "He lived up there, in the pyramid."

Marcus turned to look, as though there might be another, nicer pyramid hovering in the sky just above the one he knew. "Yeah, but…how? Why? It's a hellhole."

"Oh yeah?" Halsey squinted up at the tarnished brass siding, water-streaks like tears beneath each window. "I always thought it was still nice up there. Guess something must've happened. It used to be real fancy. I saw pictures once, in a magazine. They did a profile on Cross, and this place, just after he bought it. There was a little bit in there about how the first person to renovate the old pyramid and actually live in it was this cool hippie artsy chick and her daughter. Aiden found out about it, fell in love with the idea, and purchased the whole building. Bought her out, or forced her out, or whatever — point is, Cross wanted that quirky hipster cred for himself, so he took it. Like I said: divisive dude."

"So…what happened?" There was a distant alarm, blaring at the edge of Marcus' thoughts.

"What do you think?" Halsey shrugged.

"The maniacs got him?"

"No, the other thing."

Marcus thought about it but came up blank.

"We forget so quickly, don't we?" Halsey said. "We think, like, it's always been us versus them, but we used to *be* them. Cross turned maniac. When we first found this place — back when it was just Geraldo, Broker, Saachi, Wallace, and me — Aiden was still here."

"Whoa." Marcus was trying to pay full attention to the story, but those internal alarms of his were growing louder and louder.

"Yeah." Halsey motioned toward the pyramid. "He was holed up in there all that time. Months, must've been. It was Wallace that first went to check the place out. Said he saw Aiden all curled up in a corner, thought he was a corpse. But as soon as Wallace pried open a window, Aiden went for it like…how did Wallace put it? 'Like a dog that just saw his owner get home.' Then, whoosh — right out."

"Good god." Marcus took a step back, giving the stain at his feet a wide berth. "Was he trying to lunge for Wallace?"

"Nah." Halsey shook her head. The straw hat rustled against her scratchy poncho. "We think he was probably a carrier. One of the early ones, remember? They tried to get you to look at the spot, back when it was just a little thing. If you left them alone long enough, if they couldn't get anybody to look, they started to shut down. Eventually, they killed themselves…if they could. Aiden Cross was so far gone he couldn't manage to off himself before his body just shutdown. But the second Wallace opened that window, well…it was like he'd been sitting there, in the dark, waiting all that time just for the chance to die."

Marcus' knees were going weak. It was all the stairs, he told himself. Just out of shape.

"Like I said, I didn't see any of that. That's just what Wallace told me, later. I'll tell you what I did see, though." Halsey reached around for her sun hat, settled it atop her head, and pulled her ponytail out the back. "I was standing down here when Aiden hit. Right over there, where the tomatoes are now. And he didn't die right away. You can see it in the stain. Those streaks."

Marcus followed her gesture and examined the leading edge of the faded bloodstain. There were two protrusions that fanned outwards at the ends, each splitting up into ten smaller trails. Arms and fingers, reaching.

"As soon as he hit," Halsey said, her voice gone grim, "and I mean *the second* he hit, he realized he wasn't dead yet, and he started crawling. Over there, toward the edge of the roof. He wanted to jump again. Just didn't make it."

Halsey quietly considered the spot that Aiden had been heading for. Marcus just listened to the wind.

"Anyway, that's why we say 'hi' to Aiden." Halsey smiled, thin and brittle. "Because he was one of us. No matter what kind of guy he was in life, this was his home, too. He lived here with all of us, even if it was just for a little while."

Marcus nodded, then something occurred to him. "But how was he still alive? You guys didn't move into the tower until, what? Months after the…uh…end of…days?"

"That's as good a word as any," Halsey agreed. "But I don't know how he was still up and kicking. You've seen the Sleepers, right? Back when you and Vera were out there — before you found us?"

Marcus just swallowed.

"How were *they* still alive?" Halsey waved her hand at everything and nothing. "How are *any* of them? I know the Major thinks this thing is some bio-weapon, or virus, or something — but that doesn't work at all. What's keeping them going? What happened to the sky? You know, that's why we're all down here rooting for you guys. We know you're up there trying to get answers. For all of us."

Marcus flushed at the compliment, then those nagging internal alarms of his finally burst through. Panic spiked all across body.

"Oh god, my notes!" Marcus yelled, already running. "I'm sorry, Halsey! I was supposed to—"

He didn't bother finishing the sentence. He sprinted across the roof and slammed into the rusting double doors that led to the town square — what used to be the mid-tower restaurant, a passable Chinese place that thrived on location alone. He burrowed through a forest of stale laundry, hung on fraying lines between the two tacky lion statues that guarded the foyer. He tripped over the hostess podium — long emptied of menus, now home to boxes of powdered detergent, bleach pens, clothespins, and single socks without a mate. Chet and Tawny were posted up in the closest window booth, staring at the crumbling skyline in affable silence. Tawny brightened at Marcus' appearance.

"Hey, Marcus." She kicked Chet under the table, jolting him out of his daze. He flashed a one-fingered wave at Marcus, but his eyes were still distant.

"Sorry!" Marcus didn't slow his hustle. "Sorry, sorry, I gotta go!"

"Bathroom's back the way you came." She laughed, already returning her gaze to the horizon.

Big Ben was hanging out in what used to be the waitstaff alcove, tossing a tennis ball down the long, skinny hallway and trying to smack it on return with a battered yellow plastic oar.

"You wanna play?" he asked, but Marcus was already gone.

The kitchen was mostly counter — flat, unbroken expanses of steel running along every wall, circling the cooking island that dominated the center of the room. Every one overflowed with baskets of produce and stacks of canned goods, and Marta was there between them, sorting, chopping, opening, smelling, discarding. She looked up from her work brightly, excited at the prospect of a visitor. Then she saw it was Marcus and went back to her prep without a word. He blushed with remembered shame.

Marcus walked in on her in the shower once, and neither of them had ever forgiven him for it.

He pushed against a pair of heavy red lacquer doors that led from the kitchen to the ballroom (now part storage, part infirmary, part daycare, and thankfully unoccupied) — then raced up a half-hidden flight of stairs to the old Manager's Office.

His apartment.

Home.

There were plenty of actual living spaces in the tower proper — more than they had people, actually. But as much as Marcus would have loved it there; would have treasured the quiet; would have reaped the privacy; would have savored a little distance from his fellow human beings…Vera just couldn't take it. She slept better, hearing people banging around downstairs. She was still half-asleep when Marcus bustled through the door, swept right past her cot to the enormous manager's desk, and frantically rummaged through the many, many stacks of papers he kept meaning to deal with, someday.

He knocked over a pair of plastic horses, set opposite a weathered wooden bird with a broken wing.

"Hey, that was the Federal Bureau of Horses," Vera said, voice thick with sleep. "They were arguing with Captain Robin."

"I'm sorry, sweetie." Marcus shot her a hurried smile. "I'm in a biiiig rush, and I've gotta find my notebook. Have you seen it?"

Vera pulled the blanket up around her shoulders, all faded red balloons and dancing bears. She rubbed one eye and used the other to glare at him.

"How would I see it?" she asked. "I was sleeping."

"Fair point," Marcus conceded.

He spread a stack of notepads out across the desk and glanced at their contents. Why, for the love of god, didn't he use different kinds of paper for different subjects? Or at *least* label them? Or at the absolute minimum, why on earth did he not throw this one — an entire legal pad full of half-finished to-do lists — away?

Marcus would have to have a word with himself, when this was over.

"Will you put the FBH back up?" Vera fought through a yawn. "They were talking about cutting the power to Nakatomi Castle, like from the story."

"That's just what the Evil Count Gruber wants, though." Marcus moved on from his desk-piles to his near-desk piles, then to the sub-piles that were spillover from the near-desk piles.

"But why?" She was pure attention now; they hadn't gotten to that part in her ongoing bedtime story yet.

"No spoilers," Marcus said.

He wasn't going to find it like this. He straightened up, closed his eyes, and thought. When was the last time he wrote in his interrogation notes? It had been weeks. He'd all but given up on ever getting to ask the Chatterbox anything, so he—

"But you just did a spoiler!" Vera chided. "You told me Evil Count Gruber wanted the power cut."

A small, hateful part of Marcus briefly considered snapping at the girl, yelling for her to be quiet for *just one second* so he could think! He bit into the side of his cheek, his penance for even thinking it.

"I'm sorry, starlight." Marcus stepped around the desk and sat on the edge of Vera's cot. He snaked his fingers under her blankets and grabbed her little toes.

"Daddy!" she gasped. "Cold!"

"That's right," he said. "I've been up in the pyramid with Major Wallace, and it's real cold up there. As much as I'd like to cuddle up here with you, I have to find my notes super quick and get back up there, or Wallace will do this face."

Marcus dangled four fingers from nose like a brushy mustache and frowned as hard as he could. He squinted and made grumbling noises. Vera laughed.

"Maybe they're with John Hambo," she suggested. "Wherever he is."

"He's missing?" Marcus feigned utter horror. Her precious trio of stuffed pigs would be lost without their leader.

Vera nodded quite seriously.

"When was the last time you saw him?"

"I was playing on the ledge in the gardens, and I left him all set up there with Detective Martin Piggs and RoboHog, but when I came back, he was—"

The garden!

"We'll find him when I get back, starlight," Marcus had to stop himself from sprinting for the door, "but I just remembered where I left my notebook and I gotta go!"

"Okay, Daddy." Vera put on her best Major Wallace impression and grumbled him out the door.

On the way out, Marcus managed to duck Marta's withering glare and Tawny's forced conversation, but he caught Big Ben's flying tennis ball right in the ear. He slipped through the curtain of stiff laundry and noticed for the first time that the big double doors had been knocked closed. As hurried as he was, he still paused a moment to kick the stands back down. Marcus hadn't seen the sun in years, but the laundry didn't seem to have that problem.

Out. Into warm summer air that smelled of grass and earth and distant fire. A sheepish wave to Halsey, who returned it with trowel in hand. Then back to the stairs before his legs had time to protest. No matter how rushed Marcus was, how frantic he became, how distracted he got, nothing ever made those thirteen flights of stairs go by any faster. Marcus had been climbing for a hundred years by the time he reached the observation deck. He'd become an old man in that stairwell. He was born in there, he lived a full life in there, and he died in there. Now he was a ghost, the specter of his legs doomed to climb phantom stairs forever. He savored every second of the flat hallway between the tower stairwell and the access door, leading up, again, to the pyramid. Then he heaved it open and accepted his fate: more stairs. A short flight of crude wooden ones to the foyer, then the rickety iron spiral, chasing itself up two more flights into the base of the pyramid itself.

Only two flights, Marcus told himself.

He was not comforted.

Deep, shuddering waves of dismay broke all through his body when he saw that Major Wallace had taken the only chair.

Why was it the only chair? Why had he never gotten his own chair, in all this time?

The Major must have seen all hope die on Marcus' face. He stood up and pressed his slacks flat, took a few curt steps towards the windows, and waved irritably at the girl. Marcus settled into the hard, creaky plastic like it was the finest feather bed. He tried not to pant, but that just made him dizzy, and he wound up gasping. The Chatterbox clapped at his feeble display. The bike cables binding her wrists rattled in their moorings.

"Sorry," Marcus managed. "I…"

The girl waited for him to finish.

"Went as fast…"

Still waiting.

"As I could."

"I could tell." She winked at him. The dried blood on her eyelids crinkled.

"On your own time," Wallace snapped.

Marcus held up his notepad for all to admire. None did. He flipped through it, trying to find his most vital questions.

"What, uh…" He wiped sweat from his neck. "What are you doing here? I mean you, in particular. What brought you here?"

"What's a nice girl like me doing in a place like this?" The Chatterbox inspected her own nails, broken and filthy.

Major Wallace laughed. His version of a laugh — a churlish series of growls and exhalations of air.

"Why did you come to the tower at all?" Marcus clarified. "What was your purpose?"

"Your fingernails," the girl answered, holding up her own by way of example. "Deal?"

Marcus looked to Wallace. Wallace did not look to Marcus.

"I guess," Marcus said. "Deal."

"We saw your fires at night," she said. "We were so bored, we wanted to play some games with you. We played the stabbing game with each other to see who would get to come first, and I won!"

She lifted her shirt and showed Marcus three raw, pink scars on her abdomen. She nodded at him enthusiastically.

"We?" The Major turned. "You've never said there were others before. Where was your camp?"

"You don't get to play anymore," the Chatterbox chastised. "Hush now."

Major Wallace bristled at Marcus, raised his eyebrows, and jutted his chin out toward the Chatterbox. Marcus did not take the prompt. These were his questions now, and he was going to use them.

"What do you do when you're not playing games with people?" Marcus read the first of many sub-questions, neatly bulleted beneath the first.

Major Wallace scoffed and found the windows fascinating again.

"How about your left ear?" she said, like she was asking Marcus out for coffee.

He shuddered.

"Aw, sweetie," she cooed. "Just the earlobe? We'll start slow. We got all the time in the world."

"O-okay," Marcus agreed.

"When we're not playing games," she said, slowly, "we look for people to play games with."

Wallace growled laughter. Marcus blushed.

He searched for a better line of questions, worried that he was taking too long to find them, and asked the very next one he came across.

"Who were you, before?" Marcus could hear the Major's disdain long before the man actually grumbled it.

The Chatterbox tilted her head.

"Before the black spot and the skies and all of this," Marcus explained. "Back when you were just human, who were you?"

She was quiet for so long that he worried she was going to refuse, thus making him look even stupider in front of the Major. If that was somehow possible.

"Your bracelet," she finally said, so softly that Marcus almost missed it.

Marcus glanced at his wrist, and the series of twist ties braided together there. Most of the paper sheaths had long since fallen off. Vera made it for him, and he loved it…then she made him ten more. They were sitting in the bottom left drawer of his desk, waiting for their turn to shine.

"This?" Marcus held his wrist in the air and gave it a shake. "Really? That's it?"

"Why on earth are you trying to talk her out of it?" Major Wallace pinched the bridge of his nose. "You're somehow worse at this than I thought, and I assure you, that bar was very low."

For once, the girl didn't laugh at the dig. She always laughed when either he or Wallace insulted the other.

"I just like it," she said, so frail the words nearly fell apart. "And I didn't think you'd ask about that. Just the bracelet for the answer."

"Okay," Marcus said and twisted the wires apart. He reached out to hand it to her, but Wallace tutted.

Marcus tossed it underhand instead. The bracelet landed in her lap, and she watched it like she'd found a sick bird. Waiting for signs of life.

"I wasn't anybody special," the girl said. "My name was Aileen. I was going to be a nurse. That's all."

"I'm sorry," was all Marcus could think to say.

Even Wallace was quiet.

"Sorriest thing I ever saw!" The Chatterbox laughed, familiar cruelty biting at the edges of her words again.

Marcus asked his questions. The girl gave her prices. The tip of his pinky finger and both little toes, patches of skin from his elbows and knees, every hair on his body, his left eye, and on and on. But she gave him answers. Unhelpful ones, whenever she could, but there was always some information there, and Marcus wrote down every single scrap of it. A whole notepad full. He didn't actually remember wrapping the interview up. He couldn't recall saying goodbye to Major Wallace, or leaving the pyramid, or walking the hundreds of stairs down to the lower rooftop. If he spoke to anyone as he made his way through the town square — if Halsey joked with him, or Marta glared at him, or Cash gave him guff about his weight — Marcus did not register it. All time after the Chatterbox was spent on autopilot. Every one of Marcus' mental gears spun on their own axes, and when they did connect, a thousand new gears kicked into motion.

"Daddy." Vera poked him in the ribs.

"One second, starlight," the autopilot said.

"It was one second *forever* ago," she whined. "And you're not even *doing* anything!"

When Marcus took over the controls again, he found himself at his old overflowing desk, staring at the space between his hands. He'd left his notes from the interrogation there, and they had since been covered with a careful array of plastic horses.

"Sorry, sweetie." He shook his head. Pinched the skin on his forearm — always the same spot — until the pain brought him back to the present. "What did you need?"

"Dinner!" Vera rolled her eyes at stupid Daddy. "You missed dinner downstairs, but I brought your plate up for you, and now it's going bad so you *gotta* eat it."

Marcus appraised the pockmarked tin plate in her hands. Two raised ridges divided it into three compartments, like something out of a prison cafeteria. A spoon-shaped glob of refried beans in one, an ooze of fruit salad in the other, and the largest reserved for ten huge slices of tomato. Halsey.

Marcus smiled at Vera and smacked himself upside the head.

"Well, duh," he said. "I *gotta* eat it!"

Vera nodded in solemn agreement. It was, indeed, duh.

"Do you want my fruit salad?" He prodded a large square of pineapple. It wobbled.

"No, because I already ate at the Gershwins' table with Mr. Gershwin and Jed and Lexy."

Marcus speared a slice of tomato and forked it into his mouth. It was good. Sweet and a little sour, the outlying taste of earth and sunlight distinguishing Halsey's contribution from the sadder, canned alternatives.

"What's all this, then?" He used the back of his fork to tap each of the horse figurines on his desk, in turn.

"You remember!" Vera squirmed into his lap, ducking under one arm and carefully replacing it behind her. "It's the FBH, and they're going to cut the power to Nakatomi Castle."

"Right, right," Marcus agreed. "That's what the book says, but what they don't realize—"

"What book?"

"The Federal Bureau of Horses Anti-Count Handbook, of course. What they don't realize is that cutting the power is exactly what the Evil Count Gruber wants. Now, Princess McClane knows it, of course, and Al knows it—"

"Who?" Vera shifted in his lap so Marcus could see the skepticism on her face.

"Sorry," Marcus leaned forward to survey Vera's bed, and the toys scattered all around it. "I meant *John Hambo* knows it, but — where's Hambo?"

Vera was about to answer when Marcus remembered.

"We lost Hambo," he said, his voice as heavy as a collapsing star.

"Nuh uh!" Vera slid beneath his arm and out of his lap, romped around his desk, and dug beneath her blankets. She came up with a small stuffed pig, a red headband drawn on the felt with magic marker.

"You found him?" Marcus asked. "Where was he?"

"The gypsies had him!"

"The…gypsies?"

"The magic gypsies," Vera confirmed. "That's right, and they're our neighbors and they're reeeaaal weird, but nice, I guess. The wind came up and it blew Hambo off the ledge where I'd left him and he fell and fell but the gypsies found him because they're magic and they know where every little thing is that any other one of them has ever seen, because they can link together when their princess is around and she's—"

Vera's stories took a while to wrap up when she really got going. The gypsies were new, but the princess was familiar: everything in charge was a princess to Vera. Marcus expected the horses to make an appearance at any second. He jostled his dubious fruit salad, then opted for more tomato.

"—but she really needs us to because it's almost the end and they're going somewhere with a *lot* of people and they were making their way up the coast to get there when they saw our tower and John Hambo down on the street, so they gave him back and all they wanted for him was my laugh, which I thought was weird, but that's magic gypsies for you."

Vera ended her story with a shrug.

The tomato turned to ash in Marcus' mouth.

"They wanted something in return?" Marcus asked, trying to keep his "daddy's humoring you" voice steady.

"I guess they always want something in return because that's the game." Vera wasn't particularly interested in the details of the tale now that she'd finished. She was digging through her covers again, looking for another toy.

"And they wanted your laugh?"

"That's right," Vera confirmed. "I said you can't take a laugh, and they said, 'Let us worry about that, when it's time.' Just silly magic gypsy stuff."

"And they…what did they look like?"

Vera sensed the panic skating around Marcus' tone and turned to look at him.

"Just like normal people, I guess," she spoke slowly, thinking back on the moment. "But they had weird, bad makeup. Kind of like Mrs. Tawny does, but worse, and black around the eyes."

"Where did you meet the gypsies?" Marcus was standing now, clutching the desk with both hands just to stay upright.

"Daddy? Are you okay?" Vera began to shake.

"Yes, starlight." He smiled the world's least comforting smile. "I just need to know where they were."

"They're our neighbors," she answered, like it was the most obvious thing in the world. "They live in the floors below us."

"The floors below us are sealed off," Marcus felt some of the pressure within him ease. "How did they get up here with Hambo?"

"They didn't, silly." Vera smiled at him, happy that Daddy wasn't being weird anymore. "They were hanging out the window when we talked, and then they had me tie a rope to a bucket and lower it down so Hambo could ride up in it. They said it was okay because you knew one of their friends."

Beneath Marcus' feet, the whole world slipped away.

"They said she lived in the veeerrry top of the tower in the big pyramid," Vera finished. "Just like a princess."

Marcus considered his options. He could throw up, he could scream, or he could throw up while screaming. That was all he could really see available to him at the moment. Somehow he managed to do none of the above, but instead sat back down at his desk, like an idiot.

"Did I do something wrong, Daddy?" Vera took a few tentative steps towards him. "I didn't mean to…"

"No, starlight, no!" Marcus waved her over to him, not confident he could stand. He put his hands on her cheeks and looked into her eyes. "But you have to listen super close to what I say next, okay?"

She whimpered an affirmation.

"I have to go talk to somebody for a minute." Marcus held her gaze. "I am going to close and lock the door behind me—"

"But we never lock the door!" Vera said.

"I am going to lock it, and it is very important that it stay locked," Marcus steamrolled through her objections. "Don't open it for anybody but me, no matter what. In fact, don't even say anything if somebody else comes knocking. Quiet as a mouse. Do you understand?"

Vera shook her head furiously. She looked at her feet. Marcus squeezed her shoulders. She met his eyes again and nodded.

He kissed her on the forehead, then each cheek, and held her as tight as he dared. He was amazed when he let her go, but he managed it. He stood up and went for the door.

"Daddy?" Vera said, shaky and small.

"Yes, starlight?" Marcus couldn't turn around. He couldn't say goodbye twice.

"Is it because of me?" He heard the sobs bubbling in her throat. "Is it because of Hambo and the gypsies?"

"No, honey." He smiled, though she couldn't see it. "They were there already. All you did was warn us. If we…*when* we get out of this, it'll be because you were smart, and brave, but most all…"

"Lucky," Vera finished the line.

In countless bedtime stories about countless princesses, if they ever prevailed, it was always because they were smart, and brave, but most of all lucky.

Marcus closed the door behind him. It was reassuringly solid, heavy old wood on massive steel hinges. He waited until he heard it lock behind him, took two deep breaths, and started to run.

He took the steep, narrow stairs from the manager's office to the ballroom three at a time. Nearly skidded into a stack of toilet paper and sprinted through the double doors into the kitchen. Marta was still in there, cleaning and prepping for tomorrow's breakfast. She shot him the customary glare, but when he ran past her, wordless, pallid, she called after him. He didn't answer. Through the galley and then the restaurant, ignoring surprised calls from a half dozen people still milling about in the window booths after dinner, reading or writing or just staring.

Marcus thought about warning them, but what could he say? Vera told him a story about magic gypsies that sounded a little too familiar, and…what? Even if they believed him, what could they do?

It was pure justification. Even Marcus couldn't convince himself of anything else. He *could* stop, he *could* talk to the people, he *could* consider his words, skip over the right details in his questionable story, and get across the message that there might be maniacs in the floors beneath them. But it would take time. And every second of it was one he would spend away from Vera while she huddled, waiting and scared and crying in a locked room, without him. So Marcus said nothing.

The rooftop garden was dark, and he barked his shin on something hard enough to feel warmth soaking the top of his sock. But he pressed on. Six stories up to Major Wallace's quarters, and each flight stretched into eternity. Panic pulled his moments thin. He was on the verge of screaming when he finally burst out of the stairwell. Heavy footsteps shaking the floorboards as he barreled down the corridor and hurled his body against the door to Major Wallace's quarters. Marcus had a brief fantasy of shattering right through it, splinters exploding all around him, screaming a call to action. Instead, he felt something tear in his shoulder, bounced off, and lost his footing. He landed on his ass and sat stunned on the worn purple carpet.

Major Wallace yanked the door open and stood in the threshold, eyes wide, chin set for a fight.

"Marcus?" He goggled down at the heavyset man collapsed at his feet. "What in the green hell do you think—"

"Compromised," Marcus panted. The Major would respond fastest to his own terminology. "We're compromised."

Wallace almost laughed, then a barrier dropped behind his eyes.

"Sitrep," he commanded, offering his hand.

Marcus took it and stumbled into the apartment after the Major, who had already crossed the length of his spartan living room to kneel before a hefty metal footlocker. He pulled a chain from around his neck. A single small key dangled on its loop. Wallace popped the lock and began setting an array of increasingly worrying weapons on the floor. Pistol to shotgun to assault rifle to something that looked like a grenade launcher.

"Sitrep," Wallace snapped. "Or did you just come to paint my living room in shades of stupid?"

"R-right," Marcus spoke carefully, omitting everything that might undermine his credibility. Certainly, the princess would have to go. Possibly the pig, as well. "I have reason to believe the uh…enemy?" He couldn't recall the Major's preferred term. "The maniac…um…combatants? They're amassing in the floors beneath us."

"You got a source for this intel?" Major Wallace had been entirely replaced by training. He pulled magazines and checked chambers as he spoke.

"My d…" Marcus almost slipped a gear. "Uh…a credible eyewitness report."

Waves of doubt washed against the foundation of Marcus' resolve. But he shored up. Doubt was a luxury he couldn't afford. He'd take the hit if it turned out he was just overreacting. Anything was better than the alternative.

Major Wallace held out an industrial-looking shotgun for Marcus, and every muscle in Marcus' body went in a different direction. He tried to shrug, shake his head, take the gun, and run away at the same time.

"What's wrong?" Wallace broke his infinite stare to give Marcus a sideways look.

"I uh…I can't?" Marcus stammered. He shrugged at the gun.

"I trained you for this myself before I let you take one step in that interrogation room," Wallace said.

"Yeah, but uh…with a little guy. A nine-millimeter, right? Is that right?"

"It's the same basic concept," Wallace sighed.

"It sure doesn't look that way from here," Marcus answered.

The Major set the shotgun down at his feet, then replaced it with a pistol that looked downright friendly by comparison. This time, Marcus took it without pause.

The Major loaded himself up like he was going on a hiking trip straight into hell. Holsters and sheaths strapped to his back, chest, waist, both legs, one arm — the grenade launcher, if that's what it was, went on a sling by his hip.

"All right," Wallace agreed with nobody in particular. "I need you to evac the non-combatants, start with the bottom and work your way up. Town square all the way to the observation deck. Secure the floors as you go. Don't worry about me. There's a service ladder in the elevator shaft that I'll take up once it's all clear. Post three guards, including yourself, at the elevator doors and wait for my—"

Every word of the plan vacated Marcus' head when he heard the scream.

It came from below, far below — from the rooftop garden. It was a hot night, and the Major had his windows propped open. A breeze brought the scent of grass and flowers, smoke from somewhere distant. The mountains.

Marcus looked to Wallace for orders, but the man just shoved past him. Marcus followed.

More stairs. A lifetime of stairs. Marcus marveled at the function of his legs, still managing to haul him around long after he swore they'd fallen off. Three stories down, and another shout — this one closer. Major Wallace put his bodyweight against the stairwell door, then popped up for a quick survey through the window.

"All clear," he said, stepping away and motioning to Marcus.

"W-what?" Marcus leaned into the glass. He stared down the empty hallway. The same faded purple carpet on every floor; the same stained beige walls and stained beige artwork.

"You're on evac." The Major moved as if to leave. "You check that out, I'll get down to the garden and secure—"

"Like hell!" Marcus didn't recognize his own voice.

"Excuse me?" Apparently, Wallace shared the problem.

"I left my daughter down there to come up and get you." Marcus felt the bluster draining already. "I'm not leaving her alone any longer. You go 'check that out.' I'm going home."

"Marcus." Wallace almost put a hand on his shoulder, then reconsidered and pretended to check the action on his own rifle instead. "I can't do this without you."

"I'm not saying that." Marcus' righteous fury collapsed entirely. Reflexive shame took its place. "I'll help, just like you said. But after she's safe."

Wallace gave Marcus a look. It was an expression that Major Wallace had spent decades perfecting. He shifted his jaw to the side, narrowed his eyes, and looked at something just beyond and to the side of your eyeline. The look said, "This is very stupid, but I will pretend to think about it for a moment before explaining to you why it is stupid."

Marcus readied himself to counter a string of objections, but Wallace just nodded.

"Go, then," he said. "But if you encounter resistance, you bunker up and you wait for backup, got it? I'm right on your heels. You don't be a hero, you hear me?"

Marcus smiled crookedly.

"You really don't have to tell *me* that."

Wallace chuffed, then slipped into the hallway and eased the door shut behind him.

Marcus took the remaining stairs three at a time, forward momentum the only thing keeping him upright. He bodychecked the concrete wall at the bottom of the last flight and winded himself, but there was no time to feel it. He stumbled into the rooftop garden with stars in his eyes.

"Whoa-ho," a distant voice called. "What have we got here? Is that…?"

"Marco!" Another joined the first. "Welcome to the party, pal!"

Marcus felt the blood coagulate in his veins. Nobody called him

"Marco" except the Chatterbox. But…he didn't recognize either of these voices. He blinked, trying to force his eyes to adjust to the relentless blue light. Somebody had taken the industrial flashlight that Marta kept in the kitchen and set it on the ground just before the entrance to the town square. It was pointed right at the doorway in which he now stood, gawping like a landed fish.

Three silhouettes stood scattershot between the planter boxes. They were frozen in odd positions, like they'd been mid-sprint when god hit pause on reality. Just beyond them, between the town square and the blinding flashlight, a trio of shadowy forms reclined on the patio furniture.

"You caught us in the middle of a game, Marco," one of the reclining figures called out to him. "But you can join up, too. You'll get the rules quick. Heck, you probably played it before — check it out."

"Green light!" one of the figures hollered, this one female.

The frozen silhouettes sprang to life, charging Marcus. He flailed backward, raising his pistol and trying to aim for all three at once.

"Red light!" a third voice called, and the silhouettes stopped dead in their tracks. They'd only closed a few feet of distance between themselves and where Marcus stood, trying not to stain his jeans.

He hopped the pistol's sights from shadow to shadow, trying to gauge which target was closest.

"Marcus," the nearest one said, and he twitched.

"H-Halsey?" he ventured.

"It's us, Marcus," she whispered. "They're making us play the—"

"Hey now," the first of the reclining figures chastised, "no chatter."

He raised his hand and passed it before the beam of the flashlight, the shadow of his outstretched fingers enormous at this distance.

Halsey yelped and fell quiet.

"Greenlightredlight!" the female figure cried, words blurring together.

Halsey took a single step and froze again, but the silhouette behind her stumbled after red light was called.

The Merry at the flashlight passed his hand before the beam again and waggled his fingers playfully. A thorn of shadow sprouted from the index finger and grew into a spiky tentacle. It snaked across the ground and wrapped itself around the silhouette's foot. They started to scream. Marcus recognized the voice: Chet.

The shadow tentacle forked out at hard angles as it slithered up Chet's body, moving in hops and starts all the way up to his face. When it reached his mouth, Chet fell to the ground, thrashing and screeching and making quick wet gulping noises. Then he went still.

"Green light!" the girl called. Nobody moved.

"Okay fine." The second man laughed. "Red light. You're never gonna make it if you don't try, folks!"

Marcus tried to speak and found he'd swallowed his own voice. It took several raspy coughs to find it again.

"Do I…" He looked to Halsey's silhouette, then the other. "Do I still have to play if I'm coming towards you?"

"Whoa, big man here!" The first figure threw up his hands in faux surrender. The shadows danced, and Halsey whimpered. "You want to fight us?!"

"No," Marcus answered, slow and careful. "Just get past you."

The female figure leaned into the table, and the others joined her for a quick huddle. When they broke, the second man called out to Marcus.

"You already played a game with Aileen and lost. She's got most of your good parts. She would be pissed if we just killed you out here."

Aileen? Who was…?

The Chatterbox.

"Y-you talked to Aileen? Is she…loose?" Marcus asked.

The trio snickered.

"Not yet," the second man answered. "But she will be soon. When Herote's in the club, everyone joins the party. We know what Ai knows."

"And boy," the woman said. "We know one thing: you are fucked."

Raucous laughter cut into Marcus like sleet.

"All right, so tell you what — you can play, but if you mess up, the others pay. Cool?"

"Marcus," the second silhouette hissed. Marta. "Don't you god damn dare!"

He looked to Halsey but couldn't read her expression. In the end, he supposed it didn't matter. It wouldn't have changed things, either way.

"C-cool," he called back.

Marta swore at him in Spanish. Halsey just sighed.

"No chatter," the first man reprimanded.

Then: "Green light!"

Marcus broke into a dead sprint, lightblind and shaky, the blood crusting his sock a constant reminder of how many invisible obstacles lay between him and his destination. Halsey and Marta followed suit. Marcus wasn't a fast man, and you'd only call him "agile" in the most sarcastic tones — but somehow he made it halfway across the rooftop before the girl called for him to stop. He skidded to a halt but turned his ankle on something in the dark. Just a halfstep. He recovered so quickly. Maybe they didn't see it…

The first man laughed.

"What?" Marta asked, not daring to turn to look. "What did you do? Marcus, you son of a—"

The man's fingers danced across the light, and Marta's words turned to screams. Marcus closed his eyes, but he dared not move to plug his ears. He listened to it all.

"Green light!"

He and Halsey ran.

"Red light!"

They stopped.

Once more.

Marcus was nearly at the doors to the Chinese restaurant. He could see the frieze of faded dragons chasing along their tops. This last round, he had frozen directly alongside the shadowy trio at their seats. He didn't have enough trust in his own speed, or his skill, or himself in general to risk firing at all three at once. But the flashlight was right there — just a few feet in front of him. If they were controlling the shadows somehow, his next movement would put the light at his back. Out of their reach. Halsey must be close. She must be fingertips-to-the-door close. He could do it, one more turn.

"Greenlightredlightgreenlight," the girl paused, then, "red light!"

Marcus didn't risk running at all. But he heard Halsey stumble. The trio snickered. The first man raised his arm. So did Marcus. He fired a single shot at the flashlight, and his stomach dropped to his knees when he saw that the bullet didn't even shatter the lens. Still, it was enough to spin the casing, sending the beam slashing sideways and leaving the rooftop gardens behind in relative darkness. Marcus ran for his doors, even as he heard Halsey's slam in the distance. She made it. And so had he.

Nearly.

He hurdled the oscillating flashlight, just as the beam finished sweeping a full 180. It now cast its cold light straight ahead of Marcus — all across the interior of the restaurant. Behind him, the clatter of patio furniture being moved. The Merry were standing to pursue, but Marcus could do it. He could make it. He was already through the entry doors, past the hostess podium, nearly to the waitstaff galley. Then something flickered across the walls ahead, huge and black. A single immense finger, wagging side to side.

A black thorn broke out of its tip, slithered loose and grew, became a dark branch whose offshoots forked at right angles like circuitry. It stuttered down the wall, across the floor, toward Marcus, and he dove beneath the nearest booth. The branch split and split again, every division a new line closing in on Marcus. Now the silhouette of the hand morphed, knuckles closing, finger looping. A shadow-puppet of a dog. It barked at him, and the maniacs standing in the doorway laughed.

Marcus reached up and gripped the edge of the table. He hauled it off its heavy iron base and dropped it like a dam between himself and the approaching streams. Splitting and branching, again and again, twenty, fortysixtyeighty — a delta of black shuddering toward him in time-lapse jumps. Marcus got to his feet and straddled the bench seats, crossing booth to booth. He kept out of the light until the Merry caught on and simply shifted the beam. Black rivers surged. Marcus dove.

Something sharp and cold grazed his wrist, and then he hit the floor. Blue rubber diamonds pressed into the flesh of his cheek. The traction mat in the waitstaff galley. He'd broken line of sight, but it wouldn't buy him long. He crawled, then ran on all fours until he had enough momentum to stand. He put his shoulder through the kitchen doors, and his feet slipped on the damp tile. His wrist burned. He didn't have time to care. Into the ballroom — pausing to grab the mop Marta used (still damp; she was just here, just alive and working and she had no idea you were about to…) and shove it between the ornate, looping handles. He slipped again on the steep and narrow stairs up to the manager's office and bit his lip. He skidded to a halt in front of his apartment and knocked three times.

No answer.

Good girl.

"Starlight?" He tried to sound normal. Tried to recall what normal sounded like. "It's Daddy. Open up. We gotta go."

No response. Marcus screamed internally.

But Vera wouldn't answer frustration. When she was upset, she just shut down. She probably learned that from him. Probably learned all sorts of stupid things from—

"Daddy?" a shaky voice asked.

"Yes, sweetie. It's me."

"For reals?"

"For really reals."

"Okay…"

The lock did not clack in the frame. The door did not swing open, and Vera did not jump into his arms.

"Starlight?" he prodded.

"Who is Detective Martin Piggs' partner and best friend?"

Marcus almost laughed.

"Why, Detective Roger Murthog, of course."

A pair of muffled snaps as the locks disengaged. The door creaked open an inch. Marcus smiled down at the single eye that surveyed him skeptically.

"Good girl," Marcus said, easing his way in. "That was smart of you to check, but we're in a real big hurry and we gotta go right now so there's no time to—"

"I already packed." She held up a faded blue Jansport for him to inspect. "I remembered. From before we lived here, when we had to run all the time."

Marcus squeezed her tight and hoped she could feel all the desperate, savage pride he held in that moment. His girl: his brilliant, resolute daughter, who took this nightmare world in stride — even when her daddy failed to keep her safe.

Marcus took Vera's hand and descended into the ballroom carefully, willing himself to be still inside. Major Wallace's words throbbed in his head, and he did his best to believe them: Slow is careful. Careful is fast.

He peaked around the corner and saw his mop-handle barricade still intact. A thorough scan of the room found toilet paper and tomatoes, Ziploc bags and winter clothing, spare blankets, canned goods, batteries and water filters and crates of various other items that used to be important, back when society was still a thing that happened reliably. Some business in the lower floors had sold and shipped what sure appeared to be pure random crap, to Marcus' eyes. Fidget spinners, heating pads, essential oils, pencil holders and bicycle cable locks — the same ones they'd used to bind the Chatterbox.

The girl upstairs, whom he'd promised his flesh to, when he thought nothing would ever come of it. The girl who was probably free by now, or would be soon, or…did it even matter? There was nothing in the vast storage of the ballroom that said "maniac repellent" on the side in big letters.

Marcus tried to slow his breathing. Vera was picking up on the rapid rise and fall in his chest.

"Daddy?" she asked.

How do you tell your child you don't have a plan?

"Yes, starlight?" Marcus smiled at her. Made sure she saw every inch of it.

"What's happening?"

"The bad people — the uh…the magic gypsies you warned us about — they're here, and we're trying to find somewhere safe."

"Where is safe?"

How do you say it?

You just say it.

"I don't know."

"What are we gonna do?"

"I…uh…"

Say it.

"I don't know, starlight."

Admitting it was the worst thing Marcus had ever done. It felt like he'd taken a chainsaw to the edges of his soul. Left him ragged and wounded at the very foundations of himself.

Vera just blinked up at him, and said, "Oh."

She looked around the room some, at the windows and the roof and the door.

"What would Princess McClane do?" she wondered and wiped her nose on her sleeve.

Marcus laughed to himself. What would Princess McClane do, indeed? He had nobody to blame for that kind of thinking but himself; he'd spoon-fed generations of silly action movies into Vera with his—

He looked at the windows. He looked at the crate. Bicycle cables. Window.

"Starlight?" He nudged her. She peered up at him with eyes too big. "You're a genius."

"I know, Daddy." She smiled. "But why do you say it?"

Marcus tore open the crate and upended its contents on the floor. Every single one was wrapped in plastic packaging.

That stupid, stupid world that came before.

"Sweetie," he called Vera over, and she knelt before the pile, spreading her fingers wide to sift through all the shiny gifts. "I need you to unwrap these — as many as you can, as fast as you can. When you're done with one, you pull its end through the loop on another, and then close the lock, like this…"

He circled one cable lock through another, then snapped it shut, forming a single large link on a chain.

"Can you do that?"

She just nodded, already dutifully tearing into the plastic wrap.

Marcus crossed over to the windows and rapped on one with his knuckle. It rebounded. Not glass. Not normal glass, anyway — reinforced somehow. He'd need something sharp to break it or heavy to pry it from the—

"Maaaarcoooo," a familiar voice sang.

Marcus pivoted as quickly as his frozen muscles would allow. Framed in the porthole of the swinging door, the Chatterbox's face sported the largest, cruelest smile he'd ever seen. Thin lines of deep black bled outwards from both eyes. Marcus took it for more of her improvised makeup, at first, but she shifted her balance, and the light showed him the truth. It wasn't makeup. It wasn't anything. She no longer had eyes, just two pits dug into the foundation of reality. Dense networks of black pathways forked from her ocular cavity to her jawline, the lines running perfectly straight until they broke at right angles. When the darkness met the edges of her face, it did not fall like liquid, but crackled wildly in the air.

"Buddy!" The Chatterbox clapped. "Fancy meeting a nice boy like you in a place like this!"

"Aileen," Marcus responded, and her vicious smile disappeared for a second, flashing in and out of existence like a single missing frame in a reel of film.

"I think I like Chatterbox better!" She giggled. "Can I show you something cool?"

The crinkle of plastic ceased. Marcus looked to Vera, who had gone totally still, gaze locked to the doors. She couldn't see the Merry from her position, but more importantly, they couldn't see her. He waved to Vera using only his fingers, hoping the Chatterbox wouldn't spot the motion. Marcus caught her eye and nodded at the pile of plastic-wrapped cables. She resumed her work hesitantly.

"I couldn't do this little trick before," the Chatterbox continued, "when it was just me. There weren't enough of us in one place for Herote to live, but she's here now. You'll love this, watch!"

"Sure," Marcus ventured, shuffling to one side. Knees bent. Ready.

The Chatterbox raised the industrial flashlight alongside her head and pointed it in through the narrow porthole, pinning Marcus in a thin beam of flat blue light. She turned her head to profile and snaked her tongue before the lens. An immense shadowy tongue skated across the beam. It forked at the edges. It reached for Marcus.

He dove and felt something graze his scalp. The gush of warmth that followed. He hit the ground, rolled, ducked behind a pallet of toilet paper, felt at his skull — sure half of it was gone. But no, just a cut. Long, but thin as it was shallow.

Laughter from beyond the doors.

"Pretty cool, right?!" The Chatterbox squealed. "You just met Herote, buddy! She's a little shy. She likes to hide in the shadows. She's been here for a while now, actually — bleeding from our eyes and following the shadows up through the floors, wrapping herself aaallll around this place. She's been hiding right next to you, and you never knew! Isn't she just…"

She glanced to the side, checking something with the other Merry.

"Ain't she just dreamy?" the Chatterbox confirmed, the words falling off into a wistful sigh.

The bones of the tower shook. Marcus looked to the ceiling and caught an eyeful of dust for his troubles.

The static wrinkle of plastic paused. Marcus checked to make sure Vera was safe and still too far beyond the edge of the window to get caught in the beam. She bit her lip, waterworks brewing in her big blue eyes.

Marcus ducked back behind the pallet and whispered to her as loud as he dared: "It's okay, starlight, they can't get you where you are. Daddy is going to be just fine, but you need to keep working, okay? It is the super importantest thing."

"But Daddy—"

"What would Princess McClane do?" he chided.

"I just…" She didn't finish the thought but tore into the shrink-wrap with renewed fury.

"Whoa." The Chatterbox drummed on the porthole with her fingernails. "That was Major Wallace. Did you know he had a grenade launcher? So butch."

Marcus heard the others laugh.

"We're all connected now that Herote's here," she explained, then the building shook again. "Looks like he got Serena with that one, but hold on…yeah, he didn't get Victor. Give it just one second…"

They all waited in silence. Until Wallace screamed. So faint that Marcus couldn't swear if he'd ever actually heard it or if his brain had just backfilled the sound.

"Now Victor has a grenade launcher." She made it into a taunting little song.

The tower vibrated down its very frame. A deep thrum like a massive engine starting. Again. And again. A rain of ceiling tiles. Vera moaned, but she did not stop unwrapping, looping, clicking. There was a sharp crack somewhere in the room, and Marcus feared the Merry were finally tiring of their game, breaking down the doors. But the Chatterbox was still there, framed in the porthole, making silly faces and sweeping her light back and forth across Marcus' cover.

The sound hadn't come from the doors; it came from the windows. One of the immense panes of glass on the north wall had splintered. A frosty spider web that started in one corner, then sent shaky tendrils scouting across the surface.

Another shock. From somewhere far above, Marcus heard a whale song. An extended, draining groan that came from inside the walls. That was structural. There wasn't time.

"Starlight," Marcus tried to keep his voice soft enough so the maniacs couldn't hear, but loud enough to snap Vera out of her work trance. "Starlight!"

She looked up from her pile of cables and discarded plastic with unfocused eyes.

"Sweetie." Marcus didn't dare lean out from cover any further, just one side of his face peeking from behind an eighteen pack of Cottonelle. "You did so good. You did Princess-good: that's how good you did."

Vera risked a shaky smile.

"Now you just have to take one end of that big beautiful chain you made and loop it around that pillar right behind you — lock it back to itself, just like you've been doing, okay?"

Vera nodded and stood on uncertain legs. She wobbled toward the pillar, out of sight behind it, and emerged again to secure the cable. She looked back to Daddy, utterly uncomprehending of the plan, or what came next.

"When I say so—"

"Marco? Ol' buddy, ol' pal? You got awful quiet in there," the Chatterbox called, and she settled the beam of the flashlight firmly on his pallet. "That's boring. If you don't stop being boring, we're gonna have to come in…"

She tested the barricade, rattled the mop handle in its perch. But it held. Then both doors heaved, once — a body thrown against them, and the handle shifted. It went off balance. Started slipping out of place.

"When I say so," Marcus whispered to Vera, "you need to run over here to Daddy and bring that cable with you. Run as fast as you can, but not until I say so, okay?"

Vera tightened her grip on the makeshift chain. She opened her mouth to say something, but only a sob slipped out. She closed it again and nodded instead.

"Hey, Chatterbox," Marcus hollered. "I uh…I promised you a pinky, right?"

"Among so many other things," she cooed.

He held his hand up high, into the light.

"Come get it." He hoped he sounded tougher than he felt.

A shadow loomed on the opposite wall: Aileen's face in silhouette. The light shifted. The face crawled across the floor, up the pallet. The Chatterbox puckered her lips in an exaggerated kiss…

"Now, starlight," Marcus hissed.

Vera ran, the Chatterbox kissed, the shadows danced, and Marcus' hand lit up bright with hot pink pain. He snatched it back, out of the light, and drummed his heels against the floor. His pinky was gone, a surgically clean cut at the very base of the knuckle. Truly gone. It didn't fall to the floor, severed. It just disappeared. Something had taken it.

Roars of laughter from beyond the barricade. Marcus pulled Vera to his chest and used his uninjured hand to wrap the free end of the chain around them. He cinched the loop tight, made a note of the combination printed on a sticker at the tip, and clicked it shut.

"Marco, god damn!" the Chatterbox called. "I take back everything I said about you; you really do know how to have a good time!"

"Starlight," Marcus whispered in Vera's ear, squeezing her tighter with every word. "You remember how Princess McClane found the magic wands but didn't know what the Evil Count Gruber was going to do with them?"

He felt her nod. She was small and warm in his arms.

"Well," he gave the chain a yank. He had no clue if it would actually hold and wasn't sure what tugging at it was supposed to tell him. "Turns out Gruber had stored barrels and barrels of pixie dust on the roof of Nakatomi Castle…"

"Where all the villagers were hiding!" she gasped.

"And Princess McClane went up to save them." Marcus rose to one knee and made sure he had an unbreakable grip on Vera's collar. He used his good hand for that. His other, wounded hand, shaking and slick with blood, held the chain as best he could. "And Evil Count Gruber used the wands to curse aaall the pixie dust…"

"No," Vera whimpered.

"But Princess McClane got all the villagers out in time, and then she wrapped a golden rope around her waist, and she jumped right off that roof and swung to safety, even as the curse exploded above her."

"Daddy," Vera spoke quietly. "This isn't like in the stories…"

"Sure it is, starlight." He let her hear the laughter in his voice. "You just gotta believe."

Marcus winked at her, then barreled straight for the cracked window. He tucked his head, lowered his shoulder. The flashlight swung wildly, trying to keep him in its beam. The shadows veered and distorted.

He wasn't sure which one Herote would come from, when she came.

She came from everywhere.

Geometric black tentacles forked outward from every shadow at once, closing in on Marcus from all sides. He hopped across one, ducked another, skipped a third and then there was nothing for it but to…

Jump.

The glass shattered instantly, no resistance, went from solid plane to a thousand tiny polyhedrons in a blink. Marcus felt a fraction of terror — weightless, falling, sinking, gut in the throat panic — and then a lash of fire lit across his waist. He and Vera yanked to a stop, the momentum of the swing sending his chin cracking into the exterior window of the floor below.

Marcus gently rotated at the end of his improvised chain. He looked at a grey skyline against a pure black sky. At his own bizarre reflection, distorted by a delta of cracks in the splintered glass. Back to the skyline. Reflection again. He patted Vera, who whimpered in his arms, but seemed otherwise intact. More than could be said for him: He'd certainly have a bruise for a belt, maybe worse. The adrenaline hadn't let up enough for him to feel his damage.

Marcus glanced up at the ragged edge of the window he'd just leapt through, only a few feet above. It sure as hell felt like he'd fallen farther than that. Still: two cable lengths shorter, and their chain wouldn't have reached. Too many more, and the fall would have cracked their spines. Vera's chain was perfect. It had saved their lives. He stroked her hair, and she chewed on his collar as they waited for their idle spin to bring them back around to face the tower.

The cracks that weakened the window in the ballroom extended down, through stone and glass alike. They began three stories above, emanating out from an entire floor of shattered glass and billowing smoke, and continued out of sight below. Marcus reached out with his toes and planted one foot on either side of the window, steadying himself and trying to shift the pressure of the cable to a less sensitive spot. There was a loud snap from somewhere above, and the quality of the light changed. The Merry had made it through the doors. Marcus curled the bloody fingers of his wounded hand as best he could, still not willing to risk the good one that held Vera vise-tight, and struck the glass. Straight white pain through his knuckles to his long bones, and nothing to show for it. Shadows moved in the empty space above him. He struck again, the glass wobbling with his efforts. And again, and aga—

He wasn't actually ready for the break. The window shattered into pellets and fell away like hail. The chain wasn't long enough for them to swing into the floor below, and uprooted from his perch, Marcus could only resume his oscillations.

Footsteps from the ballroom above, coming closer.

"Starlight?"

Vera groaned.

"Daddy's going to undo the chain now, okay?" He tried to make that sound natural. Tried to sell it as a good idea, or at least *not* staggeringly suicidal. "You get a hold around my neck as tight as you can, and you don't let go no matter what, understand?"

Marcus didn't have a choice: He would have to let go of Vera. He would have to trust her grip over his own. He spun the numbers on the combination lock with his wounded hand, white-knuckling the chain above with his good one. Vera latched onto him like a barnacle. Tightened her little arms around his neck. Marcus felt the blood pool in his brain. His cheeks went flush, and a dull red roar crept in at the edges of his vision. But he didn't ask her to loosen her hold. The numbers spun slick and sloppy in his bloody fingers, his fist slid on the plastic coating of the bicycle cables, the laughter above grew louder, then a face peeked out over the side. Young, pretty, and kind — once upon a distant time — but from eyebrow ridge to cheek, nothing. A black space to rival the dead sky. Aileen smiled. He swung his weight forward. The lock clicked. Marcus screamed.

And let go.

It sure didn't feel like just a few feet. He and Vera landed on the floor below, into a scatter of shattered glass with a sound like ice cracking.

"Holy shit," the Chatterbox called from the ballroom above. "Marco, you are nuts! That was great!"

"Starlight, are you okay?" He broke Vera's stranglehold and held her face to his.

Her eyes were glossy, like she was paying attention to a sound he couldn't hear. But she nodded. When he tried to stand, the little glass pellets rolled like marbles and he tumbled down again.

"Marco," Aileen hollered after him. "I have never seen *anybody* so desperate to survive. That's hilarious! You know what? I think you deserve this win, buddy. But remember: you owe me most of your ass, and your little girl owes us her laugh. And we *all* know that now. Wherever Herote goes, every single one of us will know exactly what pieces to take from you. And there are so very many of us these days, Marco — one of us will collect. I sure hope it's me!"

"You can try," Marcus rasped, but whatever confidence he wanted to project died in his throat. It came out as a squeak and was only answered with more casual, taunting laughter.

Navigating a darkened and destroyed floor of offices while beaten, bloody, and towing a shell-shocked child — that was a challenge. Descending two-dozen flights of stairs was another, and clawing through the accumulated trash and broken furniture that blocked them was yet another. The open streets brought a new kind of fear, when every shadow could be the hidden body of some impossible monster. When maniacs who wanted to flay him alive lurked in every darkened corner. And there would be wild dogs, and disease, and fires, and worse. No distance felt safe enough. Every rest was tempered with the suspicion that something, somewhere, was using that time to gain on him. But worse was the time it allowed him to think. To remember that every one of his friends — he and Vera's makeshift family; Lexy and Cash and Halsey and so many more — had been trapped in that smoking, collapsing building. With the Merry playing their games, and the shadows coming to life.

So they kept moving.

So he told stories.

Marcus told Vera about Princess Tango and Princess Cash, and the tragic story of Princess Utah and Princess Bodhi. He told her about the merciless Princess Wick, and the epic, rambling saga of Princess Chan: the acrobatic princess who could beat up ten pigs with nothing but a stepladder, or a jump-rope, or some skis. When he wasn't telling Vera what was safe to eat, or when to hide, or how much longer to the Walled City — which all the spray-painted road signs promised was safe — Marcus told stories. Because as long as his mouth was running, neither he nor Vera would have to remember home.

Midnight Mountain

To whomever reads these words,

I apologize. You have, unfortunately, stumbled onto the last request of a dying old man. It will not be an easy one. My name is Alex Yamamoto, and these are my final words. I hope they are legible. I further hope that my daughters, Chiyo Yamamoto or Yui Hendricks, will one day read this letter. I hope it finds them in good health and that its contents do not cause them undue distress.

My last request is twofold. First, I ask that you read this carefully and considerately. If knowledge of the events recorded in this letter might help what little is left of humanity, please put them to use. That is your priority. If that is done, or there is time, I then ask another favor: please find my daughters, who have headed toward the spire of light we have seen on the horizon. It appears to be coming from the former site of the Grand Coulee Dam. That is what they have told me. They have left in that direction, believing in the safety the road signs promise them. I do not doubt they are alive. They are survivors, because I have taught them to be. And also because it would destroy me to believe otherwise.

Here are the events I wish to record. Please forgive a nostalgic old man for rambling, now and then:

I am eighty-six years old, and I am legally blind. It is unjust that I should survive the fall of mankind when so many others were more able and did not. I lived to this day in part because of what my father taught me, and which I, in my turn, taught my daughters. In no small way do I also owe my life to the kindness and sacrifices of others: Willie, Jackson,

Candace, Mal — I remember you and I thank you. I am sorry.

I have also survived largely due to sheer, blind luck.

That was a joke, of course. Because I am blind. Did you laugh? Probably not.

My late wife, May Yamamoto, once told me that I had the sense of humor of a court stenographer.

Regardless of how I survived to feel this cool and sunny morning on my skin, for the last eight months I have been living in the Larch Pine Lodge, in the shadow of Midnight Mountain, in the northeastern corner of Washington State. At first, I settled there with only my daughters, Chiyo and Yui. Then came Willie Steel, which was a stage name, who found us by the smoke of our fires. Next was Jackson and Candace Merryweather, whom Yui found during a scavenging run to the distant town of Spokane. Finally, Mal joined our ranks after initially firing on Chiyo as she bicycled down Highway 20 in search of medical supplies for a fever I had contracted. Luckily, Mal missed, and after much convincing, came to accept that Chiyo was not one of what they call "the Merry" — a lunatic that can still pass for human. If Mal had a last name, or indeed, even a full first name, she would not tell me. This was our small but close group of survivors that, over the months, became something like a family.

The Larch Pine Lodge was a nice building. It might still be. It was solid and well built, in the classic American log cabin style, though I suspect it was quite a bit newer than its facade suggested. Its insulation held heat well, and the twelve rooms originally meant for wealthy vacationers provided ample space for us. To the extent that one could be in times like these — when the skies have gone a shade of black that does not occur in nature, and bands of maniacs two hundred thousand strong roam the plains like buffalo — we were happy. Or perhaps the word is "content." Perhaps again we were just grateful for the relative safety that our extreme isolation provided.

The Larch Pine Lodge was only accessible by helipad (though we did not helicopter in, but rather walked through wild forest, snagging ankles and bootlaces on thorns and errant branches). No roads led to it. We would later find a once well-tended walking trail leading from the rear of the lodge to a nearby fire road, but we did not know it was there at the time. We, like Willie who came after us, simply followed the telltale gray smoke of a small manmade fire. Well, I should say that Chiyo and Yui followed it. I followed them, and they held my hand the entire way, warning me of hidden pitfalls and snatching brambles.

The one who made that first camp turned out to be another type of maniac, what they call a "Judge." And though it welcomed us at first, it attempted to strangle Chiyo to death when she did not rinse her cup out immediately after use, as a small typed sign on the refrigerator dictated. Yui put a bullet into his head at close range, and the poor creature was buried in an unmarked grave just beyond the border of the lawn.

Our trio, and those others I have listed above, were the only human beings who ever came to the Larch Pine Lodge after the fall of mankind. We had no visitors that did not eventually come to stay with us, and there were no more maniacs, either. It was very peaceful. Until one morning, approximately two weeks ago, when Yui happened to look out the bathroom window on the second floor and spied a twisted form amongst the ragged pines. It stood quite still, with its head pressed to the trunk of a nearby tree. It was the broken posture of a terribly exhausted person, leaning for a brief rest, but it did not move on. It did not move at all. We watched the thing for hours before approaching, and even then, not closely. We had seen a few of the Sleepers (another type of maniac — do we all use these same words? Or are they regional? Cultural?) and knew that though their natural state was one of impossible stillness, there was an invisible proximity line one could cross that would "trigger" their attack. Once set off, they moved with supernatural speed and precision, preferring to rip the limbs off of any intruders. It seemed less like they defended a space, or set any kind of conscious ambush, and more that they abhorred the very concept of movement and would only risk doing the same themselves in order to stop the hated practice in others nearby.

Both Yui and Jackson guarded and watched the Sleeper, but it did not seem to pose any immediate threat. That evening, Yui put a bullet into its head, but it did not fall. In fact, it did not react at all. We decided not to waste any more ammunition. As we slept that night — quite uneasily, I should say, with that creature lurking just outside our cabin — another of the Sleepers came. We did not see it approach, so perhaps it was already there, and we simply found another of the monsters in our midst. This newest addition was farther out into the woods but undoubtedly stationed just like the first, watching the cabin. After more searching, we found another. And another. This pattern repeated, day after day, until nearly a week later, when we found ourselves surrounded. Dozens of figures slouched in the woods to the north, south, and east of the Larch Pine Lodge — broken-backed sentries cutting off every path of escape, waiting for some unseen cue to attack. We had Midnight Mountain to our west. It did not quite rise up like a sheer cliff face, but it was still a steep grade through rough country, with many miles of wilderness before anything like a road or trail. We were, effectively, cut off. It took several days to understand why. That was when the true invader came.

Alejandra described it to me as a black and oily fog, which moved unlike any vapor she had ever seen. She said it was not like smoke, but like ink spilled in water, which then moved across the air. It advanced so slowly it was almost imperceptible, but when Chiyo climbed up upon the roof, she reported that it stretched all the way to the eastern horizon. We had not seen it advance for the density of the trees and now found that it blocked any escape we might have had, save for the treacherous slopes of Midnight Mountain itself. The Sleepers on the perimeter did not move, even as the fog overtook them, inch by inch. Alejandra said that the second the fog absorbed them, it was like they were gone. One did not see the hunched figures obscured as though in a heavy mist; it was rather like they had been enveloped by a heavy black blanket.

Willie Steel, as ever, was the boldest of us, and he took it upon himself to experiment with the fog. He threw rocks into it, and we heard each land but did not see them even an inch beyond the veil. Next, he moved in with a long pole, which had been used to clean the vaulted ceilings of the lodge's lobby. The pole touched nothing and came back clean. Yui brought Willie's attention to a small bird, flying above. My wife, May, enjoyed watching birds and would have thought to specify its type here — but I could not place it by call alone. This bird, it seems, was circling a route. Whenever its path caused it to disappear into the fog, it would come back out a moment later, apparently unharmed.

This heartened Willie.

We know better now.

He informed us that he was going to touch the fog and had Candace and Yui on standby to assist should something go awry. Alejandra described the following events to me later, when I asked what had happened. At the time, I heard only screaming and profanities. Willie extended his arm as far as he could, while holding his body at the utmost possible distance. He touched the inky surface, beyond which nothing could be seen, as though it were the very borders of existence, and immediately he cried out in pain. He tried to pull back from the fog but was held fast. It was not as though the blackness was something sticky or elastic, but rather as though it was concrete that had formed around his fingertips.

He jumped, jerked, bobbed, and heaved in his attempts to escape it but could not. The section of darkness immediately surrounding Willie's fingertips seemed to break loose, like liquid that been held back by surface tension, and was suddenly free. It flowed up his arm, across his shoulder and his face, and down the length of his body until there was only a vaguely Willie Steel–shaped patch of darkness where the man himself had once stood.

Yui thought to grab a long plank before the experiment had started and now swung it at Willie's body, attempting to knock him free without touching it herself. The wood whistled through empty air, scattering only fog, as though Willie had never stood there at all. The main mass slowly reabsorbed the Willie Steel–shaped patch, and that was the last we ever saw of him.

It was very quickly agreed that we should flee as soon as possible.

We retreated to the lodge and packed what few scattered belongings we dared, all the time aware of the advancing darkness just beyond the eastern walls. When we were ready, we slipped out the side door and began our trek up the mountain.

At this point, it should help to explain that I am legally blind, and have been for seven years, but that does not mean I am totally blind. I see shapes and shadows, when they are close. They are often blurry at the edges, and no matter how close you hold a sheet of paper to my nose, I cannot read the characters on it. But I can recognize, if it is within a few inches of my eyes, that it is paper. Or at least something paper shaped. As you can see, I have written this letter in an ordinary journal with an ordinary pen — the only difference being that the paper's lines are raised slightly, which I can feel quite well with the tip of a pen. It is in this same way that I navigate the world: I partially rely on the light, though I do not see much even on the brightest day. So I suffered the same disadvantage as the others when we slipped out of the Larch Pine Lodge at twilight, looking up a slope of shadowy and gnarled trees, without any path to speak of. Alejandra often volunteered as my guide and did so again. It seems as though she enjoyed narrating to me. I gather she had been a journalist before the end times, though something happened regarding that profession, and she did not like to talk about it. The narration, I gathered, was something that calmed her as much as it helped me. I suspect she would have done it even had I not been there, a captive audience for her every word.

That was a little joke. Did you laugh? Probably not.

Alejandra held my arm as we stumbled up the steep and uneven slopes of Midnight Mountain, whispering as best she could about the obstacles before us, which she could not see very well, either. She would tell me there was a bramble, even as she herself stumbled into it. She would warn me of a rock, even as I barked my shin upon it. We stuck very close together, moved relatively slowly, and paused at every forest noise, as though we could hear any danger and act upon that information in time to avoid it. After an uneventful while, we came to accept that there were no Sleepers lurking on this treacherous mountainside, and that was one of many mistakes we made.

It was as surprising to me as to anyone else, but I was the first to notice the presence of a Sleeper. It was the smell that alerted me, not the sight, of course. The others, looking upon its gnarled silhouette in the near dark, decided that it looked like some misshapen tree and no more. Though the Sleepers did not smell of rot, exactly, they did smell of age. They carried with them the scent of something old and long neglected. By which I do not mean filth — it was not the odor of stale sweat or dried urine or any other bodily fluid. Indeed, the human element was entirely absent from their scent. It was just dust and mold and the implacable sense of stillness that one gets from an old garment forgotten in a closet or a box for decades. I did not know what the smell was, at first, only that it was wrong. I did not think to whisper an alarm, though I doubt, in hindsight, that it would have helped Mal much. I only had time to reach out to Alejandra, who was guiding me, and grab her by the wrist, stopping her from moving forward.

There was a short, fearful shout ahead, followed by a loud, one-sided struggle, a sickening pop that I will never forget, and then the sharp metal scent of fresh blood. Another scream, and then thrashing (and much falling) as the rest of us broke and ran. We heard two more crunchy pops behind us, which reminded me of deboning a chicken, but thankfully, there was no more screaming. It was only later, when the danger had ebbed, that I wished I had thought to help, instead of flee. But that is always the way of things.

We moved more slowly after that and paused at every gnarled tree of a certain size. I mentioned the smell and became something of a bloodhound for the group. I did encounter that scent again a time or two, and I very slowly and cautiously navigated us around it. In this way, I like to think that I did my part — that I possibly made up for the handicap of my own blindness. I probably did not, but as I said, I like to think it.

That was a sort of joke. Did you laugh? I can guess the answer…

Here is a tricky thing about blindness (or should I say, about my own blindness; I cannot vouch much for the experience of others, whose abilities may vary greatly): It is not as though my other senses have been augmented, since the time when I lost my sight. I do not feel I can pick up hidden scents, or hear far-off whispers, or identify things solely by their texture, which would have at least made a good party trick. Instead, it was more that I was forced to pay closer attention to my lesser senses, because they were my only stimuli. I could smell that we were surrounded by larch trees or walking near a blackberry bush, only because I could not see that information first. So there in that dark forest, it might have seemed like I had some greater power than the others, but that is only because I had practiced not relying so much on sight (quite against my will, for the record). I say this now as an excuse, I know, for what happened next. It is what I tell myself for missing the sleeper that killed both Candace and Jackson.

We had made it relatively far up the slopes of Midnight Mountain when Yui spotted something of a rise or hilltop. We were approaching its banks when I stopped the group, believing that I had detected that mothy old smell of a lurking Sleeper. I sniffed at the air, thought long and hard about it, and asked if any of the others saw a broken tree or a twisted old shrub that might actually be a maniac in disguise. Chiyo said no, and she had the sharpest eyes of any of us, but she clarified that she was not certain and left the call up to me. I cleared us to advance again, believing my nose to be playing tricks on me. It was not.

The Sleeper was leaning its back against the trunk of a particularly large and thick pine. It was facing our ascent. In this way, it was hidden from sight, obscured by the dimly backlit tree. It secured Candace first, and before we even knew she had been taken, her screams were already fading. Jackson ran to her side, as any husband would do, and struggled with the creature for only a moment before his shouts of rage turned to barks of pain and then the broken mutterings of shock. If there was any luck on our side, it showed itself when the sleeper lunged, thoughtless and knife-quick, only to fall into a small gully between itself and the remainder of our group.

The tumble did not delay the creature long, as it righted itself with no care for any injuries sustained and resumed its attack, but it did allow Chiyo to lunge back just enough that the creature could not get proper leverage when it grabbed her by the hand. Her cry of pain was immediate and unrestrained. I am not very good at describing my emotions, but if you have ever witnessed your child in danger and heard their anguished screams, you will know what I felt. It was something akin to an electric shock, which began in my spine and quickly radiated outward into every other aspect of myself. I could not see where Chiyo and the Sleeper struggled, of course, but my inner compass was stronger than I knew. Or perhaps I just got lucky: I made my own desperate lunge and toppled into both of their bodies, sending them sprawling. This action did not delay the creature much — it resumed its work quickly and silently. It once again seized upon a limb and began to jerk and rotate, trying to pull it out at the root. The only difference was that now it was my leg and not Chiyo's arm. I had managed that much.

I would like to say I was as resolute and silent in my struggle as the Sleeper, but I did scream when my leg popped from its socket at the hip. And then there was an answering pop, much louder, just to one side. It was so loud that I could not hear for a time, as though that ear had been muffled by a pillow or suddenly submerged in water. It was the quick crack of gunfire, which I only realized when several more blasts followed. Yui acted quickly and efficiently. She had emptied an entire magazine into the creature's skull and only grazed me once, despite our proximity and the darkened conditions. I am very proud of her. I believe that I told her that, when we last spoke, but I would like to make sure by repeating it, in case this letter does find its way to her hands: Yui, I am so proud of you. And you as well, Chiyo. Forever and always.

Yui must have destroyed something integral to the Sleeper with one of her shots, because it immediately released me and then lay dormant. Perhaps because of the closeness of the firearm, or the repeating nature of the damage, it came to pass that its brain was more thoroughly obliterated than in previous efforts. Yui may have severed its spine or destroyed a specific motivating portion, or it could have been something else entirely. I wish I could be more thorough in my descriptions, but I was, and am, in quite a bit of pain. It makes focusing difficult, at times. After the attack, I did make it several steps on my own through the idiotic power of sheer adrenaline, but I soon collapsed. To my shame, I had to rely on Alejandra and Chiyo to carry me the rest of our journey, as though I had not already been handicap enough to them. I did not think to protest their efforts at that time, though perhaps I should have, but I think we all held out hope that our salvation was just beyond the crest of the next hill.

We summited that horizon just before daybreak and saw that the clearing we found there was free of suspect silhouettes, so we allowed ourselves to breathe for a moment. I made some silly joke about now using my white cane for two purposes. Can you guess how that was met? You probably can.

When dawn broke behind the blackened skies (to my eyes it was little more than a lightening of one portion of the world), I felt the mood shift. I had to remind Alejandra to narrate for me — the first such instance I ever had to prompt her. She spoke breathlessly, between squeaks of the throat, about what she saw:

A black ocean had flowed into our valley, and the surrounding hilltops barely peeked out of its inky depths. They were like islands in an absent sea. The fog extended as far as Alejandra could see to the north and halfway to the horizon on the westward side. Chiyo was first to spot evidence of its behavior on the more distant hills. There, it was already summiting and absorbing the land. It did not sink to fill the low spaces as does normal fog but climbed slowly and inexorably, even up the sheer faces of cliffs. We had not reached salvation in our little clearing but merely stood atop an obstacle in its path.

To the southwest, Yui pointed out a familiar sight: a pure white spindle of light, firing upward from some unseen point down by the Grand Coulee Dam. She had seen it before, of course, on one of her many scouting runs — and we all knew of the hastily spray-painted promises of safety and civilization that adorned billboards and boulders along the main highways. It never seemed worth the risk before, but now, the pillar seemed to stand like a lighthouse of hope amid a particularly cruel sea.

There was, of course, talk and planning for my condition: Alejandra would stay with me, while Chiyo and Yui gathered fitting branches, which they would assemble into a stretcher. They would lay me on it and pull my body — much easier now that we were going downhill, descending the lee side of Midnight Mountain — the hundred miles or so to safety, all while staying ahead of the malevolent wall of blackness that pursued them and navigating around the stilted shapes that waited for them in the forests.

I would hear none of it.

I had been a burden long enough, and there is only so much of that sort of thing a man can tolerate before it starts to degrade his sense of self. It took quite a bit of talking to persuade the others. It is not an easy task, convincing two very smart but hopelessly stubborn daughters to abandon their father to certain death. But who do you think taught them that obstinacy? I am quite bull-headed myself, and it was simply a matter of winning Alejandra over to my thinking first. I will skip over those hours of drama. I do not need to relive them, and they would contain no relevant information for you, who are reading this. Tears were shed, and it certainly sounded as though Alejandra needed to physically restrain either Chiyo or Yui at some point, which did not go well for her. But ultimately, I was left alone with my thoughts, and with Yui's pistol, which had three rounds left in it. This was a matter of further debate, as I was quite sure the fog would prove fatal enough, and the others would find a use for those bullets between here and their destination. I did not win this secondary argument, however, and my agreeing to take the pistol proved a necessity to secure the departure of the others.

This is all of the information I have for you, my anonymous reader, which might prove necessary for your survival. I know that I have rambled, and I am sorry, but I am distracted by the pain in my hip, and I am old, and I will be honest: I have always been a rambler.

If you will forgive me, I will dedicate the rest of this letter solely to my daughters, with the vain and rather silly thought that they might read it someday. Chiyo and Yui: We said our goodbyes, and they went well. But now I would like for you to know how your father spent his last hours.

I sat and I felt the sun move across the sky, and though I missed the fuzzy radiance of its light, the sensation was still beautiful, in its way. After you left, I was overcome with peace and security. Though you face insurmountable odds and difficulties I cannot even imagine, nor would wish on you if I could, I am sure that you will survive. I do not believe that thought is arrogance on my part, but rather a realistic assessment of your abilities (and yes, perhaps some wishful thinking on the part of a father). I ask that you entertain the idea of having children of your own, should mankind weather this storm, because that act has been the most true and unassailable good I have done to this world. You are my best accomplishment and have made every moment of my life a task worth undertaking.

I spent the time after your departure focusing on the sun and then writing this letter. I took breaks to listen to the birds while I thought of your mother, May, who would doubtless have told me the species of each and every one. I took heart in the thought that the birds did not seem to notice the end of the world or, if they did, did not particularly mind it. I have just removed my boots and ran my toes through the grass. I now feel a strange sort of pressure ascending from somewhere below me and believe that the fog is here. Just now, the breeze brought along flowers and pines, and a hint of that ancient decay. My time is here, and while I expected fear or uncertainty at this moment, I cannot say that I feel much of either. I am happy, because I have the sense that my job, whatever it was on this planet, has been done to the best of my ability. I gave it my best shot.

Now it is time for my second-best shot.

Because of the pistol, you see. That was a little joke. Did you laugh? Good god, humor an old man, won't you?

Sincerely,
Alex Yamamoto

Dam-Nation

The sun rode low in the sky, slipping through the gap in the shattered retaining walls of the Grand Coulee Dam like a mischievous child. Tara turned to catch the last of its waning rays on her face — well, the warmth of them, at least. She missed the sun. Like, the real sun, you know? The whole experience. Light, warmth, color, even the blinding brightness. Sunglasses were cool, you know? She missed sunglasses.

Tara used to spend whole days burning away on the endless shimmer of the Florida beaches, back before the Order came and saved her. Huge chunks of her life just idling away, doing nothing but gently cooking on the sand, watching the girls in swimsuits so small you could squint and wish them away (and hoping they were doing the same to her). It was tragic, honestly, that she'd wasted so much of her time like that, all happy and purposeless. With nothing to enforce. This new way was better. No doubt. Most if not all of those girls were dead, along with the rest of the world, and the sky was forever black, and she could feel looming hordes of monsters somewhere over the horizon, closing in by the second, and hot damn, but she missed the sun — and this was still better. Because here? Here there were rules, and they actually *meant* something.

Tara turned away from the absent sun to face the Spire of Haruk. Though its light was cold, like an arctic summer, and its expanse was somehow both totally featureless and nauseatingly dense, and all these galling concepts swam in its depths like huge ocean beasts, and she felt like screaming every second she watched it, the spire still beat the sun. Because the spire wasn't just *of* Haruk, it *was* him, and everything he represented, and he was *also* her, and she *made* him, and it was all super weird and hard to talk about it, but it was good.

She could not say she was happy — never that — but happiness is weak, and order is strong. Order defined the universe. Order made mankind what they were today, and it kept them strong and safe. And if she thought, now and again, of shallow beaches and paltry sun and frivolous girls in ridiculous bikinis, it was only leftovers. The vestigial impulses of a person she used to be a long, long time ago. Before she was better.

And it's not like it was all bleakness and harshness and "The Rules" here, in her little camp that held what was left of humanity. People could still be happy, if they wanted that kind of thing. Right? *Right!*

…right?

Tara wandered down Produce Row to prove the idea to herself. She watched the people there. An older woman in a straw-hat, gray ponytail swinging with her walk. She greeted a friend and stopped to chat, both smiling so hard their eyes went all crinkly. *Right!*

Tara slid past the older woman, and three teenagers cut her off, so lost to their own little dramas they probably didn't even see her. But they laughed even as they bickered. *Right!*

Two children darted through the shoppers' legs like little mice. A girl, younger, and a boy, older — they played like siblings, casual disdain masking obvious affection. They pinched and prodded and argued and ran. *Right!*

Tara stopped at a low plywood cart, just three crude walls built up around an old bicycle trailer. It was full to the brim with bright red apples. Not flawless, like she used to get in the stores — these were all stunted and deformed and imperfect. It bothered her, if she let it, so she didn't let it.

"How much?" she asked the shopkeep, a man about her age, with a braided goatee and two huge empty loops in his ears where plugs used to hang.

"How much you want and how much you got?" he said, then looked up from his tattered comic book and truly saw her for the first time.

"Oh," he said, straightening his posture. "I mean…nothing, for you. It's fine. Take as much as you want. Please."

"No," she laughed, "you don't have to do that. I'd love to pay what they're worth. They look great."

She flashed him a smile, the old one she used just on boys — never worked on the girls — from before, when she was a different person. He gave one back.

The younger girl, the little sister, bumped into Tara but didn't even bother looking up, much less apologizing. Tara gave the merchant a hapless shrug, and he laughed a little.

"Okay, cool," the shopkeep said. "What do you use, dollars or chits?"

"I've got a little of both," she said and probably stared a bit too long at the man's big, rough hands. She blushed and looked away, focused on the apples instead.

The merchant seemed to pick up on it and leaned into her.

"I'll cut you a deal," he said. "Because I like you — eight dollars or two chits for three. Good?"

Somewhere behind her, the little girl squealed, and her brother laughed.

"Give it back!" the girl cried.

"Come take it," the boy taunted.

"You got yourself a deal," Tara confirmed, and she gave the shopkeep a gaudy wink, even though she felt super corny while doing it. "Just gimme one second…"

Tara pivoted and drew her pistol, paused to ensure her aim, and put a bullet through the little boy's left eye. There was a quick flash of blood — never as much as you think, not like the movies showed — and the kid collapsed in the dirt, dead.

The little sister screamed, looked to Tara for the first time, then stuffed her fingers into her mouth to bite off the sound.

"Hey." Tara knelt by the girl's side and drew her eyes up so they were looking right at each other. "It's okay."

The girl shook so violently that her moans ululated with the motion, like speaking into a fan.

"Don't worry, sweetheart." Tara kept her voice hushed and calm as she stroked the little girl's braided hair. "You can let it out. It's not against the rules to scream or cry or be sad…"

The pitch of the girl's moans raised an octave.

"It's only against the rules to steal," Tara finished.

She chucked the girl across the chin in a reassuring manner, then stood and smiled at the apple merchant.

"Sorry." She shrugged and bit her lip a little. The guys went nuts for that, back in that other life, on the beaches. "Duty calls. How much were those again?"

"T-two chits for three," he said and suddenly couldn't meet her eye. "Or you could just take them. That's fine."

"No," she replied and tried not to let too much of the disappointment show. "I'll pay."

She picked three of the most uniform apples she could find and stowed them in her shoulder pack, then began the long walk back to the spire. It was probably her eyes, she thought — girls were sorta okay with them, but the guys always got skittish about her vacant eyes, the same solid, churning white as the pillar above.

Must be down to maturity, Tara figured. She tried not to take it personally.

…

Mari upends her boots and knocks them out before sliding her feet in. Old reflexes, leftover from the desert. No scorpions up here in the northwest — wait, are there? She associates scorpions with baking sun and windblown sand, not this incessant rain and these vast green spaces. These oceans of trees that march from horizon to horizon. Probably doesn't hurt to knock her boots out, regardless, and besides: everybody's probably gonna be dead soon.

"You believe it?" she asks Lucas. "All this talk?"

He doesn't answer, of course. Her little brother hasn't spoken in years, not since the day their older brother, Diego, stared at the sky too long and went crazy. Ripped a tooth right out of Lucas' head, then lit himself on fire in the driveway. Oh right, then the whole world ended.

Well, for the first time.

Lucas can nod or shake his head, sure, but he knows Mari. Knows Mari just wants to talk *at* him, not *to* him. He doesn't look up from his book, a tattered paperback, anonymous with age. Cover and first pages lost long ago.

"All these new refugees coming in," she presses on, "talking about like, monsters and stuff. It's crazy, right?"

Lucas turns a page.

"I mean, I know what some of the kids on the Snake said they saw out there before we came, and there's JR, and Ethan and his visions, but…"

She trails off, wishing she wasn't about to say what she's about to say.

"But isn't that just…shock?"

It feels controversial to even think it, but Lucas doesn't bat an eye. Doesn't even look up from his book, actually.

"Seeing monsters?" She laughs but cuts it off. "Not the monsters *we've* seen, of course."

Mari chews on the end of a lock of hair, catches herself, and spits it out.

"The human monsters. Like, people think there are actual monsters out there, Godzilla-style, and they're coming this way. That's crazy. Right? Is that crazy?"

She raps on Lucas' bunk, and he blinks at her.

"I mean, *is it*?" she continues. "After everything? The sky is gone. Everybody in the whole world went nuts at the same time, and there's those special psychos out there with the black eyes…"

Lucas dog-ears his place and rests the book on his chest.

"And there's those special psychos in here with the white ones…" Mari looks at the wall. Where a window might be, if they didn't live aboard an armored land train. She misses windows. Like, *actively* misses them.

Lucas makes big circles with his thumb and index finger and holds them over his own eyes. Mari smiles.

"I guess it's not their eyes, but where their eyes *should* be." She searches for the word Ken used on her last week — one of his special words that he holds in reserve like weapons. "Don't be such a…*pedant*."

Lucas tilts his head.

"Means like a…detail-oriented jerkface," she supplies, feeling that secondhand pride. "But I mean, are the monsters too crazy to believe, after all we've seen?"

Lucas shrugs. She knew he'd shrug. Mari plucks the paperback off his chest, flips it open, straightens out the dog-ear, and closes it again. She sends it spinning back onto Lucas' belly.

"Thanks for the help, *pedant*," she says, ignoring an eyeroll so hard she swears she actually hears it.

Mari steps out of the sleeping carriage and starts heading out. But that means navigating the crowded kitchen car, full of unattended kids trying to sneak dirty fingers through the locked Plexiglas cabinets. That Chen boy — Scurry, the other children call him — looks to be the only one successful. He grins up at her from an illicit jar of peanut butter.

She spots Ethan up by the fore exit, standing carefully removed, but not entirely absent from the looting. He's a year older than Lucas and currently stuck between cool teenage apathy and the childlike desire to join in the fray. Practically visibly wrestling with the choice. But seeing Mari tips him over the edge, and he votes to skip both options and jump right to crotchety old man.

"Can you believe these kids?" He laughs bitterly to Mari, throws a grand dismissive gesture toward the desperate scrabble. "The second the adults leave, and they're like animals. We should put a stop to this."

Mari knows what he's trying to do, and why — why he flushes red in the face whenever she gets too close; why he has to carefully position things over his lap whenever he sees her in anything less than a loose sweater. But still…

"They're just being kids," she says. "They don't get to do that much anymore. Just let 'em."

Ethan looks at the floor, seems to search for a response down there. If the traction mats have a good one for him, they don't volunteer it.

Mari can basically see him hating himself, like a black cloud pouring out of his ears, so she lays a hand on his shoulder and tries not to laugh when his whole face turns dull purple.

"*We* might be all grown up now," she whispers with a conspiratorial wink. "But don't forget what it's like to be one of them."

Ethan nods, tries to say something, and only squeaks. He clears his throat to try again, but Mari is already moving on. He directs his attention to the younger kids instead, trying to figure out the new balance Mari just gave him.

"Aaron, Ronnie, Vera," he calls, striding up beside Scurry and his ill-gotten treasure. "Come over here, Scurry's gonna share."

That seems like news to Scurry.

The three named outliers, too shy to do much looting themselves, perk up and head over. Scurry tries to escape, but Ethan has his shirt collar and is already enforcing the boy's generosity.

Mari slips through the fore exit of the kitchen car as carefully as possible, trying not to give too wide a view at the carnage within. Ken always stays with the Snake, after all, and though some of his cameras are strategically broken (and would be quickly strategically broken again, should he ever get them fixed), the guy still has eyes everywhere. She wants to give the kids a few more minutes of freedom, or at least not be the one responsible for taking it away.

Her route takes her by JR's table — the tiny nook he commandeered to do his leatherwork. Where he fixes and patches boots, holsters, and the odd jacket, but also crafts his own stuff, maybe from his people? Beautiful, wherever they're from. Intricately tooled quivers and woven moccasins, sheathes and great sweeping headbands. It smells like him, like sweat and leather and spices, and Mari feels hot in her very core. She laughs at herself a little bit — imagine her giving Ethan crap when walking by a damn table makes her go rubber-legged. But JR isn't in his nook, all bent over in the half-light with his tiny metal tools and long needles, so she keeps going until she hits the Scout's car. Mari cracks the big red lever that unseals the exterior door of the Snake and greets the city the same way she does every day: with extreme skepticism.

Far as she's concerned, Dam-Nation earns every ounce of her distrust. The psychos that live here don't just allow Judges in their midst; they give them authority. Practically let them rule over the place, enforcing the rules with all their deadly, mad brutality. Newest whispers said one of them just killed a kid for practically no reason, and dark as it was, Mari allowed herself to get excited. Figured that might be the day the civvies nutted up and asked the Snakes to help them overthrow the Judges, but no. One civilian would relate the news, and the other would ask, "Well, what did the kid do?" Like there's ever justification for plugging a ten-year-old.

Steves is adamant that this is The Spot: a place to settle down for good, make their big last stand against…well, whatever Ethan saw in his visions. The monsters, and all that. Seems weird that she's gambling everything on a pre-teen boy's nightmares, but on the Snake, Steves' word is law. Even Mari has to admit the place is pretty impressive, though. She's never seen this many people in one place, all working together — not since the skies went black and the maniacs came. It almost feels normal. They have shops here, not just traders. Like, established carts and makeshift buildings that stay in one place and have a fixed list of goods. Isn't that crazy? You need potatoes or something, you don't have to hope some wackjob wanderer has some in his backpack that day — you can go to a place and buy a thing. Maybe that's shallow, but that's the aspect that sticks out most to Mari: the normalcy and security of that one simple little practice. There are shops. There is shopping. Crazy.

There are also farms, and fresh water, and law and order (yeah: way too much), and it still all just feels…wrong. Like a big trap that hasn't been sprung yet. But nobody asks Mari what she thinks, which doesn't keep her from answering, but it sure keeps them from listening.

At least Dam-Nation only keeps a few big rules — no harming others, no stealing, obey the peacekeepers — so the Judges can't go completely nuts over some technicality and start yanking out teeth just because some poor kid doesn't eat dinner on time. But if it keeps order, it also keeps everybody on edge. This undercurrent of fear runs below everything, so deep Mari can almost taste it. Electric and metallic, like licking a battery.

You know, that's probably where this talk of monsters comes from. Scared people making up all sorts of stuff just to put the fear elsewhere — somewhere outside of their nice little town — so they can run or hide or maybe even fight it. Really, the only thing that throws a wrench into that theory is JR, and what he says he saw back in Wyoming, the day his dad died. She should probably ask him about that. And that means Mari has to do what she does best: she has to go scouting.

She flexes the fingers on her left hand and winces. Another parting gift from Diego. She can move them a little — enough to support the barrel of a rifle, enough to make a fist or grab a ledge — and that's all she needs, really.

That, and to get the hell out of this city as soon as possible. And to find JR. And maybe do some light monster-hunting, depending on how things shake out. Busy day.

. . .

Sam slapped Frankie's ass, and the man feigned the most glorious indignation this world had ever seen. He turned, he gasped, he put a hand to his chest, he wailed.

"By the stars above." He pinned Sam with a withering glare. "This unfettered perversion will not go unanswered."

"Okay," Sam said, eyes darting. "That's probably enough now."

"It is *more* than enough." Frankie pantomimed fanning vapors away. "It is the devil's work in your idle hands, Samuel Nash."

"People are looking," Sam muttered. "I'm getting embarrassed."

"*You're* getting embarrassed!" Frankie gestured around their meager stall. A fifteen-foot square with a workbench for a counter, a shade sail for a roof, and three lashed-together tarps for walls, leaving the fourth open to

Trader's Place for prospective customers.

Frankie pleaded for assistance from the passing throngs of distracted shoppers.

"Won't somebody please save me from this…*this sexual monster*!"

"You're bored," Sam sighed. "This is you being bored."

"Now he's threatening to bore me, right in my tender parts no less!"

Sam laughed a little. It had gone so far it came back around to funny again. Plus, giving in to the joke was the only surefire way to put an end to Frankie's theatrics.

"Of course I'm bored, baby." Frankie stepped around the water-warped plywood counter. "We haven't had a single customer in just about forever."

"It's been fifteen minutes." Sam smiled and shook his head. "We're actually having a good day. Do you really need such constant stimulation?"

Frankie grinned wickedly.

"Don't turn that around on me!" Sam put up his hands in surrender.

"I'll turn *something* around on you." Frankie extended his fingers as claws and readied to pounce.

"What if someb—"

"What's going on here?" A man stepped in from Trader's Place and fixed the two of them with eyes like pure white absences. Little portals straight to the sun.

"W-w-w," Sam stuttered.

"Nothing at all." Frankie beamed at the Judge. The man returned the smile, even as his hand drifted to a blood-stained hatchet at his waist.

"I thought I heard an assault in progress." The Judge scanned the store, then brightened. "Hey, this is a nice place!"

"No assault," Sam spoke too quickly, tripping over the words. "We were just joking."

"Don't joke about the rules," the Judge said automatically, plucking a small ceramic pig figurine from one of the shelves lining the walls.

"Of course not," Frankie agreed. "Our apologies."

"Hey, no problem." The man nodded. "How much is this?"

He tilted the little pink pig so it caught the light.

"It's yours," Sam said. "Thank you…for your service?"

The Judge blinked at him. He was older than Sam by at least a decade and wore deep laugh lines like an old leather jacket. Salt and pepper hair and good teeth and the kind of beard Sam associated with jolly old grandfathers.

"No need for that." The man shot Sam what would have been a comforting smile, if not for the pools of unnatural void in place of his ocular cavities. "I'm not here to shake you boys down or anything. I love your little shop. Just thought there might be a problem, and I could help."

"Of course," Frankie said. "We know that, don't we, Sam?"

He elbowed Sam, then wrapped his fingers around Sam's wrist. Frankie could feel his pulse hammering.

"Relax, darling," he said. "Everything's fine."

"Looks like it," the Judge agreed, carefully replacing the little pig like it was a revered and sacred idol. "Although if he did break a rule, if he hurt you in any way, you just let me know and I'll chop his face in half for you."

Sam's pulse beat out a frantic drum solo.

"Thanks for the offer." Frankie laughed. "I'll take you up on that in case the beast in this man comes out again."

The Judge chuckled, too, and raised a hand by way of farewell. He stepped back out onto Trader's Place and was borne away by the crowds.

"Jesus," Sam let out a breath he'd been holding since the man walked in. "Jesus Christ."

"Oh, come on." Frankie wrapped his arms around Sam's neck and nestled their foreheads together. "How long have we lived here, with them? You know how they work by now. Why do you freak out so much when they come in?"

"He was going to chop my face in half!" Sam whispered, eyelids peeled back so far he looked like a frightened little lizard.

"He was not!" Frankie laughed. "That was probably a joke. I mean, unless you'd actually assaulted me…"

"I just…what if we accidentally break a rule sometime? They kill you like they're ordering coffee."

"Don't harm, don't steal, obey the peacekeepers," Frankie recited. "Those are the only rules. The founders kept it simple because that's what keeps the Judges in line. How are you going to accidentally kill somebody? You're eighty percent marshmallow."

Frankie poked him in the paunch.

"I don't know," Sam said, adrenaline draining. "They just make me nervous."

"Here." Frankie knelt and gently shook Princess Sparklehogg awake. He hefted her tiny weight in his arms and brought her sleepy eyes up to Sam's. She dutifully licked him on the nose. "All better?"

Sam reached out and took the miniature pig to his chest, and she burrowed her muzzle into his neck.

"All better," he confirmed.

"Now." Frankie weaved around the counter and leaned out to survey the crowds. "Should we close up? The forum's this afternoon, and if we want to drop off supplies first, we need to leave soon."

"Sure thing," Sam said, bopping in place to soothe the now-fussing pig. "It's your turn to haul the cart."

"Nooo." Frankie dropped to his knees in overly dramatic protest. "I'll Baby Bjorn the Princess!"

"It was my turn." Sam frowned, then wiggled a finger in Princess SparkleHogg's ear until she squealed quietly. "But I've still got some energy to work off after that Judge…"

"You are so dramatic." Frankie grinned, standing to dust off the knees of his jeans.

"He says without a hint of irony."

"You love my theatrics," Frankie said, slipping into the worn pink harness with its faded gold stars.

When he finished doing the straps up, Sam handed him the pig, and together they settled her into place over Frankie's chest. She blinked her black and white eyelashes once, twice, and then drifted off to sleep again.

Sam opened up the rearmost flap of the stall and retrieved a small shopping cart full of assorted supplies — dented cans of food, dusty water bottles, fraying blankets. The best they could find, for today's trip. Fighting foot traffic out of Trader's Place all the way up Wall Street, to the gates of the dam, and beyond — it would take them easily half an hour. Another to distribute everything to needy refugees, and then the walk back…they'd barely make the forum. And they couldn't afford to miss this one.

Well, the thousands of people still stuck outside the city walls couldn't afford for them to miss it — it wasn't Sam and Frankie's lives on the line, after all.

…

Mari wasn't prowling for JR like some creep — honest, she wasn't, and she would clip you upside the head if you so much as suggested it. But still…where the hell was he? He didn't like the city much. They had that in common, even if it was for different reasons. So if he headed out, it was usually upriver. Across the drained reservoir and into the steep-walled canyons. But Nicko is on watch duty today, perched atop the caboose, hunched under a faded beach umbrella, boots off and feet in the sun, and he says JR headed into the city this morning. Seemed in a hurry, too.

So Mari prowls the markets and the craft shops, runs the gauntlet of merchants hawking wares she doesn't want and end-times preachers hawking religions she doesn't need, and chases Wall Street all the way up to the main gate. Not a damn sign of the boy. She pokes her head into a gap in the wire mesh and watches the assembled crowds, surging softly at the checkpoint like a human tide. Last month, there'd been dozens of them camped out there, just waiting for the Judges to clear them for entry. Last week, there'd been hundreds. Today, there might be thousands.

Their ramshackle hovels are taking on a sense of permanence now — walls being shored up, tears being fixed, hasty rows being rearranged into streets. They're settling out there, and something about that breaks Mari's heart. Whatever else she might count against the city — and there's a lot — it's still a might bit easier to rest behind the massive walls of the Grand Coulee Dam.

They'll get in, she tells herself, turning away from the pointillist mural of desperate faces. Everybody gets in, eventually. It just takes time. And that's something she can't spare any more of; the Judges wouldn't have let JR out there, not without proper clearance. So her hunt heads elsewhere.

Mari walks until her feet chafe, stops just long enough to readjust her boots, and soldiers on. She checks the trade shops again — sometimes JR likes to bother the tailors or the blacksmiths with questions about their work — and she checks the wells, kids playing in the puddles left behind by the hand-pumps. She checks the arcade (not the cool kind), and the theater (not the cool kind; wait, is there a cool kind?). Already the crowd around it is unmanageable, prodding at weaknesses in the perimeter, everybody jostling for spots for the upcoming forum. Mari doesn't find JR in the fringes, and she can't see him voluntarily wading into that press just to sit in on some local politics. The boy likes crowds less than she does.

She used to love crowds. Sweaty concerts and buzzing malls. What happened?

Crowds mean something different now, she answers herself.

Mari finally finds JR in the weirdest way. She's completing her second circle around the Heart, the Judge's walled compound that rings the huge white spire at the city's center, when she smells him. He smells like leather and the oil he uses to treat it. Earth and spice with just a touch — *a touch, mind you* — of distant fart. Not bad, empty-the-house hot dog farts or anything, but something faded. Vaguely reminiscent of guts. Sulfurous, that's what it is.

It…it isn't nearly as bad as it sounds. *Seriously.*

She follows the waft down an alley so narrow it's more like an oversight, and then looks up. Two dirty white sneakers hang over the edge of the roof above her, bopping idly back and forth.

"JR?" she whispers, and the sneakers freeze.

They disappear, to be replaced by JR's confused face, looking straight down — his long, shiny black hair framing it like a comic-book outline.

"Mari?" he whispers. "What the hell?"

"Same to you," she huffs. "What are you doing?"

"How did you find me?"

"I smelled you," she doesn't even think of admitting.

"What are you doing?!" she deflects instead, and JR flinches.

"Keep it down." He glances around, apparently sees nothing, and holds a hand out to her. "Come on up."

She's so thrown by the whole interaction, she almost offers him her bad hand. The alley's so narrow she has to edge in sideways, left side first, and JR's still deeper in it. There's no way she's lacing her messed-up fingers with his — letting him feel her scars, and the weird way her knuckles bend — so she scoots down further until she can line up with her right. She wraps it around his wrist. He pulls. She kicks off the front wall with one leg, catches the rear wall with her other, and folds up onto the roof so easily that JR falls back on his butt, expecting more resistance. He blinks at her, and she smiles, more with her eyes than anything.

"I'm a scout," she says, and when she feels herself start to blush, she adds, "idiot."

He just nods at that, then motions for her to lie down, like he had been. She drops to her belly, sun-warm metal almost burning her palms, and together, they shimmy into a foot-high gap between two of the stacked shipping containers that make up the walls of the Judge's compound. They inch forward until their faces are nearly flush with a barrier of chicken wire. There's barely enough room for them; Mari can feel her feet right up at the edge of the roof behind her. They wind up looking down into a broad and featureless sort of courtyard within the Heart itself. There's one small bench in the middle, and that's it. No plants, or sculptures, or anything. Just a bench and two figures. One sitting ramrod-straight on the concrete slab, the other pacing uneasily.

There's no law about trespassing or anything — too slippery a slope with Judges around — but still, Mari doubts very much if the pair of white-eyed figures below would be cool with this.

She looks to JR, hoping to telepathically communicate what a stupid idea this is, or failing that, at least that he'll see her glaring. He doesn't, though — he's too fixed on the scene below.

"—but how many are inside, like right now, like this morning?"

The pacing Judge is older, a mid-forties Latino guy with a deeply serious mustache and a paunch so big it strains the boundaries of his white cotton shirt.

"Updated counts? Don't have 'em yet." The seated Judge is a younger woman. Like, really young. Nearly Mari's age. Or wait, no: a few years older. She's blond and tan and thin, and Mari kind of hates her in a way she's been trying to fight recently. Doesn't feel healthy, you know?

Both of them with those trademark creepy white eyes — everything from cheek to eyebrow just gone, replaced by an impenetrable, colorless void. Razor thin white slashes run from the edges of those empty spaces, just hanging in the air like fishing line, before tracing upward to the spire above.

"There was barely two thousand behind the walls last time," the male judge frets. "And those refugees outside will be the first to go. We're not going to have enough."

"So what?" The girl cranes her head back to stare up at the spire.

"So it's the end of everything!" the paunchy Judge snaps. "He talked to that professor this morning. He got his answer. She told him three thousand—"

"Total?" the girl interrupts without looking at him.

"And that's with room for error," the man answers, "just three thousand. Any lower and he gives up on us. He'll go dark. *We'll go dark.*"

"Then that's what happens." The girl stands and makes a show of stretching as she speaks. Checks to make sure the guy is watching with barely veiled interest. "Who cares? If he wants us to end, we end. If he wants us to go dark, we go dark. Don't you trust him? Don't you love him?"

"Of course," the paunchy Judge answers automatically, his voice gone cold. "He is Order, and order is everything."

"There's your answer." The girl laughs, and she brushes the older man as she passes by him. He definitely notices.

When she's gone, mustache guy sighs so long he might be deflating.

"But he won't *be* order anymore, if we drop below three thousand," he mutters. "And neither will we."

The paunchy Judge just stares up at the spire and goes quiet. JR motions for Mari to scoot back, and she obliges. It's so good to be out of that tight space, standing feels like a privilege. She goes to talk, but JR shakes his head. He keeps them quiet all the way back down the alley and out onto the streets. They're both smart enough not to talk about it in public, so they have to walk for twenty minutes, way out onto the silt flats of the drained basin. It's hot there, and her boots sink in the sand, so she's way more tired than she should be when JR finally stops.

"So…" he says, and she waits for him to go, to tell her what he knows so she can piece together what she just heard.

He doesn't say anything else.

"What the hell was all that about?" she finally asks.

"I was hoping you'd tell me," he says.

They stare at each other, alone in the dustbowl. The shadow of some large bird skates across the sand.

…

Princess Sparklehogg oinked contentedly at the chin scratches. She kicked her stumpy hind legs in the air and squirmed in her harness. Frankie smiled down at her, then back up at the nice Latina lady with the great nails.

"Those tips, girl," Frankie said, taking her hand and stretching her fingers out. "How on earth do you manage it?"

Ali blushed and snuck her fingers back into her palm.

"It's not on purpose," she said. "I swear to god, I work. I just have strong nails."

"You have nothing to be ashamed of." Frankie laughed. "You don't have to break your back hauling supplies to be a valuable human being."

"Says you," Sam griped, wrestling the front wheels of the supply cart in the shifting dust. "The guy who never hauls supplies."

Frankie rolled his eyes at Sam, all the way around and back to Ali. She giggled, despite herself. Sam smiled at her.

"So," she leaned in to examine the contents of the shopping cart, "you're the guys who bring the water?"

"And the food, and the blankets, and whatever else we can rummage up." Frankie secured the Princess with one hand and sorted through their cargo with the other. "But we really just bring it. This stuff is donated from everybody in the city."

"Really?" Ali scanned the gathering crowd. Sallow faces, sun-beaten and tired. Dozens strong, and beyond them, hundreds — maybe thousands — more positioned just outside the walls of the dam. "I got the impression we weren't exactly welcome."

She gestured vaguely at the mass of refugees.

"No way." Sam handed a blanket to a reedy woman with a bandaged arm, too tired to thank him. "We're all trying to get you in as quick as possible, it's just the Judges…"

"And even they're trying to help," Frankie filled in quickly, afraid of what Sam might leave unsaid.

"Yeah, I guess." Sam tossed a can of beans to a child hopping for attention at the fringes of the crowd, too small to shove their way in. "Back when there was only a trickle of folks coming to the city, we set some rules about entry. We thought it was for the best—"

"Real basic stuff," Frankie said, "we wanted to make sure everyone had a place to stay, and enough food, and if you were sick, we wanted to make sure you got treatment and didn't spread it unchecked—"

"But that all takes time," Sam finished. "And the Judges won't let us change the rules once they're set. Now there's so many people waiting out here, and we all know it'd be best to set up a medical quarantine inside the walls and that most wouldn't mind sleeping in tents out in the basin until we got better homes built, but…"

"The Judges." Ali nodded. "Are they really…safe? I've never seen one before, I don't think, but they're…aren't they dangerous?"

"No," Frankie laughed, "they're kittens."

"Yes," Sam said, more quietly, "but not if you're very careful."

Frankie elbowed him in the ribs, and he jostled back.

"They have to know," Sam hissed. "It won't help them to sugarcoat it."

"Who's sugarcoating?" Frankie laughed, mostly for Ali's benefit. "Just don't break the rules and you're totally fine."

Ali smiled for Frankie, then shared a skeptical look with Sam as soon as he turned away.

A young woman dressed like an REI catalogue elbowed her way through the throng condensing around Sam and Frankie's supply cart. She was shoved from behind at the last second and stumbled too far into the circle, jostling Ali, but neither acknowledged it. The newcomer spun to find her assailant, but the crowd was too packed in for her to be certain.

"I said I'm not here to take anything!" she shouted at no one and everyone. "I just need to talk to somebody. Damn!"

She sighed and turned back to Ali, who shrugged at her. All the forgiveness needed.

"Hi there," Sam piped and gave her his best customer service smile.

She sneered at him.

"We gotta go," she said to Ali. "Now."

"What?" Ali blinked at the blankets and water bottles in her arms. "But I just got—"

"This isn't working, okay?" She jutted her chin out at the dam, looming behind them. "They're not gonna let us in. We're better moving than stuck here against a wall."

"Yui," Ali shuffled her bundle to free up a hand and put it on the woman's shoulder, "just give it time."

"She's right, you know." Sam tried his smile again, certain that, with persistence, it would erode right through the newcomer's defenses.

She answered with only a look of pure and unfiltered disgust.

"We've given it time." Yui stood on tiptoes and surveyed the tops of the crowd's heads. Apparently, she didn't find what she was looking for. "We've been here almost two days."

"Some of us have been here for weeks!" somebody snapped from the periphery of the crowd.

Yui spun like a startled lion, and whoever spoke didn't find the courage to elaborate.

"That's what I'm saying," Yui whispered to Ali. "Weeks? We don't have weeks. That…stuff up there in the hills, it might be slow, and we may have left it behind for a while, but you can bet your ass it's still coming."

Ali chewed her lip and seemed about to agree when a second jostle hit her from behind. Another woman, equally bedecked in clothing items featuring far too many pockets, peeked at Yui from above Ali's shoulder. She was younger than her counterpart, with the same low, wide cheekbones and thin lips. The same prominent eyebrows and pert, irrepressible ears holding back her glossy black hair like they were built for that purpose alone.

"Hi there." Sam loosed his smile for a third time, and the new girl's only response was a disbelieving scoff.

That cemented it: they were definitely sisters.

"Where we gonna go, Yu?" the younger one asked.

"Anywhere!" Yui snapped. "It's better than waiting here for that…that *fucking monster* to catch up with us."

"Not more of this." Frankie had finished distributing his first round of supplies and returned to the cart for more. "Honey, we're all under a lot of stress, but be sure about what you're saying."

Both sisters gave Frankie the same withering glare, to which he gasped and scanned the immediate area, presumably searching for whoever they were looking at, because it certainly couldn't be him.

"Don't you give me that face," he scolded the pair. "You keep the receipt for that face, because girls, you are taking it right back to where you got it."

They turned away from him and tried to resume their conversation.

"Chiyo," Yui started first. "What would Dad have done? Would he have—"

"Oh no," Frankie said, ostensibly to Sam, but Sam knew not to respond. This was now officially theater.

"We know what Dad woulda done!" Chiyo protested. "He told us to come here!"

"Huh uh," Frankie whispered.

Sam took a step back.

"But what *would* he have done if we got here and found it like this? Huh? Chi, you know he would've pressed on. Never trust your welfare—"

"—to a crowd," Chiyo recited. "I know, but I'm not saying we keep waiting here. Let's find our own way in. I just saw…"

"Oh, hell no." Frankie snapped his fingers between the pair of arguing sisters. "You do not get to come into our space and sass us and then ignore us."

Chiyo and Yui stumbled over themselves, racing to figure out who could argue with Frankie first.

Sam checked his side to find that Ali, too, had quietly backed out of the fray before it began. They shared a conspiratorial smile.

"So hey," he spoke to her from the side of his mouth, careful not to draw attention from the fighting trio. "Is what your friend said true? You've really seen…something else out there?"

Ali turned to answer, but Sam squeezed her wrist and she snapped back to attention.

"It is," she whispered. "I don't know about the rest of this talk, though. People here say they've seen some crazy stuff. Evil bugs the size of skyscrapers, shadows that come to life. But I know what we saw: a bank of black fog that stretched from one horizon to the other."

"That's not so crazy," Sam said.

"…that moved like it was intelligent and ate everybody in its path."

"Oh." Sam blinked. "Okay."

They took a moment to just appreciate the escalating insult war between Chiyo, Yui, and Frankie.

"So, um…" Sam risked exposure to turn and look Ali in the eye. "How far away would you say that stuff was?"

"Just over those hills." Ali nodded at the rolling green waves that swelled to the north. "It moves slow, like Yui said, but not that slow, and it was definitely coming this way. We actually figured it would be here by now. Chiyo figures it's…waiting."

"Well," Sam started to say, but he screwed up. He moved too fast. Frankie saw him privately entreating with their new enemy and spun on the pair of them. Then Chiyo and Yui followed suit.

"What do you have to say to her that we can't hear?" Frankie scolded.

"You gonna stay here with your new best friends, Ali?" Yui cocked her head like a pistol, ready to fire.

"After everything we've been through?" Chiyo chided.

Sam and Ali simultaneously raised their hands in immediate and unconditional surrender.

...

When she gets back to the Snake, Mari's so lost in her own head that she doesn't even realize Ethan's still jabbering at her. Been dogging her for three cars now. He seems set to follow her right into her bunk when she wheels toward him like a harried parent on their last nerve.

"Ethan!" She puts a finger right up on his nose. He goes cross-eyed looking at it. "Give me some space. Damn!"

"Oh, okay," he says, and she practically sees the light go out in his eyes. "I'm sorry."

She sighs, looks up at the ceiling, counts to five.

"No," she says and manages half a smile. "I'm sorry. I shouldn't have snapped at you, I'm just…I'm trying to piece something together, and I need a minute to think."

"That's fair." Ethan's so relieved that she doesn't hate him, he's almost happy to be blown off. "I'll leave you alone, but if I can help with anything — and I mean *anything* — please don't hesitate to ask."

He tries to put a little smooth on the end of that sentence, and it is basically totally adorable. But his face darkens when she laughs, so clearly, he was going for something a little more R-rated than "cute."

"I think I got a handle on it, thanks," she says.

Then Mari remembers who she's talking to. He's such a typical teen boy most times — busy getting slapped upside the head with both hands of puberty — Mari forgets about the stuff he's been through. What he might know.

"Actually," she says, and it's like the boy sat on a live wire. Whole body straightens up. "If anybody could help, it'd be you."

Hope flushes through his face.

"Of course," he says. "Anything!"

"It's about the Judges," she says.

"Oh." And somebody pulls the plug on him. "That stuff."

"Yeah." Mari knows he doesn't like to talk about it — his experience with the creepy white-haired mechanic and those empty eyes. "*That* stuff. But listen, it's important…"

"Okay." He nods. "I want to help, but it's tough to talk about, and maybe…dangerous? Mom—"

He stops short, looks around to see if anybody else heard, and course corrects.

"I mean Steves," he amends. "She said I'm not supposed to even think about it if I don't have to."

"Why not?" This is all news to Mari. She figured Ethan was just scarred by a violent episode, like Lucas — he watched his adoptive father shoot a dude practically right on top of him; gotta mess a kid up — but this sounds like something else.

"It's like…" He needs a minute to put the words together, so she gives it to him. Just a friendly smile when he seems flustered. Then he continues, "It's like that mechanic guy, he was a Judge, you know…"

Mari knows. Mari remembers finding him, sitting all peaceful on his little bench in front of that quaint small-town gas station, friendly smile on his face like a sitcom dad, only the mutilated corpses at his feet spoiling the scene.

"And he tried to explain some things to me." Ethan's brows are knit together. He chews the inside of his cheek. "But he couldn't get it right, or I couldn't get it right, so he got frustrated and he just..."

He puts his fingers to his temples.

"He just put it all up here directly." Ethan kind of laughs as he says it, embarrassed by how crazy he knows he sounds. "So now there's all this stuff bouncing around up there, about the maniacs, and the sky, and everything..."

Mari just nods, afraid that speaking might break the spell and the kid will go quiet again.

"But it's like it's behind a wall," he continues. "One my brain put up to keep all those poisonous thoughts from leaking out and ruining the rest of me. The mechanic said something to me, toward the end, about how I was *supposed* to be like him — I was just a few years too young. Like that's the only reason kids can't be crazies; they're just not old enough yet. Their brains aren't set for it. And I think that me almost being like him...that's why he was able to put that stuff in my head. And I think that's why my brain put up that wall. And I think if I keep chipping away by thinking too hard about it, trying to pull that knowledge out, even just little pieces, then the whole wall might fall. And maybe..."

He can't say it, but Mari can.

"Maybe you'll be like him?" She almost laughs but knows that would shatter everything. "You couldn't be a Judge."

"I thought so, too." He looks up to meet her gaze for the first time in a while. "Until he put this stuff in my head. Now, it's like I can feel how the Judges feel sometimes. How good it is to have things all nice and orderly, how gross it is when somebody breaks a rule. It doesn't even make you mad. You want to hurt them like it'd be doing them a favor."

"Wow." Mari puts her good hand on his shoulder, and it's like closing a circuit. Ethan snaps right out of his worries and turns back into a teenage boy. She can feel his heart pounding through his shirt. "I had no idea. Listen, if it's too tough, don't worry about it. I'll figure it out."

"No!" he almost yells at her, so desperate not to lose this moment. "I wasn't saying that. I was just saying we have to be careful, that's all."

"Well, if you're sure…"

"I'm sure."

"Okay." Mari senses that it's not the best idea to mention JR at all, so she skips most of the details of her outing. "I overheard a few of the Judges talking, just outside the Heart. And they said something weird. Something about how the city didn't have enough people, and if we fell below a certain number of survivors, 'he' would turn 'dark,' or something. And the Judges would, too. At least one of 'em was real worried about what that might mean. That ring any bells?"

She looks up to check that she's making sense, but Ethan is gone.

He's standing right in front of her, but he's gone all the same. His eyes are unfocused, and he's watching something miles behind Mari.

"Does he have the number?" Ethan asks, in a voice empty of all that is Ethan.

"Whoa." Mari shakes him, but he doesn't snap out of it. "Are you okay?"

"Does he have the number?" Ethan repeats, and Mari takes a step back.

"Y-yes," she answers carefully.

"What is it?"

"Uh…three thousand."

"How many are we?"

"Like, maybe two something thousand in the gates, and way more refugees, but they were worried the people still outside wouldn't survive…"

"It is not enough," Not-Ethan says. "He will go dark. And we are lost."

"But what does that mean?" She leans in, but Ethan picks this of all times to come back. He looks at her like she just bit him.

"W-we can't talk about this," he says, all pale and shaky.

"Just a little more," she presses and digs her fingers into Ethan's wrist. "It's important."

"It means…" He's out of breath, like he's been running uphill instead of just standing here in the hallway outside the sleeping car. "It means that if at any time there are less than three thousand surviving humans, Haruk — the white spire — will turn black. He'll be like the others. He'll stop protecting us and start killing us instead. The Judges will turn on us."

Now Mari's out of breath.

"Why?" It's all she can think to ask.

"Because he's never really been with us," Ethan says, and his voice is flickering in and out, shifting from his normal frightened teen boy self to this other, older, alien thing hiding somewhere inside of him. "He's just like the other three, Hoa, Herote, Himna — all of them are both light and dark. A concept and it's opposite. Hoa gone dark is rage, but if we saw her in the light, she'd be peace. Herote is cruelty and empathy. Himna is apathy and ambition. And Haruk is only light right now because one of them has to be, to keep the others from killing all of humanity. He's trying to keep a seed alive, leave just enough for us to repopulate, so they can come again later, thousands of years later, and harvest us again. But if we don't have enough people to rebuild — if we drop below the minimum viable population — there's no point in saving us for later anymore, and Haruk will go dark, too. In the light, he's order. In the dark, he's the worst of all of them. He's chaos."

Ethan is exhausted, seems ready to pass out where he's standing.

But when Not-Ethan flickers in, he straightens up. He looks at something far away.

"How do we stop them?" Mari swears to herself it's the last question she'll ask, and then she'll get Ethan some help. But then, she swore that five minutes ago, too…

"That's simple," Not-Ethan says. "They all come from us, from our minds. They bend our bodies to their will, and they use our energy to manifest — to become real to us. If we want to stop them, we only have to kill ourselves."

Mari slaps him.

"Jesus!" Ethan holds a hand to his face, the outline of her palm already reddening his cheek. "What was that for?"

She doesn't answer, she just hugs him tight. Oddly enough, he doesn't seem to mind.

They stand like that for only a few seconds when Mari feels something gently poking her hip, so she breaks away and starts walking back toward the scout car.

"Come on," she calls over her shoulder. "We have to tell the others."

"I-I'll be right there," he answers, turning away. "I have to get a…something from back in the…back. Of the car. Here."

Mari laughs to herself but decides not to embarrass the kid any further. She storms through the rest of the train on a mission, cracks the outer hatch to go hunt down Steves and the others, wherever they got off to, then practically knocks them over. They're all standing down there on the ground, blinking up at her in the doorway.

"What's up?" Mari says, noticing the same look on all of their faces.

"Nothing," Steves says. "Step aside, Rodriguez."

She doesn't.

"The forum," Johnson supplies. "It didn't go well. The Judges aren't letting the rest of the refugees in."

"What?" Mari looks out over their heads, back toward the city. The Heart, and the glowing white spire at the center of it all.

"Just what the man said." Steves puts a boot on the entry step and hauls herself up, now even with Mari and just a little too close for comfort. "Now step aside, Rodriguez. I have to talk to Ken. We're leaving."

Mari practically dances backwards.

"Really?" she badgers Steves. "For real this time? I've been saying since we got here, haven't I? And now you're finally—"

"Nobody likes a braggart, Mari." Ken unleashes one of his weaponized words. He's standing at the threshold of the scout car, looking like somebody just punched his dog. He's got one forearm planted on the doorway, leaning on it hard. The other one hugs his belly.

"Ken, get her started." Steves fixes Peralt with an authoritative finger. "Perry, get me a headcount. Johnson, get the internals secured and—"

"Can't," Ken interrupts her.

Everybody is stunned. Steves hates being interrupted.

"Can't what?" she snarls.

"Can't get the Snake started," Ken says.

"And why the fuck exactly not?" Steves is winding up for a tirade. Everyone in the room steps back unconsciously.

"Because it won't start," Ken says.

He removes his hand from his stomach. Reveals a wet blotch on his uniform. Holds his palm up for them all to see. It's covered in blood.

…

Frankie was handing a little portable solar lamp to a lovely older woman named Therese, who had fabulous spiky white hair and still rocked a defiant lip piercing, when Marcus tapped him on the shoulder. The big man shuffled his feet and looked at a spot somewhere on Frankie's forehead, rather than in his eyes. Frankie yelped with glee and went in for a hug which, per usual, Marcus did not return.

Well, not unless you counted two light pats on the shoulder as a return. Frankie did not.

"Marcus 'Marky Mark' Markovich," Frankie spun him around as he surveyed the man's face. No easy feat, since Marcus had at least fifty pounds on him.

"You look…" Frankie appraised. "Just *god awful*!"

Marcus chuckled sheepishly. He scratched his heavy beard and rubbed his ratty blond hair.

"Yeah," he said. "I could use a shower for sure."

"No, darling," Frankie squeezed his shoulders. "Filth becomes you. You look fantastic in dirt. This is something else."

"Listen, is uh…is Sam here?" Marcus stared a hole in Frankie's forehead. Some idiot must have taught him that trick — told him that it lets you look people in the eye without looking them in the eye. But anybody in the world could tell when you tried it. It made your forehead itch.

Frankie gave him an arch look.

"It's not that I don't want to talk to you!" Marcus protested. "It's just…I really think both of you should hear this."

Frankie pulled his lips back, gave Marcus an intentionally strange and indecipherable smile, then let the poor lummox contemplate what it meant while he went to grab Sam.

Sam was huddled up with the three new ladies: the fabulous-looking Latina girl with the great nails and cheekbones custom built for television…and the two others. If Frankie omitted a few adjectives when describing the sisters, it was only because he was feeling particularly generous today.

Frankie didn't bother interrupting politely — the sisters would just give him a look, and Sam would never call them out on that look, so Frankie would have to, and it would all just escalate from there. Again. So he pinched Sam's arm-fat instead.

"Yow!" Sam jumped and swatted at himself, thinking he'd been stung.

"Come," Frankie said and spun on his heel without further ado.

The sudden motions and loud exclamations almost woke Princess SparkleHogg, still gently snoring in the harness around Frankie's chest. So he put a fingertip to the bridge of her snout and held it there until she was properly reassured, and fell back into a deep slumber. He fought the urge to grab both sides of her furry little face and squeeze as hard as he could. Was it possible to love something so much you just wanted to kill it?

Frankie banished the thought and led Sam over to Marcus.

"Marcus!" Sam exclaimed and held his fist out for a handshake that soon became overwhelmingly complicated.

Frankie marked a point.

He and Sam loved Marcus, truly they did — especially because of his astonishing little girl, Vera. She looked like something out of a cartoon, with those layered dresses and all those frills and that plastic tiara she wore just like an actual princess. The urge to crush rose within Frankie, just thinking about her. And Marcus: a big broad boy packing a little fat around huge bones like some ancient Viking, but so shy he blushed if you so much as touched him.

The pair were inarguably adorable, and there was no limit to the amount of affection Sam and Frankie felt for them. But it was just impossible not to mess with Marcus a little bit. You could see his gears turning whenever you spoke with him, like every social interaction merited some advanced and invisible calculus. So Sam and Frankie played a little game whenever he was around. They tried to throw tiny, subtle, harmless wrenches in the big man's mental machinery. A weird smile, a complicated handshake, a bit of made-up slang that might be reserved only for black men, or gay men, or perhaps specifically black and gay men — anything to put that little wrinkle on Marcus' brow. They kept points. Frankie was winning, but Sam was getting better. Frankie had plenty of time to reflect on that fact, as the elaborate handshake was still going, and Marcus was far too fearful to break it off. He'd begun to sweat.

Frankie gave Sam a little swat — the big man deserved some mercy, after all — and Sam broke off the engagement with an explosion sound and jazz hands that poor Marcus felt obligated to copy.

"So what's happening, big guy?" Sam asked with perfect innocence.

"Oh, uh…" Marcus was out of breath from the sheer effort of stressing over that handshake.

"Right. I just…uh, I just came from the forum?"

"D-did you?" Sam blinked. "Are you asking me?"

"No, uh…sorry." Marcus shuffled in place. "I didn't mean to say it like that. It's just…it's bad. It's bad news."

"Oh, no." Frankie dove close to Sam and put a hand on his back. Frankie might show it more — *he would make a point of showing it more* — but Sam felt strongly about the refugee situation. Any sort of bad news would utterly break his heart.

"They're not letting them in," Marcus said. "Not until they can build enough housing for everybody."

"That's insane," Sam breathed. "How long will that take?"

"Two, uh…" Marcus couldn't even look in Sam's direction. "Two months."

"Two *months*?" he snapped, too loudly, then dropped into a whisper. "They expect these people to live out here for two more months?"

Frankie squeezed Sam's side, just above his ample love handles. He didn't seem to notice.

"They're doing what they think is best," Frankie said, though he knew how that would be received. "It was us who set the rules for entry to the Walled City, remember? That we'd let anybody in…as long as we had a safe space for them."

"These people won't last out here two months." Sam bulldozed right over Frankie's argument. "What if something comes this way?"

"Not…" Marcus couldn't even finish the thought.

"Not what?" Frankie prodded.

"Not if," the big man finished. "When."

"When…?"

"Tonight," Marcus said, so quietly Frankie had to read his lips to catch his meaning. "M-maybe sooner."

"They spotted something?" Sam asked. "What? Who? How many?"

That officially overloaded Marcus, and he just peered up at the dam walls, towering above them all.

"Did you hear that?!" a voice yelled from directly behind them. Sam jumped, and Frankie spun in place, ready to scold.

It was Yui, the older of the survivalist sisters.

"They're not letting you in!" she hollered, booming out over the crowd. Every head swiveled in her direction. "They had their precious meeting, and they're not letting anybody else in. Even though their scouts spotted something coming this way!"

"Jesus," Frankie hissed at her. "That will *not* help. These people will riot!"

"Hey." Sam turned to face the crowd, making eye contact with everybody he could, one by one. "Nothing is settled yet, we don't know anything, just stay calm!"

A groundswell of panic. Frankie could feel it behind his ears, electricity tickling the fine hairs.

"Maybe they *should* riot." Chiyo, the younger sister, stepped out from behind Yui. "Maybe if the people here get desperate enough, they can force their way in before whatever's coming gets to them."

Frankie leaned around the sisters to get eyes on the cheekbone girl, Ali. She saw him, but she looked away. She might not have condoned this plan, but she wasn't about to fight it.

"We have to go," Sam whispered, and Frankie moved to get the cart.

"Leave it," Sam said. "We have to go right now."

He grabbed Marcus with one arm and hooked the other in Frankie's.

The hushed shock was starting to harden at the edges. Whispers turning from fear to anger. The crowd was moving now — nowhere in particular, just agitating in place. Building up energy.

Sam, Frankie, and Marcus pushed past the cart, heading into the densest portion of the throng, back toward the gates of the dam. Ali stepped in front of them.

"Don't," she said. "That's where things will get bad first."

"We have to get back to the city," Marcus went wide-eyed. "I have to get back to Vera!"

"I know a way," Chiyo said, and five disbelieving faces swiveled in her direction. "Come with us."

"Chi, no!" Yui snapped. "We agreed: just us."

Chiyo shook her head.

"We did this," she said. "And I'm not saying it was wrong of us, but these people came out here trying to help."

"Would Dad want us to risk everything for strangers?" Yui felt at her waistband. Found the worn handle of a pistol there and adjusted it.

"Would Dad want us to screw people over for trying to do the right thing?" Chiyo countered.

Yui sucked her teeth.

"Fine," she said, already moving. "But if they hold us up…"

"I know," she filled in. "We'll cut them loose in a heartbeat."

Chiyo directed the last part at Frankie in particular, then waved for them all to follow.

Princess SparkleHogg kicked idly in her harness, her little piggy dreams turning dark with the atmosphere. At the distant, southernmost fringes of the crowd, wordless cries of astonishment went up. They were quickly echoed. Frankie didn't look back.

…

When Mari was here just a few hours ago, the Heart felt like a temple. Quiet, serious, a vast expanse of still water. Now it felt like a hive, alight with industrious and alien activity. Judges swarmed all through the place, both in clusters and alone, gathering weapons and barking commands. Something was kicking off outside, and as much as that idea terrified Mari, it also made her job easier. One thing at a time, she told herself. Deal with today before you worry about tomorrow.

Mari shimmies into the same alcove JR showed her, only this time she brings two things she'd been sorely missing before: her scouts and a pair of wirecutters. She cuts through the chickenwire, timing her snips to the quiet moments in between flurries of activity. When the courtyard below finally empties — for who knows how long — she risks three loud kicks to knock the barrier loose. It clatters to the dirt floor, and she drops in like a ninja. Rolls as she hits, practically soundless. Nicko isn't quite as graceful, and Fat Bob basically just eats shit in a semi-controlled fashion. He gets to his feet quick, though, dusts himself off, and gives her two dorky thumbs-up.

Mari holds up two fingers, points to her eyes, and then down the leftmost corridor leading out of the square. Nicko and Fat Bob head off to recon it while she takes the right one. It's empty, for now, but the heavy footprints in the loose dirt promise it won't stay that way for long. If she was hoping for some indicator — a conspicuous door, a blinking arrow, a big neon sign reading "Stolen Starter Solenoids For Military Landtrains And Also The Assholes Who Shot Ken Here" — she doesn't find it. Just a wide hall bordered by two stacks of shipping containers, arranged into a circle so that the inner edge disappears out of sight around a broad corner.

Mari looks back to Fat Bob, and he shakes his head. So it's down to luck, then. She flips a mental coin and decides on left, then joins back up with the others. They move quickly but carefully, always staggering corners and watching shadows, but they don't see anybody else. After a few hundred feet, there's a break in the shipping containers, a hole leading deeper into the Heart, so they take it. Building materials less even, here: a broke-down RV, a couple of sun shades, a lashed tarp, pallets and plywood and thick cardboard making up slapdash rooms and hasty hallways.

Mari makes tracking scuffs in the disused corners of the turns so they can find their way back through the labyrinth. She's toeing a left arrow into the dust at the point where a garden shed and a bunch of cinderblocks meet, when she hears footsteps. Fat Bob might not be graceful, but he's sharp. He hears it first and is already ushering Nicko into the blindspot left by the recessed shed door. He gives Mari a look, and she shoots back a nod. They leave their pistols holstered but draw their knives. The steps grow closer, waver for a second like they might just pass right on by…then turn in. Mari's got her blade up against the leading figure's throat while Nicko and Bob grab the two closest to them. There's screaming and thrashing and Ethan?

What?

Ethan's looking up at her with wild eyes, bouncing around his skull like pinballs. He's trying to make words but only managing syllables. She checks and sees that Nicko has a sleeper hold on little Ronnie, and Fat Bob's holding his broad paw over JR's mouth.

"What the hell are you doing here?" she hisses at Ethan.

"W-w-e-e-a-a," he stammers. She decides that Ethan is a non-functioning human right now.

She turns to JR instead, motions for Fat Bob to release him.

He does, and JR whispers, "We're following you. We came to help."

She tries, she really does, but Mari just cannot sigh hard enough to properly convey how frustrated she is.

"Sorry." JR looks at Ethan, then down at the ground. "It wasn't my idea, but they were gonna go anyway, so I figured better with me than without."

"We head back?" Nicko asks. He's not closing that sleeper hold on Ronnie, but he hasn't released it, either. The poor kid is having half an asthma attack. Mari doesn't remember if he has it, but he looks like he should. All bony shoulders and concave chest.

Mari understands Ethan following her: he's a dumb teen boy, trying to impress her in all the wrong ways. She gets JR joining in — he's an idiot, too, but he thought he'd be looking out for the other kids. Maybe he's not entirely wrong. She does *not* get why Ronnie is here. He's said two words to Mari since joining up on the Snake, and she's trying to recall if she's ever seen his whole face, without the lower half buried in one of his notebooks.

"No," she says to Nicko. "No point in heading back if we can't find that solenoid. You see those Judges? Something bad is going down, and we don't want to be here to see it. Ronnie, why—"

He knows the question is coming and starts answering before she's finished asking it.

"Somebody needs to record this. What's actually going on here. This might be it." The words rush out all at once, like he popped the cork on his brain and can't help the resulting torrent. "This might be the end of everything, and I have to write it down."

"If it's the end of everything," Mari says slowly, "who's going to read it?"

He just blinks, like it hadn't occurred to him.

"My dad," he mumbles. "He was like these ones: a Judge. I just…I have to know what happens to them. I have to write it down. Even if it's just for me."

Mari looks at the ceiling, the side of a train car with graffiti still on it. Mork Was Here, it says. She doubts he is anymore.

After counting to five and managing not to punch every single one of their stupid faces, Mari returns to the present.

"Stay low," she says. "Stay quiet, follow our every movement like you're our shadows, and whatever you do, do not make a noise. Not a word from here on out, got it?"

All three kids nod. Plus Fat Bob.

She gives him a cockeyed look, and he shrugs.

"Did you at least bring weapons?" she asks.

"Yeah—" JR says.

"What did I just say about talking?" she interrupts. She hates that JR's the one to fall for it, but an example must be made.

His yap snaps shut like a mousetrap. He reaches behind his back and pulls out an old but freshly sharpened hatchet. Mari looks to the others: Ethan pulls out a piece of metal pipe. Ronnie pulls out his notebook.

She stares at him until he blushes.

Mari takes point, and the others follow in a loose triangle formation. Ronnie is Nicko's shadow, Ethan is Fat Bob's, and of course JR is hers. They cover storeroom after storeroom — water barrels and canned food and shelves of prescription bottles and coats and light bulbs and wires and more — until they finally come across a decommissioned U-Haul, shallow pits dug into the dirt for the old, flat tires. In the back there are all sorts of vehicle parts, and she has no idea what she's looking for. But Fat Bob does. The suspension creaks a little as he gets in, and the plywood walls built up against either side of the truck crackle in protest. It takes ten minutes for him to find the part — he holds it up above his head like Excalibur and moves to dismount.

"Oh hey," a voice says from the corridor to the left. The side Nicko was supposed to be watching.

Mari spins, goes for her pistol, and drops to one knee. Locks onto a middle-aged lady with dark skin, hair back in a tight ponytail. Blank white spaces where her eyes should be. Two thin lines at their edges hanging impossibly in the air, before banking upward and disappearing into the ceiling.

"What are you kids doing here?" she asks.

Nicko is closest to the Judge, frozen in mid-crouch. One hand on the back of Ronnie's shirt collar. He looks to Mari but doesn't make a move. Fat Bob goes for his belt real slow, hoping not to be noticed.

"No need for that." The lady smiles. "No rules against trespassing. But I am going to have to ask you to follow me. I'll get you to a nice break room, and you all can have snacks while we figure out what to do with you."

"I'm afraid we can't do that, ma'am," Nicko says, low and even.

"That is a problem." The Judge frowns. "Since there *are* rules about disobeying the peacekeepers."

They're all frozen for a second, then in a single breath the Judge is on Nicko and he's screaming and she's putting her thumbs in his eyes.

Fat Bob shoots first.

She fires second.

…

Chiyo walked out front, with Ali just behind, followed by Sam and Frankie. Yui brought up the rear. The mob was restless, all dark mutterings and jabbing elbows, but panic hadn't truly set in yet. It would, though, Sam could tell. Their little group was surfing at the breaking edge of a tidal wave of fear. Everybody could hear the shouts coming from the southern fringes, even if they couldn't yet see what caused them. The cries started out as shock, awe, disbelief — but they were quickly losing the cadence of words. Slipping into raw fear. Panic moved through the crowd like a traffic jam. Sam it could feel it happening all around him. The nervous glances, the sweat on his own brow. The slow, building pressure as thousands of people tried to pull away from each other.

A sharp crack.

There was a time when Sam wouldn't have immediately known it for a gunshot.

A lumberjack type beside him broke at the noise and started thrashing about. The people nearby tried to contain him, to talk him down from it, but his nervous energy started to poison the crowd.

"Step it up," Yui called from the back.

"Aside! Aside!" Chiyo shouted, wedging herself into the press of bodies and prying them apart. "Aside, please!"

Another gunshot, and momentum took hold. The whole crowd surged like an avalanche breaking loose.

"Bunker up!" Chiyo yelled over her shoulder, then set her feet and crouched low. At the rear of the convoy, Yui did the same. Ali tried to emulate their stance, but it was clear she didn't understand. Frankie wrapped his arms around Princess SparkleHogg, who'd finally awoken and was beginning to gently protest her imprisonment. Sam didn't do a damn thing. He just gawked at the crowd like an idiot, until Yui yanked his head down.

"Keep your center of balance low. Look at the ground. Watch their feet and move with them, not against them," she recited. "When they go, your priority is staying upright and following the person ahead of you and that's it, got it?"

"What is going—"

The question died in Sam's throat. The crowd snapped. A thousand screams building together like roaring static. Nobody was looking at anybody else, all just staring, aghast, at something far to the south.

Sam was shoved by three people at once and nearly lost his balance. Yui kept him upright and pointed him at Frankie.

"Grab his belt!" she yelled in his ear, then did exactly that to him.

Sam snaked his fingers through the loops on Frankie's jeans and relayed the message. Frankie grabbed Ali in front of him, and she, Chiyo. They moved, a squat human train.

The screams grew in intensity, lashing overhead and surging forward. A portly teenager to Sam's right lost it completely and tried to climb the elderly man ahead of him. Put his hand atop the man's head, his foot on the man's back, and leapt. They both went down.

Directionless profanity and mad squeals of pain. The crowd pulsing to some unheard beat. An earthquake built on bodies. They knocked

Frankie to his knees, and he wouldn't take his arm away from Princess SparkleHogg to break the fall. Sam huddled over him, lashed out with elbows and forehead until he built a free space, and got his man back up and moving. Behind him, Yui's grip was unwavering. They stumbled and fell, redirected countless times, but never stopped, not once.

Until they did.

Sam wasn't prepared for it — bent double, eyes on the ground, feet moving with the crowd — he went face first into Frankie's butt when they paused, and Yui did the same thing to him. Sam looked over his shoulder to say something — apologize, maybe — but Yui just shoved him aside and hurried up beside Chiyo. They pressed themselves flat against a small recess in the old riverbank — a tiny pool of relative calm in the turbulent river of writhing humanity. From just a few feet outside of the press, everything looked different. Trying to navigate that throng felt like tumbling downhill in slow motion. It had taken so long. It was so hard. And yet they'd barely moved. Checking the landmarks, Sam figured they were only maybe fifty feet from where they started. From outside its boundaries, the crowd didn't look like they were panicking at all. Just jostling a bit for space. Shuffling their feet a little.

"Over here," Chiyo called, and Sam stood from his crouch to look.

She and Yui were squatting before the lip of a large concrete tube, whose entrance was blocked by a net of thick steel bars, held together purely by rust and luck. The waters of the Columbia diverted significantly when the dam broke, leaving the old riverbed all but dry. The former banks were now the walls of a canyon, twenty feet high, and far too silty to climb. Not that it stopped people from trying. Pure, blind terror led a few to claw uselessly at the dirt, bloodying their hands, eyes still locked southward on…

Sam turned slowly, tracking their horrified gazes to the horizon. Far beyond the distant edges of the refugee camp, a darker shape rose up against the black skies. Its edges were ragged and sharp, nearly serrated, its outline something like an enormous centipede standing on its hindquarters. The raised front section alone must have been forty, fifty feet tall. And to either side of its head, enormous outsized mandibles, like the arms of a praying mantis. One swept down lightning-quick, far too fast for a thing of that size to move, and reaped the crowd of refugees. Sam saw dozens of bodies lifted in the air, slashed, split in half, or just pulverized completely, cartwheeling madly through the sky to fall back to the crowd, crushing those below.

Scuttling all around the creature's base, stretching from one riverbank to the other and back as far as Sam could see, were hordes of psychopaths — the Manic, all gnashing jaws and rolling eyes. The forerunners tore into the refugees with crooked fingers and slavering teeth, and the ones behind them tore into the Manics in front, just so they could get their turn sooner. The more distant horde moved like a fluid. They flowed over hills and down banks, crashing and collapsing on each other, uncaring of the damage, so long as it brought them precious inches closer to the fleeing refugees.

Sam's mouth was dry, but his pants were wet.

"Don't look at that," Frankie whispered and stroked the stubble of Sam's cheek. "Look over here."

He brought Sam's eyes away from the horizon to meet his own. Filled with empathy and kindness and serenity.

"You're here," Frankie said. "You're with me. And we're going to be okay."

Sam feigned a smile, and Frankie traced the shape of his ears.

"Just a little further," he said.

Sam nodded and scratched beneath Princess SparkleHogg's chin. She kicked her stumpy little legs, clearly distressed, but managing. Sam aspired to be more like her.

"Got it," Chiyo grunted, pulling one of the rusty metal bars loose from its set. "That should be enough. Come on."

Yui stood at half height, arms wide, using her body to block the crowd's view of the pipe. She motioned Sam and Frankie over, while Ali stood nervously to her side. Chiyo slipped through first and disappeared into the darkness of the drain. Frankie gave Sam's hand a quick squeeze, then followed, crouch-waddling out of sight. Sam took a breath, forced himself not to think about what he was doing, what was happening behind him, or anything at all, and ducked his head.

"—I'm not—"

Sam froze when he caught part of the argument happening behind him.

"—the hell you—"

Only the loudest bits of the conversation filtered through the din. It was Ali and Yui.

"Just go, then," Ali said.

Sam turned his head to hear better.

"I will," Yui snapped. "Don't think I won't."

"I want you to," Ali said, not mad. Desperate. "Truly, after everything your dad did…I think, I know that you two need to live. He would want that. But I can't leave—"

"So you're just going to die out here?" Yui's anger lost some of its edge.

"No," Ali answered, careful and calm. "I'm going to get as many people as I can into this drain first."

"There's not enough room," Yui pleaded. "We don't even know where it lets out, what's at the other end…"

"It's better than here," Ali said. "It's a chance, and they all deserve it."

Yui didn't have a response.

"I'll give you a thirty-second headstart before I start shouting," Ali said. "And hey — maybe I'll see you on the other side."

"God damn it!" Yui spat, but she was already slipping into the tube and pushing on Sam's protruding behind.

"Get moving, tubs," she said. "We're about to have company."

…

Fat Bob's shot takes the Judge's ear off, and Mari's goes straight through her neck, but she's still burrowing her thumbs into Nicko's skull, even as the lifeblood pulses out of her with every heartbeat, splashing onto Nicko's mouth and nose. She only goes down for good when JR sinks his old hatchet straight into the back of her head. The Judge drops like a puppet with its strings cut, down on top of Nicko, who's trying to scream in between choking. Mari slides into the dust beside him, pushing the dead woman off of him, clearing the blood from his mouth, lifting his head, telling him it's over.

But not that "it's going to be okay." She doesn't lie to her fellow scouts like that, and they don't do it for her.

"JR." She looks over her shoulder at the boy, face gone pale, eyes distant. "I need you to—"

But he leans over and throws up right on the Judge's corpse. He sees that mess, moans, then has to turn away before the second round does the same.

"I need you to watch that door." She swivels to Fat Bob instead.

Barely half a nod for confirmation, he's already hustling that direction.

"Ethan," she says, and the kid doesn't even blink. "Ethan, Ethan, Ethan—"

Each iteration louder than the last, she's practically screaming when he finally snaps out of his daze, blinks at her.

"I need your help now, okay?" she says. "We need to bandage his wounds as best we can, okay? Now, I have some gauze in my left hip pouch, and I need you to get it for me, okay?"

At each "okay," Ethan nods. A bit more present every time.

Mari doesn't want to take her hands off Nicko — she's got one gently clearing away the gore on the man's face so she can see how bad the damage is, the other stroking his long, greasy hair.

Ethan walks over to her like a newborn deer — like he just found these legs ten minutes ago and nobody gave him an operating manual. He leans down, fingers trembling, and pauses.

"Is it…" he mumbles. "Is it okay if I touch you?"

Mari thinks of about twenty swears but none of them are worthy of the occasion, so she pushes down the impulse.

"Yeah," she says instead. "Hurry."

Ronnie is backed up into the farthest corner, scribbling madly in his little notebook.

"Ronnie," she starts right off with yelling, no time to build up to it. The kid jumps a full foot and drops his pen. Immediately starts scrabbling for it in the dirt.

"We got incoming," Fat Bob says, looking at something around the corner. "No eyes on them yet, but I can hear 'em."

"Ronnie," Mari tries again, "I need you to get over here and help Ethan patch Nicko up, okay?"

The magical "okay." Ronnie nods. With his nose out of the notebook, the kid is pretty unshakeable. Mari tries not to think of what he's been through to make him that way. She eases Nicko's head down into Ethan's lap — poor guy's just moaning now, "oh no, oh no," over and over again — and the boys set about bandaging his skull as gently as they can.

"Hey." She sidles up to JR. He's shaking. "First time?"

"No," he says, "but it's not easier. They say it gets easier."

"It's messed up, I know." She puts one of her blood-soaked hands on his back and rubs tiny circles between his shoulder blades. "But we're not out of this yet. This isn't good advice, and it's not healthy, but basically, I need you to put this stuff somewhere else right now. All right? Lock it in a box and shove it in a closet, because you'll probably have to do more before we get out of here."

JR is sweating and shivering at the same time. He bites his lip and nods. She hands him Nicko's pistol.

He takes it like it's going to bite him, but he knows how to hold it. His hand doesn't dip with its weight, and he instinctually checks the safety with his thumb. So he at least sort of knows how to shoot — thank god for small miracles.

"I just need you to watch our back." She uses her comforting hand to guide him around to a spot by the broke-down U-Haul. It's good cover, with a clean view of the only other entrance. "If anybody at all comes through there, just shoot. Don't warn them, don't warn us, don't ask any questions, or yell anything first — just shoot. Got it?"

JR doesn't nod this time, his eyes are already pinpricks, tunneled in on his task. Sometimes shock is useful.

Mari takes up alongside Fat Bob. She ducks out to check the hall and sees nothing, but she trusts his ears.

"How long?" she asks.

"No idea," he answers. "Tough to pinpoint sound in here, for us and for them. We might get lucky."

She sighs. Never say that.

"Sorry." He shrugs. "It's gotta happen one of these times, though, right?"

Just then the first Judge comes around the corner, an enormous barrel of a man, half fat, half muscle, easily seven feet tall, blank white eyes scanning the corridors like spotlights.

"Right," she mutters and leans out to take the first shot.

The big Judge takes a bullet in the shoulder like it's a bee sting. He steps back out of the line of fire and puts a hand to his shoulder, but he doesn't scream, or panic, or anything else that would give Mari reason to hope. He doesn't even shout for backup, but she can hear more footsteps approaching anyway. The Judges — they always seem to know more than they should. Out patrolling the city, anytime it looked like there might be trouble, more of them just kinda showed up. No radios or walkie-talkies or hand signals, it's like they just know. Fat Bob wasn't wrong with his first assessment — this place was a maze. A couple gunshots, right in the middle of it? It should've taken them a while to pinpoint the source. But here they were: first guess. Creepy bastards.

"Hey," Nicko says, real shaky.

Everybody turns to look.

"Hey," he repeats, more firmly. "Where's my gun?"

Fat Bob laughs a little, and Mari glares at him for it, but Nicko smiles.

"I don't trust your aim right now," she tells him as gently as possible, and he just nods.

"I still want it back," he says. "Drag me up into the moving truck. You all take that rear exit, and I'll hold them off here."

"No offense," Fat Bob says, "but I spot two flaws with your plan, buddy."

Nicko laughs, only a little bitter.

"I'm not saying I'll hit anything," Nicko says. "But whenever I hear them get close, I'll fire off a shot. They'll duck and cover, move in on me slow. It'll buy you time."

"Nicko, I…" Mari doesn't know where that sentence was supposed to end, but it just kind of dies out.

"Straight up," Nicko says, "do you see any way we're all getting out of here, with you dragging me *and* the kids?"

JR is looking around like everyone just spontaneously started speaking in tongues. Ethan and Ronnie are right where she left them, kneeling together in the dust behind Nicko. Fat Bob is watching the corridor. It's just her. Her call.

"Give me my gun," Nicko says, "and let me die cool, okay?"

Mari laughs a little, nods at JR. He hands the pistol over like it's both made of glass and coated in butter. They help Nicko to his feet and settle him in the back of the U-Haul. They get him pointed in the right direction, and Mari kisses him on the forehead. She gets blood on her lips. Fat Bob squeezes Nicko's shoulder once, opens his mouth twice to say something, but doesn't manage anything at all, because guys are real dumb about this kind of thing.

…

The drain was a cramped, slick, uphill waddle that emptied into an enormous concrete cylinder inside the old powerhouse. The turbine, dormant for years, took up most of the inner circle. The whole place smelled like ancient mold and fresh oil, lit sporadically from splintery cracks in the concrete walls. Sam didn't have much time to get his bearings before somebody shoved him from behind and took his place. Whoever it was apologized, just as blind and panicked as he was, and they were soon knocked over themselves, in turn. Sam felt, more than saw, the flood of refugees pouring in from the drain behind him. Deathly quiet, every one of them, each trying not to break the spell of relative safety amid the chaos and death they'd just left behind. Sam had nightmare flashes of being slowly crushed against the rounded walls of this broad, deep basin by a press of humanity, and set about to find his group.

"Frankie." It was barely above a whisper, but he still felt people jump at the noise.

"Here," he answered, closer than Sam thought.

They groped in the relative dark, manhandling a number of strangers before they found one other. A quick, cursory side hug — lest they crush Princess SparkleHogg, still strapped to Frankie's chest — and release.

"Me, too," Marcus mumbled, as though Sam might miss his hulking form. "I'm uh…I'm right here."

"Found it," Yui called, ignoring the uneasy hush entirely.

She was standing just behind Frankie, flush against the wall of basin, and waving one arm high above her head. Somebody pushed against Sam from behind, and by the way Frankie stumbled, he seemed to be getting similar treatment.

"Up," Chiyo ordered and gave him one final shove.

Sam's hands fell on cold, textured metal. He groped around, realized it was a ladder, and began to climb. They navigated most of the powerhouse that way — blind prodding and educated guessing, stumbling in the dark, cutting hands and knocking heads, the throng of desperate, unseen people at their backs. The nonstop chatter of heavy gunfire and pained screaming from just beyond the walls. Concrete dust shook loose from the ceiling, hung in the colorless light like stars in a galaxy. It took forever, and it took no time at all. Sam felt like he had always lived in the darkness of that musty powerhouse, and yet his first thought when they crested the final tunnel, emerging atop a steep hill overlooking the Walled City, was, *We're here already?*

For some reason, Sam had expected to come out on top of the dam. Perhaps it was the distance they'd climbed, or some overestimation of their angle of ascent, but he was surprised to find their long slog led to an exit point only a few dozen feet above the floor of the drained basin. It was still the highest point in the city, aside from the pinnacle of the dam itself and, of course, the spire. It was getting toward dusk, which he could only tell by the declining quality of the light, the black skies as unhelpful as ever. The stark, dividing white of Haruk's spire was almost blinding to look at by comparison, but it shed no luminance. In fact, the darks around it seemed even deeper by virtue of the contrast.

Marcus jostled Sam as he exited the penstock next, apologized, tried to move away, and found there was nowhere to go. Just a steep dirt hill with a single narrow iron stairway, switchbacking down to the city below.

"I can't believe we made it," Frankie said, half to Sam, half to the Princess.

"We didn't," Yui answered.

She pointed to the distant horizon, at nothing at all. Sam squinted and tilted his head, but he couldn't see anything of note.

"Nothing's there," he said.

"Right," Chiyo confirmed.

"So what's uh…what's the problem?" Marcus asked.

"There should be something," Yui said. "This is the very bottom of the reservoir. That's the whole point of this place. Walls of one type or another on all sides. So what's missing?"

"Everything," Sam gasped.

The steep cliffs and swollen hills to the east were gone. About fifty feet up, and they just stopped. Like they were in the process of being erased by the black skies, encroaching slowly downward.

"It's the fog," Yui explained, already looking away from the horizon and testing the rusted stairs. "That stuff we told you about in the forest. It's here, and it's coming down those hills right toward us."

"That centipede thing to the north," Chiyo said. "The fog to the east, nothing but sheer canyons all around…"

"This isn't a sanctuary," Yui spat. "It's a killing floor."

Chiyo joined Yui, both putting one foot on the topmost stair and bouncing their weight off of it. She looked to her sister for confirmation, but Yui just shrugged, and the pair started down together. The makeshift staircase squealed and shed a rain of rust with every step, but it held. And Sam didn't see an alternative. He followed. They all did.

When Sam finally stepped foot back inside the walls of the city, he released a breath he'd been partially holding for the better part of an hour. He nearly blacked out from the rush of oxygen to his brain. He held onto Frankie and laughed madly. Frankie joined him, and they spun each other around like newlyweds, dazed with relief. A third voice mingled in with theirs, also laughing hysterically. It was a stranger, a thin man wearing a heavy black hoodie despite the heat. He staggered toward them from the city proper, leaving Wall Street to weave through the narrow alley between trading stalls, pausing to lean against the walls and catch his breath.

"What's so funny?" Yui asked, her hand inching toward her pistol.

"It's just…" The man paused, a few spare laughs trickling out. "It's just you guys!"

"What about us?" Chiyo asked, circling around to the stranger's side.

"You look like you've been through absolute, unspeakable hell," he said, slowly straightening and removing his hood. "But you've finally made it here after all your trials and tribulations, thinking you've survived…"

Both Chiyo and Yui drew simultaneously.

"…and we've been with you the whole time," a different voice finished.

One of the refugees behind Sam, just stepping off of the stairs.

It was so dark, the entire trip. All through the drain, in the powerhouse, climbing up the penstock, he could only make out dim shapes and erratic shadows. Now, in the light, he could see the rest of his group for the first time. Humans…most of them. But sprinkled in all throughout the line of refugees were a dozen or so smiling faces. Ragged-edged voids where their eyes should have been.

Frankie let out a shout as he backed into Sam, who immediately stepped in front of him. Marcus was frozen. Mouth working silently like a fish out of water.

"Marco!" a chipper girl called from above. "Fancy meeting you here!"

Still two flights up the steep staircase, mixed in with the line of refugees, a pretty young woman with empty eyes leaned recklessly over the safety railing, waving enthusiastically.

The first shot made Sam jump and the Princess squeal, the second sent him and Frankie scuttling for cover. The thin man in the hooded sweatshirt went down laughing. But others were moving in on Chiyo and Yui from the cover of the crowd. Ducking low, grabbing refugees and shoving them off balance, using the kids as human shields. Yui took a few shots of opportunity, most going harmlessly wide. Chiyo didn't risk it. She holstered her gun and switched to a knife, took a low stance, and shuffled in. There was a sharp cry beside her, and a heavyset woman in a headscarf toppled over. She went hands-first into Chiyo, and the two of them sprawled in the dirt. The Merry that pushed her leapt onto her back and tore at Chiyo, trapped beneath. Her blade flashed in the half-light, but the Merry had something, too. Small and quick, drawing thin, dark lines on

Chiyo's face like a Sharpie.

Yui heard her sister cry and turned to check, only to be taken down by a falling body. One of the Merry had jumped from the third flight of stairs — twenty feet straight up — and caught Yui on the shoulder. By the sound of it, he broke both of his legs when he hit the ground, but it didn't give him pause. He crawled after Yui's prone form, got a hold of her hand, and immediately set to snapping her fingers backward, one by one. He managed three before she recovered her gun and put a bullet in his face.

Sam steered Frankie and the Princess away from the carnage, up the alley leading to Wall Street. He told them not to look back but couldn't resist it himself. Marcus was pressed flat against the smooth cement of the dam's retaining wall, his arms wide, fingers stretching, trying to climb up its surface like a gecko. The young woman who'd called out to him earlier was just working her way through the throng. One of the refugees, an older fellow with a waist-length gray beard, tried to grab her, but she stuck a finger in his nose. He was so bewildered that he released her, and she opened his throat with what looked like a miniature scimitar. She danced the rest of the way to Marcus, miming a shoddy soft-shoe, while panicked refugees bolted in every direction.

Sam watched all of this unfold with horror and promised himself that he'd go back and help, just as soon as he got Frankie and the Princess to safety. But Frankie was fighting him for some reason, pushing back against Sam's outstretched arms. Sam tore his eyes off the chaos behind and saw, for the first time, the five silhouettes blocking their escape route.

Some of them children.

Sam tried to shuffle around Frankie, to block him with his own body, but as soon as he moved, he heard an unmistakable click and looked up into the barrel of a gun.

"Their eyes are clear," the girl said to the others. "They're human."

Sam got a good look at the group for the first time: one man about his age, skinny but with a bit of a beer gut and a terrible complexion, two young white boys, and two teenagers, one looking a whole lot more comfortable with her pistol than the other did with his hatchet.

…

The chubby black guy looks at Mari like she's going to single-handedly save the world. It really pisses her off.

"If you're not going to help," she sneers at him, "get the hell out of the way."

He just nods and guides his friend past. She has to blink a few times to make sure, but the other dude's got some sort of animal strapped to his chest. It's either the cutest pig she's ever seen or the ugliest dog.

"You get these people back to the Snake." She turns to JR, shifting her eyes to include Ethan and Ronnie. Ethan looks away, Ronnie looks at his notebook. "We'll be right behind you."

"But you'll—" JR starts, and she doesn't even have to speak to shut him up. He just sees it in her eyes. He swallows hard, nods.

"Be careful," he says. "Come back."

Mari does her best not to — it really ruins the moment — but she smiles at him. Just for a second. She doesn't wait to see him off, turning to find Fat Bob already moving without her. She got to play bossman back at the Heart — it was her op, and she was most familiar with the place, so it only made sense — but now they were equals again, and there was no need for orders, anyway. You see anybody with black eyes, shoot 'em in the head. Maybe white eyes, too.

A plunk and the Merry nearest Fat Bob goes down. She takes her own shot, but the young girl after the big guy is too far away, moving too erratically. The big dude is gone in the head; she's seen that look before. He won't be able to move unless you get in there and move him, and there are two dozen refugees and god knows how many Merry in between them. Mari shoves a couple civilians out of the way, takes a potshot at a passing Merry but doesn't get to see if it lands — the crowd is stampeding now, and she's caught between them and the only exit. Something grazes her wrist, and white fire dances up her nerve endings. She jumps back to find a long, twisting slash all the way up her forearm, but nothing that might've done it. Just some strangely moving shadows.

She fords the river of panicked refugees and takes another slash on her leg. Warmth fills her boot, and the pain follows soon after. There's a break in the current, and Mari dives. Rolls on one shoulder, comes up with pistol aimed. The girl, the Merry, she reached the big guy. Doing something to him Mari doesn't really understand. Deep cuts on his face. An ear might be gone. It takes a second, but up close, Mari finally recognizes him: he's from the Snake. A recent stray, he and his daughter only joined up after the train parked at Dam-Nation. Mark something, maybe? He doesn't look like himself: his ridiculous mane has been rudely shorn. One of his arms is drenched in blood, and he's holding his wrist out like something is twisting it all the way around, but there's nothing there. Just more of those weird shadows. Then the whole hand pops right off, and the darkness swallows it.

Mari looks to the girl, sees the erratic black lines bleeding from her absent eyes, puts two and two together. She aims, fires, and the chick goes down. A flare of crackling black lightning erupting from the side of her head. The big guy collapses, like he wasn't really holding himself up. She goes to help him, but he stumbles and falls again.

"I can't," he says. "My feet."

Mari looks but can't see what's wrong with them. Big guy is wearing hearty engineer's boots up to the knee, and there's not a scratch on them.

"All my toes," he explains. He kind of laughs a little. "They're gone. One of the first things I bargained away."

Mari doesn't have time for questions, she just tries to lift the guy again, but he's easily twice her size, and he can't stand.

"It's okay," he says. "She…she took things on the inside, too. Nothing I didn't promise her. I don't think I'm gonna make it."

He seems like a good dude, if more bashful than a nervous squirrel. It sucks to lose somebody at all, but there's too much death packed into this day already. Maybe it'll hurt tomorrow, but for right now, it's just a tactical decision.

"Okay," she says. "I'm sorry."

She slides his arm from around hers, eases him to the ground, and he blinks a little. Maybe the scene played out differently in his head.

"My daughter," he says and tries to cough. It doesn't happen. Just quiet convulsing. "Tell her I love her always and…"

More spasms.

"Did you not tell her that?" Mari asks.

"I told her." His breath sounds wet. "I told her…every day."

"Then you did good," Mari says.

Big guy thinks about that for a second, then gets this huge goofy grin on his face. He tries to talk, but it's not working anymore, so he just waves Mari away, and she goes.

Mari keeps low and far the hell away from the shadows, following the gunfire. Figures it'll lead her to Fat Bob. Instead, she finds a middle-aged Asian lady with an enormous forehead and a face like a shovel. She's back to back with what has to be her sister — genetics like that just can't be a coincidence — and they're doing a damn fine job of picking the Merry off. Three bodies down in their circle of fire. But that's it. Quick mental tally says there aren't nearly enough corpses here to account for all of them. Some must have escaped with the refugees, still hiding in the panic of the herd. And Fat Bob is gone — not one of the bodies, just missing — so she figures maybe he spotted the same thing and went after them.

"Come with me," Mari says.

"Screw you," the older sister says automatically.

Mari chuckles despite herself.

"Sorry," the younger sister says, relaxing a bit now that she can see Mari's eyes. "Who are you?"

"Doesn't matter," Mari says, already moving. "But I'm leaving here to find my armored, running vehicle."

That's all the convincing she feels like doing. She keeps her pistol at the ready and breaks into a jog. A few seconds later, she hears bootsteps following her. The sisters must be smarter than they look.

...

Frankie was not built for running. And though he'd done a lot of it in the past few years, somehow it never got easier. Of course, the bouncing ball of pig strapped to his chest might have something to do with it this time.

He was desperately out of breath, sweat turning cold on his skin, a stitch lancing its way through his side, when Sam put out a hand and motioned for him to stop. Three people stood blocking the street ahead, backlit by the spotlights from that crazy military truck thing. He could see from their silhouettes that each held a beefy-looking rifle of some kind.

Frankie could hear what sounded like a babbling brook coming up Wall Street behind him. It was a hundred slapping feet — the crowd of refugees and god knew what else along with them — rapidly growing louder. Frankie scanned the abandoned stalls for a weapon, but the best thing he came up with was a plastic broom with a duct-taped handle. He tried to picture himself swinging it dramatically, mowing down foes like Conan the Barbarian, and almost laughed. He, for one, would not go down fighting. Instead, he fidgeted with Princess SparkleHogg's straps. Like hell was he bringing her down with him.

Then he saw something unspeakably wonderful: two pure white lines stretching from each shadowy figure up to the white spire above.

"They're Judges." Frankie let himself breathe. "Sam, it's okay."

Sam didn't budge.

"Is it?" he asked.

"Now," Frankie sighed, "of all times, do not be like this."

Frankie took a step forward, and all three figures raised their guns. Frankie froze. He put his hands in the air and tried to angle his face toward the light.

"We're normal," he called out. "Look at these two beautiful big brown eyes. How about it?"

"Get behind us," the Judge on the left called, and neither he nor Sam needed that particular invite twice.

The Judge who'd called out to them turned out to be a handsome Latino man about their age — a bit of a belly on him, but he wore it well. And he wore that pushbroom mustache even better. The one in the center was a shockingly young girl with platinum blond hair, all the more impressive considering he couldn't imagine her simply finding the dye lying about to keep it up. The third Judge was a twenty-something white boy with full-sleeve arm tattoos. Sam and Frankie sheltered behind the Mustache Man and watched as the refugees charged up Wall Street like a particularly desperate marathon. Frankie couldn't see their faces and would later be thankful for that minor miracle.

"Don't shoot," Sam said. "They're normal, too."

"Of course," Mustache Man answered. "You two get back to the Ouroboros. We'll keep them safe."

Sam turned to leave, dragging Frankie by the wrist.

"Be careful," Frankie called back. "Some of those black-eyed ones might be mixed in with them, too!"

Sam froze. His fingers dug into Frankie's flesh like little vises.

"Oh," the blond Judge said. "Okay, then."

She raised her rifle and began firing into the crowd. The other two joined her, staccato bursts of gunfire and careful pauses as they drew new targets. Frankie was dimly aware that he was screaming, but if you pressed him at that moment, he couldn't have told you what. Sam was pulling him somewhere, and he fought him for some reason, but he didn't win. The next thing he remembered, he was sitting on a bunk inside that bizarre tank-truck thing with a blanket over his shoulders and Sam crooning over and over about how it was going to be okay. It was utterly unconvincing, but you had to give the man points for trying.

…

When Mari finally catches up to the fleeing refugees, it's only because they're all dead. Mowed down as they ran, laid out on the street in waves. It takes her all of three seconds to spot Fat Bob among them, half his head gone. Three figures stand about fifty yards up, between her and the Snake. They're backlit, just cutouts against the brilliant spotlights of the landtrain, but she sees one swivel in her direction, and she dives for cover. She looks back but doesn't spot the two weird sisters following her. Must've jumped into cover the second they saw the blockade.

The central figure yells at her.

"What?" she hollers back, if only to buy time while she scans her surroundings.

"Hey, you normal?" a different voice calls out. Female, younger.

"Sorta," she answers, and there's a little laughter.

"Come on out," a third joins. "We won't hurt you."

"Sure hurt them," Mari says.

"Just following orders." Mari can practically hear the shrug in the girl's voice. "Steves said, 'Make sure none of those black-eyed bastards cross this line.' What are ya gonna do?"

Steves? She and Ethan warned Steves about the Judges, why would she…?

To get them away from the Snake, Mari realizes. Busywork, to buy some time once they got the solenoid back. Steves couldn't have known they'd actually see action, much less…

Mari eases out of cover slowly, keeping her weight back in case she needs to dive. But if the three figures were bluffing, they're either brilliant at it or unbelievably terrible. They've all got their rifles down, formation broken. They're not worried about her at all. She approaches slow, ready to bolt like a nervous cat. Sure enough, the trio are Judges. She spots the lines from their eyes before she even sees the voids in their faces.

"Why?" is all she can think to ask.

"Why what?" The girl turns like she kinda forgot Mari was even there. "Oh, the bodies? There were Merry in with them. Only way to be sure none crossed the line, like Steves said, was to kill 'em all."

The other two Judges nod matter-of-factly, not even the specter of debate.

Mari distinctly recalls that she has four rounds left in her magazine. The Judges aren't ready, she can—

"Oh, hey," the girl says, looking up to the white spire. "Hoa has breached the walls."

Turned like that to the light, Mari recognizes the woman. She's seen her before, back in the Heart. Her friend with the mustache, too.

"Is that it?" he asks. He sounds upset.

"It is," the third Judge answers and sighs.

All three of them stand frozen as the white spire flashes, dims, and slowly fades to black. Darkness creeps out from it, snaking down the lines — down all of them, dozens, maybe hundreds scattered all throughout the city. It surges across the six thin white wires leading to the trio in front of her, painting them black as it goes. Mari puts a bullet in the Mustache Judge's head before the darkness even reaches him. A shot rings out from the shadows beside her, and the blond Judge goes down just as her eyes flicker darkly. The weird sisters. Guess they didn't ditch her after all.

Another burst of gunfire from the opposite shadows, but it doesn't hit the third Judge in time.

His white eyes stain black, and the tattooed guy dives straight for Mari, out of the line of fire. He snatches the pistol right from her hand, puts it in his own mouth, then bites down so hard his teeth explode. He raises his own rifle and starts firing into the shadows on either side of the street, at once laughing, weeping and screaming. Mari rolls for cover, the movement apparently drawing the man's attention. A spray of bullets chases her across the narrow street and into the bushes. As soon as she's out of sight, the tattooed Judge turns and fires at the lights of the snake until his gun clicks. He buries the barrel of his rifle in the packed dirt of the street so hard it stands upright, then leaps onto the abandoned stall beside him and starts ripping down the walls.

The angry ones — the Manics — they just hate you. Like you, personally. If they don't see anybody around, they go off on these crazy internal loops, arguing with themselves and wandering about. They don't do this: they don't try to destroy literally everything, all the time.

Mari moves carefully, but it doesn't seem like the Judge, if that's what he even is anymore, remembers she's there. He just moves from one thing to the next — stall to wheelbarrow to abandoned scooter — tearing each apart with his bare hands. Mari scoots low across the corpses, finds Fat Bob, puts a hand to his chest and does…something. It's not quite a prayer. She's not that way. It's just a feeling. She gives it to him, hopes he can make use of it. In trade, she steals the starter solenoid from his pack. Keeping to the shadows, she makes it to the steps of the Snake and punches her code into the exterior keypad. The hatch hisses and thunks, starts to roll back. Only then, when the way is clear, do the two sisters show themselves. They push past her and onto the Snake, without so much as a word of thanks. Though Mari supposes that, if anything, their assistance with the Judges probably means they're even by now. So it's just as well. She's sure as hell not thanking *them.*

Mari risks a glance up at the spire, now gone darker than the waning skies. It's quickly losing its hard-edged shape, bulging out at bizarre angles. Spikes and smooth planes and bulbous tumors bursting from every inch of it. There doesn't seem to be any rhyme or reason to the transformation, aside from one: It's growing. Fast.

…

Sam left Frankie and the Princess curled up together on one of the hard military cots in the sleeping car and went in search of water. Frankie had always been so strong, so optimistic about all of this. He knew they'd survive, even as the camps were overrun in Seattle. He was all jokes and optimism, even as they lost friend after friend on the long trek down Highway 2. And when they found the fabled Walled City, and it turned out to be a broken dam full of white-eyed Judges? It was Frankie who literally slapped him out of it, kissed the stinging palm-print, and told Sam they could make it here. And now Frankie had given up. He wept until his body simply stopped producing tears, then laid down and slept. He didn't say a word to Sam the whole time. Sam hoped that time would heal those wounds, but how much damage could it possibly undo?

Sam stepped into the crowded kitchen car just hoping for some water, maybe a granola bar. Instead, he found high drama.

"—he'll get it running." The gruff blond lady jabbed a finger into the chest of the most forgettably handsome man that Sam had ever seen. He was good-looking in an almost cartoonish way — if you'd asked Sam to draw a picture of a healthy white man, this guy would've been a spitting image.

"And if he does?" The man didn't even flinch at her finger jabs. He seemed to have grown accustomed to them. "Then what? We run? Blindly, half our supplies gone, with hundreds of thousands of maniacs on our tails and that…whatever the hell that giant bug thing is supposed to be! How long are we going to hold out against fucking *giant shadow ghost bugs*?"

"We're survivors," the woman answered, but even Sam could tell her resolve was wavering. "We'll figure something out."

"We already figured something out." The man pointed to a motley assembly of soldiers, idling at the fore of the kitchen car. "You just don't want to do it."

"You saying I can't make the hard decisions?" The woman laughed. "*You*, of all people, are trying to tell me that? I can't take a shit in the morning without you whining for me to stop and weigh the consequences."

"I'm not saying that." The man sighed. "I know what you've been through. The calls you've had to make. I know you'll make the right one here, we just need you to make it…faster."

"I'll send my men out on a dangerous mission." The woman looked to the soldiers, still as statues. "That's just part of the job. But I won't ask them to commit suicide."

"Ma'am." A painfully young man stepped forward, his jaw set and head held high.

The arguing pair snapped to him with such blatant contempt that Sam could actually see the boy stagger.

"I-if you're looking for volunteers…" the soldier started, but his bravado was already waning. Sam had no doubt the man would've faced a suicide mission gladly, but he shrank all the way down into a guilty little child under the combined weight of those two stares.

"If you're looking for volunteers," a pre-teen boy sporting the most unfortunate bowl cut this side of 1984 chimed in, "you're five minutes too late."

"Ethan," the man spoke carefully. "What do you mean?"

"She went." The boy's voice cracked and dried up in his throat. "She already went."

…

Okay, so the bomb is way heavier than Mari imagined. It's maybe the size of a football, all gleaming steel and carbon fiber, so she figured it'd be light. But it's like lugging around a dying star. Maybe that's intentional, though. Like the designers had some empty space left over, so they just filled it with lead weights. As if to say that a nuclear weapon, no matter how small, no matter how targeted or low yield, should always be heavy. If only like, metaphorically.

Anyway, that's what she blames when JR catches up to her: the bomb. It slowed her down. She's not tired, or scared, or hoping desperately that somebody would catch her and make her stop.

It's just the weight of the thing.

"What the hell are you doing?" JR snaps, fully out of breath from his own sprint across the sandy grounds of the eastern basin.

As much as Mari might have secretly prayed for company, she definitely doesn't feel like being yelled at.

"Get out of here," is her only answer. She picks up the pace, forcing JR to struggle beside her.

"You can't." A pause for breath. "It's crazy, let…"

"Let somebody else do it?" Her voice is dripping with the kind of poignant sarcasm only teenage girls can summon.

"Yes," is all he says, and that brings her up short.

She turns and sees his eyes are watering. Maybe it's the wind. The dust from the dry reservoir. But neither of those explains the quiver in his voice.

"I can't." She dials down the poison a few notches, even slows to a walking pace for him. "Saying somebody else should do it is like saying the other scouts are worth less than me."

"But you're younger," JR pleads.

"So that means I deserve to live more?" She laughs. "You know that's not how it works — not for a long time now, if it *ever* did. I'm younger, yeah, which means I'm faster, I have sharper eyes, I'm quieter. I'm also less experienced. It'll be quicker to train my replacement up to my level. I'm going *because* I'm the youngest."

"Just wait," he says.

She doesn't.

"Just stop for a second."

She can't.

JR falls a step behind every time he has to talk. He goes silent and wades through the shifting sands to catch up to her again.

"You don't even know what you're doing," he tries. It's desperate and wrong.

"Sure I do," she says. "You heard Johnson. That's what the Ouroboros was built for — ford through any terrain, plant strategic, small-yield nukes, then bunker up to weather the blast. You just put in the code, flip those two switches, and watch the lightshow."

"Then I'm going with you," he pouts.

And that finally makes her stop. She looks at him sideways, checks his expression, turns it over in her head…and figures the idiot actually means it.

The core of her melts.

That's all she wanted, really — for somebody to offer.

But, of course, she has to turn it down.

"Actually, you can't," she says and hoists the bomb up along her hip. "Because I need you to do something for me."

He looks hopeful.

"I need you to take care of Lucas," she finishes. The light goes out of his eyes.

"But…"

"But you're the only one I trust to do it. I need you to look out for him like I did. He likes to just retreat when things get tough. Withdraw from people. You can't let him. You drag him back, even if he bites you. He *will* bite you."

The best it gets is a fraction of a smile.

"You've been with me when I had to do it," she continues. "He likes you, and I know you'll take care of him. And also, I need you to tell him something…"

She actually hadn't thought of any last words. For some reason the idea sends a crippling wave through her body, like she was gonna be just fine with dying so long as she never had to stop and think about it.

"Tell him," she speaks slowly. Every word seems wrong, but she's just gotta get through them anyway. "Tell him that I'm sorry I had to leave. I know he doesn't want to be alone. But the people on the Snake will be his family now, if he'll let them, and he *has* to let them. Tell him he has to live and be good because…"

The floodgates burst and tears spill down JR's face. She feels it building in her, too.

"Because I told him to, and I'm his big sister. He has to do what I say."

She shoves JR back toward the Snake before she breaks, too, and he turns to leave. The total idiot. She has to rush forward, grab his arm, and spin him around and kiss him because you have to do everything for these stupid boys. It's awkward, at first, but she kisses him until it isn't, then lets him go and walks away while he's still too stunned to protest.

It's windy, and hot, and the kind of dark Mari couldn't have even imagined back in her real life. When she lived in a house with lights, and a mom, and a dad. And she's kind of thankful that the bomb is so god damn heavy, because it keeps her distracted all across the basin, up the crumbling riverbanks, and on top of the thin land bridge keeping the waters of Crescent Bay from raging downstream and washing away all of Dam-Nation, the maniacs, and practically everything else in the whole world.

Johnson said the bombs aren't meant for wide damage, they're kind of like shaped charges meant to take out specific targets, change the landscape, clear debris — they'd have to plant this one on the inner rim of the bay, facing the dam, for the best shot at busting the levee. There's where the problem comes in. Halfway across the still and stinking waters of Crescent Bay, there's a flowing wall of blackness. Like a massive fog bank or an ash cloud churning in slow motion. It creeps steadily forward like airborne molasses, and scattered all along the perimeter, between her and her intended blast point, are the broken shapes of watchful Sleepers.

She drops to her butt right where she's standing. The bomb just falls out of her fingers, thumps in the dust. She hears Fat Bob's voice in her head, saying, "Maybe we'll get lucky — gotta happen one of these times, right?"

Laughter escapes from Mari. It bursts out of her like she's a pressurized can full of crazy. The two nearest Sleepers nearest perk up at the noise. Straightening painfully to their full height, a series of cartilage-cracks as their thick joints struggle with the sudden motion. They crane their heads in her direction. But their eyes are still closed. Alert, not attacking. She remembers the desiccated woman that nearly pulled her from that mail truck so long ago, when the world first fell apart. The Sleepers are impossibly fast, once you get them going. Mari would already be dead if she'd set them off. But she doesn't even have time to think of a plan, because that fog is rolling in, and she doesn't know what's going to happen when it reaches her, but she doubts it's going to tickle. She checks her pistol. She's got three rounds left.

Her hips hurt when she stands. Been using some weird muscles to wade through all that sand. Her back cracks like she's gotten old in the last two minutes. She tries once and doesn't even get the bomb off the ground. Hefts again, and it threatens to break her in half. She lays it across her knee, punches in the code — 1234, because in some ways, the army is extremely stupid — and thumbs both triggers. She thinks she might have a few seconds before it goes off, which she'll use to plug the two closest Sleepers, if only to give them pause while she charges past them, sticks the nuke in the dirt of the far bank like she's spiking a football, and go out in the blaziest glory possible.

None of that happens. Instead, a darkened digital display beneath the keypad blinks three times, pauses, repeats.

It's waiting for her.

It's a timer.

If she makes it back to the Snake alive, she's going to punch Johnson in the balls until he explodes from being punched in the balls too much.

…

Sam wasn't entirely sure what any of this talk meant, but the boy's revelation sure sent the soldiers into hysterics. Some of them tried to sprint right out the doors, others tried to stop them, which quickly devolved into brawling, the two in charge practically spat in each other's faces with all the screaming, and the bowl cut who set off the drama bomb, Ethan, just sat down on the floor and started bawling. Sam felt very uncomfortable just standing in the middle of high tragedy with his empty glass, so he started to back away. He was nearly to the rear door when the whole train jumped. Then it went still again, gently rocking on its suspension, before surging to life. A heavy industrial rumble thrummed through the floor, and a lunatic cheer went up from the soldiers who, having paused their fights, seemed reluctant to resume them.

"I told you Ken would get it running." The blond woman smirked. "Shooting that man in the gut isn't nearly enough to get him to take a day off."

"That was never the issue," the generic man protested, but the woman was already turning away from him, to the soldiers, some with fists still entwined in each other's collars.

"All right, you barely literate sacks of meat," she shouted, and every single one snapped to attention like they'd gotten ten thousand volts to the back of the neck. "Get to your positions and brace up. We are moving out."

"But," Ethan wailed, "Mari!"

The woman looked on him with more sympathy than Sam would have thought to credit, but then her eyes set and her posture changed.

"Nothing I can do about that now," was all she said.

The blonde turned her back on the kid and stormed away — Sam realized, with dawning horror — in his general direction. He tried to make himself small, but that just seemed to draw her attention.

"And who in the exhausting fuck are you supposed to be?" she said, eyeing him up and down and apparently not finding much to her liking.

"I'm just the water boy." Sam tried his patented customer service smile, and the woman almost decked him.

She pushed him so hard his teeth rattled in his head and left the hatch open behind her as she marched down the length of the train, shouting orders.

"Hey." Sam's guts twisted up. "Wait a minute, what about the others outside? The refugees?"

"There aren't any," a familiar voice from the corner.

Sam turned to see one of the prepper sisters — the older one, Yui — sitting on the edge of a small metal counter in a recessed alcove. She was leaned over, her weight on her elbows, her elbows on her knees, her head hung low. Nursing one mangled hand. She didn't look up to speak to him. Sam could see the other sister curled up beneath Yui, just enough room below the meager counter to shelter in.

"What do you mean there aren't any?" It was a stupid question. The muzzle flashes were burned in his brain. "There wasn't anybody with you? In the back? Another group? Nobody? The Judges got…everybody?"

"What they missed," Yui droned, "the Merry didn't. Me and my sister and another girl, one of the people who live here, we all made it. That's it."

"Your friend?" Sam asked, partly out of concern, partly to get it out of the way so he could ask what he really needed to.

"No," Yui said.

"The Merry wouldn't have made it in there with us in the first place," Chiyo said, mostly to the wall. "Not if Ali had been alive. She was…she was tougher than she looked."

"And…my friend?" Sam felt sweat break out behind his ears.

"The big guy?" Yui looked him in the eye for the first time. "No,

I'm…"

She almost said "sorry."

But she didn't.

"Vera," Sam told her. And her face twisted up in confusion. "He had a daughter, and her name is Vera. And now I have to tell her."

Yui swallowed hard, nodded slowly, and returned her focus to the floor between her boots.

…

Mari's arm is as good as gone. It's still attached and all, but she can feel the pieces jostling inside as she runs. She lost her pistol — out of bullets, anyway — and her vision keeps cutting in and out. It is literally the hardest thing she's ever done, just running across this stubborn sand. There are knives made out of fire in her hips, needles made out of ice in her lungs, and part of her sincerely wishes for an explosion to sound behind her, just so she can stop.

But she can't.

Mari decided she'd rather drop one Sleeper than stun two. She put three careful bullets in the twisted figure on the right, any identifying human feature long lost to exposure. It was a walking mummy, and she half expected dust to explode out of the back of its head — but it was just blood. Slow, dark blood. It did drop, though, so she angled around to the edge of its area of influence. Watching the Sleepers to either side, both up like meerkats at the noise, waiting for her to enter their invisible circles so they could scuttle over spider-quick and wrench her limbs off.

It was a careful, nerve-wracking balance, but she'd maintained it long enough to get in and arm the bomb. She tried to trace her own footsteps back, but this damn sand got her again. Crumbled beneath her feet, set her off balance — she didn't even fall, just stumbled a bit, then something hit her so hard she actually saw stars. She thought that was only in cartoons. The Sleeper had her on her stomach, her left arm yanked back and up, rotating it in and out of the socket.

The sand did cut her one single break: it was soft enough so she could shift, get her knife out and put it in the thing's eyeball. Or the place where it would have been. That churning void, lazily dripping a black fog that curled back, across the ground and then the water, all the way to the approaching cloud. The Sleeper didn't seem to mind having a knife in its head, so she did it again and again and again while it heaved and twisted and bright brassy notes of pain blared from her shoulder. When the creature finally slumped over, oozing slow, dark blood onto her chest, it was all Mari could do to push it off, flip those two irrevocable switches, and run.

So here she is, like something out of a nightmare. Sprinting in slow motion across what might as well be quicksand while a bomb that she set ticks down. And all that is before the tumorous black spire rotates her direction.

A sickly bulbous section breaks off and sends a multitude of thin black lances toward her. She dives and rolls, and they miss — she expects little puffs of dust to shoot up where they impact, but they just go straight through the earth, no resistance. Branches of stuttering chaos grow from the stuck lances and writhe at her heels, so she's back up and running with a brand-new kind of terror at her back. Like she needs one.

She's so close she can see the outline of the Snake behind the blinding spotlights, and one silly little part of her starts to hope. Then she hears the Snake sputter and rumble into life and start pulling away.

Mari risks a glance back. Sees a random lattice of death blooming just a few feet behind her, tendrils lashing at her fleeing bootsoles. She looks to the dam, to the gates and the most heavily populated neighborhoods. They boil with activity, an impenetrable mass of bodies howling and fighting there. Above them, stepping straight through the thick concrete of the dam itself — not breaking it, passing through like a ghost — is what looks like a giant black centipede made of knives.

Maybe it actually is a nightmare, she thinks. What makes more sense: that this is truly her life right now, or that she's trapped in hallucinations of her own making, and she'll wake up any second?

Thankfully, the loose silt of the drained basin gives way to harder-packed dirt at the edges of the city, and she picks up some speed. The Snake is slow to get moving, it's not going at much more than a walking pace for now. She's closing the distance, ignoring the unhealthy whistle coming from her own chest, focusing instead on the comforting rumble of the Snake's massive engines. She's operating on pure instinct, all thoughts blasted out of her by terror and exhaustion, and that's what saves her. She staggers away from a patch of shadow that looks like nothing, just the shapes cast by a nearby pile of junk, right before it comes to life. The darkness in there sends some kind of vile circuitry along the dirt, a mass of black pathways rapidly forking at right angles, reaching out to close off her escape. She looks the other direction, sees the same thing happening over there, and tries to find a place deep down in her bones with even the slightest bit of energy left to burn.

…

Sam didn't expect Vera to understand death so well. He tried to break it to her gently. He told her that Daddy didn't quite make it, that he got left behind, that he wished he could be there and—

"Did he die?" she said, eyes painfully clear.

"Y-yes, honey," Sam said. "I'm sorry."

She's seated cross-legged on the bunk behind Frankie's unconscious form, Princess SparkleHogg filling the space made by her legs like a porcine fluid. Sam knows from experience that the Princess is an empathy-hog — she came and curled up the second Sam sat down, then tucked her little muzzle under Vera's hand, all but forcing the pets out of her.

"I think I'll be very sad, later," Vera said cautiously. "Because it's not happening right now. Does that make me bad?"

"No, dear." Sam reached out and straightened the chipped plastic tiara atop the girl's straw-colored curls. "That's very normal."

Vera whined deep in her throat, seemed confused by the sensation, and let it pass. Sam traced small shapes in the skin of her forearm. It seemed to soothe, or at least distract her.

"Who will I live with now?" she asked, with perfect practicality.

Sam had to count to ten, measure his breaths and pinch the skin of his thigh to keep from crying. That was the last thing the girl needed to see right now.

"With us, little princess," Frankie said. His eyes were so red he might have burst something in there. He rotated gently, an operation that took quite a bit of effort on these criminally small bunks.

Vera thought about it for a moment, then nodded.

"That makes sense," she said. "Daddy liked both of you a lot."

Sam felt all of his desperate, hasty emotional barriers begin to crumble, so he stood up and walked the length of the sleeping car. He crossed the swaying rubbery threshold and picked his way through the now-empty kitchen. He paused at the entrance to the next section. The whole place looked far too busy to be bothered with his presence, so he just ducked into the empty alcove left by the main hatch and tried not to be noticed. Somewhere far ahead, the gruff woman was still shouting her profane commands. Right in front of him, there was a jumble of garbled military nonsense as ten soldiers did a hundred different things at once. Beneath his feet was a holistic rumble, like he was standing on some enormous ferry just pulling away from the dock. And to his side, a distant, muted thumping.

He looked at the hatch, a bit afraid that it would suddenly grow teeth and bite him. Sam listened and swore the metal was ringing with a decisive pattern.

"Excuse me." He waved at the nearest military-looking type, a sweaty man with a nasty scar along the bridge of his nose. "Excuse me…"

"What the hell are you doing here?" The scarred man was poking frantically at a tiny screen set into a shallow console. "Go find a seat and hold on."

"Okay," Sam agreed. "It's just that I think somebody's…knocking on this door?"

The sweaty man just shook his head in frustration, then went back to poking his screen with an inappropriate ferocity.

Sam watched the hatch for a full minute, trying to place the pattern. It sounded so familiar. Was it a…song?

Who on earth would be clinging to the side of a moving landtrain, as the world ends all around them, repeatedly tapping "Shave and a Haircut" on the walls?

It was absurd. It was insane. But then, so was everything else about this day.

There was a big red handle built into the hatch itself, surrounded by an archeological scrawl of severe warnings whose paint had long since worn down to illegibility. But a lever's a lever. He reached out, took it in his hand, and pulled…

…

Mari collapses on the floor like somebody replaced her bones with Jell-O. To make it so far, only to die on the other side of this door, it was so bad that it almost seemed inevitable. Of course that's how this would all end, why not?

She'd wailed on the door with all of her strength at first, and then she tried slow, regular knocking, followed by increasingly elaborate Morse code messages about her plight. Finally, she'd given up and just started tapping the old song from the Bugs Bunny cartoons. She fully expected to die out there, and then the hatch hissed and groaned and slid aside and she limp-tackled this totally bewildered-looking old dude who looked vaguely familiar somehow.

She tries to thank him, then warn him, then get up to close the door her damn self, but her body is having none of it. All she can do is drool on the floor and watch the horizon skate past the open hatch. The Snake isn't pointed toward the explosion when it actually happens, which is good, because she once heard it blinds you to watch it. No idea if that's actually true or what, but who wants to be the bold son of a bitch to check?

They're ascending at a pretty sharp angle, climbing the only steep, jack-knifing trail up the southern bank of the old basin. Must be taking every inch of Ken's concentration to make those crazy turns without sending the whole Snake tumbling down the cliffs. Mari watches as the leading wave surges into view and washes straight over the ramshackle buildings of Dam-Nation like they were made out of toothpicks and bubble gum. The ensuing flood looks like god's eraser: a blotch of dark water that simply insists the whole world behind it is gone. It washes over buildings, and they go away, it washes over the streets, and they go away, it washes over the dense and raging hordes at the gates, and they go away. The water froths where it meets real resistance for the first time at the old dam walls, but it soon finds the broken sections and flows through with such tremendous force that she can see the concrete begin to buckle.

The giant black centipede, however, is unaffected. In fact, it seems to spot the Snake just then, inching up the canyon walls mere meters ahead of the rising waters. It rears back one of those outsized mandibular scythes and flickers. As the flood rushes beneath it, washing away its assembled hordes, huge parts of its body just stop existing. Legs and chunks of thorax, one of those scythes, then the other. It phases out of reality one piece at a time, until it's gone. Mari remembers what Ethan told her, when she'd pushed him to remember.

They use us, and they come from us.

If we want to beat them, we only have to kill ourselves.

If there weren't enough maniacs to sustain them, did the monsters just…go away?

Mari doesn't get the answer to that question, because finally somebody is smart enough to shut the damn hatch. The bomb was small and focused, probably no great and imminent pulse of fiery death sweeping across the landscape, but still — if somebody sets off a nuclear explosion in the neighborhood, it's probably best to at least close the door.

And with that, Mari goes out. Her brain finally, finally lets her dip into unconsciousness. Oblivion is the sweetest thing she's ever felt.

…

Frankie squeezed Vera's tiny fingers as hard as he dared, and she squeezed back. He passed the crush onto Sam until the man winced and shot him an accusatory glance. Frankie reluctantly released his man and used that hand to shield his eyes from the light.

The blinding, brilliant, impossible sunlight.

He wondered how they actually survived it, before — this flaming orb firing down on them from the sky every single day. It was almost too much. But god, how he'd missed the colors.

The ungainly landtrain was parked atop a bluff just a few miles from the former site of the Walled City. Most of the survivors were standing outside, clustered in hushed groups, watching sunrise break over the shattered dam and the paint the new river below in passive purples and hazy pinks.

Sam often chastised Frankie's wide-eyed optimism. But it was at least partly an act. How can you survive if you're both hopeless? One has to bring the other up. Now worries and terrors slipped through Frankie's mind like disturbed spirits. Where would they live? How would they live? Could they rebuild? Did they want to? There would be starvation, and disease, and maybe even wars — now that the one big uniting enemy was gone from humanity. He had raw, bleeding wounds and nasty old scars all across his psyche, and so did Sam, and so did the little girl holding very tightly to his hand. Most days, Frankie felt like he and Sam could barely take care of themselves. Now they had not one but *two* Princesses to care for, and a ruined world to do it in.

But those were tomorrow's problems, and for once, Frankie felt confident there might actually be a tomorrow to address them.

...

Mari can't recall if she'd ever actually sat and watched a sunrise, back in the real world. She'd always been too busy, or sleepy, or maybe it just seemed boring. But it was amazing now. She forgot just how many colors came along with the sun. Her memories painted daylight in a kind of dusty yellow, but here there was a blaze of reds and purples and pinks and everything in between transforming the entire eastern horizon, and she wonders how on earth she'd skipped so many of these. She makes a silent promise not to do it again.

Behind her, a hardscrabble crew of dazed survivors curse, or cheer, or just break down and cry. Beside her, Lucas beams with the whole palette of the world reflected in his big brown eyes. With his hand on her back, JR shivers in the post-dawn cold. He keeps mouthing the word "wow," over and over again, periodically looking to her for confirmation. She gives it without so much as an eyeroll. This is, indeed, pretty wow.

Nevermind that her arm is probably ruined, from the fingers Diego smashed to the shoulder the Sleeper dismantled, she doubts she'd ever have full use of it again. It's only adrenaline and awe keeping her on her feet. Nevermind that her brother is too messed up in the head to even speak and probably always will be. Nevermind that she has a goofball new boyfriend (is he even that?) whom she has to both work and live with *right from the start.* And nevermind that she's looking out at the utterly demolished and totally drowned ruins of the last city on earth, and a grand new river that is definitely full of corpses. Nevermind all of it, and all the rest she can't think of and doesn't even know about, and all the things to come and all the things that passed, because right now, the sun is up.

So it's perfect.

The Last Story

"History is a curse," the Archivist said, and having put out the call, he waited for the response.

None came. The children's eyes were growing glossy, more interested in future dinners than past lessons. The solar generator sputtered and the lights dimmed, so the Archivist issued a few calculated kicks. The light and the noise resuscitated the children, if only temporarily. He repeated the call:

"History is a curse."

"Knowledge breaks it."

"That's right." The Archivist smiled at each of the children in turn. Not a single one returned it. He felt his lips droop.

"Mila." He singled out the sleepiest of their number, chin already sliding down her forearm toward the desk. "What happened to the Walled City, the last fortress of mankind?"

"You blew it up," she mumbled and perked up a little when the other children laughed.

"Not quite," the Archivist grumbled. He was hoping to catch the girl a little more off balance, so she could serve as an example to the others. "We flooded it to wash away the maniacs. And what did that do?"

He tapped on Marcus Jr.'s desk, and the boy fluttered his heavy eyelids.

"Uh…that killed all the bad guys?" Jr. straightened up, but it didn't take. He was already sinking back in his seat, tiny snags on the scarred plastic picking at his shorts.

"We're just full of 'not quite' today, aren't we?" The Archivist snickered, but nobody laughed at his little quip. "The flood took out enough of the maniacs to break the enemy's hold, because…"

He pointed at Elizabeth, who had taken his cues and now sat at attention.

"Because," she answered, "they came from us. They needed us."

"Right you are," he said and got the feeling his pride didn't buy young Lizzie any points with the other children. "What happened to the surviving maniacs?"

Every eye in the place darted away from his.

"Without the enemy's influence," the Archivist answered himself, "most of the Sleepers and the Manic simply died off. They had suffered too much in their servitude — wounds, hunger, exposure to the elements, etc. Some of the Judges and even the Merry reverted to their old selves, but…well, they didn't last long, trying to live with what they'd done."

"Mr. Mills?" Che inquired. "What time is it?"

The Archivist kept the only working watch in the classroom. He kept it on his desk, face down, so the children couldn't peek. It was only fifteen minutes past last bell. He didn't see what the big deal was. Still…

"Perhaps it is time to break for the day," the Archivist mused, then quickly held his hands up to stop the mad dash for freedom.

"But," he said, "not without repeating the rules. Marcus, would you like to start?"

"Don't forget the story," he began. "Tell it to each other and tell it to our kids and stuff."

"The actual words, please," the Archivist insisted.

The boy sighed.

"Don't forget the story. Tell it to yourself, tell it to each other, tell it to your children."

The Archivist pointed to Mila.

"Never, uh…" She picked at a flake in the wood of her desktop. "Never…don't grow too fast or too much."

She could already see the Archivist's correction coming, so she did it herself.

"Don't let mankind grow too fast or too far," she said quickly.

The Archivist pointed to Lizzie.

"Take us out, Elizabeth."

"Don't look to the skies," she recited, struggling through a yawn. "Don't listen to the stars."

"Don't look to the skies," the Archivist echoed.

"Don't listen to the stars," the children repeated.

He waved his hand at the door, and a flashflood of impatient childflesh stormed through it, screaming and pinching and pushing their way back to their respective homes. The Archivist sat at the edge of his own weather-beaten desk. His hips hurt from standing, his tailbone hurt from sitting, and his knees hurt from walking. He wasn't supposed to be this old! He hadn't cracked sixty yet, so why did he feel twice that?

He broke his own rules and leaned toward the dusty windows to look at the sky. A dying spring afternoon giving way to evening, pale blue washing into black. The first stars twinkled weakly in the fading light.

The Archivist closed his eyes and ran his fingers through his thinning hair. He allowed himself one full minute of blank relaxation, then stood to retrieve a ragged notebook from the top drawer. He flipped through it until he found the first blank page, and recorded the day's events, as he had done every single day since he was 9 ¾ years old.

History is a curse. Only knowledge breaks it.

About the Author

Robert Brockway is the author of The Vicious Circuit series from Tor Books, the cyberpunk novel *Rx: A Tale of Electronegativity*, and the comedic non-fiction essay collection *Everything is Going to Kill Everybody*. He lives in Tucson, Arizona, with his wife Meagan and their three dogs, Detective Martin Riggs, Detective Roger Murtaugh, and Penny. Penny did not make the force.

He is represented by Sam Morgan at The Lotts Agency.

Find more from Robert on his Patreon at patreon.com/brockwar, on his website at robertbrockway.net, or his Twitter feed @brockway_llc.

More books by Robert Brockway

Rx: A Tale of Electronegativity
The Unnoticeables
The Empty Ones
Kill All Angels
Everything is Going to Kill Everybody

Printed in Great Britain
by Amazon

53198105R00374